THE HAWK AND THE DOVE
TRILOGY

*For Our
Dear Fr Augustine ~
God Bless you
always !,
Much love ~
Astrid and Jim*

Previously published separately as:

The Hawk and the Dove
The Wounds of God
The Long Fall

PENELOPE WILCOCK

The Hawk and the Dove TRILOGY

CROSSWAY BOOKS • WHEATON, ILLINOIS
A DIVISION OF GOOD NEWS PUBLISHERS

The Hawk and the Dove Trilogy

Copyright © 2000 by Penelope Wilcock

Published by Crossway Books
    a division of Good News Publishers
    1300 Crescent Street
    Wheaton, Illinois 60187

Previously published separately as: *The Hawk and the Dove:* copyright © 1990 by Penelope Wilcock. First British edition 1990 (Minstrel, a division of Monarch Publications Ltd.); first U.S. edition 1991 (Crossway Books, a division of Good News Publishers). *The Wounds of God:* copyright © 1991 by Penelope Wilcock. First British edition 1991 (Minstrel, a division of Monarch Publications Ltd.). First U.S. edition 1992 (Crossway Books, a division of Good News Publishers). *The Long Fall:* copyright © 1993 by Penelope Wilcock. First British edition 1992 (Minstrel, a division of Kingsway Publications Ltd.). First U.S. edition 1993 (Crossway Books, a division of Good News Publishers).

Cover illustration: Chuck Gillies

Cover design: Cindy Kiple

First printing 2000

Printed in the United States of America

Library of Congress Cataloging-in-Publication Data
Wilcock, Penelope.
    The hawk and the dove : trilogy / Penelope Wilcock.
        p.   cm.
    Contents: The hawk and the dove — The wounds of God — The long fall.
    ISBN 1-58134-138-5 (tpb : alk. paper)
        1. Monastic and religious life—History—Middle Ages, 600-1500—Fiction. 2. Historical fiction, English. 3. Christian fiction, English. 4. Monks—Fiction.   I. Title.
PR6073.I394 H392   2000
823'.914—dc21   99-053718
                                                                  CIP

---

15   14   13   12   11   10   09   08   07   06   05   04
15   14   13   12   11   10   9   8   7   6   5   4

CONTENTS

BOOK 1: THE HAWK AND THE DOVE

BOOK 2: THE WOUNDS OF GOD

BOOK 3: THE LONG FALL

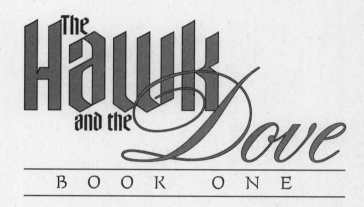

BOOK ONE

For David Bowes
with deep gratitude

I
MOTHER

I wish you had known my mother. I remember, as clearly as if it were yesterday, toiling up the hill at the end of the school day, towards the group of mothers who stood at the crest of the rise, waiting to collect their children from the county primary school where my little sisters went.

The mothers chatted together, plump and comfortable, wearing modest, flowery dresses, pretty low-heeled sandals, their hair curled and tinted, and just that little bit of make-up to face the world in. Some had pushchairs with wriggling toddlers. Together, they smiled and nodded and gossiped and giggled, young and friendly and kind. . . . But there at the top of the hill, at a little distance from all the rest, stood my mother, as tall and straight and composed as a prophet, her great blue skirt flapping in the breeze, her thick brown hair tumbling down her back. By her side stood my littlest sister, her hand nestling confidingly in my mother's hand, her world still sheltered in the folds of that blue skirt from the raw and bewildering society of the playground.

My mother. She was not a pretty woman, and never thought to try and make herself so. She had an uncompromising chin, firm lips, a nose like a hawk's beak and unnerving grey eyes. Eyes that went straight past the outside of you and into the middle, which meant that you could relax about the torn jersey, the undone shoe laces, the tangled hair and the unwashed hands at the dinner table, but you had to feel very uncomfortable indeed about the stolen sweets, the broken promise, and the unkind way you ran away from a little sister striving to follow you on her short legs. My mother. Often, after tea, she would stand, having cleared away the tea things, at the sink, just looking out of the windows at the seagulls riding the air-currents on the evening sky; her hands still, her work forgotten, a faraway expression in her eyes.

Therese and I would do our homework after tea, sitting at the tea-table in the kitchen. The three little ones would play out of doors until the light was failing, and then Mother would call them in, littlest first, and bath them in the lean-to bathroom at the back of the kitchen, brush their hair and clean their teeth, help them on with their nightgowns, and tuck them in to bed.

This was the moment of decision for Therese and me. Ours was a little house in a terrace of shabby houses that clung to a hillside by the sea, and we had only two bedrooms, so all five of us sisters slept in the same room on mattresses side by side on the floor. Mother hated electric light—she said it assaulted the sleepy soul and drove the sandman away, and when the little ones were ready for bed, she would tuck in Mary and Beth, and light the candle and sit down with Cecily, the littlest one, in the low comfortable chair in the corner of the room. If she put them to bed and left them, there would be pandemonium. Cecily would not stay in bed at all and romped gaily about the room, and Beth and Mary would begin to argue, starting with a simple remark like 'Beth, I can't get to sleep with you sniffing,' and finishing with a general commotion of crying and quarrelling.

So Mother resigned herself to stay with them as they fell asleep, and she sat, with the littlest one snuggled on her lap, in the room dimly glowing with candle-light, softly astir with the breathing and sighing and turning over of children settling for the night.

Therese and I, at sixteen and fourteen years old, had to choose between staying alone downstairs to read a book or paint or gaze into the fire; and creeping upstairs with the little ones, to sit with Mother in the candle-light, and listen to her lullabies.

Most often, Therese stayed down, but I crept upstairs to Mother and lay on my bed, gazing at the candle as the flame dipped and rose with the draught, watching the shadows as they trembled and moved about the ceiling. After a while, as we kept our quiet, shadowy vigil, I would whisper, 'Mother, tell me a story.'

I was just beginning to ask questions, to search for a way of looking at things that would make sense. The easy gaiety and simple sorrows of childhood had been swallowed up and lost in a hungry emptiness, a search for meaning that nothing seemed to satisfy. At school, I was only a number, a non-person. They could answer my questions about the theory of relativity and whether it was permissible in modern English to split an infinitive: but when it came to the great, lonely yearning that was opening up inside me, they didn't seem even to want to hear the question, let alone try to answer it. I went to church every Sunday, and I listened to what they said about Jesus, and I believed it all, I really did; but was there anyone anywhere who cared about it enough to behave as if it were true? I felt disenchanted.

I began to wonder, as spring wore on to summer in that, my fifteenth year, if I would ever meet anyone who could look me in the eye, who could say sorry without making a joke of it, who could cry without embarrassment, have a row and still stay friends. As for mentioning the word 'love', well ... it provoked sniggers, not much else. The hunger of it all ached inside me. Maybe Mother knew. Maybe she could guess what I never told her, could not even tell myself; that I was desperate for something more than smiles and jokes and surfaces; that I was beginning to wonder if it was possible to stretch out your hand in the darkness and find it grasped by another hand, not evaded, rejected, or ignored.

So I wish you had known my mother. I wish you could hear the stories she told in her quiet, thoughtful voice. I wish I could take you into the magic of that breathing, candle-lit room, which she filled with people and strange ways from long ago. I wish I could remember all of them to tell you, but years have gone by now, and I am not sure of everything she said. But for the times you, too, have a quiet moment, and need to unhook your mind from the burden of the day, here are some of the stories my mother told me. They are the stories she told me the year I turned fifteen.

Mother said these stories were true, and I never knew her to tell a lie ... but then you could never be quite sure what she meant by 'truth'; fact didn't always come into it.

II
FATHER COLUMBA

When I was a girl, a bit younger than you (my mother began) I had someone to tell me stories, too. It wasn't my mother who told me stories though, it was my great-grandmother, and her name was Melissa, like yours. Great-grandmother Melissa told me all sorts of stories, stories about my uncles and cousins, about my great-aunt Alice who was a painter and lived in a little stone cottage at Bell Busk in Yorkshire. Old Aunt Alice's cottage was one of a row of terraced cottages, all the same except that Aunt Alice's was painted in psychedelic colours.

Great-grandmother Melissa told me about my auntie's duck that had four legs—and she took me to see it too. She told me about one of my far-off ancestors, who was found on the doorstep as a tiny baby, in a shopping bag. She told me about my cousin's dog Russ, who bit off a carol-singer's finger, and about my grandfather's dog that had to be put down because it loved him so much it went out one night and killed twenty hens and piled them all up on his doorstep. She told me about how she and her sisters took it in turns to pierce each others' ears with a needle and a cork, and socks stuffed in their mouths to stop them screaming, so that their mother wouldn't find out what they'd done. All kinds of tales she told me, and all about our family. But the ones I liked best were about a monastery long ago. These stories had been handed down, grandmother to granddaughter, for seven hundred years. They came from a long ago Great-uncle Edward, who lived to be nearly a hundred, and was a very wise old man.

At the end of his life, when his blue eyes were faded and his skin was wrinkled, and his hair reduced to white wisps about his bald head (although he had the bushiest of eyebrows and whiskers that grew down his nose), Uncle Edward would while away his days telling stories to his visitors. The one who had the stories from him was his great-niece—*she* was a Melissa too. This Melissa began handing down the stories, and they came down through the generations until my great-grandmother, in the evening of her life, as she came into the twilight, would sit with me and tell me that long ago Uncle Edward's stories. And now I will tell them to you.

Great-uncle Edward was a monk, at the Benedictine abbey of St Alcuin, on the edge of the Yorkshire moors. He had been a wandering friar in the order of the blessed Francis of Assisi, and had spent his life roaming the countryside, preaching the gospel. But as time went by, and his sixtieth birthday came and went, he felt a need for a more settled life. So after forty years of preaching throughout the English shires, he entered the community of Benedictines at St Alcuin's Abbey in Yorkshire, far away from his family home near Ely, but just as cold and windy. Great-uncle Edward (now Brother Edward) was made the infirmarian of the abbey-that is to say, he took care of the monks when they were ill—for in his wandering days with the Franciscan friars, he had picked up a wealth of healing lore. He was skilled in the use of tisanes and poultices, herbal salves and spiced wines and aromatic oils, and he could set a bone or repair a wound as well as any man. So he settled down at St Alcuin's, and gave himself to the work of nursing the sick and caring for the old under the Rule of Life of St Benedict.

In the year 1303—Brother Edward's sixty-sixth—when he had been four years at the abbey, the good old abbot of the monastery, Father Gregory of the Resurrection, died peacefully in his sleep with a smile on his face, over-burdened with years and glad to enter into the peace of the blessed. The brothers were sorry to lose him, for he had ruled them gently, with kindness and authority, knowing how to mingle mercy with justice so as to get the best out of his flock and lead them in their life of work and prayer. The sorriest of all was Father Chad, the prior of the monastery, second-in-command under the abbot, upon whose shoulders now fell the burden of responsibility for the community until they had a new abbot. Father Chad was a shy, quiet man, a man of prayer, a man of few words—a gentle, retiring man. He was not a leader of men. He had no idea why he had been chosen to be prior and was horrified to find the greatness of the abbacy thrust upon him. With a small sigh of regret he left the snug prior's cell, which was built against the warm chimney of the brothers' community room, the warming room, and installed himself in the large, draughty apartment which was the abbot's lodging. Day and night he prayed that God would send a new abbot soon, and day and night he prayed that they wouldn't choose him.

It was the usual thing, when the abbot of the monastery died, for the brothers to elect from among their number the new lord abbot. The brothers of St Alcuin's prayed hard, and the more senior of the brethren spent long hours in counsel; but though they prayed long and considered earnestly, they came reluctantly to the conclusion that there was no brother among them with the necessary qualities of leadership to follow in Father Gregory's footsteps. So they appealed to the bishop to choose them a new superior from among the brothers of another monastery, and said they would abide by his choice and accept whomever he sent to rule over them.

Before too long, word came from the bishop that he

would himself be presenting their new superior to them. Since he had to travel through their part of the world on his return home to Northumbria from a conference with the king in London, he would visit them on his way, bringing their new abbot with him. The abbey reverberated with excitement, all except for Father Chad, who dreaded playing host to both a bishop and an abbot.

Great-uncle Edward did his best to encourage him; 'Put a brave face on it, Father Prior! Chin up, never say die. 'Tis only one night when all's said and done, then you'll be back to your cosy nook by the warming-room flues and leave this windy barn to the new man, God help him. The bishop gives you his name in that letter, does he?'

Father Chad looked at the letter from the bishop, not that he needed to. He had read and re-read it a dozen times this morning, and knew the contents of it near enough by heart now; but he ran his finger down the script to make sure.

'Here. Father Columba, the sub-prior from St Peter's near Ely. He says very little about him. We shall have to wait and see.'

'Ely? I was born and bred on the fens near Ely. My nephew took the cowl at St Peter's. I wonder ... Columba, you say? Columba the dove. No. No, wouldn't be him. No sane man would have named that lad after a dove!'

'You'll eat with us, Edward, when they come tonight?' Father Chad tried to sound casually friendly, but Edward knew panic when he saw it.

'I shall count myself honoured. I'll go now and get my chores done early. There's old Father Lucanus suffering with the pain in his shoulder and neck again. I must spend some time with him, give him a rub with aromatics. It eases the ache wonderfully.' Brother Edward stood up slowly and strolled across the bare, comfortless room to the great oak door. He paused in the doorway and looked back. Father Chad still sat in the imposing carved chair, staring gloomily at the letter on the huge, heavy table before him.

'Time and the hour outrun the longest day, Father Chad,' said Brother Edward consolingly. 'It'll be over before you know it.'

He set off to the infirmary, well content with the prospect of being among the first to have a good look at the new abbot.

'Columba.' He tried out the sound of the name, thoughtfully. 'Columba. Irishman, maybe? We shall see.'

When a man entered as a brother in the monastic life (my mother explained) he had done with the world and its ways and set out as though on a brand new life to try and live in every way, with a single heart, for God. He took three vows; one of poverty, that he would never have anything to call his own again; one of chastity, that he would never have a wife or a girlfriend, but all women would be like sisters to him, just as all men would be like brothers; and one of obedience, that he would submit to the authority of the abbot of the community, and obey his word in everything. When he made his first vows after six months as a novice, the monk would be clothed in the habit of the order, which was a long robe—black for the Benedictines—with a separate hood called a cowl, and wide sleeves and a leather belt.

To show that he really had finished with all the trappings of his old life, the monk was given a new name by his abbot, as if he were a brand new person. The abbot usually tried to pick something appropriate to the man's character or background. Great-uncle Edward had been christened Edward as a baby, after King Edward the Confessor, who was a good and holy king. When he entered the religious life, his abbot said he should keep the same name, since no one could hope to be more devoted to the Lord Jesus than King Edward had been. And now the man the bishop was bringing was Columba, named after the Irish Saint. Columba, the dove, the bird that represents gentleness and kindness and simplicity, as well as being a symbol of the Holy Spirit of God.

After Vespers Brother Edward hurried with anticipation to the abbot's lodging to meet their distinguished supper-guests, who had ridden in an hour ago and been welcomed to the guest house.

'Well, well!' murmured Brother Edward, as his new abbot entered the room: for it was indeed the son of his sister Melissa, whom he had not seen for years.

'Columba!' Edward chuckled to himself. 'Meek and gentle dove, eh? Well, I shall be very surprised ...'

The new abbot, whom Edward had known since babyhood, was certainly no dove. His mother, dead now, had been a proud, noble lady, and his father was a rich and powerful Norman aristocrat with a face as proud as an eagle and a grip on all that was his as fierce as the grip of an eagle's talons. When their child was born, he had a little beaky nose like a bird of prey, and a flashing dark eye quite startling in a pink baby face. His mother, laughing, called him Peregrine, and well named he was, for like a hawk he grew: fierce, proud and arrogant, with a piercing look and a hawk's beak nose. Great-grandmother Melissa said I favoured him in my looks, even all these years later.

This Peregrine had two older brothers. The elder of the two, Geoffroi, took charge of the farming side of his father's estate. Emmanuel, the second brother, went for a soldier. Peregrine, youngest, stubbornest, fiercest of the three, surprised them all by losing his proud, stubborn heart to Jesus, turning his back on the world and entering as a novice at St Peter's Abbey near Ely, to try the monastic life as a Benedictine brother.

Of course, it's one thing to love Jesus and quite another to follow him; and poverty, chastity and obedience sat about as comfortably on Peregrine as his hair shirt. Still, the brothers saw promise in him, and as much from stubbornness as anything else he grimly struggled through his novitiate year, finally making his vows and being professed as Brother Columba—a name which showed either that his abbot had a wry sense of humour or else that he had greater faith than most men and no sense of humour at all.

Peregrine was a good scholar and a devout monk, and he was ordained a priest, too. He was also a brilliant philosopher, and had inherited from his father a shrewd business mind and unmistakable qualities of leadership. He was not a popular man, because although he was just and upright and true, there was precious little compassion or gentleness about him. The fight to discipline himself, to attain all the spiritual and intellectual targets he set himself, occupied all his energies, leaving nothing to help him learn the gentler art of loving, much less of allowing himself to be loved. Still, he was valued for his abilities, even if he inspired little affection, and he was given several positions of responsibility.

When the bishop consulted the abbot of St Peter's, to see if their community had anyone who could be sent to St Alcuin's to serve as abbot, Father Columba had only recently been made sub-prior. The abbot of St Peter's suggested him at once, and so Peregrine was sent, at the beginning of his forty-fifth year, as Lord Abbot to the monastery of St Alcuin in the north of Yorkshire. The bishop was satisfied that Peregrine would serve them well. He had listened to the advice of the abbot of St Peter's, who knew the monks in his care better than they knew themselves:

'He's ruthless with himself, always has been. Drives the men under him hard too; but he's fair-minded, unfailingly courteous and astute, nobody's fool. He's a solitary man. I've wondered, sometimes, if he's lonely, but it's hard to say. Just your stiff, formal, courtly French nobleman, I think. We'll not break our hearts to see him go, and yet I shall be sorry in a way to lose him. There's a shining, honourable love of God about him that's a rare thing to see. Abbot Columba. Yes, he'll wear it well.'

So the bishop brought him to St Alcuin's, and Brother Edward watched with amused sympathy as the prior greeted them. The nails of Chad's fingers were bitten to the quick, and his left eye was twitching as he welcomed them with the kiss of peace and played host to them at the abbot's table. The senior brethren of the abbey dined with them, as did the bishop's chaplain.

Mingled in the company, Brother Edward was able to study his nephew well. Father Columba had seemed pleased to see his uncle again, embracing him with a smile of pleasure and surprise, the sudden, vivid smile that Edward remembered in him as a boy irradiating his features with unexpected warmth.

Now, as Father Columba ate and talked, unmoved by the eyes of the brethren upon him, Brother Edward observed him thoughtfully. He looked at the piercing intelligence of the dark eyes, the controlled intensity of his manner, the impatient movements of his hands. 'Like his father, Frenchman to the core,' thought Edward. 'Henri always talked more with his hands than with words. He's grown as imperious and autocratic as his father too. Columba, my eye! They should have stuck with Peregrine. Dear me, yes. Poor old Chad. This man is going to come as a shock after Abbot Gregory.'

Brother Edward thought it was a huge joke that his nephew Peregrine had been renamed Columba, and he was still chuckling at the thought of it the next day as he made the beds and washed and shaved the aged brothers in his care in the infirmary. Brother John, who was his assistant, asked him what he was laughing at, and Edward told him how their new abbot had been Peregrine, the bird of prey, before he became Columba, the dove. Brother John grinned at the incongruity. Word got round, and it was not long before it was the joke of the whole community, and the new abbot was called 'Father Peregrine' behind his back, and 'Father Columba' to his face and to visitors.

The brothers of St Alcuin's found their new superior

rather unapproachable, his remote and reserved courtesy contrasting unfavourably with Father Gregory's kindness. They found Father Peregrine's imperious face and noble carriage intimidating, though they were cautiously proud of him, too. He proved to be a good and competent abbot, and ruled over his monastery with justice and integrity, commanding the respect and loyalty of the brothers, who would not, in any case, have dared to question his aristocratic authority.

A year went by, and the brothers began to grow accustomed to their new superior. Another year and they had almost forgotten what it was like before he came. It was Easter, two years after Father Peregrine had come to be their abbot. Easter, the greatest feast of the Christian year, and all the local people had come up to the abbey, and the guest house was full of pilgrims come to celebrate the feast of the Resurrection. So many people, so many processions, so much music! So many preparations to be made by the singers, the readers, those who served at the altar and those who served in the guest house, not to mention those who worked in the kitchens and the stables. The abbey was bursting with guests, neighbours, relatives and strangers.

The Easter Vigil was mysterious and beautiful, with the imagery of fire and water and the Paschal candle lit in the great, vaulted dimness of the abbey church. Brother Gilbert the precentor's voice mounted joyfully in the triumphant beauty of the *Exultet;* all the bells rang out for the risen Lord, and the voices of the choirboys from the abbey school soared with heart-breaking loveliness in the music declaring the risen life of Jesus. Easter Day itself was radiant with sunshine for once, as well as celebration. Oh, the joyful splendour of a church crammed full of people, a thundering of voices singing 'Credo—I believe.'

The newest of the novices, Brother Thomas, known to the other novices as Brother Tom, who had just two weeks ago taken his first vows, stood almost dazed, transported by the beauty of the celebration. He had been in the community only six months, having entered once his father's harvest was safely gathered in, in the autumn of 1305. His father, a big, strapping, red-faced man, a Yorkshire farmer born and bred, had accompanied him to the abbey. His mother they had left in tears at home. She had only two children, both sons, and they were her whole life. In addition to this, the farm could ill do without the sons' labour and management. But God calls whom he will, and devout Christians both, the lad's parents respected and supported his wish to try the religious life.

With an almost oppressive sense of awe, the two men had entered through the little portal set in the massive gates of the abbey enclosure. They were put at their ease again by the kindly welcome of Brother Cyprian, the old porter, who had chatted comfortably to them as he escorted them to the abbot's lodging. His broad Yorkshire accent was something of home in this imposing place. 'Tha munnot fear Father Abbot, lad. He's not an easy man, but he's a good man for all that. Tha mun speak up for thyself, for he'll not bite thee. Through here, this is our refectory. Through yon door into t' cloister, aye, that's it. ... Now then, here we are, this is Father's house.'

What Brother Thomas remembered most of his first meeting with Abbot Peregrine (apart from the dark grey eyes that looked as if they could read his mind) was the quick, eloquent gesturing of his hands, the way he drummed his fingers thoughtfully on the table as he looked at Tom and weighed him up. In the abbot's hands all his vitality, his restless energy seemed concentrated, and the lad was fascinated by the long, fine, strong, restless fingers, so different from his own. He looked down at his own hands, broad and work-hard, rough and weathered already at nineteen years old, and reposeful with the peace you so often see in a farmer's hands. They rested on his thighs as he listened to his father discussing him with the abbot.

'. . . and you can spare him, from the farm?' the abbot was asking his father, probing. 'Only two sons, you say? You can afford to let one of them go?'

The farmer met the abbot's questioning gaze. 'He's not cut out for the land, not this one, Father. Neither use nor ornament to me is this lad, when his heart's elsewhere. Any road, we shall see. I'd not wonder if the fire dies down before long. He's a mighty trencherman—well, look at him, he's built like an ox, both of my lads are—and he'll leave a few broken hearts behind him among the lasses when he's gone. To be honest with you, I cannot see him creeping about in silence or telling beads on his knees. As demure and quiet as young ladies are some of your brothers here, and that my lad will never be. But let him try it if he will. There's always a welcome for him with his mother and me should it all come to nothing.'

This was the longest, most personal speech the farmer had ever made, and he took out his linen handkerchief and wiped the beads of sweat from his forehead as he finished. A smile twitched the corners of the abbot's mouth. He was amused by the description of his monks. He was himself inclined to be irritable with the more timid and submissive men. The abbot turned his gaze on the farmer's son, who returned it calmly, but felt somehow belittled and exposed by the aristocratic amusement with which he was regarded.

'He thinks I am a peasant, and beneath him,' he thought, somewhat resentfully, and stoutly endured the abbot's scrutiny.

'What say you then, my son?' asked Father Peregrine. 'Your father has little hope of your staying the course, it seems. It is a hard life. I shall think no less of you if you wish to change your mind.'

The abbot's aloof, ironic manner nettled the lad; the educated voice with its slight French inflection grated on him. He spoke up impulsively, with some heat. 'I doubt you could think much less of me than you do now, my lord, anyway. I am a common working man, not of your kind.'

'Eh, then. Now, now!' expostulated his father. 'That's uncivil, lad! Mind who you're talking to!' But the abbot ignored him and looked steadily at the young man, serious now.

'Well, then? You are minded to enter with us?'

'I am, my lord.'

And standing here in the sunshine and soaring music of Easter Day, Brother Thomas was glad and sure, at peace to his very soul. This was where he belonged.

'*Credo in unum Deum*—I believe in one God—oh, yes!'

The next day, Easter Monday, most of the guests were leaving, and there was much coming and going, saddling of horses, saying of goodbyes. It was next to impossible to find anyone or get anything done. The place was in turmoil. After Vespers, as the sun was sinking, Brother Edward was sent with a message in search of Father Matthew, the novice master.

Edward went into the great abbey church, determined that this would be his last task before he sat down wearily for a bite to eat with the other brothers—and then Compline and bed. He was fairly confident he would find Father Matthew in the sacristy adjoining the choir, making sure Brother Thomas knew how to set out vessels and vestments for the Mass in the morning, putting ready the Communion bread, and marking the places in the holy books for the celebrant.

Brother Edward cut through the Lady chapel—the quickest way—and although by this hour it was all but dark in the church, he walked swiftly: partly because he was in a hurry, and partly because this was his home and he knew his way about as well in dusk as in daylight.

He was striding purposefully up the little aisle, peering ahead to see if he could make out a glimmer of light from the sacristy that would indicate Father Matthew's presence within, when unexpectedly he drove his foot into a bulky obstacle across his path, and all but lost his balance. From the floor came a deep, inhuman groan of agony, like an animal, like something in the torment of hell.

Brother Edward's scalp crawled, and gooseflesh stood out all over his body at the sound. His mouth went dry, and his hands trembled as he bent in the gloom to peer at and feel the bundle at his feet. As his hand moved over it, again came that groan: hideous, wordless in anguish. Brother Edward, thoroughly shaken, hesitated a moment and then decided to go for help, and a light.

Edging his way round whoever or whatever it was, he ran to the sacristy, where he found Father Matthew, as he had expected, laying out vestments with Brother Thomas. They looked up, startled, at Edward's white, agitated face.

'Brother, for God's sake, come,' he gasped. 'Bring a light, make haste.'

Father Matthew asked no questions, but snatched up a candle and followed him, and together they hurried back into the Lady chapel, while Brother Thomas followed a little uncertainly, sensing trouble and not sure if he was expected to help or mind his own business. As he crossed the sacristy, he saw that Brother Edward's sandal had left behind a trail of marks, and the one on the threshold of the room reflected the light a little. Frowning, he bent down and held the light to look closer.

'Mother of God, it's blood!' he murmured, and carrying the light in his hand followed his superiors out into the Lady chapel.

There they found Abbot Peregrine, though his face was bruised and beaten almost beyond recognition. His body was tied and bound with his knees drawn up to his chin and his hands behind his back, the right side of his face laid open in a ragged gash that exposed his cheekbone and extended from his temple nearly to his jaw. Blood had flowed from his nose into his mouth and mingled with blood from a split lip. Two of his teeth were spat out on the floor in a sticky puddle of blood.

Appalled, the brothers looked at each other.

'Who can have done this?' whispered Father Matthew, but Edward shook his head.

'So many strangers, so many guests. Did you not hear anything in the sacristy?'

'Nothing, Brother. We came in through the main body of the church, not through here, just ten minutes before you found us. We saw no one. Whoever it was must have fled, because—'

'All right, all right,' interrupted Brother Edward. 'Brother Thomas, find me something to cut these ropes with, the knife in my belt will be too blunt to do it carefully.'

Thomas ran off without a word, and Brother Edward gently felt Peregrine's back and skull to be sure it was safe to move him. His hair was sticky with blood, and there was a swollen, spongy bruise, but his skull was intact. Thomas returned with a small knife, very sharp, filched from the kitchen, and Brother Edward took it from him and bent to cut the ropes that bound the abbot's arms behind his back.

'Lift the light a little, Matthew. I can't see what I'm doing. Oh, but what's this!?'

Peregrine's hands, tied behind him, were smashed and mangled, grotesquely broken, disfigured and bruised. Gingerly, Edward cut the cords that bound him. They moved the benches aside and carefully laid him straight, and Edward felt all over him for broken bones.

'That's his collar-bone broken. Two ribs here. No, three. Hold the light steady, Matthew, let me look at his leg. No, his left leg, that's it. His shin-bone's smashed, look at this. That'll never set straight. His knee too. Brother, what kind of devilish beast can have done this to him? And why? Dear Lord, what hatred! Nothing else broken, though. Brother Thomas, run to the infirmary and ask Brother John for a stretcher. Quick as you can.'

He sat back on his heels and looked down at the still, battered body.

'Matthew, I kicked him,' he said. 'I came through in a hurry, and I stumbled over him. The moan of pain that came from him, I've never heard anything like it. He was lying here like this, and I kicked him. Still, thank God he's alive, poor soul.'

Brother Thomas came back bringing a stretcher and with him Brother John from the infirmary. As gently as they could, they eased him onto it.

'Brother, have a care for his hands. They may be beyond repairing, but we'll not injure them further. Cross his arms so, that's right. Now then, gently.'

They carried him to the infirmary, and he lay there as still as a corpse, his eyes swollen shut with bruising, his breath snoring in the oozing blood of his nose.

Until dawn, Edward tended to the broken mess of his hands, fine, scholar's hands, shattered now. He made wooden splints, and set the bones and bound them straight, but knew with a heavy heart that those hands would never serve again to do fine lettering. He had set the leg bone as well as he could, but it was smashed, not broken clean, and he doubted if it would ever bear a man's weight again. He set and bandaged the ribs and the collar-bone, too, and then washed and bound the other wounds, salving the bruises with ointments, and laying green poultices on the places where the skin was split. The hideous wound on his face he repaired as best he could. As the sun rose on the following day Edward sank down on his knees and prayed, offering up the work he had done, beseeching the Great Physician to make it good, to bring healing where his own skill fell short.

They thought Peregrine might die. By the mercy of God his skull and his back were not broken, but the men who had beaten him had left him for dead. However, he did not die, though for a long time he lay without motion or speech, unable to open his eyes. Brother Edward and Brother John took turns to watch him night and day, and Father Chad took up the responsibilities of abbot once again.

That first day, they began by dripping water through his lips from a soaked cloth. Then after two days, as the bruises began to subside a little, they were able to feed him broth and honeyed wine; slowly, slowly dribbling it in through the split, swollen mouth. It was impossible to say if he was in his senses or not, for he made no response to them at all. All the same, they talked to him gently and reassuringly, explaining what was happening to him, words of comfort and love. He was able to swallow most of the soup and wine they fed him, which Brother Edward saw as a sign of hope, but he did not speak to them for three days. By this time the swelling had eased, and his face was recognisable as his, in spite of the bruises and the gash down the right side. Brother Edward was fearful he might have suffered some internal injury, for there was bruising on his belly and back, but though he saw some blood in his water the first day or two, he seemed to have sustained remarkably little damage. They did not attempt to lift him to relieve himself, and he had to be cleaned like a baby.

They had just finished washing him on the Thursday morning, the third day they had been nursing him, when he spoke to them for the first time. He said, 'Thank you.'

Like the other brothers, Brother Edward had respected—but had no especial affection for—their austere, uncompromising abbot, despite his blood-relationship. But nursing that battered body and fighting for him in intercession, he had come to care passionately what became of him. Day and night, he and Brother John had taken turns to watch over the suffering man.

A flood of relief and joy and love welled up in Edward as he raised his head and met Peregrine's eyes, which were open at last. He saw the look in those eyes change from a bleak gaze of hopeless pain to wonder at his own face so full of love and relief. Compassion mingled with the relief as Edward saw that the man was astonished to find himself loved. He always remembered the amazement in Peregrine's eyes as the abbot found the love he had never inspired, never won, now given him as a gift in the midst of his helplessness and pain.

In the end, it was that love which pulled him through the horror of what had happened to him, and of his helplessness. His proud, independent soul writhed at the humiliation of being fed and cleaned like a baby and recoiled from the prospect of facing life with maimed hands and a useless leg. He spoke little, and complained not at all. 'Thank you,' were the words most often on his lips.

Though he seemed calm and self-possessed, Edward, knowing him from childhood, guessed at the howling terror inside, and would sit and say the Office with him and talk to him about the comings and goings of the abbey. He sat quietly beside him at night, too, when Peregrine slept restlessly, sometimes starting awake with a sob of fear. Beyond that, Edward felt powerless to help him, did not know how to reach through his abbot's reserve to the terror inside, and comfort him.

As soon as he was able to eat, they propped him up to feed him, but he still couldn't feed himself because his hands were splinted and bound.

Brother Edward asked him if he knew why he had been so savagely attacked, and he said yes, he knew. The words came painfully.

'Many years ago now, there was one Will Godricson, who worked on my father's estate. You probably won't remember him, Edward; you were with the Franciscans by then. He killed a man in a drunken brawl. My father handed him over to justice, and he was hanged. He was a violent man to the point of insanity, and they could scarcely hold him on the day he was taken away. They bound him, in the end, bound him with his hands behind his back, his feet together and his knees drawn up to his chin. His two young sons were standing there watching; poor, scared ragamuffins, exposed to it all. They were brought up in violence, and they pledged themselves to vengeance on my father for their father's life. They never found a way to carry it out on him; you know him, well guarded and well armed, he always carried a dagger and knew how to use it. But it must have come to their ears eventually that a son of that household lived here, accessible to visitors and without defence. I suppose they came with the crowd and waited their moment.

'I had been into the sacristy in search of Father Matthew; but not finding him there, I came out through the Lady chapel, where they were waiting for me. They must have followed me into the church. They approached me, and I greeted them. They seemed vaguely familiar, though it was dusk, and they were but children when I saw them last. They had the look of their father. One of them carried a club, which seemed strange, but then visitors departing on a journey need some defence in the moors and wild places. They ... they said ....' He stopped, his voice unsteady, bit his lip and continued, 'I ... they. ...' But his voice died to a whisper, and he closed his eyes and shook his head.

Edward laid a gentling hand on his arm, 'No, no, lad, no need. Your body tells its own story.' And beyond that, the tale was never told.

The day came when he was mended as well as he ever would be, and ready to take up his responsibilities as abbot of the monastery again. The collar-bone and ribs had knitted nicely, but the leg was stiff and crooked for ever, and as Edward had predicted, the shin-bone was too damaged to take his weight, so that ever afterwards he used a crutch to get about. It had to be a crutch, and not a stick, because in spite of Brother Edward's best efforts, Father Peregrine's hands were misshapen and twisted. He had stretched them out to defend himself against the club, and to save himself as he was knocked to the ground, and in their cruel, insane vengeance, his attackers had stamped on them in their heavy labourers' clogs: not once, but again and again and again.

The brothers were unsure how to behave towards him when first he came among them again. It was as though their abbot had been taken away, and this was another man. Used to the imperious, aristocratic, decisive figure they had known, with his swift, purposeful stride and his hands gesturing impatience, they were appalled by the look of him. He had grown very thin, his face disfigured by the livid scar, his eyes shadowed with pain. His hands were good for almost nothing now, and although he did not try to conceal them, he no longer moved them as he talked, but kept them still. He went every day to the infirmary, at Brother Edward's insistence, so that Edward might massage the broken hands with his healing aromatic oils, and help him exercise them. Yet though he could feed himself, albeit slowly and with difficulty, and write, though laboriously and untidily, he would never again work on fine manuscript illumination, or sit late at night writing essays, sermons and poems. He could not even cut up his food or fasten his own sandals, and the hands tended to cramp into claws if Brother Edward left off his care of them for any length of time.

Peregrine's progress about the place was slow, lame and awkward, painful to watch. There were those who wondered if a man so broken would be fit to continue as abbot of a monastery, but they bided their time and gave him his chance. They found him changed in other ways, too. The old arrogance and self-assurance had been knocked out of him, and he was humbly grateful for the help his brothers gave him to turn pages and cut food. The constant need for help in everyday things brought him closer to the brothers, and the quietly spoken 'Thank you, brother', with an appreciative smile, were what they had gained in exchange for the imposing figure they had lost. Uncle Edward said that few of the brothers guessed just what it cost Peregrine to come among them again, disfigured and clumsy and slow.

Brother Thomas was one of those few. He had helped to carry Father Peregrine to the infirmary that Easter Monday night, and then wandered away to sit on his own in his cell, no longer needed in the infirmary, but with no stomach for company. Every time he closed his eyes, he saw the limp body, beaten almost senseless, broken and bloodied. Every time he opened his eyes, he saw the tortured man hanging on the crucifix on the wall of his cell. He couldn't decide which was worse. In the end he sat staring at the floor until the bell rang for Compline, when he rose automatically to his feet and went down to the chapel. He sat through the Office in a daze, and was glad of the shelter of the Great Silence as he walked numbly back to his cell afterwards.

Late, late that night as he lay awake on his lumpy bed, unable to sleep, he could not expunge from his mind the sight of those hands: destroyed, hopelessly mangled, swollen, bleeding, lacerated. He felt sick at the memory. He stared into the darkness, thinking of the cool self-possession of the man, the resolute, intelligent face, the eyes with their almost fanatical intensity, the proud bearing of him; but above all he thought of those quick, impatient, clever hands—oh, smashed. The brutality chilled him.

Even that memory failed to prepare Brother Thomas for the change in Father Peregrine when he came back into the community again; the painful toil of his progress about the abbey, the way his ironic superiority had been snuffed out as if it had never been. Most of all Brother Thomas looked in horror and pity at the silenced hands, scarred and twisted, which Father Peregrine did not attempt to hide, but which no longer spoke in gesture and impatience as he talked. They were still now, bearing their own mute testimony to his suffering.

'How can he bear it?' said Brother Thomas to Brother Francis, his friend in the novitiate, as they went in to the chapter house together, on the last day of April, the day Father Peregrine officially took up the duties of the abbacy again. 'How can he bear it?'

Brother Francis shrugged his shoulders. 'It is for him as it would be for you or me, Tom. He probably thinks he can't bear it, but what else can he do?'

One of the first and worst hurdles for Father Peregrine coming back among the brethren again was presiding over the community chapter meeting, held in the morning every day in the chapter house after Mass, when a chapter of St Benedict's Rule was read, and the abbot gave an address to the brothers, and the affairs of the community were discussed. Easter Day had fallen early, on the twenty-sixth of March that year, and it was on the thirtieth day of April that Abbot Peregrine took his place for the first time in the chapter house again, to preside over the meeting of the brethren.

The reader that morning was Brother Giles, assistant to Brother Walafrid the herbalist, and he read in his broad Yorkshire accent chapter seventy-two of the Rule, the chapter set for that day.

'Just as there is an evil zeal of bitterness which separates from God and leads to hell, so there is a good zeal which separates from evil and leads to God and life everlasting,' he began, confidently. 'Let monks, therefore, exercise this zeal with the most fervent love. Let them, that is, give one another precedence. Let them bear ...' Brother Giles' voice faltered, and he flushed with embarrassment. 'Let them bear with the greatest patience one another's infirmities —' he gulped, and hurried on, 'whether of body or character. Let them vie in paying obedience one to another. Let none follow what seems good for himself, but rather what is good for another. Let them practise fraternal charity with a pure love. Let them fear God. Let them ... let ... let ... let them love their abbot with a sincere and humble affection.'

Brother Giles cleared his throat and finished hastily, 'Let them prefer nothing whatever to Christ. And may he bring us all alike to life everlasting.' He sat down in confusion.

Abbot Peregrine sat with head bowed, dreading their gaze on him. Then he lifted his face, with the stark, hungry bones, the savage scar and missing teeth and dark, hollow eyes. 'The sacred text in this morning's chapter is from St Paul's letter to the Romans,' he said, "Give one another precedence". That is to say, treat one another with the deepest respect. ...' He himself hardly knew what he was saying, but he managed to speak to them calmly and lucidly for ten minutes and conduct the business of the meeting. The first hurdle was past.

The next thing to face was his pastoral work with the brothers. Peregrine was worried about his novices. Although he trusted his novice master to guide and discipline them, he knew they needed the opportunity to talk things over with their abbot, too. They had had to make shift without it long enough.

Brother Thomas was asked that morning after chapter to come to the abbot's lodging for his routine conference, to review his progress and consider his vocation. It was the first conversation Brother Tom had had alone with his abbot since the night before he had made his novitiate vows two weeks before Easter, and he found it hard to conceal his shock at the change in Father Peregrine. Those dark, penetrating eyes had never looked at him like that before; not with remote amusement, nor yet probing and challenging, but with ... Brother Thomas searched for a word, and could only come up with ... 'gentleness'. The abbot was still straight and authoritative in his bearing, still shrewd in his appraising look, still very much in charge: but the look of him was quite different.

'Grief,' Brother Tom thought. 'It's grief. The man's full of it.' Father Peregrine had been asking him a question, but he had not been listening, and now he blurted out, 'Father, I was there, the night they found you. I can't forget it. I'm so sorry, Father—about your hands. I don't know how you can bear it. Is there any way I can help?'

The abbot looked at him for a moment without speaking, and Brother Tom felt uncomfortable, and wished he had had the sense to keep quiet.

'Thank you for your concern, my son,' said Father Peregrine, evenly. 'You might remember me in your prayers. Sometimes—there are times when I hardly know myself how to bear it. But that is not what we were discussing. I asked you, if you recall, whether things are going well for you, or if you have any difficulty.'

As Brother Tom's father had predicted, the monastic life did not come easily to him. The worst of it was the food; not that the food was bad, but oh, so little of it!

Father Peregrine listened with sympathy to Brother Tom's small and natural difficulties. He liked this straightforward young man, liked his zest for life and his candid way of speaking. It steadied him to concentrate on something other than the horrors that haunted his memory and the nightmare of his helplessness.

When their conversation was finished and Brother Tom left, Father Peregrine sat thinking about him for a moment. 'That young man could save my sanity still,' he said to himself. 'Everything that is whole and healthy and good is there in him.'

Brother Tom, on the other hand, felt unhappy. Leaving the abbot's house, he had a sudden memory of his mother carrying a full basin of milk to the dairy, full almost to the brim, moving with infinite steadiness and care lest she slop it over.

'That's it,' he thought, 'he's like that. He's so full of grief that he daren't relax in case it overflows. He's the abbot. He's all on his own. Oh, God help him, poor soul.'

Brother Tom thought about it through the midday office of Sext and through the midday meal. After the meal, as he was leaving the refectory on his way to work in the vegetable garden, he was still thinking about it when he was hailed by Brother Cyprian, the porter.

'Brother! I've some letters in t' lodge for Father Abbot. I'd thank thee if tha'd spare my old bones and fetch them over to him. Will tha do it for me?'

'Gladly, Brother,' said Tom cheerfully, and walked back to the porter's lodge with old Brother Cyprian, suiting his steps to the old man's slow pace. At the porter's lodge, he stayed talking an hour or more with Brother Cyprian, who had an inexhaustible fund of stories about monks past and present, and seemed to know the history of every brother in the abbey. He was careful in his talk, giving away nothing that could embarrass or damage, but that still left him plenty. Blithely indifferent to the passing of time and to the rule forbidding unnecessary conversation, he would have gone on all afternoon, but eventually Tom's conscience could no longer ignore the fact that he was at this moment supposed to be working in the vegetable garden, and he picked up the abbot's letters and stood up to go.

'Aye, good lad, thanks for that. Th'art going by that way aren't tha?'

'I am,' said Tom, with a smile. He was now. He'd been going in the opposite direction in the first place. He took the letters, bade farewell to Brother Cyprian and strolled back across the courtyard, through the refectory and across the cloister to the abbot's house. He hesitated a moment, but the door was ajar, and he knocked shyly, then pushed it open and stepped inside.

Across the room, Father Peregrine was seated at his table, evidently engaged in study, for he had an untidy pile of manuscripts spread on the great oak table in front of him. He was not looking at them, though, nor did he see Brother Tom come in. He was sitting hunched over his table, gazing dully at nothing in particular, sitting very still, except that he was repeating one slow gesture. He was wiping the side of his scarred hand slowly across his mouth, like a little child that wipes away the crumbs of food before he runs out to play, or the old man whose frail and shaky hand wipes away the dribble of saliva from the sunken lips of his toothless mouth.

It could have been absentmindedness, could have been the unconscious gesture of a man deep in thought. But watching, Tom realised (and the realisation wrung him) that the slow, repeated movement, the slight frown, the gazing but unseeing eyes—all were nothing to do with being lost in thought or absent dreaming. The man was tortured by unbearable misery; at last he let his hand drop, and laid his face down upon it, not weeping, hardly even breathing, just tensely, despairingly still.

Brother Tom felt ashamed that his response was a strange, unreasonable resentment. His discomfort crystallised into a prayer, 'Oh God, what do I do now?'

He felt awkward about being there, witnessing the misery that lay behind his abbot's dignified and un-ruffled composure. He wanted to slip away but could not ignore the question that whispered inside: 'If it was me? If it was me—could I face it alone?' And yet he was afraid to intrude. As quietly as he could, he stole across the room, put the letters down on the pile of books, and sat down on the stool that stood before the table, facing the motionless man. He waited a moment, leaned his elbow on the table, leaned his chin on his hand. He wanted to touch him, but dared not; wanted to help him weep, but had no idea how to.

In the end, though, he could no longer concentrate on his own apprehension and self-consciousness. Instinct got the better of him, and reaching out his hand he laid it on the other man's arm without even thinking.

Father Peregrine lifted his head and looked at him. For a minute, his eyes were bewildered, unfocused in the scarred and haggard face. His lips worked a little, but no sound emerged, like a man who has forgotten how to speak.

Then, with a sigh, he smiled, and looked with attention at Brother Tom. 'I do beg your pardon, Brother,' he said quietly, in a most normal, level tone, 'I was not aware of you. Can I help?'

Tom was dumbfounded.

'I doubt it,' he said at last, bluntly. 'Not in the state you're in.'

Father Peregrine just looked at him, opened his mouth to speak, but closed it again, shook his head, shrugged his shoulders and said nothing.

Again the picture flashed in Tom's mind of his mother carrying the bowl of milk, carefully, oh so carefully. 'One jog and he'll spill the lot,' he thought, 'and by my faith he needs to spill that grief.'

'Maybe, if you could tell me, Father . . . well, perhaps I could help?' ventured Tom, unsure, feeling irritated at his own uneasiness in the face of the desolation his superior was struggling to master.

'Son, it is good of you to ask,' he said eventually. 'But my burdens are not for you to carry.' His voice was a little uneven, and the tension of maintaining his self-control was causing him to shake slightly.'My son, forgive my discourtesy. Unless your errand is urgent, might we discuss it some other time?'

Half of Brother Tom wanted to say, 'Of course, Father, I quite understand,' and beat a hasty retreat. He never knew where the other half got the courage from, but he replied, 'To be honest with you, I've forgotten why I came. But I know why I'm not going.'

Without giving himself time to think better of it, he followed his impulse, and leaping to his feet dragged the heavy table askew so that he could approach his abbot—who watched him, wide-eyed, white-faced and, Tom realised with a stab of pity, scared. Brother Tom seized the stool, placed it emphatically beside his superior's chair, and sitting on it, took the man in his arms and held him close. 'It's all right,' he said gently, 'you can let it go.' He cursed himself for a fool as he felt the awful rigidity of him, like a man of wood; but he persisted, holding him, not speaking, his thoughts racing. 'Oh well, might as well be hung for a sheep as for a lamb. Faith, I wish I'd shut the door. I hope to God nobody walks in on this. Maybe I should go now. ...'

But as Brother Tom held him and the fortress of his iron self-control was replaced at last, at last, by the fortress of the arms of someone who loved him more than he went in awe of him, Peregrine began to weep, and wept until he lost all self-control and abandoned himself to sobbing grief. 'My hands ...' he wept, the words barely intelligible, 'Oh, God, how shall I bear the loss of my hands? To have died would have been nothing ... oh, but my hands ... oh ... oh God. ...' and the words were lost in uncontrollable tears.

What comfort could Brother Tom bring but his presence and his silence and his holding him?

The bell for None began to ring, and the monotony of the bell's clang, which normally spoke peace to Tom, suddenly infuriated him. The Office? What insane futility! When a man has lost his skills, his independence and all his sense of dignity, must the afternoon Office intrude on his grieving?

But Peregrine lifted himself away from Tom's embrace, and sat for a moment, shaken, his breath coming unsteadily still. He dug in his pocket for his handkerchief, and shakily wiped his eyes and blew his nose. 'Unless I am mistaken, my son, that is the bell for None. My lateness may reasonably be excused without explanation, but I doubt if yours will. Perhaps you would spare me that disclosure and be there in good time.'

That was the nearest he would stoop to begging Tom not to tell anyone, but Tom understood well enough, and he never did tell anyone until after Peregrine's death.

Brother Tom nodded soberly and, replacing his stool, dragged the table back into position.

'Brother Thomas.' The abbot's quiet voice arrested

him as he reached the door. 'Thank you. From my heart, Brother, thank you.'

This small incident remained a living bond between the two men ever afterward, and kindled in Brother Tom a deep protective love for his abbot. As for the rest of the brothers, Father Peregrine bore their curious glances without a word, and their pity too, and knew very well their doubts as to his fitness to rule them any longer.

In the end, though, it became apparent to all the community that he had a new authority about him now. For whereas before he had ruled with a natural strength and ability over other men, now he was learning to cling to the grace of God and find his strength there. He had commanded their respect before, and it had been based on the fear of his power over them. He earned their respect in a new way now, respect mingled with admiration and love, because he had found out for himself what it was to be weak—weak enough to need his brothers' help—and his authority over them now was born of humble understanding.

Great-uncle Edward had many tales to tell of Father Peregrine, after the terrible thing that happened to him. Uncle Edward said it crippled his body, but it set his spirit free. He said that most men would have become bitter and closed in, but Peregrine did not. He used his own weakness as a bridge to cross over to his brothers, when they too were weak. Having lost everything, he gave his weakness to God, and it became his strength.

In a way, all the tales are one tale, the tale of how God's power is found in weakness. But that is the story of the whole of life, if you know how to read it right.

Mother sat for a while in silence. The candle had burned low, and the room was very quiet.

'Are you asleep, Melissa?' she said then.

'No. I was thinking about Tom. He was brave, wasn't he?'

'Mmm, yes. Yes, he couldn't be sure how it would turn out.'

'And his name—Father Columba, I mean. He did get gentle, like a dove.'

'Yes, it was a good name after all. Everyone still called him Father Peregrine, though, and he could still be pretty fierce and tough, when he needed to be. The difference was, now they weren't too scared to call him it to his face.'

Mother said in the morning she was sorry she ever started to tell me about Abbot Peregrine, because that night I woke the whole family, screaming and struggling in my sleep, terrified by nightmares of those grim vengeful thugs, stamping with indifferent cruelty on the fine, scholarly hands, flung out in helplessness on the stone chapel floor.

III
HUMBLE PIE

It was one of those hot, stifling days in late June, and the classroom was stuffy. One lazy fly buzzed monotonously, occasionally colliding with the windowpane. I looked at the fly, and at the window, and my gaze was drawn outside to the school buildings and the field beyond, where there was a row of poplar trees, graceful and slender, their topmost branches stirring even on that still day.

The teacher was writing on the blackboard, the chalk stabbing and scraping industriously. *'Tenir'*, she wrote, and *'Venir'*. She underlined them heavily, and pushed her glasses more firmly onto the bridge of her nose as she fixed us with her severe glance.

'The compounds of *tenir* and *venir* form the past historic similarly. The same applies of course to *retenir, revenir*, and so on.' She whipped round again and attacked the blackboard with the chalk once more, writing *'je tins, tu tins, il tint . . .'*

I could see the sickroom through the window, across the tennis court. I had been in there twice. It was white and bare with a calendar on the wall, and a picture of the Queen Mother. I tried to imagine the infirmary at the monastery of St. Alcuin. Perhaps its walls were built of big blocks of honey-coloured stone. The rooms would be smaller than elsewhere in the abbey, to allow for a sick man to lie alone in peace . . . in peace or in pain and fear. But Great-uncle Edward had not left Peregrine alone with his pain and his fear. He had understood, and stayed with him, talking to him gently, helping him through the worst of the horror. And then Brother Tom, greatly daring, giving him a safe place to cry. I found it easy, in my mind, to wander in the infirmary, to see the brothers bending over the sick man, caring for him: but the other ... I felt a strange shyness as I imagined that reserved, solitary man, racked with his grief, in the arms of the young brother. It seemed too intimate, too raw a thing even to think about, as though I should glimpse it with reverence, then tiptoe away ...

'Melissa, did you hear me? Are you listening at all?'

I looked, bewildered, at the teacher, my mouth slightly ajar, and struggled to adjust my blank expression to something more intelligent-looking. She took off her glasses, the better to glare at me.

'*Vint à passer,*' snapped Mrs Kerr. '*Un facteur vint à passer.*' *Vint?* I looked at the blackboard. From *venir. Un facteur?* What the dickens was that? *Un facteur* came to pass. Crumbs.

'I beg your pardon, Mrs Kerr, I can't remember what *un facteur* means.'

'*Un facteur,*' said Mrs Kerr, her black eyes glittering at me like little jet beads, 'is a postman.'

A postman. A postman came to pass. 'Please, God,' I begged, silently. I could feel the palms of my hands sweating. 'I don't know,' I said helplessly, at last.

'Melissa, you have not been paying the slightest attention to this lesson. I have just explained at some length, that when followed by an infinitive, the verb *venir à* takes the meaning "happen to". *Un facteur vint à passer* uses the past historic of *venir à,* and demonstrates this use of the verb. It means "a postman happened to pass". Now that I have explained to you what we were all concentrating on perhaps you would like to tell us what you were thinking about?'

'I ... I was imagining the infirmary, in a monastery long ago ... what it would be like,' I mumbled.

Mrs Kerr was waiting. She seemed to expect something more of me. 'It was a story,' I explained, 'about a monk who was terribly hurt and crying and the other monk loved him and comforted him.' I couldn't think of anything else to say.

She looked at me with her little black eyes. Like currants looking out of a bun, I thought.

'You must learn to apply your mind to the subject before you, Melissa. You will not learn by dreaming, or by reading sentimental novels. You will learn only if you work.' She settled her glasses back on her nose and seized the text book.

'Turn to page 131 please, girls. I want you to look at section B, which deals with the omission of the definite article in the expression *plus ... plus ...*; the more, the more as in *Plus je travaille, plus j'apprends.*'

I looked at the teacher, then down at my book. The page in front of me was full of words, but empty of meaning. Sentimental? Is that what sentimental is? When for once, instead of looking the other way, someone dares to stretch out a timid hand to comfort and to heal? I thought about Mother. She didn't seem a sentimental person. Tough as old boots, Daddy said: but she had told me the story. With that same feeling of shyness, I approached the picture in my mind again ... the heat and indignity of giving yourself up to sobbing in someone's arms, someone you didn't know very well, with your nose running and your face bathed in sweat and tears, trusting because you had to, because you couldn't carry it alone any more. ... Is it sentimental to speak about that sort of thing? Was Mrs Kerr right? I looked up at her pale, tight-lipped face and considered her rigid, ramrod-straight, thin body, buttoned up to the neck in a suit of hard, grey fabric. Perhaps it was Mrs Kerr who ... maybe no one ever ... did she sometimes—like me—bury her face in the pillow at night and cry for sheer sadness at the loneliness of it all?

'Melissa!' thundered Mrs Kerr.

By the grace and mercy of God, the bell rang.

As soon as the school day ended, I ran like the wind up the hill to the gates of the county primary school where Mary and Beth went to school. Although their day finished ten minutes before ours, the two schools were so close that if I ran, I would be in time to find Mother and Cecily, waiting at the top of the hill with the other mothers.

Halfway up the hill, I paused and shaded my eyes with my hand against the bright afternoon sun. Yes, she was still there, with Cecily and Mary and Beth milling around her. She was listening to their urgent chatter. I ran up to the top, dodging through the last straggle of mothers and children coming away from the gates.

'Hello, Cecily!' I shouted. She ran to me, and I scooped her up in my arms. Her belligerent little face dimpled with delight, and she patted my face with her grubby fingers.

'Had a good day?' asked Mother, as we set off slowly homewards.

'No. Awful,' I said. 'I couldn't concentrate on anything. I've been in trouble all day. What's for tea?'

'Baked potatoes and cheese,' said Mother. 'Why couldn't you concentrate?'

'I was trying to imagine Father Peregrine, and the infirmary, and Brother Tom. I was trying to picture them in my mind.'

'Mummy we've learned a new song!' said Beth. 'It's about water, and I can do all the first bit. Listen!'

She launched into her song, and then Cecily wanted us to listen to her sing a song, too, and then Therese overtook us as we turned in at the gate.

Therese was sixteen, pink, and plump and gentle, with her fall of brown hair like Mother's, but light blue eyes full of laughter like Daddy's. She went into the kitchen and put the kettle on.

Home, I was home. The smell of it, the peace of it! Although it was so small, and we were so many, somehow our house was like a bowl of quietness and light. As I crossed its threshold, I relaxed with a huge sigh, and the world of school dropped from me like a cloak.

The kitchen was filled with a wonderful aroma of baked potato. Therese pushed a mug of tea into my hand as I came in. Home. It closed about me like wings folding around me. Therese gave me a thick slice of bread and jam. I sat down at the kitchen table, utterly content.

'In trouble all day, you said?' Mother's voice broke in on my contentment, as she came into the kitchen. 'Thank you, Therese,' she said as she took her cup of tea. 'And nightmares last night. I think we'll have to have a different story tonight.'

'Mother, no!' I protested. 'You don't mean it? I will concentrate at school, I promise. I've been waiting all day for the story!'

'I think, maybe,' said Mother slowly, 'once you know more about Father Peregrine, you might actually work better at school. You certainly won't have any more nightmares. But listen, my dear, if I find your work suffers as a result of these stories, then no more. You must learn to keep your imagination separate, a walled garden with a little green door to go in by. Go in through the door in your lunch hour and in the evening, but when it's lesson time, you come out of the garden and you shut the door and turn your back on it. Understood?'

'Mother, I promise,' I said.

After tea, Daddy came home, and played the piano and sang to us until bath-time. Then he retreated behind a book with a mug of beer and a cheese sandwich while Therese and I got out our homework. In my mind I closed the little green door firmly, and worked single-mindedly on my maths homework for half an hour. As the little procession of clean, pink children came out of the bathroom, I slammed the book shut. 'Finished! And nothing else to do!'

The little ones went in to kiss Daddy goodnight, and then I followed them upstairs to the bedroom. They had to have their prayers first, and their game. Mary and Beth sat down on their beds while Mother drew the curtains and lit the candle. They prayed the Lord's Prayer, and Mother blessed them, and then it was time for the game.

'What does the elephant say?' asked Mother.

'Triumph! Triumph!' they shouted, brandishing their arms as trunks and stamping around the bedroom.

'And what is the only thing an elephant is afraid of?' she said.

'A mousie!' they cried, all together.

'And what does the mousie say?'

'Weakness! Weakness! Weakness!' they squeaked, scrabbling about with tiny steps and twitching noses, their hands gathered up like little claws. It was Cecily's game really, but Mary and Beth loved to join in.

'So who is the stronger, the elephant or the mousie?' Mother asked.

'The mousie!' they shouted again.

'And the elephant trumpets triumph, but the mousie says—'

'Weakness! Weakness! Weakness!' until they fell about laughing. Nearly every night they played this game. Mother said they needed to learn while they were still young that the two words belonged together.

'Go on with the story, Mother!' I begged; but she would not, not until the last elephant had trumpeted its triumph and the last mouse had pleaded its weakness and lay quiet in its bed.

Then Mother sat for a moment in her chair, little Cecily curled up on her lap with her head cradled in the crook of Mother's arm.

Beth yawned a huge yawn.

'Very well,' said Mother, 'your story. There was a story that became a legend in the abbey of St Alcuin; and Uncle Edward's great-niece, to whom these stories were first told, never tired of hearing this story, which came to be known as "Humble Pie".'

Father Matthew, the novice master, was notorious for his strictness. All the little faults and misdemeanours that most men would have turned a blind eye to, he pounced on like a cat on a mouse, and kept strict discipline and expected high standards among the novices in his charge. Brother Michael had just recently made his solemn vows, leaving in the novitiate Brother Francis, Brother Thomas, Brother Theodore, Brother Cormac and Brother Thaddeus. Of them all it was Brother Theodore who was most often in disgrace, but it should really have been Brother Thomas and Brother Francis, because they were always getting into scrapes and were inclined towards practical jokes and light, foolish conversation. Father Matthew had twice that week found them helpless with laughter over some silly tale, and had set them to tasks which kept them occupied at opposite ends of the abbey, in the hope of calming them down a bit.

Now this Brother Thomas, the same who had held the abbot in his arms and comforted his grief, was a big lad and everlastingly hungry. Sleepless with hunger one night, he had crept out of the dormitory, stolen down to the kitchen, and spirited away from the larder an apple pie, which he devoured with great speed, sitting on the stairs. He licked every crumb from his fingers, sighed happily, and crept back to his bed undetected. Tom did not believe he would ever get used to the meagre provision of a monastery table. The stories handed down to us paint a picture of monks eating and drinking like gluttons, but it was not true in that abbey, at any rate. Even the cook was thin and sour—but more of him later.

Brother Tom told Brother Francis about it as they ate their hunk of bread after morning Office, which turned out to be a foolish indiscretion, because Brother Francis told Brother Thaddeus during the time set aside for private reading and meditation after breakfast. He was unfortunately overheard by Father Matthew, who rebuked him for indulging in idle gossip and assured him this would not be the end of it.

Brother Thaddeus, on the way out of Terce, the mid-morning Office, warned Brother Tom that Father Matthew had been apprised of his misdoings, and like most men with a guilty conscience, Tom looked round for someone else to blame.

The monastic life is hard enough, you would think, but in those days it was dreadful! Discipline was strict, especially under the likes of Father Matthew! Every little fault or sin or accident was taken seriously, and must be confessed to teach the monk humility. It was not enough, either, just to say 'Sorry!' as you or I might. Not likely! The Rule of St Benedict, which was the rule by which the Benedictine monks lived, stipulated that any brother who had to be corrected for a fault, or who was in trouble with his superior had to prostrate himself on the ground at his superior's feet, and stay there until he blessed him and gave him permission to get up.

Father Gregory, the previous abbot, while agreeing with the principles that lay behind this practice, nevertheless saw that it could create problems, he himself having once tripped over the feet of a prostrate brother in passing. He therefore modified the rule slightly, and in his abbey, the practice was that any of the brothers who committed a fault, or otherwise gave offence, should kneel before the one he had offended, saying, 'I humbly confess my fault of speaking during the Great Silence' (or whatever it was he'd done wrong), 'and I ask forgiveness of you, my brother, and of God.' Father Gregory was quite firm that the offended party should not hang about, keeping the miscreant on his knees, but should respond at once, 'God forgives you, Brother, and so do I,' which blessing would be the end of the matter, and life could go on as normal. This seemed a humiliating, almost unbearable procedure to the young men who were new to monastic life, and it wasn't supposed to be easy, but it was a quick way to learn to be humble!

But worst of all, anyone who had done something wrong was supposed to kneel before the whole community and confess it, either before lunch when the brothers had said grace, or at the beginning of community chapter, before the reading of the Rule and the abbot's talk. Poor Brother Tom knew well enough that Father Matthew would have him on his knees before the whole community, confessing to sneaking a pie at midnight, and he was after Brother Francis' blood for giving him away.

At this hour of the day, which was about ten o'clock in the morning, the brothers were supposed to be about their daily tasks, but instead of heading for the vegetable garden, which was his present place of work, Brother Tom set off hastily to intercept Brother Francis on his way to the scriptorium, where the books for the library were copied and the illuminated manuscripts were painted. The work Brother Francis turned out was nothing special, but it was reasonably accurate, and it kept him away from Brother Tom, or at least it was supposed to.

Tom saw him on his way there, and the sight of Francis, walking slowly and peacefully along the deserted cloister with the air of a man who hadn't a care in the world, enraged him still further. Tom overtook him, grabbed him by the shoulder, and swung him round to face him with his back against the wall, in one violent movement.

'What have you done, you stupid blabbermouth?' he hissed. He would rather have roared like a mad bull, but his sense of self-preservation restrained him; he was in enough trouble already. He contented himself with glaring at Francis and demanding, 'Now what am I supposed to do?'

Francis' coolness was as much a habit with him as his black tunic, and he regarded Tom calmly, apparently unmoved by his red face and the quivers of rage that shook him. His eyes flickered momentarily, but he spoke with what struck Tom as heartless indifference: 'Do?' he said, 'Well, I suppose you'll have to confess it at chapter tomorrow morning.'

Tom could have hit him. He glared at him, speechless for a moment, and then spluttered, 'Fine friend you are, you big-mouthed toad! You don't care a bit, do you!'

Francis did actually care, but chose to pretend he didn't. That was the way with him. The more he cared, the more indifferent he pretended to be. The guilt and embarrassment that filled him because he had unwittingly betrayed his friend to Father Matthew he now concealed beneath a tone of defensive irritation. 'Well, it's your own fault, Brother! You shouldn't have done it. You didn't ask me to keep it a secret, did you?'

Tom launched into an indignant reply, ignoring Francis' sudden gesture intended to silence him, and warning, 'Ssh!'

'Don't "shush" me, man! I haven't ...'

'Shut *up*, Tom,' muttered Brother Francis. 'Father Abbot ...'

In spite of his distinctive gait, they had neither of them heard Father Peregrine before he saw them, and they stood helplessly as he approached. He looked at them, eyebrows raised in surprise. 'What is your dispute, brothers?'

Tom stared at him, dumbly. Francis, after a quick glance at his friend, spoke first. 'He ... I ... Father Matthew ...' he began, and then tailed off into silence, not wishing to be guilty of betraying his friend to the abbot, as well as the novice master.

This simple speech put Father Peregrine in the picture fairly well, but he thought he might as well have the details. 'Yes?' he said, looking from one to the other of them.

So poor Brother Tom had to tell what had happened, and wretchedly mumbled the whole story with downcast eyes, ending by explaining how Father Matthew had overheard it all as Brother Francis related the tale to Brother Thaddeus.

'Well, it was your own fault!' Francis burst out. 'If you lived for more than your belly you wouldn't be in this predicament.'

Tom's head shot up, and he opened his mouth to reply, but Father Peregrine silenced him. 'Enough of that,' he said. 'Brother Francis,' he continued calmly, 'it is my opinion that you owe Brother Thomas an apology for your rudeness and self-righteousness, as well as for gossiping about him. One man's sin is not an appropriate topic for another man's conversation.'

Francis looked at him for a moment and met that direct, fierce, hawk's eye, and without a word got down on to his knees before Brother Tom.

'I confess . . .' he said, 'I humbly confess my rudeness and self-righteousness, and my careless gossip, and I ask forgiveness, Brother, of you and of God.'

Tom couldn't bear this. He felt as though he was being choked. 'Oh, no, get up. Please!' he said, but Father Peregrine said, 'He has asked your forgiveness, Brother. Will you dismiss him so ungraciously?'

Tom had always found the experience of kneeling to ask forgiveness appalling. It had never occurred to him until this moment that it could be just as hard to forgive. The Rule made it clear that humble, heart-felt forgiveness was what was required, not just the form of words. For a moment, the thought of Father Matthew flashed through Brother Tom's mind again, as well as the prospect of kneeling before the community to confess his fault at community chapter, and he wasn't at all sure he forgave Brother Francis.

Francis, who could read his friend like a book, knew

the struggle going on inside him. He felt desperately ashamed of himself. 'I really am sorry, Tom,' he said in a small voice, and looked up intō his face with the disguise of indifference torn away.

Tom's heart went out to his friend. 'God forgives you, and so do I!' he said heartily, and Francis got thankfully to his feet. They looked at Father Peregrine, unsure whether they were free to go or not, and he smiled at them imperturbably.

'Now you, Brother Thomas, should go and find the cook, and confess your fault to him and ask his pardon.'

Brother Tom's jaw dropped. If there could be anything worse than confessing his sin before the community in the chapter meeting, this had to be it. The kitchen was possibly the busiest place in the abbey. Lay servants worked there, as well as two of the brothers, all presided over by Brother Andrew, a sour and irritable Scot, notorious for his impatient and sarcastic tongue. A monk would have the graciousness to pretend not to notice one of his brothers kneeling to a superior to confess a fault, but not the lay servants from the village. They regarded it as good entertainment.

'But ...' began the luckless Tom, then caught the abbot's eye and thought better of it.

His last hopes were dashed as Father Peregrine smiled at him and said, 'You can come and tell me what Brother Andrew says.'

There was no deferring until it was conveniently forgotten, then, or at least until after chapter in the morning, when Brother Andrew would already have heard his confession before the community. He swallowed hard.

'Yes, Father,' he said, and exchanged one desperate glance with Brother Francis before plodding away reluctantly to the kitchens.

'Thank you, Brother Francis. Don't let me detain you any further,' said Father Peregrine, and Francis took himself off to the scriptorium.

Peregrine then set off in search of Father Matthew and found him crossing the courtyard on his way to the gatehouse, with a bundle of letters for the porter.

'A word with you, Father Matthew,' he said pleasantly, and hesitated. Father Matthew was one of those men who had to be handled with care, for good results. 'I have just seen Brother Thomas and Brother Francis,' he continued carefully. 'They have confessed their faults to me of idle gossip and the theft of a pie, and I have given them their penance.' He wondered briefly if Father Matthew would have considered merely apologising to Brother Tom and apologising to the cook to be worthy of the name 'penance', but then, Father Matthew seemed extraordinarily unaware of what it cost them to do it. 'I do not wish to presume on your authority with the novices, Father Matthew, but I think it should not now be necessary for them to confess their faults at community chapter. I hope you approve of the line of action I have taken,' he said politely, well aware that Father Matthew had no choice but to approve.

'Yes, of course, Father. We will consider the matter closed, then?'

'I think so, Father,' said Peregrine. 'Thank you, that's all.'

Brother Tom found Brother Andrew in the frantically busy hour before lunch. Brother Andrew was vaguely aware of him as an obstacle in the congested pathways of his kitchen but took no notice of him for a moment, then nearly walked into him on his way back to the pantry with a huge cheese in his hands.

'Whatever is it you want, Brother?' he snapped.

Tom looked at him, but felt as if his tongue was stuck to the roof of his mouth, and just stood there clenching and unclenching his fists, as red as a beetroot.

'What in heaven's name ails you, man? Do you want anything or no? Can you not see how busy I am?' roared the old Scot.

'Father Abbot sent me,' whispered Tom huskily.

'Well?' said Brother Andrew, perplexed as well as irritated. 'Here, take this to the pantry; mind you wrap it well,' he said to a passing servant, handing over the cheese.

Tom fell to his knees before him, his hands clenched into fists, unable to look up. The old man's face softened, and a glimmer of amusement came into his eyes. He had noticed the absence of the pie as he went into the pantry this morning, and he guessed what this was all about. The bustle of the kitchen ceased as several pairs of curious eyes and ears gave their full attention to the scene.

'Brother, I humbly confess my fault. I . . . I came down here last night and stole a pie from the pantry and I . . . ask forgiveness of you and of God.'

Tom thought it was probably the worst moment of his life. The kitchen was utterly quiet. He felt a bony hand on his shoulder, and looked up into old Brother Andrew's eyes which were dancing with merriment.

'Brother, I esteem your courage,' he said. 'God forgives you, and so do I. Father Abbot is a very hard man.'

Tom got to his feet without a word, and stumbled out of the kitchen. Once through the door, he stood still, and took a deep breath. For the first time since eating the wretched pie, his heart felt as light as a bird. It was over.

He set off cheerfully for the vegetable garden, and turning the corner almost collided with Father Peregrine.

'I did it,' he said, exultantly.

'Did you? Well done. Let that be finished with, then, you need not confess your fault to the community,' said Peregrine, then stood there, eyeing Tom thoughtfully for a moment, as if there was something more he wanted to say. 'I was looking for you,' he said. 'What did Brother Andrew say?'

'He said he esteemed my courage,' said Tom shyly, 'and he forgave me.' He grinned at Father Peregrine. 'And he said Father Abbot is a very hard man!'

Peregrine continued to look at him thoughtfully, and Tom was just beginning to wonder if he'd said the wrong thing, when slowly, awkwardly, Peregrine knelt before him.

Tom was horrified. He knew it hurt badly for the abbot to bend that crippled leg and kneel—he didn't even kneel during the Office—and besides that, he was covered with embarrassment, anxious lest anyone should come round the corner and see his lord abbot kneeling before him.

'I humbly confess my fault, Brother,' said Father Peregrine. 'When I was a novice, twenty-five years ago, I, too, was hungry in the night, and, like you, I crept down to the kitchen, and I stole three pies, and I ate the lot. I was never found out, and to this day I've never owned up to anyone. I ask your forgiveness and God's for placing on your shoulders a burden I myself was unwilling to bear.'

Tom was utterly astonished. He could not even imagine this man as a novice, hungry, struggling with temptation and failing. All he wanted to say was, 'Oh, for heaven's sake, get *up*,' but he knew that was not what was required of him.

'God forgives you, and I forgive you, Father,' he said. 'Oh, please get up!' and he helped Father Peregrine to his feet again.

That was not the end of the story, though. That evening, in the hour before Compline when the novices had gathered in their community room in the novitiate to relax and converse, there was a knock on the door.

Opening it, Brother Cormac was confronted with Brother Michael, Brother Andrew's assistant in the kitchen, smiling at him and carrying a tray laden with pies, one for each of them, steaming and fragrant and delicious.

'Father Abbot sends these with his compliments,' he said. 'He asks me to say that he thought the novices might be hungry. Also he bids me tell you, the recipe is his own, and it is called Humble Pie. He says he has tasted some himself, today, and he finds it very nourishing.'

The candle guttered, and went out. It had burnt to the end. 'Goodnight,' whispered Mother. 'Come down for a hot drink, Melissa, if you want one,' and after laying the sleeping Cecily in her bed, and tucking the covers round her, she tiptoed out of the room.

IV
CLARE DE MONTANY

My eyes opened, and I lay still. All was quiet. I raised myself on one elbow. Mary and Beth had crept out of bed and gone to play, but Therese was still sleep, buried deep under her covers. Cecily was still asleep too, curled up with her cheek pillowed on her hand, her long, dark eyelashes resting on her soft pink cheek.

Cecily looked delightful when she was asleep. Her mouth was like a little rosebud, and her curls spread on the pillow. She was a picture of vulnerable innocence. No one could have guessed, looking at her now, what utter weariness my parents' faces wore after a morning of Cecily's company. Daddy said she was like a natural disaster, a mysterious act of God which we could only suffer patiently and pray for strength to endure. She was only two, but Mother said she felt as though she'd aged more in those two years than in all the other thirty-eight years of her life put together. From the moment those great, china-blue eyes opened in the morning, Cecily was in conflict with the world, fighting her way forward with a dauntless spirit, a will of iron and an earsplitting voice.

I lay down again cautiously. I did not want to wake her up. Today was Sunday, nearly the best part of the week. The best part was waking up on Saturday morning to the realisation that the whole weekend lay before me.

No school for two whole days. *Freedom.* But Sunday was quite good: half the weekend left, anyway. Any minute now the house would erupt into chaos as Daddy tried to get everyone ready for church, tried to find the little ones' socks and cardigans, tried to convince Mother that ten more minutes in bed was ten minutes too long, and finally lost his temper with everyone.

It was the same every Sunday. Our family would arrive at church, still slightly breathless, Mother looking deceptively serene and composed as she swept up the aisle in her voluminous skirt, finding the first hymn for the little ones just in time to sing the last verse. Nobody could have imagined, to look at her, the terrible virago of twenty minutes ago, whose eyes flashed fire and whose tongue lashed us all, who had snatched up a bellowing Cecily, slapped her hard, and dumped her unceremoniously into the car.

It was the same this Sunday. Mother took our hymnbooks from the sidesman at the door, flashing him her radiant and disarming smile, and then sailed up the aisle to our pew, with us children trailing behind her, and Daddy bringing up the rear with Cecily clinging round his neck, still hiccupping and sniffing, her tragic face peeping over his shoulder.

It is a curious thing how an hour in the swimming pool, or an hour in the theatre, is gone in five minutes, whereas an hour in church on a Sunday morning seems to drag on for eternity. The worst part of all was always Father Bennett's sermon. Never in the history of mankind had one man been able to make fifteen minutes seem so long, of that I was sure. Daddy said the trouble was he had nothing to say, but he loved saying it.

He stood up now in the pulpit and closed his eyes. Daddy gave Cecily a jelly-baby and a book about farm animals to keep her quiet.

'May the words of my mouth and the meditation of my heart be always acceptable in thy sight,' boomed Father Bennett, 'O Lord, my Redeemer and my Rock.'

He opened his eyes, and gripping the edge of the pulpit, looked down on us. "Simon, son of Jonah," he announced, taking his text from the reading we had just heard, "you are a happy man." He allowed his gaze to sweep slowly round the congregation. 'And why was he a happy man? *Not* because he was especially rich, because he was *not*. *Not* because he was especially well educated, because he was *not*. *Not* because he was especially important, because he was *not*. Yet our Lord said to him, "Simon, son of Jonah, *you*"' (here he stabbed his index finger forcefully at an imaginary figure standing a few feet in front of him, suspended in mid-air above the heads of the congregation) "—are a happy man."

I glanced at Mother. Her mouth was twitching slightly, but she sat upright in her seat, and her eyes did not waver from the preacher's face. I looked across at Daddy. He was smiling encouragingly at Cecily, slipping her another jelly-baby, a green one because that was her favourite, and silently mouthing 'Moo! Moo!' and 'Baa! Baa!' at her, as she showed him the pictures in her book.

Beth was looking at the pictures in the children's service book, and Mary was watching the little jewel-coloured pools of light that freckled the pew as the morning sunshine streamed through the stained-glass window. Therese was looking at the congregation with her eyes slightly crossed to see if she could see two of everybody.

I sighed. Father Bennett was well launched into his dissertation on the exact source of the happiness of Simon Bar-Jonah. I looked at the war-memorial plaque, with its painted relief of a golden sword stuck through a coiled red dragon, and read through all the names written there. Daddy had told me, when I was only seven, that the list of names referred to all those who had died in the services, and added that I need have no cause for anxiety since they had all been men.

I looked at the flowers, gladioli and carnations and

roses, that stood in front of the pulpit. They were quivering slightly from Father Bennett's emphatic thumps on the pulpit desk. I looked up at him with curiosity. He didn't mind kneeling down in the church service, to confess his sins to God. I tried to picture him kneeling in front of Daddy, saying, 'I humbly confess that I have bored you with tedious sermons, and made God seem very small and far away like looking through the wrong end of the binoculars.' I tried to imagine him kneeling before Stan Birkett, the dustman-a small, weary, disillusioned man-saying, 'I humbly confess that you wanted me to be your friend, but I would only be your vicar. ...' No, it didn't fit. And yet, he didn't mind kneeling down to God. Unless ... perhaps he wasn't sure God was there at all?

Just now he was beaming at his congregation with a confident smile, saying: '... and assuredly, as we confess the divinity and supremacy of our blessed Lord, we too can rejoice in his promise of blessedness, and lay hold of that coveted commendation, "Simon, son of Jonah, *you* are a happy man!" In the name of the Father and of the Son and of the Holy Spirit, Amen; Hymn 452, "Oh Happy band of pilgrims, if onward ye will tread". Hymn 452.'

'We are a happy lot this morning,' murmured Mother cynically, as she picked up her book. The congregation sang boisterously: the hymn following the sermon always had the holiday air of young cows let out to frolic in the grass after a long winter spent cooped up in a barn. We roared the words:

> The trials that beset you,
> The sorrows ye endure,
> The manifold temptations
> That death alone can cure—
>
> What are they but his jewels
> Of right celestial worth?
> What are they but the ladder,
> Set up to heaven on earth?

Mother looked down at me and smiled. 'Peregrine,' she said softly, and I smiled back; but at the time, I didn't understand what she meant.

Then came the long, long prayers. Pages and pages of them. Cecily never made it through to Communion but always had to be taken out at some point, because she insisted on banging her foot loudly on the pew, or imitating the cries of the seagulls outside. This morning, she was removed halfway through the prayers of intercession, hysterical with rage because the last green jellybaby had gone. If I listened carefully, I could hear Daddy playing 'to market, to market to buy a fat pig' with her, outside in the porch, but I forced myself to concentrate as Father Bennett's voice droned on.

'This is my body, which is given for you,' he intoned. I wrestled with the thought. How could he speak about it like that? What had it to do with us? A man, so long ago, beaten, dirty, exhausted; his face streaked with tears and blood and spit; pinned to a cross with nails through his hands and feet. What had it to do with us? The compelling defencelessness of his courage and his vulnerable love had, so far as I could see, left us unmoved. Father Bennett, whom Daddy described as a fatuous twit, had nothing anywhere about him that reminded me of the struggle and self-abandonment of Jesus. When it came to it, nor did I.

'Draw near with faith ...' boomed Father Bennett, and I got up from my knees and sat waiting until Mother stood up and we all followed her into the Communion queue. Therese had been confirmed two years ago, and I had been confirmed last autumn, but Mary and Beth were too young to receive the bread and wine, and instead Father Bennett laid his hands on their heads and blessed them.

We knelt in a row at the altar rail; first Therese, then Mary, then Mother, then Beth, then me, and I held out my hands to receive the Communion wafer.

'The body of Christ, broken for you,' said Father

Bennett, as he pressed the white, translucent wafer, with the little imprint of a crucifix on it, into my hand.

'Amen,' I said, and as I tried to swallow the dry, tasteless thing before old Father Carnforth got to me with the wine, I asked myself, 'How? How is it the body of Christ? What has happened to his hurting, his smile, his hands, his sore, dusty feet?'

'The blood of Jesus, shed for you,' said Father Carnforth in his aged, asthmatic wheeze, and I took the chalice and sipped the deep red, rich velvety wine. The delicious, intoxicating taste of it spread round my mouth, fiery and sweet. That seemed a bit more like Jesus.

I got to my feet and walked back to our pew, hands folded and eyes downcast, as Mother had taught me. In the silence before the prayers which ended the service, while the rest of the people took Communion, and then Father Bennett consumed the remains of the wine and washed and dried the chalice, I abandoned my questioning and played a whispered game of 'I Spy' with Beth.

At last it was time for the final prayers. I was itching to be out in the sunlight, and feeling light-headed with hunger.

We sang our last hymn with gusto, during which Daddy judged there was enough noise going on for it to be safe to re-admit Cecily, and then it was over.

We all shook hands with Father Bennett and said what a lovely morning it was, as we left, except Cecily who refused even to look at him; and then we went home to a huge dinner of roast lamb and new potatoes and greens, with apple pie and cream to follow.

After lunch, Cecily went up to bed for a rest, and Therese took Mary and Beth out to the park.

'I'll come and help you in a minute!' I called to Daddy. I could hear him beginning to tackle the huge pile of washing-up in the kitchen.

Mother was in the living-room, curled up in the corner of the sofa, sipping her coffee. I sat down beside her.

'Tell me a story,' I begged.

'Oh, goodness,' she said, 'my brain's full of dinner, I can't think!' But she had that faraway, meditative, remembering look on her face, and I waited hopefully.

'About Peregrine?' she said.

'Yes, please!'

She sipped at her coffee again, and then cupped her hands round the rough pottery as she thought.

Then she began her story.

The Benedictine Rule laid down that guests of the abbey, who were to be received with honour and courtesy, especially pilgrims and the poor, should always dine with the abbot. Father Peregrine found this duty particularly trying, because the awkwardness of his hands made it difficult for him to eat in the refined and tidy way such occasions demanded of him. He found the effort of concentrating on preventing his hands from letting him down, while at the same time sustaining an intelligent and witty conversation, extremely tiring. In addition, he had to try to finish his dinner at the same time as his guests finished theirs, so as to avoid a ghastly ten minutes of silence while his fascinated guests watched him struggle with the remains of his food. The mere thought of entertaining guests gave him a headache. In the end, he hit upon the plan of going into the kitchens before the meal, where Brother Andrew would give him a plate of food to stave off hunger; then he could be served a minute portion of dinner when he sat to eat with guests of the abbey. This alleviated his difficulties considerably, though he was embarrassed by the way his guests looked with alarm at the pathetic amount of food on his plate, and could later be overheard by the brothers, commenting on what a holy and self-denying man the abbot was.

It was a day of bitter cold and wind, towards the end of February. It had been raining for nearly a week and the light was weak and grey even at midday, and almost dark by late afternoon, when Father Peregrine was sitting in the infirmary with Brother Edward, who was working on Peregrine's hands with his aromatic oils. It was a good place to be, on a day like this, because the infirmary was one of the few places in the abbey which was always kept warm, and today a brazier of charcoal glowed comfortably in the room where they sat.

Brother Francis was sent to them with word from the porter that a family had arrived at the abbey requesting hospitality and a bed for the night.

'Father Chad has received them, and is seeing to their comfort. He says he will bring them to your lodging to dine after Vespers. It is a lady with her daughter and two sons, all of them between eighteen and twenty-five years of age as I judge, travelling to Iona on pilgrimage for the Easter Feast. Besides these are their servants; a groom and a lady's maid.'

'Thank you, brother. Did you enquire the name of the family?'

'Oh, forgive me, Father. I forgot. Father Chad saw to them straight away, I had no conversation with them.'

Francis left them, and Uncle Edward put away his little vials of essential oils; near the brazier he placed the little bowl which held the remains of the mixture of almond oil and essential oils he had been using, that it might slowly evaporate in the warmth, scenting and disinfecting the room.

'Terrible weather for a party on pilgrimage,' he commented.

'It is indeed. Iona is a long way in this foul rain. Still, they have a night to rest and be refreshed. Join us for dinner, Edward,' said Father Peregrine. 'You have more of a gift for conversation than I.'

'Is that a compliment, Father, or a back-handed insult?'

Peregrine grinned at him. 'As you will,' he answered. 'Now I must go to Brother Andrew and beg some bread, for I shall be fasting more or less if we have guests tonight, and what we ate at midday was nothing to compose poetry about. Thank you for your ministrations,

Brother. My hands ache, this raw, wet weather. You have eased them indeed.'

Gloomily resigned to a difficult evening meal, Father Peregrine took refuge in the kitchens, where Brother Michael was kneading a huge mound of dough. Quiet and friendly, he was a welcome alternative to the irascible Brother Andrew. He heard Peregrine's request with a smile, and found him a hunk of bread, some cheese and an apple, which Peregrine retired to a corner to eat. The kitchen staff had no leisure to watch him, and in any case were not fussy about table manners, and he ate the food gratefully and peacefully, then made his way to chapel for Vespers.

It was gloomy in the chapel, on such an evening. A few candles flickered, but in the damp air their iridescent haloes seemed to hover close to the flame, and they scarcely illuminated the dimness. Peregrine could vaguely discern figures in the abbey church, on the other side of the parish altar, but could not tell whether they would be his guests, or the usual worshippers from the village, some of whom attended Vespers as well as the morning Mass.

'*Magnificat, anima mea Dominum,*' Brother Gilbert's voice lifted in the lovely chant.

'*Et exultavit spiritus meus in Deo salutari meo,*' responded the brothers. 'My soul magnifies the Lord, and my spirit has rejoiced in God my saviour.'

'It's true,' thought Peregrine, with some surprise. 'After all the struggle of the early years, I am content now. I love this place, and these brothers committed to my charge. I am content.' He gave his mind to the chant again, which he had been singing without thinking, both words and tune being as familiar as his own skin.

'*Gloria Patri et Filio, et Spiritui Sancto . . .*'

After Vespers, as the brothers dispersed, Father Chad came round the parish altar to find the visiting family, as they sat in the gathering shadows. He led them out into the cloister, to follow Peregrine, who was crossing to his house in the persistent drizzle.

'Our lord abbot,' said Father Chad, seeing the eyes of the mother of the family watching Peregrine's awkward progress across the court.

'A crippled man?' she said in surprise. 'There must be few so afflicted who rise to become abbot of a community. He must be an extraordinary man.'

'He was not always as you see him now,' Father Chad replied, 'but he is an extraordinary man.'

They followed him into the abbot's house, and found him standing with Brother Edward before a bright fire of seasoned apple logs. The abbot's house was built with a hearth and a chimney, so that a fire might be lit to warm and cheer the guests of the abbey, though Peregrine virtually never lit it on his own account, except in the bitterest of the winter weather, when his hands, too cramped and inflexible to write well at the best of times, refused to function at all in the cold.

It was almost dark now, outside, but here the fire burned cheerily, and candles shone with a warm, soft light. The pilgrims came in gladly from the cold, and Father Chad introduced them to his superior. 'Madame de Montany and her family, Father,' he said, but Peregrine was standing staring at her, speechless, frozen to the spot.

'Clare!' he exlaimed at last.

She, too, as she saw his face, gasped with surprise and stood still.

'How came you here?' she said now. 'I had no idea ...'

As a young boy, Peregrine du Fayel and his two older brothers had been brought up on their father Henri's manor under the wide, wild skies of the fenlands near Ely. Their neighbour, Robert de Montany, also a Norman knight, was a big kindly man, married to a gentle and sweet-tempered wife, Eloise. He had a son, Hugh, born within a week of Peregrine's birth, and a younger daughter, Louise.

On the other side of du Fayel's boundaries lay the lands of the van Moeck family, Dutch aristocracy who had settled in England on land they had inherited. They felt at home there, in the flat, wet lands under the great, luminous sky. Pieter and Gerda van Moeck had two daughters, Anne and Clare.

The children of the three households grew up together, played together as infants, rode and hunted and dined together as young people, and were all friends. Privileged young things, shielded from life's hardships, with tolerant and indulgent parents all, the world was their plaything, and they enjoyed life to the full.

When he was twenty-five years old, and she twenty-four, Geoffroi du Fayel, Peregrine's oldest brother, was betrothed to Anne van Moeck. They married and settled in a manor farm given to them by Pieter van Moeck, Anne's father, on the edge of the du Fayel lands, and from there Geoffroi took charge of the farm management of his own land, and most of his father's too. Gerda van Moeck and Melissa du Fayel, having spent the last five years discreetly engineering the match, sat back complacently to await the arrival of grandchildren, at the same time having an eye to any possible developments among their remaining offspring.

Emmanuel, the next of the du Fayel brothers, dark and quick-tempered, was by nature well adapted to bloodshed, and he took up arms in the king's service, and went away to kill as many enemies of the Crown as he could lay his hands on.

Left together, Peregrine and Hugh lived the easy lives of young noblemen, more play than work, and devoted their time to hunting and breeding horses and training falcons. Louise de Montany, a docile, home-loving body, they had little to do with, and Clare van Moeck, the youngest of them all, they tolerated and teased as a little sister, until the day of her sixteenth birthday, which was 17th March 1283.

On that day, her parents gave a banquet for her,

at which all three households gathered. Anne and Geoffroi, five years married now, were there with Pierre, their four-year-old son, and their tiny, toothless, hairless scrap of a daughter, but six weeks into the world. Emmanuel was still away, but the rest of the family was assembled.

In the solar, during the hour before they dined, Gerda van Moeck was working at her embroidery in the pale, bright sunshine that streamed through the window. Hugh and Peregrine had ridden out together, ahead of their families, partly because Hugh wanted to show off the merits of his newly acquired horse to his friend.

In age, the two young men were the same, but in every other way they were different, and Gerda van Moeck, plump and kindly, sat with her embroidery forgotten in her lap for the moment, watching them with amusement.

Hugh, big-boned, blond and gentle, with a deep voice and a hearty, generous laugh, was extolling the virtues of his new mount to Peregrine. Everything about Hugh was open, ingenuous and relaxed. Peregrine, by contrast, had a gathered, flame-like intensity about him, and the watchful, fierce expression of the falcon he was named for. Just now, his face was lit with laughter as he teased his friend, mocking him for losing his heart and his wits with it, to a mere horse.

The door of the solar opened, and Clare van Moeck shyly made her entrance, in her new dress which was her mother's birthday present to her. It was a simple gown of delphinium blue, which gave her blue eyes the depth and clarity of jewels. Her mane of rich brown hair was gathered up in a gold net, and she stood within the doorway, her lips slightly parted and her cheeks a little flushed, graceful and shy in her finery. Both young men turned their heads at the same moment and saw her, and she was utterly beautiful. From that moment, and for the rest of his life, Hugh de Montany worshipped her. But as she stood a little self-consciously before their arrested gaze, it was Peregrine's eyes she sought; and reading there the candid admiration she had hoped to find, her own eyes exulted. Clare van Moeck had grown into a woman, and Peregrine du Fayel wanted her.

Gerda noted with satisfaction the impact her daughter had made. Two fish on the hook; it was well. Both the banquet and the dress had proved worth the trouble.

From that day, and through the spring and summer of the year, Peregrine and Clare were more and more together. They rode and walked and talked together, having eyes only for each other. Late in the September of the year, as summer slid into autumn, there was a day when Clare stood laughing in the russet woodland and her glorious rich brown hair fell about the green gown she wore. She looked for all the world like a dryad of the autumn woods, and Peregrine took her in his arms and kissed her. Her heart triumphed. She had won him. He was hers.

With approval, their families watched their young love blossom. Another such union between the households was welcome to both the du Fayels and the van Moecks. Hugh de Montany alone could not be glad, but he kept his heartache private, continuing a steadfast friend to them both.

It was in the spring of the following year, when Clare was just seventeen, and Peregrine was twenty-four, that all this came to an end. For some little while now, the two of them had gone further in their love than they should and, bedded in the fragrant bluebells in the woodland, or nestled in the warm-scented hay in the great barns of Pieter van Moeck's farm, they had lain together as lovers, wrapped in Peregrine's cloak, lost in each other and consumed in the ardour of their love.

But somehow, unexpectedly, irresistibly, came the call of God on Peregrine's soul. In the end there came a day when he held Clare in his arms and kissed her, and his face was sad but resolute as he told her his decision.

'Clare, what we have done is sin. What is between us

should have been saved for marriage. I have confessed it, for my part, to the priest, and I ask your pardon too.'

Dumbly, bewildered, she shook her head and held him close; held him fiercely as she felt in her heart that for some reason she could not understand, he was no longer hers.

'I have to leave you, my lady, my love, my heart.' He looked down at her blue eyes brimming with tears, and kissed her brow, her eyes, her cheeks, her hair; then put her away from him with a sudden, rough gesture.

'I am going to enter as a brother at St Peter's Abbey,' he said abruptly.

'A *monk*! You?' exclaimed Clare, her amazement for a moment overcoming even her sorrow. He looked at her, and she could not read the expression in his eyes, she who had thought she knew him like her own soul.

'Yes. Me,' he said simply.

He tried to explain to her later the burning of his vocation, the passionate longing which is greater than the love between man and woman, with which his soul cried out for God. She did not understand, and she wept, but she did not try to dissuade him. Neither did his disappointed and astonished parents attempt to argue with him—they had given that up when he was two years old. He was received into the community of brothers at the abbey of St Peter, near Ely, at the end of May in the year 1284, and Clare van Moeck never saw him again.

Until today.

Brother Edward was as surprised to see Clare as Peregrine was. He had known her well as a little girl, and even during his days of itinerant preaching with the Franciscans, he had been a frequent visitor to all three households. He had watched the offspring of the three families grow up through childhood and lost touch with them only when his wanderings took him as far away as the North Riding of Yorkshire, where he had finally settled.

He glanced at Peregrine, and seeing him momentarily incapable of speech, stepped forward with a welcoming smile to greet Clare.

'What a happy surprise, my dear! How the years have flown since last we met—and you are no whit less beautiful!'

'Madame de Montany,' broke in Peregrine. 'Then you married Hugh.' He had gathered his senses enough to smile at her. 'And these are Hugh's sons, yes, I see they are. The image of their father.'

'Hugh, and Edwin,' said Clare. 'And this is Melissa, my daughter—my first-born,' she added softly, with a slight tremble in her voice.

'Oh, forgive me,' said Peregrine, who had overlooked the young woman standing in the shadows at the back of the group. His words died on his lips, and his eyes widened as she stepped forward, looking at him out of intense, direct, dark grey eyes, set above a nose like a hawk's beak, a resolute mouth and a determined chin. It was like looking into a mirror.

'I am pleased to meet you, Father,' she said at last, and he held out his hand to her, like a man dreaming.

'Daughter, you are welcome,' he said, his voice barely above a whisper.

Clare held her breath as she watched Melissa take the scarred, twisted hand tenderly in both her own. What had happened to him? Melissa's hands were as his had been, scholar's hands, long and graceful; and they closed round his hand now, and released it again.

'I did not know,' he said, stating the obvious, looking from Melissa to Clare, and back again. 'I did not know. But come,' he recollected himself, 'sit down and eat. You must be hungry.'

From childhood Melissa had known the story of her father, and she well knew Henri du Fayel, Peregrine's father, whom he strongly resembled. As Melissa was so like the du Fayels, and apart from the mass of her brown hair she was so unlike either Hugh or Clare, there had seemed no point in keeping the story from her. Both Clare and Hugh had the generosity to portray her father to his little girl as a man irresistibly called by God, not as a lover who had used and abandoned his mistress. Now, the man she had wondered about all her life sat before her, and she could not take her eyes off him.

Clare, too, watched the man she had loved, and she wondered at the savage scar on his face, and her heart was wrenched with pity at his lameness, and the awkward fumbling of his hands. She watched the young brother, who waited on them at table, place the abbot's food before him, already cut up, as a mother might give cut food to a child too young to manage on his own. At the sight of that plate of food, the words of astonishment were out of her mouth before she could restrain them: 'Is that all you eat?'

She spoke with the forthright familiarity of an old friend, and one who had seen her lover many times come in from hunting, to devour a huge plate of food with the single-mindedness of an unusually fastidious wolf.

Her words broke the tension that bound the whole group, and Peregrine laughed. 'No,' he said smiling, 'but it is not easy for me to eat with guests, Clare, because of my hands.'

'What happened?' she asked, gently; and he told them, briefly, factually, and without emotion, how he came to be so maimed.

'I remember the man, and his sons,' she said, nodding her head. 'I remember the day he was taken away, and how he struggled and fought. It was awful. And this happened to you two years ago, you say?'

'Three years at Easter. I am used to it now.' These words were clearly intended to close the subject, and the talk was turned to old friends and family, and remembered places.

'Melissa is to be married this summer,' said Clare. 'She is betrothed to Ranulf Langton—do you remember the family? They are wool merchants from Thaxted. Ranulf is a fine young man.'

'You are ... twenty-five years old, this autumn it must be,' Peregrine said to Melissa. 'You have waited a while, then, to make your choice?'

'Mother always counselled me to wait for a man I felt I could really love,' replied Melissa. 'She says a marriage where one does not love would be a weary business.'

Peregrine glanced sharply at Clare, and she met his look steadily. 'Would you not think so?' she said.

'I think,' replied Peregrine carefully, 'that as the years go by, the same love would enrich *any* marriage as the love which builds and enriches a community of celibate monks; and that is the love which is pledged to lay down its own wants and preferences for the sake of the other. The marriage that was built on natural affection, and had nothing of such love would, in the end, sour, however promising its beginning, I think.'

Clare's son laughed. 'But you are not recommending, sir, that one should marry regardless of inclination or affection, unless one has to? That would seem noble, but not entirely sensible.'

Peregrine smiled at him: 'Edwin, heaven help me, I am a monk. It is not for me to advance opinions on marriage! All I am saying is that between any people, if their love has not that Christ-like quality of humble service, then neither is it built to last for ever.'

'Of course,' said Clare, 'even where your heart is given to love and to serve, it does not always follow that the one you love will be true to you, or to his own protestations of love. Men change, and love given does not guarantee love returned.'

Peregrine dropped his gaze before her, his face ashamed.

'No,' he said, 'I know.' He was silent.

'So you are travelling to Iona,' remarked Edward cheerfully. 'A beautiful place. Would that I could celebrate the Easter feast there with you. But you have chosen rough weather for your journey.'

Young Hugh laughed; a laugh so like his father's that

Peregrine looked up, startled; it was as though his old friend sat there with them in the person of his son.

'Brother, we do not choose our weather,' said the young man. 'Pray for us, and the one who sends the rain may relent a little!'

They talked a while longer, over the remains of their meal, and then it was time for the brothers to go to Compline, the day's last office, after which the monastery was folded into the Great Silence, and no conversation at all was permitted until the following day.

The pilgrims meant to rise early in the morning and be ready to depart as soon as they had heard Mass, so Edwin, Hugh and Melissa returned to the guest house, taking the chance to retire early and rest in preparation for their journey. Clare said she would come to Compline first, and then join them. Father Chad and Brother Edward went with the young people to the guest house to see that all they needed had been prepared for them. Peregrine set off directly to the church, it taking him a little longer than the others to make his way there; and Clare walked with him, suiting her pace to his slow and laborious progress.

'Why did you never tell me?' he said.

'Because you would have married me,' she responded sadly, 'and I couldn't bear to live my life as your second best, your dutiful choice. I kept it a secret until it could be kept a secret no longer, and by then you were clothed, and had taken your vows as a novice, and it was too late. I made them promise not to tell you.'

'So you married Hugh.'

'He offered immediately, to save me from shame.'

'And two fine sons he has given you. You have found him a good husband, I think.'

'Oh yes, he has been to me all that a husband should be,' she said softly, 'but you—'

'Clare, don't say it!' he cried, harshly.

'I have Melissa always to remind me. Every turn of her head and gesture of her hands is yours. That spring ... how could I forget?'

He flashed her one glance and then looked away. 'Neither have I forgotten,' he said quietly, 'and it does me no good, and does nothing for my peace of mind, to remember.'

They parted outside the great black bulk of the abbey church, he to take his place among the community, and she to go into the church, where visitors and parishioners sat, divided by the wooden screen and the parish altar from the brethren. She watched him go, lame and jerky on his crutch. He did not look back.

The de Montanys were ready to depart the next morning. They attended Mass in the abbey church, and made ready their horses with saddle and pack while the brothers were in chapter. By the time chapter was over, Hugh and Edwin and Clare's maid were mounted, and their groom stood holding the bridles of Clare's and Melissa's horses as well as his own. Edward came across the court to them, to bid them farewell, and Clare, after a little hesitation, went to find Peregrine in his lodging, hurt that he had not come to say goodbye.

'The time has come. We must leave,' she said. He stood and looked at her without speaking.

'Will you give me the kiss of peace?'

Slowly, he shook his head. 'I wish you peace, Clare, with all my heart; but embrace you I will not.'

'Then shake my hand, at least,' she said, her voice trembling.

'No, Clare! Do not ask me to touch you. There is too much between us still, you know it as well as I do! Go in peace, but for pity's sake, go!'

She looked at him once more, and then turned swiftly and left, without another word.

Outside, growing impatient in the steady drizzling rain, Hugh and Edwin sent Melissa after their mother to hurry her along. Melissa came to the door as her mother came out.

'A moment, and I will be with you, Mother,' she said. 'I must just say goodbye.'

Clare nodded, and went to join her family, and

Melissa, hesitantly entering the abbot's house, found him standing still in the middle of the room, his hand pressed to his mouth, and his eyes bright with tears. Struggling for composure, he stretched out his hand to her, and tried to smile.

'I'm glad, so glad we came,' she said. 'I think we have made things difficult for you, but everything is different for me, now. Before, my father was a stranger, but now I belong. And I'm sorry it hurts you so, but I'm glad you still love Mother.'

She had taken his hand in both of hers, and she looked into his face with tenderness and happiness.

'Go in peace,' he whispered. 'God bless you, little one.'

She looked at him steadily one more moment, then, 'Goodbye,' she said, and was gone.

The rest of the party was waiting for her impatiently. She hastily embraced Edward, saying gaily, 'Goodbye, Uncle Edward! I shall be back!' and added in a whisper, 'Go and help him when we're gone. He needs someone.'

Brother Edward watched them ride out, cloaked and hooded against the dismal mist of rain, then turned back to the abbot's lodging where he found Peregrine preparing parchment and inks for Brother Theodore, who was coming to do some writing at his dictation, later in the morning. Peregrine looked at Edward with a carefully composed expression of polite enquiry.

'Yes, Brother?'

'Father, there is no need to pretend,' said Edward bluntly. 'It would have devastated me, too.'

'Pray for me,' said Peregrine, and that was all he said.

They expected to hear no more of the de Montany family, at least for some while, but barely three weeks later, just before Easter, in the chill, grey evening of a cold March day, Brother Edward overtook Peregrine on his way to Vespers, breathless with hurry and agitation.

'Father, Melissa de Montany is here! She has ridden far and is in great distress. She is asking for you.'

Peregrine turned back immediately for the gatehouse,

where he found Melissa, her hands twisting in her lap, her face white and her eyes shadowed with suffering and lack of sleep. He came and sat beside her, his eyes searching hers with concern.

'What is this?' he said. 'What has happened?'

'She is dead!' Melissa blurted out. 'Mother is dead! We came to a village not three days' ride from here, and stayed at the inn there. Their food was dreadful, greasy and foul. The meat stank. We were all taken ill; it was poisoning from the meat, I think. Hugh and Edwin were tossing and delirious with fever for days. They are recovered now, but too weak yet to ride. I had eaten scarcely anything and was not too bad; but Mother died! She is dead!'

Peregrine gathered her wordlessly in his arms, and she clung to him. 'She is dead! She is dead!' she moaned over and over, and shook violently as he held her. Finally, she ceased to speak, and pressing her face to his breast, she sobbed and sobbed. Cradling her, he laid his cheek on her hair, and closed his eyes silently on his own tears.

He held her and comforted her through many such storms in the week that followed, as she grieved and wept for her mother. She leaned on his understanding love as on a rock, and when Hugh and Edwin came to fetch her, and began the sad journey homewards to bear the news to their father, the pilgrimage forgotten, she was sufficiently in command of herself to travel with them. Through the nights, Peregrine had kept vigil in the chapel and prayed for her, and during the days he had stayed with her, quietly watching over her, asking nothing, but allowing her to grieve.

She embraced him gratefully as they parted.

'Thank you, Father,' she said. 'Thank you so much. May we meet in happier times!'

He nodded. 'Greet Hugh for me. Tell him ... tell him I'm sorry.'

Edward and Peregrine stood together to watch the

forlorn little party ride away at first light on a grey, chill day, then walked slowly to the chapel for Mass.

Edward looked at Peregrine's face, haggard with exhaustion and grief. 'You have strengthened and comforted her,' said Edward. When Peregrine did not reply, Edward looked at the sad, tired face, and added gently, 'And you? Whom will you allow to comfort you in your own grief?'

Peregrine stopped and looked at him wearily. 'Surely Christ has borne our griefs, and carried all our sorrows,' he said quietly, and then groaned, 'but oh, my God, my God, it takes some believing.'

Mother was quiet.

'Is that all?' I exploded. 'Didn't Melissa ever come back? What happened next? Oh Mother, there must be more!'

'She came back. She married Ranulf Langton, and had children of her own, and some years later, just before the birth of her youngest child, she came to make her home in Yorkshire, and she visited them often. I told you, you remember, that Brother Edward told these stories first to his great-niece, who was your long ago great-grandmother Melissa.'

'Oh, but Mother, it's so sad! Tell me some more, don't leave it there!'

'Sad? Yes I suppose so. All the stories are sad, in a way. I don't believe there's a one of them without tears and struggle; but that was the life, you see. It wasn't easy. Saying sorry, and giving up your own way, and daily turning your back on your own wants took some doing. But now, help your Daddy with the drying up and I'll tell you a quick story to cheer you up again.'

As I got to my feet to take Mother's coffee cup out to the kitchen, there was a thunder of footsteps on the path outside, the front door burst open, and Mary and Beth piled in through the doorway, breathless with running, their cheeks pink and their eyes shining.

'We're home!' shouted Beth.

'Therese buyed us an ice-cream!' cried Mary excitedly, 'and it had a stalk!'

Therese was some minutes behind them. 'They can run like the wind, those two!' she exclaimed. 'Is the kettle on, Melissa? I'm dying for a cup of tea.'

'Any minute now,' I replied, and went on my way into the kitchen.

'Oh, Daddy, you've done it all! I was supposed to be helping you.'

He was sitting in the armchair in the corner, reading his paper, with the dog lying on his feet, and the cat curled up on his lap. He looked at me over the top of his glasses.

'I am among you as one who serves,' he said, in an exaggerated tone of suffering self-righteousness. 'You can make me a cup of tea, though. Once your Mother gets going, time's forgotten. I never knew such a woman, she could talk the hind leg off a donkey.'

'A donkey?' said Mary, a little uncertainly. She had come into the kitchen and was leaning affectionately on Daddy's arm. 'Why?'

'Just a figure of speech, my poppet,' said Daddy smiling at her. 'Get cracking with that tea, Melissa, you look as though you're in a trance!'

As the kettle boiled, there came an angry bellow from upstairs, 'I ... WANT ... MUMMY!' Cecily was awake. She came stumping down the stairs, only just awake, her limbs still unco-ordinated, and her face still flushed from sleep.

'I ... WANT ... MUMMY!' she roared again, but when Mother came out of the living-room, laughing at her, she was so incensed at not being taken seriously that she flung herself on the floor in the passage way, her legs rigid and her little hands clenched into fists, making a noise like rending metal.

Mother sighed. 'Heigh-ho. Back to reality,' she said resignedly. 'Oh, come on, Cecily! Do get up.'

Just then, there was a knock at the front door. Cecily leapt to her feet, crying, 'IwanttoopenitIwanttoopenit

Iwanttoopenit!' but the front door was opened before she got there, by our Grandma, who was on the other side of it.

Cecily burst into wails of disappointment and frustration, tears pouring down her crimson face, the veins standing out on her neck like cords. Grandma, confronted with this sight, looked down in astonishment for a moment, then knelt down on the floor and held out her arms. 'Cecily, my darling!' she said. 'What's the matter, poppet? Have you hurt yourself?'

Cecily was too much beside herself to speak.

'I think she wanted to open the front door, Grandma,' Therese explained.

'Oh, I see. Right-o, then.' Grandma hastily went out again, closed the door firmly behind her, and knocked on it loudly, calling through the letter-box, 'Is anyone at home?'

There was a moment's pause while Cecily wondered whether to relent. Grandma knocked again. With a hoarse cry of joy, Cecily ran and opened the front door, the noise and tears magically evaporated, her little face dimpling in an enchanting smile, her great blue eyes shining.

'Oh, hello, Cecily!' cried Grandma. 'Can I come in for a cup of tea, darling, please?'

'Grandma,' cooed Cecily. Mother shook her head and sighed.

'Make the big pot of tea, Melissa,' she said, 'and there's a new packet of chocolate digestives in the cupboard. It's hidden at the back, behind the macaroni.'

The rest of the afternoon was whiled away comfortably, chatting to Grandma and playing snakes and ladders with Mary and Beth. Grandma tried to teach Cecily how to play snap, but Cecily didn't want to put any of her cards down. She wouldn't say 'Snap' when the cards were the same, but she got cross if Grandma said 'Snap' and tried to pick them up. It was Grandma who backed down; in our family we live by the maxim that playing by the rules is less important than Surviving Cecily.

V
THE MOULTING FALCON

Therese's friend Lilian Shepherd came during the afternoon, to ask if Therese wouldn't mind helping her with her English homework. Lilian was a very popular girl at school, and always had a group of friends around her, so Therese was rather flattered that Lilian especially sought her friendship, even though there was something indefinable she didn't quite like about Lilian. Mary and Beth thought she was wonderful, because she was tall and slim and stunningly attractive, with great big eyes like a startled faun's, and a rippling mane of silky blonde hair. Mother and Daddy both disliked Lilian intensely, and Mother said all she was looking for from Therese was a brain transplant. I myself couldn't help admiring her, although she wasn't very nice to the little girls; but that might have been because Cecily had bitten her once, for no reason that anyone could tell.

Therese took her into the kitchen and made her some coffee, and as Lilian sipped it, she explained that she hadn't quite been able to come up with any ideas for her essay on Hopkins' poetry and wondered if Therese had any thoughts. . . . She had read a little, she said, and really hadn't got anywhere with it. Perhaps she would be able to borrow Therese's essay, just to have a look at it? She thought it might help to inspire her.

Therese, who loved Hopkins, was delighted to lend

Lilian her essay, and asked if Lilian would let her know what her own thoughts about the poems were, when she'd got a bit further. Lilian smiled and said she was sure her thoughts would not be half as original as Therese's, and then she excused herself and slipped off home with Therese's essay. I was bursting with indignation.

'Therese, you are a goose! She's going to copy it!' I exclaimed. 'Why did you let her have it?'

Therese looked at me uncertainly. 'You don't think she will, do you? She only said she wanted to read it. She couldn't copy it, Mrs Freeman would know.'

Mother came in with all the dirty tea things, and asked what Lilian had come for.

'What was it this time? Your Hopkins essay?'

'Mother! How did you know?'

'Because I'm not as daft as you. She's in your English class, isn't she? Be a bit more sensible, Therese. She'll get you into trouble one of these days. Don't have too much to do with her.'

'Whenever Lilian's been here,' I said, 'she always leaves an uncomfortable feeling behind. It's funny, because she doesn't argue or anything.'

'But she's my friend!' said Therese, a bit upset.

Mother began to run washing-up water into the bowl. 'Be friendly, Therese; there's nothing wrong with that, but be a bit wary, that's all. Now then, Daddy is going to run Grandma home in a minute, and take me to Evensong. Cecily can come with Daddy for the ride, but will you see to Mary's and Beth's baths for me? Daddy will do their bedtime when he gets in.'

Therese said she would, and I asked if I could come to Evensong with Mother.

'Of course you can come! Get your shoes on, though, and brush your hair, because we must go in five minutes.'

I loved Evensong. I loved the stillness of the church that enfolded the small evening congregation. The mellow evening sunshine that slanted in low through the windows in summer, the gathering, sombre shadows of spring and autumn evenings, and the profounder darkness of the winter months, all wrapped the evening worship in a mystery and a beauty that I never found in the brightness and bustle of family service in the morning.

Our church was just on the edge of the town, set in a pretty little remnant of woodland, a tiny drift of countryside still left in peace by the urban sprawl. Daddy dropped us off at the end of the church path, and we stood to wave goodbye to Cecily as he drove away. It was very important to Cecily to say 'goodbye'. If she thought she had not made her farewells properly, she would scream deafeningly until Daddy turned the car back. So we waved until they turned the corner, and then strolled up the path to the church and into the stone porch.

The great wooden inner door opened with a click as Mother pushed it. Charlie Page, the blacksmith, was always the sidesman in the evening, and his face, freckled with age, wrinkled in a smile as he gave us our hymn-books and prayer-books. Mother settled into our pew with a happy sigh. The evening service was a cherished time for her, when she could give herself to the worship without the stress of the little ones' company, or the anxiety of being late. Whenever we went anywhere as a family, however much time we gave ourselves to get ready, we were always late, and Mother hated it.

In the pew behind ours sat Mrs Crabtree; a tall, well-built, energetic, silver-haired lady in her middle seventies. She had borne six children in her time, and was still motherly through and through, wise and kind, with a rich, ready laugh. Unfortunately her singing was more out of tune than any I have ever heard before or since, and I set my teeth to endure as the organist struck up for the first hymn:

> Glory to thee, my God, this night,
> For all the blessings of the light.
> Keep me, O keep me, King of kings,
> Beneath thine own almighty wings.

I knew about his almighty wings. They were folding around us here, in the quiet of the evening, kind and everlasting and utterly secure. It was the same wings that wrapped me round in our home, in the bedtime candlelight. Sanctuary from the busy and complicated daytime, God gathered us under his evening wing, haven for all our weariness.

The evening service felt as familiar as an old friend, comfortable to be with. I knew the prayers and the responses without looking at the book. Actually, I could say them all while thinking about something completely different, which to my shame I frequently did.

'My soul doth magnify the Lord: and my spirit hath rejoiced in God my Saviour,' we sang.

I thought of Peregrine, singing the same words, but in Latin, all those years ago; wrapped like me in the contentment of evening calm, blissfully unaware of the turbulence of surprise and grief that lay around the corner ... 'No!' I told myself sharply, 'this is not the time! Come out of the walled garden, and shut the door firmly behind you, and turn your back on it. Concentrate.'

'Glory be to the Father, and to the Son ...' Mrs Crabtree sang vigorously behind me.

Father Carnforth took the evening service. His gentle, wheezy old voice led us through the prayers; the Lord's prayer, the responses, the collect of the day. I felt reassured by the humble confidence with which he prayed.

'Give unto thy servants that peace which the world cannot give ...'

What a gift! What a thing to ask for! And yet, incredibly, it is given. I knew that peace; I had been brought up with the flavour and the texture of it in our home. Peace, at the very core of things, constant, unobtrusive, like the humming of the fridge and the ticking of the clock. Peace, freely given. Beyond our making, or even our understanding. Thank you, God.

Father Carnforth was climbing slowly into the pulpit for his sermon. He read his sermons out of a book, very

fast. He was in unspoken agreement with his congregation that the preaching of sermons was an unavoidable
bore; to be endured uncomplainingly, but not prolonged. Tonight's offering was about the textual background of the Synoptic Gospels, and I strongly suspected
from the way he read it that it was as incomprehensible
to him as it was to us. He shut the book with a snap and
laid it aside with obvious relief, as he announced the
final hymn: 'The day thou gavest, Lord, is ended. The
darkness falls at thy behest. Hymn number 277.'

Mrs Crabtree gave joyful tongue behind me. Did God
mind that dreadful singing, he who made the nightingale
and the lark? Probably not. Probably it was the soul of
Mrs Crabtree he was listening to, the worshipping song
of her heart, and that rang true as a bell.

Then it was over, and we went out into the cool of the
evening. Father Carnforth smiled kindly at me, and
shook my hand in his aged hand, the joints swollen with
arthritis and the skin wrinkled and discoloured with the
years. His nose was big and red, with dark whiskers
growing from it, and he was almost completely bald. He
smelt strongly of pipe tobacco, and his cassock was not
quite clean, but even Cecily loved him, who had strong
opinions about most people. His friendship with Cecily
was helped along by the bag of peppermints he carried
in his pocket, but it was not entirely that. He called
her his sugar-plum fairy. Mary, who was always very
worried about people she loved growing old and dying,
focused her anxiety on him, as the most ancient person
of her acquaintance.

Father Carnforth looked at me with his watery old eyes.
They were brown, and small, and twinkling. Hedgehog's
eyes. Like Mother's, they looked into the middle of you
and could make you feel uncomfortable at times.

'Ah, Melissa, you do me good, you're a breath of
springtime,' he wheezed at me. 'Tell your little Mary
that Father Carnforth is still clinging to this world and
sends his love.'

He shook Mother's hand: 'Goodnight, my dear. Take care.'

Mother and I walked slowly down the pathway, breathing in the scent of the roses that grew in a hedge around the churchyard.

'I often think how odd it is,' she mused, 'that Lilian Shepherd is tall and graceful, with hair like spun gold and a face like a Greek goddess, while Father Carnforth is old and bald and fat and wrinkled; but it is Father Carnforth who is beautiful, not Lilian.'

'It's you that's odd, Mother!' I replied as I took her arm, 'and beautiful. Will you tell me that story on the way home? The one you were going to tell me.'

'Melissa, your appetite for stories is almost as prodigious as Cecily's appetite for sweets! I will tell you the story on one condition, and that is that you pester me for no more stories today.'

I promised happily. Mother picked a white dead-nettle from the side of the path and pulled off one of its creamy flowers. 'Did you know,' she said, 'that if you suck at the base of the flower, you get a drop of nectar from it—that's unless the bees have been before you, of course. Try it and see.' She showed me how to suck out the nectar, and gave me the nettle stem. I tried one of the flowers, and was astonished by the sweet, light, delicious flavour of the nectar.

'Now you know what bees eat,' said Mother, and while I worked my way through the rest of the flowers on the stem, we walked slowly out of the churchyard, and started homewards up the hill.

'It was a time when Father Peregrine was tired, and very sad,' began Mother. 'Just a minute. I've got a stone in my shoe.' She held on to my shoulder while she took it off and shook out the stone, then we walked on again.

It was only three days after Melissa had gone back home with Hugh and Edwin, and Father Peregrine had been plunged into a valley of despair: grief, temptation and sorrow. Every night during the week she had stayed with them he had kept watch and prayed for her before the altar in the chapel; and during the days he had put aside everything but the daily round of prayer to look after her, snatching an hour's sleep here and there, fasting the greater part of each day.

On the day she left, a cloth merchant and his wife who were travelling past came seeking hospitality at the abbey. Peregrine had to entertain them at lunch and supper, disciplining himself to chat about trivial matters and show an interest in the ups and downs of the cloth trade. Also, the rent re-assessment and lease renewal for the farm tenancies belonging to the abbey must be made by Lady Day, so Peregrine had spent two arduous days in conference about the rents with Brother Ambrose, the cellarer, who looked after the finances of the abbey as well as the distribution of clothing, bed linen and other necessities. They had also discussed the provision of hospitality for the pilgrims and visitors who would be guests of the abbey during the Easter Feast.

After all this, he felt weary and numb, drained now of emotion. The old wounds in his leg were aching badly, since to keep himself awake as he prayed through the long nights he had forced the unyielding knee to kneel. So his back also was tense and aching, and he had a persistent, nagging headache just to round everything off. In the end, Brother Edward insisted that he come to the infirmary and submit to having his back and leg rubbed with oils of lavender, bergamot and geranium.

'Don't be ridiculous,' snapped Peregrine. 'I'm a monk, not a lady of the court. Save your aromatics for the sick, Edward.'

'I won't have to save them long if you carry on like this,' insisted Brother Edward stoutly. 'It's you who will be ill if you don't heed my advice. This week long you've not had those hands of yours attended to. Prayer and fasting are all very well, but you're not adding common sense to the recipe. You can't possibly undertake your responsibility to this community when you're half dead with fatigue and aching from head to foot!'

'How do you know I ache?' mumbled Peregrine grudgingly.

'Because I have eyes in my head and wits to understand what I see. Now, Father, you hear sense, and come to me in the infirmary.'

Peregrine sighed and would say no more, so Brother Edward left him, muttering crossly about his stubbornness. By the afternoon, however, Father Peregrine felt ill enough to give in. He made his way slowly down the cobbled path that bordered the kitchen gardens. A few gilly-flowers grew there, perfuming the air with their intoxicating scent, and among the cobbles, little hearts-ease plants grew, and a few violets still. He leaned heavily on his crutch, and his lame leg felt like a lead weight. In the kitchen garden, the young vegetable plants were in, and Brother Tom was hoeing the immaculate beds. He watched Father Peregrine toiling down the path, looking as though he could hardly drag himself along.

Peregrine said afterwards that it was his own fault, that he should have been paying attention to what he was doing. A loose cobble turned under the crutch as he leaned on it, and it shot awkwardly to the side, tripping him so that he fell on his face on the ground.

Brother Tom saw him fall, dropped his hoe and ran to help. With his support, Peregrine got slowly to his feet, and Tom restored his crutch to him so he could stand. His nose was bleeding and the left side of his face grazed badly. He said nothing, but stood there, dazed. He blinked, and sighed. He took Tom's proffered handkerchief (which was none too clean) with stiff difficulty into his hand, and clamped it to his bleeding nose.

'Come, Father,' said Tom, 'I'll help you. Come into the infirmary and sit down.' He took Peregrine's free arm, and half led him, half supported him, to the infirmary. The door stood open and, just within, a doorway to the right led off the passage way into a room where a bench was placed near the door. Peregrine slumped onto it without speaking, his lame leg stretched in front of him, looking blackly out at the world over the grubby handkerchief Tom had given him.

It occurred to Tom as he looked at him that he looked remarkably like a moulting falcon; dishevelled and out of sorts, and with that same fierce, brooding look in his eye. Half sorry for him and half amused in spite of himself, Tom hovered beside him a moment, wondering whether to go in search of Brother Edward.

As he stood hesitating, one of the lay servants, Martin Jonson, a cheerful, good-hearted young man from the village, bustled into the room from the doorway on the other side. His arms were so full of clean linen for the infirmary beds that he could scarcely see over the top of the pile, on which rested his chin. He saw Peregrine, however, and came to a halt in front of him.

'Dear, dear, dear; what have we here, Father?' he asked jovially, using the same jolly and encouraging tone with which he was used to addressing the senile and ailing inhabitants of the infirmary. 'Whatever have you been and gone and done to yourself?'

Father Peregrine regarded him coldly over the top of the gory handkerchief. 'I fell od the stodes add gave byself a dose-bleed,' he said with icy dignity.

'Don't worry, Father, we'll put you back together in no time!' responded Martin cheerfully, and moved purposefully towards the doorway. 'I'll go and find Brother Edward for you, Father,' he said, but he never made it to the door. Peregrine's face was visible to him, but not his feet, and not noticing the stiff, lame leg that stuck out across his pathway, he tripped over it and fell among an avalanche of bedding.

Peregrine gave an involuntary yell of pain as the man's weight hit his leg, and then, his teeth gritted and his eyes screwed shut, he swore. Brother Tom's eyes widened at the string of inventive oaths that streamed from his abbot's lips. He was astonished (and delighted) to hear the words he himself used in moments of weakness in the mouth of his superior, normally so courteously and quietly spoken.

Great-uncle Edward, who had come hurrying to see what all the fuss was about, was not so delighted, and clicked his tongue disapprovingly. 'For shame, Father,' he said. 'Martin, get off his leg, man and pick this lot up. Brother Thomas, you might assist him rather than stand there gawping. Really, some of you lads are about as much use as two left feet! On second thoughts, fetch me a basin of water, when you can get through the doorway.'

Tom helped Martin pick up his pile of washing, and went for the bowl of water.

'I ask your pardon, Father,' Martin said apologetically. 'I trust you are not too badly hurt?'

Peregrine looked at him with a sickly attempt at a smile, and shook his head.

'For myself, I must say I was winded, but this here bed-linen broke my fall,' continued Martin, slightly peeved that nobody seemed particularly concerned with his own well-being.

'Thank you, Martin; just take the linen and put it away, there's a good lad,' said Edward patiently, and Martin departed, narrowly avoiding a collision with Tom in the corridor, as he returned bearing the basin of water.

'Let me look at your leg first, Father,' said Edward. 'That was a hefty weight to go crashing down on it. How is it?'

'It *hurts*,' Peregrine almost shouted at him, then sighed, 'Oh, I'b sorry Edward, but what a foolish questiod.'

'Brother Thomas, take a cloth from the cupboard there and clean his face while I have a look at this leg. Yes, that is a magnificent bruise, my friend. It will be all the colours of the sunset in a day or two, but no real harm done. You'll do.'

Tom removed the blood-soaked handkerchief, and gently washed Peregrine's face in the cool water. 'Keep your head back, Father. Your nose still bleeds slightly. Yes, that goes better.'

'What are you gridding at?' asked Peregrine, looking out of ferocious dark eyes at Tom's face bent over him.

'You!' said Tom, laughing, as he carefully washed the grit from the graze on Peregrine's face. 'You've just the same disagreeable look about you as a moulting falcon— "touch me not for I'd peck you!"'

'Brother Thomas!' exclaimed Edward. 'How can you speak with such disrespect? Recollect whom you're addressing and be a little less familiar in your speech, please! How did you come to do this, Father?'

'I fell od—hag od a bidit, let be blow by dose.' He fished in his pocket for his own handkerchief, and cautiously blew his nose. 'That's better. A loose cobble on the path by the vegetable gardens turned under my crutch, and I fell. Thank you, Brother Thomas, I feel more like a human being again. Moulting falcon indeed—I'll wager you don't speak with such impudence to Father Matthew ... I was on my way, Brother Edward, to beg pardon for my rude refusal of your kindness, and ask if you will after all give my back and leg a rub with your oils. I feel like a wrecked ship.'

They patched him up, put ointment on the graze on his face, and arnica on the wonderful bruises with which he and Martin between them had decorated his legs, and Edward massaged his hands and back and leg for him with his aromatic oils. Under the capable manipulation of Edward's strong and practiced hands, Peregrine relaxed, and as the tension flowed out of him, he fell asleep. They left him to sleep all afternoon and evening, which is what he really needed.

He was back in his stall in chapel for Compline and the night Office, and by the time Divine Office was concluded and it was time for community chapter, he was more himself again—albeit rather battered-looking—presiding over the meeting of the community with his accustomed attentiveness and authority.

The chapter began as usual, with the confession by the novices of any faults they may have committed. At Father Matthew's prompting, Brother Thaddeus came, embarrassed and self-conscious, to kneel before the community.

'Brothers, I humbly confess my fault,' he said. 'I ... stubbed my toe yesterday ...' he paused.

'Hell's teeth!' muttered Brother Cormac to Brother Francis. 'Is it an offence even to stub your toe now?'

'... and I said ... I said ... I used a most vile oath,' continued Thaddeus. 'I ask God's forgiveness and yours, brothers, for the offence.'

It fell to the abbot, on these occasions, to pronounce God's forgiveness, and Father Peregrine sat for a long moment, regarding Thaddeus as he knelt before them. Thaddeus began to sweat. Then Peregrine looked across at Father Matthew with a curious expression on his face. He sighed, picked up the crutch that lay on the floor beside him, and got slowly to his feet. He crossed over, before the puzzled eyes of the community (puzzled, that is, except for Brother Tom, who was grinning like an idiot, and Brother Edward), to where Brother Thaddeus knelt, looking up at his abbot apprehensively.

'Stubbed your toe?' he said, looking down at him. 'I trust you are quite recovered.'

'Yes thank you, Father,' mumbled Thaddeus, wondering what on earth this was about. Leaning heavily on his shoulder, Peregrine bent with a grimace of pain to kneel beside him.

'I humbly confess my fault,' he said. 'Brothers, I also was guilty of using some of the most depraved language yesterday; in the hearing, furthermore, of one of our lay servants and one of our novices. I ask your forgiveness, and God's.'

There followed a startled silence, which Father Peregrine broke by saying testily, 'I believe in the circumstances, Father Chad, it falls to you to pronounce God's forgiveness.'

'Oh! Oh, yes. I—I'm sorry!' stuttered Father Chad. 'God forgives you, my brothers, and so do we.'

Father Peregrine, leaning again on Thaddeus, rose painfully to his feet, and limped back to his place.

The novices withdrew, as was customary, leaving the fully professed brothers to continue the community chapter.

'He didn't have to do that,' said Brother Francis. 'He could have waited until we'd gone.'

'It was more honest, though,' said Thaddeus, 'and it was worth it just to see Father Matthew's face! What *did* he say, anyway, Tom?'

Tom shook his head and wagged a finger at them in mock reproval. 'One man's sin,' he said, 'is not an appropriate topic for another man's conversation: and besides, it would make me blush to repeat it!'

We turned the corner into our road, and the evening sun had transformed the window-panes of all the houses into sheets of gold.

'That was the last time Father Matthew ever insisted that one of the novices confess to the whole community for swearing,' finished Mother, with a smile. 'Run on ahead, Melissa, love, and put the kettle on.'

VI
THE ASCENDING LARK

Mary's birthday was on September the twenty-ninth, the feast of St Michael and all Angels. Last year her birthday had fallen on a Sunday, but that year, the year she was six, her birthday fell on a school day. It was a warm, clear morning, and Mary sat like a princess at the breakfast table, in a crown of marigolds Mother had made from those still flowering in the garden. She wore her best dress and her happiest smile as she looked at her little pile of presents that lay among their tissue wrappings on the table in front of her.

Mary's smile (even now she is a grown woman it is still the same) has always been a smile of extraordinary loveliness, transforming her thin, serious face into something quite dazzling.

There was not the money for large or expensive presents, but Therese and I had sewn her a doll with a pretty dress and bonnet. The fiddly bits were slightly grubby from the sweat of our concentration, and I had left a bloodstain from a pricked finger on the doll's face, but Mary didn't seem to notice. She loved it, and she loved the necklace that Mother had saved from her own childhood, and the blue cardigan Grandma had knitted to match Mary's best dress. She loved everything. I can remember thinking, with a twinge of guilt at my cynicism, how easily pleased you are when you're only six.

Mary sighed a huge sigh of contentment, and then

turned her attention to the menu for tea. We were allowed to choose whatever we liked, within reason, for our birthday teas, and usually spent weeks beforehand deciding and planning and changing our minds—yes, even Therese and I, although we pretended to be so grown-up as to be above such things.

Mary was quite sure what she wanted. She raised her small, determined chin, fixing her earnest grey eyes on Mother's face. 'I would like orang-outang pie,' she said.

Mother looked slightly at a loss.

'What did you say, Mary?' asked Therese.

'Orang-outang pie,' repeated Mary, her voice faltering a little as she read the bewilderment on our faces. 'I would like orang-outang pie.'

Mother's face cleared and she began to laugh, 'Oh, Mary! You mean lemon meringue pie!'

The wave of our laughter shattered Mary's fragile dignity, and she began to cry.

'Mary, my love, of course you shall have it,' said Mother, trying to compose her face. 'Is there anything else you would like especially?'

'Candles,' whispered Mary, abashed, 'on my cake.'

'There will be candles!' promised Mother. 'And lemon meringue pie. Now make haste to school, girls, or you'll be late.'

Therese and I took Mary and Beth down as far as the county primary school, and stayed to wave goodbye to them as they went in at the gate. Mary was happy again when we left her, still wearing her best dress and a crown of marigolds. Her eyes shone like candles, and her head was held high as she walked down the path to the school building, clutching her bag which held her birthday treasures, ready to show the teacher. We watched them go, and then continued on our way to the high school for girls.

The school motto which decorated our blazer pockets was the same as that of the Royal Air Force, *Per ardua ad astra*, exhorting us through hard work to reach for the stars. It was a school proud of its academic record, and all the lovely possibilities of that motto were ignored in favour of the one dry interpretation, 'Pass your exams.' The only stars we were encouraged to yearn for within those walls were the little gold, gummed-paper shapes that the younger pupils earned for good work.

Since it was Monday, I was condemned to failure by the time-table before I even entered the gates: geography, chemistry, French, and a double lesson of mathematics. The day was redeemed marginally by an English lesson at the end of the afternoon. I struggled through a confusion of isobars, alkaline reaction, *petits dialogues*, and trigonometry, to collapse wearily into my chair for the English lesson, with a sigh of relief. We were spending the autumn term studying the English Romantic poets, and the present focus of our attention was Shelley. We had been reading his poetry for two weeks now—or rather listening to Mrs Freeman read it. We took up where we had left off the previous lesson, halfway through the romantic wallowings of the tragic tale 'Rosalind and Helen'.

Mrs Freeman ploughed on and on through stanza after stanza, and the self-indulgent, purple language at first annoyed me, then began to seem unbearable, and finally hilarious. Mrs Freeman's voice shook with emotion as she flicked over to page 188, the class meekly following her progress in their dog-eared, ink-stained textbooks, yellowed with age.

> 'And first, I felt my fingers sweep
> The harp, and a long quivering cry
> Burst from my lips in symphony ...'

Mrs Freeman declaimed in low and trembling tones.

> '... The dusk and solid air was shaken
> As swift and swifter the notes came
> From my touch that wandered like quick flame,
> And from my bosom labouring
> With some unutterable thing.

> The awful sound of my own voice made
> My lips tremble—

'Is something the matter, Melissa?' Mrs Freeman stopped in mid-flow and fixed me with a look of withering contempt. I could no more control the broad grin on my face than I had been able to restrain the snort of laughter that had escaped from me.

'Melissa? Something is amusing you? Perhaps you would explain to the class?'

'I'm sorry, Mrs Freeman,' I gasped, trying to conquer the waves of mirth that were still rising. 'It's nothing really. It's just ... it's just ... well, the poetry's so silly!'

Mrs Freeman looked at me in silence, and I felt the tension as she weighed up in her mind whether to approach the situation with an Enlightened Class Discussion, or to treat it as a Very Serious Matter. I was lucky. She plumped for the former.

'What a very interesting comment, Melissa. Can you explain just what you mean? Shelley's poetry has been loved and revered by the learned and the great, and yet you find it "silly"?'

'It *is* silly,' I said, with a sudden flash of reckless irritation. 'He takes himself too seriously. It's as though he's forgotten how to laugh at himself, so that it's not real any more, like when Beth, my little sister, is in a bad mood and goes off into Mother's bedroom to practise making miserable faces in the mirror. And not only that; my mother says—'

I stopped. There was a dangerous glint in Mrs Freeman's eye. Maybe she wouldn't want to hear what Mother had to say on the subject of Shelley's poetry.

'Yes?' said Mrs Freeman, but her tone of voice was not all that encouraging, 'And what does your mother say, Melissa?'

'Mother says, that love is only true love when it shows itself in fidelity—um, faithfulness. She says if a person has the feeling of love, but no faithfulness, his love is just self-indulgent sentimentality. And that's what Shelley was like, isn't it? He wrote fine poems to his wife and his lovers, but he wasn't a faithful man. So how can his poetry about love be worth anything if his love in real life wasn't worth anything?'

'Well, I understand what you're trying to say, Melissa,' said Mrs Freeman, kindly, 'but you must realise, Shelley was a very great artist—a free spirit and a philosopher. He was not quite like other men. That was part of his greatness.'

I could see she wanted that to be the end of it, but I had the light of battle in my eyes now. I wasn't Mother's daughter for nothing.

'Does that mean that if I can write poetry like this it doesn't matter if I keep my promises then?' I said.

Mrs Freeman's face wore a slight frown of irritation.

'Melissa,' she said patiently, 'Shelley was a very young man, and you are very young. You still have a great deal to learn. Now, how about the rest of the class? What do you think of the poem we have just been reading? Shirley?'

Shirley looked up from the complicated doodle she was perfecting in her notebook. She cleared her throat.

'It's ... it's ... it's got some good description in it ...' she ventured wildly.

'Norma?' said Mrs Freeman coldly.

'I don't know, really,' said Norma helplessly. 'It's a bit long and complicated. Perhaps he would have been better to write a proper story.'

Mrs Freeman drew a long, deep breath, and let it go in a sigh of discouragement. 'Let's leave it there for today,' she said, in a flat sort of voice. 'You can take down your homework in the last ten minutes. I will write the title for your essay on the board. Please have the plan ready for the next lesson. It may help you to read the introductory note to *Lyrical Ballads*, which starts after the foreword and the preface.'

I felt mean, somehow, as though I had squashed something precious for her. She had been so absorbed in the

poem. It was like Mary at the breakfast table, the sparkle
in her eyes extinguished by our thoughtless laughter. I
felt horrid inside, guilty. It must be rotten to be a teacher
sometimes, to face a blank sea of faces, resisting you. It was
as though we weren't people for the teachers, and they
weren't people for us. Worse than enemies. *Strangers.*
And yet ... and yet the poem *was* silly, and dishonest
too, somehow. A lot of words without truth or goodness
behind them ... I wrote down the homework, glad of
the end of the day, but the lesson left a sour taste in my
mouth. I wished I'd never said anything in the first place.

I waited for Therese after school and we walked
slowly up the hill together. There was something kind
and sensible about Therese that always made life seem
safe and normal again, when fear or questioning or
trouble invaded me. Even Therese looked gloomy
today, though.

'Lilian did copy my essay,' she said, as we plodded up
the hill. 'Mrs Freeman was cross about it, and told her
off in class. Lilian won't speak to me at all, now.'

'*She* won't speak to *you*! It ought to be the other way
round!'

Therese shook her head. 'She's my friend,' she said
sadly, 'but come on 'lissa! Mary will be waiting for her
birthday tea! Let's hurry up.'

It was a new idea to me that you could go on being
someone's friend even when they'd done something
awful to you, even when you felt as though you didn't
like them any more. I quickened my pace to match
Therese's. Lilian didn't seem worth it to me.

As we reached the gate, the door flew open, and Mary's
eager, radiant face met us. 'Come and see my cake!' she
cried. 'It says "Mary" and there are flowers and candles!'

It was a beautiful birthday cake, iced white with pink
rose-buds. Six of the rose-buds on the top had little
candles stuck in them, and Mary's name was written
across the middle in pale green icing.

The birthday tea was wonderful, with crisps and tiny

sausages, little cubes of cheese and grapes and three kinds of sandwiches, brandy-snaps filled with whipped cream, and a huge lemon meringue pie as well as the cake. There was a big jug of Mother's home-made lemonade to wash it all down.

We ate every crumb, and drank every drop, but before we cut up the cake we lit the candles and sang 'Happy Birthday' to Mary, and she blew out all her candles in one go, with a bit of help from Cecily. After tea, the little ones went out to play in the garden, pink and sticky and content.

Therese and I helped Mother clear away the tea things before we did our homework. As Therese went down the step into the kitchen, carrying the big blue and white jug that held the lemonade, she missed her footing, and the jug shot from her hands and smashed into a thousand pieces on the tiled floor. There was a horrified silence, and Therese looked at Mother with pink cheeks and shocked eyes full of tears.

'It was an accident,' said Mother resignedly. 'Get the brush and dustpan, Therese, and sweep it up. Get every little bit, now, because Cecily runs about barefoot in this warm weather.'

Therese swept up all the pieces, and took them, well wrapped in newspaper, to the dustbin.

'It was my favourite jug,' said Mother sadly, as Therese went out of earshot, round the corner of the house, 'but there's nothing to be gained by shouting at her. Things just fly out of her hands. I have to say to myself, "She's like Brother Theo, she doesn't do it on purpose, don't be cross."'

My ears pricked up at this. 'Like who? Is it a story? Who was Brother Theo?'

'Yes, there's a story. At bedtime I'll tell you.' Therese came in from the garden, looking miserable. 'I am sorry, Mother. It was your favourite jug.'

'Darling, it couldn't be helped. Come on now and do your homework, while I wash up these things.'

I hurried through my maths homework, uneasily aware of having done some very shaky calculations, and did the reading and essay plan Mrs Freeman had asked for. The little ones came in from the garden for their baths as I was writing, and I could hear them in the bathroom, arguing about whose turn it was to sit on the plug, and Mother's tired voice growing impatient. I finished off my work quickly, and went to help her towel them dry and shepherd them up to the bedroom.

They played their game of trumpeting elephants and scuttling mice, and said their prayers, and then Mary and Beth wriggled into their beds while Cecily curled up on Mother's lap, squeaking softly, 'Weakness! Weakness!' as Mother stroked her hair.

At last the day was over. The sunset had blazed its last splendid banners and subsided to a dusky crimson afterglow. I drew the curtains on it, and lit the candle.

'You said there was a story, Mother,' I said, unable to contain myself any longer. 'You said there was at teatime; about Brother Theo. Are you going to tell us now? Is it—'

'Hush,' said Mother. 'You're filling the air with excitement. It's calm and quiet we need for a story. Yes, I'll tell you about Brother Theo; when you're ready to listen.'

We all settled down and waited, and into the silence Cecily began to sing in her high reedy voice:

> 'Free blind mice, free blind mice,
> See how they run, see how they run,
> They all run after the farmer's wife
> And cut her up with a carving knife ...'

'Hush now,' laughed Mother. 'Listen to the story. Here, put your thumb in your mouth. That's better.' Cecily cuddled in close to Mother, and a vacant, drowsy look came into her eyes as she sucked her thumb, held warm and close in the candle-light. Beth yawned a huge yawn.

'I am six now,' said Mary. 'I am a big girl. I have had a lovely day.'

'Have you, Mary?' said Mother, pleased. 'I'm glad it was a nice birthday. Snuggle down now.'

'Please, Mother,' I ventured.

'Ssh,' she said.

Brother Theodore was a novice at the Abbey of St Alcuin. He was always in trouble; he'd been in trouble all his life. It wasn't really his fault. His father had been telling him to take that look off his face ever since he could remember, but try as he might, he'd never been able to reassemble his features to suit him, and he continually aggravated and disappointed his father in a thousand other ways, too. He was slow and dreamy and inattentive, a forgetter of messages and a bodger of errands. He wanted to join in the games that the other children played, but he couldn't throw straight, and he couldn't catch a ball, nor could he run without tripping on his own feet, which were large and clumsy like the rest of him. When he was seven years old, he went to learn his letters, along with the other lads of his village, under the tuition of Father Marcus, the parish priest, but he was a poor pupil, never knowing what he had been asked to do, though his work was good enough when he did it. Taken all round, he was a child born to get under the skin of authority and irritate, and whippings and scoldings were his daily fare. Things didn't improve much when, on his thirteenth birthday, his father apprenticed him to the iron-fisted, sullen-faced village blacksmith, to learn a trade and make his way in the world. From his new master, as from his father and his teacher, he attracted nothing but beatings and derision, for the blacksmith was a surly and impatient man with neither imagination nor kindness to spare for his gangling and butter-fingered apprentice, whose incompetence was pushed to ridiculous lengths by his fear.

The one source of comfort and loving-kindness in the poor boy's life was his grandmother: a dear, wise, gentle old lady to whom he brought all his tears and his troubles from his babyhood until she died, when he was fifteen. She had been a devout woman, and from her he had learned in early childhood to love the Mass and to pray and to trust to God's goodness in spite of adversity. Her death reverberated in shock waves through his loneliness, and having no one else now in whom to confide, he clung in prayer to Christ crucified, and began more and more to long for the monastic life of prayer and service lived to God's glory.

Just after his eighteenth birthday, already world-weary, sad and sporting a black eye which was his parting gift from his father—who bitterly resented the waste of the money he had laid out on his son's apprenticeship—the young man entered the community of Benedictines at St Alcuin's. He came as much in the mood of a man seeking sanctuary as anything else, though there burned somewhere within him a small flame of hope that here, if anywhere, he would find acceptance and brotherhood, a place to belong. His name had rung in his ears like a clap of thunder in the mouths of irate parents and teachers until he was glad to hear the last of it when he made his novitiate vows and was clothed in the habit of the order, and tonsured, and given his new name which was Brother Theodore. He began his new life churning with mixed emotions: lingering grief for his grandmother, a sense of shame at his inability to succeed at anything, all mixed with a passionate longing to serve God well and to be a good monk. But for all his good intentions, here, too, he was always in trouble.

Father Matthew avowed that Theodore was the only novice who could slam a door opening it as well as shutting it. He was almost always late for his lessons, and sometimes for the Office too, however hard he tried to be in the right place at the right time. His habit was stained, torn and patched, and his hair around the tonsure looked like a crow's nest. He dreaded the days when it was his turn to wait on the brothers at table, in case a pewter plate should slip from his fingers and fall with a crash, causing the reader to lose his place and the silent monks to smile or glare according to temperament; or lest the pitcher should slip in his hands and he should splash water into someone's soup.

Poor Brother Theo. He was a thorn in Father Matthew's side; Father Matthew being neat and careful in all he did, and tidy and well groomed to the point of suavity. Father Matthew found Theodore exasperating beyond what his patience could endure, and berated him daily for his care-. lessness and clumsiness. He was determined to mould even this unpromising specimen of a novice into the quiet, unobtrusive, recollected character which was the monastic ideal; by exhortation, by penance, and occasionally even by the rod.

Theodore saw his hopes of a new beginning turn to ashes in the miserable discovery that even men who had given their whole lives to follow Christ could be irritable, sharp-tongued and hasty, to one like himself.

In spite of this sad realisation, life was not all misery, for amidst his habitual diet of failure and disgrace, Theo found in the monastery three places of refuge—sources of comfort and even of delight. The first was the scriptorium, for here, astonishingly, he proved to have an uncommon talent in the art of manuscript illumination, and a fair hand as a copyist, producing work of elegance and beauty.

He also discovered that he was musically gifted and could express in composition the same exquisite harmony and balance that showed in his manuscript work but was so disastrously lacking in all other areas of his life. So his second place of refuge was with the precentor, Brother Gilbert, with whom he spent time working on new settings for the Mass and the psalms and canticles, harmonising his clear and pleasant tenor with Brother Gilbert's baritone. Brother Gilbert treated him with friendship and respect—respect well-deserved too—and for this Theodore was grateful indeed. His family was one where there was neither interest nor pleasure in music or art, and these subjects were a new experience for him. Brother Gilbert and Brother Clement who oversaw the library and scriptorium noticed with interest that as Theodore was able to forget his self-consciousness and lose himself in the creative work he loved, so his clumsiness dropped away from him; and with ink and brush and pen and parchment he was deft and precise in all he did. They made no comment, but being artists themselves they understood, as Father Matthew did not, Brother Theodore's temperament.

Theo's third bolt-hole was the abbot's lodging, for he was often required by Father Peregrine to copy borrowed manuscripts for the abbey library, or to write at Peregrine's dictation now that his own hands served no longer for more than writing brief letters of an informal nature. It was a relief to find in Father Peregrine someone more clumsy even than himself and even more likely than he to spill food on its way to his mouth, or send a stream of ale shooting over the edge of a mug instead of safely into the middle of it. Neither did Father Peregrine glare at him, or wither him with icy sarcasm when the door handle slipped out of his nerveless fingers and the door crashed shut behind him. On the contrary, he treated him with unfailing gentleness and courtesy, and Brother Theodore found himself more relaxed and less clumsy as a consequence in Father Peregrine's company than with anyone else.

It had been some while now since Brother Theo had had the opportunity to do any copying or illuminating, or to make any music. It was the time for the hay harvest, and all able-bodied brothers who could possibly be spared from their usual work had been helping with the harvest, from the reaping until it was safely gathered and stacked, the barns filled against the lean months of winter. It had been a good year, with a warm, wet spring and dry breezy weather for the time of the harvest, so the whole community had sweated to get the hay in before the weather should break. The harvest was in now, and none too soon, for the heavy, stifling heat threatened thunder and rain.

With the barns full, the daily routine could be resumed. On the last day of the harvest, the brothers gathered in the community room after supper, weary and happy to relax for an hour before Compline.

Father Chad leaned back against the wall with a comfortable sigh, stretching his legs out before him. 'Your novices will welcome a day's rest after the work they've put in this week, Brother,' he remarked peacefully to Father Matthew, who sat beside him on the bench.

'Rest?' said Father Matthew in surprise. 'No, we shall be back to work as usual tomorrow. The lot I have at the moment are so slow with their Greek we could ill afford the week we've lost.'

Father Chad looked at him in disbelief. 'Matthew, you're jesting! They always have a day off after the harvest! Well, that is to say, when I was in the novitiate under Father Lucanus, we did. ...'

There was a slightly chilly pause. 'That possibly accounts for your difficulties with New Testament Greek, Father Prior,' said Father Matthew with calm disdain.

Father Chad, chastened, and unable to deny this deficiency, had no more to say.

The weary young men were back to work at half-past six on the following morning, with barely time beforehand to swallow their dry bread and water on which they broke their fast after the first Mass. Having kept them at their study of Greek for the better part of the morning, Father Matthew rather grudgingly gave them the three-quarters of an hour that remained after the community chapter meeting and before the midday Office of Sext for their own private reading and meditation.

Brother Theodore went up to his cell armed with a copy of Boethius' *De Trinitate* and the *Dialogues* of St Gregory. It was warm, almost hot, in his cell on this lazy summer day, and Theo could scarcely keep his eyes open as he read, his body still pleasantly aching and fatigued from the week's labour in the fields.

In the end, he laid his head on his arms ('I'll just close my eyes for one minute,' he said to himself) and slept as he sat: deep, satisfying sleep.

He awoke with a start, and listened. How long had he been sleeping? There was not a sound, nobody about. He dashed down the stairs to the chapel, paused warily outside the door and listened. They were already singing the *Kyrie Eleison*; that meant the Office was almost finished. He groaned inwardly. If he went in now, he would have to stand by himself in the place of disgrace reserved for latecomers, for the third time this week. Then would follow a cutting rebuke from Father Matthew, and kneeling to confess his fault before the abbot, to be given yet another penance.

Theodore's courage failed him. Already this week he had been in trouble for breaking a mug, for coming late to the Office and to instruction, for knocking over a stool with a terrible crash, and for singing during the Great Silence after Compline. He hadn't even realised he was singing! A new tune for the Magnificat was forming in his head, and he had sung softly without realising it as the phrases came together. Father Matthew, overhearing, had hissed in his ear, 'For shame, Brother Theodore,' and scowled at him frostily. He had been loaded with rebukes and penances and admonition until he was weary of life and of himself.

He turned away from the chapel door and plodded back up to his cell, where he sat down on his bed and stared gloomily at the crucifix on the wall, wondering what to do next. 'Lord have mercy,' he said wistfully, and then, 'Oh, God,' and sighed, and waited.

Before long the Office was ended, and he could hear the distant sounds of the brothers making their way to the refectory for the midday meal. Should he go down and slip in among them, in the hope that Father Matthew had not noticed his absence in the chapel? Not a chance. Better to go now to the scriptorium and begin his afternoon work and hope to avoid Father Matthew altogether, at least until the evening.

So Theo went to the scriptorium, sat down in his study alcove and looked at the page from the Book of Hours he was illuminating. He began to feel more cheerful at once, and was soon absorbed in his work, lost in concentration until the bell sounded for None, the afternoon Office. As soon as he heard the bell, he laid his work aside, determined for once to be on time, and bounded down the stairs to collide forcibly with Father Matthew at the foot of them, nearly knocking the wind out of the novice master's body.

Father Matthew looked at him with the expression of a man using extreme self-control. Brother Theodore began miserably to apologise, but Father Matthew cut him short. 'You were not in your place at the midday meal, Brother, nor were you present for the Office. Have you any explanation?'

'O God, O God,' thought Theodore. 'Now what?' Then it was as though all of a sudden something snapped inside him, and he heard himself saying, 'Father Abbot needed me to do some copying work for him, Father.'

'And he detained you through the Office and the midday meal?' asked Father Matthew in surprise.

'Yes, Father.'

'That's not like him,' said Father Matthew, with a puzzled frown.

'It was urgent, Father. He has a manuscript on loan that he wishes to copy before it is returned.'

'Very well, Brother,' said Father Matthew. 'It's odd, though. He usually lets me know if he has to keep one of the novices from their instruction or from the Office. It must have slipped his mind. Anyway, make haste now, or we shall be late. You'd better get yourself something to eat afterwards; you must be hungry.'

'Thank you, Father,' mumbled Brother Theo wretchedly, and followed his superior into the church.

It was in the peaceful hour after supper and before Compline that Father Matthew encountered Father Peregrine in the cloister.

'I would be grateful, Father, if you would remember to tell me when you require Brother Theodore to work for you,' he said, in tones of mild disapproval. 'He has already been in trouble almost continually this month, and I am having to watch him strictly. Today he was missing from both the midday Office and the midday meal, but when I took him to task over it, I find he was detained by yourself. Father, it is difficult enough to try to teach him discipline. If I don't know where he is it becomes impossible.'

Peregrine's eyebrows shot up in surprise, and he blinked at Father Matthew. Then he said, 'What are the things he has been in trouble for?'

'Father, the list is endless. He is careless, he is clumsy, he is late, he is noisy, he breaks things, he loses things; his behaviour is undisciplined in the extreme—why, last night I caught him singing during the Great Silence.'

'Singing, you say?' said Father Peregrine. 'I would have thought he had precious little to sing about!'

'Exactly so, Father. I have done all I can. He has been rebuked, he has been given penance, I have admonished him repeatedly. I have even resorted to the scourge.'

'Yes, I can imagine,' said Father Peregrine thoughtfully, 'and it makes it more difficult for you when you don't know what he's up to, or where he is, of course. I am too often thoughtless and forgetful. I ask your pardon. I have some work outstanding that I need him for in the morning. Perhaps you would send him to me.'

'Of course, Father,' said Father Matthew, and their conversation ended there.

In the morning, Brother Theo, by a great effort, managed to be in the right place at the right time, doing the right thing, and arrived for the morning novitiate instruction feeling cautiously optimistic, to be greeted by Father Matthew saying frigidly, 'Father Abbot requires you this morning, Brother Theodore. You are excused from your lessons.'

Theodore's mouth went dry as he received the summons, and his heart thumped as he trailed across the cloister to the abbot's house. Did Father Peregrine know? He could not tell from the way Father Matthew had spoken. It was very possible that the novice master would mention his absence from Office and the midday meal, and then of course, Father Peregrine would have exposed his lie.

Reluctantly, Theo raised his hand and knocked at Peregrine's door, which stood ajar. *'Benedicite!'* called a cheerful voice from within, and Theodore entered and forced himself to look his abbot in the face.

'Good day, Brother,' said Peregrine with a friendly smile. 'I expect Father Matthew told you, I have some illumination work I need done. It is only a text for Master Goodwin from the village. He wants it for his daughter as a present for her child's baptism.'

Theodore stared at him, dizzy with relief. He didn't know! By some miracle, Father Matthew had not asked him about yesterday. With luck he would never find out and Theo would be safe!

'Yes, of course, Father,' he said and walked to the scribe's desk in the corner by the window, where parchment and inks, brushes and pens lay ready for him.

Father Peregrine stood by his own table, selecting a book from a pile that lay there.

'What is the text, Father?' asked Theodore.

'The text?' said Peregrine absently. 'Oh, it's from the Book of Proverbs, chapter twelve and verse twenty-two: *Abominatio est Domino labia mendacia: qui autem fideliter agunt placent ei.'*

'The Lord detests lying lips,' translated Theodore slowly, 'but he delights in men who are truthful.'

He stood and looked at Father Peregrine, but he was busy with his pile of books, his back turned to him. Did he know? It was a very strange verse to choose for a child's baptismal greeting. Theodore felt that familiar, horrible sinking feeling in the pit of his stomach. What now? Should he just write out the text and say nothing? *Could* he sit there all morning, carefully writing and illuminating such words, without owning up to his own lie?

Father Peregrine turned and looked at him enquiringly. 'Is something the matter, Brother?'

Did he know? Theodore couldn't tell. He loved this man, who had always treated him so gently and so courteously, and the thought of losing his respect was unbearable. To be clumsy and careless was bad enough in a monk, but to be a liar was despicable. But if he knew ... if he knew and Theodore said nothing, he would be in even deeper disgrace than if he didn't know and Theodore told him. And if he didn't know, did not God know anyway? And what was the point in trying to please men, when you had done the thing God detested, and told a lie?

Slowly, Brother Theodore knelt. 'Father, I ... I told a lie,' he said. 'I fell asleep yesterday morning, and didn't wake up until the midday Office was nearly over. I didn't go into the chapel. I told Father Matthew ...' Theodore struggled to keep his voice firm as he spoke. To his shame, he felt a hot tear escape from his eye. Father Peregrine waited and said nothing. 'I said you had kept me here doing some copying work for you,' finished Theodore bleakly. 'I'm sorry.' He clenched his teeth and stiffened his face against the tears. He had not known how much the abbot's friendship had fed his hungry soul until now he had lost it.

'God forgives you, my son, and so do I,' Father Peregrine said gently. 'Come and sit down and tell me about this, Theo.'

When Theodore raised his eyes, he was greeted by a kindly smile. All his life he had been used to steeling himself against rebuke and censure, but the unaccustomed kindness was too much for him, and he buried his face in his hands and sobbed like a child. Father Peregrine sat down on the scribe's stool beside him and waited for the storm to pass.

'God forgive us, we must almost have broken him, poor lad,' he thought as he looked on the bowed body, shaking in anguished weeping. He thought of St Benedict's recommendation in the Rule, that the abbot should remember his own frailty and have a care not to break the bruised reed, or destroy the pot in his zeal to remove the rust. 'The abbot in this monastery wouldn't get a chance to break the bruised reed, if he wanted to,' he thought. 'Father Matthew's in there before me, trampling on it in his tactless clogs. The scourge, indeed! Oh, poor lad, you have suffered. God help me now to find the right words and bring some healing there.'

Theodore, who never had his handkerchief, scrubbed at his eyes with his knuckles, and wiped his nose on his sleeve. Father Peregrine gave him his own handkerchief, and Theodore blew his nose noisily, and raised his woebegone face to look at him.

Peregrine burst out laughing. 'Oh, Brother, it's not so bad,' he said. 'Get up off the floor, man, and tell me what's been going on.'

Theodore told him everything. Simply, and without defending himself, he poured out his pain. He told him about the misery of his boyhood, his hope of a new life on entering the community, then the lateness and breakages and the slamming of doors, his inability to please Father Matthew. Hopelessly he explained how he had tried and struggled and failed, and finally his courage had failed him.

Peregrine listened without a word. Finally he said: 'Father Matthew tells me you are careless and clumsy.'

'He tells me it, too,' said Theodore miserably, 'and it's true. I am.'

'Brother Theodore, there is no one in this community with so fair a hand as yours or such a gift for illumination. I have never known you mar your work or overlook

a mistake. I know that if I ask you to produce a document for me, it will be legible, beautiful and accurate. I
have *never* known you be either clumsy or careless in
your work. On the contrary, you make it beautiful with
both artistry and conscientiousness.'

Theo gazed at the floor, dumb and embarrassed in
his happiness. The words were like ointment on a wound.
It had always been impressed upon him that work well
done was no more than his duty, and though his work
had always been in demand, it had never before been
praised. Father Matthew felt that his soul was imperiled
enough without giving him cause to be conceited.

'Now then, get up off the floor, my friend, and get
to work on this text. Perhaps Master Goodwin would
prefer something a little less menacing. Try Psalm 103
verses thirteen and fourteen: *Quomodo miseratur pater fil-
iorum, miseratus est Dominus, timentibus se: Quoniam ipse
cognovit figmentum nostrum, recordatus est quoniem pulvis
sumus.*'

'As a father has compassion on his children,' said
Theodore, 'so the Lord has compassion on those who
fear him; for he knows how we are formed, he remembers
that we are dust.' He got to his feet, but then his heart
sank again as an unpleasant thought occurred to him.
'Father, I suppose . . . should I tell Father Matthew about
the lie I told, and confess it at community chapter?'

Father Peregrine sat looking up at him. His eyes were
twinkling. 'Brother,' he said, 'from all I hear, Father
Matthew has been zealous enough at pruning your unfruit-
ful branches for one week. You have confessed your sin. It
is done with. Put it behind you and get on with your work.'

Brother Theodore made that text a work of art. Just
at the end of it where it said, 'He remembers that we are
dust,' he painted a little lark, emblem of the soul of man,
rising up out of the dust in song.

Mother got up from her chair and carefully carried the

sleeping Cecily to her bed. 'Sleep well, little Goldenhair,' she said softly, as she tucked her in.

'I like Brother Theo,' murmured Beth's drowsy voice, 'but not Brother Matthew. Brother Matthew is a baddy.'

'Father Matthew,' corrected Mother. 'Father, because he was a priest. Don't you like him, little mouse? He was a very good monk, though.'

'He wasn't kind. Christians should be kind.'

'That's right, my love. Perhaps he was trying too hard. Perhaps he was thinking so hard about being good that he forgot to think about being kind.'

'Well, anyway, I don't like him,' said Beth conclusively.

'That's because you like the rascals! You like Brother Tom best, don't you, because he was a mischief. Enough of that now, though. Snuggle down to sleep. Melissa, are you staying here or coming down for a while?'

'I'll come down,' I decided.

'Me too!' said Beth.

'Ssh, quiet, Beth, you'll wake Mary and Cecily. No, darling, you must stay in bed now. Melissa is a big girl, it's not her bed time quite, but she'll be up soon. Night-night now. I'll leave the door open, and you won't feel lonely.'

Mother blew out the candle, and we went downstairs.

VII
TOO MANY COOKS

Beth and Cecily and I used to get the most miserable colds as children; I can still remember the feeling. My nose would be blocked, all my sinuses throbbing painfully. The area under my nose would be sore with rubbing against my hanky; my lips would be cracked and dry from breathing through my mouth; my eyes would run and my head feel as though it was full of porridge, thick and hot.

The season of colds, which ran all the way through to the end of February, started in November, when the magical, golden enchantment of autumn days (the wine of the seasons, when the year held its breath at the approach of frost and fire) turned into the raw damp of the backend of the year, clogging leaves packed underfoot and chilling fog pervading everything. If I had to draw a picture of November, I think I would draw an old man in a grey macintosh, blowing his nose. Even the smoky delights of fireworks and baked potatoes on bonfire night do no more than hold off the depression of those creeping fingers of darkness and cold.

I turned fifteen at the end of October and had no sooner celebrated my birthday than the first of November found me flushed with fever and thick with catarrh. I moped and sweated under a mound of blankets in our frosty bedroom for a day, and snuffled and dozed through a delirious night, then by the morning the fever had subsided, and I was left feeling weak and fractious with the thick-headed, mouth-breathing, runny-eyed misery of a streaming cold.

When the others had gone to school, Mother lit a fire for me to sit by and made a nest for me on the sofa. She gave me hot elderberry cordial to drink, and made me inhale steam from a great enamel jug of friar's balsam dissolved in boiling water. I began to feel more cheerful, enjoying the luxury of being pampered and waited on, and I was looking forward to the afternoon, when Cecily, who had so far escaped my cold, was to go shopping with Grandma and I would have the precious treat of Mother's company all to myself for a whole afternoon.

I think Mother was longing as much as I was for an afternoon without Cecily. I had been short-tempered and irritable all week, and Cecily was like a simmering volcano at the best of times. Feeling too unwell to summon the patience and consideration she needed, I had fallen out with her before breakfast. She was ready to pick a fight with anyone by lunchtime.

Mother's patience was wearing thin too, but she managed to humour Cecily into eating her lunch, a thick vegetable soup with hot brown rolls and creamy butter that I could not taste. Then Mother swathed Cecily in her brightly-coloured scarf, gloves and hat, and buttoned her duffle coat on over the top, then stood her on a chair in the window to watch for Grandma. She stood very still, looking with great concentration at all the passers-by. 'That's not Grandma. That's not Grandma. That's not Grandma. Grandma!'

Grandma swept Cecily up into a big hug as she came in from the cold. 'There's my precious! Are you ready? Round the shops, then tea at Betty's and back in time for bed. All right, Mummy?'

'Sounds good to me,' said Mother with a smile. ''Bye 'bye Cecily. Have a lovely time. Here, you haven't got your shoes on!'

'And how are you, Melissa?' asked Grandma, as

Mother fastened on Cecily's shoes. 'Better for a day in bed I expect. I'll pick you up some of my herbal linctus from the pharmacy. That'll frighten any cold! See you later, then, ladies. Enjoy your afternoon.'

Mother waved goodbye to them from the door, then disappeared into the kitchen and returned five minutes later bearing a tray with two thick slices of fruit cake, a cup of coffee for herself, and some lemon and honey for me. She put another log on the fire and curled up in her armchair with her coffee cupped in her hands, looking into the flames.

'Peace,' she said happily. 'Oh, this is nice. It's nice when you feel peaceful inside, and you can curl up by the fire in a peaceful house. Too much racket in the house and it frays you at the edges a bit; but if you lose the peace on the inside of you, you could be in the quietest place on earth and your nerves would still jangle.'

I ate my fruit cake slowly. It is so difficult to eat when you have to breathe through your mouth. I felt quite exhausted by the time I'd finished. I drank the lemon and honey, and snuggled under my blanket on the mound of pillows Mother had provided.

'Tell me a story about Father Peregrine, Mother,' I said. She gazed into the fire, thinking, seeing, far away. Then she smiled.

'I never told you Brother Cormac's story, did I?' she asked.

'No!' I said. 'Tell me! He was one of the novices, wasn't he?'

He entered at about the same time as Brother Theodore, two years after Father Peregrine was attacked and beaten by his father's enemies. In those days, the novitiate lasted only a year before a monk was solemnly professed (nowadays it's a matter of years). Brother Tom was a novice longer than most—he entered just over two years before Cormac, but was with him in the novitiate for six months, too. At the time of this story, Brother Tom and Brother Francis had just made their solemn profession, and Brother Theodore, Brother Thaddeus and Brother Cormac were left in the novitiate, along with a young man called Gerard Plumley, who had not yet made his first vows and been given his new name.

Brother Cormac was an Irishman. He was a long, thin streak of a lad, with a wild tangle of black hair, and eyes as blue as speedwell. He had been an orphan since he was a tiny child. His mother and father died together in the seas off the coast of England, when the ship in which they were crossing the Irish Sea was hit by stormy weather, and foundered on the rocks. A wreck always drew a crowd: some to loot, some to watch and some to save lives. Under the grim sky and against the squalls of wind and rain, men dared the savage sea and brought to shore as many of the dead and the exhausted survivors as they could find. They found Cormac, only a baby then, about Cecily's age, clutching tightly to his drowned mother, terrified and half-drowned himself, and they left it to the gathering of women on the shore to separate the two.

They also saved from the wreck an Irish merchant who had made his home in York, and had been returning from a visit to his family in Ireland. The merchant recognised the scared waif, and was able to identify the child's father among the dead. The fishermen and the other local folk had mouths enough to feed at home, and nobody knew what to do with the orphaned child. He had fought and scratched and bitten his rescuers as they prised him free from his mother's body, but he sat quietly enough now, wrapped in a blanket on a bench in the inn which had opened its doors as a refuge.

The Irish merchant had no little ones of his own, and looking down at the blue eyes great with terror and shock in the child's blanched face, he took pity on him, and being full of gratitude to God for his own deliverance from the wild sea, he took the orphan home for his wife to care for. This impulsive gesture of generosity they often regretted, for the black-haired, blue-eyed elf of a baby grew to be a wild, wayward, moody boy who brought them more headaches than joy.

When he was eighteen, the earliest the monks could take him, his jaded foster-parents steered him firmly in the direction of the cloister, feeling that they had done their fair share and more of giving houseroom to this difficult charge. They thought of the monastery, because one of his unreasonable habits was his flat refusal, since he was eight years old, to eat anything of flesh or fowl or fish or even eggs and milk. His distraught foster-mother had thought at first he would be ill without such wholesome food, but he proved healthier than all the rest of the household on his dried beans and vegetables; and besides, it was more trouble than it was worth to try to dissuade him. Early conversations had gone something like this:

'Drink up your milk, my lad.'

'It is not my milk. It is for the calf.'

'Daisy the cow doesn't mind you drinking a drop, my poppet.'

'It is not true. You have taken her calf away. She cries for her calf.'

'She's only a beast, my pet. She won't fret long. Drink up now.'

'It is the calf's milk. No.'

As he grew older, he would lecture his bewildered foster-parents fiercely about their exploitation of God's innocent creatures. His foster-father would look down at the hunk of roast meat in his hand feeling a little queasy as the piercing blue eyes fixed him with an accusing stare, and his adopted son held forth passionately on the freedom and grace of the running deer, the beauty and serenity of the mother bird in her nest. In the end, what with one thing and another, they'd had enough of him, and knowing that all the monks, except the sick brothers in the infirmary, abstained from eating the flesh of all four-footed creatures, they felt it a reasonable compromise to send him there.

He was willing, though not enthusiastic, and realising that the hospitality extended to his childhood need had now run out, he saw no alternative but to comply with their wishes and offer himself to serve and learn to love God, in return for his bed and board in God's house. He was fairly horrified to discover that there he would eat what he was given and make no complaint, and he submitted to this repulsive discipline with a bad grace and a churning stomach. He did not make himself popular in his first months with the community. He was more than a little touchy and inclined to take himself seriously and bear a grudge when anyone offended him. In truth, he was more at peace with the animal kingdom than with mankind or with himself.

The one person he did take to was Father Peregrine—fortunately, since he was entering a life that would involve vowing himself to total obedience to the abbot of the community. When first he was brought to the abbot by his foster-parents, he looked at the lean, hawk's face with its savage scar, the still, twisted hands, and he felt an unfamiliar stirring of compassion. Equally strange to him was the uneasy feeling of inadequacy that grew in him as the calm, shrewd eyes appraised him. Well used to condemning other men, he was surprised by the grudging but involuntary respect this maimed and gentle monk's unassuming authority called forth in him. As time went on, the grudging respect developed into a fierce loyalty, and the incidents of the humble pie and Brother Thaddeus' confession made their mark on him and won his affection. He was grateful, too, that Father Peregrine acknowledged his Irish origins in giving him the name Cormac.

Thus it was that Brother Cormac began to love, who had never loved; who had taken the tenderness that should have been for brother and sister and mother and father and given it instead to the birds and the beasts, because they could never be his kin, and could never hurt him by being lost to him. So he began, awkwardly, to unfold.

In his first weeks in the abbey, Brother Cormac had been put to work in the scriptorium, but his restless and discontented spirit was unsuited to the disciplined and painstaking work. After his naming and clothing he was moved to work in the kitchens, which proved equally disastrous.

He and Brother Andrew took an instant dislike to each other, and the sparks flew at every encounter. Brother Andrew provoked him by making sarcastic comments to him if his work was badly done, and Cormac, though he was not openly insolent, yet managed to convey his dislike and contempt for the old man in every look and gesture. Brother Andrew further goaded him by insisting on mispronouncing his name and calling him 'Cormick', a minor yet infuriating pinprick, but the kind of gibe that was Brother Andrew's specialty.

'Cormac,' he would say, 'my name is Cormac.' But it didn't do any good.

In the end, Father Matthew moved him and sent him to work in the gardens and in the infirmary with Brother Edward, in the hope that the contemplative outdoor work of gardening and the care of the aged and the sick would between them bring to life a little gentleness and peace of mind in him.

One of his tasks in the infirmary was to help Brother Edward with the daily task of working and massaging Father Peregrine's stiff, crippled hands. Brother Edward thought those long, sensitive Irish fingers looked as if there could be skill in them if only they could be taught a little kindness. Besides this, Edward well knew the calming and tranquilising power that lay in aromatic oils, and he thought it would do Cormac good to work with them. As for Brother Cormac, he was only too relieved to be sent to work elsewhere than with Brother

Andrew, and determined he would never cross the old man's path or speak to him again if he could help it.

It was unfortunate for him that one day when it was his turn to serve at table, he knocked against Brother Andrew's arm, entirely accidentally, while pouring ale for one of the brothers. He caused Brother Andrew to spill the spoonful of vegetable stew he was holding, and splash gravy onto his habit. Andrew growled an irritable comment under his breath at Brother Cormac, who muttered sourly back at him. Father Peregrine's attention was caught by the exchange, and he saw the ill-tempered look that passed between them. He came later to find Brother Edward in the infirmary, and asked him: 'Would you say Brother Cormac is unhappy?'

'Unhappy?' echoed Brother Edward. 'Well I can't say I've ever seen him smile. Mind you, he's better since he's been away from Brother Andrew. They came close to blows, those two.'

Father Peregrine looked at him thoughtfully. 'And that is why Brother Cormac was moved away from the kitchens?' he asked.

'Oh, yes. Brother Andrew is a contrary old devil at the best of times, but it was as tense as a thunderstorm with the two of them together.'

'I didn't know. I was under the impression that Father Matthew felt the garden and infirmary work would be beneficial to Brother Cormac.'

'Well, that's true, but it was a matter of urgency to get him away from Brother Andrew. The atmosphere between them was poisonous.'

'He'll have to go back to the kitchen, then,' said Father Peregrine. 'No, it's no good, Brother,' he insisted in response to Edward's gesture of protest. 'There's no place in a monastic community for enmity and quarrelling. Somehow or other this must be resolved.'

He discussed the matter no further with Brother Edward, but went straight along to find Father Matthew. The day following, the novice master sent Brother

Cormac back to the kitchen to work, and Gerard replaced him in the garden and the infirmary.

Cormac was to continue with only one of his former tasks in connection with the infirmary. As they were so busy at that time of year (it was a raw, damp October) with bronchial coughs and feverish colds, he was told to keep on his daily job of working with Edward on Father Peregrine's hands, at least until the winter ailments had run their course. That this was mainly for his sake, to give him a restoring space in the midst of a difficult day, did not occur to him. He was merely appalled to find himself back in Brother Andrew's company.

A picture of sullen resentment, Brother Cormac presented himself in the kitchen after the morning instruction in the novitiate, to be greeted by the sarcastic old cook's 'Good morning, Brother Cormick. Better late than never. Would you prepare that pile of chicken livers yonder for the potted meat?'

'Cormac,' the young man replied through clenched teeth and turned to his work. His gorge rose in disgust at the sight of a pile of chicken livers sufficient to feed thirty monks, and he seethed with rage and resentment that Brother Andrew should have designated this work to him. Grimly, he set to work, and a long job it was, too.

It was well on into the morning, as things were getting busy towards lunchtime, that Father Peregrine came into the kitchen. The working area was not very spacious, and the staff were hard put to fit round each other as it was, so it was with a frown of annoyance that Brother Andrew broke off from his work to attend to the interruption.

'I'm sorry to trouble you, Brother Andrew,' Father Peregrine began courteously.

'I should think you are if you want your lunch on time,' was the reply he got.

The abbot looked a little taken aback, but persevered. 'Brother, I have come to beg a favour of you. You will probably know, it is difficult for me to maintain much movement in my hands, especially as I have no form of work for them in the course of my duties but a little writing. I wondered if I might come in here and work for a while each morning, so as to stretch them a little further?'

Brother Cormac looked up from the mangled pile of poultry offal. He was mildly surprised and puzzled. He knew—they all knew—that Father Peregrine hated to draw attention to the state of his hands. As he spoke now, his stiff formality sounded awkward and reluctant, as though he was wishing he could escape from Brother Andrew's irritated glare. There was something odd about it. Cormac looked at Brother Andrew, to see how he would take the suggestion.

Brother Andrew was staring at Father Peregrine in exasperation. His kitchen was crowded, and he had enough already to plan and arrange, but a request from the abbot was an order, however politely phrased. He had no choice but to obey. He didn't, however, have to be cheerful about it.

'Father, this is my busiest time of day. I cannot stop for conversation now. If you think it would be helpful to you, then come, but you'll have to keep yourself from under my feet. This kitchen is cramped enough already. I have no space for a lame man going to and fro. No doubt I could think of something to occupy you if you'll keep to a corner out of the way; but come tomorrow early, not now, because I'm run off my feet already.' And with this gracious speech, Brother Andrew turned back to his work and left Father Peregrine standing.

Cormac, watching, saw the muscle flex in Peregrine's cheek, and saw the imperious flash in his eye, saw him draw breath to reply but then he set his lips firmly, bowed his head, turned and limped out of the kitchen without a word. Recognising in that flash of the eye a spirit as fiery as his own, Cormac's proud heart paid unwilling tribute to a self-control he knew he could not match if he tried.

It was not that Brother Andrew was really unkind, just extraordinarily thoughtless, and not always able to make the distinction between plain speaking and plain rudeness. He did, at any rate, give careful thought to what tasks Father Peregrine could reasonably do in the kitchen, and took the trouble to discuss with him at some length the next morning just what he could and could not manage, ascertaining that although he could not cut anything very hard, like a turnip, or tough, like raw meat, and could not carry anything heavy unless he could hold it in his arm, he was able and willing to try any other tasks.

And try he did, humbly and largely unsuccessfully. Brother Andrew grew exasperated with him and did little to disguise the fact, annoyed as he was that this ridiculous whim of the abbot should have been visited on him.

Brother Michael, Brother Andrew's gentle and friendly assistant, did his best to help Father Peregrine with those things that were clearly beyond him. He watched him one morning, struggling to remove the flesh from a poultry carcass for a game pie. It had taken him long enough just to roll and fasten back the wide sleeves of his habit in order to tackle the messy task. He was up to his elbows in grease and once nearly had the whole dishful off the table onto the floor. He stopped and closed his eyes, wearily rubbing his hand across his brow, thereby transferring poultry fat to his face as well as his hands. He sighed, set to work again, and Brother Michael came and stood by him quietly, helping him to finish the job.

'Thank you, Brother,' he said, but Michael caught the note of humiliation mingled with polite appreciation.

Father Peregrine did his best to minimise the hindrance he caused by his slow lameness in the busy kitchen, and mainly occupied himself with jobs that involved standing still, or sitting at a work bench, out of the bustle of activity. Even so, he did get in the way sometimes. Things were always at their worst at about eleven o'clock, when the kitchen staff were scurrying to get the main meal of the day to the table promptly after the midday Office of Sext.

On one such busy morning, Brother Andrew stood at one of the tables making a rich pastry: he was using eggs and butter, and the rare luxury of wheat flour, for a party of visitors who were staying in the guest house. He stood with the flour and diced fat in front of him, and the basin of eggs to one side at the edge of the table. He worked swiftly and deftly with one eye to the incompetent way Cormac was chopping herbs for the stew a few feet away from him.

'Chop those finer, please, Brother Cormick,' said the Scottish voice sharply. 'You're working in my kitchen now, not shovelling in the garden.'

Cormac looked up at him with undisguised loathing, and continued his work without replying. Out of the corner of his eye, Brother Andrew was aware of a pot boiling too fast over the fire, and seeing on a quick glance round that everyone was fully occupied except Father Peregrine, who had just returned from his task of sorting through the onions in the store-room, he said, 'You might come and swing this pot off the fire for me, Father.'

Peregrine, hastening to be helpful, slipped on a little cube of butter that had fallen from the pastry-making as he passed Brother Andrew's table. He shot out his hand instinctively to the table to save himself from falling, but lost his balance and fell anyway. His hand caught the basin of eggs that stood at the edge of the table, and he sat down with a jarring thump on the floor, hitting the side of his head with sickening force on the edge of the table, the spilt eggs dripping down his neck and arm. He flushed crimson at the hastily suppressed guffaw of laughter that broke out from the two village lads working across the room.

'By all the saints!' exploded Brother Andrew. 'It's worse than having a child around the place! Yes, thank you, Brother Michael, clear it up if you would. John, fetch me six more eggs from the basket, and be quick about it. I'm behind as it is.'

Brother Michael helped Peregrine to his feet and cleared up the spilt egg from the floor quickly and without fuss. Peregrine stood a moment, his head still ringing from the impact of the table, the slime of broken eggs oozing uncomfortably down his neck and sleeve. Nobody took the slightest notice of him.

'I think I'd better go and find something clean to wear,' he mumbled.

Brother Andrew looked up briefly from his pastry-making. 'Aye, I should think you had, Father, you look like an egg nog.'

Peregrine bit his lip and limped to the door which led to the most direct path to the clothing room, where he could obtain a clean tunic and cowl from Brother Ambrose. It was a little door, opened by means of a little round knob, unlike the majority of the doors with their great cast-iron handles. He could not grasp the little knob properly, and he struggled to open the door and failed. He looked over his shoulder at the bustling kitchens he would have to cross to get to the other door, decided against it, and tried again, miserably, to turn the handle; without success. The cringing humiliation and despair of the early days of living with his disablement rose up in him again, and for a moment overwhelmed him. He stood helplessly, with his hand on the wretched little knob. He didn't know what to do. Brother Michael, seeing his predicament, came instantly to help him, and opened the door. Peregrine glanced once quickly at him and limped out.

Looking up from his work, Cormac saw Brother Michael go to open the door and return to his task of seasoning and thickening the stew with distress on his face. Cormac came across to put his now extremely finely chopped herbs into it, and Michael said quietly to him, 'Brother Andrew had almost reduced him to weeping. His mouth was trembling, Cormac. He had tears in his eyes.'

Cormac scowled. 'Tears! It's a punch on the nose the old scoundrel needs. Tears won't move him!' And he took himself off to the scullery to scrub pots violently on his own.

After that incident, the tension between Brother Cormac and Brother Andrew grew even worse. A storm was brewing. When Cormac came that afternoon to work on Father Peregrine's hands, his jaw was set with anger, and he hardly knew what he was doing. Peregrine winced under his handling, but Cormac's mind was on his own thoughts, and he did not see. As he left them to go to the novitiate chapter, Edward and Peregrine looked at each other expressively.

'There goes a miserable, angry young man!' said Brother Edward.

'I know. There's more tension in his hands than there is in mine,' said Father Peregrine ruefully. 'But let it be for now. This thing must be seen through somehow.'

It all exploded on the Thursday morning, three days later, about a month after Brother Cormac had come back to the kitchen and Father Peregrine had joined him there.

Peregrine was sitting at a table attempting to cut up a cooked beetroot with a vegetable knife. It was the middle of the morning, and Brother Cormac came in from his lessons in the novitiate.

'You're very late, Brother Cormick,' said Brother Andrew.

'Cormac. My lesson has only just finished,' muttered Cormac. 'What shall I do?'

'Slice this ox tongue finely and put it on a platter for the infirmary,' said Brother Andrew.

Cormac looked at the ox tongue and was nearly sick. His hand trembled as he worked, and he prayed silently, desperately, 'O God, please don't let me vomit. Help me. Please, please.'

An exasperated exclamation from the corner of the kitchen suddenly cut across his thoughts. Half of Father Peregrine's beetroot had escaped him and rolled onto the floor. The other half lay in drunkenly cut slices on the table in front of him. The knife had slipped, and he had cut his finger. He addressed Brother Andrew humbly: 'Brother, my hand is bleeding. I'm sorry to trouble you, but have you a rag I could bind it with?'

'Aye. You'll find some in the cupboard yonder,' said Brother Andrew, 'but pick up that beetroot off the floor, or you'll be falling over that next.'

Peregrine obediently retrieved the fallen beetroot, and then limped across the kitchen, his finger in his mouth. Cormac, watching him, saw he had no hope of managing the cupboard door, the crutch and the rags, when blood ran down his finger every time he took it out of his mouth. He moved to help him.

Deep inside Brother Andrew knew it was mean, even though he was busy, to leave Father Peregrine to fend for himself. He was justifying it by telling himself that if Peregrine had come to learn to use his hands it was better to let him do so, when he saw Cormac go to help him. 'And where do you think you're going, Brother Cormick?' he asked, acidly.

Cormac's self-control finally snapped. 'My name is Cormac!' he bellowed, 'and I was going to help him, which is more than you would, you ill-tempered, uncharitable, miserable, sour old troll!' He said a lot more besides, which was even less polite, and Brother Andrew, bristling with fury, opened his mouth to reply.

Before he could do so, Father Peregrine spoke. 'Brother Cormac, that will not do,' he said firmly. 'You will beg his pardon, please,'

Cormac stood, trembling with anger, glaring at Brother Andrew.

'I said, my son, please beg his pardon.'

'I'm sorry,' Cormac muttered woodenly, still glaring, still trembling.

'Brother Cormac, please look at me when I'm speaking to you,' said Peregrine calmly. Cormac turned his head slowly to look at him, the blue eyes still icy with rage, hardly seeing him. 'Please beg his pardon properly,' said Peregrine.

'I said, I'm sorry,' ground out Cormac from between clenched teeth.

'It comes better from you on your knees, my son,' persisted Peregrine quietly.

The blue eyes blazed at him with their cold fire, and Cormac slowly shook his head. 'Kneel?' he said. 'To him? No.'

Brother Andrew again drew breath to speak, quivering in his indignation. Father Peregrine stopped his interruption with a peremptory gesture, without looking at him. His gaze still held Cormac's. 'Son, do it,' he said.

The moment of violent conflict that took place then in Cormac's soul nearly wrenched it out of orbit. Anger and rebellion and disgust at the self-abasement required of him boiled inside; but yet he had not forgotten the self-control and ability to humble himself that he had seen in Peregrine, and he knew instinctively that that was the stronger thing, stronger than anger, stronger than hate, stronger than Brother Andrew. He had a sudden intuition that if he could not kneel before his ill-mannered old adversary, it was he who would have lost the battle, not Brother Andrew, not Father Peregrine. It was the moment he made up his mind, late, that he really did want to be a monk. He knelt. The kitchen was utterly still, watching in fascination.

'I confess . . .' he said, gratingly.

'I think "humbly" is the word you're looking for,' said Father Peregrine quietly.

'I . . . humbly . . . confess,' said Cormac, shaking, dizzy with pent-up rage, 'my . . . fault . . . of disrespect . . . and . . . rudeness. I ask God's forgiveness and. . . .' He stopped, looking down at his hands, which were clenched into fists, the knuckles white. The saying of the next word seared him to the soul. He felt as though it cost him everything he had as he whispered, '. . . yours.'

He looked up, but it was Peregrine's face he sought,

not Andrew's. He was rewarded by the admiration and respect that shone in his abbot's eyes. Peregrine nodded at him, almost imperceptibly.

Brother Andrew cleared his throat, slightly shaken by the situation. There had been a moment when Cormac had looked almost mad, when Brother Andrew had realised he was more likely to get a black eye than an apology.

'God forgives you, my brother, and so do I,' he said as required, but the dry irony of his voice betrayed that it was the formula only, and his heart was not in it. So far as he could see, the rebellious and disobedient boy had been as defiant to his superior as he had been appallingly rude, and had had to be forced into submission to an extent that any other abbot would have had him whipped for. Only Father Peregrine, looking into those ice-blue eyes, had known quite well that neither he nor anyone would ever be able to make Cormac do anything: the lad's battle was with himself, and he had won it, too.

'Brother Cormac, I think it may be better if you go and help Brother Edward in the infirmary for the rest of the morning,' said Father Peregrine, and Cormac stood up, nodded his assent and was gone. The quiet hum of activity began again as the kitchen staff hastily took up their work.

'Brother Andrew, please will you come and see me one hour after the midday meal,' Father Peregrine said pleasantly. 'I'm sorry to have so delayed and hindered your work. I think I may have caused enough trouble for one morning. I'll leave you in peace.'

It was not long before the bell would be ringing for Sext, and Peregrine made his way slowly to the chapel. There was a fine mist of rain, and the winds blew in fitful gusts, driving dead leaves into little drifts against the foot of the stone walls. Inside the chapel, the air was damp, and the light dim. On the wooden stalls, there lay a rime of moisture. Winter was closing in. Peregrine sat in his stall, feeling suddenly cold and weary. He looked down at his hand. His finger was smarting, and he cautiously unclamped his thumb from where he had held it against the cut. The bleeding had ceased, but it stung. He sucked it, looking sightlessly ahead of him, his thoughts drifting.

Cormac ... Andrew ... he sighed and smiled, shaking his head. What a pair! A letter that must be written after lunch. Better eat in his own house, because he must be back from the infirmary in time to see Brother Andrew an hour after the meal ... *Brother Andrew ...* Peregrine's eyes focused on the great wooden crucifix that hung over the altar. 'What would you do with him?' he wondered. 'I have to resolve this somehow, my Lord. Help me to make him see. Poor Cormac, I can hardly blame him losing his temper. I've had to bite my own lip a time or two these past weeks. Dear Lord, he was angry. I thought he'd not obey me. Thought I'd pushed him too far. Brave lad. Brave, and very hard work. Help me to treat him right.' He gazed at the crucified Christ, the bowed head, the hands splayed back against the cross, pinned with great, cruel nails, and he shuddered. 'My God, what a price! Follow you? The thought makes me sick. Lead me, then, lead me. I haven't got what it takes to walk that path on my own.'

The bell began to ring for Sext, and the brothers were coming in silently to their places, their faces shadowed by their cowls, their sandalled feet whispering on the stone floor. 'Chad ... Ambrose ... Fidelis ... Theodore— Theodore! He's in good time, well done, lad ... John, Peter, Thomas, Edward, Cormac, Mark, Francis, Cyprian, Gilbert, Clement (must have a word with him about that new manuscript), Stephen, Martin, Paulinus—he's limping badly; his poor old knees are stiff and swollen in this weather. Matthew, Giles, Walafrid, Thaddeus, young Gerard, shaping up nicely, I think there is a vocation there, Dominic ... Denis and Prudentius both laid up with a racking cough, and Lucanus won't stir from the infirmary again now, dear old soul. No Andrew, no Michael, that's my fault, causing a commotion in the kitchens just before the meal. No one else late or absent, old Brother Basil slipping into his place, back from ringing the bell.'

'*Deus in adjutorium meum intende*,' rang out the cantor's chant.

Abbot Peregrine gave his mind to the Office.

Brother Cormac presented himself at the infirmary as instructed, and sought out Brother Edward, who was checking his supplies of medicine. 'Good morning, Brother, what brings you here? Remind me to ask Brother Walafrid for some more of his soothing brew for poor old Brother Denis. He's coughing fit to break himself apart.'

'Father Abbot sent me,' said Cormac cagily.

Brother Edward glanced at him sideways. 'Did he? Why ever did he do that?' he enquired innocently.

In spite of himself, Cormac was amused. For the first time ever that Brother Edward could recall, a brief flicker of a smile lit his face. Almost instantly, it clouded over again.

'I quarrelled with Brother Andrew,' he said. 'Father Peregrine cut his hand, and Brother Andrew wouldn't let me help him get a rag to bandage it. I lost my temper with him.'

Brother Edward turned to look fully at Cormac. He regarded him silently for a moment before he replied. Then, 'Brother,' he said, 'day by day you tend that man's hands with me. Have you not eyes to see the state of them? They are blistered with burns and sore with scalds and little cuts, and bruised too from those kitchen tasks he simply cannot manage.'

'Well, I know,' replied Cormac, 'but he said he needs to use them to keep them moving freely. I suppose he'll manage better in time.'

Brother Cormac was taken aback by the sudden flash of anger on Edward's kindly face. Edward stood, contemplating him, until Cormac began to feel uncomfortable.

'He would not wish me to say this,' said Edward slowly, at last, 'but somebody needs to tell you. He's not working in the kitchen for the sake of his hands. The damage done to those hands can't be put right by work; they're beyond repairing. Believe me, I know they are; it was I who struggled to save them when they were smashed and broken and bleeding; and every day as I do what I can to ease the discomfort in them, it breaks my heart that I had not the skill to do a better job. No, he came because he saw you and Brother Andrew had bad feeling between you and he wanted you to sort it out; but between your sulks and Andrew's ill humour he knew there would be trouble, and he thought he should be there to keep an eye on things. What else could he do? Stand in the corner with his mitre on, arms folded, tapping his foot, watching you sternly?'

Cormac looked at him, appalled. 'Are you saying,' he asked, horrified, 'that he doesn't need to be there for himself at all? That he came only for Brother Andrew and me?'

'That's about it, young man. You maybe thought, did you, that the abbot of a monastery has nothing better to do with his time than while away the morning in the kitchen, hindering the meal preparation?' Cormac just gazed at him, dumbly. 'Oh, but hark at me,' said Brother Edward repentantly, 'I sound as scathing as Brother Andrew, now; and there goes the bell for Sext and these chores not half finished. Never mind, lad. Come, let's go to chapel.'

The midday meal over, Father Peregrine came to the infirmary as usual, and Brother Cormac and Brother Edward sat in silence to work on his hands. Cormac took the right hand and Edward took the left. Brother Cormac looked attentively at that hand for the first time. Until now, he had been too full of his own problems to see properly beyond them. The cut from the morning, which never had been bandaged, was still open a little, and grubby, and getting slightly inflamed. It was on the side of the first joint of the second finger.

'That looks painful,' said Cormac.

'I had to write a letter,' replied Father Peregrine. 'The pen just catches it and makes it a bit sore.'

Cormac looked at him. 'He did it for me,' he thought. 'It's on your right hand,' he said. 'How did you come to cut your right hand?'

'My right hand was getting cramp trying to hold the knife, so I thought I'd try if I could do it better with the left. I learned to my cost that they may neither of them work, but I'm still a very right-handed man!'

Cormac straightened the fingers gently and examined the little burns, cuts and sore places. 'For me,' he thought, 'and not only that, but the sharp orders that made him look clumsy and foolish and in the way.' He remembered Brother Andrew's irritation: 'It's worse than having a child around the place!' and Brother Michael's distress: 'He had tears in his eyes.'

Cormac said nothing, but he gently salved the sore places, carefully disinfected and bandaged the cut, then worked over the whole hand as he'd been shown. This time he was seeing with his fingers, as Brother Edward had tried to teach him to do, finding the places where muscles were cramped and knotted, easing them out. When he had finished, he got to his feet and turned away without looking at Peregrine's face, and made himself busy putting away oils and salves and lint.

'Thank you,' said Father Peregrine quietly. 'Thank you for your healing love.'

Cormac looked at him a moment, then shook his head. Then, 'I'll be wanted back in the kitchen,' he said, and he left them.

'Whatever happened to him?' said Father Peregrine. 'Where on earth has this gentleness come from? Brother Edward, you've had a hand in this, I suspect.'

'I don't know,' replied Edward. 'I think it was more likely your hands.'

'Well, whatever it was, thank God for it. I couldn't have stood too many more mornings like this one. Now then, I must go and find Brother Andrew. Thank you for your care, Brother.'

He found Brother Andrew waiting for him in the abbot's house, ill at ease out of his own domain, looking older and less autocratic away from his little kingdom in the kitchen.

'Sit down, Brother, that's right. I'll come straight to the point. I know you have work to do, and so do I. This concerns Brother Cormac, as I expect you realise. To be blunt, Brother, you have treated him abominably. Your insensitivity and unimaginative dealing with him is shameful. I have never heard a monk speak with less courtesy and more rudeness than you do. You deliberately provoke him by miscalling his name, and that is inexcusable. Also, it is thoughtless and unkind to ask him to prepare meat unless it is absolutely necessary. You know well what a revolting task it is to him. Well? What have you to say?'

Brother Andrew sat rigidly still, looking down, mortified. Away from the pressure of work in the kitchen, away from the aggravation of Cormac's hostility and unwillingness, he saw his own behaviour in a different light.

'I have nothing to say,' he mumbled. 'What can I say?'

'You will confess your fault at chapter in the morning. From now on, this has to stop. If you cannot find it in your heart to love, you can at least keep a civil tongue in your head. Have you understood me?'

'Yes, Father.'

'Thank you. You can go.'

Brother Andrew forced himself to look at Peregrine and was startled to see nothing but gentleness and concern in the eyes that looked back at him, where he had expected cold rebuke.

'I'm sorry, Father,' he said humbly. 'Truly I didn't think about the meat, but for the rest, it's true what you say, I admit it. I'll try to mend my ways.'

Father Peregrine nodded and watched the old man with affection as he went on his way. 'He wants to mend his ways, Lord,' he prayed silently as Brother Andrew closed the door. 'He'll need your help, then. That the habits of a lifetime were so easily undone! But you can't help loving the peppery old codger. O Christ, be the bridge between them, stubborn men both and proud. It was a privilege to feel Cormac's gentleness, but if you could divert a crumb, just a crumb of it from me to Andrew, it would make life so much easier.' He sighed. 'And who am I, that I should be asking you of all people for an easy life? As you think best then Lord, but only, give me patience when my own runs out. . . .'

Brother Cormac had gone from the infirmary to the kitchen, which was empty now in the quiet time after the meal. He sat on a stool by a work bench, thinking, for a long while. Hearing the door open, he looked up, and seeing Brother Andrew, stiffened at once against anticipated sarcasm and hostility.

'Brother Cormac, I was looking for you,' Andrew said. 'Father Abbot has just been speaking to me. Scolding me, really. He says I've treated you rudely and insensitively. He rebuked me for miscalling your name. Brother, I'm sorry. I truly didn't think when I asked you to cut up that ox tongue. I'm sorry about your name, Brother Cormac, and for all my rudeness, I am sorry.'

Cormac was stunned. He sat and looked at him for a moment, an anxious, contrite old man, unsure of his reception, not an ogre, not to be despised. He jumped off his stool and flung his arms impulsively around his enemy. It is hard to say which of them was more amazed by his action, 'Me too,' Cormac said as he hugged him, 'I'm sorry.'

'For pity's sake, Brother,' flustered Andrew, disentangling himself, 'calm yourself! Sit you down, for heaven's sake, you wild, unpredictable, Irish whirlwind. What's all this?'

He listened soberly as Cormac recounted what Edward had told him. 'You mean he came here, not for himself, but for us? Oh, Brother, I was never more ashamed of myself in my life. Whatever should we do?'

Cormac looked at him shyly. 'Make our peace?' he suggested, with a small grin, the second in one day.

From that day onwards, Brother Andrew and Brother Cormac were friends, and there grew between them a bond of affection and understanding which transformed the two touchy, hot-tempered, and—underneath it—lonely characters. Not that they were always polite to each other.

Father Peregrine was passing the kitchen six weeks later, at the busy time just before lunch. Brother Cormac was strolling down the corridor ahead of him, late for work, and entered the kitchen as Peregrine passed.

'Where the devil have you been, you good-for-nothing Irish rascal?' roared an indignant voice.

'I came the pretty way,' came the nonchalant reply.

Father Peregrine smiled and shook his head as he continued on his way.

Mother leaned forward on her chair and prodded the fire with the long brass poker. A shower of sparks flew up and the soft white ash fell in the grate. She put another log on. Gingerly, I blew my sore, hot nose.

'He always seemed to hurt himself, Mother.'

'Yes, I know what you mean, my love,' she said reflectively. 'I think there were two reasons for that. One was simply that a man with broken hands can't protect himself, or manage tools and things as well as we can. But also, it was because he wanted so much to be like Jesus, he wasn't afraid to put himself in the place where he was vulnerable to hurt.

'Oh, Melissa! Look at the time! There'll be nothing for tea if I don't get cracking! I shall have to go and meet Mary and Beth in half an hour, and they'll all be famished in this cold weather!' And she leapt to her feet and disappeared into the kitchen.

VIII
BEGINNING AGAIN

The year had rolled to its close. New Year's Eve was a night of tingling frost, the stars shining sharp and bright in a cloudless sky, the moon riding clear and lovely in the heavens.

Huddled in my dressing-gown and a woollen shawl, I stood in the garden with Therese and Mother and Daddy, waiting to welcome in the New Year. The little ones had gone to bed late, and were now tucked up fast asleep, clutching their new Christmas dollies. They were snuggled in under extra blankets, their mattresses pushed close together so they could keep each other warm. I was sleepy too but would not have missed the magic of this moment for anything.

In the morning, we would wake up to windows decorated with frost flowers, all the grass and skeletal bushes in the garden would be stiff with hoar frost. The end of my nose and the tops of my ears hurt in the biting cold. I breathed out into the midnight air, and in the moonlight the impressive, ghostly cloud looked like a dragon's breath.

Far away, but clear and sonorous on the cold, still air, the church clock began to chime midnight. Distant, but perfectly distinct, we counted the twelve strokes and then stood there a moment on the silent moonlit threshold of another year.

'Happy New Year!' Daddy's cheerful voice lifted the

moment from solemnity and awe to party-time. 'Come indoors, ladies! I have some hot mulled wine and some goodies for you.'

We sat and sipped and munched by the fire, the room lit by candles at Mother's pleading, instead of the electric light. After a while Daddy stretched and yawned. 'I'm for bed,' he said, in sleepy contentment.

'I'll follow you soon,' said Mother. 'Warm up the bed for me.'

He and Therese took the glasses and the plates out into the kitchen, and we could hear Daddy's heavy tread going slowly up the narrow stairs, and the chinking of glass and crockery as Therese washed up. We heard her fill the kettle for her hot-water bottle, and then shortly after, she put her head round the door to say goodnight.

'Goodnight, Therese,' said Mother. 'Thank you for washing up. Happy New Year.'

'Happy New Year. I'll put the hot-water bottle in your bed, 'lissa, when I'm warm, if you're not coming up straight away.'

I smiled my thanks, and we sat, watching the fire, Mother and I, listening to Therese's footsteps mounting the stairs. There was no sound but the ticking of the clock and the settling of the glowing logs.

'What are you thinking, Mother?' I said.

She stirred in her chair and sighed. 'It's a funny thing,' she said thoughtfully, looking with wide, faraway eyes into the low, red flames. 'The thing life is fullest of is the thing we find hardest to believe in. New beginnings. The incredible gift of a fresh start. Every new year. Every new day. Every new life. What wonderful gifts! And when we spoil things, and life goes all wrong, we feel dismayed, because we find it so hard to see that we can start again. God lets us share it too, you know. Only God can give life, it's true—make a new baby or a new year—but he gives us the power to give each other a new beginning, to forgive each other and make a fresh start when things go wrong.'

She fell silent, thinking, then she started to smile. 'That reminds me—yes, I hadn't thought of that for a long time. Poor Brother Tom! Oh, that was a bad evening . . .'

She laughed, and I looked at her impatiently. Five minutes ago I had thought I was sleepy, but I felt wide awake now. 'Oh, come on, Mother, tell me, then! What happened?'

She glanced up at the clock and hesitated.

'Oh, you've got to tell me now!' I cried. 'What about Brother Tom? What happened?'

'Ssh, all right then, pipe down. I'll tell you the story. Put another log on the fire, though, first.'

She watched me as I pushed the little apple log into the heart of the fire, then she began.

It was the year of our Lord 1316. King Edward on the throne, a year of tranquillity and kindly weather. The month of June blazed with sunshine, and the brothers got their hay in early. The elder trees were loaded with blossom, promising delicious wines for the year following and a good crop of berries to soothe coughs and colds in the autumn chills and mists. The summer continued fiercely hot and dry; the water in the well ran low and the grass withered brown and dusty, but September came with a mellow, lazy warmth, kindly mists in the mornings and long, slow, dreamy afternoons.

Through the hot summer and on into the golden September days, the old brothers whose last days were spent in the peace of the infirmary were brought out to sit and doze among the herbs in the physic garden, and there they sunned themselves, lulled to drowsiness by the hum of the bees and the fragrance of the herbs, caressed by the almost imperceptible breeze.

Abbot Peregrine had ruled his flock at St Alcuin's Abbey for twelve years now, and the brothers loved him for his gentleness, humour and wisdom, and respected him for the courage and strength that lay beneath. He was in his fifty-seventh year now. The remains of his crisp, black curls were grey. All traces of youth's softness had gone now from his face, which left it more hawk-like and eager than ever. Age had done nothing, however, to dim his disconcerting grey eyes—they had lost none of their directness and urgent power.

Brother Cormac, Brother Theodore and Brother Thaddeus were all fully fledged, dignified monks now, and Gerard Plumley had become Brother Bernard, which Brother Tom said was a radical improvement. Tom himself was these days employed as the abbot's personal attendant. He helped Peregrine with the impossibilities of shaving and fastening his sandals and his belt, and he cleaned the abbot's house. He also waited at table for Peregrine when visitors came to the abbey, to cut his food and serve his guests with food and wine. Father Peregrine's maimed hands could not perform either of these tasks with any reliable outcome, and it was in any case the customary thing in those days for the abbot of a monastery to have at least one or two personal servants.

Brother Tom had been fully professed almost eight years now. He was just approaching his thirtieth birth-day, the end of his tenth year in the community, but he was still not master of his irrepressible nature, and could be as undisciplined as a schoolboy in the company of Brother Francis, whose composed and urbane exterior hid a spirit as mischievous as Tom's own.

There was a new generation of novices—Brother Richard, Brother Damian, Brother Josephus, and Brother James, who had just had his clothing ceremony and was bursting with delight at being allowed to wear the habit of the order. The novitiate was still watched over by Father Matthew's stern and exacting authority, though he was feeling his age now.

In the kitchens, Brother Andrew still ruled, with the help of Brother Cormac and young Brother Damian. Brother Michael had gone to work with Brother John in the infirmary, where his thoughtfulness and gentleness did excellent service. Although Brother Edward was more than eighty years old now, and as light and wrinkled as a withered leaf, he was still officially the infirmarian. His heart and wind were still as sound as a bell, and his mind still sharp and clear, but his sight and hearing were growing dim, and he relied more and more on Brother John and Brother Michael in the infirmary work. In the afternoons he was allowed to drowse in the sun in the herb gardens outside the infirmary in the company of the other old men, of whom he was no longer the youngest.

On this particular day, Brother Edward was sitting with Brother Cyprian to keep an eye on him lest his usual peaceful docility should erupt into one of his occasional, unpredictable fits of eccentric behaviour. Brother Cyprian had for years been the porter of the abbey—a wise, discreet and kindly man, whose job had given him a wealth of insight into human nature—but he was very old now, toothless and senile and incontinent. Brother Martin had replaced him as porter, and Brother Cyprian now dreamed and wandered and slept, propped with pillows in his chair, his veined and freckled old hands resting on the woollen rug that Brother Michael had carefully tucked around him. The experience of a lifetime was not all lost, however, and from time to time he would interrupt his vacant staring and the rhythmic chewing of his gums, to narrow his eyes thoughtfully and utter with typical Yorkshire bluntness a surprisingly shrewd and observant comment about his brothers in the monastic life.

Father Peregrine had been to the infirmary for Brother John to exercise and massage his stiff, misshapen hands, and he stopped in the garden to talk to the old brothers, telling Brother Edward news he had just received of his daughter Melissa.

'Edward, she has another child, a baby boy. She says both she and the infant are thriving.'

Melissa had been married eight years to her wool merchant, Ranulf Langton, and they had recently moved to
Yorkshire, where the fleeces of the abbeys' flocks were
renowned throughout Europe. Ranulf's business was
prospering, they were comfortably and happily settled,
and Melissa had just sent word to Father Peregrine of
the birth of her fourth child, a boy, Benedict.

Peregrine glowed with pride as he spoke of her, and
Brother Edward nodded and smiled obligingly as he
heard the details of her letter lovingly recounted. They
neither of them noticed Brother Cyprian's unfocused
gaze sharpen until he was looking with close attention
at Peregrine's face, disfigured and scarred but somehow beautiful with the joy of his love as he told Edward
his happy news.

'I don't know what 'appened to thee,' interrupted
Brother Cyprian suddenly, his red-rimmed old eyes
looking acutely at Peregrine, taking in his scarred face
and hands and the crutch he leaned on. 'Knocked all
about by t' look o' thee. Eh, but tha was an aggravating, strutting peacock when tha came! Aye, smile! Go
on, laugh if tha will, but 'tis true! Tha thought thyself
a king on thy throne. Knocked thee off, did they? Aye,
well, never mind, lad. Learned thee a bit o' sense, I
can see that.'

He blinked the reptilian lids of his hooded old eyes and
chuckled to himself. Father Peregrine stood looking at
him, startled, amused and not sure how to respond, but
the old man had retreated into his own world, chewing
and gazing. Presently he slipped into a doze, and his
mouth fell ajar as the toothless jaw slackened.

'Father—' Young Brother James' voice at his elbow
claimed Peregrine's attention. 'There is a party of folk
asking hospitality for the night whom Brother Martin
thinks you would maybe wish to greet.'

Father Peregrine turned away from Brother Cyprian,
still smiling.

'Did he give you a name?'

'Yes, Father, he bids me tell you it is Sir Geoffrey and Lady Agnes d'Ebassier.'

A shadow of weariness clouded Father Peregrine's face. The names were those of a wealthy Norman baron and his wife, landowners from just south of Yorkshire. They stayed from time to time at St Alcuin's to break the journey to Scotland, where Lady Agnes' brother-in-law owned some excellent hunting and fishing territory. Sir Geoffrey and his lady were deeply pious, good people, generous benefactors whose gifts were more than helpful to the finances of the abbey, but they were not easy guests. They liked to think of St Alcuin's as home from home and felt entitled to drop in unannounced at any time as their gifts of money to the brothers were so frequent and so large. This could be awkward at times, and besides this their keen consciousness of their own social standing and the rigid formality of their manners imposed a strain even on themselves. Father Peregrine found it exhausting. He sighed as he looked at Brother James. The joy of his letter and his amusement at Brother Cyprian had suddenly evaporated. He felt the first tightenings of his shoulders and neck that would develop inevitably into a thundering headache as the evening drew on.

'Thanks, Brother,' he said heavily. 'Yes, it would be right for me to make them welcome. Have they come with a great many servants?'

'Not so many as last time, Father. Six, only. My lady's personal maids, Sir Geoffrey's manservants and two grooms.'

'Six. I see. Very well then, see to it that their beasts are stabled and so forth, if that is not already done. My lord and lady will expect their servants to eat in the kitchens of the guest house. Would you arrange that? Thank you, Brother, I will come directly to my house to welcome them there when they are washed and rested.'

Brother James turned to go, but Father Peregrine

called him back 'Oh—Brother, if you will: when you go into the kitchen would you ask Brother Cormac to put me aside a bite of bread and cheese or something? Tell him I shall come for it before Vespers, because I can eat next to nothing with company like this to dine.'

Brother James set off on his errand, and Father Peregrine took refuge a little longer in the comfortable gathering of old men in the herb garden, discussing their ailments and reminiscing with Brother Edward. But at last he could put it off no longer, and with a sigh of resignation, he bade them farewell and limped gloomily to his own dwelling to await his guests.

As he came through the narrow passage into the cloister, he met with Brother Tom and Brother Francis, who were carrying a wooden bedstead across from the dormitory to the infirmary. Brother Fidelis had that morning put a fork through his foot in the vegetable garden, and there were too few beds to accommodate him in the infirmary. Three of the brothers had been laid low and with these three sick and the old men who lived there, the infirmary beds were filled, so Brother Francis and Brother Tom had been dispatched to find another bed.

Father Peregrine spoke quietly to Brother Tom as they came level with him: 'Brother Thomas, I shall need you tonight. I have guests eating with me. Directly after Vespers, please.'

'I'll be there!' replied Tom cheerily. 'Whoops! Mind those flowers, Francis! Glory be to God, what are you doing, man? It won't *bend.*'

'Move, then, I cannot get it into this passageway unless you—NO, TOM that's my *hand.* Look, put it down a minute. Now then, go back a bit. There!'

The journey with the bed through the gathering of ancients in the herb garden, and the negotiation of the doorways in the infirmary, had them doubled up with laughter, nearly cost Francis the fingers of his left hand, and vastly entertained the old men. They finally brought it to rest, intact, in the right place, then stayed on to help Brother John take in the old men to their beds as the heat of the afternoon cooled and the shadows began to lengthen.

'Thanks, Brother,' said Brother John as he and Tom eased Brother Cyprian into his bed. 'Have you time to do one more thing for me? Brother Cyprian needs his medicine before supper. It takes a while to give it to him. Would you mind?'

He gave Brother Tom the bottle, and Tom bent over Brother Cyprian, coaxing him to take the physic, which eased the pain of his swollen, arthritic knees and helped him sleep. The medicine was syrupy and the spoon full. It required concentration to get it into, and keep it inside, the sunken mouth. Brother Tom was intent on the task and did not see the change in the old man's gaze from vacancy to shrewd observation.

Brother Cyprian swallowed convulsively and slowly wiped at his mouth with his shaky, blue-veined old hand. His eyes, bright with interest now, studied Brother Tom. 'I know thee, tha scoundrel,' he said. Brother Tom blinked at him in surprise. 'Aye, I do. I know the spark in thy eyes too: seen it many times. A womaniser and a thief, I'll wager, before tha came t'us, and now too, it wouldn't surprise me, give thee the chance.'

Tom was speechless, and Francis, approaching from across the room, heard the remark and laughed. 'You're absolutely right, Brother Cyprian, scoundrel he is. You know us all. It's the wisdom of God in you. Pray for him then, and the Lord Christ may make a saint of him yet.'

But Brother Cyprian was wandering again, and did not respond. The Vespers bell began to ring, and Tom straightened up, shaking his head. 'The old reprobate!'

'Reprobate yourself. It's true. He's seen that spark that's in your eye many times, he said so. Women I know nothing of, but light-fingered I can vouch for!'

He ducked the hand that shot out to cuff his ear and grinned affectionately at his friend; 'What's more, you'll

be late for Vespers if we don't make haste. Brother
John, are you coming?'

After Vespers the brothers ate together in the refectory.
Then there was an hour of relaxation before Compline,
when they were free to rest and converse, sitting in the
community room which was lit by a fire in winter and
the last rays of the evening sun now at the end of the
summer.

Brother Cormac came in late from his last chores in
the kitchen, to snatch a little company and conversation.
He crossed the room to where Brother Tom and
Brother Francis sat in dispute with Brother Giles and
Brother Basil as to the best method of tickling trout.
'Ought you not to have been helping Father Abbot with
his guests tonight, Tom?' Cormac asked in surprise.

Brother Tom froze in his seat and looked at Cormac,
wide-eyed and utterly still. He took a deep breath. 'Holy
saints! I forgot! Did no one stay from the kitchen when
they took the food over?'

Cormac shook his head. 'No. They assumed you were
on your way, I suppose.'

Tom gulped. 'He'll have my blood! He can't do a
thing! Not pour the wine, nor serve them, nor even
manage his own food. Oh I'm for it now.'

'Would his guests not help?' asked Brother Giles.

Tom shook his head. 'No, that's not the point. You
know what our abbot is, as formal and particular as they
come when it's a question of courtesy and hospitality.
He'd as soon ask them to clean out the cows as pour the
wine. Oh ... oh, how could I forget? Who are his guests,
Cormac, do you know?'

Cormac grinned at him. 'Yes. I do. His guests are Sir
Geoffrey and Lady Agnes d'Ebassier.'

Tom closed his eyes and groaned, then he opened
them to stare hopelessly at Brother Cormac. 'What in
the name of heaven am I going to do about this?' he
asked.

'Could you not go over now?' suggested Brother Francis tentatively, but Tom withered him with a look. 'That would add insult to injury, I think. No, I'll just have to go and kiss the ground after Compline and hope he doesn't break my head with his crutch. Ah, by all that's holy, why me?'

They had no more heart for conversation, and after a few desultory exchanges sat in silence, listening to the anxious drumming of Tom's fingers on the side of the bench. And at last the sand in the hour glass ran out. Brother Basil got creakily to his feet and shuffled off to chapel to ring the Compline bell.

Father Peregrine walked to the guest house with his distinguished visitors.

'God give you good night, Sir Geoffrey, and my lady,' he said. 'It is an honour and a pleasure to be your host once more.'('And God forgive me the lie,' he added silently.) After exchanging a few more pleasantries, their conversation was ended by the ringing of the Office bell. Father Peregrine took his leave of them and set off for Compline. Lady Agnes lingered a moment to watch him go, then followed her husband in to the guest house.

'He is such a dear man,' she said dreamily as she closed the great oak door behind her, 'so courteous, but so natural. He makes one feel so at home; so ... wanted.' She paused a moment, then added wistfully, 'He truly listens.'

'What? Oh yes, good fellow,' barked Sir Geoffrey absently.

The dear man, meanwhile, was limping with angry jerks across the cloister towards the chapel, his mouth and jaw set hard.'I'll kill him. I'll kill him,' he was thinking.

He had waited and waited for Brother Tom to arrive after the lay servants from the kitchen had brought the food in dishes ready to be served, and departed leaving him stranded with his guests. Their visit, unannounced as it was, had found him rather unprepared, and he had not invited any of the brothers to eat with them, so there was no one to serve the food but himself and his two aristocratic guests. Eventually, unable to delay the meal any longer, he turned to Lady Agnes with a disarming smile and said 'Madam, I am in a little difficulty. Our brother who would normally wait upon us has evidently been detained. I would gladly wait upon you myself but ... as you see, I cannot. It distresses me to ask it, my lady, but I wonder—would you be so kind as to serve our food?'

Lady Agnes, having never lifted a finger to do anything for herself since the day she was born, was quite taken with the idea. Lifting the lids from the dishes, she sniffed with appreciation the fragrant steam, and proceeded gaily to serve the two men and herself.

Father Peregrine's heart sank as she placed before him a mighty portion of food. His head ached as if it would split open. Inwardly cursing his intended humility in having only one brother to wait upon him he smiled radiantly at Sir Geoffrey: 'My lord, could you— would you—I must ask you to pour our wine. I regret, that also is beyond me.'

'What? Oh, by all means, Father!' the baron blustered, embarrassed by Peregrine's disability and his own failure to notice the need. Father Peregrine put him at his ease with another dazzling smile, and they began their meal. They talked of this and that, Lady Agnes asking after various of the brothers, and Sir Geoffrey enlarging on his plans to stock his sister-in-law's larder with venison and fish as part of his holiday relaxation.

He was just in the middle of a long and tedious anecdote which was mainly designed to show off his prowess as a huntsman, when his wife interrupted him: 'I beg your pardon, my dear, for breaking in upon your story. Father, I am so sorry. I did not think. I can see you are having trouble with your meal. I hope you will not mind my asking—would you like me—will you permit me—to cut some of that meat for you?'

Sir Geoffrey cleared his throat and took a deep drink of his wine. 'Good stuff, this, very good,' he mumbled.

Peregrine looked at Lady Agnes, his face burning. Her eyes were fixed on him in anxious appeal, fearing that she had made an indiscretion. He smiled at her. It was the costliest smile of his life. 'That would be very good of you, my lady,' he said, 'the brother who waits on us would normally cut my food for me.'

Lady Agnes relaxed under the kindness of his smile, happy to have said the right thing after all.

'Do carry on with your story, dear,' she said. 'You were just saying how the boar broke suddenly from the undergrowth, right at your feet.'

'Ah, yes. Hmmph. Great big fellow. Glittering eyes and massive shoulders. Well, of course, there was only one thing to do. . . .'

Peregrine submitted to having his food cut for him, and struggled to eat it, conscious of the lady's eyes on him, trying not to spill anything, trying to hurry, trying at the same time to convey rapt attention to the interminable tale, glad that at least somebody was talking and he did not have to think of anything to say himself.

All things come to an end, and the meal was over at last. Having taken his leave of Sir Geoffrey and Lady Agnes, he came in to Compline, trembling with fury and humiliation, sick with the throbbing pain in his head.

Brother Tom watched him come in. Father Peregrine did not so much as glance in Tom's direction, but sat down in his stall with elaborate composure, looking straight ahead, giving nothing away. Brother Tom, looking at the set line of his superior's mouth, was as apprehensive as he was remorseful.

The chant rose and fell in the shadows of the evening, lovely in its peace. The tranquillity of the Office concluded in the blessing, and the brothers slipped away in silence to their beds.

Father Peregrine remained where he was in his stall, looking straight ahead. He neither moved nor spoke as Brother Tom, who also stayed behind, stood reluctantly and walked slowly across the chapel to face him. Tom waited. At last Father Peregrine's gaze shifted to look him in the eye. Brother Tom looked down, unable to endure the anger that was turned on him.

'Where were you?' said Peregrine coldly.

Brother Tom looked up, but only for a pleading instant. His head bent, he mumbled almost inaudibly, 'I forgot. I just forgot. Oh, Father, I'm—'

'You *forgot*?' Peregrine leaned forward, shaking. 'You *forgot*? I have just spent the most humiliating and embarrassing evening of my life and you can come and face me here and tell me you just *forgot*? No, *don't* you kneel to me, I don't want to hear your apologies, Brother.'

'Father, I—'

'What was I supposed to do? I had to ask Lady Agnes to serve us at table and Sir Geoffrey to pour our wine. Brother, you—' He broke off, white with rage, glaring at poor Tom. 'Oh, go to your bed, get out of my sight,' he concluded, spitting out the words with biting anger.

Brother Tom turned to go, took two steps, but stopped and turned back again. He stood at the entrance to the abbot's stall a moment, and then knelt there before him. 'I cannot go,' he said miserably. 'It is the Rule, Father. The Rule for you as well as me. Do not let the sun go down on your anger. Be reconciled. I . . . oh, Father, I'm sorry. I'll never, never do it again. Forgive me, I—'

'Again? *Again!* As I live, you will not! Brother Thomas—' He stopped and looked at him, Tom finding the courage somehow to meet his eyes. 'Can you not imagine what it is like to be imprisoned by these useless, useless hands? To be the object of the pity of those . . . those . . . of Sir Geoffrey and his wife?'

He shut his eyes and leaned back wearily in his stall. 'God forgives you, and so do I, Brother,' he said flatly, after a moment. 'Go to bed.'

But Tom, hesitantly, stretched out his hand, which was muscular and brown and workmanlike, with blunt, strong fingers. He closed it gently over Peregrine's hands.

'Please don't say useless,' he whispered. 'You don't know how ... ask Cormac, ask Theodore ... not useless ... so much I—I don't know how to say it, I ... no ... not useless. Oh, Father, I'm sorry.'

But his abbot did not move or speak, and Tom withdrew his hand and crept wretchedly to bed.

Peregrine sat, completely still, weary and frustrated as the anger ebbed away. The events of the day flowed through his mind. He thought of Brother Cyprian: 'Tha thought thyself a king on thy throne. Knocked thee off, did they?' Of Lady Agnes, smiling, happily and inexpertly dismembering a fat roast fowl, and the touch of Tom's hand on his own, 'Not useless ... not useless. ...'

He opened his eyes. The chapel was all but dark now, but he could still make out the shape of the figure on the great cross.

'What imprisons me, then? My hands or my pride?' he thought sadly. He remembered his words to Tom: 'The most humiliating and embarrassing evening of my life. ...' Gazing at the cross, he shook his head. He thought of Jesus, blindfolded by the soldiers, beaten and mocked. 'Prophesy then, prophet! Which of us hit you?' Father Peregrine groaned in his shame and bent over, burying his face in his mutilated hands.

'Oh ... oh, Brother Thomas, forgive my pride,' he murmured. Holy Jesus, crucified one, if my hands are useless, what are yours? Oh ... oh no ... forgive. ...'

After a while he straightened himself and sat looking at the dim shape of the cross, emptied and tired.

'Aggravating, strutting peacock ...' Brother Cyprian's words came back to him, and he began to smile. 'Amen,' he said, ruefully.

He stood up, bowed in reverence to the real presence of Christ, and went to his bed.

In the morning, Brother Tom came to shave him, after the morning Office of Prime, and was much relieved to be greeted with the usual friendliness. He stood at the table, assembling soap and blade and water, while Father Peregrine sat in his chair and waited. After he had been waiting a few moments, struck by the intense quietness, he turned his head to look at Brother Tom. He watched with curiosity as Tom stood very still, the linen towel in his hand, his eyes closed.

'What are you doing?' said Father Peregrine.

Brother Tom started guiltily and opened his eyes. 'I—I was praying,' he said, flushing slightly as Peregrine continued to look enquiringly at him; 'I was praying I'd not cut you.'

Father Peregrine burst out laughing. 'Oh, forgive me, Brother! Am I so intimidating? It was in haste and anger I spoke last night. My pride was wounded.' As Tom tucked the towel round his neck, Peregrine leaned back in the chair looking up at him. 'My pride can do with some denting,' he said quietly. 'Oh, but Brother—for the love of God, don't forget again.'

Brother Tom bent over him, and shaved him carefully—it was quite an art shaving that scarred face—then dried Peregrine's face and throat and stood back to survey his handiwork.

'Brother Cyprian', said Peregrine with a wry smile, 'described me yesterday as an aggravating, strutting peacock. He said I thought of myself as a king on his throne.'

Brother Tom grinned as he contemplated him. 'Well, I'll not tell you what he called me! There, you look beautiful, my lord. I'll clear these things away now and be gone. I'll see you at the midday meal. Without fail, I stake my life.'

It was with a sense of sweet relief that Father Peregrine bid God speed to his guests after the noon meal, and he stood in the abbey courtyard to watch them go, his hand raised to his eyes against the sunshine, absorbing the still, gentle warmth of the mid-September afternoon. Then he let his hand fall and made his way slowly to the infirmary, where Brother Michael worked on his hands for a while with the aromatic oils. Father Peregrine closed his eyes and relaxed. After all these years, the sensations in his hands were still odd; they were in places numb, in others tingling or painful to touch. Still, all in all it was a soothing and comforting thing, Brother Michael's quietness and the gentle firmness of his touch.

'Father, I beg your pardon—' Peregrine opened his eyes at the sound of Brother James' apologetic voice. 'I'm sorry, but another visitor has arrived and is asking to see you.'

'Oh, no!' he groaned. 'Oh, Brother, no! Who is it?'

'It's a woman with a little baby—I forget the exact name she gave. A Melissa Langforth? Thornton? Something like—'

'Melissa!' Father Peregrine's face lit with happiness and he snatched his hand out of Brother Michael's and, stooping, fumbled on the floor for the crutch that lay beside him. 'She's my—she's my—she's a relative of mine,' he said to Brother James as he limped out of the room with jerky haste to find her.

She was walking down the cobbled path to meet him, and she laughed at his eagerness and joy as he greeted her.

'Welcome, daughter, oh welcome! We heard your joyful news, dear heart, but I never thought to see you so soon. So this is the littlest, a son. Bless him, look at that yawn! By the saints, what a great, cavernous mouth he has on him! And a roar like a lion, I'll be bound. But come, dearest, let me find you a place in the guest house where you can rest and be comfortable. You must be mortally weary; you should not have travelled so soon. Would to God that all our visitors were as welcome as you!'

She stayed with them for a week, and she would sit in the gardens outside the infirmary, her baby on her knee, talking to Uncle Edward, and the old brothers who sat out in the sun with him, and to Peregrine when he could snatch the time. It was one of those brief spells of complete happiness that come once in a rare while, an unlooked-for gift of God, when the forces of darkness, of sorrow and temptation seem miraculously held back, a breathing-space in the battle.

On the third day of her visit, Peregrine stole an afternoon to be with her, and they sat together in the deepening golden peace of the afternoon sun, Melissa suckling her child and telling all the news from home.

She lifted up the baby, drunken and replete, eyes drowsing shut, a dribble of white milk trickling from his slack mouth. Holding him up to her with his head nestled on her shoulder, she stroked his back as they talked. The baby gave a huge, satisfied belch, which made them all smile.

'Father, would you like to hold him?' she said.

Peregrine looked at her, and looked down at his hands, and then at Melissa again, and the wistfulness and sadness in his eyes went through her like a knife.

'Of course you can hold him!' she exclaimed. 'Here, I'll lay him on your lap, so; rest his head on your hand.' Gently she straightened Peregrine's fingers under the downy head. The baby looked up at him, and gurgled and smiled—the little, confiding noises of baby conversation, the endearing, dimpled, toothless smile of innocent happiness.

Peregrine gently stroked the delicate skin of the child's forehead, smiling back at his grandson, his face radiant with vulnerable tenderness.

'Thus was Jesus,' he whispered, 'and thus all the little ones whom Herod butchered. Oh, God protect you in this world, dear one. God keep you safe from harm.'

Melissa watched the tiny, pink hand grip round Peregrine's scarred, twisted fingers, and sadness welled up in her for sorrow to come, for the inevitable harshness and pain.

'You can't ask that, Father, and you know it, of all people,' she said gently. 'But let him travel through life with his hand gripping Jesus' scarred hand as tight as it now grips yours, and the storms will not vanquish him.'

The baby yawned hugely, and Peregrine looked up at Melissa, delighted. 'Wearied by theology, God save him, at eight weeks old! Oh Melissa, you have brought me joy!'

She came and stood beside him, leaning against him, her arm resting around his neck, her fingertips stroking absently, tracing the scar on his face as she smiled down at her baby son.

'It's a wonderful, wonderful, sacred thing; this perfect little life, a new beginning born out of my body, out of Ranulf's and my love. It must be hard, to live without family life. Did you never think you missed your way, maybe, being a monk?'

'Missed my way? No, not me. Did I choose it, or did God choose me? I would make the same choice again tomorrow. Although ... sometimes my skin is hungry for tenderness of touch as you touch me now. Yes, that I miss: but no one is guaranteed that loving tenderness, and look, I have found it in the cloister, where others starve for it among their own kin, at their own hearthside.'

A sudden grimace of distress crossed the baby's face, and he opened his gums wide in a trembling cry of protest. Melissa stooped and lifted him, held him against her, patting and rocking him gently. He drew his knees up and cried again, then belched enormously, and relaxed, content.

'He is not yet baptised, Father. I saved that for you. Will you baptise him for me this week?'

'Need you ask? I am honoured! Benedict, you said you were naming him, did you not? What brought that on?'

'Well I wanted him to be named after you, but Peregrine is such an outlandish, ridiculous name, and none of the brothers here ever call you Columba—your kitchen brother says you may coo over the baby, but you're still no dove. So I didn't know what to choose. But I've been reading the Rule of Life that St Benedict wrote, and all he says the abbot should be sounds just like you, so I thought Benedict would do, because his Rule has shaped your life.'

Peregrine said nothing for a moment. She could not read his expression. His eyes were very bright in his lean, intent face as he looked at her.

'That is all right, isn't it?' she said.

'Yes. Oh yes. I was just a bit overcome by the compliment you've just paid me. There, Brother Basil is ringing the Vespers bell.' He raised his voice. 'Wake up, Edward!'

Brother Edward started awake from his peaceful doze.

'Eh? What is it? Vespers already? Forgive me, Melissa, sleeping. My old age overwhelms what manners I ever had, these days.'

He yawned and stood slowly. The three of them walked together up the cobbled path, Melissa holding her baby close and peaceful against her: four generations. At the guest house they parted company, and Melissa went in to lay her drowsy baby in his bed.

Peregrine and Edward continued together to the chapel.

'God has been so generous to me, Edward. The sin of my youth is covered by his forgiving love, and all that is left of it is his gift of a daughter, and grandchildren. His generosity is more than I can comprehend.'

They entered together the cool dimness of the chapel and went each to his own stall.

Motes of dust floated in the rays of sun that slanted through the narrow windows. The brothers' voices lifted in the sixty-second psalm. Peregrine closed his eyes and allowed his soul to be lifted on the beauty of the chant. 'Is this worship,' he wondered, 'or is it self-indulgence?'

He joined in the singing of the sixty-third psalm: '*Quoniam melior est misericordia tua super vitas, labia mea laudabunt te* ...—For your loving-kindness is better than life itself: my lips shall speak your praise ...'

He opened his eyes, and his gaze fell on the great wooden crucifix, and then his attention was caught by a movement. Brother James, the newest of the new generation of novices, was still struggling with endless rules and regulations, and was creeping in late, standing wretchedly with downcast eyes, in the place of shame set apart for late-comers. Little darts of disapproval were flying his way from Father Matthew, who had seen him, too. Ah, well, life goes on ...

'*Quia fuisti adjutor meus. Et in velamento alarum tuarum exultabo* ...—Because you have been my helper, therefore in the shadow of your wings I rejoice ...'

'Bear up, Brother James, three months now and you'll be professed, God willing, and then it will be me you have to deal with, and not Father Matthew. God grant I may not be over-indulgent with you, because you *are* undisciplined for all your heart's in the right place ...'

Father Matthew, perfecting his withering look at the unfortunate Brother James, flared his nostrils and inhaled more dust than he had bargained for, which caused him to sneeze, violently. Peregrine lowered his head, glad that the cowl hid his face, burying his delighted grin in the pages of his breviary:

'*Gloria Patri et Filio, et Spiritui Sancto* ...'

Repentantly, Peregrine composed his face, and gave his attention to the prayers. Wise old Benedict had laid down in his Rule of Life that at the first Office of the day and in the evening at Vespers, the abbot should pray aloud the Lord's Prayer, so that the day should begin and end with the remembrance that we are forgiven, and must in our turn forgive, and so all differences between the brethren be laid to rest.

Abbot Peregrine raised his head and led the prayer in his firm, clear voice:

'*Pater noster, qui es in caelis, sanctificetur nomen tuum* ...'

Then the Office was ended, and the brothers were

dispersing quietly. Brother James came and knelt before Peregrine, humbly awaiting penance.

'Say a *Miserere*, my son, and try to be in good time tomorrow,' said Father Peregrine mildly.

Then with a light heart he set on his way to meet Melissa and Brother Edward at his house for supper, and smiled at the sight of Brother Tom, hastening ahead of him, anxious not to be late.

'And that's all,' said Mother firmly, looking at the clock. 'There were plenty of other stories, though, to keep us going in the New Year.'

She smiled and stretched and yawned, and uncurled reluctantly from her armchair.

'Bed time, I think, my darling. Happy New Year.'

We took one candle to light our way upstairs, and blowing out the other one, left the dying fire, its embers faintly illuminating the night.

Shivering in the unheated bedroom, I decided it was too cold to wash and clean my teeth, so I slipped off my dressing-gown and crept quietly into my bed, careful not to disturb my sleeping sisters. It was warm and cosy under the blankets; Therese had left me the hot-water bottle there. I lay for a long time in the darkness, listening to my sisters' regular, peaceful breathing, punctuated by the little sighs and murmurs of sleep: thinking, remembering, imagining ... and then finally thinking drifted into dreaming, and I was asleep.

Those are some of the stories then, that Mother told me the year I turned fifteen, so many years ago now: stories of my long ago grandfather, Peregrine du Fayel, and his Uncle Edward, and his daughter Melissa, named for Melissa du Fayel, Peregrine's mother. Down the ladder of seven hundred years they have climbed, preserved by grandmother and mother and daughter, told at the firesides of our family through all those generations. My mother, my wonderful, magical mother, weaver of dreams, with her dark, compelling eyes, her wild mane of hair, and the soft blue folds of her skirt: she made them come alive for me, and they fed my hungry soul, and they changed everything for me. They have been stored away in the garden of my imagination, walled away since I was a young girl, until I have opened the green door and taken you in to wander in the garden. And the stories were there waiting, surprisingly fresh to my memory after all. ... Well, but Peregrine was unforgettable, wasn't he? So now I have told some of them to you. I hope, I really hope, they fed your hunger too. I wish you had known my mother, for she would have told them better than I; but there it is. Like you, I make the best of what I can do.

BOOK TWO

*For my friend
Margery May*

I
ABOUT THESE STORIES

I will never forget my friend Maggie dying. Word came to me on the Saturday afternoon that there had been a fire at her house and she was in hospital. I cancelled my plans for the evening and went straight there. I was not allowed to go in to her, the doctor was with her, so I sat down to wait in a room where chairs and bits of furniture were stored. Presently a plump, fair-haired, rather anxious-looking priest appeared in the corridor, looking for a nurse. He turned out to be Father Michael, one of the priests from the church Maggie attended. We sat in the small, cluttered room together, waiting, exchanging what news we had, what little we had heard, giving details to a nurse to fill in a form about Maggie; the sparse pitiful details of her lonely life.

Then we saw a nun walking briskly along the corridor, her veil flowing behind her. She marched straight up to the door of the intensive care unit. Maggie was there, and she intended to be with her. It was Sister Kathleen, the Irish nun, one of Maggie's friends from the convent. They wouldn't let her in, so all three of us sat together and waited, bound into a strange intimacy by the tension of the situation.

The doctor came to see us. She was very poorly, he said. She had seventy, maybe eighty, per cent burns. The right leg—most of the right side—was gone. He suggested we should not go and see her. The nurse agreed with him. It was not a pleasant sight, she said, even for a nurse. I felt glad enough to go along with the advice. What could we do, after all? She was unconscious. The priest, also with some relief, agreed with me. Sister Kathleen said nothing. The doctor went away, saying he would bring us more news later. Not until he had gone did Sister Kathleen speak: 'Should you not anoint her, Father?'

Of course. Of course he had to. We found the nurse again and explained. There were prayers that must be said: she must be anointed, blessed, absolved, before she died. Sister Kathleen said firmly that she would like to be there at Maggie's bedside to join in with the prayers. Me too. I knew it then. Just to creep away would not do. The nurse said she would go and ask. Where did Father want to anoint her? The forehead, he explained, was the usual place. The nurse looked doubtful. 'There's not much of her forehead left,' she said.

She went away and returned a moment later. Yes, there was a little place. It would be possible. The priest and I looked at each other. He did not speak, but there was a sort of barely perceptible wobbling about his face. I think he felt the same cold nausea of horror that I did. I don't know what Sister Kathleen was feeling. We trailed in the wake of her intrepid resolution, through the ward into the sideward where Maggie lay on her back under a sheet. Only her face was showing, and she was attached to all the tubes and drips of intensive care.

I don't know what I expected to see. I thought she would look like a piece of toast from what they said. It was Maggie, that's all. Maggie, with her face swollen and her hair singed, some of her skin burned away, the rest of it discoloured. But it was Maggie. I could see her soul.

I don't mean my eyes saw a shining thing or anything like that. I mean that my spirit perceived, knew, beheld, the childlike, sweet reality of Maggie's real self, radiating from the still, burned body on the bed. Father Michael anointed her, and we said the prayers, and went home.

She was still alive in the morning. I was angry with myself for not having stayed with her. Maggie, who was so afraid of dying alone. I went back to the hospital and asked to sit with her.

'You can hold her hand,' said the nurse. 'Sit on this side. There's a bit more of this hand left.'

Again the cold, sick clutch of horror. What would it look like, the remains of that hand? The nurse lifted the sheet, and there it was, Maggie's hand. That's all it was; it was her hand. Burned, yes, and a lot of the skin gone, but it was Maggie's hand, and I held her hand till she died.

I have always been grateful for the clear-headed courage of that Irish nun, not discouraged by medical professionals or intimidated by unfamiliar territory and the instincts of fear and dread, remembering the human essentials. Maggie needed us; she needed us and she needed God, and in some strange way those needs were not separate but the same.

I walked away from the hospital down to the sea, wanting to be by myself, not ready to go home yet. I watched the waves crashing onto the pebbles as the tide came in, seeing and yet not seeing the foam and surge of the sea; half there and half still standing in the presence of death's mystery; fear, reverence, awe … My lips still remembered the cold, dead brow I had kissed in farewell. My eyes still saw the sharp outline of her face, no longer softened by colour or blurred by the constant under-current motion of breath, pulse, life. Once, just once, the fingers of her hand had moved while I held it, while the respirator still held together the last shreds of her life's breaking thread. Had she heard my voice? Talking so quietly, not wanting the nurse to hear: 'Forgive us, Maggie. Oh forgive us.' Maybe things would have turned out differently if I had stayed with her, been there to avert the last fatal stupidity: the spilt brandy, the dropped cigarette. I didn't know. I wished I still had my mother to talk it over with. Mother always understood my questions, spoken or unspoken, and my grieving—even this grief all numbed by regret. I remember how I used to come home to her with my troubles when I was a girl, and she always understood. I picture her now in the kitchen, washing up maybe, or slicing .potatoes, or stirring custard. She would listen quietly, and as often as not she would ponder my words for a few moments, then say, 'I know a story about that.' She would tell me stories, wonderful stories, that teased out the tangled threads of my heartaches and made sense of things again.

It was a monk Mother used to tell me stories about; a monk of the fourteenth century called Peregrine du Fayel. He was a badly disabled man with a scarred face and a lame leg and twisted, misshapen hands. He was the abbot of St Alcuin's Abbey in North Yorkshire, on the edge of the moors. He was a man whose body was shaped by the cruelties of life, but his spirit was shaped by the mercy and goodness of God. He couldn't do much with his broken hands, but he discovered that there were some precious and powerful things that could be done only by a man whom life had wounded badly. He was loved and honoured by the brothers who served God under him, and there were many stories told of his dealings with them, the things he said and did. These stories were never written in a book, but they have been passed down by the women in my family, from one generation to another.

The one who first collected the stories was a woman

like him. In actual fact, although he kept this to himself, she was his daughter. Before he entered monastic life, he had a love affair, and unwittingly left his sweetheart expecting a baby. The baby, Melissa, was brought up by her mother and stepfather, and not until she was a young woman did she accidentally come across Abbot Peregrine, her real father. Finding him brought her a sense of completion and belonging, and she used to visit him in his monastery, and grew to love him very much, treasuring the stories about him that she gathered from the monks.

One of the stories they liked to tell her was the story of his name. His name in religion, the name his abbot had bestowed on him when he took his first vows and severed himself from all that he had been up until then, was 'Columba'. It is the Latin word for a dove. The abbot had been named 'Peregrine' by his mother, because even as a baby it had been evident that he was going to inherit his father's proud, fierce, hawkish face—and he did. The brothers of Abbot Peregrine's monastery found the incongruity of the name 'Columba' very amusing. They called him 'Peregrine', his baptismal name. They thought it fitted better. Melissa liked that story too, but she liked it because she saw both in him, the hawk and the dove. He was fierce and intimidating at times, it was true, but there was also a tenderness and a quality of mercy about him that he had learned in the bitter school of suffering. 'Columba' had been a good choice, after all.

My name is Melissa. It is a family name. There has been a Melissa every now and then in our family for hundreds of years, since Abbot Peregrine's daughter. The last one before me was my mother's great-grandmother. She died the year I was born, and Mother didn't want the name to die out in our family, so I was christened Melissa too. I don't know what she'd have done if I'd been a boy.

The stories and the name were passed down through our family, grandmother to granddaughter, all the way to my mother's great-grandmother: hundreds of years. My mother's great-grandmother told them to my mother, and Mother loved the stories. She told them to me in my turn, when I was fifteen.

She waited until I was fifteen, because they were not children's stories. They were stories of men who had faced disillusionment and tasted grief and struggled with despair. Mother waited until I came to that time when I was no longer satisfied with the convenient and the pleasant and the comfortable; when I had seen enough of the shifting sands of appearances and wanted to stand firm on the truth, and then she began to tell me the stories that long ago Melissa had remembered and treasured about Abbot Peregrine, her father. He was an aristocrat, the son of a rich nobleman, and I must confess I liked that too: it's been a long time since we had one of those in our family. My own mother and father never had two ha'pennies to rub together, but that might have been because, with more faith than wisdom, they had five children.

When I was fifteen, my sister Therese was sixteen and my little sisters Beth and Mary were eight and six. My youngest sister Cecily was only three then, but she certainly made her presence felt. Daddy said she was like an infant Valkyrie, and words failed Mother to describe her adequately. She would just shake her head in silence. All three-year-olds are a force to be reckoned with when they get going, but I've never met anyone like my sister Cecily. She's not all that much different now, actually.

We lived in a small terraced house near the sea, which is the place my mind goes back to when I tell these stories, the stories Mother first told me there, the year I was fifteen. My sisters liked stories too, but not as much as Mother and I did. We lived with one foot in reality and one in fantasy, and sometimes we forgot which foot was which. I still do.

I went to school at a girls' High School. I have heard it said that 'schooldays are the best days of your life', but the best of my schooldays was the day I walked out of the gate for the last time and turned my back on it for ever. I used to feel as though my life was made up of weekends separated by deserts of weekdays, a bit like the beads on a rosary that come in clumps separated by bald stretches of chain. Perhaps I was a difficult person to teach—well, I know I was, they left me in no doubt about that—but if I gave my teachers trouble, it was nothing to the misery they caused me.

Have you ever been given one of those horrid joke presents, a big, inviting, exciting box, which when you open it contains only another box, and inside that another box, right down to the last one which has nothing at all inside? That's how my schooldays were. Day led onto day, a meaningless, hollow emptiness, the promise of learning no more than academic exercises wrapped around nothing.

I can see my headmistress' face now, the permed waves of grey hair rising from the domed forehead above those eyes that so remarkably resembled a dead cod, and the sort of embossed Crimplene armour she wore under her academic gown.

I learned very little. I have no idea where the Straits of Gibraltar are, and not until last weekend did I learn the square root of 900. But the day I opened the last package in the sequence and found it was an empty joke, I mean the day I pulled up the drawbridge of my soul for ever, and never learned another thing from those teachers (though I was at the school two years more) was the day I got my English exam result. I was not good at many things at school, but I was good at English and I *knew* I was. I tried my best in the exam, and I hoped I'd done well. When the results were given out, I got 54%, which just scraped a pass. I can remember it now, sitting in the classroom; the wooden desks with their graffiti, the high Victorian windows, and the teacher explaining to me that she had given me no marks at all for the content of my exam. She had given me marks for my punctuation and for my spelling, but that was all, because the content was, she felt, immoral. She had thought, she said, when she began to read it, that it was going to be a love story, but it turned out to be about God.

It seems funny (odd, I mean, not amusing) to think how that hurt me, then; how the shutters of my soul closed for good against the school that day. I know now what that poor, starved woman cannot have known, that not only my essay but the whole of life is a love story, about a tender and passionate God.

So my life was lived in the evenings and at weekends, and the greater part of my education was not geography or mathematics, but the wisdom my mother taught me, wrapped up in stories her great-grandmother Melissa had taught her.

Here are some of those stories.

II
WHO'S THE FOOL NOW?

Stories and songs are for wet days and evenings, and for camping. You could offer me a mansion with central heating and every luxury; top quality stereo systems, colour televisions and ensuite bathrooms, and I would not exchange it for my memories of campfires under the stars.

I remember my little sisters, Mary and Beth and Cecily, dancing to the music of Irish jigs piped on a recorder, their silhouetted shapes leaping and turning in the firelight. I remember Mary's eager smile as she stretched up towards the flying sparks that floated high in the smoke. Fire-fairies, she said they were. I remember their breathless voices as they sang 'Father Abraham had many sons ...', hopping and jumping the actions to the song.

Round the fire, sitting on the big stones that ringed it, were friends and family. Mother and Daddy, Grandma, my uncle and auntie, Grandad sitting in his camp chair with a pink towel draped over his head to stop the midges biting him. Familiar and commonplace in the daylight, as the dusk fell and night drew on they became folk-tale figures, mythological beings from another age.

The kindly light of the fireglow hid the irrelevances of whether Grandma's anorak was blue or white and Auntie's trousers were fashionable, and revealed different things: the kindness of Grandad's face, and the serene wisdom of Grandma's. Daddy's face with its long beard looked like an Old Testament story all by itself. People think you can see more by electric light, but you can't. You see different things, that's all. You can see to read or do your homework or bake a cake by electric light, but you see people more truly by candlelight and firelight. 'Technology is man-made, and has no soul,' my mother used to say.

'You're a pyromaniac!' Daddy would say to her. 'Candles, bonfires, campfires, fires on the hearth at home. Why can't we have central heating like everybody else?'

'Everybody else? Who's that?' Mother would reply. 'If there really is a faceless grey "they" mumbling, "There's safety in numbers," what is that worth to me? I need fire and earth and wind and waves as much as I need food. I'd go mad living in this wired-up, bricked-up, fenced-in concrete street if I didn't dose myself with fire and weather and earth and sea. My soul would get pale and thin. I don't want a pale, thin soul.'

'Okay.' Daddy knew when to give in. 'No central heating.'

Our camping holiday was an important part of our dose of the elements. We used to go to a place in the Yorkshire hills, sheltered by tall, whispering trees, beside a shallow stream where brown trout swam among the stones under the dappling of sunlight shining through leaves.

Sometimes the sun shone and we lay out on the grass reading comics and books, eating peaches and french bread and chocolate. Sometimes it rained and we lay in bed at night listening to the drumming of raindrops on the canvas, careful to let nothing touch the edge of the tent. On rainy days we warmed ourselves up with mugs of tea and chips from the chip shop, and watched, as the clouds cleared, the beauty of the wet hills holding the transparent, washed loveliness of the light like cupped hands holding the eucharist.

You don't see rainfall in a town. Oh, you can see that it's raining and you can get wet all right, but there is not the space to see the mist of rain blowing, the approach of rainfall across a valley, the majestic breadth of the sky with its gathering fleet of clouds. In the town, it is sunny or it is not. It is cold or it is warm. The gold of autumn and the silver of the rain has no meaning. Where I live now, I have a view from the front of my house of a large rendered wall painted grey, its flat surface relieved by an extractor fan, a flat blue door and a small window. From the back I can see a clutter of washing lines, sheds and greenhouses. But I remember the holidays of my girlhood by the stream and under the stars, and I still do as Mother did and take regular doses of fire and water, earth and air, to stop my soul getting pale and thin.

Daddy always said there was not much difference between camping and staying at home for us, because we girls slept on mattresses on the floor at home, too. Five of us children in a two-bedroomed house made mattresses a practical option. On winter nights we pushed them close together and kept each other warm. So camping had no sense of hardship or roughing it for us. Grandad brought his Tilley lamp and his calor gas camping stove, and Mother had her campfire in the evening.

We sat beside the fire one evening at camp, Mother and I. Daddy was putting the three little ones to bed, telling them the story of how the sky fell on Chicken Licken, and Therese had gone with Grandma and Grandad to buy some milk. It must have been early on in the week, because I don't think Uncle and Auntie were there that night.

'You haven't told me a story about Father Peregrine and the monks for ages,' I said. It was a clear, warm night and we had spent the early part of the evening gathering brushwood and fallen branches from among the trees, for the fire which was going beautifully now.

'I haven't, have I? All right then. Let me think a moment.'

You remember Brother Thomas? Remember how, when Father Peregrine had been beaten and crippled, his hands maimed and broken, he struggled so hard to keep his fear and horror and grief hidden inside, and almost did; but it was Brother Thomas who plucked up the courage to put his arms round him and gave him the jog he needed to spill his grief, his misery and despair. Brother Thomas never forgot it either. He kept the memory in the tender, mysterious place at the very centre of his soul, and he never spoke about it, because none of us can speak easily about the things that lodge in the very heart of us like that. He admired and respected his abbot for his justice and his natural authority and he loved him for the gentleness and mercy that was in him too. But at the very core of his love was the memory of Father Peregrine sobbing out his despair—'Oh God, how shall I bear the loss of my hands?'—as Brother Thomas held him in his arms.

Well this story concerns Brother Thomas, although most people called him Tom. Even Father Peregrine did in the occasional unguarded moment. Brother Tom was, as you remember, a vital and hearty young man, who hugged life in a mighty embrace and was given more to laughter than to tears. He had a deep appreciation of wine, women, song and good food, and he found the life of a monk very, very hard—at times intolerably hard. None the less, he loved the Lord Jesus to the bottom of his soul and was determined enough to follow his calling. But he did wonder, at times, if God should

ever ask of him that he be removed elsewhere, to serve
over the sea, or in another monastery, whether he could
bear to leave his abbot, because although it was God who
called him to the monastic life, it was Father Peregrine
who kept him at it, or that was the way Brother Tom saw
it. Then again, as he told himself, God's will was for him
to serve in *this* monastery *here*, so maybe loving his
superior was part of loving God, although ... but here
Brother Tom's brain wearied of the complications of the
issue: he loved his abbot, and he understood his vulnerability as well as his strength. Truly, the two of them had
been through some harrowing times together. In the
course of Brother Tom's novitiate there had been an
unfortunate incident with a young lady, which is a story
all of its own, and had it not been for the way Father
Peregrine dealt with Brother Tom and pleaded for him
with the ancients of the community, Tom would have
been turned out for good. Indeed, love his abbot though
he might, Brother Tom caused him more trouble than
all the others put together. He was on more than one
occasion in disgrace for raiding the larder under cover
of night, and his irrepressible streak of mischief combined with Brother Francis' inventive sense of humour
to cause chaos and disapproval again and again.

Father Peregrine had so often to plead for him and
bail him out, to admonish him, listen to him, talk things
through with him, pray for him and have him beaten,
that he wondered from time to time if it wouldn't have
been better for Tom simply to call it a day, give up
struggling against the grain to be Brother Thomas, and
return to farming the land with the family who had
grieved to give him up. It amazed them both when
Brother Tom at last came to the end of his novitiate
(which was twice as long as it should have been, because
of the young lady) and the community agreed to receive
him for life and he made his solemn vows. Father
Peregrine, who did not trust Tom out of his sight for too

long, gave him the job of being the abbot's esquire, his own personal attendant. Brother Tom cleaned his house for him, waited on him at table, and did for him those tasks that his broken hands could not accomplish, for example, shaving him, buckling his belt, and fastening his sandals and tunic. Things went reasonably well for a while after he took his vows. The consideration that he was now a fully professed Benedictine monk had a sobering effect on Brother Tom, and he spent nearly six weeks after his solemn profession affecting an unnatural dignity that made Father Peregrine smile, and drew derision from Brother Francis who had made his own life vows three months previously and was now recovered from the awe and apprehension that went with it.

It didn't last. As inevitably as the flowering of blue-bells in the spring came the temptations of the flesh that regularly assailed Brother Thomas. After a week of fasting and praying, and scourging himself mercilessly in the privacy of his cell, he stole the key to the cellar, sat down by the biggest cask of wine he could find and got blind drunk. Brother Cormac discovered him there, and attempted to remonstrate with him, unwisely as it turned out, for black gloom had descended on the miscreant by then and Brother Cormac got nothing but a bloody nose for his pains. Brother Andrew, Cormac's superior in the kitchen, reported the matter to Father Peregrine in bristling indignation, and Father Peregrine, mortally weary of Tom's misdemeanours and exasperated beyond measure, had them souse him with a bucket of cold water and lock him up in the abbey prisons to sober up overnight.

Red-eyed, sneezing and penitent, Brother Thomas was brought to stand before the Community Chapter Meeting in the morning and receive his penance, which in these rare and unhappy circumstances was the standard one of a flogging.

Father Peregrine hated to see a man flogged, and he was upset as well as angry with Brother Tom, so spoke with more heat than he might normally do as Brother Thomas knelt down before him: 'Brother Thomas, you are a *fool*. You have the goodwill of this community and you *spit* on it. You have the trust of this community and you throw it away. You're a fool, Brother, because goodwill does not last for ever. You betray our trust, you betray your vocation, you betray the good name of this house with your silly capers. You are a fool!'

He glared at Brother Tom, and Tom humbly bent his aching head before his abbot's wrath. Both of them felt sick at heart, because in each of them the love for the other hurt like a splinter, like a sharp thorn. Father Peregrine was angry with Tom because he loved him, because he wanted him to be true to his vocation, because he didn't want to give the word to have him flogged. And Tom was ashamed and miserable because he'd failed again, because his abbot had spent so much time and kindness on him and he'd let him down once more.

Brother Clement, chosen for the job because he worked in the scriptorium and library, and therefore had little to do with Brother Tom and was as impartial towards him as any of the brothers could be, stood with the scourge in his hand. Brother Tom unfastened his tunic and undershirt, and bent low as he knelt before them, exposing his back to be beaten. Peregrine sat in his stall, his eyes downcast, the slight frown of distress that he could not help belying the sternness of his face.

'Father . . .' Brother Clement hesitated. Brother Tom's back was already a mass of purple welts where he had used the scourge savagely on himself in his battle against temptation.

'Ah, no!' said Peregrine, seeing it. 'Let that be finished with, Brother. No, no, I've no stomach to lay wound upon wound. Let him be. Resume your place, Brother

Thomas. For your penance you may eat only dry bread and water these three days, and that you must take on your knees in the refectory, set apart from the brethren.'

It was on the third of these three days that Brother Tom came in to the abbot's lodging to sweep the floor and generally tidy up, and found Father Peregrine seated at his table, thoughtfully gnawing his lip as he frowned at a letter he was holding in his hand. He glanced up briefly at Brother Tom, grunted a response to Tom's pleasant 'God give you good day, Father', and went back to the perusal of his letter.

Brother Tom, as he swept the room, watched out of the corner of his eye as his abbot laid the letter down at last, and sat deep in thought for a while, then picked it up again and looked at it once more. It was written in an elegant hand on the finest vellum.

'The cunning devil!' Peregrine announced suddenly. 'Here, read this, Brother. 'Tis from Prior William of St Dunstan's Priory. You know, the Augustinian house. He invites me, in terms of the most friendly courtesy, to take part in a conference—a debate—concerning the nature of God, whether his supreme manifestation be in justice or in mercy.'

'What's wrong with that?' asked Tom, reaching out his hand for the document.

'Only that he hates me like poison, and that St Dunstan's Priory is three days' ride to the southwest, and his conference begins in three days' time. If Prior William bids us to conference he's up to no good somewhere. It's not like him to waste the substance of his house on hospitality if he can help it, and he doesn't intend me to be there for sure. It means leaving on the instant and riding half the night to be there in time. Why this sudden interest in the mercy and justice of God in any case? It never troubled his mind before that I recall.

'No ... he's up to something and he counts on my

absence to work it. He's a manipulator of minds and a
good politician, but he's no theologian. Whatever he's
cooking up, he wants me out of it because he knows I'll
have the better of him in theological debate.'

He sat frowning in thought a while longer as Tom
scanned the letter, then he exclaimed, 'No, I don't trust
him! We'll go. I want to know what he's hatching.'

Brother Tom looked up from the letter in surprise.
'But Father, how are you going to—I mean, can
you . . . ?'

'Sit a horse without falling off? Yes? Well, we shall see,
shan't we? Find Father Chad and Brother Ambrose.
Have three horses saddled, prepare for ten days' absence.
Make haste. Yes, you're coming with me. I don't trust
you out of my sight, you drunken fool.'

The preparations were quickly made. It was agreed
that Father Chad, the prior, should travel with them,
leaving Brother Ambrose, the wise old cellarer, who was
also the sub-prior, to rule over the community in their
absence.

Brother Peter, who cared for the horses, considered
Father Peregrine's situation carefully.

'You've been a good enough horseman, it'll not matter
about your hands, but can you grip with your thighs?
These two years near enough you've been limping about
on a crutch. Your muscles will be wasted. Not only that,
but that stiff knee. I'm not sure. . . . Better not to arrive
plastered in mud, I would imagine. How do you feel
about being tied to your saddle? No, don't answer that. I
can see by the look in your eye how you feel about it.
Would it not be for the best though, truly?'

They did in the end strap him to his saddle as well as
they could, and by noon they were on the road. They
rode late into the night, that first night, slept under the
stars in the lee of a hedge, and were on the road again
before first light. The second night they begged food
and lodging of a house of Poor Clares, who received

them with warmth and kindness. They ate a hearty meal
in the guest house there, and finished just in time to join
the sisters for Compline. As they made their way to their
beds, Brother Tom broke the Great Silence to whisper,
'Shall I not attend to your hands before you go to your
bed, Father? Brother Edward has given me some oil,
and said I mustn't forget to massage them every day. I
neglected to do it yesterday. Will I not see to them
tonight?'

Peregrine shook his head. 'Not now. We are in silence,
and we need all the sleep we can get. We must be away
early. Thank you, but leave it.'

'Father ...'

'Leave it. We are in silence.'

With a sigh, Tom abandoned the conversation. He
knew his abbot well and had seen how his proud spirit had
balked at being tied to his horse like baggage on a mule.
Peregrine had been touchy, on his dignity, all day, and was
not about to have his independence eroded any further.
He carried himself stiffly, and Tom guessed how the lame
leg must be aching. Father Peregrine had not ridden since
his leg bone was smashed. He looked weary. Tom glanced
at him anxiously and tried one last plea: 'Father ...'

'No.'

And they went to bed.

The kindly sisters made them a food parcel for their
journey, and they were on their way directly after Mass.
They had made such good time the first two days that
they were assured of arriving at St Dunstan's before
Vespers. Brother Tom and Father Chad rode side by
side, enjoying the change of scenery and each other's
company. Father Peregrine kept a little apart from
them, speaking rarely and clearly on edge. They stopped to eat and water their horses at noon, and sat awhile
to let the horses crop the roadside grass.

'Father, shall I not see to your hands?' Brother Tom
ventured again.

Three days of holding the reins of a horse had left them more awkward than ever, and it had not escaped Tom's notice that it was with more difficulty than usual that Father Peregrine broke his bread and meat as they ate.

'Not now. We must press on. I want to be there before evening. Prior William is a heartless, cunning fox. Whatever this conference is about, it'll not be what it seems. He feels obliged to invite me to give credibility to his appearances, but see how he's left it so late that I can reasonably be expected to get there late or never, without actually being able to say I was not asked in time. Depend upon it he'll force me out of the debate in Chapter, and away from the meal table conversation if he can. Well, we shall see.'

'He knows then, does he, that you can't—that you no longer—that you are thus disabled, Father?' enquired Father Chad.

'Not from me, but yes, no doubt he knows. The only thing that takes more care to inform itself than love is hatred, and he hates me with a thoroughness that unnerves me a little, I confess. I've worsted him in debate before, and that he will not forgive. Anyway, enough, we must be away. We'll not be late.'

They rode in at the large grey stone gatehouse that straddled the moat surrounding the impressive priory of St Dunstan just after the afternoon office, dusty and tired. They were received with all civility, and news of their arrival was sent to Prior William, who came out to meet them as their horses were led away to be stabled and rubbed down.

Prior William greeted first Father Peregrine, then Father Chad with the kiss of brotherhood. Brother Tom, who carried their pack, he barely acknowledged. As the formalities of greeting were exchanged, Tom studied the prior's face. Narrow, mobile and intelligent, with thin lips and very little colour, its most striking feature was his eyes, which were of a very pale blue beneath silver eyebrows. The premature whiteness of his hair added to the impression he gave of coldness and austerity. Tom reflected that though his lips curved in a smile as he addressed Father Peregrine, his tone as he spoke was like frostbite.

'A chamber is being prepared for you upstairs in the north wing of the guest house, Father Columba,' he said. His voice was as soft as a woman's; as soft as velvet.

'Upstairs?' butted in Brother Tom. 'My lord, there must be some mistake.'

'Let it be, Brother,' said Father Peregrine quickly, but Prior William's attention was caught.

'Is that inconvenient, my son?' he asked, in his soft, gentle, dangerous woman's voice. He turned to look at Brother Tom as he spoke, and Tom had a sudden feeling of panic, like a small, tasty animal caught in the predator's hypnotic death stare.

'He's—he's lame, my lord, as you see,' Tom stuttered.

'I had thought,' the prior purred, smiling faintly, 'that a man who could make such good time on horseback must be less disabled than I expected.'

Father Peregrine and Father Chad said nothing, but Tom's mettle was up.

'If that be so, my lord,' he said, 'why did you not send him word earlier?'

The eyelids flickered momentarily over the cold blue eyes, but the prior did not stop smiling.

'Shall I instruct my men to prepare your chamber at ground level then?' he asked, fixing his gaze on Peregrine. Peregrine's face was grim as he met Prior William's look. Like an eagle confronting a poisonous snake, thought Tom.

'No, thank you,' said Father Peregrine. 'The upstairs chamber will do well.'

Prior William raised one sardonic eyebrow. 'If you are sure, my brother,' he murmured.

'I am sure,' said Father Peregrine. 'Please let us not detain you, Father Prior. I remember the way to your guest house well enough.' The two men bowed courteously to one another, and Prior William turned his attention to another small party of men who were riding in at the gatehouse, while Father Chad, Father Peregrine and Brother Tom made their way to their lodging.

'Father ... forgive my asking ...' Father Chad hesitated, daunted by the grimness of his abbot's look.

'Yes?'

'Forgive my asking you—how *are* you going to get up the stairs?'

'Backwards,' said Peregrine tersely. 'Unobserved, please God,' he added, with a flicker of a smile.

The stone stairway of the guest house was narrow and steep, but did not pose any great problem. Father Peregrine ascended it sitting on the steps, using his good leg to move him up one at a time, while Father Chad held the wooden crutch and Brother Tom carried their baggage. Tom could not help the grin that spread across his face at the undignified procedure, and Father Chad rebuked him. 'Brother, for shame, it is nothing to laugh at.'

But Peregrine smiled. 'Don't scold him, Father Chad. There'll be little enough to laugh at these four days if I judge right.'

Father Peregrine would not eat that evening with the company gathered after Vespers at Prior William's table, though he insisted that Father Chad and Brother Tom go.

'Keep your wits about you, listen to what's said and note who's here. I'll see you later. I'll sup on the remains of the bread and meat the good sisters packed us for the road. I'm too stiff and sore to keep company.'

Tom took a deep breath. 'Father, *please*, when we return, will you permit me to see to your hands?' He looked in appeal at Peregrine, and somewhere in his gut, compassion clutched him as he read the look on his abbot's face, saw how his sense of dignity was cornered and mocked by his helplessness.

'Thank you,' said Peregrine quietly. 'If you would. I can scarcely move them.'

'After supper, then,' said Tom, cheerfully, and turned to follow Father Chad out of the room.

'Brother.' His abbot stopped him. 'You are quite welcome to say "I told you so".'

Tom grinned at him, understanding how fragile was the dignity with which he protected his disability. 'I wouldn't dare,' he replied. 'I wouldn't dare.'

Most of the men who sat round the long, carved table in Prior William's great hall that evening were unknown to Brother Tom, but Father Chad discreetly pointed them out.

'Abbot Hugh from the Cistercian House to the east of our place, you know already. That's his prior with him, whose name I forget. The dark, bearded man I know not, though judging by his habit he's one of us. The slight, nervous fellow beside him is Abbot Roger, a Cistercian from Whitby.'

'Who is he?' asked Tom, nodding his head towards an enormously fat Benedictine monk, whose clean-shaven chins shook with laughter as he listened to a story his neighbour was telling him.

'He? Do you not know him? He has stayed with us before. It is the Abbé Guillaume from Burgundy. He has known Father Abbot since childhood, I believe, and esteems him highly. An incomparable scholar and a wise and holy confessor.'

'Mmm. Good trencher-man too, by the look of him,' observed Brother Tom.

There were in all seven superiors of prestigious houses seated round the table. Father Robert Bishopton, the Cistercian from Fountains Abbey was there, and the abbot of St Mary's in York. Three of them had brought their priors too, and there were half a dozen other monks of less elevated status, but of scholarly renown, rising stars. So there was a good company gathered round the magnificent oak table.

Prior William's eyes rested meditatively on Father Chad and Brother Tom, and he drew breath as if to speak to them, but thought better of it and merely smiled at them, inclining his head in greeting. Thereafter he ignored them. They were glad of each other's company, neither of them being much at ease among the learned and the great. They were weary, too, from three days' hard riding and it was a relief when the meal was ended, Compline sung and they could turn in for the night. When they returned to their room in the guest house, Father Peregrine wanted to know just who was there and what was said. He heard their account of the company as Brother Tom worked over his hands, gently flexing and stretching the stiff fingers, probing and rubbing the cramped muscles. He listened, and then said, puzzled, 'I still don't understand why Prior William has summoned men of this calibre here to debate whether God's mercy is greater than his justice or the other way about. If it had been Abbé Guillaume I could have understood it. The night could pass and the sun come up and he never notice if he was absorbed in debating the things of God, but Prior William ... they bear the same name, but you could hardly find two men less alike. Ah, what's he up to? I'd give my right hand to know. Not that I'd be missing much. Thank you, brother, you have eased them wonderfully. It takes a day or two to get them right again once I've let them get this bad. They don't ache so much though, now.' He yawned. 'Forgive me, brothers, you're falling asleep where you sit. To bed then.'

The august gathering met in the Chapter House after Mass the following morning, and there the day's business of the community was briefly despatched and the debate began.

It quickly became clear that Prior William, whatever his reasons, wanted the group of eminent men to conclude that God's justice outweighed his mercy. Brother Tom gazed around the room, drowsy with boredom as the men rose one by one to speak, citing the Church Fathers, the Old Testament and various Greek and Eastern philosophers he had never heard of. His attention was recaptured by Prior William's silky voice as he began to wind up the talk for the morning. 'It is on the cross that we see the final, ultimate vindication of God's justice, for God must remain true to his own laws, and requires a sacrificial victim for sin. His demand, yea thirst, for vengeance of his wrath aroused by our corruption requires a victim. Victim there must be, though it be his own Son. The price must be paid. Though the fruit of the cross is mercy, yet its root is justice, for it is a fair price paid, gold laid down for the purchase of our redemption.'

There was a silence at these words; a depressed, uneasy silence, broken by Abbot Peregrine's firm, quiet voice as he rose to his feet and stood leaning on his crutch, his hands hidden in his wide sleeves, his eyes fixed on Prior William's face.

'No, my brother, it is not so,' he said. 'The root of the cross is not justice, though its fruit be mercy, as you say. The root of the cross is love, and what is laid down is more than gold, it is blood, life: given not with the clink of dead metal, but with the groans of a man dying in agony. No yellow shine of gold, but the glisten of sweat, and of tears. Justice is an eye for an eye, and a tooth for a tooth, for every sin a sacrifice. But Christ, the sinless one, is he whose broken body suffered on the cross, and the holy God in Christ who suffered hell for our sin. That is more than justice, my lord Prior, it is love. Nor is it merely a just love. It is a merciful love.'

He remained standing as Prior William rose to his feet to confront him. 'Are you suggesting,' purred the velvet voice, 'that God is not just?'

Peregrine shook his head. 'No. How should we know justice if God were not just? But I do say this: God's justice is subordinate to his love, for his justice is a property of his character, but his love is his essential self. For do not the Scriptures say, "God is love," but never, "God is justice"?'

Brother Tom had no idea which of them was right, if either, and was not sure what the point of the argument was anyway, but Prior William's smooth, disturbing voice, that spoke of victims and wrath and vengeance and gold and corruption, made him feel a bit sick. He felt on firmer ground with Father Peregrine's talk of suffering, merciful love, and to judge by the atmosphere of the meeting, he was not the only one.

Abbé Guillaume rose to speak, and the two men broke the look that locked them in combat and resumed their seats to hear him.

'Le bon Dieu, yes he is charité. But he is perfection, is he not? And is not perfection the essence of justice? The precise, appropriate purity of verité—n'est-ce pas? Is not justice as we conceive of it none other than that which approximates to perfection? Eh bien, in the incomprehensible perfection of God, where all is a radiance of pure light, all crookedness is made straight, is not love swallowed up in the manifestation par excellence of justice—that is perfection?'

'No!' Peregrine was on his feet again, his eyes burning. 'No, good brother. For God loves me, even me; and though Satan parade my sins and weakness before me, yet am I saved by the love of God in Christ Jesus, from which nothing can separate me. Justice would separate me from the love of God. By my sins do I justly perish. But I am redeemed, reborn, recreated; I am held and sheltered and restored by the love of God. Mon père, I cannot call that justice. It is grace, free grace. It is the most prodigal generosity. It is all mercy.'

Brother Tom glanced across the Chapter House at Prior William. The prior was gently caressing his chin with his hand, and his eyes were fixed on Father Peregrine with a cold, calculating, thoughtful look. Tom had never before seen such pure hatred, unmixed with passion or anger or any such agitation. Ruthless, single hatred. He shivered. The company were murmuring their assent to Peregrine's assertion, but Père Guillaume took it serenely. To him, winning or losing was immaterial. He saw debate as a lovely thing in itself, a sculpture of truth chiselled out by the cut and thrust of argument. He was well content.

It was at this point that the Chapter Meeting broke for High Mass, and Tom sighed with relief to be able to stretch his stiff limbs and move again. After the suffocating boredom of the morning's debate, the liturgy with its colour and music seemed like a night out at the inn. Despondency descended on him as they returned to the Chapter House to pursue the debate after Mass. He decided that four days of this would be more than he could endure, and resolved to make himself scarce after the midday meal.

Meanwhile, the talk batted to and fro, concerning the perfection of justice, the perfection of mercy, the essence of perfection, whether or not perfect mercy is a form of justice, the essence of God—all substantiated by long quotations in Latin which Tom couldn't understand properly, and references to bits of the Athanasian Creed which he couldn't remember. Eventually he dozed off to sleep.

He cheered up considerably at lunch time. The table was laden with the choicest roast fowls in rich sauces, vegetables beautifully prepared, dishes of fruit and cheese—a feast to make a man's mouth water. The normal rule of silence was suspended on this occasion, so that the talk might continue on an informal basis. Brother Tom didn't care what they talked about. There was enough food here for him to eat as much as he wanted for once in his life, and as soon as the long Latin grace was said, he applied himself to it with great relish.

The men who sat down to eat were divided roughly according to status. Prior William presided at the head of his table among the scholarly and eminent men he had invited to conference. Lower down the table were those like Father Chad, men of importance but not of the first rank—abbots' priors mainly. Brother Tom sat with the small fry at the end of the table; young monks like himself who were their abbots' esquires. He felt a little uneasy at being separated from his abbot. Once again he had not had chance to attend to his hands, nor opportunity to speak to the lay brothers who served at table here, to ask them to help Father Peregrine with his food. Still, his abbot had common sense enough, and was used to coping with these situations. No doubt he would prefer to avoid having attention drawn to his disability.

Brother Tom investigated the wine that had been poured for him. Like him, the young men among whom he was seated were used to watered ale at table, and his neighbour turned to him with a smile of pure contentment as he set down his elegant, silver goblet. 'That,' he said, 'is like the fire in the heart of a ruby. I think I could find a vocation to this community with very little persuading.' It *was* good wine, clear and dark and smooth. A glow of well-being spread through Brother Tom.

'Faith, yes, I could see off a barrel of this,' he replied happily. 'But it would take more than that to tempt me to live my life in the chill of that miserable icicle of a man.'

His neighbour laughed and glanced up the table towards Prior William. 'Endearing, isn't he? Never mind, he knows where to purchase his victuals. Have you tried this cheese?'

Though there was a fair number of men there, they were used to eating in silence; not only without talk, but without unnecessary scrape and clatter. Their conversation was a discreet hum of sound, and it was easy enough for Prior William to raise his smooth, soft voice just sufficiently loud to be heard by all the company: 'Ah ... I crave your pardon, Father Columba. It had never occurred to me that the mutilation of your hands would render you so ... incapable. What an oversight! You are used perhaps to having your food cut up for you?'

Brother Tom's hand stopped halfway to his mouth and slowly sank down to his plate again. The morsel of cheese he was holding dropped from his fingers forgotten. He watched Peregrine's mortification as the attention of the whole table was inevitably turned towards him. He had spilt some of his food, but not much, and had been struggling with his knife to cut a piece of meat. It was unwise to attempt it, but he was hungry and the food was delicious. The knife had turned in his awkward grasp, and there was gravy splashed on his hands and on the fine linen tablecloth. Brother Tom looked anxiously at Prior William as he reclined in his graceful chair, holding Peregrine in the cool taunting of his gaze.

'Don't,' whispered Tom. 'Oh, please don't.' It was unbearable.

'Perhaps you would prefer to have your food cut up for you?' purred the spiteful voice. The pale eyes watched him relentlessly. The eyebrows were raised and the lips curved in their mirthless smile. Father Peregrine returned his gaze, his face flushed, his jaw clenched. The men nearest them stirred uncomfortably and tried in vain to keep their conversation going.

Father Peregrine looked down a moment at his food. Then he looked back at Prior William. The pale blue eyes shone with malicious mockery. 'Father Columba?' he prompted. Brother Tom held his breath.

'Yes, please,' said Peregrine humbly. 'I would be grateful for that assistance.'

Tom's breath sighed out of him as the tension was broken. He felt like standing on his chair and cheering. 'What a man! What a man! To so humble himself to that cruel devil!' he rejoiced inside. But his rejoicing was numbed when he saw how Peregrine's hand was shaking as he reached out for his goblet of wine. It had cost him dear.

'Oh! Alas!' came the hateful, gentle voice again. 'Father Columba has spilt his wine now. You do normally feed yourself, Father? I never thought to ask.'

'I do,' said Peregrine, almost inaudibly.

'Ah well, never mind,' the prior's voice persisted. 'The boy will mop up the mess you have made. Boy! See the mess he has made: there ... yes and there. And there. Thank you. Replenish his wine.'

The cut food was replaced in front of Father Peregrine, and he murmured his thanks but scarcely touched it after that. His wine he drained like medicine, and he drank heavily throughout the rest of the meal, speaking to no one, his confidence shattered. And all the while, those pale, malevolent eyes returned to look at him complacently. The company rose from their meal in time for the afternoon office of None. Peregrine swayed as he tried to stand, and leaned on the table for support. Brother Tom hastened to his side.

'Are you not well, Father Columba?' came the heartless voice. 'Perhaps you have taken a little too much wine? We shall quite understand if you wish to be excused from the Office.'

'Oh shut up,' muttered Brother Tom under his breath, and he took his abbot's arm and looked round for Father Chad.

Between them, he and Father Chad manoeuvred their abbot and his crutch out of the prior's house and back across the cloister to the guest house. They were

kindly ignored by the other guests, and Brother Tom
was relieved to catch a glimpse out of the corner of his
eye of Prior William departing for chapel.

'Now for the stairs,' said Father Chad dubiously, as
they came to the guest house door. Peregrine raised his
head.

'Chad, go to chapel,' he ordered abruptly. 'I don't
trust that weasel out of my sight and hearing. Go to
chapel. I'll join you later.'

But he leaned on Brother Tom as he spoke, and his
speech was very slurred. Tom doubted very much if he
would be going anywhere but his bed, although getting
him there would be another matter.

Some of his escapades with Brother Francis proved
good practice for this occasion for it was not easy
manhandling a man, both lame and dead drunk, backwards up the narrow stairway. Peregrine complicated
matters by refusing point-blank to relinquish his crutch,
which he clung to as the last symbol of his independence.

They made it though, and Tom helped him into his
chamber, where he collapsed onto a chair and sat staring
moodily at nothing.

'Let me unfasten your boots, Father. I think maybe a
sleep would do you good,' suggested Brother Tom, and
squatted at Peregrine's feet to untie the thongs that
laced his boots.

Resting his hand on his abbot's knee, he looked up
into his face at the bleary, unfocused eyes and uncharacteristic sag, and could not resist a grin. 'Faith, man, you
have drunk well,' he said. Peregrine looked at him
morosely, and nodded in assent.

'Who's the fool now?' he said bitterly.

But Tom's look of amusement and affection penetrated
the fog of alcohol and misery that enveloped him, and
he managed a lop-sided smile.

Brother Tom coaxed him into his bed, where he slept
like the dead until morning.

The next day, in the Chapter meeting, Father Peregrine
was determined to make up for the ground he had lost
by his absence from the previous afternoon's debate.
Père Guillaume spoke of all the Old Testament history
in which God's justice was the sign of his presence, the
manifestation of his love. He spoke with impressive and
detailed knowledge, and Prior William sat nodding with
satisfaction in his chair as he heard him. But when
Peregrine stood to speak, their eyes were all upon him.
His absence had not gone unremarked the day before,
and the men were curious to know what he would say
now; how he would conduct himself, having last left
their midst too drunk to walk alone.

'It is true, what you say, Abbé Guillaume,' he said. 'It
is true that judgement and authority, the instruments of
justice on earth, are authenticated by the command of
God. It is true that God shapes the lives of men in the
ways of justice, and that the righteous find expression of
his Spirit in the paths of justice and of peace. But justice
is a path, yes a way; it is not a home. It is a framework, or
a setting, but it was made to carry another jewel. Justice,
like John the Baptist, is the forerunner, clears the road,
for the coming of the Christ himself. And when he
comes, he is compassion. He is love. Remember the
words of the psalmist *"Hodie si vocem ejus audientis, nolite
obdurare corda vestra."* Harden not your hearts. Today, if
you want to hear the Lord's voice, harden not your
hearts. Oh God forbid that our lives display the sterile
correctness of men who have learned what justice is, but
never tasted mercy.'

The gathering of men listened spellbound to the
urgency of his voice, as he clung like a terrier to a rat to
his insistence on God's merciful love as the one, central,
all-supporting fact of life.

The prior watched him without emotion, biding his
time. In debate this man was magnificent, but he was not
invulnerable, it seemed. There were other ways of

discrediting him. Prior William smiled complacently as they went in to eat after the midday Office. He waited his moment with pitiless detachment. There was entertainment to be derived from seeing this accomplished and scholarly aristocrat grow increasingly uneasy as he tried to ignore the sadistic patience of his host, tried not to lose his nerve under that unpleasantly speculative gaze. There was pleasure in the waiting, but not too long. Once grace was said, the men were seated and the meal was underway, the cruel, gentle voice began.

'Oh, but we mustn't forget to cut your food up for you, Father Columba. Ah, it is done. Can you manage— or not really? Alas, how thoughtless of me to provide insufficiently for you. Look, Father Columba, you have dropped a piece of meat. It seems a shame to soil your garments so, does it not? Perhaps you should have a towel tied about you, as a child does who is learning to eat, yes? That would answer your requirements, would it not? Fetch a towel, boy, a large one, and tie it about him.'

The conversation at the head of the table had ceased in the embarrassment of this baiting, and the men occupied themselves self-consciously with their food. Father Peregrine withdrew his hands from sight and hid them in his lap, protected from view by the wide sleeves of his habit. Mute and still, he waited for the next gibe as the boy came towards him with the towel, and Prior William leaned forward to speak again, his victory shining softly in his eyes.

'Mais non, laissez-le tranquil, mon père. Ca suffit,' murmured Abbé Guillaume unhappily, but the prior did not heed him.

'Thanks, lad. There now, here is the towel. Shall he not tie it about you, my friend?'

Peregrine looked round at the boy standing there with the cloth in his hands and then at the sophisticated men who sat hushed in unwilling fascination at the sight of him caught in his clumsiness and helplessness. It was more than he could bear.

'No!' The harsh pain of his cry splintered the tension of the atmosphere. Tom thought the loneliness of it would have bruised a heart of stone, but it did nothing to disturb Prior William's placid smile. He scarcely even blinked. Peregrine groped on the floor for the crutch that lay beside him, and pushing back his chair with a violence that sent it crashing to the ground, he stumbled blindly to the door. One of the serving-boys assisted him in his ineffectual struggle with the latch, and he escaped.

Brother Tom sat frozen in his seat, appalled. The prior looked down the length of the table at him, his eyebrows raised, his eyes mocking. 'He seems a temperamental, unstable man, your lord,' he remarked in the silence. 'Does he ever complete a meal both sober and in good humour? Or have I said something to upset him?'

The blood was pounding in Tom's ears like thunder. He stared, speechless with rage, at this cruel, smiling man. His heart remembered those weeping words from long ago, 'Oh God, how shall I bear the loss of my hands?', and he lost his temper.

Slowly, he rose in his place. Father Chad took one look at him and buried his head in his hands. Brother Tom walked with measured deliberation to the head of the table, and stood looking down at the prior, who returned his look with scornful amusement.

Tom took a deep breath, and with an effort kept himself from shouting. 'It is easy, easy, sir,' he said, his voice unsteady with restrained rage, 'to humiliate a man and make him look foolish. Why, all it takes is this . . .' Quick as lightning, Tom shot out his arm, seized the prior by his silver hair and smacked his head down into his dinner. He stood shaking with anger, oblivious to the murmurs of some and the stunned silence of others. Prior William lifted his dripping face from the table. His left eyebrow was decorated with a blob of parsley sauce. The boy who held the towel hurried to his side.

'It's not so easy to win a debate, nor to humble yourself before another man!' Tom bellowed at him. 'That takes intellect and courage. You, my lord, have made it plain that you have neither!' He stood glaring at him for a moment, then said in contempt, 'Ah, you sicken me. I would rather be the cockroach that crawls on the floor in the house where my abbot is master than be the greatest of those who serve under you.'

It might even then not have been so bad had not Father Roger from Whitby added a quiet 'Amen'. That was the last straw.

'Take him away,' snapped Prior William, his face a mask of fury behind the remnants of sauce. 'Let him cool his head in the prisons until his master is in a fit state to give permission for his flogging. I had heard the Benedictine houses were sliding into decadence, but now I see it with my own eyes.'

It was not until after the afternoon's discussions had been concluded and Vespers said that Father Peregrine caught up with Father Chad.

'Where's Brother Thomas?' he asked, with some trepidation. 'What's he done now?'

'I regret he made a spectacle of himself at the table after you left, Father.' Father Chad shook his head sadly. 'He pushed my lord prior's face down into his dinner. He said it took no more than that to humiliate a man and make him look foolish. He said it took courage to humble oneself before another man, and intellect to win a debate, and that my lord prior had neither. His implication was that you, Father, have both, though he left that unsaid.'

He raised his face to look at his superior, sorry and ashamed, but Peregrine was grinning at him incredulously.

'He did so? He said that? Well God bless him. That

redeems a few insults. Courage to humble oneself and intellect to win in debate. And I was about to run away. What have they done with him then?'

'He was confined in the prison, Father, until you should be with us again to give permission for his flogging.'

'Flogging for what? Not I! They'll not lay a finger on him!'

The confrontation came in the Chapter meeting the following morning, as part of the business before the theological debate. Brother Tom, dishevelled and defiant, was brought to stand before the gathering to face the prior enthroned on his high-backed, intricately-carved chair on its dais. Prior William regarded him with cold dislike (as much charity as a man bears towards the slug on his salad, thought Tom).

'You deserve to be flogged, you young fool,' said the suave, smooth voice, 'for your gross and brutish manners. You give your permission, I am sure, Father Columba, for his beating?'

The velvet voice permitted itself a shade of triumph. He had caught them. Disgraced them. Discredited them. But Father Peregrine replied, 'I do not.' He rose to his feet. 'In my house,' he said, 'we do not flog a man for loyalty, nor for love, however inadvisedly expressed. We treasure it. However, neither do we permit discourtesy and violence to go unchecked. Brother Thomas, you must ask his forgiveness.'

Brother Tom looked at his abbot, who returned his look calmly, confident of his authority with his own. Tom knelt before the prior.

'Father, I humbly confess my fault of grave discourtesy and unseemly violence. I ask God's forgiveness for my offence, and yours, my lord.'

Prior William looked down at Brother Tom, his pale eyes bulging with rage. He had no idea how they'd done it, but they'd turned the tables on him somehow. For how can you humiliate a man who humbles himself, or disgrace a man who willingly kneels? There stood that insufferable cripple, with the bearing of a king, and there knelt his loutish boy, humbly begging forgiveness, with not even a trace of cynicism or rebellion to his voice that one could fasten on to condemn.

'You are forgiven. Go in peace,' the prior spat out, after the custom of his house. The beautiful words almost choked him. 'Go to hell' would have been more in line with the look on his face.

Peregrine spoke again. 'I recommend for your penance, my son, that you be returned to your cell, for it seems I cannot guarantee your self-control when you are provoked to anger. I suggest you fast there on bread and water until we return home.'

'So be it,' snapped the prior, and irritably dismissed Brother Tom with his long, white, bejewelled hand.

So Tom finished the week as he had begun it, fasting on bread and water, in narrow escape of a severe beating. There were three prison cells, grim stone hovels whose only light was the rays of the morning sun shining through the small barred window set in each of the heavy doors. In the cell adjoining his was one of the local men, a farmer, kept there until his family should pay off an outstanding debt to the priory, for right of way across the canons' land. He and Tom whiled away some of the hours of their imprisonment in talk. They could converse tolerably well if they raised their voices and stood with their faces up against the barred apertures in the cell doors.

'He's a grasping old tyrant, is the prior,' the farmer ruminated, when he had told Tom the story of his troubles and his debt. 'Well, that's plain enough. Look at this conference, up to his tricks again. "Enough" is a word beyond his understanding.'

'What? I thought this business was all theology, spiritual stuff.'

'Spiritual? God save us, nothing's spiritual here but the servants' wages. No, he wants the fishing rights of the river.'

'*Fishing*? What has that to do with his conference?' Tom was bewildered.

'Justice and mercy, isn't it, all this talk? Am I right? Ah, I thought so. Well, young man, justice, in Prior William's terms, is that all the fishing of the whole stretch of the river that runs through his lands, four miles of it, nigh on, is his. He can turn off any of the villagers who seek a little fishing there, and fine any poachers. Mercy means that a man of the cloth like him should look kindly on the rights the villagers have enjoyed for years, and let them have a little pleasure and a few fish dinners at his expense. Now then: which is a man of God? Just or merciful? Prior William's notion is to have justice win the day, so he can lean on the Bishop to back him up when he petitions the sheriff to enforce his fishing prohibition. Eh? Are you still there?'

'I'm here, but ... stone the crows! The greedy old ... ! Is it true what you say? *Fishing*!'

'Aye well, you monks eat a lot of fish.' The farmer chuckled appreciatively at Tom's indignant snort.

'Any road, that's the story. Eh up, here comes my vegetable broth and your dry bread. Mother of God, you must have almost a quarter pound there. Is it a feast day?'

Father Peregrine also finished the conference light-headed with hunger, surviving the nightmarish meals where, for the glory of God, he humbled himself to be tied in a towel like a child. He also finished triumphant in debate, having established beyond all doubt in the minds of his hearers what they should have known anyway, that it is mercy which is the power of God.

So Prior William, having spent hand over fist on hospitality to prove the opposite point, lost his case, had his suit rejected by the Bishop, and lost his fishing rights too. He did not come out to bid Father Peregrine farewell on the morning they left, Tom having been released from imprisonment, eaten heartily and shaved his abbot with loving care.

But as they rode out, Abbé Guillaume hailed them from across the court where his own party were making ready. He came running breathlessly.

'Adieu, mon frère,' he said, taking Peregrine's hand tenderly. 'It is an honour to have engagé in debate with you once more.'

Peregrine bent down in his saddle and gave the abbé the kiss of brotherhood. He stood, still clinging to Father Peregrine's hand, his chins quivering with emotion.

'*Qui se humiliaverit, exaltabitur, non?* The man who humbles himself is exalted. God will not forget. Moi non plus. Adieu.' And he kissed the twisted hand. Standing back from them he waved in salute.

'Adieu, Frère Thomas! Would I were loved by our young brothers as well as your abbé is loved by you! Adieu, Père Chad! Au revoir!'

They rode home with almost the same urgency of their outward journey, thundering across the moorland turf of the last few miles, Peregrine longing for the haven of his own community. When they arrived, they were greeted by the porter opening the gate with the news that there were distinguished guests staying in the guest house, Sir Geoffrey and Lady Agnes d'Ebassier. Father Peregrine shook his head. 'Father Chad, you and Brother Ambrose must be their hosts tonight. I'm not eating with *anyone*—I'm too hungry.'

Mother pushed the wood together on the fire. A little flame sprang up out of its dying glow. Sitting on the stone in the firelight, wrapped in a shawl, the folds of her blue skirt falling around her feet and her unruly hair tumbling down her back, she looked as though she didn't belong in this century any more than Peregrine did.

'That was a horrible, horrible man,' I said. '*Nobody* could behave like that.'

'Don't you think so?' She was still not satisfied with her fire, and rearranged it until it was burning well again. 'That's better.'

'Well, I've never met anyone like it.'

Mother sat crouched on her stone, her chin in her hand, watching the fire. The flames illuminated her face. Around us, dusk was deepening into night. 'Cruelty,' she said, turning her head to look at me, 'is part of human nature. An acorn is like an oak. The small, acceptable cruelties you and I might get away with are not much different from Prior William's spite.'

'How depressing,' I said gloomily. 'I don't want to be like him.'

'Well, that's all right. When you have no mercy to give, you can always ask for more. For all our cruelty and heartlessness there is a prayer, "Lord Jesus, have mercy on me, a sinner." His mercy takes root in us. Grows like a weed if you give him the chance. Where's your father? Not still putting Cecily to bed?'

'No, here he comes. Oh good, he's got a bottle of wine! And Therese has some crisps.'

Mother smiled and stretched out her feet to the fire's warmth. 'Songs and stories and wine by a campfire ... people who stay in hotels don't know what they're missing.'

'Mother,' I said, as I reached my hand out for the plastic beaker of wine Daddy offered me, '—thank you, Daddy—what was that you said about Brother Tom and a young lady?'

'I said he got into trouble in his novitiate year, after he'd taken his first vows.'

'Will you tell me that story?'

'Some day. Not tonight. Remind me another evening.'

I did remind her, every evening we were at camp, but the little ones stayed up later and later, playing in the stream and singing songs round the fire, so there were no more stories until the holiday was over and we were home again.

III
KEEPING FAITH

Therese had finally been enlisted to help with the Sunday School. Mrs Crabtree had been trying for a long time to persuade her, and in the end she had given in.

She sat in our kitchen on Saturday morning with her feet up on a stool, the table strewn with papers, preparing a lesson for the seven- to ten-year-olds on the theme of friendship. When I came in to make myself a cup of coffee she was talking about it to Mother, who was sitting in the easy chair topping and tailing gooseberries for dinner.

'And what did they say?' Mother was asking as I came in.

'Lilian says a friend is someone who is always there when you need them. Daddy says a friend is someone you can trust. Susanne says a friend is someone who likes you. I've got down here, "A friend is someone you like being with." I can't remember who said that. Jo Couchman says a friend is someone who always understands. Beth says a friend is somebody you know. Mary says a friend is someone you play with.'

'Did you ask Melissa?'

'No, not yet. I'm asking everybody for my Sunday

School thing, 'Lissa, what they think a friend is. What do you say?'

'A friend is ... crumbs, let me think. Someone who sticks by you, I think. Someone who won't let you down.'

'That's good; thanks. Make me a cup of coffee, too, will you? Oh, Mother, you haven't said. What do you think a friend is?'

Mother frowned thoughtfully and carried on nipping the little stalks off her gooseberries without replying. She said eventually, 'Well ... I've had friends who've disappointed me. Sometimes, even the ones who loved me have let me down, and not understood, and betrayed my trust. That's only human nature, isn't it? I daresay I've done as much to them. No, I would say ... I learned it from a story great-grandmother Melissa told me ... I would say that because we all have our failings and weaknesses, because each of us is only human, a friend—a good friend—is someone who helps you to persevere.'

'What?' said Therese.

'A friend is someone who helps you to persevere. When the going gets tough and you're on the point of jacking it all in; by the time you reach my age, Therese, you will be able to look back at lots of times when you nearly gave up and walked away from a difficult situation; and the people you will remember with thanks and love are the ones who helped you, in those moments, to persevere.'

'Okay, okay, I've got it; don't preach a sermon at me, Mother,' said Therese. 'A friend is someone who helps you to persevere. I bet they won't even know what "persevere" means.'

'Well if they don't,' said Mother drily, 'it's time they learned. It'll come in handy.' She finished her gooseberries and took them to the sink to wash.

'What was the story, then, Mother? Here's your coffee, Therese.'

Mother looked over her shoulder at me and smiled.

'Come for a walk after dinner, up on to the hill, and I'll tell you the story. There's not time now, and anyway I've got to make this pudding which needs thinking about because I've never made it before.'

It was a warm, lazy day and Cecily fell asleep after dinner. Somebody needed to stay at home and mind her, and Daddy wanted to read the paper, so he was very glad of the excuse she gave him to stay at home. Mary and Beth went along the road to play in a neighbour's sandpit, and Therese was still struggling with her Sunday School lesson for the following day.

'Looks like just you and me then, Melissa,' Mother said after the dinner things had been washed up. 'Do you still want to go?'

'Course I do! I've been waiting for that story since before dinner!'

We took the dog and set off up the hill to where our road forked. Leaving the houses behind, we took the left-hand fork and followed the narrow unmade track to the heath at the top. It was a clear, warm day, and the breeze smelled of the sea. After five minutes' walking the sound of traffic was no more than a hum in the distance.

We were in a place of seagulls and gorse, rabbits and sea-pinks among the rocks and wiry grass.

We walked in silence up the hill; it was steep enough that you needed your breath for climbing and had none to spare for talking. Our dog ran ahead of us, his tail curled over his back, a flag of happiness. He trotted in zig-zags, his nose snuffing the track of rabbits along the ground.

As we breasted the rise of the hill, Mother paused to get her breath back and look out over the sea. The other side of the hill fell away sharply from the plateau of gorse and turf on the top; a cliff face that dropped down to the sea shore. From where we stood, we could see for miles. On the one side the pebbly beach lay below, where

the fishing boats were drawn up and their nets spread to
dry near the wooden shacks where the fishermen sold
their catch. On the other side spread the patchwork of
allotments, and the parish church, and the winding
terraces of houses that clung to the hillside.

'Let's sit down here for a while,' Mother puffed. 'I'm
still too full of dinner and it's too hot to walk far.'

We sat down on the grass near the gorse bushes at the
cliff edge. Mother reclined on her elbow, shaking back
her mane of hair. I noticed for the first time that it had
strands of grey in it here and there.

'The story,' I prompted.

'Oh, just a minute, let me get my breath back!'

We sat there for a while, listening to the long pull of
the surf, and the cry of the gulls overhead, watching the
bees visiting the gorse flowers, industrious and content.

Then she began her story.

Brother Francis finished off the little red dragon he had
painted at the foot of the page. He had intended it to
glower at the reader with an intimidating scowl from the
margin of Psalm 102, 'For my days are consumed away
like smoke and my bones are burnt up as it were with a
firebrand. . . .' Francis looked doubtfully at his dragon, a
perky little beast with an endearingly quizzical expression on its face. He didn't understand why Brother
Theodore's illuminations reflected the passion and loveliness of the sacred text, but his own always managed to
introduce a note of unseemly comedy. The problem was
not restricted to the art of manuscript illumination
either. Since first he had entered the community,
Brother Francis' irrepressible cheerfulness had caused
consternation to Father Matthew, the master of novices,
who took his responsibility of watching over their souls
with a seriousness bordering on obsession.

'I must answer for them before God,' he said earnestly
to Father Peregrine. 'I must account for them on the

judgement day. And how I shall account for Brother Theodore and Brother Thomas and Brother Francis, I do not know. I have rebuked them, exhorted them— "Brethren be sober, be vigilant, because your adversary the devil goeth about as a roaring lion, seeking whom he may devour!" And Brother Francis says to me, "Yes, Father Matthew," as if butter wouldn't melt in his mouth, but there is a twinkle in his eye and I can't get rid of it.'

Father Peregrine hoped desperately that there was no such damning twinkle in his own eye, and did his best to adopt a suitably grave expression, but he couldn't be sure. The thing that was worrying Father Matthew above all else about Brother Francis was the way he walked.

'Have you seen him, Father?' he demanded of Peregrine, shaking his head in bewildered sorrow. 'He crosses the cloister with a step that is as merry and light as a Franciscan friar! It's not dignified, it's not edifying, it's not right.'

'He has a naturally sunny temperament, that's all,' Father Peregrine consoled his novice master, 'and I'm glad he's happy here.'

'But he shouldn't be so happy, that's just it. He should be reflecting on his sins and the awesome judgement of God. He came here to live a life of penance and prayer, not to enjoy himself.'

'And does he not pray?'

'Yes indeed, I have no complaints of his diligence in prayer or in work. On the contrary; but the more he prays, the worse he gets.'

Peregrine bent his head in an attempt to disguise the smile that tugged at the corners of his mouth.

'I think, Father Matthew, you worry yourself unnecessarily,' he said finally. 'Your conscientious vigilance will save him from much levity, and much mirth, I am sure.'

Father Matthew looked at his abbot with a glimmer

of hope in his troubled eyes, 'Do you really think it might?'

'I am sure of it,' Peregrine replied solemnly, but there was something in his manner that caused a faintly suspicious look to cross the novice master's face. 'You don't think I am too hard on the novices, Father?'

'Well—now and again, maybe,' said Peregrine gently.

'But their souls, their young souls that are constantly tempted to sin!' Father Matthew leaned forward in his chair, his eyes glowing like coals.

'Yes ... yes, I know. It's not easy.' Peregrine nodded sympathetically. 'They—we all—respect your devotion to God and to your duty, Father. But don't lose too much sleep over Brother Francis. I think his vocation is secure enough.'

Francis, who had no wish to cause offence to anyone, did his best to comply with Father Matthew's attempts to mould and discipline his character, and struggled to adopt an air of appropriately sober monastic recollection. The effect was more that of adding an easy urbanity to the original impish good humour; a sort of charming serenity which Father Matthew could never be sure was an improvement or the reverse.

Brother Clement, an artist and a scholar, in whose charge were the library and the scriptorium, had no fears for Francis' soul, but was frustrated by his manuscript illumination. He looked in vexation at Francis' alert and interested little dragon.

'Brother, the text you have copied well enough—your hand is not excellent, but it will do, it is passable. But this! Have you read the thing you are illuminating? Your purpose is to *illuminate*, not to obscure, the text. Here, where the psalmist says, "*Percussus sum ut foenum, et arnuit cor melim; quia oblitus sum comedere panum meum.*" Do you not know what that means? "My heart is smitten down and withered like grass so that I forget to *eat.*" He goes on, "I lie awake and moan." The man is in pain, Brother Francis, not in fairyland.'

Francis looked chastened. 'I know,' he admitted. 'I didn't mean it to look like that. It was supposed to look threatening. I could do its eyebrows a bit blacker after the midday meal, perhaps.'

But the dragon was spared his cosmetic surgery, because after the midday meal Brother Dominic, the guestmaster, waylaid Brother Clement. 'Brother, I wonder if you could spare me a pair of hands from the scriptorium for the guest house? We're almost rushed off our feet there, what with Brother Stephen laid up sick and a great party of folk that's just arrived today.'

Brother Clement's eyes brightened. 'I'll send you Brother Francis directly,' he replied.

That evening, the visitors from the guest house dined with Father Peregrine, as was customary. There were one or two travelling south to Canterbury on pilgrimage, and a family who were passing through and had asked hospitality and help because one of their horses had gone badly lame. There were two little children in the family, who had been left tucked up asleep in the guest house, but the mother and father and their two older children supped with the abbot. Their eldest was a girl of sixteen, Linnet, a vivacious, pretty girl with dark brown eyes and rosy cheeks. She had glossy black hair which was coiled demurely in a net, but wisps of it escaped to curl on her neck and brow. Her brother, four years her junior, excited and proud to be included in adult company, sat beside her, and they chatted happily to Brother Edward who was seated opposite them.

'You're all settled in, then, and comfortable, over the way?' he asked them kindly. 'The brothers are looking after you, I hope?'

'Oh yes!' Linnet smiled at Brother Edward, causing two delightful dimples to appear in her rosy cheeks. 'Oh yes. Brother Francis has been looking after us. He's made us very welcome. I like him, he makes me laugh; he's got a lovely smile—like sunlight dancing on the water.'

Turning her head to speak to her brother, she did not see the look Brother Edward exchanged with Father Peregrine.

As Compline ended that evening, and the brothers in silence filed out of the chapel, the abbot stretched out a hand to detain his novice master.

'A word with you, Father Matthew. Have you sent Brother Francis to work in the guest house?'

Father Matthew looked surprised. 'No, Father, but Brother Clement may have done so. They are very short there just now with Brother Stephen sick. No, I never send any novices to work among the guests, as you know. Such worldly contacts do them no good.'

'Is there anyone else who could go in his stead? One of the older brothers?'

'Well ...' Father Matthew looked thoughtful. 'There's Brother Denis. He's usually helping Brother Mark with the bees just now, but maybe ...'

'The bees?' the abbot interrupted him. 'That would do admirably. Brother Denis can go and help out in the guest house, and Brother Francis can help Brother Mark with his bees.'

Father Matthew looked doubtful. 'Brother Mark is very particular about his bees, Father. He won't let any of the novices but Brother Cormac near them normally. He says the others don't know how to talk to them. Brother Cormac can handle them bare-handed and without veiling his face. They like him, but the others get stung.'

'Send Brother Francis to help with the bees,' said the abbot firmly. 'It would be no bad thing to have his glory veiled for a few days. If Brother Mark has any objections he can bring them to me.'

So after their studies in the novitiate the next morning, Brother Francis walked along as far as the vegetable garden with Brother Tom. Tom worked in the vegetable patch, which lay between the abbey buildings and the orchard. The orchard was the bees' kingdom.

'The bees?' said Tom in surprise. 'Brother Mark won't want you near his bees.'

'No, I know,' Francis replied. 'I don't understand it either. It was only yesterday they sent me down to the guest house, and I was enjoying that. I here's a beautiful girl staying there. She took quite a shine to me, too.'

There was a silence. 'What's her name?' asked Brother Tom casually.

'Linnet. She—oh, *no*, Tom. No! Put it out of your mind. There now, go and recite the psalms at the cabbages and forget I said it.'

Tom grinned at him. 'Try your charms on the bees, then. Brother Cormac said to tell you they like the 23rd Psalm and Gaelic love-songs.' He went in to the great sun-trap where the vegetables grew, protected from the wind on three sides by stone walls, and on the fourth by the lavender hedge which grew alongside the path to the infirmary. 'Linnet,' he murmured to himself, 'that's a pretty name. Heigh-ho. Those were the days.'

'Ah Brother, there you are.' Brother Paulinus came hobbling up the path, elderly and arthritic, a small, tough, sinewy man, whose brown eyes were bright in his weathered face. A gnome. No, a robin, thought Tom.

'Brother, we've a party of guests in the guest house, and that means horses! Would you take the handcart down to the stables and see what they've got for us, please? I want some muck for my vegetables before Brother Fidelis has it all for his roses. Bring it down this way when you return and I'll show you where to make the new heap. There's a good lad.'

Five minutes later, Brother Tom stood in the stable doorway entranced by the sight of the loveliest girl he'd ever seen crooning a song to her lame horse, stroking its ears, playing with its mane.

'By all that's holy,' he breathed, 'I never thought I'd wish I was a horse.'

'Oh! Brother, you made me jump!' Linnet looked at him. 'What did you say?'

Tom shook his head and smiled at her. 'Saying my prayers,' he said. There was a pause and Linnet shyly dropped her gaze.

'My horse is lame,' she said. 'She caught her foot in a rabbit hole on the moor. It hurts her, I think.'

'Let me have a look,' said Tom. 'I used to care for the horses on the farm where I was brought up. Oh, yes, they've poulticed it and bound it right. Not too bad a sprain, I should think, but it's swollen and I expect it . . .' he looked up at her, '. . . aches.'

He released the horse's leg. 'Have you come from far?'

'We were returning to Chester. We've been visiting with my auntie. It's a shame Blanchefleur went lame, but I'm glad we came here. Everyone's been so kind and friendly. Mother says I'll have to ride pillion with Father and leave Blanchefleur here if she's not fit to ride in a day or two. Uncle would come for her, and keep her till he comes down our way. What do you think?'

'Two days?' said Tom. 'Two days? I should ask your mother to make it three. We might well have got somewhere by then. Two days seems a very short time.'

He looked at her over the mare's back, his fingers absently fondling the coarse hair of her mane, when Linnet's hand caressing the beast's neck touched his hand. The contact went through Tom's whole body like an electric shock. They both withdrew their hands. Linnet blushed, and Tom stepped backwards.

'I should go,' he said. 'I should go. I ought to be doing my work.'

'Where do you work?' Linnet enquired with a smile,

dimpling her cheeks enchantingly, looking up at him through the sweep of black lashes that fringed her dewy-bright eyes.

Tom stared at her. 'I work ...' he said slowly, 'in the vegetable garden.' Inside his heart was saying, Yes, oh yes, come and find me. I cannot come to you, come and find me. Forgive me, God, I haven't promised for life. Not yet. No, but I've taken my first vows. I shouldn't be doing this. Forgive me, my God. Oh, but you're beautiful.

'Brother Thomas!' Brother Paulinus' voice was calling from the stable-yard. 'Brother Thomas! Have you not got that muck loaded yet?'

'Coming!' Tom called over his shoulder. He looked back at Linnet. He tried to smile, but couldn't. 'Goodbye,' he whispered. 'Three days. If you can. For the mare.'

'Goodbye, Brother Thomas,' she smiled.

And he was gone.

Two weeks later, Father Matthew came in great agitation to the abbot's house.

'Father, Brother Thomas has gone.'

'Gone? Where?'

'Left us. He was not at Matins, nor Lauds, nor first Mass. His bed was not slept in. He has gone. Nobody knows where he is.'

'Where is Brother Francis?'

'Brother Francis? In the scriptorium, I think. Brother Mark wouldn't keep him with the bees once he could have Brother Denis back.'

'Send him to me.'

'Father, I've asked all the novices; none of them have any idea—'

'Send him to me.'

When Francis stood before him, Father Peregrine asked him bluntly. 'What's happened?'

'Father, I can't be sure,' said Francis cautiously, but the fierce hawk's gaze gripped him.

'Don't give me that. You know him like your own self, Brother,' said Peregrine. 'What's happened?'

'Well, he said nothing to me, but ... the guests who were here last week, with the lame horse ... the young lady. I think he ... well, he fell in love with her.'

In the silence that followed, Francis shifted uneasily.

'And how did he come to meet the young lady?' Peregrine asked him quietly.

'He met her in the stable, with the horse. Brother Paulinus sent him to the stable.' There was another moment's silence.

'So why is that troubling you?' asked Peregrine.

Francis flushed. 'I ... I also told him about her. I told him her name. It was indiscreet of me, and foolish. I may already have sowed the seed in his mind. I never thought—I'm sorry.'

The abbot nodded. 'There are reasons for silence. Hardly ever has a man regretted his silence, but there are thousands who have regretted their words. Still, it can't be helped. He said nothing to you, then, about going?'

'Nothing, Father. I don't think he meant to go. I think he just couldn't bear it.'

Peregrine sighed. 'So be it. Thank you.'

Later in the week, Brother Tom's mother came up to the abbey from the nearby farm where his family lived, to return his black tunic, the habit of the order. He had called in to his family to beg some clothes and food, and to borrow some money and a horse. He would tell them nothing, but asked them to return his tunic to the abbey. She was sorry.

The summer slipped away, and Tom did not return. Autumn came and went, its fogs and chills deepening into the harder cold of winter. November ... December ... and Tom had been gone four months. The brethren for the most part had ceased to wonder about him.

December 10th, and a bitter cold night; the ringing of the night bell to wake the brothers for the midnight Office shattered the frozen, starry skies like splinters of ice.

Abbot Peregrine's eyes opened, and he lay for a moment in the warmth of his bed, gathering the courage to brave the frosty night. He lay there a moment too long, and his eyes began to drowse shut, his body longing with a deep, sensual craving to slide blissfully back into the depths of sleep. Sleep. . . .

He was pulled back to wakefulness by his personal attendant, bending over him, shaking his shoulder. Peregrine levered himself up on his elbow, and swung his legs out of bed. He fumbled to put his habit on, and after a moment said in exasperation, 'I'm sorry, Brother, I need your help. My hands are as much use to me as lumps of wood in this cold.'

The young brother helped him to put on his tunic and cowl over his under-shirt, buckled his belt for him, then knelt to fasten on his feet the night-boots of soft leather.

Stiffly, Peregrine smiled his thanks, and he reached down for the wooden crutch which lay at the side of the bed. Together they went out into the cloister and along to the huge abbey church, floodlit by the silent white moon in the frozen sky.

Father Chad joined Father Peregrine at the door of the choir, and they waited there in silence while the brothers shuffled past in file, led by Brother Stephen carrying the lantern. The last brother passed in before them and Brother Basil ceased tolling the bell. Then Father Chad and Father Peregrine followed into the choir and took their places. Abbot Peregrine gave the knock with his ring on the wood of his stall, and the community rose and began the triple-prayer and the psalms. The day had begun.

The brothers appointed to read stumbled over the words, their lips stiff with cold as well as sleepiness.

Brother Theodore, giving the candle into Brother Cormac's hand as he came up to the lectern to read the fourth lesson, dripped hot tallow onto his thumb, and Brother Cormac swore, softly but audibly, causing Father Matthew to glance at him furiously. Brother Cormac was too sleepy to see or care. Father Peregrine watched his face as he returned to his stall from the lectern. It was wooden with weariness and cold, and the piercing blue eyes were dull with sleep. Brother Stephen, walking the rounds of the brothers with the lantern, stopped by Brother Thaddeus, who had dozed off to sleep, held the lantern in front of his eyes and shook him awake. Thaddeus took the lantern from him, as the custom was, and took his turn to carry it, treading slowly round the choir, watching that the brothers kept awake.

It was not easy, Peregrine reflected, that first year of monastic life. The young men came to the point of despair and defeat, not once, but many times, as they learned the endurance and humility that was required of them even when every nerve was at screaming pitch, suffering from cold and hunger and tiredness, from strict discipline and the rigours of penance and prayer. Not easy to turn their backs on despair and renew determination again and again, learning to continue in patience and peace, to offer all the trials up as a prayer. It never surprised him when a young man gave up on the life, came to the end of his stamina. But Brother Thomas ... Brother Thomas had had a vocation, the abbot was sure of that. He wondered what had become of him.

Matins ended, and the brothers had ten minutes to stretch their legs in the cloister if they wished, while the bell tolled for Lauds. The abbot crossed the choir to where Brother Andrew remained in his stall, telling his beads as he waited for the Office to begin.

Peregrine bent down to speak quietly in his ear. 'Brother, will you serve the brethren a bowl of hot gruel each with their bread, when they break their fast? It is so bitter cold. Some of these men look in need of a little comfort. You may be excused from Prime to prepare it.'

'Aye, Father, it'll be no trouble,' the old Scotsman replied, and the abbot returned to his stall as the brothers came back in silence to their places, the cowled figures slipping like shadows among shadows in the dim and uncertain light of the candles and the lantern.

When Lauds was over, the community went back to bed for the few hours left until daybreak and the Office of Prime.

'It's insane,' grumbled Brother Cormac to Brother Francis, breaking the rule of silence as they crossed the cloister to wash themselves and comb their hair after Prime. 'It's barbaric. Is heaven offended if a man has a good night's sleep before he prays? There's not an inch of my flesh but groans in protest when that infernal bell breaks in on my sleep. It's no help to go creeping back after Lauds and shiver till morning either. It ...'

'Brother Cormac,' Father Matthew's whisper reproved him, 'you have no leave for conversation.'

Cormac knelt before his novice master, saying more irritably than penitently, 'I humbly confess my fault of talking when I should be in silence, and I ask forgiveness, Father, of God and of you.'

He rose to his feet as Father Matthew blessed him. The novice master continued on his way across the cloister.

'The whole place should be towed out to sea and sunk,' muttered Brother Cormac in Brother Francis' ear. 'The only one of us who had any wits was Brother Thomas.'

Francis smiled at him and nodded; there was nothing to do with Cormac but humour him first thing on a winter's morning. Francis wondered about Tom. He missed him. He was never mentioned. They never mentioned anyone who left; but Francis had never ceased to pray for him.

Father Peregrine also had continued to pray for Brother Tom. His thoughts were on him that evening as he sat in his house after Vespers, peering over his work in the candlelight, huddled in his cloak. The room was barely warmed by the meagre fire that glowed in the hearth.

He looked up and called out '*Benedicite!*' in response to the hesitant knock at his door; and Tom came in, and stood before him. His body was tense and his face grey with cold and weariness. There was a shadow in his eyes that was new.

The abbot looked at him, and observed the pinched look that came from cold and tiredness. He also read and understood the shadow in Tom's eyes. Disillusionment. Heartache. Sorrow. He'd seen it often enough in this room.

He met Tom's gaze steadily, and in the quietness between them a little of the tension eased out of the young man.

Tom bit his lip. He stepped forward, and his hands gripped the edge of the great oak table. 'Can I come home?' he asked huskily, into the silence.

'Sit down,' said Peregrine, 'and tell me about it. I've waited for you long enough.'

Outside, the first drifting feathers of snow began to fall. Tom sat down wearily on the stool by the abbot's table. He had a long ride behind him, and a fair walk up from his parents' farm, whence he had come on foot after he had returned their horse.

'I've broken my vows,' he said sadly.

'Did you find your Linnet?'

Tom nodded. 'Linnet, little bird; yes I found her. It was a long ride and then a long search, but I found her.' He sat with his head bowed, utterly dejected, until the room seemed to fill with his hopelessness.

'Would she not have you?' Peregrine asked him gently, at last.

'Oh, yes. Yes. She . . . I think she loved me. Her family made me welcome. I was with them for two months. Yes, she would have had me.' His words came slowly, and so quietly, Peregrine had to strain to hear him.

'It was like a dream. It was a dream. Linnet, little bird. Such brightness . . . such sweetness. And she would have had me.'

'Then . . .?' Father Peregrine was puzzled. Tom raised his head and looked at him out of his despair.

'I *promised*,' he said. 'The brethren and the Lord Jesus, and you. I had made my first vows. Father, I am a monk. How could I stand before God and vow myself Linnet's man, when I am already vowed to holy poverty, holy obedience . . . holy chastity? I mustn't . . . mustn't break my promise.'

'Did you tell Linnet this?'

Tom nodded miserably.

'And you really want to come back to us? Is it that you feel constrained by your vows or is it a thing of your heart?'

'Father, this is my home. This is my life. There is nowhere else for me. This is where my peace is. Will you have me back?'

Peregrine considered the young man before him. 'It is a grave thing you have done,' he said at length. 'The brethren will need some convincing. For myself. . . .' His grey eyes searched Tom's. 'God knows, we all stumble, we all fall. One thing I must ask, take it not amiss. Linnet: you are sure you have not left her with child?'

Tom shook his head. 'No. I did not—we did not—no. She could not be with child.'

Father Peregrine weighed it in his mind one more moment, then stooped down and gathered up his wooden crutch. 'Come to the kitchen, then,' he said as he pushed back his chair and stood up. 'You look hungry and bone-weary. Eat well, and sleep here in my house tonight. Tomorrow you must begin again, asking to be admitted

here. I cannot promise the brothers will have you back,
but I will do what I can. If they will receive you, it hardly
needs me to tell you there would be room for no more
such mistakes. Come now, eat heartily and sleep well.
We will see what tomorrow brings.'

The ritual of begging admittance to the abbey was
almost, but not quite, a formality. The aspirant had to
stand outside the great gates of the abbey and beat on
them with his fist. The man in question would, of
course, have been to see the abbot long ago, and be
expected in the community. The form was that the
abbot and his prior would open the gate to him, and ask
him, 'What do you ask of us?' The man at the gate
would then ask, according to the custom of the abbey, 'I
beg you for the love of God to admit me to this house,
that I may do penance, amend my life and serve God
faithfully until death,' and the abbot would welcome
him in. There were occasions though—and this was one
of them—when the community had reason to be unsure
of the man begging admittance at the gate. They then
tested the sincerity of his intentions by the simple but
surprisingly effective method of keeping him waiting.

The morning after his arrival back at the abbey, Tom
was still sleeping off the exhaustion that followed weeks
of troubled nights and conflicting emotions, while Father
Peregrine was addressing the community Chapter
meeting.

'Brother Thomas has returned to us,' he said, and
took note of the guarded expressions, the slightly pursed
lips of some men, the surprise and interest of others.

'I cannot, under the circumstances, take it upon
myself to admit him here again without the goodwill of
the community. I have talked with him, and I will vouch
for him that he comes with a pure intention, burdened
with no mortal sin. He is wiser by his experience, and
truly sorry for his conduct. In my judgement, his return

to us is the return of a man submitting to a true call of God. Brothers, I beseech you; be merciful. Think· on your own weakness, and be not over-hasty to condemn. You have today and tomorrow and the next day to pray and consider. The day after that I will take counsel of you and we will come to a decision. I ask only this: that you seek God's wisdom and you search your own heart; but let no man presume to discuss the matter with his brother except at the Chapter meeting today or tomorrow morning. Has any of you a question to ask?'

'I have.' Old Brother Prudentius rose to his feet. 'It is true, is it not, that Brother Thomas left because of a woman?' A slight murmur rippled through the community. Peregrine, sitting imperturbably in the great abbatial chair, listened to it. Embarrassment, he detected, and disapproval. He inclined his head slightly in assent, but said nothing.

'Four months is a long time,' continued Brother Prudentius. 'Why has he come back? Has she jilted him? Is he weary of her? Why the change of heart after so long?'

'It is a long time, Brother, I agree. No, she did not abandon him, nor did he weary of her. He came back because of his promises to Almighty God. He would not make a marriage vow, having once vowed himself to serve God as a monk, in his first vows here.'

'But Father, surely he has broken his vows?'

Father Peregrine took a deep breath and let it go in a sigh. He looked down for a moment, then lifted his gaze to meet Brother Prudentius' eyes.

'And which of us has never done so? Is there a man here among us who can boast perfect poverty, perfect chastity, perfect obedience? God have mercy on me, I make no such claim. But I have promised and therefore persevere. His was the weakness of youth and vitality. Our weakness as his pastors was that of negligence. We failed him no less than he failed us. He offers us the grace of trying again. Most good shepherds seek their lost sheep. We are lucky. Ours has returned of its own accord.'

And I couldn't really push them harder than that, Peregrine reflected as he returned to his house after Chapter, to find Brother Tom, having woken, washed, dressed and found himself some breakfast, awaiting further instruction.

'Have you eaten well?' asked Peregrine. 'Are you sure now? Then borrow my cloak, for you'll need it. You must go out of the gates and seek admittance again. Be of good courage.'

Tom walked out of the abbey, through the little postern door set in the great gate and heard it click shut behind him. He stood on the road, looking up at the turbulent sky, banked with cloud of deepening tones of grey. The wind was sharp as a knife and he wrapped Peregrine's cloak around him, glad of its protection. The snow that had fallen in the night was mostly melting, but the puddles that lay in the wheel-ruts and pot-holes of the road were frozen over.

Tom thought of Linnet, the last sight he had of her, standing very still, silent tears rolling down her cheeks, her eyes drinking in everything about him and storing it away in her heart. The dreariness and hostility of the weather suited his mood as he turned again to face the great door, asking himself, 'Am I really going to do this?' Then he raised his hand, clenched hard into a fist, and beat on the abbey gate. There was no response. He raised his fist again, and thundered on the massive door. There was still no response. Tom stood, nonplussed, for a moment, then remembered Father Peregrine's words, 'Have you eaten well? Are you sure now? Then borrow my cloak, for you'll need it,' and he understood. They meant to make him wait.

He wandered about a bit, leaned on the wall and gazed out across the valley, looked down the road towards the village, watched the rooks squabbling in the trees at the roadside. He bent down and picked up a little stick that lay on the road, peeled the bark off it, broke it into bits and threw the pieces away, one by one. The wind was stinging his ears, and he covered them with his hands, but that left his cloak flapping free, so he wrapped it about him again. How long does this go on for? he wondered.

He went again and beat on the door, but no one came. Feeling slightly foolish, he turned away and sauntered about. He tried to whistle a tune, but the wind snatched the breath from his lips. 'Mother of God, it's cold,' he muttered, and moved close to the shelter of the abbey wall.

After a while a cart came up the road on business at the abbey. The carter stopped at the gate, glanced at Tom in curiosity, then went through the postern to seek admittance from Brother Cyprian, the porter. The great gate swung open, and the man came out and led his horse through. The cartwheels rumbled across the flags of the yard and the horse's hooves clattered loud on the stone. Brother Cyprian, closing the gate, nodded to Tom standing there, but had neither word nor smile for him. The noise of the gate as it clanged shut leaving Tom outside echoed through his head, his heart, his soul. He thought of his mother and father. They would be at home now, eating a hearty meal before a roaring fire. And Linnet? Baking maybe, or sitting with her mother and little sister at the hearthside, spinning or sewing. He wondered if she thought of him too. In the abbey now, the midday Office and meal would be over, the brethren going quietly about their work. Francis would be blowing a little warmth back into his numb fingers in the scriptorium. He would be through with that Book of Psalms now. Tom wondered how much of the illumination of it Brother Francis had accomplished himself, and how much Brother Clement had rejected in favour of Brother Theodore's superior artistry. He could imagine Brother Clement's face, frowning in irritation as he perused the book, the mediocre lettering, the uneven quality of the illumination divided between Brother Theodore's and Brother Francis' efforts, the parchment grubby with sweat and worn with too much erasing. The months of work would likely be dismissed with dry disfavour—'I doubt if this is one for posterity, Brother.' Fortunately Francis was used to it, and his good humour was equal to it. It would be good to see Francis again. Tom was not a solitary man. He liked company and conversation; he liked to work alongside other men. The loneliness outside the abbey seemed as final and chilling as hell. The leaden despair of it took hold of him and filled him. 'Sing something,' he said to himself. 'What shall I sing? A psalm, anything.'

He began to sing, and the words that came to his lips were the words of the Misere: '*Misere mei Deus, secundum magnam misericordiam tuam. Et secundum multitudinem miserationum tuarum, dele iniquitatem meam.* Have mercy on me, O God, after thy great goodness: according to the multitude of thy mercies, do away mine offences.'

As he sang the mournful chant, sorrow welled up in him, and though the words came of their own accord to his tongue, his mind was not on them. I've broken my vows, disgraced myself, and they may never have me back, he thought. Oh, if they won't have me, what then?

'*Cor mundum crea in me Deus: et spiritum rectum innova in visceribus meis. Ne projicias me a facie tua: et spiritum sanctum tuum ne auferas a me.* Make me a clean heart, O God: and renew a right spirit within me. Cast me not away from your presence and take not your holy spirit from me.'

His throat ached with forlorn misery, and he abandoned the chant.

The heavy catch of the gate was lifted from within with a clang, and Tom turned towards it, hopeful. But it was only the farmer, bringing his horse and cart home.

Tom turned his face away, sick at heart. He would not look at the farmer, though he felt the man's eyes on him. They were not well acquainted, but they knew each other, and Tom had no wish to submit to his questions, or his banter. The abbey gate swung shut and the cart was on its way. The gloomy day began to darken with the shadows of evening, and Tom wondered what time it was. Three o'clock maybe. Half past. The woollen cloak was no longer much protection against the cold. Desperately he beat again on the door, then stood humiliated in the indifferent silence.

It was getting really dark now. Brother Stephen would be bringing the cows in for milking, and soon it would be time for Vespers.

'Faith, I'm hungry,' Tom muttered to himself. 'I could even face Cormac's bread and count it a blessing.'

The bell rang for Vespers. Faintly, intermittently, he heard snatches of the brothers singing the Office in the abbey church in the moments when the wind dropped. It was completely dark now, but there were no stars visible. They were all hidden behind the mass of clouds.

Tom looked up at the great looming bulk of the abbey that towered beside him. I've been here *hours*, he thought. He hesitated a moment, then stepped swiftly to the door and raised his fist, hammering and hammering on the rough, wet wood. The thunder of his knocking echoed in the black silence. There was no response.

The postern door set in the gate opened presently, and one or two of the villagers who worked in the abbey came out, returning home to their families. Tom drew back into the shadow of the wall, unwilling to be discovered by the light of their lantern. He heard Brother Cyprian's cheery 'God give you goodnight!' and was seized by the most abject, engulfing self-pity that he had ever known. He sank down onto his haunches, squatting on his heels, huddled into his cloak in the scant protection from the wind that the abbey wall offered. 'Oh, come *on*,' he groaned aloud. He had never been so cold and hungry and tired in his life. He seemed to have fallen into a pit of icy black timelessness.

The bell rang for Compline, and again he heard distant drifts of chanting. After that, the utter profound stillness of the Great Silence descended on the abbey, and a new thought spread like a dark stain of incredulous horror through Tom's soul. Oh God, they're not going to leave me here all *night*?

It was then that it started to snow.

Tom looked up at the sky, and the snowflakes settled on his eyelashes, melted in his eyebrows, settled softly onto his face, little dreary kisses of cold wetness. He hunched his shoulders, wrapped his arms about himself, shivering, and bent his face down into his body warmth. Crouched thus in the corner of the gateway to glean what pitiful shelter he could, Tom passed the night dozing fitfully. The cold seemed to have seeped through to his bones and hunger gnawed at him mercilessly. He clung to the hope of the morning when the gate would open, 'What do you ask of us?' and the nightmare would be over. He fell asleep towards dawn, but was woken by the sound of voices. Two of the villagers who worked in the kitchens were coming along the road. Tom shrank back against the wall, drawing into the blackness of his cloak, and was thankful to escape the men's notice as they passed through the inset door.

The Office bell began to ring. The snow had ceased for the time being, but the air was still and the sky hung heavy with cloud. The occasional snowflake still drifted down. Tom rose stiffly to his feet and stamped about a bit, clapping his arms against his sides. The pain of the cold in his feet, especially his toes, was acute, and his ears ached in the wind.

After a time he heard the door of the porter's lodge as Brother Cyprian came back from first Mass. The sun rose, its first faint flush of pink swelling to a crescendo of crimson glory in the east. The blush of beauty faded as the day wore on, hour after hour, until the sun was suspended, a white remote ball of light in a leaden sky.

Straggles of the faithful trudged up from the village to the abbey church for ten o'clock Mass after Chapter, and Tom kept out of sight as best he could. He watched them return again down the hill, bundled in shawls, wearing stockings over their clogs so as not to slip on the icy roads. His eyes followed them until they turned the bend in the road and were lost to view, and then he watched the rooks squabbling in their high, precarious nests, listened to their disconsolate cawing. He looked down at the puddles in the pot-holes, white where air was trapped under the ice, and grey where water touched the frozen surface. One or two blades of grass poked through the flatness of the ice. Far away a dog yelped, its cry carrying in the cold, and a blackbird cackled in alarm in the hedgerow at the top of the road. Into the hopeless eternity of the day, the abbey bell tolled for the midday Office. The sun hung overhead, its glory contracted to a wintry sphere of severity.

Through the afternoon, Tom either squatted in the corner of the gateway, leaning against the wall, or else he walked to and fro, beating his arms about his ribs to try and keep warm. Sometimes he whispered the words of the prayers the brothers would be saying in the chapel. He thought back over all that had happened in the last few months, remembered that first casual conversation with Francis, standing in the summer garden—What's her name? Linnet—oh no, Tom, put it out of your mind . . . It seemed a lifetime away. Even his thoughts ran sluggishly, frozen. He felt as though he'd been there for ever. Once or twice he beat with his fist on the door, but less often, and with less conviction.

A few callers came and went. Tom bent his head and would not meet their inquisitive gaze. Then the sun was sinking again in a wide glow of ochre light. Darkness,

and the Vespers bell, and he sank down hopelessly and
sat with his arms tightly round his knees, his head resting on the top of his knees, trying to conserve what ves-
tige of warmth he had. His head ached with hunger and
he was thirsty too. After a while he stretched out his
hand and scooped up some of the snow that had drifted
against the wall, and ate it. He satisfied his thirst with
snow, and felt the coldness penetrate inside him.

The Compline bell rang, and then came the deep
silence of the night. 'No ...' Tom whispered to himself.
'No, not another night. Oh, please, no.'

By the middle of that night, Tom could no longer dis-
tinguish between the ache of the cold, the ache of
hunger and the aching of his cramped body. It snowed
again in the night, a light, persistent snowfall, and he felt
the dampness oozing through the thick woollen cloak.

In the early hours of the morning, he stood up clumsily to stretch his cramped and aching limbs.

I've had enough, he thought dully. I'm going home.
He trudged fifty yards down the road, then stopped.
What if they opened the gate now, after all this waiting,
and found him gone? He turned back, running and
stumbling up the road to the silent black mountain of
the abbey. 'This is my home,' he said aloud.

But what if they never open the door to me? he
thought. He searched his memory, trying to think if he
had ever heard of anyone who had not even been
rejected, but simply ignored, left outside, forgotten. In
the lightening grey of the dawn, he sat down again on
the abbey threshold and resumed his weary, aching vigil.
Just before sunrise, he heard the click of the postern
door, and scrambled to his feet, wild with hope. It was
old Brother Andrew from the kitchen. 'I've permission
to bring you this,' he said. He held in his hands a steaming bowl of soup. Torn between bitter disappointment and abject gratitude, Tom reached out his hands

without a word. He drank the soup greedily, spilling some, his hands and mouth clumsy with cold.

'Thank you,' he said, as he held the empty bowl out to Brother Andrew, 'that was grand. I thought maybe you'd all forgotten me,' he added with an attempt at a smile.

Brother Andrew shook his head. 'No, lad,' he said, 'we've not forgotten you.' Then he took the bowl and went back inside. Tom resisted the temptation to beg him to wait, to come back. Oh God, would it never end? It was like a bad dream.

That day he sat, most of the day, motionless against the wall, no longer bothering to hide from those who came and went, colder than he had ever thought it was possible to be. The wind cut through to his marrow. He felt bone-cold, as cold as stone. He couldn't imagine ever being warm again and he tortured himself, conjuring up memories of the blaze of logs in the warming room fireplace. His head ached in a constant dull throb, and he shivered in his damp clothes.

Evening came, and nightfall and again the snow, and still they left him there. By morning he lay on his side in the snow on the threshold against the abbey gate, shuddering with cold and fever, numb and half-delirious, simply enduring.

Inside the abbey, as the community was gathering for Chapter, the abbot with his prior, Father Chad, and his infirmarian, Brother Edward, went and opened the great gate. Tom looked up at them, and raised himself on his hands, awkwardly, until he knelt, after a fashion, at the abbot's feet. Through the dizzy waves of fever that clouded his head he heard Father Peregrine saying to him, 'What do you ask of us, my son?' and that firm warm voice spoke hearth and home to him, journey's end.

'For ... the ... love ... of ... God ...' Tom's lips felt

like slabs of clay, robbed of all feeling. 'For ... the ...
love of God ... Father ... I can't say ... it. No ... admit
... me. ...' He looked up at Father Peregrine and was
overwhelmed by the blaze of love and compassion that
met him there.

'Help him,' said Peregrine abruptly. 'Father Chad,
Brother Edward, help him to his feet.'

'Father, he's in a bad way. He's burning up with fever
and his clothes are sodden. Should we not take him
straight to the infirmary?'

'No,' said the abbot. 'Bring him to Chapter.'

Father Chad and Brother Edward half-supported,
half-carried Tom to the Chapter House, where the
community was gathered.

The abbot took his seat in the great carved chair and
looked at Tom as he stood, held up by the infirmarian
and the prior.

'Thank you, brothers. Let him stand alone,' he said.

'But, Father ...' protested Father Chad.

'Let him stand alone,' repeated the abbot. 'Father
Chad, Brother Edward, go to your places.'

As they left him, Tom swayed on his feet for a
moment, his teeth chattering and his body shivering
uncontrollably, the room swimming before his eyes.
Then his legs gave way under him and he fell on his
hands and knees to the floor.

'What do you ask of this community, my son?' the
abbot asked him calmly.

'I beg of you ... for the love of God ...' the words
came slow and slurred, 'to forgive me ... and admit me
again ... to this house ... here to do penance ... amend
my ... life ... and serve God ... faithfully ... until
death. ...'

Tom tried to raise his head, but it felt like a lead
weight. He knelt on the floor, his arms, which were
shaking with fever and fatigue, braced to prevent him
from collapsing altogether.

'I think under the circumstances, brothers, it would be unreasonable to ask this man to go and wait outside while the community votes.' The abbot's voice was aloof and dispassionate. He paused, allowing them to listen for a moment to the shuddering, almost sobbing, labour of Tom's breathing.

'I ask of you, brothers, will you have him back? Those in favour, please raise your hands ... and those against ... thank you. My son, we welcome you into this house. May God grant you grace so to amend your life, to do penance and serve him faithfully until death, as you have requested. *Deo gratias.* Brother Edward, Brother John, get him to bed.'

Floating in a light-headed haze of fever, Tom submitted gratefully to the care of Brother Edward and Brother John in the infirmary. They stripped him of his wet clothes and rubbed him dry. They gently chafed the feeling back into his hands and feet as he sat wrapped in a blanket before a glowing fire of sweet-smelling apple logs. They dosed him with infusions of elderflower and peppermint, and gave him warm milk and honey to drink.

'I know you're hungry, lad, but it's no good you trying to eat in this state. Just take this for now, then a good sleep and we'll see.'

They warmed a shirt for him by the fire and dressed him in it, and tucked him into bed like a child, having washed his hands and face and combed his hair. There was a hot brick wrapped in cloths at his feet, and one at his back, and Tom lay in a peaceful daze, contentedly smelling the lavender of the infirmary sheets as he sank into the blissful relief of sleep.

'I think he'll be all right in a day or two,' said Brother Edward quietly to Brother John. 'His chest is clear at the moment. Keep him warm and watch him, and don't let him eat too much too soon. God bless him, he's a brave lad. We'll let him sleep now. That's the best thing for him.'

They went softly from the room and closed the door. Brother John stood with his arms full of Tom's wet clothes, his face troubled.

'That was a heartless way to treat him, Brother. I don't understand it. To have him kneel before us all—poor soul, it was cruel.'

Brother Edward chuckled. 'Come and dump his wet things in a pail before you're soaked yourself—and treat them with respect. That's Father Abbot's good winter cloak you have there, if I'm not mistaken. Heartless, you think? Don't you believe it, Brother. Father Abbot would give his life for that lad. You just wait and see who comes and sits at his bedside as he sweats out his fever through the night. How were you intending to vote when you came to Chapter?'

'I wasn't sure. It was a serious thing he'd done. I don't know even now—but seeing him kneeling there—poor soul, what he'd been through! I'd not the heart to vote against him. It could have killed him, three nights in that bitter weather.'

'Not him, Brother John, he's as strong as an ox. It would take more than an east wind and a fall of snow to snuff that lad out.'

'Aye, maybe, but it was hard-hearted. Father showed him no pity at all.'

Edward shook his head, smiling. 'No, no, that's not the way it is. Brother Thomas has a welcome in this house again and it would have taken nothing less to win it for him. He's a man in a thousand is our abbot, Brother John. He knows what he's about. And he holds this community in the palm of his hand.'

I lay on my front in the grass, absentmindedly pulling apart a daisy, watching the seagulls wheeling over the harbour. There was a fishing boat out at sea on its own.

All the others were drawn up on the shingle at this time of day.

'I like Brother Tom,' I said. 'That was a good story.'

'Yes, it was one of my favourites when I was your age. But I liked Father Peregrine best. It's a skilled job, that,' Mother said thoughtfully, looking out at the solitary fishing boat coming in towards the beach, 'bringing a boat safely into harbour. Especially on stormy nights when the sea is rough.'

She yawned and stretched her arms above her head.

'It's a good story, but a long one. I could sit here all day, but I expect they'll be wondering at home where we are, and wanting their tea. Let's go back.'

'When you began,' I said, linking my arm in Mother's as we started down the lane home, 'I thought it was going to be a story about Brother Francis. It started off about him.'

'Francis? Yes. He and Brother Tom tend to turn up in the same places. Although actually Brother Francis' story is quite different from that, at least, in some ways. He had his struggles too, but they were different from Tom's.'

'Will you tell me Brother Francis' story? Will you tell me it tonight?'

Mother laughed. 'Not tonight, no. I've had enough story-telling for one day, and I've promised Mary I'll read a whole chapter of *The Wind in the Willows* before bed tonight. Tomorrow, maybe.'

'Tomorrow,' I said firmly, 'for sure.'

IV
THE POOR IN SPIRIT

Cecily had put something up her nose. She came running in to Mother from the garden with an air of great importance, to communicate her news.

'There is a stone inside my nose,' she said impressively.

'Oh, no! Let me look. Come here, into the light by the window. Oh heavens, there is too. Just a minute, let me get my tweezers.'

Mother went for the tweezers that she kept hidden away in her box of private things. She would never let the little ones play with them, because she said some pairs of tweezers were better than others, and having in the past wasted her money on tweezers that wouldn't work properly, she didn't want to lose a good pair. She kept them for plucking out the bristly hairs that grew on her chin. In general, Mother was in favour of hair, and refused to shave the hair off her legs or under her arms like Therese and I did. But then she wouldn't go swimming at the sports centre because she was embarrassed to be the only lady with hairy legs and armpits. She didn't mind the beach, because you can get away from people there. So what she thought about it wasn't quite straightforward. As she said herself, you can't always close the gap between what is and what ought to be. Anyway, she drew the line at bristly chins.

She poked about in Cecily's nose with the tweezers, but the stone, though it was low enough to be seen, was too high up and too well-lodged to be freed with the tweezers.

'I daren't push it at all in case it goes even further. Beth, fetch me the pepper. Honestly, Cecily, you really are the end.'

Beth brought the pepper and Mother shook some onto the back of her hand.

'Here, sniff this,' she said, holding it up to Cecily's nose. Cecily obediently sniffed it, and sniffed it some more. Her eyes watered a bit, but nothing else happened.

'Oh dear. Bother it. I'd better phone your daddy. He'd be coming home in half an hour anyway. We shall have to take you to the hospital.'

Mother phoned Daddy at the book-binding place where he worked, and he said he would come home straight away and take them in the car up to the hospital.

'Therese, will you give Mary and Beth their tea if I'm not back in an hour?' said Mother. 'You can heat up the stew from yesterday, and there's an apple pie in the cupboard. Open a tin of evaporated milk. I don't know when we shall be home. You know what it's like waiting in casualty. You could grow old and die before ever you saw a doctor. Come on, Cecily, don't start crying. You'll be all right. Fetch a book to look at and a dolly to play with.'

'Can I come too?' I asked.

'We'll be a long time, Melissa. Are you sure?'

'Yes, I can bring my homework.'

I wanted to see what the doctor would do.

Daddy came home, and we bundled Cecily, who was

whimpering by now, into the car, and set off for the hospital, leaving Mary and Beth waving in the doorway.

The hospital was a large, dingy building constructed of flat expanses of pale blue stuff and plate-glass windows. There were no spaces left in the car park, so Daddy went in search of somewhere to park while Mother and I took Cecily in.

Cecily and I sat on two of the chairs that lined the corridor while Mother gave our details to the receptionist who sat behind a glass panel in the wall.

A wide doorway led out of our corridor into the next corridor. That was also lined with chairs and people sitting on them, waiting. A notice over the doorway said 'X-RAY' with an arrow pointing one way and 'FRACTURES' with an arrow pointing the other way. The walls were painted with buff-coloured gloss paint. Under the plate-glass window that looked out onto the car park stood an old-fashioned radiator, and in front of it a low coffee table stacked with back copies of *Country Life*. Someone had pushed a cardboard box with some rather dirty toys in it half under the table. On the wall opposite me stood a fish tank. There was coloured gravel in the bottom of it, out of which grew two pieces of water weed. I counted the tropical fish swimming among the weed. I could not be sure because they were very small and kept disappearing from view, but I think there were about five.

Mother came and sat down beside us. 'I do hope we won't be here too long,' she said. 'Come and sit on my knee, Cecily. I'll read you your book.'

Cecily shook her head. 'It hurts in my nose,' she said. 'I want the stone out now.'

A doctor (I suppose he was a doctor; he was wearing a white coat with the buttons undone) came walking along our corridor, out into the next corridor where the other people were sitting. He stopped beside a rather prissy-looking lady with a little girl, about five years old. The little girl's arm was encased in a plaster.

The doctor looked down at the little girl. 'Hello,' he said, in a jolly sort of way, 'how are you?' The little girl stared at him, and didn't say anything. The doctor had short, frizzy black hair except for a bald bit on top. He was wearing glasses with gold rims. He kept his hands in his pockets, and he had a clipboard tucked under his left arm. He smiled at the little girl, but she didn't smile back. He took his hand out of his pocket, and took hold of the clipboard and read the papers on the front of it for a minute.

'Well, Mrs er ... Robbins,' he said in a brisk sort of way, looking up from the clipboard at the lady, 'this shouldn't take a moment. We'll just take her dressing off and have a look at her. All right?'

'Thank you, doctor,' murmured the lady, but the silent little girl came to life quite unexpectedly.

'No!' she cried out. 'No! You can't! No!' She sounded quite panicky. The lady with her looked embarrassed and cross. 'Don't be silly, Sarah,' she said sharply.

'Oh, don't you worry,' said the doctor. 'We'll have that dressing off in no time.'

'Stop it, Sarah. Don't be such a naughty girl.' The lady's voice was rising in irritation over the top of the little girl's voice. She was screaming incoherently, 'No! No! No! You can't take my dress off,' and starting to cry.

'Now come on, Sarah. If you'll just bring her along here, Mrs er ... we'll have it off in no time,' said the doctor.

They disappeared down the corridor out of sight, the little girl still crying and protesting, her mother still telling her off.

Why didn't he listen? Why didn't he think? What was the matter with him? I looked at Mother, who was shaking her head in disbelief.

'I'll bet you that child's never heard the word "dressing" before,' she said. 'Her mother will *always* have called it a plaster. Somebody needs to tell these young men that unless you listen and observe, and use your imagination to get below the surface of what you see, you're not fit to be trusted with other people's lives. Silly fool. That was our name they called there, wasn't it? Come on, Cecily. Now you must be brave, and very, very good. If you want that stone out you must do exactly as the doctor says. No crying and no fuss.'

Our doctor was a lady doctor. She had a small office in a cubicle at the edge of the ward. It had a big poster on the wall, covered in colour photographs of all the different kinds of injuries it was possible to do to your eye, and underneath each picture the information about appropriate treatment.

Mother sat down with Cecily on her knee, and I stood in the doorway, because there was no room for another person. Mother explained what Cecily had done and the doctor listened quietly.

'Can I have a look in your nose?' she asked Cecily. Cecily nodded, solemnly. She tipped back her head, with a tragic look on her face. I think she was enjoying it, really. The doctor had a pencil-shaped torch to peer into Cecily's nose.

'Oh yes, I can see it quite easily,' she said. 'Stay like that and I'll see if I can get it out.'

She had a long, fine steel instrument with a circular loop at the end, and she used this as she tried carefully to hook out the stone. All she got was a bit of snot. She sat back thoughtfully.

'Mmm. . .' she said. 'I'll have another go, and if that fails we shall have to try something else.'

But Cecily suddenly drew in her breath and sneezed an enormous sneeze. The little stone shot across the table and ricocheted under the doctor's desk.

'That thing tickled my nose,' she said.

When we got out into the corridor again, Daddy was sitting there, flicking through a copy of *Country Life*.

'Look, I've found the house for us,' he said. His thumb was marking a page with a picture of an old farmhouse. It had a thatched roof, and its sloping lawn ran down to a duck pond. There were big oak trees dotted about here and there in its garden. Mother smiled. 'One day,' she said.

The doctor had given Cecily her stone wrapped up in a tissue, and Cecily showed it to Daddy, and to Mary and Beth and Therese when we got home. They all admired it respectfully.

I told Daddy, in indignation, about the little girl and her plaster. He listened and nodded.

'When you grow up, Melissa, my dove,' he said, 'remember that little girl. You can go to university and train your intellect. You can go to college and learn all sorts of skills. You can be an apprentice and be taught a trade. But, understanding ... you yourself must listen to the wisdom of life itself to learn understanding. They can't teach you that in university, or medical school, or technical college, or anywhere in the world. Now then, I don't know about you, but I fancy a bit of cheese on toast.'

At bedtime, Cecily's stone was put in a jam jar on the mantelpiece, and I carried her up to bed while Mother checked Mary's and Beth's teeth in the bathroom.

Mother read them a story and they played their bedtime game and had their prayers, then she tucked them into bed.

'Mother, you said you'd tell me about Brother Francis,' I said when they were snuggled in.

'Yes, I know. I haven't forgotten. Draw the curtains and light the candle. Dear me, it's been a long day. Ah, that's better. Settle down now, Cecily. Stop wriggling like that.'

Well then, this is Brother Francis' story. What do you
know about him? Not much, I think, except that he was
Brother Tom's friend and made him laugh. The two of
them had grown up together in the same neighbour-
hood, and they both came from farming families, but
Brother Francis' family were richer, and of considerable
social standing. So although they had been acquainted,
it was not until the differences between them were
ironed out by their shared life of simplicity and poverty
in Christ's service that they discovered each other as
friends. Of course, a man in monastic life was supposed
not to have any particular friendships, being given as a
friend to all men for love of Christ, but set apart from
intimate relationships, again for love of Christ. But
understanding flourished more readily between some
men than others, and in that abbey natural affection was
seen as a grace and a gift, provided it did not begin to
develop into the kind of friendship that made other
people feel shut out or unwanted. And Brother Tom
and Brother Francis got on well. Any time you wanted
to know how Brother Tom was, you could ask Brother
Francis and he could tell you at once, because he loved
him and understood him, and also because Brother
Thomas was a straightforward kind of man who shouted
when he was angry, wept when he was sad, and fell
asleep when he was weary—whether that was in bed, or
during the long psalms of the night Office, or in the
middle of Father Matthew's Greek lessons.

Any time you had asked Brother Thomas how Brother
Francis was, though, he would probably have said, 'All
right—I think. He seems cheerful enough.' Because
Francis always did. He was courteous, he studied hard,
he prayed earnestly, he had a smile for everyone, and he
kept his own counsel regarding his private thoughts and
feelings. He was cheerful at all times, and had an
irrepressible sense of humour which, along with a
tendency to get into conversation at the wrong times, got

him into disgrace now and then. Brother Francis made himself pleasant to everyone and was well-liked. If he had a dark side, it was not obvious. If he had troubles, no one knew; and everyone was well content with this state of affairs, except Father Matthew.

'He's like the froth on a wave, that young man,' he would say to Father Peregrine. 'There's something insubstantial about him. All this light-heartedness is pleasant enough, but he seems insincere to me. He's not a minstrel or a court jester, he's a man of prayer and he ought to behave like one. He's too happy. You mark my words, this eternal smile of his covers an emptiness within. He needs sobering up, that lad. We must be more strict with him.'

The abbot considered the matter. Father Matthew, though admittedly not the most sensitive of men in helping the novices in his care through their struggles, did have, one could not deny it, an uncanny ability to spot and expose their weaknesses. If he said Brother Francis was too happy, he probably was too happy. He was certainly getting under Father Matthew's skin.

'I'll talk to him,' Father Peregrine said finally one Wednesday evening when Father Matthew had button-holed him on the way out of Vespers. 'I'll see him after Chapter tomorrow.'

The abbot thought about Francis as he waited for him the next day. It was a fresh, chill day in early spring, when the snowdrops were out and the jasmine growing on the wall was tentatively blossoming, but not the primroses yet. Father Peregrine liked Francis, though he did not believe Brother Francis had ever really taken him into his confidence. 'Insincere ... an emptiness within....' The abbot pondered Father Matthew's words. The judgement seemed a bit unkind and dismissive.

He recognised Brother Francis' firm, quick knock at

the door, which stood ajar. The knock was like the man: confident, but not arrogant.

Father Peregrine pushed back his chair, deciding not to sit behind his great table full of books to talk to this young man. He picked up his crutch from where it lay beside him on the floor, and stood up to cross the room. Again the knock, not growing impatient, rather its assurance diminishing. The abbot hastened to the door. He kept it ajar when he was not in private conversation, partly to be welcoming, and partly because the heavy iron latch on the door was not easy for his broken hands to manipulate.

'Come in, Brother.' He smiled at Francis as he pulled the door open. 'Come and sit down over here. Are you cold? Would you like to light a fire?'

'A fire?' Brother Francis hesitated at the prospect of this unfamiliar luxury.

'Yes? The things are there at the hearth. Your hands are abler than mine; I shall fumble it if I try to light it.'

The abbot settled himself into one of the two low wooden chairs that stood near the fire place, and watched Brother Francis as he set about making the fire. His movements were deft and brisk, economical.

There were some men it was easier to talk to by the fire. There were those who could not easily look into Peregrine's eyes and tell their troubles, but who unwound as they looked into the dancing flames and relaxed in the warmth. Father Peregrine thought it might well be so with Francis.

It was a long time since Brother Francis had had occasion to build a fire. Dry sticks and cones over a twist of dried grass. Some rosemary twigs cut in the summer saved for the sweet-smelling winter kindling, that catches well. Then the little apple logs, gnarled and speckled with blue lichen. An old candle stump on top of the pile to encourage it along.

Father Peregrine watched him. I like him, he thought. His bearing is composed but modest. Yes, there's no swagger to him. Alert, intelligent face and plenty of humour there. Well, he needs that, no doubt. It's not an easy life. The abbot felt a bit like Pilate, looking for a fault and finding none, saying desperately to the Jews, 'But I find nothing wrong in this man.' There was a little nervousness about him maybe, a certain tension around his shoulders and neck, and his fingernails were well bitten. Having got his little fire going, he sat back on the hearthstone and looked up at Father Peregrine. The ready smile that caused Father Matthew such foreboding flashed a bit too quickly maybe, but then ... being required to discuss his vocation with his superior was unlikely to set him at his ease.

'There, you've made a better job of it than I would have. Sit for a while and enjoy the warmth now. I'll not keep you too long. Brother Clement will be missing you in the scriptorium.'

Brother Francis laughed. 'Yes, like a headache, I should think.'

'Does he dislike you? He has never complained of you.'

'It is my illumination work that is his sorest trial. "Will you look at the knowing smirk you've done on the face of Our Lady, Brother Francis," he says to me, and, "What is this monstrous being here? Is't an *angel* with this lewd wink and cunning leer? For shame, Brother, it is a holy thing you've rendered thus like a brutish yokel in a tavern, three parts drunk!"'

Peregrine was laughing in spite of himself at Brother Francis' exact mimicry of Brother Clement's refined dismay. Francis grinned at him.

'No, he bids me stick to flowers now, for flowers have no expressions to disgrace their faces. I doubt if he sighs much over my absence this morning. He must think the good Lord has given him an unexpected holiday.'

Father Peregrine shook his head. 'I must see these works of art for myself one day. I remember him speaking of a thing of the Last Judgement you had painted that went somehow amiss.'

'Oh that, yes. He had me erase it and give it to Brother Theodore to finish in the end. I thought it was coming on quite well. I'd to paint a scowling devil glaring over the souls of the damned, and I was thinking of Brother Cormac first thing in the morning when Father Matthew berates him for his Latin; and it was shaping quite well I thought, black-browed and a kind of ugly look in his eye, but Brother Clement didn't like it at all. "It looks like an Irish pedlar with the belly-ache!" he exclaimed, which made me smile, because I'd got it more true than I intended. "And what is this simpering Christ like a silly lass sighing for her sweetheart? Brother, no more! Your lettering is adequate, but these caricatures give me a pain," he said. Yes, that was my last judgement.'

He laughed and looked into the fire, pushed the little logs together and watched the sparks fly. Peregrine could see that his conversation would not be to Father Matthew's taste. 'Apart from your disasters in the scriptorium, how are you finding the life, my son?' he asked him.

Brother Francis smiled. 'When I'm not too hungry to raise my thoughts above my belly, I get a glimpse of heaven now and then.'

'You don't have enough to eat?'

'Oh, I didn't mean it really, no, no. The food here is good, and it drives us to prayer, you know—"Of your goodness, dear Lord, have Brother Andrew make the bread today and restrict Cormac to the vegetables." Left alone in the pantry I should eat more, I confess it; but no, I have enough. I'm just greedy.'

'Poor Brother Cormac. Is his bread so bad?'

'You haven't noticed? Father, you're a saint! He made

the bread yesterday. Did it not sit in your gut like a stone?'

Father Peregrine forbore answering that question, and changed the subject.

'How are you finding the rule of silence, Brother? Some men find it disturbing and hard to live with at first.'

'Well ...' Brother Francis glanced up at the abbot with a grin, then looked away into the fire. 'It wasn't so bad in the middle of winter, because my lips were too cold to move then anyway, but I ... um ... you must know I'm always in disgrace over my tongue—it has a life of its own it seems. Not only that, it chatters what's little worth hearing. "Half-witted and facetious babble" were the words Father Matthew used, and on that particular occasion I own he was not far wrong. I talk too much and jest too much—speak first and think later.'

'Well, that's honest,' said Father Peregrine. 'But silence—when you are silent—does not oppress you?'

Francis laughed. 'It is formidable at times, but then I am small-minded. I lie like a child in the night, counting sheep until I fall asleep at last, and then the bell is clanging and I am stumbling down the night stairs to Matins, drunk with sleep and cursing the day I ever heeded God's call. The silence then is a happy necessity, for if I were permitted to speak it would be only a drivel of self-pity and complaint!'

'Yes ...' Father Peregrine nodded thoughtfully. 'It's not easy to get used to the night prayers and the broken hours of sleep.'

'Get used to it! By my faith, I had ceased daring to hope there would ever be a time when I'd get *used* to it! Will I?'

'Oh yes, you will adjust. Granted, it would be pleasanter to stay in bed, but it is not always as weary a business as at first.'

Brother Francis smiled. 'Then God be praised,' he said. 'I'll look forward to that.'

'Your fire is dying,' said Father Peregrine. 'Put some more wood on it.'

I must make this lad talk to me seriously, Peregrine thought as he watched Brother Francis placing the little logs on the fire. Things are not all roses. He has a low opinion of himself. He knows he's a trial to the man he works under ... he thinks himself greedy ... small-minded ... a chatterer. There must be some conflict in a young man who bites his nails to the quick and can't get to sleep at night.

'I imagine,' he said, 'that the vow of celibacy you have taken is at times a stony path?'

Francis was silent for a moment, fiddling unnecessarily with the fire. He looked up at Peregrine with a wry smile, then he dropped his gaze again.

'I have learned,' he said eventually, 'to sit on my hands and say "*no*" and then ten Ave Marias and then "*no*" again.' He grinned sheepishly at the abbot, hugging his arms round his knees as he sat on the hearthstone. 'But stony, as you say.'

'That can be the least of it,' said Peregrine quietly. 'The hardest lesson is the learning to bring your capacities for tenderness—the heart of you—into a communion of trust with the other brothers. A celibate monk must learn how to be fruitful in his dealings with others—how to open himself to them in truth, and bear the pain of letting himself be seen, be known. Yes, your heart must truly have an unlocked door, or celibacy will sour you, wither you. It is not only a matter of the physical urge, though God knows that is not to be belittled.'

Francis raised his eyebrows. 'You're saying, in effect, "You think it's bad enough now, my lad, but you wait!"'

Father Peregrine smiled at him. 'Not exactly that, but

no, it is never easy. There are ways, though, to lift this renunciation up out of the realms of mere denial into a beautiful giving of your self; a way of peace.'

The fire spat out a spark, and Francis moved back a little, and flicked it back into the flames. He sat tracing his finger through the ashes on the hearthstone as he took in this thought. Composed and quiet, half-smiling, his face gave nothing away.

I can't get near this young man, Father Peregrine thought as he watched him. He has made himself a fortress. Amusing, courteous, responsive, but too well-defended for his own good. Father Matthew's right, there is something about this eternal cheerfulness ... a rebuff ... no, maybe not. Maybe he is protecting something ... a wound somewhere. ...

'Brother Francis,' he said, 'are you aware that you have turned aside my every enquiry with a jest?'

Francis looked up in consternation. 'No, I—I'm sorry,' he stammered. 'I didn't mean to be rude, I—'

'You have not been rude. But I can be of no help to you if you keep me for ever at arm's length with flippant remarks and an armour-plated smile. Now tell me honestly, since you are evidently not too troubled by any of the things I have asked you about, is there anything you *are* finding difficult?'

'Not ... not really,' said Francis slowly after a moment's silence.

Father Peregrine shook his head. 'Let me put the question another way. I would be ten times a fool if I let you assure me that it is all plain sailing. What is it that you find hardest about your life here?'

Brother Francis stared at the ashes in the hearth, his face fixed into a slight, strained smile. He had hidden the secrets of his heart from others for so long it was not so easy to put his hand on them himself now when he wanted to. He did not speak for a long time.

'The constant criticism,' he said at last. He looked up

at Father Peregrine, his face still protecting his heart
with the habitual pleasantness of his smile. The abbot
was observing him quietly and seemed not about to
speak. Brother Francis swallowed. 'I know I have a long
way to go. I know I talk too much. I know I am sinful
and proud ... and foolish. But, oh God I do try!'

His smile was gone suddenly, and the surface of his
face was distressed with little twitches of nervous
muscles that didn't know what to do now they were no
longer employed in guarding his soul with the shield of
a smile. 'I have studied and practised and done my
utmost to please, but it is never enough. I am hemmed
in by rebuke and censure until it seems there is nowhere
left to stand. There is no place for me. I can *never* be
good enough.' The words tumbled out and stopped
abruptly. Quivering in the unaccustomed exposure, he
looked at the abbot, his brown eyes full of distress.

Father Peregrine considered him carefully. 'Francis,
you try too hard,' he said.

The young man responded with something halfway
between a laugh and a gasp of indignation. 'Let me
know when I've got it right and I'll stop,' he said bitterly.

'No, that's not it. It is the effort itself which is your
undoing. It makes you unreachable. Father Matthew
now, he feels as though you are, somehow ... insincere
... in some way false, maybe.'

Brother Francis said nothing, his face was quite still.
I've hurt him, thought Peregrine. He was not ready for
it. It went too deep. Help me now, good Lord, or this
will close him up even more.

Francis looked away, gazing into the fire. 'Insincere?'
he said quietly. 'Am I?' Slowly and absently he crushed
one or two tiny sparks that lay on the stone, then he let
his hand lie still. 'You have met my family, haven't you.'
It was a statement, not a question. 'My father's wife is his
second wife. She is not my mother. I was not quite seven
years old when my mother died. My father married

again not long after, and my stepmother brought me up after that. She did her duty by me, fed me and kept me clean, but ... I suppose I was as irritating then as I am now. More so, if that be possible. She said no end of things to me along the lines of, "Why can't you ... ? Will you never learn to ... ?" and "For the hundredth time, child!" It must have been the hundredth time, too. It certainly felt like it.'

He paused and pushed the logs together on the fire, took another from the pile and placed it among them. His thoughts were far away. 'My mother, my real mother, I will never forget her. She was beautiful. I tried to paint her face when I was painting the picture of the Virgin that Brother Clement took such exception to—she with the offending smirk. She had gentle brown eyes, my mother, and she was always merry and kind. She had the kind of laugh that made you laugh with her. She used to say to me, "Always do your best, my son. Be a good boy," and she'd rumple my hair and smile at me.'

He was silent, then, and Peregrine waited; waiting for the memories that hurt and haunted the silence to be spoken and released.

'She got ill a long time before she died. I don't know what was the matter with her. They didn't tell me then, and no one ever spoke of her after my father married again. It was as though she'd never been. They took me in to see her, the evening they knew she was dying. She'd grown so thin, her eyes big and her face white. She could scarcely speak. Just a whisper. She smiled at me though, even then. She looked as though the illness was hurting her badly, but she was smiling, for me; looking at me and her eyes were shining and kind still. She was not afraid. My father was standing behind me. I can remember it, because I wanted to go and kiss her—it was the last time—but he had his hands on my shoulders and restrained me. I suppose she was too ill. She stretched out her hand and touched my cheek, and she said, "Be a good lad for Mother now. Do your very best." They sent me out of the room then. It was late—dark— but I was sent to play in the garden. I stood out in the garden, looking up at her lighted window. I was cold. The next time I saw her she was laid out for burial.'

The sense of his suffering swelled out now that the protective layer he had covered it with was stripped back. The air was tense with his pain. His body was rocking slightly in the rhythm of rekindled grief. Softly, he said, 'And I *have* done my best. But somehow it is never good enough.' He grew still, very still, his face a mask of sadness.

'It may be,' he said at last, 'that my soul is ... lightweight ... not worth very much perhaps, but I give you my word, Father, I am not insincere. I have done my best.'

How odd it is, Peregrine thought, that men think the soul is invisible. Times like this, a man's soul sits about him like a mantle for all to see. I wish Father Matthew was here. He'd not now scorn this man as insubstantial froth.

'Your soul, my brother, is of inestimable worth,' he said. 'It is also of great beauty and nobility. It is only that you have kept it hidden from us. You have not under-stood. Your best *is* yourself. You are not a dog or a dancing bear that you must do tricks and search out ways to please us. The gift of yourself in trust—that is your best. You need courage to make that gift to us, because we also are weak in our humanity and will sometimes deal with you clumsily, as Father Matthew has, as Brother Clement has, as I have just now, without understanding, bruising you. Brother, please forgive us. Please trust us. There is nothing, nothing, nothing amiss with your conduct or your attitude. There is no rebuke here. But, be at peace. Breathe a little more easily. Allow us to see you, to know you. When you are bewildered and bowed down under discipline and hard words, weep—don't laugh. Father Matthew is not unkind, but he takes you as he sees you, and he believes he sees light-hearted indifference.'

'I can't weep!' Francis' voice was sharp with pain. 'How must I weep? I couldn't bear to weep. There is no one . . . it hurts too much . . . I could never stop . . . I can't weep.' His hand moved in a gesture of hopelessness, and he got up from the hearth and knelt before the abbot.

'Father, I confess my fault. I ask God's forgiveness and yours.' The words were torn wretchedly from the centre of him, little shreds of his soul ripped away in pleading need. He was trembling, his head bent, his hands clasped together.

Peregrine looked at him in perplexity. He's getting tighter and tighter in this pain, he thought. God help me, I'm not breaking it for him. What is it he fears? What is it he needs me to do?

'My son, what is it you want me to forgive? Are you asking me to *forgive* the pain of your heart? God knows—'

'*Me*,' Francis broke out in anguish. 'I need you to forgive *me*. I want to be clean. I want to be true . . . I want to belong to God. . . I want him to forgive *me*.'

Father Peregrine looked at the young man, the tightness of his hands, his shaking despair, the rigidity of his bowed shoulders and neck and bent head, and wondered what to do.

'I don't want him to leave me alone.' Peregrine heard the note of shame, of reluctance, and understood that this was the heart of the thing.

'I am so terrified he will abandon me. I don't deserve him, I'm not good enough, I'm not clean or pure or holy. I dread his coldness, his turning away . . . Oh, I'm so afraid of burning in hell. I would do anything, I . . . I am a desert place, useless and poor. Oh God, forgive me . . . forgive me . . . not only my sins, but *me*. Oh, do not leave me alone, don't abandon me. . . .'

'This is what you fear?' Father Peregrine asked him gently. 'Francis, look at me. This is the thing you fear? That God will abandon you?'

'Yes. How should he not? What is there of worth in me?'

Blindly, almost cringing in his need, he reached out his hands to Father Peregrine, and creeping forward he buried his face in the abbot's lap and allowed the brittle shell to shiver into a thousand pieces.

God of love, help me to drive out this fear, thought Peregrine as he stroked the young man's head and brooded over his grieving. However can I reassure him? He had seen many men weep in release; seen it bring them comfort and ease their sorrow, but this man's weeping was bitter agony. There was no peace in it, only pain. He thought of Father Matthew—'This eternal smile of his covers an emptiness within,' and resolved to listen to him more often.

'My child ... my poor child,' he murmured. He did not know what else to say. He knew the futility of smothering this fear with platitudes about God's mercy and love. It is a thing a man needs to know deep in his heart, an understanding with God himself. That is what faith is. It cannot come second hand.

'It hurts too much. It's going to break me!' Francis gasped in terror. 'It's like a great black wave, towering too high. If I let it fall, oh God ... I'll be dashed to pieces! It will destroy me!'

On the quivering shoulders Peregrine rested his hands, frustrated at their crippled immobility, wishing he could spread his fingers, hold the man through his fear.

'It will destroy you if you try to contain it,' he said. 'You must allow it to break. If it destroys you, well, I will be with you. There is no more holding it in, my child.'

There was a moment when the abbot felt the power of that black tide of grief rising in Francis' soul; when the two of them were arrested in the awe of the moment before it crashed. Then Francis' whole body convulsed like a man vomiting, his hands gripping desperately in the folds of Peregrine's tunic. His mouth was forced wide open in a silent cry of agony, his eyes screwed shut as the thing ripped through him. It left him sweating and shuddering, his mouth slack and trembling, his eyes dazed and dully oozing tears. He moaned softly like a labouring woman. Then, in the wake of the first crashing wave, poured out the flood-tide of his grief. The pathetic bravery with which he had fought it so long lay splintered like matchwood, floating dispersed on the dark sea that swept him away. There was no way now to combat the bitter sorrow or master the pain. It was too much for him.

'Oh . . .' Francis groaned in misery as he sat back on his heels, struggling unsuccessfully to compose his face and stop the tears. 'Forgive me the liberty. I . . . oh . . .' he hid his face in his hands, unable to contain his grief, bent double with the anguish of it. Looking down at him, Peregrine realised then and for ever that faith and peace come not from believing in God, but from the secret of God's love hidden in a man's heart. Surely, my God, he prayed sadly, you will fill this child's emptiness, have pity on his torment? Father Peregrine watched as Francis fought with his subsiding grief, finally managing to control it, straightened up with a sigh that was half a sob and spread his hands on his knees.

'There you are, then. This is me,' he said, with an attempt at a smile that wrung the abbot's heart. 'What now?'

Father Peregrine looked at him. He could think of nothing to say.

Francis turned his head aside and looked into the dying embers of the fire. 'The brotherhood of this community,' he said, his voice flat and tired in the sad, bruised finality of defeat, 'is like a lighted room in a house. There is the warm fire of life and fellowship on the hearth, and the brothers are gathered safely round it, and outside it is night. Out in the night is the lonely place of darkness and danger and fear. Do not bad men prowl in the darkness, and wild beasts? Out in the darkness, where no light is, you can stumble and fall on the stones, and the cruel thorns tear at you. I am here in the light and warmth of the house, but I belong in the darkness. I can't forget the darkness, it draws me. This light, this warmth, this brotherhood—it's not for me. I don't deserve it, it isn't mine. I'm here on false pretences. I don't belong.'

He looked desperately at Peregrine. He is tortured by this, the abbot thought. I've got to say something to help him.

'If you cannot put the darkness out of your mind, my son,' Peregrine said slowly, 'maybe you should face it. Open the door of the lighted room and go out of the house and look at the darkness. What is there?'

Francis hesitated. 'The restlessness of night. The silence, and strange sounds in the silence. Then—out there in the night, someone ... a long way out into the garden, under those big whispering trees somewhere ... there is someone weeping ... sobbing ... groaning. Father, there is someone m such trouble out there. I want to go and see!' His eyes widened. He was really seeing it.

'Go on then.' It seemed so real that Father Peregrine felt as curious as Francis did.

'Oh! There are stars. The darkness is not as black as I had thought. I had forgotten the stars. It's a garden with shrubs and trees, dark shapes. I can smell the perfume of the flowers. And someone is crying in the darkness in bitter distress. I can't find him. I'm searching for him, looking everywhere. Wait—there, under the trees. A man, crouching, bowed down to the ground. Oh, the loneliness of him. He's *broken*. He's—he's afraid. I've never seen a man in such despair ... I must go and ... oh, God, it's *Jesus!* Out here, all alone. Jesus ... he was out here even before I came out. He was out here all the time, in the lonely plate where abandonment and fear belong. He has always been here. I think it ... it is Gethsemane.'

'What are you going to do?' asked Peregrine in fascination. Brother Francis looked at him incredulously. 'Do? Stay with him, of course. I can't leave him alone in this distress. I couldn't just abandon him. Jesus, my heart, my love . . . his courage is the hearth for the night. As long as he is here, the darkness is home. The outside has become the very centre. Jesus . . . my Lord, and my God.'

The tension and pain had drained out of him; his face was soft and rapt, lost in the vision. His eyes, no longer haunted, were brimming with wonder and tenderness.

There was something Peregrine wanted to know. He hesitated, reluctant to intrude on Francis' contemplation. Then he said, 'The door of that house—did you shut it behind you when you went out?'

'No. I was scared to go out. I wanted to leave a way back in. You can shut it behind me now. I'll be all right here.'

He knelt a moment longer, and sighed deeply, amazingly at peace. For a few seconds, time had tipped over into eternity, and they were in the place where angels come and go. Then Brother Francis looked up at his abbot with a grin.

'There's the Office bell now. My foot's gone completely dead, kneeling here. I'm going to have the most wonderful pins and needles when I stand up. I'll limp along to chapel with you if that's—oh I'm sorry, Father, that was tactless.'

Brother Francis blushed as the abbot bent to pick up his wooden crutch, stood up and leaned on it. Peregrine laughed at Brother Francis' mortified face as he scrambled to his feet.

'We'll limp together then, my son,' he said.

As they walked along the cloister, Father Peregrine glanced at Francis' face, which had the same intelligence and humour, the same firmness—everything the same but for red eyes and a red nose—but resettled now into a new context of peace. The same but all different. The same man but reborn.

'The Christ you saw,' said Peregrine quietly, 'that is the Christ I love. All his life he lived pressed on every side by human need, and he met the weariness and testing of it with a patience and humility that silences me, shames me for what I am. But in Gethsemane, I see Jesus crumple, sobbing in loneliness and fear, crushed to the ground, pleading for a way out. And there was none. I cling to that vision, as you will. That sweating, terrified, abandoned man; that is my King, my God. Such courage as I have comes from the weeping of that broken man.'

Brother Francis reached out one finger and gently touched the abbot's hand. They went into the chapel in silence, each to his own stall. Father Peregrine pulled his cowl up over his head, and sat gazing as he always did at the great cross that hung above the altar. 'How did you do it?' he prayed in silent wonder. 'How did you do so much without doing anything? How did you lift the man out of that torturing agony of grief and fear just by consenting to bear the same torture, the same lonely agony? Suffering God, your grace mystifies me. You become weak to redeem me in my weakness. Your face, agonised, smeared with dust and sweat and blood and spit, must become the icon of my secret life with you. The tears that scald my eyes run into your mouth. The sweat of my fear glistens on your body. The wounds with which life has maimed me show livid on your back, your hands, your feet. The peace you win me by such a dear and bloody means defeats my reason. Lift me up into the power of your cross, blessed Lord. May the tears that run into your mouth scald my eyes. May the sweat that glistens on your body dignify my fear. May the blood that drips from your hands nourish my life.'

Father Peregrine watched Brother Theodore take his

place beside Francis, saw him rest his hand gently a moment on Francis' shoulder, having seen in his face the signs of recent tears. The abbot watched the shyness of the smile with which Francis acknowledged Theodore's gentleness. Ah! Yes! He has allowed himself to remain vulnerable, the abbot rejoiced. Then as the cantor lifted his head to begin the chant, Peregrine sped one last private prayer to the Almighty—'And of your goodness, dear Lord, help me to think of some sensible explanation to offer Father Matthew.'

'*Deus in adjutorium meum intende*,' and the brothers responded '*Domine ad adjuvandum me festina*.'

Mother fell silent then. I looked at her, sitting in her chair in the candlelight, her hands folded quietly in her lap, her eyes still seeing people and places far away as she gazed at the candle flame.

'What do those Latin words mean?' I asked.

'Mmm? What?'

'Those Latin words you said at the end of the story. What do they mean?'

'They mean, "Oh God, come to my assistance. Oh Lord, make haste to help me." It's the versicle and response from the beginning of the Office.'

She sat a moment longer, thinking, then she said, 'I have always loved that story. It was that story which first taught me that we can offer no solutions, no easy answers, to other people's tragedies. We can only be there. It is Jesus they need, not us, and even he offers no answers. He offers himself. It is when people find their way through to him that the pain of their life becomes the pain not of death, but of birth. A thing of hope. Hark at me, rambling. It must be late—look, this candle was a new one and it's half burned away. Let's go downstairs. Therese and Daddy will be thinking we've fallen asleep up here.'

V
BEHOLDING THE HEART

'Tell me a story, Mother,' I said one Sunday afternoon. We had been doing a jigsaw puzzle while the rest of the family were out walking the dog on the hill after lunch. 'Tell me a story about Father Peregrine.'

But the telephone rang just then, so I went into the kitchen to answer it. It was my friend Helen, wanting to know about our geography homework, what it was and whether it had to be in on Monday or Tuesday. While I was talking to her, there was a knock at the front door. I heard Mother opening it and saying, 'Hello, Elaine! This is a surprise. Come in.'

My heart sank, because I knew once Elaine got going she would probably talk for ages and ages. After I had finished my conversation and put the phone down, I went and popped my head round the door.

'Shall I make coffee, Mother?'

Mother nodded, but didn't speak, because Elaine was talking already. So I made three mugs of coffee and took them in. I thought that if I was there too she might go a bit sooner.

Elaine looked a bit pink-eyed and sniffy, as though

she'd been crying. She was telling Mother that she had decided to leave our church.

'I didn't want to go without saying a word to anyone,' she said. 'Keith and I have prayed and prayed about this. Every time we open our Bible, it falls open at the book of Jeremiah, about how the people of God are deceived and idolatrous. I think God is trying to tell us something about our church.'

'Maybe ...' said Mother cautiously. 'Of course, the book of Jeremiah is very near the middle of the Bible. It probably would keep coming open near there.'

Elaine shook her head sorrowfully. 'I wish I could think it was only that, but this morning in my Bible notes, the reading was from Jeremiah. It said, "Of all the wise men among the nations, in all their kingdoms, there is no-one else like you. They are senseless and stupid, and they are taught by worthless idols." I don't think I can ignore it any longer. God's word to us is so powerful and clear. Keith and I have been longing—you know we have—for months and months for our church to move on with God, and it just isn't. The Holy Spirit isn't there. It's so dead. We have to face the fact that God has moved on and left us behind, and Keith and I want to move on with him. So we're going to start worshipping at Hill Street Baptist Church. We've been there a few Sundays, and the Holy Spirit is really moving there.'

Mother sipped her coffee. 'Do you really think God has left our church, Elaine?' she asked.

'I don't think he was ever there. Just look at it! Father Bennett's so awful and Father Carnforth's so old. We never sing anything but dirging hymns. We should be dancing and singing and raising our hands to God in praise. The Bible says we should.'

'Well, why don't you then?'

'Oh, don't be silly. You just *can't*. It's so inhibiting, so dead. You understand really, I know you do.'

'In a way, yes. I do like hymns though, and I can't see

why Father Carnforth being old means that our church is dead, but I can see that Hill Street would suit you and Keith better.'

'It isn't a question of what we want for ourselves. If it was only us, of course we'd stay. It's what *God* wants that counts. It's been such a hard decision for us.' Elaine's nose went very red, and her eyes filled with tears. She blew her nose, and carried on, 'I haven't been able to sleep a single night this week, but God is moving on and he won't wait for ever. Either you move with him, or you get left behind, and our church just isn't moving with him.'

Mother looked a bit sceptical, but she didn't say anything. She drank some more of her coffee.

'I've been thinking about what Jesus said to his disciples,' Elaine went on. 'He said that if anyone would not listen to their words, they must shake the dust off their feet and move on. Keith and I have been to Father Bennett and challenged him about the baptism of the Holy Spirit, and he was very rude to us.'

'You talked to Father Bennett about baptism in the Holy Spirit?' said Mother. 'My hat! What on earth did he say?'

'He just dismissed it. He said it was all a fad. He said all Christians had the Holy Spirit or they wouldn't be Christians.'

'Well, you have to admit, there is something in that,' said Mother.

'In a way, but *you* know there's more to it than that. It was you who first taught me about the Holy Spirit. So anyway, Keith and I have challenged him, and he has been confronted with God's word and rejected it. So we're shaking the dust from our feet and moving on with God.'

Elaine went quite soon after that. She didn't stay as long as usual. As she was leaving, the rest of the family came home, and then it was teatime and after tea Mother went to church.

At bedtime I went up and sat with her as she put the little ones to bed. I sat on the floor, watching the candle flame as it moved in the slight draught.

'Is it true what Elaine said, Mother?' I asked, once the little ones were settled down in bed.

'About what?'

'That God moves on, and won't wait for us. If we can't keep up with him, he'll leave us behind.'

'No. It's not true.'

'How do you know?' I needed to be sure. I felt a bit afraid at the idea that I had to keep up with God.

'I know because ... well, if God moves on like that, who is it that picks me up when I stumble and fall? Someone does, and it feels a lot like Jesus. What about the story you wanted, Melissa? Shall I tell it to you now?'

'In a minute,' I said slowly. 'With the Bible ... it is God's word, isn't it?'

'Yes,' Mother replied firmly.

'Well then, Elaine might be right, mightn't she? Jesus did say that thing about dust.'

'He said it, yes, but he said a lot of other things too that Elaine might more usefully take note of. A funny thing happens with the Bible, Melissa. It acts a bit like a mirror. People who come to it resentful and critical find it full of curses and condemnation. People who come to it gentle and humble find it full of love and mercy. The truth of God is not a truth like "cows have four legs" is true. God's truth is him, himself. There are no short cuts. You have to get to know *him*. If you try to use the Bible like a fortune-telling game, it just bounces your own ideas back at you. God won't let us use him like that. It's all right, Melissa. He understands our weaknesses and our mistakes. He does love us. He'll wait for us to catch up—even Father Bennett. He's not going to dump us like that.'

I sighed. 'Tell me the story. Whose story is it?'

'There's a bit of everyone in this one. Brother

Theodore and Father Peregrine and Father Matthew mostly.'

'I like Brother Theo. Go on then.'

I lay down on the floor with my head on Beth's mattress, watching the candle flame as Mother began her story.

People have different ways of protecting themselves. Brother Francis had chosen to protect his vulnerability with a smile. Brother Cormac was like a hedgehog, making his soft belly invisible and exposing to the threatening world a back full of spikes. Both those ways are quite good ways of protecting yourself. They help you to cope when life's upsets seem more than you can face. But to protect yourself like that has a few drawbacks when the soft, vulnerable part of you has a wound. The hedgehog is wise to bristle against attack, but if his soft belly is wounded, sooner or later he needs to uncurl and let someone salve it, dress it, heal it. The one who, like Francis, hides his vulnerability with a shield, a mask, a smile, is protected more or less from wounding, but not of course from the wounds behind the shield—the wounds he already has. Sooner or later he has to lower the shield, to let the physician see and touch the sore place, if he wants it to be cleaned and bound up and soothed.

Father Peregrine's defence was his dignity of office— there was a certain refuge in being the competent, authoritative abbot of his community—but he too, for his soul's health, and for the sake of truth, needed from time to time to allow someone to see him, know him in his weakness and his human reality. There are, though, some people who—for whatever reason—cannot seem to protect themselves successfully, and Brother Theodore was one of those. He grew up through a miserable childhood in a home where he was a misfit, beaten and disliked; and he never found an adequate way of protecting himself. Francis had his smile, Cormac had his fierce bad temper, Peregrine had his aristocratic authority. Theodore had only his clumsiness. It was as though misery had numbed him. When a man's fingers are numb with cold or illness, he drops things, blunders, becomes butter-fingered—and that was Brother Theodore. Father Peregrine had found and touched and gently bandaged the wound behind the clumsiness; but of course we are what we are, and not even Father Peregrine could wave a magic wand for Brother Theo and change him instantly. For those like Brother Francis and Brother Cormac, once someone has been let near the hurting place, and allowed to touch it and help the pain, then their ways of protecting themselves against more hurt are quite useful.

But poor Theo and his disastrous clumsiness drew rebuke and trouble constantly, adding humiliation to pain, and insult to injury. Because, of course, his *soul* was not numb or impervious to hurt. He came perilously near to giving up on life, sinking into defeat, existing utterly without hope. Worst of all, in that most ugly face of despair, the despair of receiving love and affirmation, the little green plant of tenderness inside him all but withered and died, so that he could no longer *give* love. The wound almost cut too deep, and cut off life.

He was saved from this final despair by the joy of his work as a scribe and a musician, in which creativity his artist's soul flew free and rejoiced; and also by the understanding of his abbot, who kept him going. Father Peregrine patched up the cuts and bruises Theo's soul endlessly sustained, comforted his confused misery, delighted in his artistry, beheld his grief. It was a wonderful thing to Brother Theodore, that beholding. In his private meditations he would read the words of Psalm 139: '*Domine probasti me, et cognovisti me*—Oh Lord, you have searched me and known me,' and he would kneel down in the solitude of his cell whispering his prayer. 'Look at me, oh, look at me! Look at my sin, my failure, my stupidity. Oh, look at me and heal me.' And it was as he allowed his secret grief and shame to be looked at, touched and beheld by his abbot, that he was healed. It was not anything Father Peregrine did or said that healed Theodore so much as knowing that the abbot, whose body bore the scars of his own suffering, really did behold his grief. That somehow made it bearable.

For the period of his novitiate in the community, Brother Theodore and Father Matthew, the novice master, were each other's cross to bear. Father Matthew, that upright, stern, deeply religious pillar of monasticism was determined, though it cost him everything, to train Brother Theodore into an admirable figure of recollected piety. Brother Theodore, so far as Father Matthew was concerned, went from the novitiate into full profession as one of his failures. The mere sight of Brother Theodore was enough to pucker Father Matthew's austere brow into an unconscious frown of irritation. The encounter was indeed a costly one, but Father Peregrine knew what his novice master never understood: that it was Brother Theodore, not Father Matthew, who paid the price.

The abbot was, of course, a man of his time, and whereas a modern superior might have found someone kinder than Father Matthew to be the master of novices in his community, Father Peregrine accepted the severity of Father Matthew's régime as an important, if sometimes excessive, discipline. He contented himself with tempering its effects with his own mercy. He also suspected that much of Father Matthew's unyielding spirituality was made more of plaster than of rock, and to humiliate him by depriving him of his post might bring the noble edifice of his assurance to dust.

This particular day, which was a day when Brother

Theodore was nearly, but not quite, through the tunnel of his novitiate year, had seen a good morning so far for both Brother Theo and Father Matthew.

The novice master had spent the greater part of the morning in the parlour with a family: mother, father and their son, who meant to try the life at St Alcuin's. They had come humbly for Father Matthew's guidance and counsel, which they received with a reverence and respect that was the more gratifying because they were of a lineage and descent that would have put them as far above Father Matthew's social aspirations as the sun in the sky, had he remained in the world as the fourth son of a struggling merchant. So St Alcuin's master of novices was feeling well-disposed towards all men as he emerged into the courtyard with his little party of visitors. Their talk had gone well. The lad was full of the wild hopes and ideals proper to a nineteen-year-old heart, and Father Matthew had smiled benignly on his avowal of vocation. He had smiled on the lad's parents too, for their coffers were lined with as much gold as silver, and more estates than any man could reasonably require. The abbey stood to receive a fair gift at their hands if their youngest son chose to make his soul as a monk in its cloisters. Even Father Matthew, whose vision was set unwaveringly upon heaven, could not help but notice these material benefits out of the corner of his eye, and feel a modest glow of satisfaction that their meeting had run so favourably.

He came into the courtyard with the three of them, and together they made a striking group indeed. Father Matthew's erect and ascetic dignity was enhanced rather than eclipsed by the fashionable elegance of his wealthy guests. Yes, things had gone well, and the small frisson of exultation he permitted himself was only diminished, not utterly extinguished, by the sight of Brother Theodore approaching, one sandal flapping awkwardly on a broken strap, the hem of his habit trailing and a

smudge of livid green ink on his left cheek. Theodore
was bearing in his hands a jug of beer from the kitchen,
which was one of the ingredients of the ink he was
mixing for his new project in the scriptorium ('*Beer?*'
Cormac had said in the kitchen. 'Theodore, this had
better be true') which was just now absorbing him heart
and soul.

He had one morning last week been summoned to the
abbot's house, and found Father Peregrine seated at his
table with a book lying before him in a little clearing
amid the landscape of manuscripts and letters that
cluttered his table. The abbot had greeted him with
friendly courtesy, and then after a fractional hesitation,
a split second of indecision, had taken the book between
his hands. 'Brother, I would like you to look at this. It is
a book of Hours that has not been completed. Do you
think you can finish it for me?'

Brother Theodore heard the slight diffidence, almost
shyness, and realised this was something special. He
took the book and opened it. It was indeed something
special. It was three-quarters completed, with fine and
graceful lettering, and illuminations of subtle beauty,
paintings of flowers and birds, of mythical beasts and
intricate designs; a courtly dance of colour, balanced
and harmonious, yet of uninhibited and arresting vitality. There were touches of gold shining on its pages, but
used with restraint. This was not a vulgar riot of scarlet
and gilt, but a sophisticated marriage of colours, and it
was wanting a few pages still. As he turned over the
parchments, which lay loose in a stack, unbound as yet
because unfinished, he found there were two or three
blank at the end, and one or two with the design
sketched out, but not lettered or painted. There was one
half-finished page with the lettering complete and the
capital, but the margin half-done, started with the
soft blue that was the theme colour for the page, but
interrupted.

'Father, this is a beautiful thing,' said Theodore, holding it in his hands, handling it with the curious mixture of confidence and reverence which denotes the true artist. 'It is ... it is ... I've rarely seen one so lovely as this. Indeed I would be honoured to complete it if you think I can, but where have you come by it?'

Father Peregrine had been watching Theodore closely as he examined the book, but now he looked down at the table, unnecessarily moving his pens, the ink, the seal.

'I had thought to continue it on the next Tuesday,' he said, looking up abruptly, his voice studiedly light. 'I had begun the painting of that last page on the Wednesday, then left it, with reluctance I confess, because the claims of Holy Thursday, Good Friday, Easter Eve and Easter Day left me with no leisure for anything. Then on the Monday night, they destroyed my hands. I put it away at the bottom of the chest over there, and it has stayed there this long time. Brother, will you be my hands? Will you finish it for me?'

Brother Theodore laid the little book on top of a pile of manuscripts on the table and turned over the leaves until he came to the half-painted one. He took it into his hands and studied it carefully.

'You think I can do justice to this?' he asked. 'If I had made a thing of such beauty as this, it would be no small sacrifice to turn it over to another man to finish.'

'These long months I have locked it away,' Peregrine said. 'It begins to look a little as though I thought it my own private property, which it is not. It is the community's, not mine to sit on like a dragon guarding its hoard. Of course you can do it justice. Your work is equal to mine. Besides, even if you could not, what of it? It is only a book.'

Brother Theodore had need to put a brave face on too much heartache in his own life to be fooled by this. He put the parchment back carefully among the others.

He cleared his throat. 'In the eighth Psalm,' he said, speaking in rather a hurry, his ears a bit red, embarrassed at seeming to preach to his superior, 'it says that God has put all he had made, all the works of his hands, into our care. I have often wondered what God felt— feels—when the beauty he has made and given us on trust is indifferently regarded; when men trap the singing lark and cut out her tongue for a dainty meal; when we beat little children with belts and sticks and let them creep hungry to bed to nurse their bruises; when we smoke out the bees and destroy them to rob them of their honey. God must have his head in his hands and weep sometimes, I think, in the heartbreak of our negligent misuse of his artistry, the work of his fingers. You understand what I'm saying to you? He knows, and I know, how you feel about this, even if no one else would. Can I take all of this away, not just the pages waiting to be done, so I can study how you've gone about it? Then I can do my best to make the whole thing a unity. Will you also write down for me the recipe for this blue ink, and I will try to mix some like it.'

Father Peregrine took a scrap of parchment from a little pile of torn scraps he used for jottings, and wrote down the proportions of the blue mixture. Theodore watched the toiling progress of the pen as the abbot formed the crabbed, unsteady letters. It was a laborious business: time and again the pen slipped in his crippled grasp, but the result was legible. He gave the slip to Theodore.

'Can you read my staggering script?'

'I can read it.' Theodore paused, then gathered his courage to say, 'To be your hands, that is a humbling thought, for your hands have more skill than you know. They have erased a lot of the black and ugly scenes from my heart and painted some fairer, brighter colours. Father, I will do what I can.'

So Brother Theodore had spent the week studying

the little book, getting the feeling for its design, planning and preparing the last pages, practising lettering in the style Peregrine had used, and now he was ready to mix his inks and begin to paint the remainder of the half-finished page. It was to be a work of love, and the trust given him he hugged like a treasure to his heart—'Brother, will you be my hands?'

As he walked along carrying the jug of beer to make his ink, his mind was filled with the vision of the page as it would be when it was done. The soft blue; blue of the Virgin's cloak, blue of the morning, blue of the woods in spring, of a child's eyes, of the harebells nodding in the summer fields ... blue of all things gentle and beautiful and ... Theodore looked up and saw for the first time the little knot of gentry standing in front of him. He was suddenly uneasily aware of Father Matthew's eyes upon him in the sort of mild disapproval that Brother Theodore knew from experience could be kindled into wrath as easily as dry grass in the drought of summer can be set ablaze. He felt the familiar flutter of panic at the base of his throat, the clutch of apprehension in the pit of his stomach, the tightening of his chest.

It was at that moment that Father Peregrine came limping out into the courtyard to find Father Matthew, and to extend his own greeting to the guests. He saw the family standing there making their farewells. He saw Theodore pause, then nervously approach with his head bent in an attempt to render himself invisible as he passed them on his way to the day stairs leading up to the scriptorium. He saw the expression on Father Matthew's face as Theodore stumbled over his broken sandal strap, shot out his hand to save himself, and dropped the jug he was carrying. It was smashed into tinkling fragments on the stone, in a puddle of warm fizzing beer that splashed my lady's elegant gown and my lord's embroidered shoes. There was a moment in which the universe stopped to allow for Brother

Theodore's mind to reel in dismay, Father Matthew's expression to change from mere resentment to red-hot rage, and my lady to step back with a little, affected 'Oh!' of alarm.

Theodore, speechless, went down on his knees in haste, gathering up the pottery fragments, dropping them again, cutting his finger on the broken shards. Father Matthew, his lips tight with fury, drew himself up to his full height and towered over the offensive wretch grovelling in the beer at his feet. Then Theodore's soul shrivelled under the excoriating shower of rebuke that the novice master released upon his head—his clumsiness, his discourtesy, the order and dignity of the abbey: it went on and on.

Smiling at the familiar scene (had he not often and often occasion to bawl out his own serfs?) my lord took his lady's hand that she might step across the pool of beer, and the family moved discreetly away to allow Father Matthew to finish his scolding.

Theodore crouched on the floor, his hands filled with broken bits of pot and dripping with blood and beer.

Father Peregrine, when his novice master paused for breath, said quietly, 'Go gently, Matthew—he's shaking. There now, you neglect your guests. Leave him to me.'

After one last scalding reprimand, Father Matthew consented to rejoin, with a profusion of apologies, his guests thus abused by the clumsy foolery of his novice. They dismissed his apologies with gracious good humour as they moved away towards the gatehouse buildings across the abbey court. None of them looked back, except the boy. He glanced over his shoulder to see the abbot stooping down, trying with his twisted and awkward hands to pick up the last fragments of sticky pottery, and the young monk on his knees remonstrating with the abbot, dropping what he held already in his attempt to gather up what he had missed.

With an amused smile, the lad turned away and followed his parents into the gatehouse.

Father Peregrine pulled his handkerchief out of his pocket. 'Here, Brother, you have hurt yourself. Put that pile of pieces there to this side. Go and wash the cut on your hand and then you can find something to gather up these in. There now, don't distress yourself, it couldn't be helped. Swill away this spilled ale and there will be nothing left to remind Father Matthew of the offence.'

In mute distress, Brother Theodore did as he was bidden, and Peregrine went after Father Matthew and his guests to offer them the courtesy of an abbatial greeting.

When Theodore had disposed of the broken pot, and collected a broom and a pail of water, he returned to find Father Matthew standing there, balefully surveying the scene of Theo's disgrace.

'You will confess your fault of rude clumsiness at Chapter in the morning, Brother. I trust you are planning to wash this mess away. Have a care to leave no little shards of pot. What's this?'

He picked up a scrap of parchment which lay on the stone flags. Theodore thought at first he must have dropped his ink recipe, it was a little torn-off slip like it; but his recipe was safely tucked away in the scriptorium. It could not be. There was something written there, though. As Father Matthew read the writing on the little chit, his eyes widened and his eyebrows rose higher and higher. Brother Theodore watched him apprehensively. At last, the novice master looked up at him.

'Do—do you recognise this hand?' he spluttered. 'Whose drunken scrawl is this? Can a brother of this house be responsible for this . . . this . . . this . . . well, read it!'

So overcome was he with horror and disgust, that he held out the thing to Theo, who took it and read it with some curiosity. It was a poem, written in Latin. Father Matthew, having second thoughts, twitched the parchment out of Theodore's hand. 'No, no, you should not be reading such filth. Heaven bless us, what a thing!'

But Theodore, who spent all his days working with Latin texts in the scriptorium, had scanned and understood what he read, which roughly translated was this:

> This vigil is long.
> What time I have sat here,
> Watching the candle flame's
> Slow, passionate exploration kiss the night.
> The blind and gentle thrusting tongue of light
> Finds out the secrets of the dumb receptive dark.
> Her sensuous silence trembles with delight.

He did indeed recognise that drunken scrawling script. He had referred to it a dozen times that afternoon as he mixed up his pot of blue ink.

Father Matthew crumpled it in his hand. He was really shocked by what he had read.

'Did you recognise the hand, Brother?' he asked. 'To think that a monk should pen such words!'

'Maybe.' Brother Theodore hesitated. 'The young man who came to see you this morning stood here some while, Father. This is the kind of thing that young men sometimes write.'

Father Matthew was visibly relieved. 'Ah yes, it must be so! Then I shall give it to his father. The young lad's priest should know. His soul is in danger if he is prey to such sensual and lascivious ramblings.'

'No! Um ... no, Father. Perhaps I should take it to Father Abbot. He should see it, surely? It may be that one of the brethren wrote it, after all, and besides, the lad plans to enter our cloisters. Father should know, don't you think?'

'Yes. Yes, Brother, indeed. I will take it to him after we have said Office. You are right.'

'I could take it,' said Theodore hastily. 'I am going there directly I have mopped up this floor. I—I won't look at it again, I give you my word. I'll just take it to him.'

Father Matthew looked suspiciously at Theodore. Theo looked as innocent and submissive as it was in his power to do.

'I should like ... I should like to confess to Father Abbot that I caught a glimpse of those words, and seek his counsel,' he murmured. It worked.

Father Matthew nodded soberly.

'Very well, but I charge you under obedience not to read it again.'

And he gave the incriminating verse into Theo's care.

Brother Theodore swilled away the spilled beer, his gut still swarming with butterflies as Father Matthew vanished from sight. Returning the pail with all speed lest the novice master should think better of his decision, he hurried to the abbot's house, and found Peregrine just setting off for chapel.

'Father, please, have you a moment? The bell's not rung yet.' Peregrine looked at him in surprise, and stepped back to admit him into his lodging. 'Yes, Brother?'

'Father Matthew found this in the cloister. I think you might have dropped it when you pulled your handkerchief out of your pocket this morning.'

He smoothed the crumpled parchment in his fingers as he spoke, and gave it to the abbot who took it and looked down at it. Peregrine took a deep breath.

'Father *Matthew* read this?' Never before and never afterwards could Brother Theodore recall seeing his abbot so completely disconcerted.

'What—what did he say?' Peregrine enquired, red faced.

'He was not too—he didn't appreciate its beauty, but he was generous enough to believe that no brother of ours could have written such a thing. He was happy to swallow the suggestion that the young lad who came this morning might like to write poetry.'

'You have read this?'

'But briefly. He asked me if I recognised the hand, showed it to me, then thought better of it, fearing to corrupt my innocence. He consented to let me bring it to you, and put me on obedience to look at it no more.'

'Yes. Well, he was right.' The abbot turned away and took the crumpled poem to his table, and put it inside his box of sealing waxes. 'I will burn it later.'

'No.' Brother Theodore shook his head. 'Don't burn it. He may have been correct, but he was not right. He doesn't know what life is; he doesn't know. He hasn't known what it is to be in black darkness, and won, revived by the tender wooing of light. He doesn't know. The filth is his; the poem is not filth. Don't burn it.'

'Filth? Is that what he said?' Father Peregrine pondered the judgement. 'I hadn't meant it so. It seemed a thing of wonder, that silent, lovely mating of the darkness with the light. A hallowed thing. I am sorry if I have degraded that loveliness.'

'Father ...' Theodore begged, 'can I read it once more? Please. It was beautiful.' The abbot looked at him, torn between propriety and the understanding that lay between them. Then, 'Why not?' he said. 'You have read it once. The harm is done, if harm there be.'

Theo retrieved the shabby scrap and read it through. 'I'd like to put this at the end of your book of Hours. It is lovely.'

'You'll do no such thing! Put it away, Brother, the bell is ringing for Office. We must go. Thank you for saving my blushes.'

Theodore smiled. 'You've shielded me often enough. I need no thanks.'

When the midday Office and meal were over, Father Matthew went in search of his abbot. Peregrine braced himself for the interview as he heard the knock at the door.

'Father, might I have a word with you?' The abbot's

stomach tightened into a knot at the discreet, confi-
dential tone of his novice master's voice. He managed a
pallid smile.

'Be seated. Have you come to talk to me about this
verse you found?'

'You have seen it then? I trusted Brother Theodore to
bring it straight to you. He is a sore trial, but he is
honest, I believe. I was shocked and ashamed to discover
evidence of such lewd and inflamed imaginings in this
holy place. Brother Theodore wondered if it might be the
work of the young man who was here this morning. If you
think it may be so, I will take it upon myself to inform his
confessor. The thought that it be not his, but may be the
shameless fantasy of one of our brethren is almost too
much to contemplate. Did you know the script?'

'Yes.' Peregrine looked at him helplessly. He
moistened his lips with his tongue.

'Brother ... the poem is mine.'

The weights and balances of all the world readjusted
in the incredulity of Father Matthew's silence. A
hundred angels shut their eyes tight and stopped their
ears and held their breath in dread of his reply.

'*Yours?*' He was absolutely thunderstruck.

'Yes. I'm sorry it so distressed you. It ... please believe
I had not intended any lewdness. There is a place, in the
mind of a man of God, for reverence of carnal love in its
beauty, surely? As there is a place for Solomon's love
canticle in the canon of Scripture.'

'The Song of Songs,' said Father Matthew coldly, 'is an
allegory of the love between Christ and his church.'

'Well, I don't know ...' Peregrine demurred.
'Solomon was a long time before Christ. It reads a bit
more lively than that to me.'

Father Matthew shook his head sorrowfully. 'Sacred
Scripture is then to be taken thus lightly? Compared
with such verse as this thing you have written?'

'No. No, of course not. I didn't mean my scribblings

were of that standard. Matthew, I'm sorry, I'm very sorry to have offended you. I don't know what else to say. I beg your pardon. It was not meant for anyone's eyes but mine. I'm sorry.'

'Sorry you wrote it, or sorry I saw it?'

It is possible to push a man too far. A flash of irritation shone a warning spark in the abbot's eye.

'Sorry you saw it, since you ask. I would never willingly offend you, you know that, but don't you think you are being a little bit prudish?'

A tremor shook Father Matthew's upright frame.

'I strive for purity in my innermost being,' he replied.

Peregrine sighed. 'Well you've achieved it in good measure. Father Matthew there is nothing else I can say. I'm sorry, I beg your forgiveness. Is there anything further you wish to discuss?'

Poor Father Matthew. He retreated from his abbot's house a saddened and disillusioned man. He came that evening into Compline, and sat scowling in thought in his stall. What was the world coming to? His eye fell on the candle flame as it moved in the slight draught. He watched it, intrigued, as it dipped and swayed, swelled and pointed, shivered and moved in the air current. He watched the hungry urgency of the flame push against the gathering dark, and a tingle of unfamiliar life stirred somewhere inside him. 'Heaven help us, he's right,' he acknowledged reluctantly.

He paused by the abbot's stall as the brothers filed out of chapel, and almost spoke; but they were in silence, and it would not do to break the rule. Father Matthew lay awake in his bed for some time that night, troubled by a dim uneasiness. It was the closest he ever came to understanding that 'he came that we might have a proper code of behaviour' is not the same as 'he came that we might have life'. But he chose in the end to take refuge in sleep, murmuring the words from the 139th Psalm, '*Proba me Deus, et scito cor meum: interroga me, et cognosce spiritas meas. Et vide, si via iniquitatis in me est, et deduc me in via aeterna* ... Examine me, O God, and know my heart: probe me and search my thoughts. Look well if there be any way of wickedness in me, and lead me in the everlasting way.'

The words that Theodore clung to for healing, Matthew scoured his soul with before he tidied it away, clean, to sleep. God, in his unfathomable silence was content for them each to find what they could in his book. No doubt he also heard the abbot's last silent meditations from the same Psalm.

> For all these mysteries I thank you:
> For the wonder of my being, the wonder of your works.
> You know me through and through.
> You saw my bones take shape
> As my body was being formed in the secret
> Dark of my mother's womb.

It had never struck me before, the sensuous, very physical intimacy of those words, but as Mother spoke them, I could almost feel it, see it; the close, fluid world of the foetus, turning in the darkness that changed from red gold to deep red, to velvet blackness, depending on where the mother's body was. The silent dance of creation, a symphony of mysteries woven together; bone, sinew, skin. The hands of God hidden from sight, working from the spirit outwards with absorbed tenderness, creating toes, shoulders, shaping the cranium, the long curve of the spine, the delicate intricacies of the lungs. Not to be despised, a human being, in all its weakness and helpless desire, its clumsiness and frailty. A thing of beauty, a work of God's hands. I glanced up at Mother, but I felt shy to put into words the things that were stirring in my soul. Instead, I said, 'I'll never look at a candle flame in the same way again!'

She smiled. 'No,' she said, 'but you'll look at it more attentively.'

VI
GOD'S WOUNDS

Mother and I walked slowly up the hill to church. It was a warm, still evening. The sun was sinking behind the trees. Their leaves had begun to turn yellow and a few were falling. Our church was built on the edge of the common land that led up to the cliffs, on the outskirts of the town; a little oasis of countryside undisturbed by the spread of housing estates.

The bell was tolling slowly for Evensong as we strolled along the church path, and the tower clock chimed the half-hour as we settled into our pew. Mrs Crabtree was there, and the Misses Forster, elderly twins who dressed the same in pale green macintoshes and grey suede shoes. Two rows in front of us sat Mr and Mrs Edenbridge, very upright and correct. She was very smart, as always, in a coat with a fur collar and a rather expensive hat. He was immaculately turned out in his grey suit, the bald dome of his head, above the snow white hair that fringed it, shining pink in the lamplight. Across the aisle, Stan Birkett the dustman was hurrying into his pew as Father Bennett swept out of the vestry, paused to bow ceremoniously to the altar, and then turned to face us, booming, 'Hymn number three hundred and eighty-one: "Crown him with many crowns." Hymn number three eight one.'

That was an ambitious hymn for Evensong, long and loud. I was glad Mrs Crabtree was sitting in front of us and not behind us as the congregation started to sing, and the enthusiastic dissonance of her voice made itself felt.

> Crown him with many crowns,
> The Lamb upon his throne ...

A late wasp droned lazily across the church, its aimless, floating path carrying it to the pew in front of us. It settled there and walked about a bit. It stopped to wash its face.

> Ye who tread where he has trod,
> Crown him the Son of Man,
> Who every grief hath known
> That wrings the human breast,
> And takes and bears them for his own ...

The wasp took off again, drifting towards the front of the church. Its flight carried it up towards Mr Edenbridge's right shoulder, and he suddenly became aware of its buzzing. He must have been one of those people who are afraid of wasps, because in instinctive recoil, he ducked his head and gave a little, hoarse, hastily-muffled cry, flapping his hymnbook at his shoulder. The wasp veered away, and dropped from view into the pew behind him. Mrs Edenbridge, who stood on her husband's left, was looking at him in surprise. He, oblivious to her astonishment, continued peacefully with the singing of the hymn:

> His glories now we sing,
> Who died and rose on high;

> Who died, eternal life to bring
> And lives that death may die.
>
> Crown him the Lord of peace …

The wasp arose from the pew again, ascending behind Mr Edenbridge's head. He could hear it, but not see it. He spun round in panic, beating the air about his head with his hymnbook. His wife stared at him in amazement. The wasp had changed course and was now sitting quietly on a pillar.

Mr Edenbridge resettled his glasses on his nose and glanced at his wife. 'Wasp,' he mouthed, silently. 'Wasp.'

She looked at him in blank incomprehension. Father Bennett, aware of an undercurrent of commotion among his flock, was eyeing Mr Edenbridge with disfavour over the top of his hymnbook.

'Wasp! Wasp! There's a wasp!' whispered Mr Edenbridge loudly to his wife, who was rather deaf. She look around, looked down behind her, looked behind him. He too began to look around for the wasp. It was nowhere in sight.

Then it came sailing across in front of Mrs Edenbridge, and she jumped backwards in alarm. Mr Edenbridge lashed out at it hysterically with his hymnbook, but it dodged him and flew away.

> Crown him the Lord of love;
> Behold his hands and side—
> Rich wounds yet visible above,
> In beauty glorified …

'Hrrmph!' Mr Edenbridge cleared his throat, and applied himself to the hymn again. He had seen Father Bennett watching him, suspiciously.

> All hail Redeemer, hail!
> For thou hast died for me;
> Thy praise shall never, never fail
> Throughout eternity!

The wasp was sitting innocently on the rim of the lamp overhead, washing itself.

'Dearly beloved ...' began Father Bennett in forbidding tones. I picked up the prayer book and looked hard at the words of the prayer, quelling with an effort the giggles rising inside me.

'Whatever was the matter with Mr Edenbridge tonight?' asked Mother as we walked down the church path afterwards. I looked back up the path. Father Bennett, standing on the doorstep to bid his congregation 'Goodnight' as they departed, was offering Mr Edenbridge a distinctly cool handshake.

'Oh, Mother, didn't you see it? There was a wasp!'

'Is *that* what it was? No, I was concentrating on the hymn. It's one of my favourites: "Rich wounds yet visible above, in beauty glorified." I love that one. So it was a wasp. Poor man. Father Bennett was looking rather sourly at him by the end of the hymn.'

'Father Bennett couldn't see it. Mother, will you tell me a story? There's time, walking home.'

'All right then. I'll tell you a story if you make me a cup of tea when we get in.'

'Mother! I always do!'

'I always tell the stories. Have I told you Brother James' story? No? I didn't think so. He wasn't Brother James yet, at the time of this story. It was before he took his first vows. His name was Allen Howick. It was singing that hymn tonight that reminded me of this story. It's about the wounds of Christ.'

Allen Howick was born in the year 1295, and throughout his childhood was loved—adored even—as the only child of his father and mother. He grew up into a fine, handsome, young man, whose mother denied him nothing, and whose father, a silversmith, a master craftsman, intended to bequeath to his son all his treasure, all his skill and all his business acumen. Allen

enjoyed a privileged status in the small society in which
he lived (the parish of St Alcuin's on the edge of the
Yorkshire moors, served from the Benedictine abbey of
that name). He was a wealthy, well-fed, well-favoured
young man. By his twentieth year, he was a much
coveted prize as a husband, and there were no fewer
than five lasses making sheep's eyes at him at Mass on
Sundays and dreaming about him in bed at night. In
short, he was a big fish in a small pool, thoroughly
spoiled and wanting for nothing. He had everything.
Life had nothing left to give him that he hadn't already
got, and he was peevish, discontented and bored. The
village lasses, eager to win him as a husband, had tried to
put a little on deposit by securing him as a lover. He'd
had them all and they were nice, but he had to confess,
with a certain sense of amazement, that even sex bored
him now.

He came up early to Mass, one Sunday morning. He
was out of sorts and more than a little hung-over from a
party the previous night. It had been his birthday and
he had celebrated in style. Now he had twenty years
behind him and a foul taste in his mouth.

One of the brothers (it was Brother Francis) was
opening the great doors of the abbey church as Allen
walked up the stone steps. Allen had never really
noticed Brother Francis before, but he supposed he
must always have been there. Francis, on the other
hand, well knew Allen and his family, knew it had been
his birthday and was surprised to see him out of bed at
all. One glance told him what Allen had been doing the
night before and that its legacy this morning was a thick
tongue and a muzzy head. He grinned at him. 'Fine
morning,' he said pleasantly. 'Been celebrating?'

There was something in the innocent enquiry that
caused Allen to look at him suspiciously. He flushed
slightly, put on his dignity by the twinkle in Brother
Francis' eye.

'Yes, if it's any of your business,' he retorted, and stalked past him into the church.

He sat hunched up in his family bench, and watched Francis as he walked purposefully up the aisle, his cheerfulness evidently undented by Allen's rudeness. Francis disappeared through a door in the north wall of the church, and Allen was left on his own.

The spring sunshine streamed gloriously through the great window at the eastern end of the church, and he could hear birds singing. From further away the bleating of sheep carried on the wind. Otherwise, all was quiet. Allen looked around the huge, empty building. Usually among the last to arrive and the first to leave, he had never been there on his own before. Lord, but it's peaceful here, he thought, as he gazed about him. Wonder how much it cost to build it?

As he rested in the great hollow shell of tranquility and light, listening to its silence, it dawned upon him that 'empty' was the wrong word for this place. It was as full as could be: full of silence, full of light, full of peace. There was something about it that was almost like a person. It had—almost—its own speech. He lost the sense of it as people began to arrive in dribs and drabs, and the speaking silence was erased by their murmured conversation, the creak of the benches, the occasional stifled laugh, the shuffle and tap of shoes on the flagged floor.

The Mass was attended by the well-to-do and the respectable; farmers and merchants for the most part. They came in their Sunday finery, their wives on their arms, their sons and daughters around them. Their servants were expected to attend first Mass at five o'clock, and were busy making Sunday dinners and doing the household chores by this hour of the day.

Allen's parents came into the church and sat down beside him. It was not like him to be early to Mass, but they knew better than to ask questions. Rosalind

Appleford, the wool merchant's daughter, shot a coquettish glance in Allen's direction as she passed. 'God give you good morning, Allen Howick,' she whispered, pouting her lips just a little for his benefit. Allen raised a wan smile, then looked the other way. His obvious rejection stung her, and Rosalind began to regret last Wednesday evening, which she had spent in his arms.

'*Dominus vobiscum*,' the cantor raised his voice in the chant.

'*Et cum spirito tuo*,' responded the brothers in the choir, and the people of the parish in the nave.

Allen yawned. He found the Mass tedious. It was a question, in the main, of trying to avoid reproachful feminine eyes and enduring pangs of hunger. He sat or stood or knelt with everyone else through the rite of penance, the liturgy of the word, the abbot's homily; but his mind was sunk in indifference, in the contempt of familiarity.

'*Pax Domine sit semper vobiscum.*'

'*Et cum spirito tuo*,' responded Allen automatically. Then, like a far away song, like a weak shaft of sunlight on a December day, something roused in his soul. '*Pax Domine sit semper vobiscum.* The peace of the Lord be always with you.' Peace. Peace. He thought of the huge serene peace of the building as he had sat waiting for the people to arrive. Was it then possible to have that vast peace *inside you*? He had always assumed the words of the Mass to be a polite ritual, designed to humour a remote deity, keep him happy, keep him remote. But this—'the peace of the Lord be always with you'—this invited the far-off God right *in*. Peace. Allen was not sure what peace was. He was not sure if he'd ever known it. He wondered vaguely if his father would permit him to convert the guest bedroom into a chapel, maybe pay the abbey to send one of the monks there to say Mass for him, so he could have that peace on hand, at home when he wanted it. It would be good to spend a spare moment sitting in the quiet, enjoying the peace of God.

One of the lads from the abbey school was singing the *Agnus Dei*, his voice trembling slightly in the dread of public performance.

'*Agnus Dei, qui tollis peccata mundi, dona nobis pacem.* Lamb of God, who takes away the sins of the world, give us your peace.' Allen felt as though something was wringing the inside of him. Suddenly, angrily, hungrily, he knew he didn't have peace. He had everything else, but he didn't have peace. He thought of Brother Francis; that cheerful, purposeful manner, unmoved by his own surliness. Peace, yes, it sat about that monk like it clung to the stones of these walls. How had he come by that peace? What had it cost him to get it?

Allen went up with the straggle of communicants and took the bread on his tongue, the body of Christ. 'Give me your peace,' he prayed. Sitting on the bench through the final prayers the words repeated in his mind: 'Oh Lamb of God, who takes away the sins of the world, give us your peace.'

He spoke to no one as he left the church and walked home. All his life, whatever he wanted, he had asked the price and it had been his. What was God asking for his peace? Lamb of God, you take away the sin of the world ... that, it seemed, was his price. He wanted Allen's sin, in return for his peace. It seemed like an easy bargain. Allen thought over the past week. Wednesday night with Rosalind. Well, that was sin. Pleasant, but sin. He thought of his party the night before ... luxury, drunkenness ... the wasted food thrown to the dogs. In fact, the more he thought about it, the harder it was to think of anything in his life that did not bear the taint of sin. Did God want the whole of it, then, before he would part with his peace?

Allen was irritable all that day. He slept little

that night, and on Monday morning sat pale, moody and silent at his workbench in his father's shop.

'What's biting you?' asked his father, as he set out his tools at his own bench. 'You look like a jilted lover.' He glanced questioningly at Allen. Maybe one of the lasses had made her mark. It was about time. He picked up the trinket he was working on, and bent his head over it.

'It's not that,' he said. As he looked at his father, Allen felt a fluttering of apprehension. What he was about to say was unlikely to be well received. 'It's not that,' he repeated, a little louder. There was an edge to his voice that his father had not heard before, and Master Howick looked with attention at his son. Allen cleared his throat nervously.

'I'm going to be a monk at St Alcuin's,' he said.

His father stared at him in disbelief. 'You've lost your wits,' he said at last.

Allen shook his head. 'No.' His father was still staring at him, waiting for him to explain.

'I want God's peace,' Allen said, feeling foolish.

'God's peace? Can't you have it here at home? It's free, isn't it?'

'Is it? Have you got it?'

His father blinked. 'Me? Yes, of course. Well, I don't know. Peace? I never thought about it.'

There followed two weeks of arguments and scenes, but in the end Allen's determination overrode his mother's tears and his father's hurt bewilderment. His heart was set on the monastic life, and he meant to have it, as he'd had everything else he took a fancy for.

Allen went to see the abbot. He did not enjoy the interview. Trained to the craft of the silversmith, Allen's hands were dexterous and precise tools, and he found the sight of the abbot's maimed, almost useless hands disturbing, revolting. The long scar that extended all down the side of his face looked horrible too, and his jerky gait as he limped along with the aid of a battered wooden crutch, the foot of it padded with leather to silence its tapping progress, reminded Allen of the bogey-man of his mother's nursery tales. His wounds and the fierce hawklike look of his face, with its dark eyes that seemed to pierce a man to the soul, frankly terrified Allen, but he made his request and was told that he, like any young man, was welcome to try the life.

So Allen Howick kissed his girlfriends goodbye, and dutifully embraced his parents. He would prefer to walk up to the abbey alone, he said. There was nothing to be gained from their company. He turned, embarrassed, from his mother's tears, and filled with an almost intolerable mixture of elation and dread, he walked away.

His mother and father watched him go, their only child.

'It's worse than if he'd died,' his mother whispered. 'How did we fail him? We gave him everything.'

'Not peace,' replied her husband, with heavy sarcasm.

Their son turned the corner of the road without looking back.

Allen found life at St Alcuin's gruelling. The night prayers, the meagre food, the hard work and the silence all combined to make him irritable and weary beyond endurance. The other young men in the novitiate, Brother Damien and Brother Josephus, had both taken their first vows and seemed to know their way about and behaved with an easy nonchalance that grated on Allen's strained nerves. He could not wear the habit of the order until he too took his novitiate vows, but he was given a plain, coarse, black tunic similar to the brothers' clothes to wear, and his own soft wool and fine linen were given into Brother Ambrose's care, in case he should change his mind and leave. Neither a brother nor the worldly lad he had been, Allen was alone in a no man's land between two worlds. Father Matthew, the novice master, he hated. Allen had never bothered much with his studies, knowing that his passage in life was assured, and he felt degraded by Father Matthew's detection and scrupulous exposure of his academic and spiritual weaknesses. The bitterest pill of all was the very public business of confessing his faults, kneeling on the ground, begging the brothers' forgiveness for such trifling matters as offending against holy poverty by losing his handkerchief.

He lay at night, sleepless on the rock-hard straw bed. 'Peace!' the night mocked him, astir with Brother Thaddeus' earth-shattering snore and Brother Basil's troublesome cough, and the gibberish mumblings of Brother Theodore's dreams; 'Peace!'

In spite of it all he sensed something. He didn't know quite what it was, because he didn't have it himself, but he sensed something in some of these men: an assurance, humour, tranquillity—hang it, peace! How did they get it? Allen ached for it.

He could feel it in the abbot, though he was afraid of him. He could not analyse it. In the brief moments of the one or two occasions he had dared to return the gaze of those dark grey eyes, Allen had glimpsed unfathomable depths of sadness, resignation, warmth ... a mixture of things, and behind them all an extraordinary vital gladness that didn't fit with the lameness and disfigurement. Somewhere, Allen reflected, as he worked in silence at his task of book-binding, that man is saying 'yes' where I am saying 'no'. But yes to what?

'How did Father Columba get his scars?' he asked Brother Josephus one evening as they sat in the novitiate community room for the hour's recreation after supper. He had been only eleven years old when the abbot was crippled and his hands were broken, and he had not been interested in the village gossip of adult life in those days.

'Who? Oh, Father Peregrine. He was beaten up by

enemies of his father's house eight—no nine—years ago.'

Allen digested this information. He wanted to ask another question, but hated to look uninformed. His curiosity got the better of him eventually: 'Why do you all call him Father Peregrine?'

Brother Josephus grinned. 'Well—does he look like a hawk or a dove?'

'What?'

'Columba—his name in religion—it's the Latin word for a dove. After Saint Columba, of course, but that's what it means. His baptismal name was Peregrine.'

Allen thought about it. 'He ... he scares me,' he admitted, surprising himself with his own truthfulness.

Brother Josephus looked at him in astonishment. 'Father Peregrine scares you? Why?'

Allen began to regret his honesty. 'I—I feel as though he can look right into my heart,' he mumbled.

Brother Josephus laughed. 'It's not him you're scared of then. You're scared that what's hidden in your heart will be found out. What are you hiding?'

Allen stared at him for a moment then looked away. 'I think I'll go down early to chapel and be in good time for Compline,' he said stiffly, and made his escape.

In the choir, one or two of the brothers knelt in prayer in the twilight gloom. Father Peregrine was sitting in his stall, the scarred face shadowed by his cowl, his maimed hands resting still in his lap. Allen couldn't tell if his eyes were open or closed. He hurried to his own place and knelt there. The silence of the choir seemed oppressive, a great, swollen stillness, weighing down on him. He was glad when, ten minutes later, the bell began to ring for Compline and the community filed in and filled the shadows with the music of their chant.

Then, silence again, the deep, deep silence of the night, the Great Silence that took a man down with it and would not let him ignore the doubts and fears that daylight business crowded out.

Allen slept fitfully, as always, and felt bone-tired in the morning. After first Mass he trailed up the stairs to the novitiate schoolroom. Father Matthew greeted him with the information that Father Abbot wished to see him that morning to discuss his progress. Allen turned round and plodded back through the scriptorium where the scribes were already busy with their copying and illumination work, and down the day stairs to the cloister. He met Brother Theodore on the stairs. One of the fully-professed brothers beyond the small world of the novitiate, Allen didn't know Theodore very well, but the quick appraisal of Theodore's glance discovered his weariness, and there was something comforting in the smile he gave Allen as he passed.

Allen was relieved to have escaped a morning studying the latest arguments for and against pre-destination, but he was not looking forward to being alone with the abbot. He hesitated outside the door of the abbot's lodging, which was as usual ajar, then knocked. He walked into the large, sparsely furnished room and shut the door behind him. The abbot was at his table, reading through some documents.

'A moment, and I shall be with you, my son,' he said, and glanced up at Allen momentarily. Then he looked up again, his attention arrested. 'Faith, boy, you look weary. Don't sit on that stool. Fetch the chair from the corner there. You need something to lean on, by the look of you. I won't keep you but a minute.'

Allen fetched the chair and sat on it, watching Father Peregrine's face as he finished the perusal of his documents and then put them aside. The abbot smiled at him, and the kindness of his smile, in that fierce, uncompromising face, took Allen by surprise.

'Well? Hard going?'

The frank sympathy with which he spoke brought

sudden, completely unexpected tears to Allen's eyes. Hard going? By all holy, it was hard going! He blinked the tears away furiously, but didn't trust himself to speak. He stared hard at the inkstand on the table, determined not to betray his exhaustion and turmoil.

'My son, why did you come?' asked Father Peregrine, quietly. That, at least, Allen could answer, and the moment perilously close to tears was over.

'I came to find God's peace,' he replied.

The abbot nodded. 'Have you found it?'

Allen looked at him, wearily. This man could see right into him. He could see that, couldn't he?

'You know I haven't found it.'

'Do you want to go on looking, or have you had enough?'

Allen thought. To go home ... home to a good fire, a soft bed, a bath whenever he wanted one. Home to his mother seeing to all his needs, to lying abed in the mornings sometimes ... to an undisturbed night's sleep.

'But if I go now ...' Allen paused. 'Well, where would I go? I can't spend the rest of my life walking away from it, can I? I couldn't bear it. I don't ... I don't really feel as though I have a choice. Apart from that, yes, I've had enough. More than enough.' He felt the lump rise in his throat again and thought he'd better stop talking.

'If it's any consolation,' said Father Peregrine, 'which it may not be, I felt very much as you do. And ... God turns no one away. He will give you the peace you crave.'

Allen leaned forward in his chair. 'When did you— how did you find it?'

The abbot smiled. 'It'll give you little comfort if I tell you. I found the peace of God, really, surely, for always found it, just nine years ago. I was forty-seven. And I wouldn't recommend anyone to find it the way I did.'

Allen looked at him in horror. 'Forty-seven!'

Father Peregrine laughed at him. 'I'll pray for you,

my son, every day, until you find the peace of God. I know what it is to hunger for it, believe me.'

He talked to Allen a little longer, asked some more questions, let him talk a while, then said, 'Father Matthew will be chiding me if I keep you longer from your instruction. He says ... he feels you can do with as much schooling as you can get.'

'Thank you, Father.' Allen got to his feet, and returned the chair to its corner. He felt obscurely encouraged. This rather alarming man seemed to know, and care, how he felt.

'Forty-seven,' he said as he put the chair down. 'God's wounds, that's a long time to wait.'

He turned towards the door.

'Just a minute.'

Allen looked back at the abbot, and was startled. Father Peregrine's eyes were ablaze with anger, his mouth set like a trap. He looked furious. Allen's jaw dropped. He stared in astonishment.

'If I *ever* hear you speak of the wounds of Christ again with such blasphemous levity, I will have you flogged, I give you my word.'

'Oh. Sorry,' said Allen, stupidly.

'That is not how we say it here,' replied his abbot, still angry but not quite so furious.

Allen knelt hastily on the stone floor. 'I humbly confess,' he said, as he had learned to do, 'my—my blasphemy. I ask your forgiveness Father, and God's.'

'No doubt God forgives you, and so do I. Now get up off your knees and hear this.' The abbot was still very angry. Allen stood up bewildered. Whatever had got into the man? It was only a figure of speech.

'Christ Jesus your God,' said Peregrine, fixing him with the fierce eyes that had made most of the brethren quail at one time or another, 'was mocked by the Roman soldiers. They blindfolded him and beat him with sticks, laughing at him, saying, "Who hit you then, prophet?"

They stripped him naked and then dressed him up as a king. They crowned him with a cap of thorns. They flogged him until he bled, and they had him carry his cross on that bleeding back through the streets of Jerusalem until he fell under it. He lay on the torn skin of his back on the cross, and stretched out his arms and suffered the soldiers to hammer nails through his wrists. Nails that hurt him so ... that convulsed his hands into claws. Have you ever wounded your hands, boy?'

Allen shook his head. He had never wounded anything, beyond the grazed knees of childhood.

'It is *hideous* pain. It is *agony*. Do you remember what he said—Jesus—the words he prayed as they hammered nails into his hands on the cross? Well? What did he say—or have you forgotten?'

Allen moistened his lips nervously. 'He said, "Father forgive them."'

'Yes. Would you have said such a thing in that moment? No. Well may you shake your head in silence. Nor would I. Five years, ten years later maybe, but not then. The pain of it ... I would ... I would have begged, not for their forgiveness, but in terror, for mercy. I ... did. They hoisted him up on the cross. A crucified man, my son, dies of suffocation from the weight of his own body. Three hours he hung there, shifting his weight from the nails through his feet to the nails through his wrists, scraping his flayed back on the wood of the cross. He did it because he loved us. He chose it, wanted it. It was the price of our peace. I say again: if I *ever* hear you make light of his wounds with your blasphemy, I will have you beaten until your back bleeds as his bled, and leave you to imagine the rest.'

'Father, I'm sorry. I didn't mean to offend you. I didn't think. I ...'

'Whatever have you been thinking about while you've been here then?' Peregrine roared at him. Allen stood, silent.

'Well? What have you been thinking about?'

Allen felt as small and scared as a five-year-old. His well-fed, well-dressed, handsome, popular self seemed as far away and unreal now as something from a dream. Trembling in his coarse black robe in the blaze of this frightening man's indignation, he felt utterly wretched.

'I suppose,' he said, in a very small voice, 'I've been thinking about myself.'

'Tell me then,' said Peregrine, the quietness of his voice no more reassuring than the roar of the moment before, 'about yourself.'

Allen felt a trickle of sweat run down his back. Whatever was he supposed to say? The dark, fierce eyes were holding him, compelling him.

'I thought if I gave God my sin, he would give me his peace. It says it in the Mass, that the Lamb of God who takes away the sins of the world gives us peace. But—all my life seemed to be sin. I gave it to him by coming here.'

'So. That is what you thought and what you did; but you, tell me about you. You, whom Christ died for. You've been thinking about yourself, you say. Tell me then.'

Allen looked at him helplessly. 'I don't know what to say.' The abbot's silence gripped him like a huge pair of hands, and shook him.

'I ...' he began huskily, 'I used to think of myself as something special. My mother and father dote on me. I had everything: clothes, money, horses, everything I wanted. Women, too. There were several ... five—there were five girls. I used them shamelessly for my pleasure. I used my parents too. There was not ... never has been ... any gratitude in me. Nor reverence. Nor respect. But I didn't see it. You want to know what I am? I couldn't have told you until now. I'm a spoiled brat.'

He stopped, caught unawares again by the lump in his throat and the tears in his eyes.

'Thank you for answering my question,' said the abbot. 'As far as I can see you have answered it truthfully. You can go, then.'

Allen looked at him in horror. The tears threatened to overflow. Don't leave me like this, he wanted to plead. You've stripped me of everything. I can't face the brothers in the shame of this nakedness.

Father Peregrine met his look, looked right into him. Allen had never met a man who could look at him like that, unwavering, unembarrassed, without any inhibition at all.

'If you're going to weep, weep,' said the abbot. 'All of us do, sooner or later. You can forget any foolish notions you may have about your personal dignity when you stand as you are before Christ. Weep, then. Let him heal you of your ingratitude, and your heartless abuse of love, and your using us to achieve your own selfish spiritual ends.'

Allen wept. The bluntness of the rebuke pushed him off the edge of the composure to which he had been so precariously clinging, and he fell down and down into the loneliness of his shame. First reluctantly, then miserably, then in an abandonment of shame and disgust, he faced himself and his own sin. Not even a villain, much less a hero, just a conceited, self-centred, ungrateful lad; unexceptional, lazy and spoiled. All his vanity and artificial dignity crumbled into ruins about him, leaving him wide open, unsupported, undressed. The world he had always known seemed to draw away from him, until he stood in a great empty tract of desolation. The nothingness, the falsity of all he was, bled out of him until it filled the vast, bleak desert of his loneliness, and he was engulfed in emptiness, hopelessness; lost. There was nothing left but the abandonment of his sobbing, which embarrassed him in its uncontrolled noisiness, until not even that mattered any more.

He had never felt so alone in his life, as he stood in the middle of the stone floor in the great, comfortless room hearing the noise of his weeping, hot tears coursing down his face, consumed in loathing of himself and all he had been. All the while he was aware of the presence of the abbot, neither condemning nor consoling him, watching and understanding the depths of his shame, such utter abasement, such a seeing of his own sin and strutting foolishness. Even to be stripped naked and stood in the market-place to endure the sniggers of passers-by would not have exposed him as the roots of his soul were now exposed. It felt as if it would never stop. He would have thought it was unbearable, except that he was too filled with shame to think anything about it at all.

'Help me.' The words came out brokenly, indistinctly, through his tears. He was unsure if he was addressing the abbot or God. Neither of them answered him, and in the end came the weary misery of the moment when his weeping had finished and there was nothing to do but find his handkerchief and blow his nose, dry his eyes and raise his head at last to meet the eyes of the man who sat in silence watching him. He was no longer sure what he was, who he was. Gutted of all that he had affected, all that he had taken for granted, he had nothing left but his wretchedness, his tired, hungry body, the coarse simplicity of the tunic that clothed him and the distressed unevenness of his breath. So he allowed his eyes to meet the abbot's grey eyes, and saw there profound sadness, and deep kindness, and a compassion that clothed him again, gave the nakedness of his soul some protection against the harshness of pain and humiliation. Allen drew in his breath and let it go in an exhausted sigh. He drank in the comfort of the abbot's compassion, of his evident understanding, but he could think of no words to say now. He could not begin to know how to move forward from the holocaust he had fallen into and start to live again; speak, act, move.

'Sit down,' said Father Peregrine. He picked up the wooden crutch and got to his feet. 'Sit down and gather yourself together again. Wait for me here. I'll not be long.'

Allen watched him as he limped across the bare austere room, his jerky gait, the awkwardness of his twisted hands as he leaned on the crutch and with both hands grappled with the great iron handle of the door. It occurred to Allen that this man had good reason to understand humiliation, and was well acquainted with suffering. Formidable he might be, but the most imposing man in the world would be overwhelmed at times by that level of disablement. While he was wondering whether to help him, Peregrine conquered the door handle, and glanced across the room at Allen before he went out. Allen's soul, stripped and washed clean, was still plain in his eyes, as clear and clean as a new sheet of parchment ready for use. The first thing written there was concern for Peregrine as he struggled with the door. Nothing patronising; insight. There was a flash of understanding between them as their eyes met again. Each had glimpsed the other's humiliation, met it with compassion, felt it as his own.

'Wait for me,' said Peregrine again, and left Allen sitting alone, trying to make sense of all that he had just been through. It was as though he had just crossed the rapids of a turbulent, flooding, wild river, and was cut off for ever from the further bank on which he had lived his whole life until now. He felt as tender and naked as a newborn; as exposed as a creature that had lived all its days underground and then found itself astonishingly, painfully, in the air and dizzy light of the mountains. No doubt about it, it was a costly, hurting thing. His soul, used to covert ways and sly disguises was sore in the breeze and brightness of its new climate, but

... there was something about the very pain of it that was more exhilarating than anything he had found in the comfort and ease that had padded his life so far. Allen gave up trying to understand it, and waited, wrapped in a sort of light-headed tranquillity of exhaustion.

It was not long before the door opened again, and Father Peregrine entered, with Brother Cormac in his wake carrying a large slab of pigeon pie and a mug of ale. Cormac glanced round the room and, locating Allen in his chair in the corner, brought the food over to him. He looked down at Allen's blotched and swollen face with a cheerful grin. 'Hungry?' he said. Hungry? Allen was becoming so accustomed to feeling hungry that he had almost ceased to notice it, but as he caught the smell of the food, he felt ravenously hungry, and his mouth watered for it.

He devoured the pie and downed the ale, which was not diluted this once, with single-minded absorption, while Brother Cormac chatted comfortably to Father Peregrine about the progress of planting in the vegetable gardens behind the kitchen.

'Thank you,' said Allen gratefully, as he gave the plate and mug back to Cormac, having chased up every crumb of pastry and drained every drop of ale. Brother Cormac took them with a smile, and there was something in his look which made Allen feel that here was someone else who understood very well indeed what he had been through, and knew just what it felt like. Allen returned his smile, wondering fleetingly if it was in this that brotherhood and peace had their roots, the losing of everything.

Father Peregrine had returned to his chair behind the table with its untidy heaps of books and parchments. 'Thank you, Brother,' he said to Cormac as he disappeared with the crockery, then he turned his attention back to Allen. Allen felt as warmed and fed by the kindness of that look as he was by the pie and ale that comfortably filled his belly.

'Now go to bed,' said the abbot, 'and go to sleep. Sleep all you need. Get up when you're rested.'

Allen looked at him in amazement. His whole body longed for sleep, *ached* for sleep, but he couldn't quite believe his ears.

'But—Father Matthew ...' he said doubtfully at last.

'Father Matthew is not the ogre he seems. Nor, incidentally, am I. Leave me to speak to Father Matthew. You go to bed.'

Allen went to his cell and collapsed in sweet relief onto his hard bed. He felt drained and utterly spent, and he fell asleep instantly.

He was woken by the Office bell. He went down the night stairs to the choir, to discover to his amazement that it was time, not for the midday Office, but for Vespers. It was nearly supper-time. He had slept all day.

Brother Francis was the reader for the day. It seemed a long, long time since that Sunday morning when Allen had met him at the church door before Mass. He was reading from the book of Isaiah.

'*Ipse autem vulneratus est propter iniquitates nostras, attritus est propter scelera nostra; disciplina pacis nostra super eum, et livore ejus sanati sumus.* He was pierced through for our transgressions, crushed for our iniquities. Upon him was the punishment that brought us peace, and by his wounds we are healed.'

Allen felt as though the words were turning him inside out. Now he was rested and fed, he was able to look beyond the confusion of misery and shame that weariness and hunger had compounded into abject desolation.

'Upon him was the punishment that brings us peace, and by his wounds we are healed.' Timidly, hungrily, humbly, Allen's spirit reached up, yearned towards God. Wave upon wave upon wave of peace swept through him, cleansed him, comforted him, healed him. As he walked out of Vespers to the refectory for supper, he was bathed in peace, alight with peace, overflowing with peace.

Father Peregrine smiled as he watched him go.

After supper, Allen went up to the community room where he found Brother Josephus and Brother Damien. Brother Damien broke off his impersonation of Father Matthew discoursing on the beatitudes to look at Allen in amazement.

'God's wounds!' he said. 'Whatever happened to you?'

'Oh, don't say that,' said Allen. 'I'm sorry, I don't mean to sound like an abbot's chapter, but don't swear by God's wounds, Brother Damien. He ... they ... the wounds of Christ are the most precious thing the world ever saw. Don't make a blasphemy out of them.' He blushed, embarrassed and shy; it was so thoroughly unlike himself that the two young brothers stared at him.

'I'm sorry,' said Brother Damien, 'I didn't know it mattered that much to you.'

We had reached our house before Mother came to the end of her story, and sat down on the steps to finish it uninterrupted. We stayed a moment longer, without speaking, watching the splendour of the sun going down, and then both looked round as we heard the sound of the front door opening. It was Daddy, holding his car keys.

'Oh, there you are, you two. I thought you'd got lost; I was coming to look for you. What on earth are you doing there?'

Mother got up and smiled at him.

'Enjoying the peace,' she said. 'But I'm ready for a cup of tea.'

VII
HOLY POVERTY

Mother stood in the kitchen, reading through the letter Beth had brought in from school. She looked anxious and harassed as she glanced up and caught my eye. She waved the piece of paper at me.

'They never let up, do they? Beth's class is going on an outing to the estuary to see the geese and the other waterfowl, and just look how much money they want for the cost of the trip! Pocket-money recommended, for heaven's sake! Dear, oh dear, I don't know. She'd not get more than that for her birthday! What else? Some sensible outdoor shoes and a waterproof coat; a packed lunch and a warm jumper. Well, I can manage the lunch and the jumper, but she hasn't got a waterproof coat, and she's only got sandals. She hasn't grown out of those yet. I was hoping to wait until the weather gets a bit colder before I buy her winter shoes. If I get them now she'll outgrow them before the spring. Do your wellingtons still fit you, Beth?'

Beth shook her head glumly.

'No? Your feet must have grown, then. It doesn't show so much with sandals. Oh, goodness me, Melissa, she'll have to borrow your kagoul and roll the sleeves up. That's waterproof. All that money, though! Why, it's as much as it costs me to feed her for a week. How many children are there in your class? Thirty-two? They're going to spend all that money taking you to see some ducks on a puddle of water; and we live by the sea! What's wrong with seagulls, for heaven's sake? A whole month's housekeeping that would be for me.'

She sighed wearily. 'You'll have to wear your sandals and they can just lump it. You can take some spare socks in case you get yours wet. I suppose your class has an outing too, Mary, and Cecily's playschool. All right, never mind. You'll probably come home with a photo-copied outline of a duck to colour and a vivid memory of someone being sick on the bus, but I daresay your teacher has spotted some educational value in it that I can't see. Out you go into the garden to play for a little while. I'm not quite ready with tea yet.'

There was never any money to spare in our house. We had two meals a day, apart from our breakfast porridge, and bread featured very prominently in one, and potatoes in the other. Mary and Beth came home from school for dinner in the middle of the day, because Mother said she could feed them at home cheaper than either school meals or sandwiches. Daddy said Mother was the only cook he knew who had hit upon the novel idea of using meat as a garnish. Our clothes were almost always second-hand, and so were our books. The little ones had some money for sweets on Saturday, I did a paper-round for pocket-money and Therese worked on Friday evenings at a local supermarket, filling shelves. We didn't mind not having much money, but I hated Mother having to be anxious about school trips and new shoes, and getting through the last week of the month before Daddy was paid.

'It's all right,' she would say, 'but choosing between baked beans and toilet rolls defeats me. They go together, don't they?'

Worst of all were the weeks before Christmas, when she would be nearly in despair trying to get together enough Christmas presents for all our relatives and friends.

'What a *silly* way to celebrate Jesus, homeless in a manger,' she said crossly. 'Although, I don't know. We're more or less down to milk and hay ourselves by the time we've paid for all this lot.'

Yet somehow, we always managed. 'There is nothing in my life,' Mother said, 'that has taught me so much about the kindness of God and the reality of his love watching over us as not having enough money. He has never let us down. Never. Well, sometimes we have to ring up and say we'll pay next week, but nothing worse than that. I don't know what we'd do without him.'

'Without God?' Mary asked, puzzled. 'We couldn't do anything without God because we wouldn't be here at all.'

My mother was a resourceful woman, not easily defeated, but worrying about money was one of the few things that would reduce her to tears. More often though, when she was anxious, she would be bad tempered, irritable and sharp with us all. It was at the end of a week like that, that Beth's letter about the school outing came.

I got out the loaf of bread and the pot of blackberry jam for tea while Mother read through Beth's letter again.

'It's not bad really,' she said, 'and it's a month off yet. Perhaps she'll be able to have some shoes.'

'I wish we were a bit richer,' I said, getting the margarine and cheese out of the fridge, and bringing knives and plates to the table.

'I don't,' said Mother. 'I know it sounds odd, but I don't. I couldn't bear the thought of people who have no homes and are cold and hungry, if I always had enough. I know I get cross and upset about it, but I would be no better off for covering up my weakness with money. It's good for me to know the places where my soul falls down, and it's good to have to lean on God and ask for his help. I know it's not very nice for you when I'm ratty, but maybe it will help you to understand people better than you would have if you'd been too protected from the realities of life. There's another thing of peanut butter if you look at the back of the cupboard.' Mother poured tea into mugs for everyone except Mary and Cecily, who had glasses of milk. 'I know a story about poverty. I'll tell you it after tea, if you like. Call the girls in now. Where's Therese? In the living room? Oh, I didn't hear her come in.'

After tea, the three little girls had their bath, and then I read Cecily the story of the Great Big Enormous Turnip. Beth and Mary had heard that story too many times, so they went upstairs for a chapter of a book with Mother. Cecily made me laugh, her blue eyes getting rounder and rounder as I said, '. . . and they pulled and they pulled and they pulled and they *pulled* and they PULLED!' Without her realising it, her mouth was silently mimicking my mine as I spoke the words of the story.

'. . . and the little mouse came and pulled the cat, and the cat pulled the dog, and the dog pulled the little girl, and the little girl pulled the little boy, and the little boy pulled the old woman, and the old woman pulled the old man, and the old man pulled the *turnip*, and they . . .' I looked down at her, and she said the words with me: '. . . pulled and they pulled and they pulled and they *pulled* and they PULLED, and . . .' Cecily looked at me, her eyes dancing with delight. '*Up came the turnip*!' she shouted with me. 'And they all had turnip for tea, all of them, all of them. I hate turnip!'

I hugged her, but she wriggled free and raced upstairs to Mother. In the bedroom, Mother took her on her knee. 'Prayers, Cecily,' she said. Cecily put her hands together and shut her eyes so tightly that her face was trembling with the effort of keeping them shut.

'Gentle ...' Mother prompted.

'Jesusmeekandmildlookuponalittlechild,' gabbled Cecily. 'Pity ... pity ... pity mice ...'

'Pity my simplicity. Suffer me to come to thee,' Mother finished off for her. 'There, into bed.'

She drew the curtains and lit the candle as Cecily nestled into her bed. 'Go away, Cecily,' muttered Beth irritably as Cecily snuggled up against her.

'Lie still now,' said Mother. 'Ssh. I'll sing you a song.'

She sang them some songs, an Irish folk song and two hymns, and they were quiet and drowsy when she had finished.

'Story?' I said.

'Oh yes. About poverty. This is not a story about the sort of poverty where people are in rags or starving. It's about holy poverty, monastic poverty.' Mother laughed. 'I once knew a girl who went to stay with some Poor Clares in their monastery. She came back all big eyes saying, "They live in such poverty! They only have *one* towel in the bathroom."

'"It must get very wet," I said. "Oh, no," she said, "they've got lots of bathrooms." Yes, holy poverty is different from the ordinary sort. It's simplicity, really. Having a humble and frugal way of life for the sake of Jesus because he was poor and like a servant. To live in holy poverty is one of the three monastic vows. The hardship of holy poverty is almost the opposite of ordinary poverty. With the ordinary sort, the worst thing is having no choice, being trapped in it. With holy poverty, the hard thing is being faithful to it, having chosen it.'

'Anyway, this is the story. It's one that Father Peregrine's daughter Melissa used to love especially.'

'I 'ave brought a little cask of wine with me, mon père. Exquisite, beautiful wine. If one of your young men will bring it to your house, we will sample it together. I made the mistake of drinking your wine last time I was here, bon Dieu! Hedgerow vinegars made of every curious root and flower the wilderness spawns. Sacré bleu! Your father would turn in his grave to see what you have descended to! And the foul mixture you drink with your viands—your ale and water—ah, Lord have mercy! There is time enough for purgatory. I have no wish to begin it now.'

Père Guillaume from Burgundy had come to pay Father Peregrine a friendly visit while he was in England. The two of them were walking across the great court of the abbey from the guest house to the refectory, which was the point of entry into the cloister buildings. Brother Martin, the porter, watched them from the gatehouse with a smile as they went slowly across the court, for they made an extraordinary couple; Guillaume strolling in corpulent magnificence (twenty-one and a half stones, Brother Martin decided, would be a very conservative estimate), and Peregrine's spare, nowadays slightly stooping, frame jerking along with the aid of his wooden crutch. To Brother Richard, the fraterer, who had caught sight of their approach through the window of the refectory and opened the door for them, they presented an equally amazing sight. Père Guillaume's voice was suave and educated. His eyes took in everything around him with quick intelligence, missing nothing. Great waves of rich laughter rumbled up from his enormous gut, shaking his immaculately shaven chins as he took Peregrine to task for the severity of St Alcuin's simplicity. His elegant white hands gestured articulately as he spoke.

At first glance, Father Peregrine's ungainly figure seemed unlikely company for such a man. That Peregrine's ascetic preferences and the frugality of his house horrified the abbé was the first thing obvious from the words that rolled across the court before him in the deep and fruity accents of his confident voice; the voice of a man used to commanding, used to imposing, used to power. But as they drew closer, Brother Richard saw that there was more to it than that. Père Guillaume bent his head and listened with close attention to Father Peregrine's quiet replies, and looked sideways at him with a sort of fascinated respect. And well he might, thought Brother Richard, as he held the door open for the two abbots to pass into the refectory, looking at the lean, uncompromising lines of his superior's face, disfigured by its cruel scar, illumined by the disquieting penetration of the dark, direct grey eyes. Well he might.

Father Peregrine stood aside to allow his guest to precede him through the doorway. 'Mais non, après toi, mon ami. I must follow my betters!' The abbé stepped back, raising his hands in deprecation, then courteously but firmly put his hand to Peregrine's elbow, steering him ahead of him through the door.

Abbot Peregrine smiled his thanks at Brother Richard standing holding the door for them and Père Guillaume stopped to acknowledge him too: 'Ah, now; see how your sons love you, mon père! In my house they slam the door in my face. "Let the old pig root for his own truffles," they say. Yes, mon fils, 'tis true, I swear it!' He nodded at Brother Richard's startled face, then put a plump hand on his shoulder, the gold of his ring glinting in the sun that slanted through the doorway. 'I am jesting, maybe, but I speak the truth when I say that I am not loved as this abbot of yours is loved. The reign of God is in your love here. I love him too.' He patted Brother Richard's shoulder, and continued on his way into the room, where Peregrine stood waiting for him, watching Brother Richard's reaction with amusement. But the abbé stopped short. 'Mon Dieu!' he said, the sweeping gesture of his hand inviting them to look at their refectory. 'Look at the bare wood of this place! Have you no linen for your tables? Have you nothing

better than stone for your candlesticks? Ah, but they are
beautiful candles. I remember Frère Mark and his bees.
Beautiful candles! They tell me, mon père—can it be
true?—they tell me that these Englishmen are barbaric.
Come, you are a Frenchman, you can tell me if it is true!
They tell me it is impossible—but impossible—to stop
the English from wiping their knives and blowing their
noses on the tablecloths. It is true then, mon père. It
must be true, for you have taken their tablecloths away!'

He stood in the middle of the room, his eyes wide in
mock horror and amazement, his hands spread and his
eyebrows lifted in enquiry. Peregrine laughed at him.
'For sure it is true, but I didn't take them away. Our
novices stole them to enable them to escape over the wall
at night, driven to despair by the insupportable harshness of our regime. Come now and revile me in my own
house. Stop offending the silence of our cloister, Alas, I
have only bare wooden chairs to offer you there too, but
I see you've thoughtfully provided your own cushioning
as well as your own wine. Brother Richard, if you have a
moment to spare, would you be so kind as to bring us
from the guest house Père Guillaume's cask of wine? I
have nothing he can bear to drink. Even the water in
our well is rank, though it be sweet enough for our
degraded palates.'

'Ouf! Touché!' the abbé chuckled. 'Very well, then,
let us tiptoe across your cloister. Let me amaze you with
the revelation, we too keep silence every now and then. I
can bear to cease my chatter till we are within your
parlour.'

So saying, he folded his hands reverently within the
sleeves of his habit, and proceeded with regal dignity
along the cloister, his face composed into a grand
abbatial solemnity which went oddly with the gleam of
mischief in his eye.

Brother Richard brought the wine, and broached the
cask. He poured it out into the simple pottery beakers

that were all the abbey could boast for drinking vessels. Father Peregrine saw the expression on Père Guillaume's face as he looked at the beakers, and forestalled his comment. 'Guillaume, it *suits* us to make pots. It keeps our idle hands from mischief. We make them, and then because we are barbaric as you say, and have but the clumsy manners of peasants, we drop them and break them. Then we can make some more and it saves us from mischief again. If we drank from silver vessels, we should have nothing to do but drink all day, and nothing to drink anyway, but ale and water. Thank you, Brother Richard. Your very good health, my brother, my friend. May God unite us in peace.'

'Amen, mon ami. Bon santé!'

'Oh, but Guillaume, this *is* beautiful wine. You have brought me the best. I am not so boorish yet that I cannot appreciate this. It is *beautiful* wine!'

Abbé Guillaume smiled in satisfaction, and looked affectionately at his friend. 'I have looked forward with impatience to this visit with you, mon frère. I carry you in my heart, though I see you seldom. It is an honour to be your guest.'

There was a knock at the door, and Brother Tom entered quietly. Brother Richard had sent him: 'He has a guest, Tom. Someone important, I think. He may need you to wait upon them.'

Père Guillaume looked round to see who it was who had entered the room, and when he saw Brother Tom, he put down the beaker of wine which looked so incongruous in his elegant hand, and heaved himself to his feet.

'Frère Thomas! Mon ami! You remember me? You, I shall never forget, never! I see you as if it happens *now* before my eyes, standing like a prophet of God over that Augustinian snake, storming at him as the gravy dripped from his furious face. Ah, Sancta Maria, that was a moment to remember! Let me embrace you, mon fils!'

He enfolded Tom in a mighty hug, soundly kissed him on both cheeks and stood back with his hands on Tom's shoulders, beaming at him fondly.

'"I had rather be"—what was it? A beetle? Mais non, a cockroach! "A cockroach that crawls on the floor in the house where my abbot is master than be the greatest of those who serve under you!" Formidable, eh? I salute you, Frère Thomas. It does my heart good to see you again. May he have some wine, mon père? Is it permitted? Un tout petit peu?' He turned in enquiry to Father Peregrine, who hesitated.

'Truly, Guillaume, this is not how we usually spend the afternoon; but yes, why not. Sit down and share some wine with us, Brother.'

'Let me pour you some, mon fils, into this enchanting little pot. It is not at its best; it should settle, it should breathe, but never mind. Voilà. I have given some to your abbot, to draw the English damp out of his soul. The fog has penetrated him. He has become a little chill, a little grey. This will put the laughter back in his eyes— eh bien, look at him! You see! That frozen pond of austerity is melting at the edges. You will drink some more of my wine, mon père? But a little. Non? Un soupçon?'

'Guillaume, this will not do. You can afford to roll unsteady into the Office, but I lurch like a ship with the side stove in as it is. Leave me with a rag of dignity to cover my foolish soul. I'll not go down to choir drunk, breathing fumes of wine with every phrase I sing. Oh, don't look at me like that. I meant no rebuke. We'll drink some more wine over supper.'

Abbé Guillaume nodded mournfully. 'It is as I thought. You have seen through me. "'Ere is a man," you say to yourself, "with all the virtue of a cracked pot." Fear not, mon frère, the comparison suggests itself to me quite unbidden. There is nothing amiss with this one. "He has suffocated his spirit, which was, alas, noble, in folds of flesh, and I must be wary of the contamination of his gluttony. What is more, I must shield this young monk from the debauchery of his ways, and in no way seem to condone them." N'est-ce pas? Eh bien, tu as raison, mon ami. Your abstinence is my reproach.'

He smote his breast and hung his head sadly, then burst into roars of delighted laughter at Peregrine's discomfited silence.

'Ça va, mon ami, je comprends. I will leave you to your dreary labours until supper-time, but you must promise me then to put aside your dignity of office and be my companion, my old friend, not my judge. I have a conscience of my own to make me uneasy—yes, still, I swear it—I will not be needing to borrow yours. You have finished, Frère Thomas? How do you find my wine? Ah, it has lit in your eyes a little candle. Pleasant? Yes, I think so too. Perhaps your good abbot will send you to France to visit me one day. I have a whole cellar full. What did you say, mon père? What was that very ungracious muttering? You think not, is that it? Ah, well, Frère Thomas, you would have been welcome. Tant pis, uh?

'With your permission, mon père, I will feast on the delights of your library until Vespers. I will behave impeccably, as solemn and recollected as your extraordinary novice master. À bientôt. You will be with us later, Frère Thomas? Yes? Bon! You make an excellent cockroach! À bientôt.'

As the abbé left the room, taking his colour and laughter with him, and Brother Tom followed him out, Peregrine was left alone. The abbé reminded him of all the world he had left behind; the wealth and sophistication of his youth. To leave it all had seemed a clear call, to which he had responded with an unhesitating 'yes', but ... it was true, maybe he was a little chill, a little grey ... a bit negative, perhaps.

For the first time in years, his single-hearted conviction

wavered. Oh God, if it were all a hollow edifice, this life he had built. If the gamble of faith were a losing bet, and the temple he had made of his life prove only an echoing vault, an empty house of death; all the sacrifice of chastity, poverty, obedience be no more than frustration, denial, loneliness. He shook the doubts away. There was work to be done. He must go to the infirmary to spend an hour with the aged bedridden brothers. There he forgot himself for a while in their company and conversation, but his mood of uncertainty and uneasiness descended again as he made his way slowly to chapel before Vespers.

He sat in his stall in the choir, the abbot's stall, centrally placed in the position of dominance for the man who carried the weight of status and power. When first he had come here, there had been a certain thrill in occupying that place. Pride ... ambition, I suppose, he thought sadly as he sat there now. What a struggle it has been. What a struggle to fight the pride of my spirit on the one hand and the rebellion of my flesh on the other, and still to lead with confidence—to teach and shape the men given into my trust. He sat motionless, unblinking, looking back over the way he had travelled. What am I become now? he asked himself. The sour defender of my own crabbed asceticism? Is all that I have endured in the name of humility only the symptom of my own vain pride?

He thought of the merciless indifference with which he had driven himself in the early days: the hair shirts, the scourgings and fastings, the perverse satisfaction in his body's miserable craving for softness, for comfort, for pleasure, for tenderness. What was it for? And then, the bleak and barren desert in which he had fought to come to terms with his disablement, the grim tenacity with which he had striven to prove again his competence, his ability to rule, to lead.

He thought back on a day, one among many, when with a certain cruel detachment, he had very deliberately knelt to pray, brutally forcing the shattered knee to bend, letting the sickening waves of pain force his self-pity and distress into the background, so that the dizzy sweat of it hurting won a savage victory over threatening tears. Why? Systematically he had stripped the life of his community of all pretensions, all luxuries, all self-indulgence, seeking the poverty that God had promised to reward with the kingdom of heaven. He saw again the suffering of men he had held to his own standard: Brother Tom, half-frozen, prostrated on the threshold of the abbey in the biting winter dawn; Allen Howick, now Brother James, drowning in his shame, his poverty of being. 'I thought it was for you, my Lord,' he prayed uncertainly in an anguish of self-doubt. 'Was it not so? Was it the conceit of my spirit? If so, the most cowardly sensuality would have been a better choice. Let me not be a sham, my God. I had thought I had shaped a place of peace. I want your poverty.

'Oh, a pox on it all, I am tired of trying. Cling to me now, my God, for I have lost the will to cling to you.'

He tried to concentrate on the psalms, the prayers of Vespers; tried to ignore the insistent questions—'Why? Why? Why can I not be as Guillaume is, to laugh and drink and eat and forget? Why can I not forget the poverty of Gethsemane, of the cross? Nails! Nails! Oh my Jesus, my Lord . . . your love has won me . . . and how should I forget?'

At supper with Père Guillaume that evening, he toyed absently with his food, and he had little heart for conversation. Brother Tom, seeing his superior out of sorts, made himself as unobtrusive as possible as he waited on them. Père Guillaume observed his old friend shrewdly. He loved him. He had never understood his brooding intensity, but marvelled at his hunger for truth, for simplicity, for holiness. He tried to lift his friend's mood, to entice him out of his despondency, but without success. In the end he decided to take the bull by the horns.

'Is it your heart, your liver or your soul that is afflicted, mon frère? Your good brother has made us an excellent repast—these delicious little cheeses, this crisp salad—it is not all suffering under your roof. But you do not taste them. You are looking at your supper as if it has done you wrong, and you are pausing only to decide whether to flog it or excommunicate it. Will you not tell me what troubles your heart? You have the face of a thundercloud. You will give yourself indigestion.'

Peregrine did not reply. He tried to pick up his beaker of wine, but failed, as he often did, to straighten his fingers sufficiently to get them round the vessel. He gave up the attempt, and lifted it to his mouth with both hands. Brother Tom realised that both he and the abbé had stopped breathing as they watched him struggle and fail. Tom hurt for his abbot as he took the thing into his hands. I never knew a man hate his own weakness so much, he thought.

Peregrine looked at Père Guillaume over the rim of his beaker as he drank. The stormy intensity of his eyes made the abbé stir uneasily. They had been the best of friends from youth, but despite all the years he had known him, the depth of passion he saw in Peregrine's eyes still made Guillaume feel uncomfortable, almost afraid. Peregrine set down his wine and pushed his plate of food away.

'Guillaume, am I a posturing fraud?' he asked abruptly. 'No, don't smile at me. You have mocked me this day long for my efforts at holy poverty. What humility I have, I tell you straight, is too frail to bear the weight of many gibes.'

Abbé Guillaume looked at him with dawning comprehension. 'Ah, so *that* is what it is! Mon frère, I apologise. Would that I had the quickness of compassion you have, to see another man's distress. I had never intended that my idiot buffoonery cause you pain.'

'It's not your idiot buffoonery that hurts. That just

makes me laugh, and heaven knows I can be melancholy enough. You do me good. No, it's not that. It's the thought that all I had hoped was humility, might be no more than my own stiff-necked pride. That's what hurts. Am I a Pharisee, a—a shell of religion, a loveless hollow of vanity?'

'No,' said Brother Tom, very quietly. It was not his place to speak, but he couldn't help it.

'Ah! Listen to your cockroach!' said Père Guillaume. 'Let his wisdom comfort you! Speak, Frère Thomas.'

Peregrine looked up at Brother Tom. 'Yes, you may speak,' he said.

'I cannot presume,' Tom mumbled, self-conscious, 'to tell you what you are. All I can say is that I love you very much. Whatever you may be, it is not in me to love a man who is a proud hypocrite. And I think you should eat your supper.'

Father Peregrine smiled. 'Forgive me. I am behaving like a child. It is indulgent self-preoccupation on my part. Of your goodness, overlook my discourtesy. Your jesting has unsettled me, Guillaume, for you, as well as I, are vowed to holy poverty.'

'Mais oui, *holy* poverty. To renounce all ownership; to say the tunic on my back, the sandals on my feet are not mine—that is holy poverty. To own no estate, no gold or silver, to dress in simplicity and say of nothing, "This is mine,"—that is holy poverty. But the warmth of a good fire on a chilly night, the savoury juices of a sucking pig roast in honey, the delight of old, rich, red wine—these are the bounties of God's immense kindliness! Why should we throw them back in his face? Me, I do not like a leaking roof, or the draughty east wind whistling round my hams, or the lifeless frigidity of water at table. Mon Dieu, there must be some pleasure in life! Our flesh cries out for it!'

Peregrine did not reply at once; then, 'I thought we were supposed to crucify the flesh,' he said quietly.

'Ah, mon père, moderation! You ask too much! Your self-imposed penury is not holy poverty. It is like the poverty of the world. It is ...'

'Too much like the real thing, you mean?' interjected Peregrine wryly.

'Non, non, ce n'est pas ça ... you wallow in it, mon père. That's what it is.'

'Wallow in it?' Peregrine grimaced thoughtfully, pondering the words. 'I suppose I do. Jesus wallowed in it, did he not? To choose a stable, not a modest mansion; a cattle trough, not a plain, respectable crib; a cross, not a clean, unexceptional death-bed. How do you judge that? Was it an ostentatious waste of his glory? Does it matter? He said, "Follow me" and that I mean to do. Our life here is not the poverty of the cross. We do not pretend to it. We are not naked, we are not thirsty, we do not bleed, but we try at least to find the poor carpenter of Nazareth in all that we do—whatever the folly. You think it an unreasonable bargain to lay aside earth's pleasures to win heaven? But he laid aside heaven to win the sons of earth.'

Guillaume leaned back in his chair regarding Peregrine with amusement. 'You have not changed, mon ami. Your rhetoric is as impressive as ever. But you are wrong in one thing. You are too late to win grace, or heaven, or strike any kind of bargain with God. It is not a prize to be won, or a deal to be negotiated. It is a gift, already given. Tu comprends? A gift. Receive it and be glad. Celebrate a little now and then.'

'I ought not to have said we win heaven. It is, as you say, a gift. The free grace of God, the treasure of his love, precious beyond words, it is pure gift. We do know celebration here, Guillaume. I have seen men's faces alight with peace, with joy, content. Good, wholesome food, and enough of it, we have that. All right, it's a bit chilly, I grant you, and we are frugal, but we do not go without. But the dainties of the rich, platters of silver, and line linen; in the church, altar frontals of cloth of gold, a chalice studded with jewels—such things would shame our vows.'

'Your purity condemns my self-indulgence. You make me blush, mon pÈre!'

'Guillaume, it's not funny. Why do you mock our simplicity? Am I pretentious to insist on it? No, no it cannot be right to live like kings when we are supposed to be like Jesus. Can it?'

'Ah, my very dear friend, it is because you are a little crazy that I love you so. Le Seigneur, yes, he laid aside everything, and became poverty for us. But we are not Jésus. You over-reach yourself. Be realistic. We—'

'*Are* we not?' Peregrine leaned forward, his eyes burning, urgent in his intent face. 'If we who are the body of Christ are not Jesus, who will ever be? The world has need of the presence of Jesus, in the word of the gospels, in the holy bread and wine and in us. Somewhere in all the cynicisms and disappointments that bind and stunt their lives, men need to find a living Jesus, one who can hear their pain and understand their grief and shame; someone to be the love of God *with* them. It has to be a poor man ... doesn't it? To touch and heal the pain of men's poverty? I mean all kinds of poverty: the poverty of their need and their brokenheartedness, of their sin. ... It would need a man poor in spirit and poor in means to comfort the loneliness of the poor. It is not possible for a rich man's hand to dry the tears of the poor—is it?'

'How should I reply? I admire you. In a way, you are right, mon frÈre ... but ... who can live like this? It is not sensible. What would you have me do with my altar frontals? Give them to a peasant who is short of a blanket? What shall I do with my chalices? Distribute them to beggars, that they may fill them at the horses' trough? And what shall I tell my bishop, my patrons, mes frères?' He leaned forward and spoke with a frown of vehemence, serious enough now: 'The poor carpenter of Nazareth, he would not stand a *chance* in the grand machinery of the church, mon ami. We also have a stable on our estate. He would be at home there.' He looked at Father Peregrine, shaking his head, as he relaxed back into his chair. He speared a small piece of cheese with the point of his knife, and as he put it in his mouth and ate it, he looked thoughtfully at Brother Tom.

'What do you say to all this, Frère Thomas?'

Brother Tom had been sitting patiently, wondering if this involved discussion would never end and marvelling that his abbot could become so engrossed in thought as to become indifferent to a plateful of good food. He looked up at the mention of his name.

'What do I say?' he echoed uncertainly.

'Mais oui. To follow Jesus, must a man live stripped of everything as your abbot would have me believe, or can he without sin enjoy the good things of life if his heart is thankful?'

'Jesus ...' Brother Tom struggled for an intelligent answer. 'Well, who is your Jesus? I can see Father Abbot's Jesus in the gospels, but who—where is yours?'

There was a silence, broken by Abbé Guillaume's bellow of laughter and his fist crashing down onto the table.

'Mater Dei! You two together—you are *dangerous* for the gospel! You have caught me in my own folly as you caught that filthy Augustinian, you young rogue! Ahhh, you have finished me! Pour me some more wine, mon frère. Let me drink to your answer.

'Eh bien, enough! Let us turn our talk to other things or you will have me kneeling in tears, promising to distribute the substance of my house to all the vagabonds of France. I know you of old. You will lead me out of prudence into your own wild extremism.

'There is a book in your library, mon père, a valuable book. Our library is impoverished for lack of it. Will you lend it—see, I do not ask you to give, though you are rich and I am poor, in the matter of this little book—only lend it, that my scribes may copy it?'

'What book?'

'Aha! Is this the man upon whom earthly things have no hold? Why do you enquire "What book?", mon ami? What is that to you, who have left all to follow Jésus, the *real* Jésus of the gospels, not the vain idol worshipped by worldly men like me!'

'I didn't say you worshipped a vain idol, nor yet that I am free of worldliness, though I wish to God I were. What book?'

'But a little book, though valuable to me. A little text of Aelred de Rievaulx, a book of sermons I have not seen before. You know the book I mean. I see you do by the possessive glint in your eye!'

'You want to borrow that book of homilies by Abbot Aelred, written and bound by his own hand?'

'Oui.'

'For how long?'

'How long? Since it must be only the spiritual substance of the text you value, and not the book itself, I would have thought you could preach your own homilies the equal of Abbot Aelred's, mon frère. It is a book, only a book. Maybe you will let me keep the original. I can have a very nice copy made for you. Our Frère Jean has an excellent hand ...'

'Stop it, Guillaume! How long do you want it for?'

'Three months.'

Peregrine hesitated.

'Oh! Regards, Frère Thomas! Quelle avarice!'

'Oh, very well. You can borrow it. I know you will take care of it. Three months only, though. I will hold you to it.'

'Three months. I will return it myself, guarded in my bosom as though my life depended on it.

'Is that your Compline bell already? Mon père, I am

sure that bell has a little crack in it somewhere. It sounds like a bucket . . .'

'*Guillaume*! No man would find silence a hardship if he had you to live with. 'Twould be sweet refuge from the endless abuse. Come then to prayers.'

The Abbé Guillaume held the door open with all courtesy for Abbot Peregrine to pass through, and winked at Brother Tom as they followed him out into the cloister.

In the autumn of that year, as the evenings were drawing in, and the nights were beginning to tingle with the threat of frost though the afternoons still basked in gold, Brother Tom came one afternoon to Father Peregrine's house with a package that Brother Martin, the porter, had asked him to deliver.

'Who has brought this? This is from Père Guillaume. Stay a minute.' He undid the parcel, which contained the little book of Aelred de Rievaulx's homilies and a letter. Peregrine read through the letter swiftly, and looked up at Tom.

'Do you read French? No? Let me tell you what he says, then. He sends you his greetings. He remembers you with affection; says he has no cockroaches in the whole of his house; he has searched it nostalgically. Enclosed, the book—his apologies for keeping it these six months. He is sure I am not surprised. (No, I'm not. I'm surprised to get it back this soon.) He would have brought it himself, but his circumstances have changed. He could not forget our conversation here, and when he went back he proposed the sale of all the treasure of his abbey. All of it! Oh Guillaume, bless you, you never did anything by halves. They laughed him to scorn, he says. He resigned himself to accepting their rejection of his proposal, tried to forget the whole thing, but could not. He's made an enemy of his prior and upset the bishop. Dear heaven, that was rash. He has left his community, and gone to live with the Carthusians at St Michel. He says their library is second to none, especially now it has a copy of Abbot Aelred's sermons in it, and he has his own little garden with bees and vegetables. He is rearing a little pig—his mouth waters every time he looks on it. It is good wine country, he says, but not the best, which he laments. He has made some friends among the peasants there, who bring him cheeses and olive oil. How did he manage that, I wonder, in such seclusion? He's bending a rule somewhere if I know him! He has a peach tree in his garden. He says he also has peace in his heart and loves us for what we said. He bids us share a pot of wine by a good fire to remember him, and guard against chilblains in the abominable English cold. The poor carpenter of Nazareth, he says, is teaching him the tricks of his trade. He ends, *Quasi tristes, semper autem gaudentes: sicut egentes, multos autem locupletantes: tamquam nihil habentes, et omnia possidentes.* In our sorrows, we always have reason to rejoice: poor ourselves, we bring wealth to many: penniless, we own the world.

'Guillaume de St Michel. Oh Tom, I hope he's done the right thing.'

'What do you mean?'

'Well, he's given up all he had—status, comfort, wealth. The Carthusian Rule is very austere.'

'And he has exchanged it for peace in his heart. I thought that was the bargain you urged him to make.'

'It was. Yes, it was. What looks like sacrifice is the richest treasure of all. I know it, I know. I have chosen Jesus to be my heaven, and him in all his poverty, all his grief. It's just that sometimes I get cold feet.'

In the quiet bedroom, I listened to my sisters breathing and the wind blowing round the roof of the house outside.

Mother leaned down and picked up the tall candlestick from the floor.

'They're asleep,' she whispered. 'Shall we go down-stairs?' I nodded. We tiptoed out of the room and went quietly down the stairs. As I opened the door of the living room, and the lamplight shone out into the passage, Mother blew out the candle.

VIII
THE ROAD CLIMBS UPWARDS

Father Carnforth, the retired priest who acted as curate in our parish, had come to tea. He sat in the middle of our sofa, by the fire, Mary on one side and Beth on the other. Cecily had already greeted him, and her conversation with him had been, as usual, brief, factual and to the point: 'Have you got any peppermints today?'

Father Carnforth smiled at her, and laughed his wheezy laugh. Beth liked to watch his face when he smiled. 'A thousand, thousand smile wrinkles,' she said to Mother, 'are hidden in his face. Then he smiles and you can see them all.'

Father Carnforth had no objections to Cecily's straightforward method of approach. Mother said he was one of the few adults who could have a conversation with Cecily without Mother having to stand there saying, 'Hush, Cecily. Don't be rude, Cecily,' every five seconds like a parrot.

'I have a new bag of peppermints in my pocket, as a matter of fact,' he said. 'I had an idea when I woke up this morning that today I might be needing some. So I went to Mrs Sykes' shop and I said, "Mrs Sykes, I need half a pound of peppermints. Not a quarter today, Mrs

Sykes. Half a pound. If you please." Why do you ask? Would you like one?'

'Two,' said Cecily.

'Here you are, then. Two, and one for luck.'

There are some grown-ups who offer you sweets and you'd love one, but somehow all by itself you hear your voice saying, 'Oh, not for me, thank you.' Father Carnforth was not one of them. We were soon all sucking peppermints happily, watching the fire blaze up.

'Ah, I do like a log fire, my dear,' he said to Mother. 'My housekeeper will only buy coal, I regret to say. She says it burns hotter, which is true of course, but what evil, sulphurous smoke it has. This is like incense by comparison.'

Mother had baked scones for tea, which we had with strawberry jam and cream cheese, and she had made an enormous fruit cake and some coffee meringues. We ate everything, the whole fruitcake even. Nobody spoke much while we were eating except to say things like, 'Yes please,' and, 'Pass the butter.'

Afterwards, Father Carnforth wiped his mouth with his napkin and sighed contentedly. 'I think I could just manage one more cup of tea, my dear,' he said. 'Would it offend you if I were to light my pipe?'

Father Carnforth smoked a lovely fragrant blend of pipe tobacco. Mother said she had sometimes been tempted to follow him up the road just to go on sniffing it.

'My doctor says I should give this up,' said Father Carnforth as he held the match flame to the tobacco and drew at his pipe. 'He says my wheezy chest is all down to smoking. I expect he's right. "You're going downhill this year, James," he says to me, but I *am* eighty-three. What can you expect? "If you mean my chest is worse," I said to him, "I will accept your judgement as a medical man, but don't tell me I'm going downhill. The road climbs upwards, upwards to the light. It must do. It wouldn't be such hard going if it was going downhill." You have to be positive about this life, my dear; you know that. Bother it, it's gone out already. Pass me my matches, Mary, my sweet. That's it. My dear wife, God rest her soul, used to tell me that this was the filthiest, most time-consuming way of wasting money she could possibly think of. She was right, of course; she was right. But there we are; it has given me a lot of pleasure. Good food and good conversation, and a pipe by the fire: what better riches could life have to offer? What's that Cecily? Still room in your tummy for one more peppermint? Here you are, then. One more, and one for luck.'

Mary snuggled up closer to Father Carnforth. He was the oldest person she knew and she was always afraid he was going to die. She often asked him about it. He put his arm around her now, and looked down at her, smiling a kindly reassurance.

'What have they taught you at school this week, little Mary?'

'We are doing a project on dinosaurs. Mrs Kirkpatrick has been telling us what the world was like in prehistoric days.'

Father Carnforth laughed so much he began to cough.

'Dear me, dear me,' he wheezed. 'That must be useful to you. And how does Mrs Kirkpatrick know what the world was like before history began?'

Mary looked nonplussed. 'She does know. She tells us all about it. About the dinosaurs, what they did and what they looked like, and how people used to have tails and lots of hair.'

Father Carnforth looked at the dark grey hair growing on the back of his hand. There was a lot of it.

'Ah, yes,' he said. 'Some of us have progressed less than others, I suppose. I daresay it is a sign of the times that people teach little children with confidence and authority what they cannot possibly know anything about, and have nothing to tell them about the true meaning and development of life. Don't you think, my dear?'

Mother nodded. 'A lot of what they teach them now is above their heads. Mary came down on Tuesday morning saying she would like some vitamins for breakfast. We live in an age of intellectual sophistication and spiritual darkness, I'm afraid. Mind you, I'm glad I don't have to teach them. The spiritual darkness is more in evidence in the classroom than the intellectual sophistication from all I hear.'

Daddy leaned forward and picked up the poker to prod the fire. 'I like Mrs Kirkpatrick,' he said. 'She has more about her than some. Beware of toppling her from her pedestal. Little ones respect their teachers enormously, and it's right they should.'

'Respect is fine, but not mindless acceptance,' said Mother, 'however young they are.'

'Have no fear, my dear. Your children are nothing if not strong-minded. Isn't that so, Cecily? Well now, it's my turn to say Evensong, so I must tear myself away from your fireside. Pull me to my feet, Beth and Mary. Thank you. Thank you so much, my dears. I have enjoyed myself immensely. I expect I shall see you all on Sunday.'

Daddy helped him into his coat, and stood with Mother at our door, watching him walk up the hill towards the parish church.

'We shall miss him sorely when the time comes,' said Mother as she closed the door and came back into the living room to curl up on the sofa by the fire. 'Father Bennett's all right if you can stand it, but I do love that old man.'

She sat there, watching the fire, while Daddy and Beth cleared away the tea things. Mary went with them to help wash up, and Therese got into the bath. She was

going out in the evening, to the cinema, and wanted to
wash her hair. The lovely scent of her bath stuff drifted
through the house. Mother sniffed it. 'Mmm. This has
been an afternoon of nice smells,' she said. 'Where's
Cecily? It's very quiet.'

I went to look. She had fallen asleep playing with her
toys upstairs in our bedroom.

'So you could tell me a story, Mother,' I said as I sat
down again by the fire. Mother glanced through the
window at the overcast sky and drizzling rain. 'It's a
story kind of day,' she said, 'not fit for much else.'

'Tell me a story about Father Peregrine with Melissa
in it; Melissa and her children.'

'Melissa . . . she doesn't come into many of the stories,
you know. The monks told the stories to her, so she
wasn't part of the stories. But there are one or two times
she was there, so had her own memories to pass on.
Melissa . . . . Now then, there was one story, yes. Put
another log on the fire, my dove. Yes, I remember it
now.'

Melissa had brought her children to the abbey to stay
through the last watch of Lent and celebrate the Easter
feast. She never saw very much of Father Peregrine
when she came at Easter; there were too many other
demands on his time. Already the guest house was
almost full with visitors and pilgrims who had come to
share in the resurrection festival. Still, she liked to be
there with him following the long, sorrowful journey of
Holy Week, and the explosion of triumph as the tables
were turned on death itself on Easter Day.

There was another reason, too, why she came at
Easter. It was on Easter Monday eleven years ago that
Father Peregrine had been beaten and disfigured, his
hands maimed and his leg crippled. It was a time of year
when the sharpness of memories pressed painfully upon
him, and old terrors stirred. Melissa knew that. She

knew that most of the brothers would be rushed off
their feet caring for guests and carrying out the rites of
the Easter liturgies, on top of the round of work and
prayer that was a daily necessity. They would likely be
too busy to glimpse the horror and panic that sometimes
came very close to the surface in Abbot Peregrine on
Easter Day. She had asked him once, straight out, 'How
is it for you, Father, at Easter-time? There are some
bitter memories there for you.'

He had sat in silence a long while before answering
her, and when he did speak, it was hesitantly, reluctantly.

'Holy Week is not too bad. I ... Jesus in Gethsemane
... I ... he ... that is the source of all my peace. There
have been, there's no point in trying to hide it, times
when I've thought I would go under in the fear and
helplessness—despair really—that overwhelms me some
days. I have held myself together, just, but ... the dread
of breaking apart before the whole community, I can't
tell you. His terror and distress in Gethsemane ... you
can see his soul writhe ... it answers, more profoundly
than I could express, the intolerable ... how can I
explain it? The words go round and round in my head,
"I can't bear it, I can't bear it," behind all I am saying or
doing, filling all my silences. It steadies me to hear his
humbleness, "Lord, if it be possible—take this cup from
me." Then I know what courage is, where to find it.
Good Friday, and the cross ... nails through his hands
... oh, God! ... Melissa, *nails* ...'

Peregrine paused and shook his head, his face
contorted at the horror and pain of it.

'Nails through his hands! On Good Friday morning I
kneel before the crucifix in my chamber and I stretch
out my hands to him, and I say, "Crucified one ...
beautiful one ... Redeemer ... Saviour ... Lamb of God
... you heal us by your wounds. Can you make something of these broken, ugly hands ... put them to some
use?" But Easter Day—Easter Day is another thing.

Christ is risen and I know, I *do* know, that is my salvation. I understand that it is my glory, and my hope. Without his rising, our suffering would embitter us beyond redeeming, I know it. Only . . . he is in glory, and I am still in Gethsemane. He is in triumph and I am still pinned to my cross. On Easter Day he leaves me behind. Besides all that, it is our busiest time, and I do wonder at times, I confess it, if one day among the crowd, they will come again and finish their vengeance on my body. For they meant to have my life. I greet the pilgrims, and I must smile at them, and welcome them lovingly as I should. But all the while I am watching, wondering. Well, no, not all the while. I exaggerate. But the old terror is still there. I feel sick with it sometimes. It's hard to control. Don't mistake me, death I do not fear . . . but pain, infirmity, helplessness. When I walk through the church and I hear someone behind me, I am cold, sweating, terrified. I have tried to overcome it. God knows, I have prayed. I am ashamed to have so little joy in Christ's most glorious day. It is not for want of trying.'

He sat looking down at his misshapen hands. The craftsmanship and costliness of the abbot's ring decorated the right hand incongruously, its opulence mocking their ugliness. They showed starkly against the unrelieved black of his tunic. Melissa wondered how often in a day he looked down at his hands, and if there was ever a time when he thought nothing of it, being merely accustomed to their brokenness.

He raised his eyes to look at her. Usually his gaze was full of warmth, of love; the heart of his giving, passing on the peace of God. But for once he let her look into him and see just what he was; his sadness, his pain, the frustration that raged in the man trapped inside the living prison of his disabled body.

'It's a poor thing, isn't it, that the abbot of a monastery should be so . . .' He paused, searching for the word he wanted.

'Human?' she said.

She did not forget the conversation, or his sadness and his sense of shame, and she tried when she could to be there at Easter. When she came, she brought her children too. They were growing fast. The youngest, Benedict, was almost two, and his days were one long disaster of joyful exploration. Nicholas, her oldest child, was just eight years old. In between came Anne, a little more than a year younger than Nicholas but twice his age for wisdom and common sense, and Catherine, who was just four, candid, passionate and therefore a continual source of embarrassment to her parents.

As soon as they arrived at the abbey, the children made for the kitchen and Brother Cormac, who was their hero. They were a little bit afraid of Brother Andrew, the fierce old Scot who was the cook and monarch of the kitchen's self-contained kingdom, but Cormac told them stories and fed them tit-bits, and took them to see the lambs and the calves in his free time. Cormac also knew where the birds and the field mice nested, and won their undying admiration by being able to spit a cherry-stone even further than Nicholas, who had been practising for weeks. It was Cormac who made them a swing and climbed to a dizzy height in a tall elm tree to secure it to a branch. It was Cormac who took them sledging in the winter on the steep hill that sheltered the guest house and played hide-and-seek with them among the straw bales in the barn. He showed them how to call the owls at night so that they would answer, and he played fivestones with them in the summer dust, and they loved him dearly.

'Don't plague the life out of the kitchen brothers, now!' Melissa called after them as they vanished across the abbey court, 'and mind Benedict near the well!' They were not listening. She watched them go, and then turned back to the guest house. She felt happiness bubbling up inside her, a pressure of joy. She loved to be

at the abbey. It was a harbour of peace for her, a place
to rebuild her strength. There are not many places where
a woman with four small children is welcomed with
unfeignedly joyful hospitality, but this was one of them.

She stood leaning her back against the rough stone
wall of the guest house, looking across the flagged court
at the huge abbey church rising like a great rock of
strength and assurance. She sighed contentedly and went
in at the guest house door. She saw Peregrine before he
saw her, limping slowly across the hall. He had come in
search of her, having been sent word of her arrival.

'Father! God save you, you look tired to death!'

His face lit in a smile of welcome and he hugged her
to him. 'It's good to see you, dear one. Oh, I've been
looking forward to this! Have you lost all your babes to
the kitchens already? Well then, come and share some of
Brother Walafrid's blackberry wine with me, and we've
been given some figs that are good. We can have a
moment of quiet together. Oh, but forgive me, selfish.
Maybe you are too weary after your journey? Would you
rather rest first, dear heart?'

Melissa smiled at him, loving him, soaking up the
luxury of being cherished, made to feel special. 'It's
you I've come to see,' she said happily. 'If you've a
spare moment, I'm going to seize it before someone
else does. I can rest later.'

The children found Brother Cormac finishing the
preparations for the cold evening meal that the community would eat after Vespers. He was pleased to see
them, but he looked slightly harassed.

'Oh, ho! ho! It's you, you demons! Search in the store,
little Annie, and you'll find apples and honey—you know
where the bread is. If you'll take some out to the cloister to nibble, I'll come presently and take you to see the
new foal and the bats in the church tower. I mustn't

come for another few minutes yet though. Brother
Andrew's turned into a dragon today and he'll scorch
me with his fiery breath if I stop working for one
moment. Find yourselves something to eat and skedad-
dle, there's good children. I'll come out to you when I
can.' And with these words he disappeared into the dairy
to fetch the pitcher of milk from its cool stone shelf.

Catherine moved closer to her sister. 'Has Brother
Andrew really turned into a dragon?' It did not seem
unlikely.

'No, stupid. Cormac just means he's in a bad temper,'
said Nicholas scornfully. 'Come on, let's get some bread
and honey and apples before he comes.'

They sat out in the cloister which gave a fair shelter
from the chill March wind, and ate the things they had
found. Benedict transferred most of his honey, gener-
ously ladled out by Nicholas, from his bread to his hair
and clothes, and then turned his attention to rooting
up the flowers that were Brother Fidelis' pride and joy.

'Glory be to God!' gasped Cormac as he finally
emerged from the kitchen and caught sight of Benedict.
'Is that a child or a compost heap? Let me give you a
scrub, for mercy's sake or your mother will be scolding
me, and I've been scolded enough already for one day.'

He seized Benedict and holding him well away from
himself, he carried him through the kitchen to the yard
at the back, and set him down on the cobbles beside
the well, ignoring the little child's indignant yells of
protest. The other children trooped through behind
him. 'Fetch me a towel, Annie,' said Cormac. 'You'll
find some back in the cloister, in the lavatorium, next
to the refectory. Nicholas, a bucket of water if you will.
Thank you. That will do nicely. Now then.' He kept a
firm grip on Benedict as he spoke, and stripped his
clothes from him and sluiced him thoroughly under the
icy water. Not brought up to monastic asceticism,

Benedict roared with pain and rage when he could get his breath back. Brother Cormac took not the slightest bit of notice, but briskly rubbed the little body with the towel Anne had found until Benedict was pink and glowing; then wrapped him up in it and proceeded to rinse his clothes.

'Stop screaming, child. Think you you're a worm or a mole that you can go burrowing in the earth and come up clean? Come now, that's the worst of it off. Let's go and rummage in your bags in the guest house and try if we can find some clean clothing before your mother sees you. Here, I'll carry you. Nicholas, bring his clothes. We'll set them to dry before the fire. I've wrung them well, but they may drip still, so mind you hold them away from you and don't get yourself all wet. That's it.'

Cormac took them as he promised up into the bell tower of the abbey church and showed them the bats hanging in the dimness, and to the stable to see the spotted foal, very young, bedded with her mother in clean straw. They collected the eggs from the henhouses, and carried them back to the kitchen, brown and snow white and speckled, and one of a pale, rosy beige, which Cormac said was laid by Dame Cluck, the sovereign of the poultry yard and the cockerel's favourite wife. He took them into the warming room to say hello to the two or three brothers there who had come down from the scriptorium to warm fingers that were numb with cold at the great fireplace. Just before Vespers he returned them to their mother, and she thanked him warmly.

'Brother Cormac, you're an angel! Many, many thanks. Look at them: tired and happy. All I need to do is feed them and put them to bed. Oh—what happened to Benedict's clothes?'

Cormac grinned at her. 'An angel, is it? By'r lady, I shall need to be this week. We've that much work in the kitchen it's beyond mortal man. His clothes you will find drying by the fire, not entirely clean, but recognisable now. I'll take the children to see the lambs tomorrow, but not till the afternoon. There's the Vespers bell now, I must be on my way. The thanks are all mine; I've loved their company.'

He kissed Benedict and handed him over into his mother's arms, rested his hands lightly a moment on Anne's and Catherine's heads, nodded to Nicholas as one man to another, and was gone. Melissa took them to eat their supper in the guest house refectory after they had washed their hands and picked the straw out of their hair and clothes. A bowl of new milk had been set for each of them, and a small loaf of fresh bread, wrapped in a linen cloth. There was a pat of rich, yellow butter on an earthenware plate, some soft, white cheese, salted slightly and delicately flavoured by the herbs that had wrapped it, and a wooden bowl of sweet yellow apples from the store, polished until they glowed in the firelight like lamps.

'Brother Dominic says the abbey is supposed to reflect the peace and order of heaven,' said Melissa to her children as she sat Benedict on her lap and helped him with his milk, 'and it does. I can't think of heaven being much different from this.' She smiled peacefully.

'That's because,' said Nicholas, tearing a large piece of bread off the loaf and spreading it vigorously with plenty of butter, 'you haven't heard Brother Cormac and Brother Andrew arguing in the kitchen.'

Melissa looked at him with a little frown of irritation. 'Nicholas, don't put so much food in your mouth at once,' she said sharply. She did not want her dream shattered. 'I'm sure they don't argue.'

'They do. They're terrible, worse than us. Brother Damien says you could light a candle from the sparks that fly between them. It's because Cormac's cooking's so awful and he doesn't like doing the meat and the fish. Brother Andrew says to him, "What would you like me to do with these rolls, Brother? Will I put them on the table, or are you saving them for sling-shot? But half of one of these would slay Goliath nicely," and Cormac glares at him from under his eyebrows and mutters. He *swears*. Yes he *does*, Mother, I've heard him.'

'Nicholas, I'm sure you're making all this up. *I've* never heard Brother Cormac swear. Father Abbot says those two love each other like father and son. Now stop talking and eat your supper. Look, Catherine's falling asleep over her food.'

'They may love each other, but it doesn't stop them . . .'

'Nicholas! Enough. Don't speak with your mouth full either.'

When they had eaten everything in sight and left nothing but a sprinkling of crumbs and a scrape of butter, Melissa shepherded them upstairs and into bed.

'Brother Cormac,' said Catherine sleepily, as Melissa tucked her and Anne into the bed they shared, 'knows what the rabbits think. He knows what the words are of the song the thrush is singing. It is saying, "*Can* . . . *cantabo* . . ." what did he say Annie?'

'*Cantabo Domino in vita mea*,' Anne recited carefully. 'But I don't know what it means.'

'I will sing to the Lord as long as I live,' said Melissa softly. 'Is that what Brother Cormac says the thrush is singing?'

She told Father Peregrine about it as they sat together over their evening meal, and he smiled.

'Brother Cormac, yes, it wouldn't surprise me at all if he understood the song of the birds. He loves the wild creatures. He used at one time to love birds and beasts more than he loved mankind. It distresses him to see anything wounded and killed. He likes them to be free. I've seen him in the kitchen preparing a fowl for the pot. Brother Andrew will be standing there with the bird dangling by its feet, neglected in his hand, as he issues orders or corrects someone's work, and he'll dump it on Brother Cormac—"Pluck this and gut it please, Brother." Brother Cormac will take it into his hands with its poor dead head supported on his wrist, and carry it to the workbench so, and lay it down reverently, and strip it of its feathers as tenderly and gently as a woman laying a sleepy babe to rest. It irritates Brother Andrew no end. Ah, no doubt about it, the kitchen work is a hard discipline for Brother Cormac sometimes.'

'Couldn't he do something else—work in the garden or something instead?'

'Yes, he could—now he could. There were reasons for keeping him to the kitchen at one time. He helps in the infirmary and he helps Brother Mark with his bees, but he likes to work with Brother Andrew. They have a good understanding. Brother Cormac had no family of his own, and Brother Andrew has come to be like a father to him; answered a need in him somehow. There was no love lost between them in the early days, though. Two of a kind, they are. A bit too much alike for comfort sometimes.'

'Brother Cormac's good to my children. He took them to see the bats in the church tower today, and he says he'll take them to see the young lambs tomorrow when he can escape from the kitchen in the afternoon.'

'Maundy Thursday, yes, the brothers are fasting before the evening Mass. He'll maybe find some free time. He needs some. He's been carrying most of Brother Andrew's work lately. Brother Andrew is feeling his age. He's been tired, very tired and a bit breathless of late. He has a look sometimes as though he's in pain, but he'll not admit to it. Brother Cormac has been doing all he can to spare him in the kitchen.'

'Oh, then . . .' Melissa looked concerned. 'Should he be spending this time with my children? I don't want them to be a burden.'

'No, no.' Peregrine shook his head. 'Brother Cormac

delights in your children. They have extra help in the kitchen during the Easter feast. Brother Damien is there, and Brother Mark. Let it be.'

In the morning, when her children went out to play, Melissa cautioned them, 'Don't go bothering Brother Cormac, now. This afternoon, he said. You must wait until then. Go for a walk down to the infirmary and say hello to Uncle Edward.'

But Catherine stole away, and appeared at Cormac's side in the kitchen, where she stood in solemn silence as she watched him gutting fish for the midday meal.

'Is that a fish?' she asked at last.

'It is,' he replied shortly. He hated the job and it put him out of sorts to do it. He cut the head away deftly with the sharp knife, and slit the belly, flicking out the spilling mess of guts with the knife point.

'Oh, Cormac,' said Catherine in a shocked voice, 'you've cut off its face.'

Cormac closed his eyes and swallowed hard. He felt distinctly queasy. 'Catherine!' Anne's voice called from the doorway. 'Catherine! Mother says you're not to bother Cormac in the morning. You've got to stay with us.'

'But Cormac is cutting the fishes' tummies open and throwing their insides away,' protested Catherine. 'I want to stay and watch.'

Cormac put down the knife and wiped his hands. He picked Catherine up and carried her to the door. He deposited her firmly outside.

'You do as your mother says,' he said, and closed the door behind her.

'You didn't do anything naughty, did you, Catherine?' asked Anne, anxiously. 'He looked a bit cross.' But Catherine was already running across the cloister, heading for the infirmary.

Brother Cormac returned grimly to his task, stuffed

the fish carcasses with herbs and butter and left them packed in neat lines in a covered dish ready to be baked.

Brother Andrew called him from the other side of the room: 'Brother Cormac! It's time you did those fish. You've not got all the morning.' He sounded tired and irritable.

'But I ...' began Cormac.

'"But" nothing, Brother. There's bread to be baked for tomorrow and they need a hand in the guest house kitchen, so will you set about it and get them done.'

'But, Brother ...'

'Brother Cormac, it *needs doing*!' Andrew shouted at him. Cormac's black brows were gathering in a frown and his blue eyes were as cold as frost.

'Come *on*, Brother Cormac!' roared Andrew.

'I have done the fish,' Cormac said from between clenched teeth with slow and deliberate fury, glowering at the old man.

Brother Andrew clicked his tongue in exasperation. 'Then why the devil didn't you say so?' he snapped.

Cormac looked as though he was about to boil over. The kitchen staff kept their heads bent to their work. Neither Brother Andrew nor Brother Cormac was the most patient of men, and minor confrontations were a common occurrence. For a moment the two of them glared at each other, then, 'Whatever *ails* you today?' said Cormac more gently. 'You're like a bear with a sore head. I've done the fish. Shall I make a start on the bread or go over to the guest house?'

'I—*oh*!' Brother Andrew clutched at the table where he stood, gasping with sudden pain. The colour drained from his face and beads of sweat stood out on his brow.

Cormac was across the room to him in an instant and Brother Andrew turned to him and gripped his arms convulsively, bent over in pain.

'Get Brother John,' said Cormac to Brother Damien, who left at a run. 'Where does it hurt you?' he asked

Brother Andrew, looking anxiously at the old man's face as he tried to stand erect. It was deathly pale, the lips blue and set in a tight line of pain.

'It—*ah*!' Andrew gasped and clung to him. 'Like a great hand squeezing my ribs. Like . . . bands of iron. *Ah*! It's not been this bad before.'

'Lie down,' said Cormac. 'Here, on the floor. Come, rest your head on my lap, so. There now, Brother John will be with us from the infirmary.' The old man could not keep still, but writhed in his pain. His hand gripped Cormac's knee fiercely, and he pressed his face into his thigh. Brother Cormac could feel the agonised contortion of it, and the old man's trembling passed through into his own body. Oh John, hurry, he thought, desperately. Oh Jesu, mercy.

Brother Andrew drew up his knees in pain and groaned. Sweat was pouring from him. Brother Mark bent over them offering a cold, damp cloth. Cormac took it without looking up, and tenderly wiped the old man's head and neck and as much of his face as he could get to.

Brother John came hurrying through the door and knelt beside them. 'All right, we'll carry him to the infirmary. Two of you men here, make a chair for him with your hands. We'll carry him so.'

'I'll come with you,' said Cormac.

'You . . . will . . . not . . .' gasped Brother Andrew, fighting for breath. 'You'll get . . . the meal . . . to the table—and Brother—don't . . . burn . . . the bread.' Then he screwed up his eyes and clamped his mouth shut as another wave of pain engulfed him. He looked very old and shrunken and frail as they carried him out of the door. Brother Cormac watched them go, his face almost as white as Andrew's, but as the door closed behind them, he turned resolutely to his work.

'Put the fish in to bake, Brother Damien. John, fill the pitchers with ale. Water it, but not so much as yesterday;

they were grumbling. Brother Mark, take the bread from its proving and knead it again. Luke, Simon, go down to the guest house and see what you can do.'

He himself continued the preparation of a green salad that Brother Andrew had begun, his face taut with anxiety, his hands trembling. Brother Damien came up quietly behind him and put an arm around his shoulders. Cormac shook him off irritably.

'Come *on*, Brother. Have you done that fish? Good. Watch the pot of beans on the fire. They're nearly done. They mustn't overcook or they'll go to a mush. Drat, there's the Office bell. You go, both of you. I can finish off here. Is the bread ready for its second proving? Thank you. Cover it with a cloth before you go. No, set it to rise there, near the fire. Yes, yes. Go now, then.'

When the Office was over, Cormac listened to the soft slapping of the brothers' sandalled feet coming along the cloister, and the indefinable whisper of their robes as they passed the open door, the splash of water in the lavatorium as they washed their hands. Oh, hurry, he pleaded silently, please hurry. But they filtered through into the refectory with their usual dignified calm.

Brother Cormac made the kitchen tidy, and saw the meal to the table. He did not join the brethren to eat, but restlessly paced the kitchen floor, listening to the drone of the reader's voice and the subdued background sound of the meal: pottery on wood, metal on pot. Then pot on pot and metal on metal as the servers stacked the bowls and collected the spoons and knives. Cormac served the kitcheners, the reader and the servers with their meal as they came through into the kitchen from the refectory, and then he left them to it and ran to the infirmary. In the ante-room he found Father Peregrine sitting with Catherine playing at his feet. Anne sat beside him, very quiet, her eyes gravely fixed on Brother Cormac as he hastened through the door and stopped, looking helplessly to Father Peregrine for reassurance.

'Is he—?'

'They could not save him,' said Peregrine gently. 'He was gone by the time they got him to bed.'

'No ...' whispered Cormac. 'For God's sake, *no*. Where is he?'

'Just through there.' Father Peregrine watched him stumble through the door. The room Cormac entered was airy and chill, filled with the cold light of spring. It was utterly silent except for the faint squeaking and tapping of leaves outside crowding against one of the windows. There was no one there but the motionless form on the bed, laid out straight in his habit and sandals. His hair was combed, and his rosary placed among the fingers of his hands folded on his breast. Cormac looked at Brother Andrew's body, white and frozen in the absolute stillness of death; at the toes like carvings and the sculpted silence of his hands, his jaw, his nose. He stood by the bed in the pale spring light and looked down at the deserted house, empty dwelling, that had been his friend. He lifted his hand and caressed the cold forehead and bony cheek.

'We served the meal on time,' he whispered. He took one last long look, stooped and pressed his warm lips to the cold, still brow, his eyes closed. Then he turned away and left the room and closed the door behind him.

'Come and sit down.' Father Peregrine's voice penetrated the daze of shock, and Cormac sat on the bench beside him, his elbows resting on his knees, his hands clasped together, seeing nothing.

'I wish I'd been with him,' he said at last, tonelessly.

Catherine looked up from her game on the floor. 'Cormac, why are you crying?' she asked curiously. 'Is it because of Brother Andrew?'

'I'm not crying,' said Cormac dully, without looking at her.

'Shush, Catherine,' said Anne, but Catherine was not to be put off. 'You are,' she insisted. 'Your nose is

running and your eyes are full of tears, like Nicholas'
when he's trying not to cry. There's a tear running down
your face now. I can see it.'

Peregrine stretched out his hand and laid it on
Cormac's hands which gripped together till the
knuckles were white. Cormac groaned and his head
went down on the abbot's hand. Anne darted to his side
and spread herself over his shoulders like a bird.
Catherine got to her feet and crept close to Peregrine,
frightened by the sight of adult grief. 'Is Cormac's heart
breaking?' she asked in an awed voice.

Peregrine nodded. 'Yes, Catherine,' he said quietly,
'his heart is breaking. It will take a long time to heal. Go
and find your mother now, children. Tell her what has
happened. There, Annie, your love has done him good,
but let him be now. Go and find Mother.'

They buried Brother Andrew's body on Easter Eve in
the morning, pushing the bier slowly up the winding
path under the dripping beech trees to the brothers'
burial ground in the wood; a sober and silent procession
of cowled black figures shrouded in the grey morning
mist. At the graveside, Cormac stood and watched as
they shovelled in the wet earth, his face pale and remote
in the shadow of his cowl.

He went about the duties of the day in silence. The
kitchen was enclosed in a pall of silence. The absence
of Brother Andrew's sarcastic Scots rasp was as vivid
among the men there as if they could hear him still.

At midnight the brethren gathered in the choir for
the Easter vigil; the moment of solemn joy and mystery
when death is turned back, and the victory of the grave
disintegrates in its own ashes, for Christ, Morning Star,
is risen. The massive church was filled with pilgrims,
the rustling dark alive with the excitement of their
expectation. The Easter fire was set alight in the darkness, and the Paschal candle lit from it, the light

illuminating the watch of the night, the ranks of brothers in the choir, the crowd of men and women and children in the nave.

Silent and numb, Cormac stood in his stall, grief welling up in him until he could no longer contain it. Tears ran unchecked down his cheeks as he stood watching Father Chad help Father Peregrine to take the great Paschal candle into his scarred and twisted hands. Father Chad stepped back and the abbot lifted up the candle.

'*Lumen Christi*,' his firm voice sang out the triumphant chant, and '*Deo gratias!*' came the thunder of response from all around the church. The light of Christ: thanks be to God. There was, obscurely, hope in the candle held aloft in those maimed hands, the light of Christ.

Is this your healing? Cormac prayed silently in the bitterness of his soul. To waken my heart to love and friendship and then flood it with this pain? Is this your light, your gift, your way—this agony?

He did not expect an answer. He was filled with the anger and desolation of his loss. He was unprepared for the word, whispered deep in his soul, from somewhere as far outside himself as the stars, yet as near as his own shuddering breath: 'Yes.'

The Long Fall

BOOK THREE

For
Mark and Gill Barrett

'The worst of partialities is to withhold oneself, the worst ignorance is not to act, the worst lie is to steal away.'
Charles Péguy

I
THE LAST OF THE SUMMER

July 22nd. The blackberries are in flower. Pink. They are
pink, and I thought they were white; but these new,
tender, thrusting shoots are burdened with clusters of
tight, grey-green buds, and here and there a flower of
sharp pink.

The raspberries grow thick and luscious this year, all
that rain. It's raining now: fat drops of rain spattering into
the languid warmth of the evening, hissing in the flames of
the bonfire. The honeysuckle sprawls over the fence, its
sweet, heavy scent mingling with the woodsmoke. The
fragrance of it in the warm, damp stillness of the evening is
decadent, feminine, overpowering.

The sage is in flower, its purple-blue petals shining
brighter as afternoon drifts into dusk and the sun fades.
The borage flowers too are bright stars of blue, and the
dropping clusters of pink and blue comfrey flowers hang
motionless from the thick, hairy stems. The elderflower is
nearly finished now, the umbels of dense blossom give way
to a plentiful load of berries. The roses are still a mad
profusion of beauty, a good promise there too of fruit.
Rose-hip syrup, elderberry cordial—there'll be plenty for
the winter.

In the physic garden, the feverfew is a mass of yellow
and white, and the calendula growing up radiant among
it. Flowers, everywhere flowers. What a summer it's been.

The hay was half-ruined in the rain, just a bit left standing to come in. The grain harvests look good now, though, and the beans are looking healthy, which is just as well. There was nothing to them last year, and what we dried was scarce enough to eke through the winter months. Ah, but the honey will be good this year! The flowers ardent with life on their stems, nothing faded or limp. There should be enough nectar in there to put a smile on any bee's face.

Evening coming down now: a rumble of thunder threatening in the distance. The sound of the cows lowing as they come down from the pasture to the byre. Brother Stephen was late with milking again, then. He needed more help, really, this time of year. Further away, the voices of the sheep on the hills. What must it be like to live where there are no sheep; not to hear the sound of the ewes calling their lambs, and the lonely cry of the curlew overhead, and the sweet, rising song of the lark?

Brother Tom forked the last wayward straggles of leaves over the smoking fire. The Office bell was ringing for Compline. The wind changed, and the smoke from Tom's bonfire engulfed him suddenly. He turned away choking, his eyes stinging with it.

'Serves you right, standing here dreaming when you should be on your way to chapel,' he told himself. He left the pitchfork leaning against the fence, and walked down through the garden to the abbey buildings. The bell had stopped ringing, but he was not hurrying even now. It just wasn't that kind of evening.

At thirty-three years old, Brother Tom had been a fully professed brother of St Alcuin's Abbey on the edge of the Yorkshire moors for eleven years now, serving God under the Rule of St Benedict, learning the rhythm of spirituality which sees prayer as work and work as prayer. He had had his early struggles, like most men, but he was contented in the life now. His time was for the most part occupied with his duties in the abbot's house, but he was a big, brawny man, raised on a farm, and there were not many days he let pass without doing some work out of doors in the garden, or on the farm, or up on the hill pastures at lambing time.

He looked with satisfaction at the patch he had weeded, as he strolled down towards the cloister. He paused to tie up a white rose that was straggling across the path, the slender stem bowing under the weight of its blossom. He rummaged in his pocket for the end of twine that was in there somewhere, cut it in half with the knife that every brother kept in his belt for a hundred and one uses, and tied the rose back neatly. He bent to breathe in its perfume before he left it and disappeared into the passageway that led through to the cloister. There was a little door in the wall of the passage, through which he entered the vestry and sacristy of the abbey church.

Tom stood for a moment, accustoming his eyes to the change as he left behind the dim fragrance of the summer dusk, and stepped into the chapel with its smells of stone and beeswax and incense, the echo of its silences widening out about him, an immense, deep cave of breathing dark.

In the choir, the tranquil chant of the psalm was ringing. Tom listened carefully: '...*frumenti, vini, et olei sui multiplicati sunt. In pace in idipsum dormiam...*'

'Faith, they're on the last verse already,' he muttered to himself. 'I'd better move.'

The reading from the Rule at the morning's Chapter had been concerned with punctuality at the Office, and the abbot's homily on the chapter they had heard had dwelt at some length on punctuality as a golden rule of courtesy, and courtesy as a jewel in the crown of Christian charity.

Brother Tom had not listened to the homily with the closest attention, being familiar through long experience with this particular bee in his abbot's bonnet. Anything that Father Peregrine took to be a necessity for courtesy was insisted upon punctiliously. Brother Tom, having held the obedience of abbot's esquire for eleven years now, had heard a great deal in the course of time on the subject of courtesy and punctuality.

He moved briskly across the Lady Chapel into the choir, and slid into his place with an appropriately submissive air just as they were singing the final phrase of the Gloria from the first psalm. He could not, then, technically be said to be late, but it was only by the skin of his teeth. He could feel his abbot's eyes on him, and risked a glance at him. Father Peregrine was shaking his head at him in disapproval, but the amusement and affection in his face were plain enough. Brother Tom knew better than to presume on it though, and bent his head meekly, joining in the chant of the psalm: *'Non accedet ad te malum: et flagelum non appropinquabit tabernaculo tuo. Quoniam angelis suis mandavit de te: ut custodiant te in omnibus viis tuis...'* ('Upon you no evil shall fall: no plague approach where you dwell. For you has he commanded his angels: to keep you in all your ways...')

Brother Tom had often wondered what his abbot made of the promises of that psalm, and all the other promises like it that were scattered throughout the Scriptures. How did Father Peregrine feel when he sang those words, Brother Tom wondered; Father Peregrine whose left leg had been lamed and his hands crippled by an attack of thugs. He had borne the disablement thirteen years now, limping about the place on a crutch, struggling with the handicap of his awkward, deformed hands; yet he sang those promises in the psalm with equanimity.

Brother Tom wondered if the abbot's soul ever raged against God, *'Where was your protection when I needed you? Where were your angels for me?'* Probably; but he kept such things, like most things, to himself. Brother Tom sighed. He loved his abbot, but being his personal attendant was no easy job. He was not an easy man, with the storm and fire of his moods, the quick flare of his temper, and his high standards of spirituality. Still, Tom knew no one like him for compassion and tenderness when a man was broken by grief, or weariness, or defeated by weakness and despair. It was that particular quality of his gentleness with men in trouble that betrayed the nightmare of his own suffering. But—did his soul ever rage against God? Tom wondered. Maybe not. Father Peregrine's favourite text from the whole of Scripture was Pilate's brief sentence *'Ecce homo'*, 'Behold the man'; spoken as Pilate brought out the flogged and battered figure of Jesus, decorated with Roman spittle, crowned with thorns. Behold the man, Emmanuel, God with us. Tom had heard Father Peregrine recall the minds of the brethren again and again to this living icon of the love of God. Maybe he regarded his sufferings as some kind of offering to this wounded deity.

'He is the God of the broken heart,' the abbot would tell his monks, 'the God of the bruised spirit, and the shattered body. Those are his shrines where the power of his presence dwells, not the relics of the dead or the altars built by human hands.'

Tom looked across the chapel at him now. He looked weary. He always looked weary. Last night when Brother Tom had got out of bed at the ringing of the bell for the Night Office, he had looked for his abbot, whose chamber he shared, and found his bed not slept in. As he passed to the cloister through the great room which was Father Peregrine's centre of operations, he found him rising stiffly from his table spread with plans and accounts relating to the abbey farm. It was the same in the morning when the bell was ringing for Prime and the morrow Mass.

Brother Tom had scolded his superior as he washed him and shaved him before they went into Chapter.

'You're fussy enough about everyone else keeping the rules, you should keep them yourself. Any other brother in this house that drove himself as you do, and wasn't in his bed where he ought to be at night, and you'd be on his back like a ton of bricks. What's so special about you?'

'I'm the abbot of this community; that's what's so

special about me. If I don't get all this business about the farm buildings right, we shall be into debt again, and have I not worked these fifteen years to get this community back into solvency and keep us that way?'

Brother Tom washed the last traces of soap from his abbot's face.

'You look a wreck. Your eyes are that shadowed you look as though you've been in a fight. You're losing weight. You look horrible. You're sixty years old this September, you can't go burning the candle at both ends at your time of life. You'll make yourself ill—you *will*, don't look at me like that. You're a monk. You're supposed to be humble and put your trust in God and go to bed at night and eat up your dinner like a good lad. If I were your superior instead of you mine, I'd bawl you out for your flouting of the Rule.'

'My superior? Since when have you waited to be my superior to bawl me out? Hark at you! Brother Thomas, I swear living with you is like being married without any of the fun. Peace, man, for pity's sake. Come now, will you carry some of these documents to Chapter for me? I'll be here with them today with Brother Ambrose and everyone who knows the details of it, but I must give some indication to the community of what we're about.'

After the Chapter meeting, where the bare bones of the situation had been laid before the brethren, the abbot met with Brother Ambrose his cellarer, Father Chad his prior, Brother Stephen and old Brother Prudentius from the farm, and Father Bernard who was learning the difficult and complex job of the cellarer with a view to taking it over from Brother Ambrose who, though as shrewd and competent as ever, was none the less getting very old. One of the abbey's tenant farmers, who helped with the farm management in lieu of part of his rent, was also with them; and Brother Tom had the job of fetching and carrying plans, deeds and letters as required.

The plans under discussion concerned some of the farm

buildings, which had for some while been in need of repair. The need was becoming urgent, but the coffers of the abbey had been heavily bled by Papal taxes and the King's war taxes in the past year. In addition to this, the hay harvest had all but failed throughout the region in the rains of the early summer, which meant buying and transporting in hay from elsewhere for the winter months.

Brother Thomas had listened to all this with some interest. The business talk of his superiors usually failed to engage his attention at all, but the subject of farming was one near to his heart, and he understood it well.

'... in addition to this, we lost fifty-eight ewes from the blowfly after we moved them down from the hill pasture to the orchard. That wasn't our fault. We had to move them because of Sir Geoffrey d'Ebassier's wretched hunting dogs harassing the sheep. The Cistercians at Mount Hope will sell us some ewes in lamb this autumn, when we have the money from the wool we sell of this summer's shearing. Theirs is all good stock, but we can expect no favours. We shall have to pay through the nose for them.

'Brother Stephen is adamant that we must replace the beasts' field shelters here... and here. The repairs to the byre will have to wait. We must pray for a good winter, that's all.

'Another call on our finances is the urgent repair to the masonry of the main drain from the reredorter. That can't wait. The morale of any community is only as good as its latrines.

'There is also the matter of the repair of the tower at the church of St Mary the Virgin. The tower, Brother. It was damaged in the gales during the spring, if you recall. So was the roof at the east end of the church. Father Chad said Easter Mass for them with drips of rain dancing on his pate, which entertained the people vastly no doubt, but we have responsibility for repairs there, and also we are liable for the priest's house.

'Further to that, Bishop Eric and his retinue will be

here for six weeks in February; that means fires, and winter feed for his horses, and a mountain of provisions at the leanest time of the year.

'Also, we are bound to send at least two of the junior monks to university this year. We won't get away with pleading poverty another year. Brother James, probably, and maybe Brother Damien. I'm not sure. I have friends at Ely who will put them up in the abbey's hostel at Cambridge, which will cut down the expense a little.

'We could look at increasing the rents again, but that'll go down like a dish of toenails as usual. Other than that, I don't know. I'm hoping you have some suggestions for me. But if they include building a barn with three threshing floors like the one at Barlbridge Manor and a new dovecote, which is what I've heard rumoured, you can forget it. Brother Stephen?'

Brother Stephen cleared his throat. 'Well...with all due respect, Father, I do feel the dovecote is a matter of some urgency. We left it last year, and the year before that. The pigeons do us very well for meat all through. As you just pointed out, the bishop will be here, and we shall have to feed him. If half the birds have died of cold, it'll only mean slaughtering more sheep or cockerels. If we rebuild it, and build larger, we can accommodate more birds, which we really ought to do.'

Father Peregrine sighed. You're too tired, thought Tom. You can't think straight, can you? He watched the tension around his abbot's eyes, the persistent twitching of the left eye. Your head's aching, and you feel sick with it.

'Oh, very well. Does it truly have to be rebuilt? Can we not repair it?'

Brother Prudentius shook his head. 'The roof has been in holes through several winters. Some of the timbers have rot, and the nesting boxes the same.'

'Yes, but if we repair it, the rot will stop, won't it?'

Brother Prudentius said nothing, meekly lowering his eyes.

'Won't it?' snapped the abbot.

'Yes, Father,' Brother Stephen responded resignedly.

'Thank you. The roof, I grant you, must be repaired. We can do that.

'The field shelters, then. Brother Stephen?'

'The one out on the hills...here...is tumbling down. It needs rebuilding, but it is all stone. Brother Thomas and I can do that after the harvest, if you will spare him for me. This one also is in a bad state. The great ash tree fell on it in the spring gale. Again, those timbers and the stonework are not beyond us, but I shall need Brother Thomas. We can make new piers for it I should think, wouldn't you, Brother?'

Brother Tom nodded. 'I've done it before.'

Brother Stephen smiled encouragingly at his abbot, who did not respond, but sat scowling in thought at the plans of the abbey estate in front of him. Brother Stephen exchanged a quick glance with the farm manager, and then embarked cautiously on the proposal about which he had the least optimism: 'If you'll look at the outlying buildings to the west there, Father—there near the boundary. I doubt if you have been out there yourself for some years.' It was said respectfully, but it was a barbed shaft designed to get Brother Stephen his own way, and it made its mark. The tension in Peregrine's face increased, and the tightness about his mouth and jaw was a warning with which Brother Tom was all too familiar.

'Yes?' There was not much that the abbot could not accomplish, disabled though he was, but it was true he had not ventured out to this steep and rough terrain since he had been lame. Brother Stephen, Tom thought, was unlikely to win himself much sympathy by rubbing his abbot's nose in his disabilities.

'The shelter shed there is large, and in need of extensive repair. Not to put too fine a point on it, it is falling down. The barn has worm in some of the aisle joists. The lift is rotted through, and the pigs and poultry from the neighbouring land can come and go as they please. Also, if we took it down now, while some of the timbers will still serve us, and built a larger barn with two, maybe three, threshing floors and a porch with a granary over, we could cut down on transport of feedstuffs and straw—'

'Brother Stephen.' The abbot spoke quietly. 'Over my dead body will you tear down a perfectly good barn to pursue some grandiose scheme of your own. May I remind you we are sworn to holy poverty. It is not the most convenient building, and I am prepared to consider enlarging it if that is within our means when all the repairs are done; but that is all. The joists and the lift to keep out the animals, we will replace.'

Brother Stephen said nothing. The farm manager opened his mouth to speak. Peregrine looked at him, silently. The man closed his mouth, and nodded.

The atmosphere in the room as the men rose to attend midday Office, was not entirely happy.

Things did not improve after the midday meal as they got down to close inspection of financial possibilities.

'My Lord, we could always' (Peregrine raised one eyebrow in sardonic response to Brother Ambrose's obsequious approach) 'sell corrodies, as we used to—'

Save your breath, thought Tom, in the split second before the abbot thundered, '*No!* The years I laboured to reclaim this abbey from its debts! I am not now going to encumber it with unwanted inhabitants mingling with the brothers to their spiritual detriment and weighing round our necks for ever, just to raise ready money now!'

Brother Ambrose raised his hands. 'So be it, so be it. We are back to pulling our belts in and raising the rents, then.'

'Yes. Yes we are, until we have achieved the stability we need to afford the improvements we would like— always providing those are sufficiently modest to be in keeping with our vows of poverty.'

They had finished before Vespers, Father Peregrine insisting on restricting all expenditure to the most frugal necessary repairs. The men were disappointed, but they trusted and respected him, and accepted his judgement with the best grace they could muster.

Brother Tom was left alone with the abbot as the others went their way. Peregrine sat staring at the accounts and plans spread before him.

Tom seated himself opposite him, in the chair Brother Prudentius had vacated.

'Have you ever noticed, Father,' he said, 'what an ill view of life a man has when he is dog-tired, and his head is throbbing, and his headache has made him feel sick so that he's hardly eaten for two days? Have you ever noticed how short with his brothers a man like that can be, speaking sharply to them and not having the kindness, as he normally might, to hear out their points of view?'

'Brother Thomas, are you lecturing me?'

'Would I dare to? I simply wanted to remind you that a man without sleep, food and leisure is indistinguishable from a man without charity, patience or a sense of humour.'

'Well, thank you very much. Now, I have some work to do with these accounts. No doubt you also have some work to be getting on with.'

'Perhaps I should have said, "...without charity, patience, a sense of humour, or any other kind of sense, including common sense".'

'Brother Thomas, that is impertinent. You are presuming too much upon my goodwill, and you are testing my patience sorely. That is enough. Go and weed your garden, or whatever it is you want to do.'

Brother Tom gave up, and left him to it.

Now, as Peregrine sat in chapel at Compline, his face was drawn in hard lines of weariness, his eyes and mouth tight in tension and pain.

After Compline, the brethren retired to bed in silence.

Tom gave his abbot ten minutes to return to his house, then rose from his knees in the chapel and followed him in. He found him seated once again at his table, the accounts spread out. Tom sat down opposite him. Peregrine raised his head. He lifted his eyebrows in enquiry. He did not speak. They were in silence now.

'Go to bed,' said Brother Tom.

Peregrine frowned. 'Brother Thomas, we are in silence.'

'Please; go to bed.'

The abbot hesitated. 'Brother, to tell you the truth, I don't feel very well. I must get this straight in my head before I go to bed, in case I have a fever or something in the morning. I promise you, after I have done these last few things, I will spend a day or two searching out my lost common sense, not to mention my sense of humour and all the rest. I can hardly keep my mind to it as it is. You go to your bed. I shall be finished before Matins. I will get some sleep before morning.'

The brothers had to be abed early if they were to be up for the Night Office at midnight, and it was still no later than ten o'clock when Brother Tom unfastened his sandals and his belt, took off his habit and climbed into bed in his drawers and undershirt. The Rule laid down that the brethren must sleep clothed saving the knives in their belts which might wound them as they slept, but Tom had no intention of going to bed in a habit on a hot summer night. Outside, dusk was only just deepening into night, though it was dark enough in the chamber of the abbot's house, with its tiny slits of windows.

Tom kicked off his blanket. It was sultry weather, and oppressive even in the cool of the monastery buildings with their thick walls of stone. In the distance, he could hear a low rumbling of thunder. He could not get comfortable in his bed, and lay shifting about restlessly for a while. 'Wish it would rain,' he said to himself; 'I can hardly breathe.' The few, fat, heavy drops that had fallen earlier had come to nothing, and the night waited in sullen

stillness for the storm. Tom lay on his back, his knees
drawn up and his hands clasped behind his head, staring
into the dark. 'I'll never get to sleep on a night like this,'
he thought.

He was woken by a tremendous rending crash of
thunder. Lightning flashed blue through the narrow window, and the air was full of the sweet freshness of rain.
Tom lay listening to the torrential wetness of it on the
sloping roof of the abbot's chamber, built on as a single-
storey after-thought projecting from the rest of the building. He rolled onto his side, raising himself on one elbow,
listening. The deluge of rain and the rolling of thunder
were loud enough to obscure the sound of anyone's
breathing, but he was sure he was alone. Another flash of
lightning illuminated the room; a split second, but long
enough for him to see his abbot's bed, empty and
unruffled. Tom frowned. 'Whatever's he doing?' he muttered.

He slid out of bed and pulled on his habit, fastened his
belt, then went through into the main room of the abbot's
house. The great oak table was a litter of plans and
accounts still, but Father Peregrine had gone.

The door into the cloister was closed, but someone had
opened wide the little door at the back of the room, beside
where the scribe's desk stood under the window.

Brother Tom crossed the room and looked out through
the low, narrow doorway into the streaming dark. Peregrine was standing on the flagged path, leaning on his
wooden crutch, his face held up to the pouring rain. The
thunder growled and crashed around him, the flashes of
lightning intermittently illuminating the path awash with
rain and the wet leaves of the birch tree tossing in the
storm.

'Come inside, you crazy fool!' Tom called. 'What the
devil are you doing?'

Peregrine turned round at the sound of Tom's voice. In
the momentary illumination of the lightning, Tom saw his

face radiant with exultation, laughing in the wildness of the storm.

'Man, truly I wonder if you're quite sound in the head,' Brother Tom grumbled at him as he came and stood in the doorway, the fringe of hair around the tonsure plastered to his skin, the whole of him drenched, from head to foot. Tom stared at him incredulously. 'Father, I...oh, you witless...witless... Here, let me go fetch a towel: don't you dare cross that threshold till I'm back.'

He went out through the main door of the room, that led into the cloister, and down to the lavatorium beside the kitchen entrance, where the stack of towels lay neatly folded for the morning. He grabbed two from the top and hurried back to the abbot's house.

Peregrine stood in the doorway still, his back turned to the house, looking out at the deluging night.

'Come and dry yourself now; you'll be catching your death of cold. Look at you, just look at you! No, wait; let me come to you—you're wringing wet, and it's me, not you, will have to mop this floor in the morning.

'Oh, Father, the state of you! You're wet to the skin! I'll have to find you something dry to wear. Have you a habit in your chest in the chamber?'

Peregrine was rubbing his head with one towel while Tom scrubbed him down with the other, having peeled his dripping clothes from him and flung them in a soggy bundle onto the doorstep. Peregrine looked at Tom, his eyes dancing, his face still full of the wildness and jubilation of the storm. 'I don't know,' he said. 'You're my esquire. You're supposed to know about that sort of thing.' He grinned at Tom happily. 'It was the joy of the rain,' he said apologetically, 'the passion and grandeur of the storm. I didn't mean to put you to any trouble.'

'It'll be no trouble to me at all, Father. You'll have to go to Chapel naked if I can't find anything, that's all.'

Tom lit a candle and went back into the chamber. He opened the chest against the wall, setting the candle down beside him so he could see well enough to rummage for some clothes.

'Your old habit is there,' he said to Peregrine as he returned. 'It'll do till morning. Patched and stained it is, this one, but never mind, it's dark, no one will see. There's an undershirt here too, about fit for a scarecrow, but it'll serve for now. Drawers you'll have to live without until the morning. Come and sit in this chair then, so you can put that crutch down.'

He helped his abbot into the dry clothes, and dried his belt and sandals with the towel.

'I've no idea what the time is. Should we go to Chapel or back to bed? Oh, there's the bell now. There, you look reasonable, which is more than you are. Let me fasten that door before we go. Did you get your work done?'

'I did. It's sorted in my mind now. I can see how to do what's needful within a year without incurring debts. I'll go through it with Brother Ambrose and Father Chad in the morning. But hush now, we're breaking silence shamelessly. No more talk.'

'Except—Brother Thomas, thank you. For everything, I mean.'

During the Office, in the long chanting of the Gospel, Brother Tom watched the abbot's eyelids drooping irresistibly; the little shake of his head as he fought valiantly to stay awake. He lasted through to the end of Matins, but by the time the bell was ringing again for Lauds he leaned sideways in his stall, his head lolling, fast asleep.

Tom left his place in the choir and crossed over to Father Peregrine. He shook his shoulder gently. Peregrine sighed and stirred, opened his eyes and looked up sleepily at Tom. 'Mm?' His eyes were drowsing again.

'Father—' Tom bent over him, his hand on his shoulder. Peregrine would be deeply embarrassed to be caught dozing once Lauds had begun. 'Father—'

The abbot's head rolled and he murmured something, then his body sagged completely, sliding down in his stall.

Tom squatted down beside him, taking hold of his arms: 'Father...Mother of God, he's convulsing...'

He looked back over his shoulder, and saw with relief Brother John coming into Chapel. The infirmary brothers were not always there for the Night Office. Whether they were free to come depended on whom they had in their care.

'Brother John!' Tom spoke urgently, but not loud. Even so, his voice overrode the whisper of robes and the shuffling of sandals as the brethren made their way back into the choir for the second Office of the night. All round the choir, cowled heads lifted, and Brother John strode to his side in the stillness of a watching, listening silence.

'He's in some kind of a fit—I don't know—he's convulsing...'

'Let me squeeze past you. Yes, hold on to him. I want to try and get a look at his face. Look, if I lift under his arms, will you take his legs? Lay him on his side, not on his back. Can you manage?'

The calmness of Brother John's voice eased Tom's fear. They lifted him down from his stall, and laid him on the ground.

'No vomit in his mouth. His eyes are all over the place, look. Face very grey. Hmm. He doesn't look too good, Tom. Can I come where you are? Let me have a look at his body. Oh...yes. Can you see how all this right side is awry? And his face, look—twisted the same. I've seen seizures like this before. He might well come through...but...there, the convulsion has stopped now. Breathing very, very slow. Faith, he's a horrible colour, isn't he—even by candlelight.

'We'll carry him to the infirmary. Bring the bier round from the parish side. We'll take him on that. Send someone ahead of us to the infirmary to give Brother Michael word to expect us—someone sensible; Brother Francis or someone. And Tom! Tell Father Chad to start the Office, will you? This silent audience is giving me the creeps.'

The chapel was full of heaviness as the tense, despon-
dent silence of the gathered community roused itself into
the ancient duty of worship. They had already seen death
that year: Father Matthew, in the spring, and old Father
Lucanus six weeks after him, in Whitsuntide. The
brothers' voices rose and fell with the chant, but their
thoughts were with the unconscious form of their abbot as
the bier trundled out of the south door of the choir to the
infirmary, under the sombre speculation of their gaze.

In the infirmary, night-lights were burning in the still,
warm dark. Brother Michael had made ready for them,
prepared a bed already in a room where no other patients
slept. Like Brother John, he moved in unruffled efficiency;
he was used to men, fearful and ill, needing his reassuring
calm as much as they needed bones splinting or fever
physicking, or muscles rubbing. It was part of the nursing
care the infirmary offered, and Brother Michael, aware of
Tom's agitation, made available to him the soothing peace
of his own competence.

Tom hovered anxiously, watching Brother John's face
while he and Brother Michael put the abbot into a clean
bed and stripped him of his habit. Peregrine's body was as
limp and unwieldy as a corpse now, offering neither co-
operation nor resistance. His eyes were open, but rolling
independently, and his breathing rasped slow and stertorous. Brother John's face, observant and purposeful,
gave nothing away as he went about his work.

'That's his old tunic,' Tom explained. He was aware of
his voice gabbling nervously, but not able to slow it down.
'He went out in the rain tonight and got himself wet
through. That's an old undershirt too. I couldn't find him
any drawers, it was the middle of the night. I was expecting to find him some presentable clothes in the morning.
He—'

Brother John looked up at Tom. 'It's all right. He won't
be needing to wear drawers here for a while. He won't
need his habit either, and we've a whole cupboard full of

undershirts. Don't worry yourself, Brother. I suggest you go and get a bit of rest. If there's any change, I'll send you word. He may be quite a time like this, and then it could go either way. Be prepared for that.'

'I told him. I told him he was working too hard and he'd be ill if he didn't slow down.'

Brother John shook his head. 'It probably would have happened anyway, Tom. He's not getting any younger. These things can sometimes be hastened or delayed—but not by very much. We'll do our best for him, don't fret.'

Brother Tom nodded, and stood there a moment longer. 'I'll go then,' he said. 'There's nothing else I can do. Let me know.'

As he went back out into the night rain, he was gripped by a sense of deep loss. There had grown between himself and Father Peregrine over the years a bond of trust and love. Prepare yourself, Brother John had warned. It would not be all that easy to prepare himself to lose the dry wit and warm compassion, the honesty and courage and faith, of the man he had come to know so well.

Brother Tom did not return to his bed. He went back to the chapel. There was nothing he could do, but he could pray, and sleep would be an impossibility. It was the sight of Peregrine's eyes that haunted him: rolling in the grey, sagging face. Sleep would be exiled by that memory. He pushed open the door, and walked slowly back into the choir.

There he found the rest of the community, who in silent unanimity had remained in prayer. They stayed there, united in anxious intercession, until the morning.

II
THE WAKE OF THE STORM

'It would make more sense for you to be on the farm than working in a job like this, wouldn't it?' asked Father Chad.

'Yes. It would. I'd like to be on the farm just now.' Brother Tom stood before the great oak table in the abbot's house. Father Chad had it considerably tidier than Father Peregrine ever had. He had been Father Peregrine's prior for so many years now, and the community was now so stable both economically and pastorally, that he had been able to step smoothly into the role of abbot, filling his superior's place in time of sickness. Brother Tom looked down at the tidy table, and at Father Chad supplanting Peregrine in the abbot's chair. The resentment he felt was, he knew, the danger of particular friendships. As part of his vow of chastity, keeping his heart guarded against human affection, he ought now to contemplate the prospect of another man filling Father Peregrine's place with equanimity. He did not. There was no point trying to deceive himself.

'Thank you,' he said. 'I think I'd rather be on the farm. There are two strips of hay still standing because of the rain in June. They need to get it down and stacked as quickly as possible, and they need someone to thatch the ricks besides Brother Stephen. We want to begin work on the field shelters in the least sheltered places before harvest, too. Once the harvest is over and the fall is on us, the weather will be more uncertain, and we shall need to get started with the ploughing, and—'

'All right, Brother Thomas! I can see you're itching to get underway. I'll ask Brother Josephus and Brother Thaddeus to take your place here. It's not really advisable to have just the one attendant these days anyway; people expect at least two. I know Father liked to keep to just the one—humility and poverty, and so forth—but there are lots of good reasons why having two is more practical. You have done good service here, Brother. I have often thought it was hard to keep you to the obedience of abbot's esquire when your heart is for the land, but Father would have it so. He relied on you as he relied on no one else. The change will be good for you. You can go up to the farm this morning if you like. I've no visitors. I shall be eating in refectory with the brethren at midday.'

'Thank you, Father.'

Father Chad smiled at Tom, and Tom obliged with a smile in return, but his heart was sore. It was true, all summer he had fretted to be out on the farm, as he always did, but now he had what he wanted, there was no joy in it.

Earlier in the summer, in June, when they had been struggling to harvest what hay they could before the rain defeated them, his obedience had weighed like chains. Most of the able-bodied men had been out in the fields all day, and he had been able to snatch only a couple of hours in the afternoons. The rest of his time had been taken up in the abbot's house, where a seemingly endless procession of wealthy pilgrims availed themselves of the abbey's hospitality, day after day. He had chafed under the tedious restriction of waiting at table, standing unobtrusively to one side to pour wine. Father Peregrine had seen it.

'Would you rather be on the farm, Brother Thomas?' he had asked.

'Yes,' Tom had responded shortly. And he had watched the familiar tightening of tension about his superior's jaw as he replied evenly, avoiding Tom's eyes, 'Brother, it would be the work of a moment to release you to the farm. I can have Brother Francis or someone to help me here.'

Eventually Tom's silence had forced the abbot to look him in the eye, revealing the anxious vulnerability of his incapacity. Tom knew that anyway. He knew how Peregrine needed someone who was very familiar with the limitations his disability imposed on him, to smooth the path with guests, and to a certain extent with the brethren. He knew, too, that Peregrine needed someone who could read his moods, see through his defences, to help him live with his own stormy spirit, its occasional moods of anguish and blackness.

Tom had shaken his head. 'Don't distress yourself. My work is here. I'll help with the ploughing in the fall. That'll do me.'

And Peregrine, who with anyone else would have dismissed it, sent them to the work they were best fitted for, sat with the anxiety twitching his mouth, looking at Tom, helpless, his eyes begging understanding. 'Thank you,' he had said stiffly, at last. He needed Tom. Both of them knew that.

Tom plodded away from the cloister buildings, and up to the farm. Only a week. It did not seem possible. Only a week, and the gap was closing behind him...another man in his chair...another man's rule making little changes...another man's style in the abbot's chapter at the morning meeting. It was as though he'd died. Worse, maybe.

It was four days since Tom himself had been to see Father Peregrine in the infirmary. There was nothing to go for. He lay mute and paralysed, beyond communication.

The first day of Peregrine's illness, Brother Tom had been at the infirmary at six o'clock in the morning, as soon as he had eaten his breakfast; and that had stuck in his craw like sawdust, as he ate in anxious haste.

Martin Jonson, the village man who came every day to help in the infirmary, greeted him at the door.

'Good day to you, Brother Thomas. Have you come to see how Father Columba is?'

'What? Oh—yes.' Columba was Peregrine's name in religion; the name he had been given when he took his monastic vows. His brothers all called him Father Peregrine, which was his baptismal name, agreeing that Peregrine the hawk was more in keeping with the man than Columba, the dove; he could be gentle and merciful, but he was no dove. Even his compassion burned with the fierce ardour of his spirit. No dove. But as a matter of propriety, outsiders to the community knew him as Father Columba.

'Yes. Can I see him?'

'Well...' Martin pulled a long face. 'I wouldn't, not if I were you, Brother. I don't want to upset you, but he's not right, like. He's as limp and floppy as a stick of wilted rhubarb; his eyes turned up in his head, and as helpless as a baby, too, if you know what I mean. There's no point in speaking to him, not really. He'd not know you.'

'I see. Thank you.' Brother Tom turned away. He could not now remember the rest of that day. The events of it all gave way to the dull pain of sadness. It must have been like any day, shaped by the round of prayer and work, but all he could remember of it was lying in his bed in the abbot's chamber that night, listening to the regular breathing of Father Chad's peaceful sleep; wanting to cry, and telling himself not to be so silly, wanting the familiar comfort of Peregrine's grey eyes watching him shrewdly as he poured out his troubles.

'This is a big one, Father,' he whispered into the sleeping dark. 'I need your counsel to help me through this.' And he remembered the senseless anger and indignation he had felt that Peregrine was not there, now when he needed him.

At Mass in the morning he had sat in his stall gazing up at the great wooden crucifix, as he had seen Peregrine do, times beyond counting. But it was nothing, only lifeless wood. God seemed as far away as the sun in the sky, shimmering in remote, impassive glory on the half of the world that was not engulfed in the night of sickness and confusion and distress.

After Chapter, where he had listened with aching resentment to Father Chad, sitting in the abbot's chair, giving the abbot's address, he had gone again to the infirmary, and found Martin Jonson sitting out in the morning sunshine, sorting through a great bag of absorbent sphagnum moss.

'Good morning to you, Brother Thomas! Not much change I'm afraid, if it's Father Columba you're asking after. He's a little better, maybe. Not so limp today, but his right side is all stiff: apoplexy, Brother John says it is. They've only just started on washes and physic dosing and what have you. Truth to tell, you'd be wasting your time waiting. We'll let you know.'

'Thank you,' Tom had said miserably, and trailed slowly back down the path to the cloister buildings. That day he could remember. He remembered sweeping the floor in the abbot's house, moving out his bed into the dorter upstairs, because Father Chad did not need him in the night to help him dress and fasten his shoes, as Peregrine had.

'You don't think he'll be back, then?' he had asked Father Chad, trying to keep his voice casual, trying to make it sound like a friendly enquiry. The sick pain of sorrow that wept inside him was too private to share with anyone. He did not want Father Chad to see it. He thought of all the times he had come into the abbot's house, in perplexity, in heartache, in temptation— 'Father, can I talk to you?'—and Peregrine putting aside

his work, looking at him affectionately, perceptively—
'Tell me about it.'

Father Chad shook his head doubtfully. 'Brother John
thinks not. He's paralysed all down one side, you see, and
he can't speak. They think he can see and hear, but...no,
Brother. I'm sure he won't be back.'

'No,' said Tom. 'No, of course not. I'll move the bed.'

He remembered waiting on Father Chad at table, the
concerned enquiries of guests, and Father Chad's discreet,
reassuring answers: 'Not too well—overwork—complete
rest for a while. No, we're not at all sure...yes, he will be
delighted to know you were here and greeted him. Yes, I
will pass on your good wishes with all my heart...no; no
visitors, I'm afraid.'

When he was free to go, Tom went early into chapel for
Compline. He sat in his stall, thinking nothing, holding
the sadness inside him like a great weight; sitting very still
lest the rolling weight of sorrow topple his equilibrium
completely.

Suddenly aware of someone beside him, he looked up,
into Brother Michael's face. Brother Michael, Brother
John's assistant in the infirmary, had been with Brother
Tom in the novitiate for a short while, and they had the
ease between them of men who had trained together, even
though years had passed since those days.

'Are you not coming to see him, then?' Brother Michael
asked. His gentle friendliness undermined most men's
defences. Tom felt the tears welling in his eyes.

'I came. Martin said...' he couldn't finish the sentence.

'Martin Jonson sent you away?'

Tom nodded.

'I'm sorry. He had no business to. Come in the morning, after High Mass.' Brother Michael paused. 'And
what about you, Tom? This must be distressing you. Have
you talked to anyone about it?'

'No.' Brother Tom replied dully. 'There's no one I
want to talk to.'

Brother Michael looked at him, quietly taking in the harshness of pain in his face.

'You know where to find Brother John and me, if you need us. I'll see you in the morning then, yes?'

Brother Tom nodded. He did not trust himself to speak. The Compline bell was ringing, and the chapel beginning to fill up. He did not want to make a spectacle of himself here. Brother Michael pressed Tom's hand gently, then took his place in his own stall.

In the morning, as soon as Mass and Chapter ended, Tom hurried up to the infirmary. He went in, and found Martin carrying a tray of drinks out to the old men who were sitting in the sun in the physic garden.

'Can I go in and see Father?'

Martin smiled at him cheerily. 'Yes, I don't see why not today. You'll have to wait a minute though, the brothers are washing him and whatnot just now. There's a bench there outside his room if you'd like to sit yourself down till they're finished. He's not so bad this morning. They think he's going to pull through. He's not like he was that first day—grey as a corpse he was, gave me the shivers! Brother John thinks he's all there and understanding us now, though I must say I can't see much sign of it. His eyes have righted themselves, but that's about all. Brother John says we have to keep talking to him, chatting like. "Chin up, never say die!" I say to him, and, "Look on the bright side!" Well, it's important to keep sick people happy, that's true enough. Sit you down then. They'll not be long.'

Tom went and sat on the bench outside the room. The door was ajar, and he could hear Brother John's voice talking quietly to Brother Michael. Years, those two had worked together now; they were a good team, understanding well the blend of hygiene, discipline, compassion and medicine that was needed to promote healing. He listened to the calmness of Brother John's voice.

'We'll leave the sheet for now. He may need a clean one

later anyway. Has he passed water this morning? Yes? Recently? Good. Bowels open? No? Still not? That's three days. Hmm. We'll have to do something about that then. I don't want to be messing him about with enemas. You dosed him, yes? But no luck. Let's have a look then, and clear out whatever's necessary. Pass me the jar of ointment there.'

Tom listened to the gentleness and kindness of his voice as he spoke to his patient, soothing.

'Father, we've to look and see if you need to relieve yourself, or you're going to be in pain. I won't hurt you. We'll roll you on your side over to Brother Michael, and I'll check if there's a stool formed needing removing, and take it out if there is.'

Silence.

'Ah, yes, I thought so. That's impacted there. He needs it out.'

Squelching. A whimpering moan.

'Oh God, will you never finish with this man?' Tom's spirit groaned. 'How much more are you going to put him through? How much more pain and infirmity and humiliation have you got in store for him?'

He leaned his head back against the cool stone of the wall behind him, and closed his eyes. 'It's not fair,' he whispered. 'It's not fair.'

Jesus, whom Peregrine worshipped and clung to as a suffering, broken Lord, was determined, it seemed, to make him bear the same grim cross, endure it to the bitter end. 'What a wonderful friend you are,' Tom muttered.

'There, that'll do for the moment. You should be more comfortable now, Father. Hold him like that a minute, Brother while I wash my hands, and I'll give him a quick wash, then we'll leave him in peace.'

Silence. Water splashing. A nailbrush. Silence.

'Good, that's done, then. There, we'll leave you alone now, Father. I'll come back later and see if you can manage something to eat at midday. I'll take the pot and empty it, Brother, if you'll take the water and towel and shaving things.'

They came out of the room.

'Hello, Brother Thomas! I didn't know you were here. I hope you haven't been waiting long. You can go in and see him if you like. He's not saying anything, but I think he's with us, taking it all in.'

Tom stood up and made himself smile at Brother John. 'Thank you,' he said, and went into the room.

It was cool and dim, a west-facing room that missed the morning sun. A table. A capacious wooden chair. Against the wall another chair, the jordan, with a circular hole cut in the seat and a chamber pot on a shelf below the hole. A low stool. The bed. Tom looked at the bed. He felt his throat constricting in the apprehension. You look small in that bed, he thought.

He went nearer, stood beside the bed looking down at Peregrine. Oh God, he thought; oh my God, what have you done to him?

Saturday morning, shaving morning; they had just shaved him, washed him, combed his hair. This was as good as he was going to look. The right side of his face with its disfiguring scar, sagged tonelessly. His eyes had righted themselves, but they had lost all their lustre of life, staring—no, not even staring, only gazing, blankly. Tom could not be sure that those eyes saw him at all. There was a mute, bleak, stillness about that face, except for the lips that vibrated and spluttered loosely and noisily with every outbreath. Every breath in grunted and rasped in his nose. Tom stood looking down at him. 'Oh God,' he whispered. 'Oh suffering Jesus... Father of mercy... oh my God...'

The door pushed open, and Brother Michael had returned, entering softly. He came and stood on the other side of the bed.

'Here's Brother Tom come to see you, Father,' he said lightly. 'He's been before, but now you're well enough to see him, and looking very clean and presentable. You put me to shame indeed! Your first visitor; and if you're very lucky, he might even say "Good morning" to you.'

Tom looked up at Brother Michael incredulously. What was the point in saying anything to this...?

Brother Michael returned his gaze with a challenge in his eyes. 'Please,' his lips mouthed silently.

Tom swallowed. He put out his hand and laid it gingerly on Peregrine's head, his thumb caressing his brow. 'Good day to you, Father,' he said. He looked up desperately at Brother Michael.

'Better not stay too long, not today.' That same light, easy tone, as if there was nothing wrong; as if he'd been visiting a man with no more than a cold in the head. How does he do it? Tom wondered. He let his hand drop to his side. Not a flicker of response from those dull, gazing eyes. Those eyes...such compassion, intelligence, laughter, anger he had seen burning in those eyes, dark grey brooding eyes. And now...now nothing, shallow emptiness; the bright lamp of the man's spirit snuffed out to a charred and smoking wick. He turned away, and walked to the door.

'Tom.' He looked back at the sound of Brother Michael's voice. Brother Michael indicated with a slight nod the still figure in the neat infirmary bed. Peregrine had turned his head. The lifeless grey eyes were following him. They bore no spark, the song of the spirit was extinguished, but they were watching him go. Tom looked back a long moment before he left the room.

Brother Michael followed him out, walked with him out onto the path, where the bright sunshine stabbed their sight.

'He's going to die, then?'

'No,' said Brother Michael, 'we don't think so. Not now.'

'You mean, he's going to live? Like that?'

Michael hesitated. 'It's impossible to say. He should improve—Brother John thinks he will improve, and so does Brother Edward. He should be able to get out of bed, sit in a chair.'

Tom looked at Brother Michael. 'That's wonderful,' he said bitterly.

'It may be better than that. He may recover his speech.'

'Speech? He'll have to recover his mind first!'

'We don't know that his mind is gone, Tom. It's better not to jump to hasty conclusions.'

'How long will he live, like this?'

'We don't know. It could be years, months, hours—we don't know.'

'But he's not going to die.'

'We don't think so: but it's impossible to say. We don't know.'

'Don't know much, really, do you?'

Brother Michael did not reply at once. He plucked a leaf from a bush of lemon balm that grew at the side of the path, and crushed it absently in his fingers. 'I love him too, Tom,' he said quietly. 'So does Brother John. It's not easy for any of us.'

'No. I don't suppose it is. I'm sure you look after him admirably. I won't hold you up any more.'

Brother Michael sighed as he watched Tom walk away. Which would I rather have, he wondered: the luxury of turning my back like that, or the privilege of facing it?

He went back into the building. The old men needed an opportunity to relieve themselves, and there were three men to be bathed before the end of the morning, and half the beds still to be made.

Brother Tom went straight up to the abbot's house, not seeing, not thinking, his memory harrowed by the vision of that empty, foolish, blowing face, like a derelict house with the shutters broken and the door swinging loose. He came in to Father Chad and requested bluntly to be transferred to the farm. He half-wished Father Chad had it in him to look at a man with shrewd compassion, 'Tell me about it;' but Father Chad was not one to probe too deep. Tom looked into amiable, accommodating brown eyes; not astute grey ones that saw through to the soul.

'It would make more sense for you to be on the farm than working in a job like this, wouldn't it?' asked Father Chad.

'Yes, Father. I'd like to be on the farm just now.'

And now he came into the farmyard, and stood listening for clues of Brother Stephen's whereabouts. The farm track wound up through the farm buildings—a barn, the cow byre, the milking shed with a dairy attached to the back of it.

This dairy was the occasion for many caustic remarks by the kitchen brothers, whose own dairy, at the back of the kitchen, was a spotless model of cool, scrubbed cleanliness, pleasingly stocked with wide bowls of cream set to rise, and dripping nets of curds destined to become soft, delicate white cheese, and pats of yellow butter, and stoneware pitchers of milk. The farm dairy, by contrast, was more or less swilled down each day and brushed through, but it was a comfortable haven for bats and spiders, and never scoured so viciously as to disturb the corners. A large, rough table stood in the centre, and that was well enough scrubbed. On it, the milk pails and water pails were stacked side by side, and the barrels in which the farm brothers transported the milk down to the kitchen, to be poured out for using fresh or making cheese, or left in the barrel to be churned for butter. Along one wall of the dairy ranged the capacious feed chests of grain and dried beet, which kept the cows happy during milking. Strictly speaking, these had no place in the dairy, but it was the most difficult building for the cows to plunder, so there they stayed.

On the far side of the milking shed was a foldyard and a byre. After milking, the beasts went through into the yard, where they stayed in colder nights, and daytimes as well in the depths of winter.

In the summer, they were released into the pasture

beyond the yard, but it was still useful to send them out through the foldyard, because any beast with mastitis or a cut leg could be kept back for treatment when the rest of the cows went out to pasture.

Past the milking shed, the track curved uphill still to an apple orchard enclosed by a stone wall. The pig sties formed part of the wall, and these apples grew mainly for the benefit of the pigs. They also fed on the beechmast and acorns that fell from a row of trees planted in a curve around the upper side of the orchard, sheltering the farm buildings from the north and east winds.

This year the two sows had fourteen piglets between them, and these Brother Stephen was nurturing carefully for the bishop's visit in the spring. He fed them on kitchen swill and wild plants, sow thistle, comfrey and dandelions, with the added luxury of a pail of milk thrown over their barley meal in the morning. The littler boys from the abbey school hunted snails on wet afternoons when lessons had finished. They took a gruesome pleasure in watching the pigs' eager, abandoned greed as they snuffled and crunched their way through a pail of them.

Beside the pig sties a stout stone shack with a thick, heavy oak door that fitted snug to the ground with no space beneath it, housed various of Brother Stephen's veterinary implements and animal medicines. From this shed there suddenly erupted the most appalling cacophony of noise; a deafening racket of screaming and squealing which Tom could attribute to only one thing. Brother Stephen was castrating the piglets. Brother Tom cast a nervous glance up towards the orchard. Where were the sows?

His question was answered the instant he looked. The two of them, in furious haste, came belting down the orchard to the gate in response to the screaming panic of their offspring.

Tom knew from experience that they could lift the orchard gate off its hinges as if it were no heavier than a milking stool. The pigs, if they could get their noses under the stone sinks in which they were fed, tossed them carelessly aside as though they weighed as little as a wooden pail.

Once in the farmyard, they would not be able to get at Brother Stephen about his bloody work: that was why the door had been so carefully fitted, too nicely seated to admit any pig's snout. Their enraged motherhood would therefore wreak its vengeance on whomever their small, livid eyes caught sight of. A full-grown pig provoked to wrath can crush a man's limb between its teeth with astonishing ease. Tom knew. He had witnessed it.

He stood frozen for one moment as the two sows thundered down the orchard to the gate, then, 'Sweet mother of God!' he gasped, and fled to the milking shed. He dragged the door shut behind him, sweating and cursing the accumulation of straw and cow dung that clogged around the foot of the door, and the rust that bound the hinges. The cows were staid old beasts, used to the routine of milking. They had no objection to it provided there was a manger of cereal in it for them, and they entered the shed in placid procession every morning and evening, each strolling peaceably to her own tethering ring, awaiting her pail of food. Those cows weren't going anywhere. No one had had need to close that door for years.

Brother Tom heard the orchard gate go with a crash. 'Oh, God, my God!'

He was shaking as he got the door to and dropped the heavy iron latch. Within seconds two dewy, whiskered pink snouts were snuffling and questing under the door. Tom watched in awe as the two of them heaved and the tall, wide door shifted a little. The hinges were made like those of all the farm buildings' doors, so that the doors could be lifted off if they were needed elsewhere or needed replacing.

'Dear heaven...' Tom murmured as he watched the hinges creak and shift. He didn't believe even the two sows together could take the weight of that door, and yet… 'Oh no, you're not having me for breakfast, sweetheart,' he said, and went through the milking parlour into the dairy. This time the door presented no problems, being always secured to keep the beasts out of the feed. Tom went in and shut it behind him. The latch was on the dairy side of the door, accessible from the milking parlour by a round hole cut in the wood of the door. Cattle had too much of an aptitude for mastering latches with their noses for a farmer with any sense to attach the latch where they could reach it.

On the table in the centre of the room a pail of milk and a pail of barley meal stood waiting. When Brother Stephen had finished with the piglets, he would release them out of the shed to their indignant mothers, wait until both piglets and sows had calmed down and wandered away, then restore their confidence in him and tempt them back to captivity with this extra feed.

Tom scrambled up onto one of the feed chests, and waited. Even after the ear-splitting discord of the terrified piglets had ceased, he did not dare move.

Eventually, he heard the scrape and creak of the milking shed door. Common sense told him it was Brother Stephen, but still he did not dare move. Pigs, after all, were intelligent and resourceful animals. Then unmistakably human fingers reached through to the latch of the dairy door and lifted it. Brother Stephen entered the dairy just in time to catch Brother Tom climbing down from the feed chest.

Brother Stephen stopped in his tracks, gazing at Tom in blank surprise. 'What on earth are you doing?' he enquired in amazement. Brother Tom found the question, and the foolish look on Brother Stephen's face, intensely irritating.

'I thought,' he replied with biting sarcasm, 'that the peaceful pastoral setting of this hillside would be an ideal environment for some private meditation. What do you think I'm doing, you fool? I got here just as you started work on the pigs.'

A slow grin spread over Brother Stephen's face, and he began to laugh. 'You were hiding from the pigs?' he chuckled.

'Is that so perishing funny? I only just got in here in time.'

'Well, well. What are you doing up here anyway?' Brother Stephen lifted the pail of milk and the pail of meal from the table. 'Come and show your face to the pigs.'

'I've permission to come and work on the farm now.'

'For good?' Brother Stephen looked at Tom in pleased surprise.

'For good.'

'How comes that, then?' asked Brother Stephen as they walked across the farmyard. 'Lift the gate back onto its hinges, will you? Here, pigs! Piggy, piggy! Here pigs!'

He tipped the meal and milk into one of the stone troughs that stood in the orchard, and banged the bucket on the side of it, calling. In a cloud of dust, the pigs came bustling up the farm track, and hurried greedily into their orchard, all trauma forgotten before the happy prospect of food.

Brother Stephen shut the gate on them, and he and Tom stood watching the grunting, hasty delight of their feeding.

'Father won't be out of the infirmary again,' said Tom. 'Father Chad is willing to have someone else for his attendant. Attendants. He wants two.'

'Yes, well that's sensible enough. It's a job for two men, for all so much of the time is employed in standing about.'

'Father didn't think so.'

Brother Stephen glanced at Tom's face, and decided against pursuing that conversation.

'So,' he said brightly, 'you're up here with us. Well I don't need to tell you how glad I am. One more day to dry that hay out, and we'll mow it tomorrow, God willing, if the fair weather holds. I need your hands, and I need your sense. We've Brother Germanus since he took his simple vows, but that's only been six weeks, and you wouldn't think he'd ever been within hailing distance of a cowshed, to watch him work. You couldn't have come at a better time. Wish we'd had you for shearing.'

Brother Tom did not reply for a moment. He leaned on the gate, staring gloomily at the pigs.

'Shall I milk tonight, then?' he said after a while, without enthusiasm.

'Yes, please. Brother...' Brother Stephen paused.

'What?'

'I know how you feel about Father Abbot—'

Brother Tom interrupted him savagely. 'Do you?'

Brother Stephen tried again, hesitantly, searching for the right words. 'I'm sorry about it. That's all I wanted to say. It's all I can say. We all know how close you are to him. It must be very painful for you.'

'Yes. Well, there's no point crying over spilt milk, is there? I'll do the cows, if you like, this evening. What about this afternoon?'

Brother Stephen sighed. It seemed Tom wanted his heartache kept private.

'Thank you. We'll start the hay first thing tomorrow, then, as soon as the dew's off the field. If you'll milk tonight I would be grateful, and in the morning, please. This afternoon I'm sharpening and greasing the scythes, and looking over the hay wagons. Then I'm going up to the hay field and the top barn to make sure all's ready. I'll have Brother Germanus with me, but you can come along if you like.'

Brother Tom pulled a face. 'No thanks. Don't fancy his company. I'll go and help Brother Paulinus get his beans in, and pod them tonight after Vespers. They've cropped well. He needs help. Oh, 'struth, there's the Office bell already.'

The two of them walked back down the hill in silence.

Tom did not spare a glance at the infirmary buildings as they passed them on their way to the cloister buildings and the abbey church.

The choir was full of sunbeams, and the whispering quiet of the movement of the brothers' robes and their sandals on the floor, the quiet undertow of sound that served only to emphasise the stillness of the river of light and peace that flowed at all times in the chapel.

Brother Tom was grateful for the silence as the brethren gathered to pray, each one motionless in his stall, his cowled head bent reverently.

Tom sat down in his own familiar place. Brother Francis, who had been close to him since novitiate days, took his place in his stall beside him. Brother Cormac had the stall on the other side, but his place was empty. The kitchen brothers rarely all made it to the Midday Office, occurring as it did during the preparations for the main meal of the day, any more than the infirmary brothers managed all three to attend the Office. Tom looked for the infirmary brothers. Old Brother Edward was there in his place, so bent and frail these days, he looked as though a puff of wind might blow him away; and Brother Michael, just slipping into his place now at the last minute, as the cantor rose to sing the versicle.

'*Deus in adjutorium meum intende.*'

Tom felt suddenly weary of the whole business as he rose to his feet with the rest of the community. '*Domine ad adjuvandum me festina.*'

He sang the words of the Office numbly, automatically; but the duty of worship, that usually sat so comfortably on him, today seemed too tedious to bear. Tom looked at Father Chad; the prior, but so naturally filling the abbot's place, sitting in his chair. It rankled. Why couldn't they have left his place empty, allowed his absence as the reminder of his presence, let his empty chair stand for a silent hope that he was not finished, not dead? I'm being unfair, Tom told himself. They have to fill the office. They don't pretend to replace the man. And besides, he is finished. Not dead maybe, but over, done with.

The Office ended, and the brothers filed out into the cloister to wash their hands at the lavatorium, then into the refectory to stand before their places for the long Latin grace. They sat down to eat: fish, beans (again), bread, fruit.

The reader stood at the lectern reading some interminable ramble from the Church Fathers. This could go on for ever, Tom thought. An endless, suffocating round of days; beans, porridge, bread, prayer, watered ale, silence. When I die, he thought, I shall go to heaven and St Peter will say, 'And what have you done with your life, my son?' and I shall say, 'I have been to chapel seven times a day, my Lord, every day for years and years and years. I have got up in the middle of the night to pray, every night, for years and years and years. I have choked down Brother Cormac's bread—uncomplaining, mark you my lord, give me credit at least for that—and I have eaten beans and pottage, pottage and beans, dried beans, fresh beans, stewed beans, boiled beans, baked beans till the thought of them turned my stomach.'

And St Peter will look at me in horrified pity and say, 'Is that true, my son? Is that what you did with the life you were given? Well, that's a shame, because you only have one. You won't get a night's sleep, or roast beef in heaven, you know. Ah well, chapel's along there. Have a nice eternity.'

Brother Francis, whose turn it was to wait at table, was removing Tom's dish from under his nose. It was not like Brother Tom to leave half his food, and Francis paused, looking questioningly at Brother Tom. Tom came out of his reverie, and looked at the dish of beans and bread sopped in fish juices. He shook his head. Francis smiled at him, and took the dish.

Brother Tom spent the afternoon in the vegetable garden, picking beans.

'I thought we'd take the haulm down and burn it today, but it's still going strong, isn't it?' he remarked to Brother Paulinus. 'We shall be in beans up to our necks all winter. Oh, joy. Here, I'll take this lot and shell them this evening after Vespers.'

As soon as Vespers was sung, Tom went swiftly up the hill to the farm, and brought the cows in, milked them, brought the milk down the hill on a hand barrow ('Whatever did you do that for?' asked Cormac in astonishment, in the kitchen. 'You'll kill yourself. Use the pony, for heaven's sake; that's what we keep it for.'). Then he went back to the garden and podded beans until the Compline bell rang as the sun was sinking.

After Compline, he went to his bed in its little cell, the wooden, partitioned cubicle in the dorter that had been allocated to him on moving out of the abbot's house. The air was lifeless and stuffy. He tossed and turned in his bed and could not sleep.

In the end, he sat on the edge of his bed with his head in his hands, and prayed, silently. 'I don't know what you want,' he prayed. 'I thought I knew you, but I don't understand you at all. Lord God, your loving kindness is supposed to be better than life. What have you done to my friend? He loves you. Don't you know that? Have you forgotten him? Well let me tell you something: you'd better remember him now, because I can't bear to think about him any more. I'm going to forget him. It hurts too much to see him like that, because I love him, God, and there's nothing I can do. Nothing. You're the almighty one, not me. If you love him too, you—you who know everything—then you do something about him. You know what to do. I don't. If I could make a miracle to make him well again, I'd do it; but there's nothing, nothing I can do. So it's up to you now. I can't stand any more. I'm out of it.'

After that, Tom had no more words, no more thoughts. He sat among the sounds of night; Brother Peter's whis-

tling snore from the next cubicle mingling with Brother
Thaddeus' awesome snoring from further down the dorter, Theodore's mutterings, and someone making a most
extraordinary noise, rapidly smacking their lips, a sound
like a dog chasing fleas in its fur.

Then the bell was ringing for the Night Office, and
Tom got wearily to his feet. 'You heard me, God?' he
whispered, just before he left his cell. 'You remember him,
because I'm going to forget him. I can't bear to think
about him any more.'

Morning came, and Chapter Mass, then Community
Chapter, and Father Chad attempting to counsel the
brethren on secret sins of the soul, how, according to the
Rule, a brother must confess his secret sins to the abbot or
a spiritual father, who could discreetly go about healing
the wounds of others, seeing they knew how to heal their
own wounds.

Do they, indeed? thought Tom bitterly. Does he know,
my abbot, how to heal the wounds of his soul and mine
too? Oh, shut up, Chad. What do you know about it?

Then the business of the day. Father Chad laying
before the brethren the position now with their abbot. No
improvement...serious condition...time going on...look-
ing at permanent invalidity...time to consider election of
a new man. And Brother John getting to his feet, 'May I
speak?' Yes, assuredly.

'Brothers, please don't write him off. I have seen men
before recover from seizures such as this, but they need
time, and hope. Something to work for. I beg your
patience. Father Chad can stand in for him very well. Give
me till the spring to work with him. Let's elect a new
superior at Easter-tide. Things will run smoothly enough
till then. Give him his chance. Please.'

Idiot, thought Tom. Blind idiot. Wishful thinking. He's
finished.

Then the community expressing doubt. They thought
he was finished too; thought Brother John over-optimistic.

Father Chad overruling; 'Until Easter, Brother John. We know his amazing resilience, the power of his spirit. We grant him his chance.'

Tom shook his head in disbelief. Some people never knew when to let go.

He was glad to get out of the Chapter House and up to the farm. The weather was holding fair, no more than a lacy veiling of white cloud adorning an azure heaven. Tom stood in the hayfield in the sunshine, rolling and fastening back his sleeves, kilting up his habit into his belt. Every year of his life his spirit had lifted in joy at the blue and gold of harvest, but this year he was indifferent to its loveliness, lost in a dull misery that would not let him go, would not let him forget, would not let his soul out of its pain into the singing freedom.

The only hope and gladness in it was the opportunity the harvest offered to work himself into the oblivion of exhaustion, taking out his anger and unhappiness on the standing grass, slaying it in methodical sweeps of the scythe.

'All right,' he said to Brother Stephen, 'let's start. We'll have it mown and turned before dark.'

There were four of them to mow the hay; Brother Prudentius and Brother Germanus as well as Brother Stephen and Brother Tom. It was not many, but there was little hay still standing. They had no need to call on the rest of the community until the larger affair of the grain harvest. There was enough hay for the four of them to have their work cut out though, and they went at it at a gruelling pace, sweltering in the heat of the climbing sun. Brother Germanus, though he came of a farming family, was an aristocrat and had never laboured in the fields until he came to St Alcuin's. He handled the scythe clumsily, though he learned quickly, and he was left further and further behind the others as they mowed in a steady line along the meadow. By the time the bell rang across the hillside for the Midday Office, he was trembling with weariness, his palms bloody with broken blisters.

'Never mind,' said Brother Tom unsympathetically. 'You haven't held us up too much. We're three parts done. It'll be as hot as hell out there this afternoon. The grass'll be dry enough to turn before night. Bind your hands with a rag. They'll soon harden.'

'Easy, Brother,' protested Brother Prudentius. 'He's too young, and I'm too old. You work like a madman if you will, but don't forget, work here is supposed to be prayer, not frenzy. We can hardly keep up with you.'

'Let's not turn it yet, Brother,' said Brother Stephen. 'It needs to be well dry. We'll trust providence and leave it a day. There's no sense half-killing ourselves to rush it in, only to have the rick burst into flames a month from now because the hay wasn't dry when it was stacked.'

Tom shrugged his shoulders and grunted his assent.

The brothers went down the hill to eat their midday meal in the refectory. Once the cereal harvest had got underway, they would be given permission to dispense with this midday interruption, but this final day's mowing was a minor undertaking, and they had been given no dispensation from the Midday Office and meal. They finished the mowing in the afternoon, though it meant skipping Vespers, and stood leaning on the scythes, looking with satisfaction at the swatches of grass lying in neat lines along the meadow.

'Cows'll be up,' said Brother Tom. 'I'll milk again tonight.'

'Brother, you're a saint,' Brother Stephen responded warmly. 'My back's fit to break in half, and my legs are melting. I'll be hobbling down that hill like old Father Cyprian. Look at that sky now, coming crimson. Fair weather tomorrow. We shall get this last lot dry and stacked, God willing. Give me your scythe, then, Brother Thomas. I'll put it away for you. You can do the cows with my blessing.'

Tom gave Brother Stephen his scythe without a word, and set off down to the milking shed. The other men watched him go.

'What's eating him?' asked Brother Prudentius.

'What d'you think?' Brother Stephen replied.

'Aye, well...it's hit us all hard.'

'What has?' asked Brother Germanus curiously.

'He's breaking his heart for Father Abbot, is Brother Thomas,' said Brother Prudentius. 'He's taken it hard, poor lad.'

'Yes,' said Brother Stephen. 'Going to make life hard for all the rest of us too, by the looks of it. Still, he's more use working than he would be sitting about moping. Let's get these scythes away and grab a bite to eat before Compline.'

Brother Tom sat on the milking stool in the dusk of the milking shed, his forehead leaning into the hollow of a cow's flank, his hands wet and greasy with milk, rhythmically squeezing and pulling the teats. The whiskery hairs of the firm udder against his hand as he grasped the teat, the warm living bulk of the beast against his head, the gurgling of her belly, and the shifting of her flank as she moved her foot, the inquisitive blowing of her breath as she swung her nose round to inspect him, getting impatient as he stripped down the last of the milk; it made a world. He took refuge in the solid, living presence of her comfortable benevolence.

The milk was finished. Tom rubbed his face against the cow's warm rough flank, yearning for the comfort of her sensual, unquestioning being. Then he swore and fell back, knocked off his balance as she shifted impatiently, lifting her foot and planting it firmly in the pail of milk.

The sunset was fading by the time he had finished milking, turned the cows loose, swilled down the milking parlour and fed the pigs. He brought the milk down in the hand barrow, the muscles in his shoulders burning, his legs protesting with every weary step.

He ate a hasty meal of bread and cheese and ale in the kitchen as the Compline bell was ringing, tramped wearily to chapel, then fell into his bed and slept like the dead until the insistent clamour of the bell roused him for the Night Office.

After that, his days were a blur of work and weariness. They stacked the precious hay, and thatched the ricks with straw against the rain, the days still holding fine.

Brother Stephen and Brother Tom sweated to get the field shelter out on the hills repaired before the early plums needed harvesting.

Then the cherries were ripe and had to be picked before the birds had them all, and the last of the beans harvested and shelled, spread out to dry for the winter soups and stews, and some saved for sowing next time round.

Apart from that, there were all the little jobs; filling the water butts for the milking parlour, and the cattle troughs, from the spring above the orchard; teaching Brother Germanus to milk the cows, sharpening and greasing the scythes again ready for the corn harvest, clearing the ditches, mending the flails where the leather had perished, patching the hen-house where the fox had got in.

And every night and every morning the milking, and swilling down the shed, scrubbing out the pails, carting the milk, and checking that Brother Germanus had fastened the hens in securely at night, and the geese. Brother Stephen could be trusted not to forget his pigs.

'I don't know what we did without you,' said Brother Stephen with frank gratitude as he and Tom started work on the timbers for the second field shelter. 'You've done the work of three men. I never thought we'd get these done before harvest. At this rate we might attempt the dovecote ourselves before the cold weather comes. We shall have a breathing space before ploughing.'

And gradually, as he immersed himself in the work of the farm, Tom succeeded in blotting out the guilt and helplessness of his thoughts about Peregrine. He ceased to grieve, ceased to wonder if Father Peregrine knew enough to miss him, ceased to notice the ache of it. At first he had to force himself to think only of the farm, but now it came easily.

When he walked past the infirmary on his way down the farm track to chapel, he looked the other way at first; then, when that brought him the view of the back of the abbot's house, he walked with his head bent, setting himself to think of the milk yield, the egg yield, anything. And he did love the farm. Peregrine's absence, illness, became a familiar background ache, displaced from the fore of Tom's mind as he became involved in the work with the beasts and the land.

August passed in shimmering, coppery heat. Tom watched with satisfaction as the fields of grain turned red-gold, white-gold in the sun, the fat ears rustling in the stirring of a breeze at evening. It would be a good harvest, providing the weather held.

The boys from the abbey school turned out to help harvest the plums, which was the usual noisy business of shrieking and laughter, as the boys did battle with the geese in the orchard, climbed the trees, fell out of them, ate the plums, gathered them in baskets, golden and green and purple, sweet and full, with Brother Prudentius fussing to and fro, beseeching the children to handle the fruit with care.

The fleeces from the June shearing all sold, and Brother Tom went with Brother Stephen to the Cistercian abbey higher up in the hills at Mount Hope, to buy some new ewes to replenish their flock.

'Thirty beauties,' said Brother Stephen happily, as they unloaded the sheep from the wagon. 'Beauties. And a good bargain too. Come with me again next time, Brother. You drive a harder bargain than I ever could. They always strip my purse to the lining.'

Tom shrugged. 'We should have waited and got them in lamb. We'd have paid more, but got a better bargain.'

'Oh, I don't know. Our ram's willing enough, and his seed comes cheap.'

Tom shook his head. 'Their pure stock's the best. You can't beat it. Still, never mind. We've not struck a bad bargain, as you say. Help me get the milking shed doors down before Vespers, if you will, to keep the cows out of the rick beside the farm track. They'll spoil it before we have any good of it at all, if we don't look out.'

'Get the shed doors down? That'll take some doing. The hinges are rusted. Don't you ever stop? I was looking for a rest in the sun, admiring these ewes, this afternoon.'

'They're not rusted solid. I oiled them and eased them before we went. They'll slide out easy.'

Brother Stephen sighed. 'Oh well, if you're doing the milking. But that's my last job today. That trip up to Mount Hope about rattles my bones loose. We usually take a week over it and drive them home. It was madness going in the wagon. Oh, I know, don't bother to say it; it saves time. For mercy's sake, will you slow down, Brother Thomas? You'll be the finish of me. I can't keep up this pace. You're like a man trying to run away from his own shadow.'

III
PICKING UP THE PIECES

Brother Michael walked into the milking shed. The seven milk-cows that served the needs of the community had been brought in and tethered in their stalls for the morning milking. They were munching contentedly on the pail of oats and dried beet Tom had emptied into the feed trough that ran the length of the wall beneath the iron tethering rings.

The regular hiss and splash of milk squirting into the pail revealed Tom's presence in the shed.

'Brother Thomas.'

Tom leaned out from the flank of the fifth cow in the line.

'Hello,' he said, surprised. 'I mustn't stop now; can you wait while I've finished? They'll be restive if they've finished their food too long.'

'I'll wait.'

Tom stripped out the milk carefully, then appeared from behind the cow, with the pail in one hand and the low milking stool in the other. He went through into the dairy, and Brother Michael heard him pouring out the milk into a larger vessel. He returned with the pail rattling in his hand.

'Two more to go. I won't be long. Beautiful day, isn't it?'

'Lovely.' Brother Michael did not sound particularly communicative.

Tom picked up the pail of water that stood by the wall, and began to wash the sixth cow's udder with the cloth he fished out of the pail. 'Holy saints, this is filthy! Ugh! Did I say I wouldn't be long? I take it all back. You disgusting beast, you're crusted in it! Just a minute, I'll have to change this water.'

Brother Michael waited. He waited in silence, while Tom milked the last two cows and disappeared whistling into the dairy with the last pail of milk.

Tom unhitched the cows from their tethers, and slapped the first cow, the one nearest the door, on her rump.

'On your way, Petal,' he said affectionately. The cows lumbered slowly out of the shed, into the foldyard.

'Now then, I've to swill down in here and take them up to the top pasture, but that can wait five minutes. There's nothing wrong, is there?'

'I want to talk to you.'

Brother Tom looked at him. 'Come out into the sunshine. That sounds ominous. It's not—Father Peregrine's all right, is he?'

They walked across the foldyard and leaned on the gate, looking down the hillside towards the abbey buildings.'That's what I want to talk to you about.'

'What is it? Is he—?'

'Is he what? Dead? Worse? Better? Do you care?'

Brother Michael turned his head to look at Tom. 'Are you never coming to see him again?'

Tom plucked an ear of wild grass that grew high beside the gate. He twirled it in his fingers.

'I suppose I ought to. Would it make any difference?'

'Don't you *want* to see him any more?'

Tom stripped the little seeds from the stem, and broke it into tiny pieces with his fingernails.

'No. I don't. He…the thing I saw in the infirmary five weeks ago wasn't him. He'd gone. I wish he'd died. It was hideous.'

'He's got a lot better since you saw him. He's out of bed. He's still paralysed down his right side, but he's got a bit of tone back in his face. He's no longer so incontinent. He can speak, just a little; mainly "yes" and "no".

'He likes the kittens. He has a length of string tied to his chair, with a little piece of wood on the end. The kittens come and fight it and play with it. He likes to watch them. It makes him smile, and there's precious little that does. They climb into his lap and curl up to sleep there. He strokes them, broods over them. You know, I believe he prays for them, fleas and all.'

Tom couldn't speak. He stared at Brother Michael, appalled. That this man, with his intellect, his fire, the power of his spirit, should be reduced to playing with kittens, and find joy in it too. Brother Michael looked at his face, read his silence. He nodded.

'I know. But that's the infirmary work, Tom. To make the best of the circumstances. They bring us their own despair. Our job is to steal them a crumb of hope. Anything. Anything that will rouse a man from the profound grief of his infirmity is worthwhile. There is no healing without hope. Despair is life's direst enemy. Despair is living death. At the moment, he is entirely gripped by it. You know him. You will see. Humour, hope, interest in the day's events, the need to be with others—he's lost it all. The kittens help. They are a ray of sun in his prison. They don't sit in embarrassment wondering what to say to a man who gets angry because he can't reply. They don't remind him of the humiliation of his helplessness. They come to him, and they're glad of him, and it takes him out of himself a bit.

'Won't you come and see him?'

Tom threw the shredded pieces of stalk away, one by one.

'If you think I should.'

'Yes, I do think you should. He's very low in spirits. He's shattered, obviously he is, by what's happened to

him—as anyone would be. After all, he's well nigh helpless. But there's something more than that.' Brother
Michael paused, looking out across the hillside.

'When we open the door and come into the room—any
of us—he looks up; and then...it's as though he's disappointed. He looks away again, listlessly. I think, Brother
John thinks, he's looking for someone, waiting for someone. Tom, I think he misses you terribly.'

'He didn't even recognise me when I came to see him
before.'

'Didn't he? Didn't he? How do you know that?'

'His eyes. They were so blank and dead...'

'Oh, for pity's sake, man! He's *ill!* He's been dreadfully
ill. What did you expect him to do? Get up and dance a
jig?'

Tom said nothing.

'I'm sorry. I shouldn't have said that. It must have
been upsetting for you. But if you can bring yourself to get
over it a bit and consider his feelings as well as your own,
will you come and see him?'

'I've said I'll come. I can't drop everything and come
just right now. We've started to reap the corn now, we're
halfway through the oats, I can't just vanish. Still, maybe
if I put in most of the day here—we've plenty of help from
the brethren and the neighbours, and the school, not that
the boys are much use for reaping or stooking—I'll come
this afternoon, after the Office.'

'Thank you. Thank you, Tom.'

Brother Michael put his hand on Tom's shoulder with
a smile of real warmth. Tom managed a wry smile in
return, then shook his head and looked away.

'You don't know what you're asking,' he said.

'Maybe. At least I'm not asking any more of you than
I've asked of myself.'

'It's different for you. You do it every day.'

'Easier then, you think?'

'Yes. That is what I think.'

'In some respects, perhaps. There's nothing easy about watching someone you love eating his heart out because his friend's abandoned him.'

Tom sighed, impatiently. 'Don't start on me again. I've said I'll come. Is that all, then? The cows are standing waiting in the foldyard.'

'That's all.'

Brother Michael watched the defensive hunch of Tom's shoulders as he tramped back up to the milking shed. 'Help him out a bit, Lord God,' he prayed as he turned and walked back down the farm track to the infirmary. 'A bit of grace, and a bit more compassion. Help him find the Christ in himself.'

Brother Tom opened the foldyard gate and watched the cows stroll out to the pasture. Nothing hurried the stately, sensuous, matronly sway of their going; they had their own ponderous grace, from the great, luxurious curve of their bellies to the slender delicacy of their ankles, picking their way out of the foldyard into the open field.

He closed the gate behind them, and set off up the hill to the cornfields. The weather was set fair. The oats they had cut and stooked yesterday would be drying nicely. Three weeks of this and we shall be home and dry, Tom thought, with satisfaction. But not if I have to be spending half my time in the infirmary.

'You don't know what you're asking,' he had said to Brother Michael, but he could not fully admit, even to himself, the horror he felt at sickness and the decay of infirmity; at the memory of the vacant gazing of those empty, lustreless eyes. It was easier to bury it under resentment—call it a nuisance, an intrusion, a waste of time; anything but look steadily at the frightening, nauseous reality.

Up on the hill, Brother Stephen had already begun. The tenants of the abbey farms were too busy with their own harvest to spare hands to help, but all the monks he could beg or coerce to help him were out on the hill.

Brother Francis and Brother Peter; Fidelis, Paulinus, Prudentius, Mark, Walafrid, Germanus. Brother James was there too with some of the older boys from the abbey school. Oh, we shall get this in easy, if only the rain holds off; Brother Tom's spirits recovered as he put from him the disturbing encroachment of memories and fears, bringing the focus of his attention back onto his chosen course with relief.

He joined the men and boys coming behind the reapers, gathering the fallen corn and bunching it into orderly blond sheaves secured with oatstalks twisted together and bound about the waist of the sheaf. The stalks must all butt in neat conformity at the ends, and achieving this needed the skill of experience. Brother Germanus, his hands blistered from handling the scythe, was trying the sheaf-making, attracting covert smiles of derision from the older monks who worked alongside him, which burned his pride as much as the climbing sun burned the back of his neck and the top of his shaven head. Brother Tom, who was not in the mood for pity, shamed him even more by working twice as fast as his own very best attempts; shaping, fastening and stooking his sheaves with effortless precision and relentless rhythm.

The work was killing, worse than the hay harvest, because the hay, although it must be raked and turned, did not require this endless, back-breaking slog of stopping to gather the corn and standing to form the sheaf; endlessly stooping and standing.

Brother Germanus spat out the little prickles of chaff that had found their way into his mouth, gritted his teeth and narrowed his eyes against the dust and flying chaff. His ankles were scratched sore by the spears of stubble, and sweat poured down his back under the heavy, coarse fabric of his tunic. And I came here to pray, he thought incredulously, as he straightened up, dizzy in the heat, pressing a hand momentarily to his aching back.

The triple-pattern of the choir bell tolling for the mid-morning Office of Terce carried up the hillside, and the brothers laid down their scythes, completed and propped their sheaves. This was the time for the schoolboys to have a break from work, hunting fieldmice nests and satisfying their thirst with the watered ale in stone bottles that was keeping cool in the stream which ran through the copse at the field's edge. There was bread and fruit for them too, wrapped in linen and hidden in the shade of the hedge.

With nods and smiles of farewell, the monks left them to their hour of play. After Terce and Mass and Chapter, the brothers would work through on the fields until Vespers, bringing food up with them for their midday meal, but there was no dispensation from Mass and Chapter. Brother Germanus marvelled that the day should have come when the Chapter meeting formed a cool oasis, a tranquil respite of grateful sitting.

Brother Tom walked down the hill beside Brother Stephen. 'I've to knock off at None,' he said, regretfully.

Brother Stephen glanced at him in surprise. 'Why so? Something amiss?'

'No. I've promised Brother Michael I'll come down to the infirmary to see Father.'

'Would not this evening have done?'

Tom was silent a minute. 'I dare say. I've promised him now though. I'm sorry. He wanted me to go this morning.'

Brother Stephen snorted indignantly. 'And whence comes the oatmeal for the infirmary if all the harvesters are visiting the sick? Do they stop and ask themselves that?'

'It's my fault, if I'm honest,' Tom said quietly. 'I should have been before. I'll milk, anyway. Don't you stop for that. I'll milk after I've been to the infirmary. I'll not be taking that much time out really.'

They came dusty and sweaty into chapel, some like Brother Germanus who was new to hard physical labour, and Brother Prudentius who was old, grateful for the opportunity to sit down in the coolness of the church. Others, like Brother Tom and Brother Stephen, found the interruption of the work a tedious discipline. Either way, after ten days' harvesting, it was not easy to keep awake during Chapter.

'This morning's Chapter exhorts us, "Do not be overwhelmed with dismay, and run away from the way of salvation," and promises us that as we persist in the life of faith and monastic observance, our hearts will be made larger, or opened up...'

Do I want my heart ripped open? Tom asked himself, as he listened to the beginning of Father Chad's homily. I've had a taste of that, and I don't like it. Faith and monastic observance are fine, but I don't want to have my heart torn open. What's Father Chad going to make of that, I wonder?

Tom could remember Father Peregrine speaking to the brethren on the same chapter of the Rule a few weeks before they had watched the cut hay ruined in the rain.

The rain had been streaming relentlessly outside the Chapter house that day, and he had begun with a smile, and some ironic quip about the patient suffering that this particular chapter recommended.

But then he had spoken to them about the sufferings of Christ that the chapter urged them to share, talking quietly about the necessary pain of having your heart ripped open that was part of following Jesus.

Tom frowned, remembering. What had he said? Something about the broken heart being the most intimate place of communion with God...and the psalm, the verses from the Miserere he talked about...about the sacrifice of God being a troubled spirit...the humiliated, aching heart a precious offering in his eyes. And it had carried conviction. When he had paused from time to time, the only sound had been the endless wet falling of the rain, not the ceaseless muted whisper of fidgeting that accompanied Father Chad's homilies.

He had told them that the road of God would of necessity bruise their feet, and sometimes have them on their knees in the mud and the nettles. 'There are some hellish deep potholes on the road our Lord has set us to walk,' he had said with a smile, and he had added, 'That's why we need each other. Sometimes we fall in.' Well, he had fallen in now all right, up to his neck. Tom stirred, irritably. Oh do get on with it, Father Chad, he thought, chafing to be out, to get done what he could in what was left of the day.

Then came the business of the day. Brother James would be going to university, at Oxford. Brother Francis had a vocation to the priesthood, and would be going away to the seminary for a while. All the piecemeal news of the community. Is this really necessary? Tom wondered, tetchily.

At last they were through, and climbing the hill again, carrying their packages of bread and cheese for the midday meal.

Brother Tom glanced in amused sympathy at Brother Germanus plodding with stoical weariness along the farm track beside him.

'Don't be discouraged,' he said, on a sudden impulse of kindness. 'You'll feel just grand when it's all in and stacked in the barn, and when you stand in the mill watching sack after sack of grain pouring down the hopper, and the blisters have healed on your hands as you break the bread.'

Brother Germanus looked at Tom in grateful surprise, warmed by his friendliness.

'I'm sorry my work is so slow,' he said. Tom shook his head. 'If we've made you feel bad about it, the fault is ours. You're giving your best. It's me and Stephen, impatient, making hard work harder.'

Then, suddenly, he regretted opening himself to the young man's need of friendship and approval. He did not

want a lad's dog-like affection tagging him, and he withdrew into his shell of uncommunicative silence the rest of
the way up to the field.

In the grass beside the track, harebells grew, and purple vetch and wild scabious, and at the edge of the copse
the blackberries were beginning to ripen, and the cob nuts
forming green on the bushes. The smell of summer, the
dusty fragrance of grass and the sharp scent of chamomile
lay distilled on the arid air, too familiar to be remarked,
but none the less part of the beauty of the morning. They
worked through the heat of the day, stopping to eat the
food they had brought and pass round the stone jar of
watered ale at midday when the Office bell rang from the
abbey. By the time the bell was ringing again, for None at
four o'clock, most of the strip of oats was cut and stooked.

'You'll be through this patch by Vespers,' said Brother
Tom as he gave his scythe to Brother Stephen. 'There, you
can take a turn with the scythe again; I must be away.'

Time to face it, then. He walked down the hill alone,
and the day with its larksong and nodding poppies,
ripened fields and clear blue sky almost lifted his mood of
uneasy apprehension; but not quite. He looked down on
the abbey buildings as he walked, at the honey-coloured
stone, gentle on the eye, and the lazy drifts of woodsmoke
from the kitchen chimney. He could not find a way back
into the satisfied contentment the scene usually brought
him. He had a disturbing sense of having been pushed out
of the nest; having left behind easy tranquillity and familiar peace; as though, like Brother Germanus, he was being
required to break his back and bloody his blistered hands
on a new, demanding task.

He went into chapel looking for courage, seeking peace
in the daily round of the chant. Doubtless the founding
fathers had never intended the Office to be treasured for
the anaesthetic value of its familiarity, but it often was.

The Office of None ended at half-past four when the
west end of the chapel was suffused with tawny light

pouring through the tall, narrow windows. The choir, at the east end of the church, on the other side of the parish altar, was dim at this time of the day. Now, in early September, it was a warm, golden, dusty dimness, almost languorous in its tranquillity.

The chapel emptied gradually, the novices going to the novitiate Chapter meeting, and the fully professed brothers going about their afternoon work. Only Brother Tom sat in the luminous silence of the choir still; and he was sitting with his forearms resting on his knees, his back hunched and his head bowed, his hands clasped together. He had to admit it now. He was afraid.

'I don't want to see him,' he whispered into the stillness.

The silence of the chapel was never an empty silence. The air had a perpetual sense of hopeful expectancy, of radiant peace. 'I'm always expecting to catch a glimpse of wings, a shine of gold there,' Peregrine had said to Tom, smiling, one day in the early summer of the year. 'It is so pregnant with life and glory.'

'I don't want to see him,' Tom whispered in fear. 'God help me, I don't want to see him like he is.'

It was almost five o'clock before he finally gathered his courage and stood up to go. He stood for a moment, looking up at the great wooden crucifix that hung above the rood screen. 'You should do something about him,' Tom muttered. 'He's a friend of yours.'

Resolutely he tramped through the choir and the Lady chapel, out of the little door in the south wall into the afternoon sunshine, and up to the infirmary.

Outside the infirmary buildings, in the sheltered fragrance of the physic garden, four or five aged monks were tucked up in blankets, sitting in their chairs in the sun. Why do they live so damned long? Tom thought. Why don't they just die like people everywhere else? Brother John looks after them too well. He should let them die. Look at them. What have they got to live for?

He looked for Peregrine, but Peregrine was not among them. Brother Tom passed through them without speaking, into the cool peace of the infirmary. In the little anteroom, Martin Jonson was strewing fresh herbs on the floor. Their pungent, antiseptic aroma smelt clean and good.

'I've come to see Father Peregrine,' said Tom.

'Good, good, good! They like to have a visitor, cheer them up, tell them all the news. Brother Michael said you would be coming. Brother John wants a word with you first. I expect he wants to explain to you about Father—he's a bit peculiar you know. Temperamental, like. Not quite right in his head, between you and me, though Brother John won't have it said.'

'Where is Brother John?'

'Just along the way, in the linen room, Brother, folding the sheets.'

Tom went along the wide passage to the linen room and stood in the doorway.

'You wanted to see me,' he said.

'Yes.' Brother John laid the sheet he had folded into a neat square on the pile that lay on the table, and slipped two stems of lavender, from a bunch that lay alongside, between the folds of the sheet.

'Here I am.'

'Yes.' Brother John turned to face him. He folded his arms and stood looking at Tom. 'About time too, isn't it? You should be ashamed of yourself.'

Oh, here we go. I could do without this, Tom thought.

'I've already had this ticking-off from Brother Michael,' he said defensively.

'Is that so? Well now you've got it from me. Whatever have you been thinking of, never coming near the place all this time?'

'All right! I am ashamed of myself! I know what you're saying—it's written on my heart, as it so happens! I'm a coward, I couldn't face it, I was upset, I stayed away. It

was selfish. I know. I know I should have been to see him
before this. I know. I couldn't bear it, that's all. I don't
want to see him witless and drooling. It twists me up
inside. I can't...anyway, I'm here now. I'm sorry, and
I've come. All right?'

Brother John regarded him thoughtfully.

'Who gave you the idea he was witless and drooling?
Martin Jonson been talking to you? Yes?' Brother John
snorted derisively. 'Witless he is not. He gets impatient—
but then he always did, as I recall. He can't make himself
understood. Can you not see the frustration of that? It's
resulted in a few scenes, yes. He threw his dinner across
the room on Tuesday and he bit Martin's finger this
morning, but—why are you staring at me like that?'

'I'm sorry. Just for a moment I thought you said Father
Peregrine bit Martin Jonson.'

'That is what I said. He did bite him. Will you give me
a hand folding these sheets while you're here?'

'He *bit* him? His mind must be affected, then.'

'Why? There's nothing wrong with his mind so far as I
can tell. You should never underestimate the frustration of
being unable to communicate, Tom.

'Look what you're doing—take those two ends. Martin
misjudged his man, that's all. You know what he is, all
"there's a good lad" and "whoops-a-daisy". He patted
Father on the cheek and chucked him under the chin once
too often. He had hold of his chin and gave it a playful
little shake. He's always doing it. He said, "How are we
today, then?" and Father sank his teeth into his finger.
Serves him right. I'm surprised nobody's bitten him
before. I fancy he'll approach him with a little more
respect in future. Well, caution at least.

'I'm particularly glad you agreed to come today.
There's no one free here but Martin this afternoon to sit
with him, and he needs someone, but not Martin. It's like
a red rag to a bull.

'He can't read now, and the old men in here are too

senile to make the effort to converse with him. I've tried
sitting him with them in the afternoons, but he doesn't like
it. We ask him if he wants to sit outside with the others.
"N-o," he says, like that, "n-o." So we leave him in peace.

'He needs some company though, he's that morose and
miserable looking. It'll do him the world of good to see
you. Read to him or something. Tell him what's going on.
Thank you, I'll manage these on my own now. You know
where he is?'

'Yes, I know where he is, but wait a minute: how can I
talk with him if he can't speak?'

'He can speak. Who told you he couldn't speak?'

'You did. I thought you said…'

'He has very little predictable speech. He can say "yes"
and "no" reliably. Other words are usually too difficult if
he thinks too hard. But he says quite a lot really.'

'I misunderstood. I thought he could only say "yes"
and "no", and the rest was all garbled.'

'Oh no; it's a struggle, but he can make himself understood if you'll be patient. Sometimes he comes out with
something as clear as can be. In French usually.'

'In *French?*' Tom looked at Brother John in blank
bewilderment.

'His family are French, aren't they? It will have been
the language of his childhood. It's a strange thing, this
kind of illness. I've seen it before. Memories, words,
thoughts—they all jumble into a rag-bag mixture, and
you never know what will come out; sense or nonsense, or
a bit of both. Mostly "yes" and "no" are the only things
he can say clearly, and he sometimes gets those the wrong
way round, but just now and again the odd phrase comes
through perfectly. This morning, he had his breakfast—
I'd left him to get on with it—and he was muttering to
himself as I went past the doorway. I stopped just outside
to listen to him. I was intrigued. "Merde…incroyable…"
he was saying to himself, and, "…dégueulasse," Cormac's porridge. I went in and tasted it. He was quite right,

it was appalling. Grey and lumpy, and no salt that I could detect. But if I'd asked him, he couldn't have told me in English—nor in French either. Just sometimes the odd phrase slips through, that's all. I do mean odd, too. "Merci, chéri," he said to me last Saturday after I'd finished shaving him. I think he was as startled as I was. You can see why he doesn't want to sit with the others. It's embarrassing for him, and a bit frightening I think.

'Anyway, you'll see. Take him as you find him. He's in the same room as before. Thanks for your help with the sheets. I'm glad you've come.'

Brother Tom walked along the passage to the room where he had last seen Father Peregrine. He was still afraid. He stood outside the room with his hand raised to the door. Then he heard footsteps approaching further along the passage, so he pushed open the door and took two steps into the room. Peregrine was seated in the chair, near to the bed.

Tom had never seen him sitting like that; his left hand resting in his lap, idle; no books, no letters, doing nothing. Just himself, alone in the chair, the length of knotted string to amuse the kittens dangling forlornly to the floor.

The warmth and mellow light of the afternoon sun lit the room, but it had the lifeless air of a sickroom. There was no hope in that room. Even the wooden crutch, faithful companion, symbol of independence, was gone. He no longer needed it, of course.

His body sagged dispiritedly. As he raised his head and looked at Tom, his face was blank, shuttered. John's mistaken, Tom thought, his mind has gone.

They looked at each other in silence. Tom looked at Peregrine's face, the scarred right side of it still drooping slightly in paralysis. He was sitting askew in the chair, his useless right arm and hand awkwardly tucked into the side of the chair, pushed out of sight among the cushions. By himself, no doubt. Brother John would never have left him sitting like that. He liked his patients to look tidy.

What a mess, Tom thought. What an awful mess. He tried to think of words to say. Some news, Martin had said, to cheer him up. What news was there? Tell him maybe that most of the brethren felt he was finished for good now, and it was time to choose a new superior? No, not that news. 'Make him smile if you can,' Brother Michael had said. 'Try to rekindle some hope.' Hope. For God's sake, hope? There was nothing to say; nothing.

A moment later Tom wished he had thought of something, anything to say; because Peregrine spoke to him. It was just a jumble of sounds. Should I go and fetch Brother John? he wondered, nervously. Then Peregrine spoke to him again, urgently this time.

'I—I can't understand you...' Tom faltered. Anxiety clutched him. It was rubbish the man was talking; Tom had no idea how to respond, what to say. Inadequacy felt like fear, tightening his gut, making him want to leave, run away from this predicament. Peregrine was glaring at him, talking heatedly, beads of sweat on his face. He leaned forward, his eyes compelling Tom, willing him to understand; and Tom could not understand at all, stood dumb, uncomfortable, completely baffled. Peregrine raised his hand in desperate agitation, and crashed it down in frustration into his lap. Then, abruptly, he turned his face away. He held his head away from looking at Tom, in rigid misery.

'What? Whatever is it?' Stupid question, thought Tom, as soon as the words were out of his mouth. All he can say to me is more of the same. Then suddenly he saw the spreading, splashing puddle of urine under the chair. Maybe if I was Martin, he thought numbly, I could make a joke of this, ease his embarrassment. Then maybe if I was Martin, I'd be able to see something funny in it.

'I'll get Brother John,' he said. 'We need to clean you up. I'm sorry.'

Once outside the room, Brother Thomas stood, sick with the guilt and shame of his relief to be getting out of that room, finding someone else, not having to be left alone with Father Peregrine.

'Brother Michael!' Tom saw him passing the end of the corridor and hastened after him. 'Brother Michael, can you help!'

'Is something the matter?' Other people's agitation flowed off the infirmary brothers like water off a duck's back. It was too commonplace. In the infirmary, full of the sick, the infirm, the dying, occurrences that felt like emergencies were too numerous to count, and actual emergencies were almost unheard of.

'Father Peregrine's wet himself!'

Brother Michael smiled at Tom's appalled face.

'Has he? What do you want? Something to mop up with?'

Tom stared at him, aghast. 'Me? I...no...no! Please come and see to him. I can't deal with this. It's no use, the whole thing gives me the creeps. He doesn't need me. I'm no good at this sort of thing; I can't...I...I'm going.'

Brother Michael stood listening to him in mild surprise.

'There's no need to get upset. He's a bit incontinent— that's quite normal. Help me change his clothes, and then stay for a chat with him.'

'Oh, you're joking! Michael, I'm going.'

'All right, but hang on a minute, don't run away. When are you coming back? He might want to know.'

'I'm not. Don't look at me like that; I'm not like you are. I can't bear this sort of thing. I've simply got no stomach for it. He'll understand. Just give him my love— tell him I'll pray for him.'

'Tell him *what?* I'm sure he'll be really delighted to hear that! Don't be ridiculous, Tom—' But Tom shook his head, turned on his heel and left.

He strode up the track to the farm, where the cows were already queueing placidly outside the milking shed. He

called them in, rattling their cereal in the bucket, overwhelmed with gratitude at the reassurance of their vac-
uous, undemanding stolidity.

His hands were trembling as he tethered the beasts in
their places; but as he went from one to the other, resting
his head against the warm, impassive bulk, moving his
hands in the rhythmic, sensuous physicality of the milking, the turmoil died away, and he was calm again.

After he had milked the cows and turned them out to
pasture once more, Tom walked the half-mile to the mill,
and spent an hour meticulously clearing out the millrace,
scraping all the accretions of moss and slime from the
wheel. He ignored the Vespers bell, and did not return to
the milking shed and take the milk down to the kitchen
until the sun was setting, having no wish to run into
Brother Michael or Brother John.

By that time the kitchen was deserted. Tom rolled the
barrels of milk into the dairy, and took out the empty ones
from the morning milking in solitary peace. He helped
himself to some bread and cheese and plums, then he
barrowed the empty barrels all the way back up the hill to
the farm again. The stars were coming out and the Compline bell ringing by the time he came down from the
farm. After Compline, the abbey would be folded into the
Great Silence, and all conversation of any kind forbidden.
Even if Brother John managed to get to Compline, there
would be nothing he could say.

Brother Tom had laboured too hard that day to lie
sleepless in his bed. He lay five minutes in the darkness,
wondering if the moon shone into Peregrine's room, and if
he slept or lay wakeful, but he could guess the answer to
that; then he turned his back on the whole thing and took
refuge in sleep.

In the morning, he slipped out of the choir and up to
the farm as soon as first Mass was ended. He breakfasted
on oats and barley-meal from the cattlefeed boxes, and
warm new milk from the cow.

'Take the milk down to the kitchen for me, will you? There's a good lad,' he hailed Brother Germanus as the men came up the hill to begin the day's work. 'I'll take your scythe.'

Delighted by this unexpected reprieve, Brother Germanus agreed readily, so Tom kept well clear of the cloister buildings until the bell rang for Terce and Chapter Mass. Brother John came into Chapter, but Tom refused to catch his eye, and concentrated on disciplining himself not to fidget through Father Chad's meandering discourse on Cenobites, Anchorites and Hermits. After the Chapter meeting ended, he slipped out as quickly as he could.

'Brother Thomas, wait a moment! I'd like to talk to you.' Brother John put a hand on Tom's shoulder as he was leaving the Chapter House. Tom scowled at him mutinously. He would gladly have knocked Brother John unconscious if it would have given him a way out of this conversation.

'I've no permission to talk.'

Brother John smiled at him. 'I've never known that to stop you. I've asked permission of Father Chad. He says we can talk in the little parlour.'

Tom shrugged his shoulders in ungracious assent, and the two of them walked in silence along the cloister, among the other silent monks who were going about their daily business. Away from the claustral buildings, the brothers were not so particular about silence, a certain amount of conversation being necessary on the farm, and good in the infirmary, though they were not permitted to stand in idle gossip anywhere; but here in the heart of the abbey, talking was kept to a bare minimum, and only in the abbot's house when a brother had come to seek counsel, or in the little parlour tucked away beside the day stairs, could any conversation of length take place, and that only with permission.

Brother John came into the gloomy little parlour after Brother Tom, and shut the door behind him.

'Sit down,' he said.

They both sat on the wooden chairs that were provided there—chairs, not stools, for visitors occasionally used this parlour too.

'Now then. What's this Brother Michael tells me, that you don't intend to come back and see Father Peregrine again?'

'That's right.'

Brother John sat in silence, looking at him.

'Oh, don't try your unnerving infirmary manner on me! I came, it was awful, and I'm not coming again. That's all there is to it. Is that all you want to know? Can I go? I'm supposed to be reaping the oats with Brother Stephen.'

'Tom, stop it! How long have we lived in community together? Can't you trust me? Tell me about it.'

Tom's head shot up, and he glared at Brother John furiously. 'Don't say that to me! Don't you *ever* say that to me!'

'Ssh now, peace.' Brother John held up his hands. He was not in the slightest perturbed by Tom's raised voice and furious face. He was too accustomed to the unpredictable moods of senility and the undermined emotions of sickness for that.

'What did I say to upset you? I didn't intend—oh, I see. That's one of Father Peregrine's sayings, isn't it? "Tell me about it." Yes.

'Brother Thomas...why are you making such a *fuss* about all this? It's like trying to get a nervous horse through a gate! He's your friend, he's sick, he needs you. Why isn't it simple for you, just to spend some time with him? A little while in the evenings would do, if you're needed on the farm in the day.'

'Oh...' Tom sat hunched and miserable, not wanting to talk. 'You don't understand.'

'Explain to me then! *Tell me about it!*'

Tom stared at him angrily. 'I told you...'

'Oh, never mind what you told me! You're behaving like a spoiled child! Come on. Talk.'

'He...I couldn't understand him, John. He tried to tell me, got angry with me; but it was all just rubbish, what he was saying. I don't know what to do. What could I say to him? I didn't know what he *is* now. He's destroyed, he's all different. If he'd died, I would have grieved, I would have cherished the memory of him, but...this—this is *horrible*. Can't you *see?*'

'Well, yes. I can see it from your point of view. Now, maybe you could try to look at it through his eyes?

'He's been ill, it's taken a lot out of him. He desperately needs the comfort of familiarity to find his bearings again. He's lost his work, his status. He's helpless. He's stuck in the infirmary, can't go anywhere, can't read, write, talk. Tom, think about it. It's *horrific,* isn't it? And what's the one link that he could have with the way things used to be?'

Tom looked at him. 'I...I suppose I am.'

'Quite so. He would have wanted you anyway—he loves you, Tom. But having lost everything else, he needs you quite desperately. He's watched for you, waited for you, pinned his hopes on you coming, *all this time.* And then yesterday you came, and everything went wrong. Brother, have you no pity? Can't you imagine how he must have felt—the embarrassment, and the distress, and the pain when you walked out and didn't come back? The sickness hasn't destroyed him. Far from it, he's all there. It's you that's destroying him.'

'Ah, that's not fair!'

Brother John shrugged his shoulders. 'That depends how you look at it. Speech is not everything. Mobility is not everything. Besides, his speech will return if he will work on it. He has a little, it's not all gone—he can swear well enough! It's grief, despair, unhappiness that's making him an invalid. He won't even let us take him out of his room. He won't *try*. Tom...it's true, this has changed him.

You can't be this ill and it not change you, but he's still himself. At the moment, you're looking at the sickness, not at the man. If you can find enough grace, enough charity, to look past the paralysis and the muddled speech, you'll find him again.'

Brother Tom sat looking at the floor in a torment of indecision. He rubbed his hand nervously across his face.

'Oh God, Tom, is it so difficult? *Please*. I *beg* you to come. You've *got* to come back.'

'When?'

Brother John sat back in his chair with a sigh of relief. 'Today. Now!'

'Brother Stephen's waiting for me up at the farm.'

'Father Abbot's waited for you five weeks, and I can tell you he needs you more than the farm does. I dare say Stephen can wait an hour or two.'

'*An hour or two?* You want me to spend more than an hour with him? Saying what for mercy's sake?'

'Oh Tom, half an hour, ten minutes, anything. Just come.'

They walked along the cloister together. 'I wish Brother Bernard wouldn't hang the washing out in the cloister garth,' Tom muttered crossly. 'Makes the place look such a shambles.'

Brother John smiled, but did not reply. He had beseeched God to send Tom to see Peregrine; it seemed unreasonable to expect even the Almighty to send him in a good humour.

Brother John escorted Tom closely into the infirmary, and along the passage to Father Peregrine's room.

'Go in alone,' he said, very quietly. 'It would hurt him to know I had to fetch you.'

Tom nodded and put his hand to the latch. Brother John walked away, and Tom stood there summoning his courage a short eternity. He felt sick.

He lifted the latch and pushed open the door. For a moment, oddly, he had a sense of being given another chance; a sense that today was yesterday all over again, because in this room nothing had changed, except that the sun had not yet moved round to fill the room with golden light. Peregrine sat, just as yesterday, immobile, slumped uncomfortably awry in his chair, enduring the passing time.

He lifted his head a little at the sight of Brother Tom, something like interest lightening the leaden dullness of his eyes. But he did not speak.

'Father...' Tom came fully into the room, and stood; uneasy, tense. He hoped desperately that Peregrine would not say anything to him. Not just yet. He wondered what he would do if yesterday repeated itself. Suppose he needed to relieve himself again? Even if I managed to understand him, what would I do then? How does he do it? What should I do to help him? Why didn't I ask Brother John?

Why me? Tom asked it of God in silent panic. Why me?

He moistened his lips, became aware of his fingernails digging painfully into the palms of his hands. This is ridiculous, he thought.

Peregrine was saying nothing, watching him. He looks sad, Tom thought. Sad and...wary. Apprehensive. He's finding this as hard as I am. It's as though we were strangers. Worse. I've got to speak to him. He moistened his lips again.

'Please bear with me. I don't know what to say...'

He pulled the low stool over and sat down beside Peregrine, self-conscious under the silent, brooding gaze of his abbot's eyes. Shyly, he took his hand. He held it in between his own hands, gently rubbing it with his fingertips. Peregrine suffered him to do it.

'I'm sorry about what happened yesterday.'

Peregrine said nothing. An unreasonable irritation seized Tom. He's not exactly making this easier for me, he thought resentfully. If he would only—only...what?

What could a man do with one crippled hand? He saw

then that Peregrine's silence was the best thing he could offer, the best he could do to ease the situation. He's not holding out on me, he's giving me time, Tom realised; time to come to terms with this... purgatory. There was a certain wonder in that insight for Tom, testing the ground of an unfamiliar form of communication, reaching in to the other man's wordless presence, groping for an understanding of the language of his silence, like a blind man's fingers exploring the surfaces of an unseen face.

What would he say. if he could speak? Tom cast his mind back, pictured again the times he had come into the abbot's house, bringing his burdens, his perplexities to this man. Sometimes no doubt Peregrine had troubles and heartaches of his own, but he usually had time to listen. Tom remembered it so vividly; the man sitting at his table, the comfort there had been in his acceptance and affection, the amusement and penetration of his eyes— 'Tell me about it.' Maybe that's what he would say now, Tom thought.

It occurred to him that such disability had a terrible honesty. It left no possibility of social niceties, the smooth, conventional exchanges by which men assuaged their loneliness without ever compromising their isolation. In this silence and stark deprivation, a man was pared down to the bedrock of his humanity. There were no pretensions here. If there was to be any communication at all, it would have to begin at that level. It would have to be the truth.

'They want me to help you to smile again,' Tom said. His fingers moved lightly on the unresisting hand. 'But there's nothing to smile about, is there? This hand, this poor, broken hand is all you've got left. It chokes me. God alone knows what it does to you.'

There was a cautious answering pressure from Peregrine's hand.

'I'm thinking,' Tom said very quietly; 'I'm thinking it's like it was once before. Maybe you need to allow yourself to weep before you can think about laughing again.'

He looked into Peregrine's eyes, looking for the answer of his silence. He found his answer. It was like looking into a chasm of misery. No defence met him. He saw right in to the grey, barren hell of despair. It was overwhelming. Tom looked down, away from the intolerable unhappiness of those eyes, at the maimed hand he held in his. Peregrine's lack of speech meant that conversation was no longer a common ground. Tom also had to come in to the place of silence if they were to meet as equals. He had to find a way in silence to bring his friendship, his love, a crumb of comfort. He let the tentative shyness go from his touch as he held and caressed Peregrine's hand with uninhibited tenderness, trusting his love to be received, a human reality flowing from hand to hand.

'Do you?' he said softly, then. 'Do you weep?'

Peregrine nodded, slowly. The words came slow and muffled. 'Oh, y-es.'

Tom looked up into his face. Peregrine looked back at him a moment, then closed his eyes. He was silent. Then, 'Y-es,' he said again.

'Alone? At night?'

'Y-es.'

'And...does it ease things a bit?'

Another silence. Tom held his hand, waited.

'N-n...n-o.'

There was something very final about that. Tom cast about in his mind for something else to say.

'I've missed you,' he said in the end. He glanced up at Peregrine's face. The dark grey eyes were open again, watching him very intently. By my faith, Brother John was right, Tom thought. There is nothing wrong with your mind.

'Have you—have you missed me?'

The twisted hand gripped Tom's hand. 'Y-es. Oh, oh y-es.'

Tom looked down at Peregrine's hand, holding his tightly. 'That...um—that sounds like real heartache.'

'Y-es.'

Tom tried to look up at the grey eyes again, but could not. He felt too guilty. There was no backing out of this conversation now, though. That would be another evasion, another stealing away, and it would not do. Tom was in no doubt now that this was by no means a one-sided conversation, even if he had all the words and Peregrine had only 'yes' and 'no' at his disposal. His abbot was putting him on the spot as unerringly as ever.

'I—I've got no excuses. I was frightened. It was because you couldn't speak, and I didn't know what to say to you. I knew you'd be all churned up inside. It was too big for me to face. I felt so helpless—'

Peregrine snatched his hand out of Tom's, and Tom looked up, startled. Peregrine beat his hand against his chest, his face contorted with emotion. A stream of muddled words poured out, none of them intelligible, then he stopped, glaring indignantly at Tom, who tried not to smile, but couldn't help it.

'All right. I understood that. That was anger. And pain. Something like, "*You* felt helpless! What about *me?*" Yes?'

The misshapen hand came down onto Tom's hand again, and the fingers curled round his.

'Y-es.' The relief at being able to communicate some of the anger and hurt that tore at him was immense. Peregrine felt the sickening mass of despair that filled him, sometimes till he choked on it, faintly eased. Tom was aware of a slight relaxation of tension, and realised that some of it had been Peregrine's apprehension and fear, not his own.

'So! Do you forgive me?'

'N-o.'

Tom looked at him nonplussed. Peregrine smiled, an extraordinary, lopsided smile with the side of his face that had escaped paralysis. If you could see yourself, Tom thought.

'Why not?' he demanded.

Peregrine lifted his hand and beat it three times against his breast in the ritual gesture of the penitential rite from the mass—*mea culpa, mea culpa, mea maxima culpa;* my fault, my own fault, my own most grievous fault.

'*Your* fault? What's your fault?'

'N-o.'

'Then...' light dawned. 'You—are you asking me to apologise?'

A silence. The smile waning, a little bit shamefaced. 'Y-es,' very quietly.

'Oh, my Father—you'll make a good monk of me yet!'

Tom knelt on the ground beside his abbot, and took his hand again, his head bent.

'Father, I confess my fault,' he said. 'You needed me, and I knew you needed me, and I stayed away. I confess my fault of cowardice, and of hardheartedness, selfishness. I humbly beseech the Lord Jesus to restore the trust between us; and I ask your forgiveness, and God's.'

Father Peregrine blessed him, a jumbled sentence full of tenderness. 'Y-es,' he added, just to make sure.

Brother Tom sat back on his stool again, and looked again into Peregrine's eyes. 'So that's what was wanted,' he said softly, 'to rekindle a small flame of hope.'

He drew breath to speak again, then hesitated. Peregrine spoke to him. A question. Again, imperatively.

'What was I going to say? Yes? I'm not going to get away with much, talking to you, am I? You're worse than you were before. I was going to say, Brother John thinks—has he told you this?—he thinks you may recover your speech, at least in part. He says that the paralysis will probably be with you always, but you should expect to get quite a bit better. He thinks, by the spring—it's early to tell yet, but by the spring—you could be able to...well, at any rate to work again. Did he say this to you?'

'Y-es.'

'Well? What do you think?' Foolish question, thought Tom, as soon as he'd said it; as if he could tell me.

'N-o.'

'No what? Don't you believe him?'

'Y-es.'

'You don't think you'll work again?'

Peregrine held up his hand, broken, twisted, his left hand (and he was such a right-handed man, Tom thought). He shrugged his shoulder. 'N-o.'

The abbot's work: working with guests, important church officials, government officials, local dignitaries; entertaining; leading the brethren in pastoral counsel, spiritual direction, homilies; presiding over the Community Chapter, leading the Office; orchestrating the huge network of the community's business affairs: no, Brother Tom couldn't see it either. What else, then? Peregrine met his gaze, and nodded.

'Y-es,' he said slowly, and made a gesture of wiping clean with his hand. Finished.

Tom took a deep breath. Hope, Brother Michael had said; but this man was no fool. He was not going to be duped by false hopes or jollied along by shallow optimism. This was a time for honesty.

'No,' he said. 'I can't see it either.' Tom looked into Peregrine's eyes. Warmth. Gratitude. Affirmation. That man preferred the truth. He did not want to be patronised with kindness.

'All right,' Tom said. 'Let's look at the worst. You could be like this for years. Paralysed. No speech. Helpless. Just like now. That's the worst, yes?'

'Y-es.'

'Can you bear it?'

The briefest of pauses. 'N-o. N-o.'

'What then? Are you afraid of dying?'

'N-o.' No hesitation there.

'Have you thought about dying?'

'Y-es.'

'And is it...have you wished you might die?'

'Y-es. Y-es.'

'Do you want to go on living—like this?'

'N-n-o.'

'Father...shall I help you out?'

The abbot's eyes widened. He grew very still, looking at Tom. And I thought nothing would ever shock him, Tom thought.

Peregrine looked down, away from Tom's gaze. He was silent. When at last he raised his head and met Tom's eyes again, he looked so vulnerable, so wide open, that it hurt Tom almost physically.

'N-o,' he whispered.

'Because, when it comes to it, you fear death?' Tom hated himself for the brutality of the questioning, but he persisted.

'N-o.'

'What then? Do you really believe, deep down, that there's a chance you'll get better?'

'N-o.'

'Is it because it is forbidden to take life?'

Peregrine looked at him, unhappily. 'N-o,' he whispered.

'That makes you ashamed? That you would take your life, against the laws of the Church?'

'Y-es.'

'What then? You can't bear this shadow of living, but you don't want me to get you out of it, because...?'

Peregrine looked at Tom, waiting. Oh God, he wants to tell me, and I've run out of guesses. Help me. Help me to see.

'Maybe...is it just that life is sweet? That there are kittens, and sun, and the scent of rain in the morning. And maybe...having someone to talk to makes it a little bit worthwhile?'

'Y-es...T-om.'

So that was it. It shook Tom to the core to see the power that had been in his hands.

'Let me be sure of what you're saying. Do you mean...my coming to see you has made the difference between wanting to die...and wanting to live?'

A long, long pause. Even now it was terrifying to reveal his need of Tom's friendship, how he had ached for his company, wept at his absence. Like a man confessing a secret, shameful guilt, hanging his head he whispered, 'Y-es.'

Brother Tom sat in silence, looking down at the hand he held between his own.

'Do you know,' he said, 'it *hurts,* loving you. You turn me inside out.'

IV
OUT OF SILENCE

'You're very quiet today.'

Brother Stephen passed Brother Tom the stone jar of ale as they sat leaning against the hay rick, sheltering in its shadow from the midday sun.

'I'm supposed to be quiet. I'm a monk.'

Brother Stephen looked at him sideways.

'What are you looking at me like that for? You know, we really should have some mugs up here for this ale. Drinking it straight from the jar, all of us, and eating bread at the same time, it's like porridge before we're halfway down the jar.'

'Got something on your mind, have you?'

'Me? What makes you think so?'

'You're very quiet today.'

Tom rubbed his hand over his chin reflectively. 'I've been thinking about Father.'

'Peregrine?'

'Yes. Do you know, for all he can't converse, when Theodore came in to say Mass with him the other day—'

'Theodore?' interrupted Brother Stephen. 'Oh yes, *Father* Theodore! Sorry, go on.'

Theodore had been priested in the spring, and made Master of Novices when Father Matthew died, but it took the brethren a while to adjust to his new status. The notion of Father Theodore saying Mass and hearing confessions still had an aura of comical novelty about it.

Tom smiled. 'Yes,' he said, 'Father Theodore. As soon as he said, "*Dominus vobiscum,*" Father responded, "*Et cum Spirito tuo,*" as smoothly and easily as can be; never faltered. He said it without thinking, just automatically; "*Et cum spirito tuo.*" I'm sure, you know, that all his speech is there locked away still . . . dammed up somehow.' Tom looked at Brother Stephen with a grin. 'Another thing, he swears faultlessly! Again, Brother John says that's because a man swears *before* he thinks, not afterwards.

'The words are there still, and the physical possibility of saying them. What's gone is the carry over from an idea to a sentence.

'I think . . . maybe it's a question of reestablishing a flow; you know, like a melody—so he can get the thoughts through to words again . . .'

'Can he not use the sign language of the Silence?'

Tom shook his head. 'Not really. He was never that good with it, because his hands are so inflexible. Before all this, he used to speak to me rather than sign if he had to tell me something in the night. But anyway, now, even when he tries to indicate something with his hand . . . it's funny, that comes out garbled too. He points to the wrong thing. Points to his mouth when he means his eye . . . it's as though—well, the problem is not speech, just. It's communication altogether. And yet . . .' Tom paused, frowning.

'What?'

'I don't know how to say it. He can't say anything much. He can't share his thoughts. Half a face and one mangled hand isn't much to communicate with, especially when what you want to put across comes out all muddled anyway, but . . . it's like a light shining in darkness instead of daylight . . . the light is all the brighter for the depth of the night. Himself. He can share himself—with absolute honesty and clarity too. Stephen, he's shown me—it's possible to have communion even without communication. If you don't hold back; if you don't withhold yourself.'

'Is that so?' Brother Stephen yawned and stretched his arms over his head. 'It's all a bit deep for me, I'm afraid. Time to stop withholding ourselves from that strip of rye, I should say. Brother Germanus will be thinking we've fallen asleep. You've answered my question, though: I can certainly see why you've been so quiet!' He got slowly to his feet. 'Ooh, my back! All this bending will kill me yet.' He rubbed his hands on the small of his back and stretched, to ease it. 'Come on, then; one last push.' He reached his hand down to Tom and pulled him to his feet. 'If we don't slack this afternoon, we'll have the whole field done, and tomorrow we can begin carting the oats home.'

The feeling at the end of the day, looking back along the strip they had cut, the golden stubble shining in the afternoon sun, the neat stooks of corn, was beyond words. Brother Tom put his arm goodnaturedly across Brother Germanus' shoulders, and waved his other hand expansively, taking in the broad sweep of the fields.

'Does your heart good, eh? The wind and the sun, and the good earth, and all that lot, bread and cattle fodder . . . beautiful.'

He clapped Brother Germanus on his aching back. 'How do you feel now?'

Brother Germanus smiled. 'Like you said,' he replied. 'Grand.'

'And tomorrow we can start bringing it in,' said Brother Stephen as they walked down the farmtrack to the abbey, the Vespers bell tolling across the fields, calling the brothers in at the end of the day. 'This makes up for the ruined hay.'

As he stood in his stall singing the responses at Vespers, Tom's mind wandered back to Father Peregrine. He shouldn't be in that stuffy room all day long, he thought. It isn't healthy for any man to be shut away from the fresh air and the sunshine. Not to see the grass on the hill blowing back in the breeze, and the lark tossing against a blue heaven, and the sun going down at evening; or the mist lying in the ditches of a morning, and the first sweet light of the day. I've got to get him out.

He sat when the others sat, stood when they stood, but his mind was on other things. If I could get his interest in something outside himself again... the farm maybe....

When Vespers had finished, Tom followed Father Chad along the cloister. 'Father Chad! Can you spare me a minute after supper?'

'Most certainly.' Father Chad was surprised, and pleased. it was the first time since Father Peregrine's illness that Brother Thomas had shown any inclination to talk to him at all. He received him with some curiosity in the abbot's house when the evening meal was over.

'Father Chad, can I borrow the maps of the farm that Father was using to plan the building work? I thought I might look at them with him in the morning; thought it might lift him out of himself a little, encourage him to go outside, take an interest.'

Father Chad smiled at him kindly. 'What a good idea! Yes, by all means take them. I have been more sorry than I can tell you that he had not the opportunity to let us know his scheme for the financing of the things we need to do. I'm no good at that sort of thing at all, I regret to say. Maybe it will come back to him. I haven't liked to trouble him about it, poor man.'

As he spoke, he got up to search in the heavy chest of documents that stood against the wall. Tom waited, looking round the familiar room. His heart was tugged with sadness for times irrecoverably gone. He put his hand out and stroked the surface of the great oak table. His eyes wandered over the ink, the seal, the box of sealing waxes, all of them clearly visible beside Father Chad's neat pile of letters waiting his attention.

Tom remembered with a smile Father Peregrine

searching irritably for his seal underneath a spilling riot of letters, accounts and books, accusing Tom of having lost it, and then snapping a rebuke at him for his indignant reply.

The scribe's table, under the window to catch the best light...Theodore had sat there so often, peaceful in Father Peregrine's company. The fireplace, not used since last winter: Tom had himself swept it clean and furnished it with a little pile of kindling: pine cones, dried rosemary and sage, knotted twists of dried grass. The times he had come into this room in the depths of winter, and Father Peregrine, embarrassed at the luxury, had asked him to light a fire; 'For my hands, Brother Thomas. They're so stiff in this cold.'

Apple logs; he had always asked for apple logs. Everyone else chose ash for firewood if they could get it, but Peregrine loved the smell of the applewood burning. There were one or two apple logs still, lying in the box at the side of the hearth.

Father Chad had the accounts and plans relating to the farm, and leaned on the open chest as he got up from his knees on the stone flags of the floor. 'Eh, it's a long way up! I must be growing old. Yes; here they are. I think you'll find they're all here in this bundle, though I must admit, his documents were not very orderly, especially the things he was working on. Let me know if there's anything else you need—and how you get on. No hurry to have them back; I shan't need them for a week or two.

'How about you, Brother? The harvest is coming in well ahead of time with your help, I hear.'

'Yes. Yes, we've done well. We start bringing it in to the barns tomorrow.'

'They've been glad to have you on the farm. How does it feel to be back in this room again?' He smiled, friendly.

Tom looked at him. 'Oh...well...' he said, and shrugged his shoulders. 'Thank you for the plans. I'll take them to him tomorrow.'

Tom was milking in the morning, and then busy with the preparations for carting home the corn. The first they had cut had stood more than two weeks in the fields now, with never a break in the weather. In the pouring heat of the afternoons and the breezes of the evening it had dried well, and needed to be in. Brother Stephen received Tom's request for time off to go down to the infirmary after Chapter with less than enthusiasm.

'Brother, you are needed here, you know. You have been going in to see him after Vespers. What's wrong with that?'

'I wanted him to get a look at the plans in daylight. I'm hoping I might persuade him out of doors. I—oh, please, Stephen.'

'You'll be back here after the midday break?'

'Yes; I promise.'

'You can tell Brother John I'll be needing another pair of hands for the farm if he's filching my men for the infirmary. No, go on, I'm pulling your leg. We'll manage. It's good to see you looking a bit less like a thundercloud than you have been. Greet Father for me.'

Brother Tom came down from the hill and collected the documents, taking them along to the infirmary. He paused and snapped off a sprig of rosemary, rubbing it between his fingers to release its fragrance as he strolled through the physic garden and into the low infirmary building. Peregrine raised his head and greeted him with a smile of surprised pleasure as he came through the door of the room with his bundle of plans, the smells of earth and air and herbs clinging about him. He had not expected to see Tom until evening.

'I've brought the farm plans. I thought I'd show you which bits we've been able to repair. Want to see them?'

'Y-es, s'il te plaît.'

'What? Oh, right.'

Peregrine looked up at him amiably, seemingly unaware he had said anything unusual. Tom suppressed a smile, and laid the plans on the table. Does he know, he wondered; does he know when he speaks French? Sometimes, maybe. Brother John had said Father was taken aback by saying, 'Merci, chéri.' But even then, had he known it was in French, or had he simply been embarrassed because he thought he'd said, 'Thank you, darling'?

Tom glanced down at the table which stood beside Peregrine's chair. Two books lay there already, a copy of John's Gospel, and a breviary.

'Brother John been saying the Office with you?' Tom asked, as he smoothed the plan on top of the books.

'N-o. B-Br-B...oh!...F-Fr...n...'

'Francis?'

'Y-es.'

'D'you know, I haven't spoken to him in an age. Dawn to dusk I've been up on the farm. And he's going away to be priested soon.'

'Y-es.'

'And Brother James off to Oxford.'

Peregrine reacted to this piece of news with an explosion of consternation, ending in an incomprehensible question.

'I beg your pardon?' Tom looked at him blankly. 'I didn't get any of that. Do you object to Brother James going to Oxford?'

'*Y-es.*'

'Why? I thought you set up for him to go to university.'

'Y-es.'

Tom frowned at him, puzzled, then his face cleared. 'Oh! Cambridge, wasn't it—for the cheaper accommodation? I suppose Father Chad forgot. Anyway, he's going to Oxford now.'

There followed a long muttered grumbling from Father Peregrine, which required all Tom's self-discipline to keep a straight face, then Peregrine sighed and dismissed it.

'Ainsi soit-il,' he said, and turned his attention resolutely to the farm plan.

Looking at the plans was not a success. Peregrine leaned over the map with interest at first, but his initial eagerness faltered as Tom pointed out to him the field shelter they had been working on, the harvest fields and the mill. He shifted restlessly, shadows of bafflement and unease gathering in his face as he studied the plan. He rubbed his hand over his eyes and looked at the map again, struggling to make sense of it. Tom, absorbed in his favourite object of thought, did not notice his disquiet at once.

'We've built the ricks here... and here. Brother Stephen wants to build a new shelter up here because of the stream; then we could pen the ewes in at lambing, and there'd be water on hand. It seems the ideal place to me; what do you think?'

Peregrine licked his lips. He was trembling. 'Y-es.'

'What's the matter? Are you all right?' Tom looked at him, concerned. 'Haven't you understood what I was saying?' he asked gently.

'Y-es,' said Peregrine hastily, frowning at the plan.

'Are you sure? You can remember when we looked at these to decide on the repairs and rebuilding?'

'Y-y-es.'

'Start here, then. This is the abbey. The chapel, look, and the cloister. Can you see the infirmary?'

The uneasiness was turning into outright fear in Peregrine's face. However hard he looked at the plan, it would not unlock its mysteries to him. Stalling for time, he rested his head on his hand, obscuring his face from Tom's gaze.

'Here's the infirmary. Look, trace your finger with mine. The infirmary here... and the path up to the farm. Do you remember?'

'Y-es,' Peregrine lied.

'All right. So this is the orchard where the pigs are, and

beyond that, the field of oats and rye. Now then ... up here
the pastures ... Yes? You remember?'

'Y-es.'

'And the outlying buildings to the west, where the
aisled barn is and the field shelter with a foldyard. Yes?'

'Y-es.'

'So then. You've got that?'

'Y-es.'

Tom looked at him, not at all sure he was telling the
truth.

'Can you show me then, on the map, the place by the
spinney, where Brother Stephen wants to build the new
shelter? No, not there, it's north-east of that, above the
long meadow. Do you see?'

'N-o,' Peregrine whispered hopelessly, his face shocked
and ashen pale.

'Let me tell you about it then,' said Tom gently. He was
not sure what had gone wrong, but judged this not the
moment to ask, and tried to speak tactfully, wondering
how to abandon the project without the total humiliation
of conceding defeat.

'There's a spinney up there on the hill; lovely in the
spring. The primroses grow there, and the bluebells. Violets too. It rings with birdsong on a May morning. Behind
the wood is the source of the stream which runs down
through the spinney, coming out beside the pasture. This
is the lower pasture here, where we bring the ewes down
when their time is coming in March. Up till now, we've
brought them into the foldyard and the byre for lambing,
because the cows are out to grass by then, but Brother
Stephen wants to build a new shelter there, so we shall be
able to take in the ewes that are about to give birth,
without disturbing them too much. What do you think?'

Peregrine pondered the question. It was a relief to be
released from the map, but he felt shaken still, his confidence undermined.

'Y-es, b-b-b ... m ... wh-wh ... oh ...' He sighed wearily.

'A good idea, but some reservations; yes?'

'Y-es.'

'What are the reservations? Too cold for the sheep?'

'N-o.'

'Unnecessary?'

Peregrine smiled. 'Y-es...N-o.'

'You mean yes, but that isn't what you meant?'

'Y-es.'

'What then? The expense?'

'N-o.'

'What then? It's a lovely sheltered spot. Perfect I would have thought.'

'Th-th...m...S-s-s...G...m..Sj...oh!' He strove desperately to shape the words, but the attempt was utterly futile, and Tom had run out of ideas to help him. Peregrine explained again, but Tom shook his head, helplessly. 'I'm sorry, Father, I'm stumped. I just can't make out what you're saying.'

Peregrine glared, exasperated at him, redoubled his efforts to make himself understood.

'I'm sorry, Father. I'm sorry. I can't make out head or tail of that. Try again.'

Peregrine waved his hand impatiently. 'Oh, n-o,' he said.

'Please. We'll get there in the end.'

'N-o.' His mouth was a grim line and his eyes were glowering as he looked at Tom.

'Come on, you'll never get anywhere if you don't try. Start again, slowly.'

'N-o.'

'Oh, you obstinate old man! Will you not just *try?*'

'N-o! N-o! N-o!' Peregrine lost his temper, shouted the words at him, beside himself with fury born of frustration and fear. He stopped himself, still breathing heavily, but the turmoil was too much to bear. He would not look at Tom and sat shaking his head from side to side like a wounded animal, then with a roar of anger and frustration he swept the plans and books from the table beside him with a violence that sent even the heavy Gospel flying. They crashed to the floor, scattering everywhere, and the binding of the Gospel split as it fell open and hit the wall. One or two of the pages were torn loose. Peregrine sat, trembling, his head bowed, refusing to look at Brother Tom.

Tom looked round as the latch clicked, and Martin Jonson appeared through the door. Martin viewed the scattered books and documents on the floor with alarm.

'Dear, dear me!' he said. 'What's been going on here? Are you all right, Father? I thought I heard some kind of a commotion. What happened? Has he been taken bad again, Brother? He looks bad.'

'He's all right,' said Brother Tom. 'I'll pick these things up. Don't worry yourself.'

'Well, if you're sure, Brother. Call me if you need help.' He looked apprehensively at Peregrine, who did not lift his head, did not move.

'N-o!' he ground out through clenched teeth, as Martin left the room.

'No what?'

'N-o! N-o!'

'Do you mean you don't want me to pick the things up?'

'N-o!'

'You do want me to pick them up?'

'Y-es.'

'No what then? What else did I say? Do you mean you're not all right?'

'Y-es! N-o!'

'Oh, for the love of God!' Tom ran his fingers wearily through his hair and across his tonsured scalp.

'I'm sorry. I didn't understand you. I can't promise to understand you. I'm sorry. Does it make me entirely a failure?'

'Y-es!'

'Thank you. So you hate me, yes?'

'Y-es!'

'Drop dead, Brother Thomas, is that it?'

'Y-es.'

'Get out of here, and never come back?'

'Y-es.'

'Would you do me the courtesy of looking me in the face when you say that?'

Peregrine didn't move for a moment. Then he lifted his hand and pressed it to his mouth; and Tom sat there an intolerable, harrowing eternity, listening to him trying to stifle the shuddering of his breath, watching the tears trickle down the back of his twisted hand; a painful, scalding grief of inadequacy and defeat, sparing nothing.

Eventually, Peregrine stole a glance across the room at the mess of plans and parchments, and raised a stricken face to Brother Tom.

'M . . . b-b . . . n-b-b . . . oh! merde!! . . . b-b-ook.' And he smote his breast in the ritual gesture of penance, *mea culpa*. Tom looked at him, torn between pity and exasperation.

'Yes. As you say; book. Your nose is running and your face is a river of tears. Have you a handkerchief?'

'Y-es.'

'Use it then, while I gather up this shambles.'

He gave Peregrine enough time to recover some measure of composure, busying himself with the reassembling of the plans and letters. The intact Office book he placed with them on the table, and he took the torn Gospel onto his knee as he sat down again on the low stool.

'What did you say this was? Can you say it again?'

'N-o.'

'Try.'

'N-o.'

Tom sat with his elbow on his knee and his chin in his hand, regarding Father Peregrine in amused vexation. Peregrine blew his nose and looked back at him, shamefaced, but not giving an inch. Tom shook his head, and took the Gospel into his hands.

'You said that. You said "book". If you will at least try to
say it again, I will take this Gospel *most discreetly* to
Brother—oh, I beg his pardon, Father Theodore, and get
him to mend it, no questions asked. If you will not even *try*,
then I swear by this book I will tie it round your neck, and
I will stack you on a barrow and take you to Chapter in
the morning for you to make your confession there of your
destructive tantrum; so help me, I will. Now then!'

Peregrine stared at him, incredulous, furious, horrified.
'Y . . . Y-y-ou . . . y-ou . . .'

Brother Tom dissolved into helpless laughter.

'Abbot Peregrine du Fayel, you are the most obstinate
mule of a man God ever created. If you can say that,
surely to goodness you can say "book". Say it! Try!
Please.'

'Mm-b . . . b . . . b-ook! B-ook.'

'Yea!' Tom waved his fists in triumph, Peregrine
watching him in an attempt at dignity which cracked up
into a grin.

'Can you say it again? Book.'

'Book. Boo-k.' He tried to look nonchalant, casual, but
his eyes laughed at Tom in excitement.

'You can! If you can say that, you can say anything.
Says it in the Scriptures, doesn't it? In the beginning; one
word. I'll wager God's word cost him as much struggle and
tantrums as yours did, too. Can you still say it? Book.'

'M . . . b-ook. Boo-k.'

'Ah, you're wonderful. I knew you could do it. Now I
don't know how long I've been here, and I've promised
Brother Stephen I'll be back up at the farm by midday,
but I've been wondering, won't you come outside with me
one of these mornings? It's beautiful out there, Father.
You can smell the year turning, the ripening, joyful smell
of the autumn, and the hills are just breathtaking in the
morning light.'

Some of the laughter died out of Peregrine's eyes; he
withdrew a little into himself again.

'N-o.'

'Don't you miss the trees, the dew...the sky?'

'Y-es. M...s-s-st—oh!' He shook his head irritably.

'The sunshine?'

'N-o.'

'What then? Won't you come outside, just for a while? It's a lovely morning!'

'N-o.'

'Why is it? Don't you want people to see you?'

'Y-es.'

'Who's to see? Old men in their second childhood— they can hardly see anyway, most of this lot.' Tom looked at him, encouraging, but Peregrine appeared quite adamant.

'You don't want to go out then?'

'Y-es.'

'You *do?*'

'Y-es. M...b...s-s-st—Ah!' He thumped the arm of the chair, angrily.

'All right, don't lose your temper again. There's something you want to do?'

'Y-es.'

'Something you want to see?'

'Y-es.'

'Outside?'

'Y-es. Y-es.'

'Shall I take you out now, then?'

'*N-o.*'

'Well...' Tom was perplexed. 'This afternoon?'

'N-o. *N-o!* N...n...s-s-st—oh, merde! s...' He waved his hand at the ceiling, gesturing all around.

'The sky?'

'Y-es. *Y-es.*'

'You want to see the sky?'

'Y-es.'

'So let's go out and see it then.'

'*N-O!!*' Peregrine screwed his eyes up, furious, grinding his teeth in helpless rage.

'Father, stop it! I can't help it. Don't be so impatient. You make me feel all harassed. You want to go out. Yes?'

'Y-es.'

'But now now.'

'Y-es. N-o.' Peregrine sat looking at him, his face twitching with impatience, the dark grey eyes burning with the words he couldn't say. Tom looked back, utterly baffled.

'Not this afternoon.'

'N-o.

'Later?'

'Y-es. *Y-es. Y-es!* S-s-st...'

'You...oh, sweet heaven, you want to see the stars!'

Peregrine closed his eyes and relaxed in relief, nodding.

'*Y-es.* Y-es. Y-es!'

'Stars.'

'S-s-st-ars.'

Tom smiled at him. 'I'll take you. Tonight, I'll take you outside to see the stars.'

The infirmary had two contraptions, designed and built by Brother Peter, for moving its patients who could sit up but not walk. The design was a mutation of a barrow and a chair; either a barrow with no front and an upright back, the wheels being at the back and two legs at the front, like the opposite of a wheelbarrow: or a low chair with wheels instead of back legs—it depended how you looked at it.

Into one of these singular creations Brother Michael and Brother Tom lifted Father Peregrine after Compline had ended, and dusk descended into darkness. Brother Tom had begged permission of Father Chad to be late from his bed, and Brother Michael was up anyway, because the infirmary was never left unsupervised.

They padded the barrow with pillows, and lifted Peregrine into it, their hushed voices and the low-burning night-lights of the sleeping infirmary adding to the sense of adventure that attended the occasion. Brother Tom pushed the chair along the passage, carefully over the low sill of the threshold; Brother Michael closed the door behind them, and they were out in the aromatic darkness of the physic garden.

It was a fine night, the moon reigning proud and fair in the heavens, bathing the gardens in an unearthly beauty of light. A breeze freshened in the night air, but scarcely enough to stir the leaves of the herbs or the laburnham tree that grew beside the path. Peregrine gazed ravenously at the high, immense expanses of the moonlit sky and the silent brilliance of the stars.

What a relief it must be, Tom reflected, to be away from the geometry of man-made things, feeling the wild, anarchic beauty of the night wind's caress and seeing the random flung scattering of the stars, to a man who has lost the ability to interpret patterns, who has been baffled and defeated by codes and schemes these long, dismal weeks. It must have been like putting down a great burden to come out here where there was no pattern, no code, only the wordless immediacy of life. Tom thought on the times in his own life when everything had seemed to be disintegrating. There had been such a healing reassurance in the rhythm of natural things. Maybe, he pondered, maybe it was not that it had no pattern, but that human beings were part of the design, and couldn't look at it because it didn't exclude them, only restored them to themselves.

Day and night, the dance of the stars, the cool fingers of the breeze...it wove men into its purpose like single threads. Even the broken ones could be woven together with the others to make the whole thing beautiful. There had to be a pattern, surely, because it was not empty of meaning, all this. It made more sense than anything. It was just that the pattern was not so much of a code...more like a dear, familiar face.

'Are you all right?' Tom asked quietly, releasing his

hold on the handles of the barrow and resting his hands lightly on Peregrine's shoulders.

'Y-es. Oh...T-om...th-th-th...s-s-stars.' His voice was filled with the sweet agony of his yearning delight. 'I l-l-lo...m...'

'Yes. I know. You love the stars.'

In silent consummation Peregrine drank in the beauty of the night; the wide enchanting wilderness of stars, the close enfolding of the secret dark, losing himself in the music of loveliness. He closed his eyes and lifted his face hungrily against the exquisite kiss of the night air. 'Oh, le bien,' he sighed. 'Oh mon Dieu, comme c'est bien...'

Tom stood a long while, perfectly still, unwilling to intrude upon this silent communion. Then he took the handles of the chair again, and pushed it along the path, slowly, among the scented plants. He stopped beside a rosemary bush that had grown out across the path so that it brushed against them. Peregrine leaned over and buried his face among the thrusting young shoots.

'Oh, mon Dieu...' He breathed in the heady, resinous aroma; 'Oh le bien!' He reached out his hand and rubbed the fragrant leaves against his face until the air was suffused with the scent.

'Smells so clean and good, doesn't it?' said Brother Tom. 'It makes you feel more alive.'

'M...y-es. Oh y-es.' He righted himself in the chair, and they continued slowly through the fragrant paths of the physic garden.

'D'you think you can face the cobbles?' Tom asked him, as they came to the end of the flagged path that wound among the herb beds, and looked along the cobbled path that skirted the vegetable gardens and led to the cloister buildings.

'Y-es.'

'Here goes then, but it'll shake you up a bit. I'll go onto the grass where I can.'

The barrow, with its narrow metal-rimmed wooden

wheels, clattered and bounced along the path, and it was a relief to reach the flagged passage that led from the back of the cloister, between the Chapter House and the church to the cloister. Tom pushed the chair through the passage, and they stopped and looked at the deserted cloister garth lit with white moonbeams. Nothing stirred there, sheltered as it was from the wind. Brother Fidelis' rose bushes stood in immortal stillness, bathed in the silver light.

Tom hesitated. He wondered whether to walk round the cloister, past the abbot's house. Deciding that the pain of that might spoil the delight of the excursion, he turned the chair round, and pushed it back into the passageway towards the small door in the south wall of the church.

'I think this is not too wide to go through the Lady Chapel door. Let's see.

'Oh, somebody's oiled the hinges. Wonders will never cease. Now...yes, we can do it.'

He pushed the barrow past the vestry and sacristy door, through the Lady Chapel and into the empty choir, straining his eyes to see by the faint gleam of moonlight that filtered through the windows.

Beside the altar, the perpetual light glowed in its lantern of ruby glass. Peregrine looked up, but it was too dark to see the cross above the rood screen.

'He's hidden in the darkness,' Tom whispered, 'but he's there.'

'Y-es. L-l-lum...'

'*Lumen Christi?*'

'Y-es.'

'*Deo Gratias.*' He pushed the chair up to the sanctuary steps, the altar dimly discovered in the shadows by the moonbeams and the warm, patient shining of the perpetual light. They rested without speaking in the holy presence of the dark that bent over them and wrapped them round.

'Have you missed being here?' whispered Brother Tom. Then, when Peregrine did not reply he said quietly, 'I'm sorry. That was thoughtless and stupid. Your absence has ached among us, too.' He paused. 'One day...one day, when you feel ready, I'll bring you to Mass. When you're ready.'

Peregrine said nothing, gazing at the dear familiarity of the altar, the silver cross, the rood screen, sick with loss.

'Come on then. I must take you back.'

And Tom wheeled the chair round, and found his way carefully through the Lady Chapel and out into the cloister passage.

'If we go through the kitchen, we can come round by the orchard and the vegetable gardens, and avoid the cobbles. What do you think?'

'Y-es.'

This proved less simple than it had sounded. Tom had forgotten the cobbles in the kitchen yard, and the chair nearly overturned in the uneven ground of the orchard, but he returned Peregrine in one piece to the infirmary, and with Brother Michael's help undressed him and got him back to bed.

'Goodnight, Father. I'll come tomorrow, after Vespers. Sleep well.'

'Y-es.'

Brother Michael went with Tom to the door.

'Was that a success?'

'Yes. Yes it was. We went into the chapel, and I think that made him feel a bit sad...but to be outside and see the stars, smell the herbs, yes, that was good. I'd like him to come out in the sunshine though.'

'So would we all. It'll come, now he's ventured out. Don't rush him. Thank you, Tom. Goodnight.'

Brother Michael closed the door, and Tom walked back through the herb garden, along the cobbled path to the cloister, where the night stairs led up out of the passageway between church and Chapter House to the dorter. Brother Peter, carrying the lantern round, nodded to him in greeting as he passed. Tom went into the little wooden

cubicle where he slept, and sat on his bed to take off his
sandals, his belt and knife.

'Father God...' he whispered, as he sat on the edge of
the bed, feeling the coolness of the stone under his bare
feet; 'just his speech. We can carry him, nurse him, dress
him, but we can't speak for him. Because of your loving
kindness, give him back his speech. And make him be able
to hold his water long enough to get through Chapter. We
can do the rest.'

He pulled back the covers on his bed and climbed in.
He lay with his hands behind his head, gazing into the
dark.

'Please,' he added, before he fell asleep.

Throughout the next day, Tom's mind teemed with the
possibilities for developing Peregrine's speech, helping
him to come out of his reclusive existence in the sanctuary
of his infirmary room.

'How can I persuade him to really *try?*' he asked
Brother Stephen, as they trudged up the hill after Chapter.

Stephen pondered a while. 'With animals,' he said at
last, 'if you want to train them or persuade them to do
something, you offer a reward—rattle a bucket of cereal,
or tempt them with some corn. Maybe it's the same with
people? Teachers sometimes reward children with sweet-
meats for a lesson well done, don't they?'

Brother Tom turned over this idea in his mind. 'Yes,'
he said finally; 'I think that might work. I've waited on his
table long enough. I know better than the infirmary
brothers what his likes are. I'll try a visit to the kitchen
before Vespers and see what that turns up.'

He appeared in Father Peregrine's room after Vespers,
carrying a tray with a bowl and spoon and a little jar. He
had a very purposeful expression on his face.

Father Peregrine, sitting in the last warm light of the
afternoon sun, absently stroking the tabby kitten that lay
curled asleep on his lap, looked with interest at the tray;

then the interest in his face gave way to misgiving as he saw Tom's determined expression.

'Now I've some beautiful, sweet blackberries here for you, and I've wheedled my way round Brother Cormac to spare me a little pot of cream so thick you could stand the spoon up in it. You've got to earn them though. Brother John thinks that if we really work at it, you might get most of your speech back; all of it even.

'You said "book" yesterday, beautifully, and "stars"; you can say "yes" and "no" well enough, and the odd word here and there, and you can swear with great fluency in two languages; methinks it's time we developed your vocabulary. I want you to try repeating some words after me. Yes?'

Peregrine's eyes wandered to the fruit Tom had put on the table. He swallowed. His mouth was watering for it. He sighed. 'Y-es,' he said resignedly.

Let's try something you know really well; maybe the flow of it will help you remember: *"Pater noster qui es in caelis."* Try *"Pater"*. P-P.... Go on: P....'

'P-P-P-shlastr—oh, *merde!*'

'*Try!* P-P-P-Pater n-n-n-noster.'

'P-ater n-n-n-n NO!'

The kitten leapt down from his lap in alarm at his raised voice, its ears flattened back, scampering for safe shelter under the bed.

'Try. You did it. Just this one sentence. Try. Pater noster....'

'N...b...b...'

'P-P-P-'

'P...P...'

'P-a. P-a. P-ater'

'P-ater n...n...n...'

'Pater n-n-n-noster. Try.'

'N-os...n-os...oh! P-ater n-os-n-oster!'

'Very good. Try "qui"; qu-qu....'

'N-o.'

'Try. Just this one short sentence.'

'N-o. N-o. N-o-o.'

Peregrine glared at him defiantly, but Tom held the winning card. 'Don't then. But I'll take this fruit away and tell them not to bother, you didn't want it. Well?'

'N-o.'

Tom shrugged indifferently, and took the bowl of black-berries and the little pot of cream. As he reached the door, he couldn't resist a glance back to see Peregrine's reaction. He sat, the bitter disappointment and humiliation written plain on his face, his lips pressed tightly together to counter the treacherous trembling.

It was a moment not like any other in Tom's life. Without warning he was in the howling place of storm, the fearful meeting ground of the tortured and the torturer, the betrayer and the betrayed, the powerful and the powerless, those who have and those who have nothing; the still place of knowledge in the eye of the storm. The look on Peregrine's face filled that hateful, howling desert, assaulted Tom with the violence of a blow. In unendur-able, stabbing accusation, Peregrine's eyes helplessly filled with tears. He bent his head, in a futile effort to hide his face, dismayed that Tom should see him so childishly upset over such a little thing.

But Tom was across the room in two quick strides, and dumping the fruit and cream on the table he fell on his knees by the chair and hugged Peregrine to him, his heart torn open in an agony of pity and shame.

'No, no, no,' he moaned. 'What was I thinking of? Oh, what was I thinking of? Father, forgive my cruelty...'

In that moment, Tom detested himself beyond bearing. He had never dreamed that he might play a part in driving home the nails, hoisting the cross, in this particu-lar crucifixion.

He pressed his lips against Peregrine's face, tasting the salt of his tears as he drew back to look at him, his hands holding his shoulders, his eyes beseeching his forgiveness. 'Oh, my God, I'm sorry.'

Tom had known the blissful security of a mother's arms and the intoxication of being in love; but here, in the anguish of wounding and forgiveness, was a steep, austere intimacy; knowledge beyond ordinary loves. Such unconditional encounter demanded no lesser honesty than the humble, painful disclosure of his naked soul. He bent his head and closed his eyes, suffering the pain of it to sear through him and through him, a merciless, costly compassion.

'I haven't been much of a friend to you, have I?' he mumbled.

In the tenderest gentleness, he felt Peregrine's finger trace lightly across his cheek.

'Y-es. Oh y-es. Thank you, T-om.'

Tom lifted his head and looked at him in amazement. 'What did you say?'

'Th-ank you, T-om.'

The scarred, tear-stained, crooked face lit up suddenly in a most mischievous grin: 'Th-ank you, T-om.'

'You... terror! You can say that perfectly! Since when have you been able to say that? Ah well, it's a nicer thing than *"Pater noster qui es in caelis"*. Come on then; are you going to eat these blackberries?'

'Y-es.'

'I'll put the cream on. Can you manage the spoon if I hold the dish?'

'Th-ank you, T-om.'

'What *is* this? Have you been practising saying that?'

'Y-es.'

'You crazy fool! You let me go through all that *Pater noster* rigmarole and you never told me you'd been working on something else!'

'Y-ou d-did-d...n...m...'

'I didn't ask?'

'Y-es.'

'No. I didn't, did I? Well there you are. That's one more homily on courtesy you've notched up to your credit.'

Tom knelt beside him, holding the bowl. He watched Peregrine's awkward progress, carefully scraping with the spoon the dribbles of blackberry juice that escaped from his mouth, painfully anxious not to let the spoon twist in his clumsy hand.

Tom made no comment. Questions ached in his silence: why does it have to be him? God in heaven, couldn't you have found some slob who couldn't care less to strike down? Or would that have been less fun?

He smiled at Peregrine as the last scraping of blackberries disappeared. 'You've made a neat job of those. Good, aren't they? You know, blackberries make a beautiful sauce for roast pheasant. There should be some pheasants worth eating any time now—grouse too. Yes, my mother used to roast them with honey, and serve them in gravy and blackberry sauce, with parsnips and turnips...it was good, that. We used to eat two each.'

Peregrine lifted his hand and wiped away a dribble of saliva from the side of his mouth that still drooped in paralysis. Tom grinned at him. 'I'm sorry. Am I setting your digestive juices flowing? Is that what you'd like, some roast pheasant in blackberry sauce?'

'Oh, mon Dieu...y-es.'

Tom laughed. 'I'll see what I can do. I'll talk to Brother Cormac. He'd do anything for you anyway. Now then, I'm sorry to go so soon, but I need to have a word with Brother John before Compline, so I'd better be moving. I'll leave this bowl here if you don't mind it. It can go back to the kitchen with the things from here in the morning.'

He stood up to go. 'Goodnight, Father. I'll see you tomorrow.'

'Y-es. Th-ank y-ou, T-om. G-G-G...m..G-o...m...b-ble...Oh!'

'God bless you too. Goodnight.'

Tom closed the door behind him, but did not walk away at once. He felt upset and ashamed still, that he should have pushed Peregrine to the point of tears. Two months ago, if he had hurt someone that much, he would have gone to Peregrine and knelt before him, and confessed it; but now...who? He had no intention of telling Father Chad about the incident. Brother John, then. Tom walked slowly down the passage. So much turmoil, he thought. I get so exasperated with him, and I feel so sorry for him, and I need him still; his faith and wisdom. I'm so angry with him for being ill and needing me, when I still need him.

Brother John would likely be setting out the medication for the night at this time of day, while Martin and Brother Michael made the old men comfortable in their beds. Tom walked along to the little room where the medicines were kept, a small room full of the fragrance of aromatic oils and herbs, furnished with a stout workbench and two stools, and lined with shelves full of innumerable jars and pots and phials.

Tom stood hesitantly in the doorway.

'Have you a moment to spare, Brother?'

Brother John was preparing the evening medicines; sedatives, sleeping draughts and pain relief. He had several bottles of physic on the workbench in front of him, and three pots of liquid heating slowly on a tiny brazier raised on wooden feet on a block of stone. He looked round at Brother Tom standing in the doorway holding the doorhandle.

'No, not really. Not if I'm to get done in time for Compline. I've skipped Chapel so many times this week I shall be earning a scolding if I'm not careful.

'However,' he added, looking again at Tom's face, 'I might make a free minute, provided you can help me give out these doses?'

'Yes. Yes, of course.'

'Sit down then. Excuse me if I carry on with this. What's troubling you?'

Brother Tom sat on the stool without speaking. Brother John finished his medicines in silence. He was familiar with this kind of communication. It came with the infirmary work. He had learned by now to understand as much from men's silences as he did from their words. It was time-consuming though; he privately resigned himself to missing Compline for the third time that week. He swivelled round on his stool and sat opposite Brother Tom, his hands loosely clasped in his lap. He waited until Tom was ready to speak, and in the end Tom asked him, 'You taught Father Peregrine to say, "Thank you, Tom"?'

'Almost. I taught him to say "thank you". He could already say "Tom".'

'Why did you teach him to say that? How did you go about it? Was it a struggle to get him to do it?'

Brother John smiled. 'Been arguing with him, have you?'

'Not exactly.' Tom hesitated. 'I think it would be fairer to say I've been bullying him. I didn't intend to...at least...oh, I don't know. I thought I'd try and build on his speech, teach him some words. Brother Michael said you told him that could be done. I tried him with *"Pater noster qui es in caelis"*, because of it being so familiar. He managed *"Pater noster"* and point-blank refused even to try further than that. I'd brought him some blackberries. I told him I'd take them away if he wouldn't try. I made to take them away, but...his face—he looked so...reduced. Degraded, stripped—I can't put it into words. He looked like a child. As though I'd robbed him of his adulthood. Such power, such abuse of power. I'm afraid to have such power. He wept, John. For blackberries and cream. Wept.'

Brother John looked down at his hands, sensitive to the uncertainty and dismay in Tom's voice.

'Not quite for blackberries and cream, I would think,'

he said, speaking with the same reasonable calmness he used on his patients when they were anxious or distressed. 'The humiliation of powerlessness like that is very hard to bear.

'It is not easy for us who can choose and determine so many basic things—feeding ourselves, relieving ourselves, talking, walking freely—to appreciate at all what it must be like, such broad deprivation. His emotional balance seems, to us, rather precarious, until you remind yourself of how the world looks from where he is. Blackberries and cream—well, you were able to go and get them, weren't you? And you could just as easily go and get some more. Him, he might as well long for the moon. Unless someone takes the trouble to decipher what he wants, and bring it, he has to do without. Don't be too hard on yourself, though. Be content to learn from it.

'As to the speech, I think no one could teach him better than you, but a few tips might help you do it better. "Thank you" is two words of one syllable each; an easy and rewarding target. Also, it's something he desperately wanted to say to you. He wanted me to say it actually, but I said no. It's taken him two days to learn to say, "Thank you, Tom," reliably. Two days. *Pater noster qui es in caelis* is a bit of a mouthful, and it may not be something he really wants to say himself. If he does, he'd probably sing it more easily than say it, incidentally.'

'I thought—Brother Stephen suggested it—I thought it might be possible to teach him by rewarding him; like you do with children and animals.'

Brother John could not help the broad grin that spread across his face, in spite of the crestfallen tone of Tom's confession.

'You didn't tell him that? No, I should think not. Sancta Maria, that would have made him spit!

'You have to bear in mind, Tom, he's very afraid of failure, of making a fool of himself. His sense of humour only takes him so far. He needs to feel that he's being treated with respect, courtesy—his watchword! Did you say sorry to him?'

'Yes. Yes, I did.'

'I'm glad you did that. That goes a long way. Is that all, then?'

'Yes. Thank you. It's a relief you don't think what I did was too cruel.'

'Did I say that? It was cruel indeed. I think it would have reduced me to tears if I'd been in his place. The look you saw on his face was your best guide to how cruel it was. The degradation of punishment, you know. Brother, I'm not blaming you, because I've done the same kind of thing myself, too often. There is the most terrible power attached to this job, and I don't always use it wisely myself on days when I'm tired or distracted. A sharp word, a hasty rebuke from me sears them to the soul. I've learned to say sorry, and say it humbly. It helps to rebuild some of the fragile structures I so thoughtlessly destroy.

'Now Tom, I really must get these medicines out.' He strained some of the steaming liquid infusing in the pots into small beakers as he spoke. 'Can you take this for Brother Denis, and this for Brother Cyprian—there's hyssop, coltsfoot and honeysuckle in it for his wheezy chest.'

'What's in Brother Denis'?'

'Sleeping draught. Chamomile and limeblossom. Take Brother Cyprian's first—he ought to have it hot. When you've done that, would you come and help me turn Father Aelred, please?'

Tom took the two beakers and went into the dorter. The rooms were smaller here than in the main body of the abbey, to allow for a man to be isolated in cases of infection or insanity, or if it seemed better for any reason that he should be alone.

Brother Cyprian and Brother Denis shared a room, and there was also one empty bed in with them. When Brother Tom came into the room, he found them both neatly tucked into their beds, ready for the night. He set down

Brother Denis' beaker by his bed, and moved round to Brother Cyprian, who was already asleep. Tom stood looking down at him. 'Brother Cyprian,' he said, quietly.

Brother Cyprian's eyes opened instantly, and Tom found himself met by a gaze of the most piercing wisdom. They looked at each other for a moment.

'Have they mended it yet?' asked Brother Cyprian irritably in his broad Yorkshire accent. Tom blinked at him, taken aback. 'Mended it?' he echoed. The shrewd old eyes continued to watch him. Clearly an answer was required. 'I don't think so,' he said. 'They're terribly behind with the repairs.'

Brother Cyprian clicked his tongue impatiently. 'Aye well, that's nowt fresh, is it? Where are we off then? Into town?'

'Um...no, it's bedtime, Brother. I've brought you your medicine.'

'Bed? Have I to stay in bed? I don't want to go to bed. I have to stay here hours and hours and hours. Don't be like that, lad. Let me get up.'

'But Brother, it's night-time.'

'Nay, don't say that to me. What's that you've got there?'

'It's your medicine.'

'Oh, I can't have that, lad.'

'But, Brother John said...'

'Nay, nay...I should never have done it. I let them poison me, and I died last Monday, and I've to do it all backwards now, if you catch my drift; to get back again. Why are you looking like that at me? Is it some kind of wizard or necromancer you are?'

'I'm a monk, Brother Cyprian.'

'A what?'

'Oh, glory be to God—a *monk!* Same as you. Please drink this medicine, or I shall catch it from Brother John. You've to have it while it's hot. Let me help you sit up.'

Brother John came into the room. 'Aren't you done yet?

Being awkward, is he? All right I'll do it. Give Brother
Denis his. Come on, Brother Cyprian, sit up.' He slipped
his arm under the old man's shoulders and raised him up
to a semi-sitting position, holding the cup to his lips.

'Nay! Nay, Cedric, I don't want that, it tastes nasty!'
the old man protested.

'Behave yourself, Brother! Get this down you!' retorted
Brother John sharply. 'There, that's right. All of it now.
That's better. You'll breathe easier now. Go to sleep.'

'You'll not put the light out, will you, Cedric? Leave me
a light—please. I hate the dark.'

'Ssh, go to sleep. When have I ever left you in the dark?
The night light is burning here. Hush now.' Brother John
stood with the beaker in one hand, smoothing the old
man's brow with his other hand. 'Ssh, ssh...go to sleep.
Be at peace. Ssh.'

Then he turned quietly away from the bed and joined
Brother Tom who was waiting for him at the door. He
glanced back across the room, which was darkening now,
the small flame of the night light beginning to glow in the
shadows. He held out the empty beaker to Tom, tiptoed
back to Brother Denis, and tucked his blankets in firmly.

'God give you goodnight,' he whispered. Then, satisfied
that his charges were comfortable, he was content to leave
them.

'How came it Brother Cyprian drank that stuff for you
when he wouldn't for me?' said Tom as they left the room,
leaving the door ajar.

'Ssh, don't disturb them now, for mercy's sake. He's a
naughty old man, that's why. Half his mind doesn't work,
and the other half works all too well, the old devil.'

In the next room four men were settled in their beds.
Brother John put his head round the door to see that all
was well with them, then Tom followed him along the
passage past the linen room to the little room where
Father Aelred slept.

'Why is he all alone here?' asked Tom.

'You'll see. Light the candles from the night light, will you, so we can see what we're doing. That's right. You go that side of the bed. We have to turn him so he doesn't get bed sores. We'll check if he's wet, and if not it's just a matter of turning him onto his other side.'

The old man was sound asleep, his face peaceful with the rapt innocence of a child. John looked at him, smiling. ''Tis pity to disturb him,' he said softly, 'but it has to be done.' As Brother John lifted back the blanket and sheet, Tom was assaulted by a nauseating, overpowering reek of sweat; the sickly stench of a body that was old and unwell and needing a wash. He grimaced, revolted. Brother John glanced at his face.

'We'll bath him tomorrow,' he said quietly. 'He's not well. It's a job to keep him fresh. He's wet, look. On the chest over there are some pads of sheeting and a pillowcase stuffed with sphagnum moss. Two pads please, and the pillowcase. That's right. Put them ready here. Now, roll him over to you.'

As Tom took hold of the shrunken, bony old body clothed in the standard infirmary issue of an undershirt and grey woollen socks, Father Aelred let out a high, wavering shriek of pain or distress so wild and piercing it made Tom's flesh crawl. 'Aaagh! No! No! No!' he cried. 'Oh please, no! Oh leave me alone! Please, please! Aaaagh! No! Aaaaagh!'

'Hush, Father Aelred,' said John soothingly. 'We won't take long.' He looked up at Tom's appalled face with a grin. 'That's why he sleeps on his own.'

The loud quavering protest continued unceasingly as they changed his bed and turned him and repositioned his pillows. It only diminished as Brother John rubbed his hip and shoulder with ointment to guard against sores, talking to him gently for a while.

Then John tucked the blanket in firmly, whispering, 'Goodnight, Father Aelred.'

'Goodnight,' replied the high, loud voice with startling,

hysterical clarity. They gathered up the wet sheets, blew out the candles and left him. He had not once opened his eyes in all the time they were in the room.

'I'll wager you thought we were negligent not bathing him oftener until you heard that,' said Brother John as he pulled the door to behind him. 'We'll take those along to soak until the morning; there's a tub out at the back. I'll show you.'

Outside the building in the yard, where the washing hung drying in the dusk, a thrush was singing, the out-pouring glory of sound filling the twilight. Tom paused to look for the bird while Brother John took the sheets from him and pushed them with a stick into a vat of soaking sheets waiting to be washed in the morning.

'Beautiful, isn't it? Will you take the pad with the moss, and empty the moss out on the heap yonder for burning? Thank you. The pillowcase can go in soak. There. We can wash our hands here—we've our own lavatorium.'

'Brother...' John hesitated, rubbing his hands dry on the linen towel. Tom looked at him enquiringly, shaking the drips from his hands.

'Brother, you should never look at a sick man with disgust on your face. Even someone like Father Aelred whose stink makes your gorge rise, and whose mind is gone. You can't be sure how much they know, how much they understand. Never let them see if the care of them revolts you. It fills them with shame, confirms their worst fears, seals them into their distress. It's important to look at a sick man with love in your eyes. Always.

'There's the Compline bell now, and I thought we'd miss chapel. Brother Michael will be on his way over. I'll walk along with you.'

He laid the damp towel over a bush of lavender that grew in the bed bordering the yard.

'It dries smelling of lavender there if the dew falls on it and then the heat from the sun dries it out.'

Tom spread his towel on the next bush in the border,

sweet-smelling southernwood, and the two of them went round the back of the infirmary building to the cobbled path.

'I'd like to get Father out into the sunshine before the days turn chill,' Tom said to Brother John as they walked along the path.

'You will. Now he's begun to master his speech, he'll get it back quickly. That's what'll give him the confidence to go out. It won't be long now. Ah—there's Brother Michael. God give you good evening, Brother. All's well. I'll be in after the morrow Mass, so you can go to Office and Chapter Mass as soon as we've got them up.'

Michael smiled, and nodded a greeting to Brother Tom.

'Thank you. Father Theodore said to tell you he will be coming after Chapter to say Mass with Father Peregrine and bring the others the sacrament. Goodnight, then.'

'Goodnight.'

The bell ceased tolling as they took their leave of Brother Michael, and they quickened their footsteps, hastening into the choir just before Father Chad gave the knock and the men rose to begin the last Office of the day.

V

A PROMISE

Still in September the days continued fair. The blazing heat of summer had faded and the dusk came earlier, the sunrise born in low-lying mist and heavy dews. The apples had almost ripened, the trees bowed under their load of fruit, and the grain was nearly all into the barns, a few strips still waiting the reapers, and some corn still standing in stooks, drying in the fields.

It was the busiest season of all on the farm, and Brother Tom had had little time to spare for the infirmary. He called in every evening, but only for a brief while, to bring news of the harvest, and to let Peregrine know he had not been forgotten. He did not sit down to talk, and sometimes, if he managed only to snatch ten minutes before Compline, Peregrine would already have been put to bed.

'When the harvest is all in,' he said to Peregrine, 'I'll come and see you properly, I promise. You—you do understand, don't you? I'm not running away, it's just...'

'Y-es,' Peregrine had said, and smiled for him, to set him at his ease. 'Y-es.'

And now the grain was in, and the weather could do what it liked, and Tom had a little more time until the ploughing began.

So he came into the infirmary after Vespers on the evening they had seen the last of the grain under cover, and found Brother John preparing to put Peregrine to bed.

He had undressed him and washed him, and he sat in his nightshirt and drawers, and his grey wool socks, while Brother John folded his habit neatly for the morning and cleared away the washing things.

'Hello, stranger,' said Brother John, as Tom entered the room. 'It must be near on a week since last we saw your face here for more than five minutes at a time. Still, I told Father, all I've seen you do in the Office and Chapter Meetings this week is sleep, so I reckoned you'd been working hard.'

Tom smiled. 'You were right. The barns are full. We've a good harvest. The rain can come now. But I've missed you, Father. I've been thinking of ways we might work on your speech while I've been breaking my back in the fields. Am I intruding? Can I stay for a while? You're early with bedtime, aren't you?'

'*Y-es,*' said Peregrine, and Brother John laughed.

'You're intruding if you're here to make him more rebellious than he already is, Brother Thomas. Maybe I'm a quarter of an hour early, but no more than that. I've had more grumbling than a quarter of an hour deserves though, you may take my word for it. No, it's just that I have to trim the toenails of one or two men tonight. It's easier to do it at bedtime than any other time, so this poor soul has missed his usual privilege of being last to bed; and left me in no doubt of his objections.

'You should be tired, anyway, Father. You've been working all day and every day to get your speech back under control; I'm surprised you're not glad to go to bed.'

'Have you?' said Tom. 'You've been working on it? What have you done?'

'I think you found Father Theodore's pictures helpful, didn't you, Father?' said Brother John, as he pulled back the blanket on the bed.

'Father Theodore's pictures?' Tom felt a sudden stab of resentment. He really had been too busy to call in during the last few days, but he felt put out that Theodore had taken his place, and irritated with himself for his own unreasonable resentment.

'Yes. Father Theodore spends a lot of time here with Father.'

'*Theodore* does? Why?'

Brother John chuckled at Tom's defensive tone. 'Maybe you thought you were the infirmary's only visitor? Father Theodore came every day when Father was first ill. Just to spend time with him, talk to him, hold his hand. Good thing somebody came, wasn't it, Tom?'

Brother Tom said nothing.

'T-om. A-a-re y-ou j-eal-ous?' The slow, blurred voice was full of affectionate amusement. Tom flushed.

'That was a very advanced sentence for someone of your disability,' he said acidly.

Peregrine grinned at him, happily. 'I'v-ve b-een pr-a-ac-tis-ing w-ith F-a-th-er Th-e-o.'

Tom stared at him. '*Have* you?'

'M...y-es.'

'You didn't tell me.'

'N-o. I w-w-anted t-o s-urpr-ise y-ou. *A-a-re* y-ou jea-l-ous?'

'No! Of course I'm not! Why should I be?'

Tom looked from Peregrine to Brother John. They were both laughing at him.

'Hmm...' Brother John considered him critically. 'Not only jealous, but too proud to admit it, I should say, wouldn't you, Father?'

'N...n-o...n-ose d-ef-in-ite-ly ou-t of j-oint.'

'All right! Have you two had enough? What pictures, anyway?'

Peregrine started to tell him, but his speech scrambled hopelessly. After one or two attempts he waved his hand in a gesture of defeat: 'I...I...oh...t-ti-r...ed...J-ohn.'

'I'm not surprised you're tired. You've done very, very well.

'The pictures, Brother, were some illuminated Gospels

and books of Hours that Father Theodore had done. He brought them to show Father, and then thought he might use them to help him communicate the things he wanted to talk about, or that he'd been thinking about, by finding and pointing out the pictures. Then they practised the words and sounds that seemed relevant to the picture, and the related thoughts it inspired.'

Tom digested this information in silence.

'T-om? T-t-ell m-e.'

Tell me about it. The relief and emotion that flooded Tom's heart at hearing those words again were inexpressible.

'Tell you about it? I was just wondering how it was that Theodore had thought of that and I didn't.'

'Th-at's ea-ea-s-sy.' The dark grey eyes were smiling at him, teasing. 'H-e's-s b-b-ri-ight-er th-an y-ou a-re.'

Tom looked at Brother John. 'We'll get this rascal into bed, shall we, before he heaps any more insults on my head?'

'Yes, indeed. I must get Brother Denis' toenails pared. He'll be wondering what's become of me. Yes, if you'll lend a hand, Brother Thomas, it'll save Brother Michael a job.'

Brother John plumped the pillows on the bed, and arranged them to provide the right support. He came and stood behind Peregrine, his hands on his shoulders.

'Are you ready, then, my lord?'

'H-ave I a ch-ch-oice?'

'No.' He squeezed his shoulders gently. 'No. I'm sorry. Brother Thomas, if you can take his legs, please.' Brother John moved his hands down to a firm grip under Peregrine's arms. 'Lift, then. On his right side.'

'N-o. On m-y b-b-ack.'

Tom looked questioningly at Brother John. 'Yes, Tom, if he wants.' They laid him on his back on the bed. 'I can see,' said Brother John, as he deftly stripped Peregrine of his drawers, pulled up the sheet and blanket and tucked

them in with firm precision, 'that I'm going to have
nothing but trouble with you now you can speak to us!

'There now, are you comfortable? Good. I must get on.
I'll bring your night light. It's almost too dark to see in
here already. Are you staying a while, Tom?'

'Just a few minutes, yes.'

'Good. I'll bid you goodnight then, Father. I'll call in to
you before you go to sleep. Here's your jar, and your bell.'

'G-oodn-n-ight.' Peregrine watched Brother John as he
gathered up the washcloth and bowl and dirty linen,
casting a quick glance round the room to check that all
was in order before he left.

'H-e...h-e's a g-ood m-an,' commented Peregrine as
Brother John left them.

'Yes.' Tom fetched Peregrine's chair over to the bedside
and sat down beside him. 'Father...now that I have a bit
more time, will you let me take you out of doors, while the
fair weather lasts? Please.'

'Wh-ere?' Peregrine sounded doubtful.

'Not in the thick of everything. Up to the farm, maybe.
Up to the field below the burial ground; it's quiet there,
and sheltered by the beech trees.'

'Mmm.' Peregrine considered this. 'I'm n-n-ot s-sure.
H-ave y-ou as-ked Br-oth-er J-ohn?'

'Yes, he thinks it's a good idea. What are you worried
about?'

'N-oth-ing.'

'Then will you let me take you?'

Peregrine hesitated. 'Y-es,' he said finally.

Tom smiled at him. 'You'll enjoy it, you wait and see.
I'll come for you in the morning, before you have time to
change your mind.'

Peregrine returned his smile, but Tom thought he
looked anxious.

'I'll leave you to go to sleep,' he said. 'Father, I'm
amazed at the way your speech has come on. I think it's
wonderful.'

Peregrine's smile this time was genuine, happy. 'Th-ank y-ou, T-om. G-oodn-ight.'

Before he left the infirmary, Tom sought out Brother John again. He found him just setting out with his tray of medicines.

'Brother, I won't keep you but a moment. I've talked Father into coming out of doors with me for a while in the morning.'

'Oh, *good*. After all this time! If you come after Chapter, that would be a good time.'

'He seems worried about it. I said I'd take him to a quiet place, away from everybody, but he seemed...anxious. Said had I asked you. What is it he's worried about? Do you know?'

'Yes: almost certainly, I should say, he's afraid of wetting himself.'

'Oh.' Brother Tom looked taken aback. 'I hadn't thought about that.'

'No. Well, of course, that's just what he's worried about. On the one occasion when his incontinence intruded on your life, you fled the building, if I remember rightly.'

'I don't know how to help him. I can push him around in a chair, but...it's a bit beyond me, this infirmary stuff. What do you do with them?'

'Tom, it's common sense, more or less. They simply need whatever help is appropriate to do what anyone else does. If it goes wrong, and there's a mess, we clear it up. What else would anyone do with them? What else would you do?'

Tom grinned at him. 'Me? That's easy. I'd bring them to you.'

'How kind. No, all you need to do for him is take a water jar with you, and don't delay if he needs help with it. He can manage it on his own with a bit of fumbling, but obviously it's no easy task with that crippled hand of his.

Once he sees you feel comfortable about it, I think his worries will be laid to rest too.

'My guess is, that's all that's bothering him. I'll tell him I've talked to you about it, if you like.'

Tom nodded. 'And that's all I'll need? A water jar?'

'Well... not quite. A water jar and a sense of humour. All right? See you in the morning, then.'

Every day after that, Tom took Peregrine out in the sun and breeze, sharing his delight in the freedom and space, the clean, good scent of the air. The warm dry days continued unbroken, and they spent long afternoons out on the farm, or in the field on the hillside below the burial ground enjoying the sunshine, and talking. As Peregrine talked, his speech improved. As he struggled to put into words the store of thoughts that had burdened his heart during the past weeks, he gained more confidence, and won his way back to coherent, articulate communication. Each word was slurred and slow, every sentence had to be fought for, but it was there. He had overcome the barrier, and the words came with more facility every day.

One evening, after they had put him to bed, Brother John commented to Tom how much good it had done Peregrine to go out, to find an interest in life again, to be able to talk.

Tom nodded. 'It has been good,' he said. 'Good for me too. It hasn't just been a case of me doing him a favour. I thought I'd lost him, thought it was a death within a life; grotesque. But now I'm wondering, you know, wondering if I ever really knew him. Whatever's happened to him has closed some doors—that's plain enough to see—but it's opened some too, somehow; windows into his thinking and into his heart. As if we'd mourned the loss of the sun when the night came down, but without the darkness we'd have never discovered the stars.'

Brother John smiled at him. 'That was very lyrical for Brother Thomas!' he said. 'I think some of his poetry's rubbing off on you.'

'Wouldn't surprise me. He's talked enough this last week to make up for the six weeks that went before it twenty times over. I meant it though. It really is like that.'

'Yes. Yes, I know. I've thought it myself. *"Et dabo tibi thesauros absconditos et arcana secretorum; ut scias quia ego Dominus, qui voco nomen tuum."* '

Tom looked at Brother John in surprise. A smile curved his lips as he softly translated the words, as if he had glimpsed something very precious. ' "I will give you the treasures of darkness, riches hidden in mystery, so that you may know that I am the Lord, who calls you by name." Oh John...that...where's that from?'

'Isaiah.'

'Isaiah? Well, if this has made a poet of me and a theologian of you, there must be some strange, divine workings in it somewhere!'

Brother John hesitated. 'Yes...Tom—be ready. You're right in what you say, more right than you know. Be ready. The work of God...all his paths lead through the cross.'

Tom nodded. 'True; but this is resurrection. Father's had his crucifixion.'

John was silent a moment. 'Maybe. But I didn't mean him. I meant you.'

The hills cradled the abbey buildings so that the porter at the abbey gate, or the faithful leaving the west door of the church, looked out across the valley, the road winding down from the abbey to the village nestled below at the foot of the hills; but the back of the abbey was sheltered by the protective curve of the hills. Behind the abbey buildings to the east a track curved up to the farm, and to the north another path led up beyond the church to the burial ground within its low stone wall.

A drift of woodland, a patch of ground which had been allowed to remain a wilderness, protected the burial ground from rough weather. Beyond the wood, the abbey

farm spread out over the curve of the hills, petering out
eventually as the upper ground gave way to the moors.
Below the burial ground a row of beech trees lined its
approach, and a sweep of greensward sloped down to the
abbey school and church.

It was here on this field below the burial ground that
Tom and Peregrine had been sitting talking together one
afternoon in the second half of September. The wood
behind the graveyard was a haven for birds and wild
creatures, and the two men had listened to the birds
singing when there was a lull in the cawing of the rooks
that nestled in the taller trees, and amused themselves
watching the antics of squirrels and rabbits that strayed
out of the cover of the trees.

Tom had lifted Peregrine out of the wheeled chair and
helped him down onto the grass. That was not too hard. It
was getting him back in again that presented the difficulties. But for the moment they were peaceful in each
other's company, each quiet in his own thoughts, Peregrine lying on his back gazing at the slow drift of clouds
across the evening sky, and Tom sitting beside him, looking down on the abbey spread out below them, basking in
the rays of the sun.

'It's a ted-iou-s busin-ess...d-ying.'

Tom looked down at him startled, his own ruminations
forgotten.

'Dying? What d'you want to talk about dying for?
You're not going to die.'

'Oh, T-om. L-ove gives l-ife, b-but not f-or ever.
Brother J-ohn said...'

Tom felt a sudden chill of foreboding. 'Yes? What did
Brother John say?'

'He said tha-at sei-s-sei-zures like th-is come ag-ain,
soon-er or l-ater. Th-is ti-me is a br-ief gr-ace. Sw-eet,
though.'

Tom sat very still, gazing into the distance across the
sprawl of buildings. Above him were the yellowing leaves

of the beech trees and the clouds fanning out across a sky
tinged now with the gold and pink of evening. The beauty
of the day shone all around him, but its glory was blighted
by those words.

'Is that true? You could be ill again the same, and all
this...all this be undone?'

'Y-es.'

'Oh...God.'

'Y-es.'

'And...I suppose you might even die, then—if you
were ill like that again.'

'I h-ope so.'

'I don't. When you were ill, at first...I wished you'd
died. I...I wanted you to die. It was too horrible. But
now, no. The...I...oh, what shall I say? It's meant so
much, taught me so much, these weeks. If you did have
another seizure and went right back again, even to incontinence and not being able to speak and blank gazing, I'd
want to start again.'

'O-h, th-ank you v-ery m-uch! T-om, I c-ouldn't d-o it.
Being p-aral-ysed l-ike th-is is...h-ell. I h-ate it. This is
wh-at I said, a gr-ace, but...en-ough is en-ough, *non?* I
mean, is-n't it?'

Tom said nothing. Overhead the beech tree stirred and
rustled in the warm breeze. A few leaves loosened by the
movement floated down. Higher up the hill, a sheep called
mournfully. The sun, low in the sky now, slanted across
through the branches of the trees above them. Tom moved
his hand restlessly, tugging at the grass, absently uproot-
ing and throwing aside some of the wiry little stalks. Then
his hand ceased to move.

'I don't think I could bear to lose you, that's all,' he
said quietly. It was an admission of the very core of his
heart, belonging to the same place of silence in which he
had first learned to communicate in total honesty. It came
clothed in the overwhelming silence of that honesty, and
Peregrine accepted it in the same way, in the truth from

the place beyond words. The sky, the fields, the light, the very air became a bowl of silence, cupped hands receiving the breaking pain of love.

'I don't know how you can talk about it like that, anyway,' said Tom eventually.

'L-ike wh-at?'

'Matter of fact. "Dying is a tedious business." You sound as though you're talking about the weather.'

'Wh-at sh-ould I s-ay? Th-at I c-contempl-ate th-e f-uture and th-e earth op-ens out in a ch-asm of terr-or in fr-ont of m-e? Th-at I cl-utch fr-antically f-or cour-age l-ike a lunatic tr-ying to gr-asp a wr-aith of m-ist? Th-at panic rises up unt-il it is ch-oking m-y th-thr-oat? Wh-at?'

Tom shifted irritably. 'Was that a poem or a speech? There's no need to make a three act tragedy of it. All I meant was—'

'Th-th-thr-ee a-a-act...T-om! I am n-ot dr-ama-tis-ing it. I am s-erious. M-ust I coll-apse in t-ears bef-ore y-ou ev-ery *day* bef-ore y-y-ou w-ill...w-ill...oh, n-ever m-ind it. Dr-ead also h-as a c-ertain tedium if it g-goes on l-ong en-ough. The m-ost appall-ing r-ealities ev-entually l-ose th-eir n-ovelty. Th-ere is a time of dr-ab gr-ey horr-or wh-en y-ou acc-ept that th-is r-eally is h-appen-ing to y-ou. It is pr-ecisel-y wh-at you s-aid: a m-atter of f-act.

'Th-at m-oment of acc-eptance turns y-ou to ice, T-om. It's l-ike dead m-en's f-ingers str-oking y-our s-oul. Th-e w-ay out of th-e pl-ace I am in is a sev-ere, n-arrow pass-age.'

'*Stop it!* You're making my flesh creep. "Dead men's fingers"! You...stop it!'

'Y-ou w-on't all-ow m-e ev-en th-e indulg-ence of a l-ittle m-orbid s-elf-pity th-en?' He grinned at Tom, but Tom, looking into his eyes, saw no laughter there. Death was teasing him like a cat with a mouse, playing with his life, a mirthless, taunting game. He was weary of it.

The day had begun to turn chill. The warmth of the afternoons no longer burned with the heat of summer. The lazy golden length of sunbeams belonged to colder evenings, longer nights. The shadows of the trees lay across the meadow, and the pink sky began to deepen into a wash of rose. A little cloud of gnats danced their incessant aimless ritual on the evening air. In the tall trees behind the burial ground the rooks were cawing and flapping, their racket suddenly loud in the stillness that steals upon the day and draws it down into dusk, silence, night.

The two men lingered in the waning day, the afternoon warmth prolonged here in the shelter of the low wall that separated them from the burial ground.

'T-om.'

'Mm?'

'I w-ant y-ou to p-p-romise me s-om...um...so-...oh!'

'Something. What?'

Tom turned his head to look at Peregrine. He had mastered speech well enough not to get stuck on a word these days, unless he was very tired, or under some sort of emotional pressure.

'Y-ou s-s-aid once th-at...if I w-w-ant-ed...y-ou wou-would he-lp m-e out.'

'Yes. I said that. But...'

'If...whe-en i-t h-ha-hap-pens ag-ain...d-on't l-eave m-e in it. I c-ould-n't, T-om, c-ouldn't go th-thr-ough it a-gain.'

Tom said nothing. He had deliberately not thought about the future. The present had seemed daunting enough. He chewed his lip anxiously, the months to come opening out ominously ahead of him now.

'Th-ere are h-h-ard time-s ahea-d. N-o sh-ort-cut-s on th-is r-r-oad. I am n-not af-raid to d-ie, and...en-ough is en-ough. P-rom-ise me, T-om.'

'Help you out? How?'

'H-em-lock...a p-ill-ow o-n m-y f-ace...I d-on't m-ind. B-ut if y-ou lo-ve m-e, d-on't m-ake m-e end-ure it ag-ain.

'T-om?'

'I'm listening. Believe me, I'm listening. Do you know

what you're asking? This is mortal sin you're talking about—um—hell. For both of us.'

'There is n-o such th-thing as h-ell for-r two people.'

'What?'

'Hell is f-ull of p-eople who a-re p-p-pur-suing th-eir p-pers-onal gain. Ev-en person-al s-alvation. L-ove anti-dotes hell. If y-our f-ear of h-ell ou-ts-trips y-our com-pa-assion, th-en y-ou have r-un to m-eet h-ell. M-ake hell w-ait; forg-et you-rself.'

'I hope the bishop hasn't checked up on your theology lately.'

'T-om. Pr-omise me.'

Tom shifted uneasily. Until now, the shadows of this level of reality had never lengthened over his life. Their chill carried a sense of gathering dark. When he finally replied, his voice shook in spite of himself. 'If you're sure it's what you want.'

'P-romise me.'

'I will.'

'*S-ay it.*'

'I promise that if you have another seizure, and you are as helpless as you were before, I will...finish it.'

'Th-ank you, T-om.'

'I hope you don't regret this when it's too late, that's all.'

'If I d-id, the c-consequ-ences wo-uld be no bl-eaker.'

Tom blew out his breath in a long sigh. 'Well, no. I suppose not. Look, I'm not easy about this, Father. It seems...it seems such a pity to risk forfeiting heaven when you're...well...knocking on the door, more or less. God is patient and merciful, but he has his rules, doesn't he?'

'God. Wh-ere is this G-od of y-ours, T-om?'

'Where is he? What do you mean, where is he? He...well, he's enthroned in heaven, isn't he? With Jesus at his right hand.'

'V-er-y p-retty an-d c-lean. Wh-at does he do?'

'What are you getting at? What do you mean, what

does he do? God keeps everything going, neither slumbers nor sleeps.'

'In a w-orking d-ay, th-ough; h-ow does your God s-pend his t-ime? S-ending men to h-ell, b-urning the ones who w-ere too af-raid to s-ee their nightm-ares th-rough?'

'Well, no, not all the time, but... I suppose that's part of what God does.'

'And th-is is the God in wh-ose image y-ou h-ope to be perf-ected, y-es? Th-e butchers in I-taly wh-o are b-urning the F-ranciscans... are they antic-ipating heaven then, or h-ell? If the G-od of h-eav-en b-urns people... a-nd people burn in h-ell... h-ow will you kn-ow the dif-ference?'

'Father! That's *heresy!*'

'M-y-es, I kn-ow. I h-ave stud-ied th-e Ch-urch F-ath-ers t-oo.'

'I don't know... I don't know about God.'

'Sh-ould do. You're a m-onk.'

'Tell me what you think then, about God. Where do you think he is?'

Peregrine did not speak for a minute. He drew breath, then paused. 'I...'

'Well?'

'Th-is m-ight h-urt you.'

'Go on.'

'When I w-as first sick, a-nd you d-idn't come to s-ee me, I w-as s-o w-wound-ed. As e-ach day ende-d... V-esp-ers, C-ompline, night, I t-urned my f-ace to the w-all and w-ept. I was l-onely and afr-aid. I n-eeded y-ou. After a wh-ile, I re-alised y-ou really w-ere not c-oming. When I f-aced th-at, someth-ing d-ied in m-e. It w-as tr-uly m-ore than I c-ould bear.'

'I'm sorry.' Tom's voice was husky with sadness and shame. 'I'm sorry.'

'N-o; w-ait. I w-ept before G-od, and I s-aid to him, "Where are you? Wh-y have y-ou aba-ndoned m-e?" I s-aid to h-im, "Y-ou have p-ermitted th-is. Y-ou s-uffer-ed me to be cr-ippled. Y-ou suffered me t-o b-e s-tripped of all dignit-y. Y-ou suffer-ed me to b-e p-aralysed and dumb a-a-and t-ortured. Could y-ou n-ot…God, in whose h-hand is th-e g-ift of all our d-ays…could y-ou not h-ave left me my friend? Wh-ere is your mercy? If it is true y-our v-ery be-ing is love, *where a-a-are you?*" T-om, I h-ad p-lenty of t-ime to th-think.'

'And?'

'I r-emembered the creat-ion s-tory. G-od m-ade Adam f-rom the d-ust of th-e earth. God the artist, s-tooping, kneeling in the dust, tend-erly, absorb-ed, h-is h-ands f-orming A-dam. W-e make th-em t-oo. Statues, im-ages fashioned with a-artistry and love, but G-od wanted more th-an that.

'H-e st-ooped and p-ut his mouth on Adam's mouth, a-nd closed his eyes, a-nd b-r-eathed in-to Ada-m l-ife. S-o Adam became a living being; not w-ith the dumb l-ife of the flesh, d-ust th-at g-oes down to d-ust, but with the breath of God.'

Peregrine struggled up onto his elbow to look at Tom, the spark of eagerness rekindled in his eyes.

'The thing—Holy Sp-irit—that m-akes God divine, is the same as th-e th-ing th-at makes m-an h-uman. H-umanity and deity share one br-eath. Just as man and w-oman are th-e s-ame b-ut d-ifferent, a-nd it is th-e d-ifference in th-eir unity wh-ich is th-e secret delight o-f th-eir love; "At last! Fl-esh of my fl-esh, b-one of m-y bone"—rememb-er? So it is th-at G-od's r-eality is found in our human-ity. D-o y-ou f-ollow m-e?'

'Um…no.'

Peregrine sighed in exasperation. 'It's my f-ault, I don't th-ink so cl-early n-ow. L-ook; God did not *w-atch* m-e w-eep, watch p-art of me die in m-isery. We sh-are one br-eath, he and I. G-od also w-ept, g-roaned, d-ied. He carries my w-ounds in h-is body. M-y gut clenched in s-obbing, a-nd it w-as the h-eartache o-f G-od. All my fear and d-efeat are s-cars that he w-ears on h-is breast.'

'But…God lives in eternal bliss. God can't die. Surely

that was the point about Jesus; he came so we could have life—to put an end to death. God's supposed to lift us up! It's a poor do if our miseries drag God down in the dirt too, isn't it?'

Peregrine smiled. 'Oh, T-om; don't tr-ample on all m-y th-eories w-ith your common s-ense. Wh-y do you h-ave to be r-ight all the t-ime? Y-ou'll n-ever m-ake a poet.'

'You don't think I am right though, do you? Don't smile at me like that. I want you to explain it. I don't understand the way you see it. Talk to me about it. After all, you might drop dead next week, and then I would never have understood. The dying bit. Tell me what you mean.'

'W-ell...th-e soul of us; our hum-anity, is th-e breath of God. If y-ou expose a h-uman being to too m-uch h-orror, too much agon-y, h-is spirit is w-ounded; s-omething in him dies. If a ch-ild is bullied a-nd beaten, h-as nowh-ere to turn, n-o refuge, his h-umanity is murdered. He becomes h-imself cruel, inh-uman. The im-age of God in him is s-oured: th-e v-ery breath of G-od in part dies in h-im. In m-e, p-art of m-y humanity is def-aced...des-troyed. Speech, th-ought, movement: I am not c-omplete an-y m-ore.'

Tom shook his head, protesting his denial.

'N-o, w-ait, T-om. 'Tis tr-ue. I h-ope th-e part of m-e that l-oves, tr-usts, forgiv-es, is still f-unctioning, but not even a f-ool would pretend th-at all of m-e is. And I conf-ess it to y-ou; h-ope has died in m-e a little; terror h-as advanced, and h-ope retreated. I th-ink th-at might be a s-in, but I can't h-elp it. I am v-ery afr-aid, n-ot of death, but of l-ife. But, our f-aith is n-ot in immortality; n-ot th-e immortality of h-uman endeavour, or of th-e hum-an s-pirit. We die: s-ome in sw-ift r-acking agony, l-ike Jes-us, some piecemeal, like me: but all of us en-tirely die. Wh-at I believe in is th-e resurrection of th-e dead. Th-e m-an whose childh-ood innocence h-as b-een wrung, str-angled, he w-ill see it r-isen. Th-ose like m-e, for whom h-ope is n-o longer realistic, we will f-ind a r-isen hope, bec-ause God is bound up w-ith us. H-e h-as thrown his l-ot in w-ith us; desc-ended into h-ell for us; h-arrowed hell ev-en m-ore thoroughly th-an hell has harr-owed us.'

'You're not entirely a heretic, then; you do believe there is a hell.'

'M-e? T-om, how c-an y-ou s-ay...I *kn-ow* it. I have tas-ted in m-y own b-ody th-e ag-ony of th-e d-eath o-f God. Sw-eating in f-ear I h-ave cried out to h-im, oh l-ose me n-ot utterly; do n-ot l-et go of m-y hand. He is with m-e. Odd, isn't it? God wh-o is l-ife, he is f-ound in death. It is th-e cr-oss, not th-e empty tomb wh-ich is th-e symbol of our f-aith. Th-e empty t-omb is tom-orrow's story. Th-e cross is the ch-apter of our day.'

'So where is all this leading?'

'The l-ove of G-od is not s-omething that stands over agains-t us. Th-ere is a j-udgement, b-ut it does not look on our despair d-is-passion-ately, w-eighing righteous-ness in the b-alance, and r-ecking no-thing of our an-guish. Th-e justice of G-od holds us in h-is arms in in-timate em-brace.

'What i-s G-od? Well, wh-at is it th-at makes h-umanity precious? What is th-e love by wh-ich I w-ept for you, and y-ou h-eld me c-lose wh-en I w-as in ang-uish, if it is n-ot the b-reath of God?'

'Human life is sacred.'

'Y-es.'

'Even so, you aren't God! It's not for you to take life until it's yours to give it.'

'N-o. I u-nderstand. B-ut, if wh-at m-akes m-e a l-iving be-ing is the b-reath of God, then what will he s-end to h-ell? T-om...I asked it of you n-ot as the p-roduct of th-eologic-al logic ch-chopping, but because m-my c-ourage f-ails at the pr-ospect of end-uring it ag-ain. By what c-razy, cr-uel ethic is it r-ight to s-end a lad of ei-ghteen to d-eath in b-attle, but needful to d-eny a t-errif-ied, c-rip-pled old m-an rel-ease?'

'Don't ask me. You're the theologian. You're making my head ache. It's getting cold, and Brother John will cut my liver out if I let one of his little chicks catch a chill. Let's get you home to bed. Don't worry about it any more. I've promised you. I don't like it, but I've promised. You can rest easy.

'Do you need to use this jar before we go? Yes? Go on then, while I get the chair turned round and sort out your pillows.

'Faith, there's quite a breeze when you stand up where it blows above the wall.

'I'll empty that, shall I?

'Here we go then, I've got your chair ready.'

It was a difficult manoeuvre, and it required all Tom's strength to heave him without help into the chair. The procedure was not always completed without mishap, but today it went smoothly enough.

'I don't know about you dying, you'll be the death of me. I'm sure you're putting on weight.

'Nay, not really,' he added quickly, seeing the discomfiture in Peregrine's face. 'Come, let's see what they've got for your supper.'

That day proved to be the last of the summer warmth. In the night that followed it, the wind got up, bringing rain in the morning, and there were no more days mild enough to sit outside. The rain came in squalls and the wind tossed the trees, tearing down the dying leaves and laying about the last of the summer flowers, except for Brother Fidelis' roses in the security of the cloister garth.

Occasionally, when the rain held off, one or other of the hardier inhabitants of the infirmary would be loaded into a wheeled chair and trundled around the paths for a short walk, but they felt the cold more quickly than active men, and such excursions had to be short and rare now.

'We'll be lighting fires in the rooms not much after Michaelmas if this gloom doesn't lift,' said Brother John.

'The place is as damp and dreary as a vault. It's taken me three days to dry Monday's washing.'

Michaelmas Day dawned in grey clouds and puddles, depressingly chill, the wind blowing from the east, discovering every chink in doors and windows and aggravating every ache of rheumatic old age, in spite of the shelter of the hills ranged about the abbey to the north and east. The rain fell in showers, depressing deluges that eased off after a few minutes to a blowing mist of drizzle. The summer was gone.

On that day every year, the daily rhythm of the abbey altered. The central section of the day, incorporating the Office of Terce, Chapter Mass, Chapter, work, the Office of Sext and the midday meal remained the same, and the brothers still rose for Matins and Lauds at midnight: but None, Vespers, and Compline were said earlier, they ate supper earlier, and they rose later for Prime and first Mass, which gave them an extra hour's sleep before midnight, and an extra two hours after midnight.

The morning after Michaelmas Day was a blissful lie-in, as the brothers, used to the brutal clamour of the bell shattering sleep in time for Prime at five o'clock, slept on for two hours, and rose with a comfortable sense of having rested well.

Brother Tom felt well-disposed towards everyone on the day after Michaelmas Day. He was never sure whether Brother Cormac's cooking tasted better on that day because of his own good humour, or whether in fact Cormac cooked better for being well-rested and relatively cheerful. This year, as always, Tom felt contented on Michaelmas Day, in spite of the rain and wind.

His spirits were slightly dampened by the day's reading from the Rule at the Chapter meeting. It was not the most encouraging Chapter in the Rule in any case, being a stern warning against the harbouring of forbidden lust and desire, with a reminder that death lurks near to the gate of delight, and that the deeds of the brethren were at regular intervals reported in humourless detail by watching angels to a God who was already keeping a strict eye on them.

On that particular day Father Chad, who had chanced to overhear Brother Thaddeus remark to Father Theodore that Father Chad's sermons sent him to sleep, took it upon himself to rub the brothers' noses thoroughly in the shameful depths of their own inescapable original sin. He chastised them in what for him were extraordinarily savage terms for the slothful, perilous indulgence with which they, like all men, were inclined to regard the stirrings and yearnings of the flesh.

He urged them passionately to root out every thought which offended against holy chastity, and every immodest word or look, adding that they must no more wink at such evil in others than did Christ in his purity who held the keys of death and hell. The brothers were slightly startled at this uncharacteristic outburst, but in the main received his exhortation with due humility and resolved to try harder in case the severity of their superior might be Christ in his purity giving the keys of death and hell a little rattle for their benefit, rather than a mere recurrence of Father Chad's chronic indigestion.

After Chapter, Brother John overtook Brother Tom as he was trudging through the rain along the track that led past the infirmary, on his way up to the farm.

'Have you time this afternoon to spend an hour with Father Peregrine?' he asked, squinting at Tom from under his cowl in the blowing rain, his shoulders hunched against the weather.

'Yes, it would be no trouble at all. I'm not especially busy today. Why? Is something amiss?'

'No. But the nights are long and often wakeful for him with his disabled body and active mind. Michaelmas Day is not as welcome to him as it is to the rest of us; even longer nights to lie alone with his thoughts. He'd be pleased to see you ... delighted even.

'Also, he bade me tell you his friend Père Guillaume in

France has sent him a cask of good wine, and he wants you
to share a cup of wine with him before he does as he
should and surrenders it to the abbot's table. It *is* good
wine too—he gave me some this morning. Father Chad'll
be wringing out the dregs, I fear, by the time we've all
begged a sample.

'I'll tell him you'll come, then? After the midday meal?'

'That would suit me well, yes; I'll come then.'

'Thank you kindly, he'll be grateful. That Chapter took
the skin off our souls, did it not? Whatever do you suppose
brought that on? We haven't had a going over like that
since you ran off with a woman in the novitiate.

'I wonder if he's planning to terrify the novices with it
in their Chapter this afternoon? Theodore will need to
pick up the pieces of a few stricken consciences if he does.'

Tom smiled. 'He's right, though. We are inclined to get
slack. I'll see you after dinner, then,' and he raised his
hand in farewell as their ways parted.

Tom spent the morning threshing oats with Brother
Stephen, showing Brother Germanus how to use a flail. It
was hard work, and cold, the barn doors propped back to
allow the chaff to fly in the wind.

He was ready for his dinner by midday, and applied
himself with pleasure to a large helping of roast capon and
green salad, followed by plum tart and cream.

He felt on good terms with life as he strolled over to the
infirmary, looking forward to a beaker of first-class French
wine.

Peregrine greeted him with a smile. 'It's g-ood of y-ou
t-o c-ome, T-om. W-ill y-ou sh-are s-ome w-ine w-ith
m-e?'

Tom could not help but notice the slightly glazed look
of his eyes, and judged that Peregrine had probably had
enough already, especially in view of the fact that his
dinner lay untouched beside him on the table.

Tom felt some sympathy for him in the rejection of his
dinner. It seemed likely that it had been concocted from

the same ingredients as his own meal, but that it had been macerated with milk into a broth-like substance, and the bread that had accompanied it torn up and put to soak in the liquid. The kitchen staff had, it seemed, grasped only too well that most of the residents of the infirmary had dim sight, aging tastebuds and no teeth. Beside the unappetising savoury dish stood another bowl bearing well-stewed greengages that had been vigorously mixed with custard to a pale green curdled pulp. This offering Peregrine had also ignored.

'I'd love to share some wine with you,' said Brother Tom, and he poured himself a beaker.

'D-on't g-ive m-e an-y m-ore,' said Peregrine, to Tom's relief. 'I've h-ad m-ore th-an w-ill b-en-efit j-udgem-ent or discr-etion.'

The atmosphere in the room was not entirely happy. The day scarcely lifted the light in the room above a damp grey dusk. Peregrine's face sagged in lines of despondency, his eyes fogged with wine.

'Aren't you hungry?'

Peregrine glanced in contempt at the meal on the table beside him. 'I w-as unt-il I s-aw th-at.'

Tom could think of no answer to this. He sipped his wine. 'This is good, at any rate. I'll wager you've enjoyed it.'

'Y-es. T-oo m-uch.'

They both looked up at the click of the latch, and Martin put his head round the door.

'Have you finished with those crocks? Oh, for shame, Father, you bad lad! You haven't touched your meal at all! Whyever not, now? They went to no end of trouble to mix it up for you. It should have been just what an invalid needs—hot and soft and wet.'

Peregrine looked down at the mess of shredded bread soaked in broth. It had long gone cold, and globules of yellow grease floated on the liquid and washed up on the surfaces of bread.

He looked up at Martin and contemplated his wagging finger of disapproval for a moment. Then, leaning forward in his chair with an expression of bland, almost empty-headed, innocence, he said to him, 'Th-e o-only th-th-ing th-at i-s h-h-ot a-nd s-s-oft a-a-nd w-w-et I ev-e-er h-ad a l-l-iking for, I l-e-eft beh-h-ind wh-en I e-nt-ered th-e cl-oist-er.'

Brother Tom choked on his wine and put it down, coughing and spluttering. Martin smiled tolerantly at Peregrine.

'Eh, what was that, Father? Perhaps we could get you some if there's something you fancy? Tut-tut, that *has* gone down the wrong way, Brother Thomas. Let me clap you on the back—that's better. Now then, what was it you fancied, Father?'

'No!' said Tom hastily, when he could speak. 'No, Martin, he'll be all right. You be getting on. I'll find him some supper.'

'Oh, very well then. Thank you very much, Brother; if you're sure. I'll take this bowl with me. That's a naughty lad though, wasting good food when it's given to you!'

Peregrine blinked slowly, like a disdainful, rather befuddled bird of prey; he did not reply.

When they were alone again, Tom sat looking at Peregrine, waiting for him to meet his eyes, which eventually rather shamefacedly he did.

'Father!' said Tom. 'I'm surprised at you.'

'H-e pr-ov-okes m-e bey-ond end-ur-ance,' Peregrine muttered guiltily.

'Even so, that was a most distasteful remark.'

Peregrine flushed, and looked away from Tom's disapproval.

''Tis tr-ue th-ough,' he mumbled, mutinous, and he added, 'I *hate* th-is inf-f-irm-ary sl-op. I h-ate be-ing p-atr-onised. I hate th-e w-eath-er. I th-ink I ev-en h-ate b-eing a m-m-onk. I w-ant a d-ec-ent d-inner a-nd s-ome g-ood c-omp-any.'

'Thank you, Father. You're so appreciative.'

Peregrine glowered at him. 'Wh-y do y-ou have to b-e s-o self-r-r-ighteous?'

'I'm not! I—'

'Y-es, y-ou are! Y-ou r-em-ind m-e of F-Fath-er M-atthew.'

Tom stared at him in astonished indignation, but Peregrine was not looking at him. '"Oh, f-or sh-a-ame, F-ather, you b-ad l-ad,"' he mimicked Martin to ludicrous effect in his slow, difficult speech. 'D-on't laugh at m-e, h-e m-akes m-e s-ick. Wh-o does h-e th-ink I am?'

'I wonder,' Tom replied. 'Why? Who do you think you are? Or is that the trouble? Aren't you sure anymore?'

Peregrine glanced up at him with a quick frown of pain. The question had touched surely on a wound.

'M-e? I know wh-at I am n-ow. Wh-at h-e s-aid; invalid. I'm a cr-ipple, an obj-ect of pity. I sp-ent years fighting n-ot to b-e, b-ut n-ow ...' He shrugged impatiently and turned his face away. 'It s-ticks in m-y thr-oat, th-at's all,' he muttered.

'And taunting Martin with lewd remarks? That restores your self-esteem?'

Peregrine's mouth twitched in irritation. He lifted his head and glared hopelessly at Tom. '*A-all r-ight, I'm s-s-orry!*' he shouted at him. 'B-ut d-o y-ou h-h-ave t-o be s-o s-s-sanct ... um ... s-sa-a ... *oh merde!*'

'Sanctimonious?'

'Y-es.'

'You think I should just indulge your lapses of propriety, do you? On account of you being an object of pity, maybe?'

Peregrine did not reply. Tom leaned forward and encased Peregrine's hand in his own grip. 'It is not my pity you have earned, but my respect, my fealty, my love. I will tell you who you are, in case you have forgotten. You are my lord Abbot, and I depend on you still, for your counsel, your wisdom, your example.

'So please don't say anything like that again, because it made me laugh—and I ought not to have—the angels are watching.

'Now, my Father, put it behind you, and tell me what you'd like for your dinner. Let me see . . . if I can lay my hands on some cold roast capon and a little salad . . . maybe a large slice of plum tart and some cream . . . something of that order? Yes? A man after my own heart! Wait for me—I'll see what I can do!'

Tom begged a laden tray of food from the kitchen.

'Cormac, why do you send him that repulsive mush?' he asked.

'It's what Martin asks for. Isn't it right?'

'Oh, come on—you know what kind of food Father likes. He's still the same person. The only good thing about that slush is that it makes life easier for Martin. He doesn't have to cut it up, and Father's less likely to drop bits.'

Brother Cormac looked thoughtfully at Tom.

'Yes, I can do that. I can send him over anything he likes. You're upset about this, aren't you?'

Tom held the tray as Cormac filled it with plates of food. 'Yes,' he said. 'It seems such a little thing to do, and it means so much. All the while he hasn't complained, no one's thought of it. It . . . it's not fair. It's like forgetting he's a person.'

Cormac nodded. 'All right. I won't forget. I'll see he gets what he likes.'

Tom carried the tray back to the infirmary room where Peregrine's eyes brightened at the sight of it. Tom cut it into manageable pieces and set it on his table within reach.

'Now I'm going to tread on the toes of Holy Poverty by finding some candles to wage war on this gloom,' he said.

'It n-ever f-ails t-o am-aze m-e,' Peregrine said to Tom, as they sat together contentedly by candlelight in the satisfied companionship that follows good food and good wine, 'th-at a m-an, m-ade b-y G-od t-o b-e l-ittle l-ower th-an the ang-els and cr-owned w-ith gl-ory and hon-our, c-an b-e brought d-own to th-e l-ev-el of a b-east, s-unk in d-espair and s-elf-pity, by d-isappointm-ent, or h-unger, or loneliness.

'I hardly kn-ow whether t-o be ash-amed or m-oved to w-onder, but y-ou h-ave f-ed m-y *s-oul* w-ith th-is g-ood f-ood . . . and w-ith y-our company.'

'If you ask me,' said Brother Tom, 'it's not such a bad thing to be a little lower than the angels. I wouldn't swap with the angels for love nor money if they have the job Father Chad said they did today. Roast capon . . . Père Guillaume's wine . . . Oh, heavens, the angels don't know what they're missing!'

VI

SORE

Brother Tom woke up on the third of October with a feeling of well-being that he could not at first account for. His soul was happy in anticipation of a good day, and he could not remember why.

Then, as he sat on the edge of his bed, fastening his boots and buckling on his belt and knife in the murderous clangour of Brother Thaddeus ringing the handbell to rouse the brothers for Prime, he remembered. Today was the beginning of the ploughing.

The sense of well-being swelled into a blithe melody of joy as he came down the daystairs into a morning clear of rain, the dawn promising well for a fine day after so many days of wet.

Tom loved the ploughing better than anything else on the farm. The sight of the neat rows of earth, good dark earth, well manured, turned back in straight, true furrows, was deeply satisfying. The steady purposeful work of following the plough, maintaining the rhythm by singing the chants of the psalms and the Mass, expressed for Tom as perfectly as anything could, his faith; a simple glad rejoicing in the earth and its Creator, a grateful fusion of adoration and hard, satisfying work. And all of it under the wide, happy skies of a fine October day, bracing and blowy; the exhilaration of a light fall frost without the biting stone-cold of winter.

Gladly, wide-awake for once, he joined in the Morning Office and the morrow Mass. Happy and hungry, the breakfast of a hunk of yesterday's bread and a beaker of well-water seemed almost appetising.

After breakfast, the Great Silence ended, and the absolute prohibition of speech lifted. It was now permissible for brothers to indulge in necessary conversation, though idle chatter and gossip still had no place in their lives.

Brother Tom stood with the others, stooping to wash his face and hands in the icy water of the lavatorium. He rubbed himself dry vigorously with a towel from the pile there, and combed his hair after a moment of indecision. I'll look like I've been dragged through the hedge anyway after a day on the farm, he thought. Still, may as well start out beautiful.

As he left the cloister buildings and set off for the farm, Tom saw Brother Josephus walking down from the infirmary. Only Brother Edward of the infirmary brothers had managed to get to Mass, a sure sign of a difficult night and a busy morning. Sometimes, if one of them was sitting up through the night with a sick man, the infirmary brothers would be given permission to sleep through the night and miss the Night Office and morning chapel to enable them to work shifts and catch up on sleep. Brother Josephus had not been in chapel either. Probably he had been conscripted to help with getting the old men out of bed and feeding them their breakfast.

'Brother! Can you spare a minute?' Brother Josephus hailed him as Tom waved cheerfully from the path that led to the farm.

Josephus broke into a run across the grass and joined Tom on the path.

'Tom, Brother Michael sent me to ask you, could you give them half an hour in the infirmary? Please.'

Tom looked at him, dismayed. 'Not really. We're starting the ploughing today. I've promised Brother Stephen. We'll be busy all day.'

Brother Josephus looked more harassed than normal. 'I can't give them any more time. Father Chad has people in after Chapter; I've to clean his house and get some refreshments sorted out for his guests. Just half an hour, Brother.'

In Tom's experience, there was no such thing as just half an hour. He resigned himself to saying goodbye to a whole morning with the best grace he could muster. Brother Stephen, he knew, could manage perfectly well for a morning without him. He could get started with Brother Germanus to help him; everything was ready to go. It was only.... 'Oh, all right then. What's wrong?'

Brother Josephus looked relieved. 'Brother Michael said that if you could just come in and spend half an hour with Father, he'd be so grateful. He needs someone to talk to, and Brother Michael just hasn't time. Oh, thank you, Brother Thomas. I know he'll be so grateful.'

Tom nodded, and walked slowly across the grass to the infirmary path, as Brother Josephus hurried away to his chores in the abbot's house.

Still struggling with resentment, he came into the infirmary and found Brother Michael renewing the dressings on Father Denis' purple, ulcerated legs. He glanced up and, seeing Tom, straightened up and smiled.

'Oh, it's a relief to see you, Tom. Did Brother Josephus tell you? Thank you for sparing the time. I know you're busy. We're all walking on egg-shells this morning. You'll find his lordship *very* much on his dignity—what's left of it.'

'Why's that then?'

'Brother John has told him he's got to spend two weeks lying on his belly in bed, to let the sores on his behind heal. They all get them, sitting in the same position all the time. This he rebelled against, and they had a right old ding-dong this morning. I just kept out of the way. Brother John walked out in the end and left him—he hadn't the patience to reason with him. Poor John, he's exhausted; been working all day yesterday, up all last night with Father Anselm, and now it's Martin's day off. Brother Thaddeus will come in this afternoon to help Brother Edward, but we're a bit stuck at the moment. Anyway, there's been nothing but scowls and short answers from Brother John since he fell out with Father Peregrine this morning, and Father I haven't been near. I'll come in later to put him on the jordan before the midday meal, but I thought I'd leave him a while to calm down.'

'What's the matter with Father Anselm?'

'Oh, it's his chest, nothing new; he's wheezy. Most of them get like it when they're in bed or sat in a chair all day. But it flares up in an infection every now and then. One day we'll lose him that way, and Brother John's fond of him. He sits up nights with him when he's bad, feverish, like this.'

'So I'm to pour oil on troubled waters with Father Peregrine, is that it?'

Brother Michael smiled. 'If you can! Do your best to talk him round to the idea of lying on his front a few days. We could do a lot for him if only he'd let us. So much of this black melancholy can be shifted with simply a bit of comfort; the reassurance of discovering that his body can be eased of its aches and sores. It's not just a question of falling down and down into worsening disintegration and helplessness—which is what he thinks at the moment. Poor soul, you can't blame him, he's fallen far enough, but there's no need for him to be quite so uncomfortable. Bleeding sores do nothing for anyone's temper, do they Brother Denis? No, that's right. You could tell him, couldn't you? He needs to get off them till they're healed up, then he can sit in his chair all day until he grows some new ones if he likes.'

Brother Tom grimaced apprehensively. 'I see. So I've to convince him of the need for common sense. I shall expect a hundred and fifty days off purgatory for this mission. I know this man's temper! I shall walk into that room feeling exactly like Daniel walking into the lions' den saying, "Here Pussy, Pussy," waiting to be shredded.'

Brother Michael laughed. 'I wish you all the best of it. Now then, I must get on with this. If Brother John finds me here talking in his present humour, I shall be gaining an extra day of purgatory, starting now.'

Although Tom would rather have been out helping Brother Stephen and Brother Peter with the ploughing on this windy October day, the infirmary was a pleasant place to spend time, being one of the few places in the abbey that were heated. As he entered Father Peregrine's room, the pleasant sight of a fire glowing on the hearth met him.

Brother Tom had spent some time the previous spring raising that hearth, because it had smoked badly and could only be used when the wind blew from the south and they had least need of a fire. Tom had built the hearth up to two feet off the floor, and fashioned a hood to fit in the chimney, and it served well now. Today, the little logs from the smaller branches of an old, diseased pear tree that had come down in the spring gales were burning on the hearth, warming and scenting the air. He glanced appreciatively at his handiwork as he came into the room, then braced himself to encounter Father Peregrine's state of mind.

'Oh, those smouldering eyes!' The words were out and Tom was laughing before he could stop himself. 'Is it as bad as all that?'

Peregrine looked at him without speaking. Angry falcon, feathers ruffled. Don't go too near it, Tom thought. 'Haven't you even a "Good day, Brother" for me? Really, anyone who didn't know you could be forgiven for thinking you were insane. You look like Saul brooding in his tent, plotting to kill King David.'

'It would be a c-omfort to Father Matthew to know

you'd learned your Old Testam-ent history so w-ell.' Peregrine roused himself to speak, his voice as morose as the expression on his face.

'H-ave you come here s-imply to unburden yours-elf of your impertin-ent wit at my expense, or is there s-omething I can do for y-ou?' he added, acidly.

Tom sighed. The prospect of gently persuading Peregrine into a more amenable outlook seemed suddenly too wearisome. He spoke with less patience than he had intended: 'Outside, the wind is blowing, the sun is shining and Brother Peter is taking the oxen out to start the ploughing. In here it is dark and stuffy, with you glowering in the corner like a bad-tempered owl perched in the roof of a barn. No, there is absolutely nothing you can do for me. By the sound of you, there's not much I can do for you today either.'

He could have bitten his tongue off as soon as he'd said it. No apology would serve to mend it. Peregrine looked away, his mouth twisting in bitterness.

Tom fetched the stool and sat down beside him, waiting for Peregrine's wounded pride to recover sufficiently for it to be possible to have a conversation with him.

'Y-ou don't have to st-ay.'

'No.'

'Y-ou were looking forw-ard to the pl-oughing.'

'Yes.'

Peregrine forced himself to look at Tom; sore, offended, hurt. He knew that if he said the words that naturally followed ("Go then"), Tom would get up without a word and go. He had to say it if he wanted to preserve his self-esteem, but he couldn't bring himself to say it, so he dropped his gaze again, saying nothing.

He wanted Tom to help him out, make a way forward for him, but Tom, longing to be out of doors, disinclined to spend a morning coaxing Peregrine out of a foul temper, decided against smoothing the path for him. He allowed the silence to continue, feeling a certain callous desire to

see how Peregrine would go about climbing down, asking
him to stay, and he felt shame too at his own merciless
waiting.

'W-ould y-ou pr-efer to g-o, then?' asked Peregrine,
icily, at last.

'Yes.' Tom stood up promptly and picked up the stool.
Just because you're having a bad day, he thought, justifying himself, it doesn't give you the right to wreck everyone
else's day. He replaced the stool, very precisely, and
walked to the door.

'T-om.' Even now that his speech had almost perfectly
returned, Peregrine had never reverted to the formality of
address, 'Brother Thomas', that he had insisted on before.
'Tom' he called him, always, still; a frank admission of his
intimate dependence. It was also an acknowledgement of
the no man's land in which he lived; outside status,
peripheral to the life of the community, a marginalised
limbo life.

Tom looked back enquiringly, his hand on the door.

Peregrine met his gaze, reluctant, mortified. 'Will y-ou
h-ave me m...beg y-ou?' he asked stiffly.

'No. Civility will be adequate for me.'

Peregrine nodded. It was hard to say it. 'Pl-ease. Will
y-ou st-ay?'

Tom came back into the room, laid another log on the
fire, brought the stool again and sat down resignedly.

'Out of sorts, then?' he said, mustering his patience,
aware that his unwillingness was all too apparent to Peregrine, which would not help.

'Y-es.'

'What's biting you? Tell me about it.' What a long,
ignominious fall, Tom thought, that he should need to tell
his troubles to me, as once I used to tell mine to him.

'I h-ave been pond-ering.'

'On what?' He did his best to sound interested, without
much success.

Time was that Peregrine would not have spent two

minutes sharing his private thoughts with someone who had no inclination to listen. His abhorrence of scrounging other men's time burned him, but his need outstripped his pride. Today found him clinging with his fingertips to faith and rationality. He was desperate for someone to talk to. He would not look at Tom's face; had no wish to see his longsuffering boredom.

'Have y-ou time to l-isten?' he asked quietly, 'I c-an hardly... I'm s-orry to b-e a nuisance.'

'Father,' said Tom, penitent, 'I have as much time as ever you had for me. As much time as you need. Tell me.'

'When a m-an c-omes here...' Peregrine paused, searching for words. 'When he j-oins th-is commun-ity, he l-earns a discipline o-f silence, and it is s-ilence in the f-ace of th-e presence of G-od. That w-ill b-e what Father M-atth-ew t-old y-ou in the nov-itiate, non? I mean, isn't it? Th-at all our l-ife here in the cl-oister is prayer, a self-offering lived out in the f-ace of God's presence. He said th-at to y-ou?'

'More or less. It wasn't quite so poetic the way Father Matthew put it, but yes, he said something like that.'

'M...y-es. Now, here am I, f-ound m-yself d-umb. Sh-ould th-at not have b-een a p-erfect silence, a f-inal self-offering, true prayer at l-ast?

'And y-et, Br-other John and Th-Theo-d-Theodo...oh! Theo, and y-ou, have all d-one your b-est to help m-e speak again. There is l-ess silence in m-y life than before, wh-en I c-ould speak w-ell. Don't y-ou f-ind that amus-ing?'

No, thought Tom, and nor do you. He waited in silence for Peregrine to continue.

'Wh-why is it? Wh-y do we always dem-and of ours-elves the difficult, p-ainful things; espe-cially in the n-ame of God? To speak wh-en we are dumb, to be d-umb when we c-an speak.

'I h-ave wondered if G-od is p-unishing me. M-aybe my words bef-ore had s-ome worth, and he h-as silenced m-e,

th-at I may not r-aise the head of m-y hum-anity in pr-ide
before his deity. Has he cr-ushed my human-ity so that my
words w-ill be inv-alid…m…inva-alidated, like m-e?'

Tom smiled. 'Sounds like a bad attack of self-pity to
me. You might be confined to bed, but there's nothing
crushed about your humanity. Besides, God—well, isn't
it a bit arrogant to suppose that your humanity posed a
threat to *God?*'

'Y-es; very arrog-ant.'

'As for being told to be silent when you could speak,
and to speak when you had only silence, well that's life,
isn't it? Ironic, but not significant. You're brooding, that's
your trouble.'

'Oh, is th-at all? Why didn't s-s-someb-body t-ell m-e?'
retaliated Peregrine angrily. 'I th-ought there was m-m-
ore to it th-an th-at. S-ince I was tw-enty-four I h-ave
s-erved God in the cl-oister. How l-ong is that? Th-irty-six
years, non? All those years I h-ave s-erved him, y-earned
f-or him, hunted him down, and now that he has f-inally
turned and sh-own me his f-ace, I am t-errified. M-y
Jesus, the Lord of Misf-fortune, the King of th-ose who are
sn-apped in two, th-ose whose grotesque rem-ains enact a
pitif-ul surv-ival of disease, abuse, tr-agedy. I offered h-im
m-y homage, and now he has taken m-e f-ully as his
subject. I vowed him I w-ould live in poverty, and oh, m-y
God, this is p-poverty. I said I w-ould l-ive in ch-astity,
and wh-at w-oman—forg-ive me, but what w-oman
would w-ant me n-ow, this th-ing I have bec-ome? I promised obedience, and h-ere I am: I cannot eat or def-ecate
or even get fr-om the chair to the b-b-bed without h-elp,
permission. "T-ake all of m-e," I said to h-im, and I
approached w-ith my head held high, m-eaning to kneel
gracefully, lay down m-y life at his f-eet. Instead of th-at,
he h-as reached d-own and t-aken it out of my hands.' He
laughed, bitterly. 'Damn it, he has *t-aken* my hands! He
h-as taken my gift w-ithout ceremony, an-nd thro-wn it
aside. I am a n-aked soul, abased before him, stripped of

m-y offering. I have n-o life to offer h-im any m-ore, and his thr-one which gl-glowed so invitingly fr-om far away is a bl-aze of terror, scorching m-y face now. The pr-esence of God, surely it should bring deep peace, home-coming, comf-ort; n-ot an agon-y of bitter tears and an endless des-ert of despair.

'T-om! I am afraid of God! Has he n-no pity? M-y sacrifice is not l-ike the s-acrifice of Jesus. Th-at bought r-redemption for mankind. M-ine is empt-y, v-alueless. My life was w-orth something to *me*. Of wh-at use c-ould it be to G-od, that he sh-ould snatch it fr-om me l-ike this? He has taken my life, heedlessly, and cr-ushed it und-er his heel in the mud, gone on his w-ay. He has l-eft me. M-y Lord...he has rejected m-e.'

'Father, you're not making sense,' said Tom gently. 'You're saying God has rejected you, left you; and you're also saying he has made you fully his subject. You're not being sensible about it—'

'Oh *God*, T-om, *help me!* I am in despair! I c-an't lift up this weight of bl-ackness. I f-eel as though there is n-othing left of m-y soul but a split, sw-ollen br-uise...oh G-od...help me...T-om...'

Tom looked at him. Plainly this was not an agony that could be placated with kindness. I suppose I should feel honoured, he thought, that he trusts me with his heart-ache. Honour apart, what can I say to him? God help me! For Christ's sake, don't abandon both of us!

'Can you not use your theology now to fight this despair?'

'*Theology?* Th-eology is n-o use to anyone! It is an intellectual's t-oy, an elegant f-encing f-oil, a usel-ess courtly g-ame.'

'All right. Forget theology. What about God?'

'Well, y-es; wh-at about G-od? I don't know. I th-ink I must h-ave off-ended him. Wh-ere is he in all th-is...mess?'

He waved his maimed hand in a gesture of hopelessness

and disgust, baffled by the tangle of pain and doubt. Tom tried again.

'Father, do you remember talking to me earlier this fall, out in the field below the burial ground, about God's breath? Yes? And you said that God is not outside, watching, but in the middle of all the sweat and turmoil, with you. Remember?'

'Y-es.'

'Do you still believe that?'

'It is st-ill m-y the-ology, y-es. It remains th-e only w-ay I can m-ake sense of anyth-ing.'

'Will you tell me more about it?'

'About wh-at?'

'About God being with us, in us. I'm not sure I properly understood.'

Peregrine looked at Tom very carefully. He felt fairly sure this was nothing more than a ploy to draw him out of himself, but Tom's face was giving nothing away.

'It is only basic incarn-ational theology. Y-ou should have it by h-eart from your novitiate studies. Th-e Christian religion p-pivots around a b-elief in incarna-tion. Its central ten-ets f-orm a dual st-atement about G-od and about man, s-pringing fr-om the person of J-esus. Th-ere are various things to b-e l-earned fr-om that. F-irstly, v-ery important, is th-at tr-uth is essentially p-ersonal. Tr-uth does not exist in the abstr-act: y-ou could s-ay, truth has to be inca-arnate. Jesus said it b-etter, m... "I am the way, th-e truth a-nd the l-ife." G-od is tr-uth, and truth is pers-onal because the v-ery *heart* of God, his c-entral r-reality, th-at he is love, is to d-o w-ith r-elating, giving of h-imself, embr-acing.

'I th-ink the reason God forb-ade the making of idols, gr-aven images, is th-at the image of God is personhood in intim-ate relation; m... Adam and Eve, to y-ou. M-ust be breathing, loving, vulnerable to pain, ar-oused to life, to b-e the image of G-od. Everything a statue is n-ot. Statues are the image of everyth-ing that is not God. They are f-orm without personhood. He is personhood without f-orm. I hope I...tell me tr-uth, Tom; am I boring y-ou?'

'Go on.' Tom smiled. He was none too sure that he knew what Peregrine was talking about, but there were signs of eagerness in the man's face, a flicker of something better than misery. You need your job back, Tom thought sadly. Your faith would burn as bright as ever if you had to teach in Chapter again.

'So, truth is p-ersonal. That is why h-ypocrisy is so great a s-in, because it is anti-truth. It is the statement of truth without the body of truth, so to sp-eak. It is m-ore important to *be* truth than to t-ell truth.'

Tom listened, fascinated to hear the impediment in Peregrine's voice lessen as his distress lessened and he grew absorbed in thought.

'Wh-en God cast Adam and Eve out of the garden, his image was l-ost, defaced. There was no way through to him any m-ore. Truth was all bottled up in God again, and nowhere could fl-ow out cl-early, until Jesus.

'Jesus showed us God again; b-ut also, Jesus, because he is the true likeness of the F-ather, showed us for the f-irst time since Adam, hum-anity. Je-sus is wh-at he s-aid he was: the revelat-ion of the Fath-er. We don't take h-im s-eriously. H-e als-o is th-e revela-tion of hum-anity. B-efore Jesus came, we h-ad not s-een God, a-nd we had n-not seen man either. We th-ought we kn-ew man, but...u-tter humanity, br-eathed by the mouth of G-od...we s-ee tha-at in Jesus.

'Man, the living image, had been lost in sin. Jesus r-estored to us a vision of God and a vision of humanity. Better than that even, he gave us a w-ay back; to our God, and als-o to our humanity.

'B-ut what an awesome vision, non? We w-ere used to the tradition of God as power and m-ight, glory and m-ajesty. But remember, the only images we h-ad were defaced images; sin-distorted, abased. Therefore our conc-ept of pow-er and majesty, learned from what we s-aw of earthly kings, was also corrupt. W-e th-ought power and majesty were self-protective, comfortable, luxurious, remote. That is because we saw their reflection in images all burdened with sin. Then J-esus, startling Messiah, the first true man—I mean true like a line is true or an arr-ow speeding to the target—showed us a true p-icture of m-ajesty and glory. Remember his words: "Father, the hour has c-ome. Glorify your Son." What an hour of glory...flogged and derided, n-ailed up...oh...G-od...

'He showed us that the shekinah of G-od, his radiance in creation, does n-ot rest where we looked for it, in pomp and pr-ocessional, in riches and state and inv-estiture of power. N-o, the fragrance of his presence is f-ound in the broken, suffering ones. The beggar at the r-oadside, we have to kneel to see his f-ace. The newborn child and the torn, exhausted body of the labouring w-oman, the midwife m-ust kneel to deliver. Brother Michael describes to m-e how he kneels at Brother Cyprian's side, helping the old man l-ost in his dementia to eat his oatmeal, sw-allow his m-edicine. 'Tis true, we still kneel before his glory. But we do not recognise it, least of all wh-en our own hour comes and his gl-ory is agonisingly born in our selves. F-ather, the hour has come. Glorify your Son. Oh the torture of Geths-emane, the prospect of his inheritance, the gl-ory of God...' Peregrine shook his head, his face stilled with sorrow.

'Father, that day...that day...you remember that awful day with the blackberries and cream, when you were just starting to speak again? Is it like that, you mean? Remember? I knelt and...took you in my arms. The glory of God in your...weeping and...humiliation.'

Tom felt his gut writhe with embarrassment to speak such words; to expose to scrutiny that humiliation and grief. Silence, those things belonged to silence; not to conversation.

Peregrine looked at him, intrigued by his shyness. 'Y-

es,' he said. 'Y-ou, and I, at that mom-ent, found ourselves reduced to the raw m-aterials of our humanity.' He
smiled. 'V-ery raw. It w-as a painful m-oment, as I recall.
But for the angels, what did th-ey see? Perhaps a m-an
kneeling in homage to God who is love, expressing the true
f-ealty of his heart, that he will serve love and gentleness,
not indiff-erence, detachm-ent. M-aybe to th-em, a man
whose heart is wrenched with pity does not appear
qualitatively diff-erent from a m-an whose heart is m-oved
to adore the Most High…and, maybe it is n-ot.'

'Father…' Tom hesitated. Now for the difficult bit.

'Mm?'

'If that's true, then…we owe it to each other to allow
ourselves to be comforted, nursed—even when it feels
humiliating. If what you say is right, then to let other
people help us allows the glory of God to shine in our
helplessness, and lets them pay homage to his presence.
Doesn't it?'

Peregrine looked at Tom suspiciously, waited for what
was coming next.

'Doesn't it make you ache, sitting in your chair, not
able to move?' Tom met Peregrine's gaze with what he
hoped looked like a kind of artless candour. He was rely-
ing on Peregrine's gratitude for company and conversation lowering his defences enough to make him open to
persuasion.

'M…y-es.' He sounded wary, but he was not disposed
to shut Tom out completely. 'It w-ouldn't be so bad if I
could get some lever-age with m-y leg, but one being paralysed and the other l-ame…this elbow is n-ot enough to
shift my weight. I…straight answer is y-es; I f-eel as
though I've been beaten.'

Tom looked down, innocently examining his fingernails. He knew he could not steal a march on Peregrine
and look into his eyes at the same time.

'Couldn't you ease it a bit by shifting your position in
the chair?' he asked, with childlike, ingenuous concern.

Peregrine looked very hard at Tom. He was not sure how loaded this question was.

'No,' he said shortly. 'I...I've s-ores from s-itting. They hurt. I...it m-akes my eyes w-ater to sh-ift the tiniest bit.'

Tom met his gaze levelly then. That admission would have eroded Peregrine's resistance almost entirely. A little gentleness now should disarm him completely.

'Well then...will you not lie on your belly awhile and let them heal?' he asked softly. 'Someone could rub your back and your legs, ease them a bit of the aching. Give those sores a chance to heal up.'

'Oh y-ou w-ily tr-aitor! Who told y-ou?'

'Brother Michael. Come on now. Have some sense.'

'S-o, I am r-educed in the end to comm-on sense. Ah w-ell, I have av-oided it l-ong enough, I suppose.' He was fencing, delaying the mortifying capitulation. But Brother Tom would not release him, waiting relentlessly. Peregrine looked down, away from Tom's eyes.

'To s-it upr-ight...it's all th-e dignity I h-ave left.' It was a mumbled, wretched confession, and the pain of it raged in Tom as if it were his own so that for a moment he could not speak.

'Father,' he said then, gently, 'think of all you've just told me. Nobody, nothing, can rob a human being of his dignity. A man on his belly, aching and sore, is the house of the dignity of God. It's only our corrupt understanding, our *tradition* of dignity you stand to lose. No one can take real dignity away from you.'

If all this had taught me only one thing, Tom reflected as he waited for Peregrine to reply, it would be that silence has many qualities. It is not colourless and plain. It has all the richness and variety of a stained-glass window. Silence is full of speech. This one is a battlefield.

Eventually, Peregrine spoke to him out of that struggling silence. His voice was almost inaudible, he could hardly bring himself to say it. 'I expect Br-other J-ohn would be busy now,' he muttered, beaten.

'Man...you don't need to sound so utterly defeated. Look at me. You've fought your pride and won; and as you well know, you've more pride than most of us. Oh, thank God; I do believe that was almost a smile!

'Let me go and find Brother John then. I'll not be long.'

Tom vanished hastily from the room before Peregrine had a chance to change his mind.

He found Brother Michael taking Father Denis outside to sit in the physic garden. 'You can take your little bell with you, and if you feel too cold, ring it and I will come, or tell Brother Edward and he will fetch me. It is chill, but we shan't have much sunshine now. You might as well make the most of it. Hello, Brother Tom. Success?'

'Yes. He's had enough. He consents to be given a rub over and take to his bed with his tail in the air. Grudgingly.'

'Ah, bless you, you master of tact and diplomacy! Will you bring Father Denis' blanket off his bed—the thick, soft one; no—yes, that's it. Thank you. And his water jar. No, no I don't mean water to drink, the other one. That's it. Bring it outside for me if you will. Oh, and he'll need the pillow from his bed I think—bring it in case.'

Outside in the garden, two or three old monks sat dozing in their chairs, well tucked in with blankets, and wearing woollen bonnets under the hoods of their winter cloaks. A picture of cleanliness and tranquillity, they were Brother Michael's *opus Dei*, the means by which he expressed his faith and devotion. He came to chapel when he could, and attended reverently at Mass, but the infirmary was the place of his true worship, and he made his communion with Christ in his dealings with the senile and helpless men who had been entrusted to his care.

The end and object of his devotion was to produce the result he had now, an expression of peace and contentment on the face of the man he was tending. He patted

Brother Denis on the shoulder. 'There you are then. I won't leave you so very long. Here's your little bell, look, and your jar. You'll have to have help if you need that, you're that wound up with woollies. Happy? See you later.

'Come and speak to Brother John with me, Tom. Oh, sorry, were you hoping to go?'

Tom shook his head. 'It doesn't matter,' he said. 'Let's spend the whole day persuading crabbit monks out of their sulks. Why not?'

Brother Michael smiled. 'It's worth it in the end. You stay long enough to see the change we can bring about in Father Peregrine once we get him comfortable. It's the most satisfying thing in the world. Brother John should be in here doing the medicine. Ah, yes. Brother—'

Brother John looked up from the workbench where he was grinding a pile of slim, shiny leaves into a hideous green pulp with his pestle and mortar.

'Good day, Brother Thomas. Are you through with washing and feeding yet, Brother Michael?'

'Yes. Um...Father Peregrine is willing to allow you to dress that sore for him, and take his weight off it.'

Brother John grunted irritably and added another leaf to the mush in the mortar. 'How gracious of him. Right now, I suppose?'

'It might be wise, Brother, since he's asked.'

Another irritable grunt.

'Oh, come on,' said Brother Tom. 'I've given up this morning to wheedle him into complying. Strike while the iron's hot, for mercy's sake.'

'It so happens,' Brother John inspected the mess he had ground, poked at it with the pestle, and put it down satisfied, 'that I have just finished pulping this heal-all for a green poultice for him. I had an idea from his temper this morning that he'd about reached the end of what he could bear. But he'd better not try any more nonsense with me, because I've had enough too. Let's get him back onto his bed then.'

It struck Brother Tom as he looked at Brother John standing, arms folded, glaring down formidably at Peregrine in his chair, that Brother John's authority created the supportive structure which made Brother Michael's kindness possible. It could be no easy task trying to nurse Father Peregrine, but he looked suitably chastened under Brother John's unswerving, intimidating gaze.

'You'll consent to lie on your bed and let this thing heal then? Sure?' He turned to Brother Michael. 'Very well, let's have his clothes off. I'll clean the sore, anoint it with some of Brother Walafrid's marigold ointment, and lay a green poultice on it for today. Tomorrow morning we can wash it and paint it with egg white.' He knelt down as he spoke, unfastening Peregrine's sandals, unbuckling his belt. Tom thought how crumpled and fatigued John's face looked as he glanced up at Brother Michael. 'Should heal rapidly, but he will need to lie on his side or his belly, day and night for several days—two weeks maybe—because the flesh will be fragile there even after it heals.'

'H-ow is F-ather Ans-elm?' Peregrine asked the question timidly, aware that his own conflicts and unaccommodating behaviour had contributed to Brother John's weariness this morning. He could not quite bring himself to apologise, but he wanted to make amends.

'Twice as ill as you are, and half the trouble,' Brother John dismissed his question shortly. 'Do you need to pass water? No? Open your bowels? No? Tell me *now* if you do, because I'm dead on my feet. I need some sleep, and once I've gone to my bed there's only Brother Michael and Brother Edward here today. No? Thank God for that.'

He pulled Peregrine's tunic up to his thighs. 'Lean forward on my arm then. Brother Michael, take this habit up over his head. There, that can go to the wash, he'll not be needing it for a few days. He can keep his shirt and stockings on. You take his legs, Michael. All right? Lift. On his right side for now. That's fine.'

He leaned over Peregrine's body and undid the string of

his drawers. 'Now then, let's see.' He clicked his tongue impatiently. 'I'm not going to be able to get these drawers off easily, there's that much blood and serous fluid glueing them to the flesh. Oh, Sancta Maria, this is going to take for ever.'

Brother Tom watched Brother John's face, dark with weariness, but careful, attentive still, as he tugged experimentally at the fabric, glancing up quickly at Peregrine's sharp, shuddering, hastily suppressed intake of breath as the cloth pulled at the sore. 'Did that hurt you? Brother Michael, this will have to be soaked off. Warm water, with a little salt in it. I'll need some oil too, and aromatics—lavender and rose—to ease out the general aches. Snap to it, come on! I'm all about worn out.'

'Brother John,' Michael was shaking his head at him in a mild, smiling rebuke. 'Go to your bed. I can finish this. I'll clean the sore place, dry it, anoint it, poultice it, dress it. I'll rub him over with oils, and he'll be as right as rain by the time I've finished with him. Brother Thomas can help me if I'm short of a pair of hands. You go and get some rest. Father Anselm may need you again tonight. Please.'

Brother John stood in hesitation, and Michael took his elbow, propelling him gently towards the door.

'I'll stay till you're back,' volunteered Tom.

'Thank you. Thank you. All right.'

Brother Michael closed the door behind Brother John, then came and stood by Peregrine's bed, looking down at him lying on his side in his undershirt and socks, and the drawers caked in sticky blood and serum. Michael considered him for a brief moment, then sat on the edge of the bed beside him and laid his hand on Peregrine's head, stroking over it as he spoke to him.

'You,' he said quietly, 'have a look on your face like a child who's been whipped. I think you feel thoroughly scolded...and confused...and afraid of the way your body keeps betraying you. Am I right? I think the thought of lying on your belly in nothing but an undershirt, smeared with ointments, exposed to whoever walks in, is more appalling to you than pain. Yes? I also think you probably do need to use the jordan, make yourself comfortable, and there's plenty of time for that.' He sat, observing Peregrine quietly, stroking his head all the while.

'Father...you know the weight and weariness of responsibility. You know how tired John is. This morning, you've been frightened and in pain, and he's been extremely tired. He'll probably want to apologise to you himself later on, and you were none too civil to him yourself in the way you spoke to him earlier. Maybe you'll want to say sorry to him. Anyway, that's up to you. But whatever, it's nothing to get upset over. It's easily enough put right.

'I think I'll cut these drawers off that you're wearing, so you can sit on the jordan a while, relieve yourself if you can. Then I'll soak free the cloth that's stuck to you and do something about the sore place. How about that? Does that sound good?'

'Th-ank y-ou.' Peregrine sounded relieved, but he still spoke stiffly, and Brother Tom, looking at him, thought how old he looked. Old and bewildered and defeated, his spirit withdrawn somewhere deep inside him in an ineffectual evasion of indignity and loss of privacy. Tom looked down at his own hands and arms, muscular and browned by the sun and wind, resting on his knees as he sat on the low stool. I don't want to grow old, he thought. Nobody can take the terror out of this kind of stuff, not even Brother Michael. I don't ever want to see the day when I can't walk or hold my water, sit mumbling milky oatmeal and talking rubbish, humoured and coddled by young men, a toothless bundle of sores and creaky old bones.

'Brother Tom?' Michael had cut away the drawers with his knife, and was ready to move Peregrine. 'You were a thousand miles away then. Help me move him, would you? It might be easier if you bring the jordan over by the bed. So, what were you thinking about?'

'I was thinking that I don't want to grow old. It doesn't look easy.'

'Different for different people,' said Brother Michael.

Peregrine said nothing.

'You take his legs, Tom, under the knees. Lift when I say. Ready? Lift.'

'Now then, Father, you just sit here and see if you can go. We'll go and get the things you need and be back in a while. No rush. There, I'll put the blanket over your legs so you're covered. See you in a while.'

Brother Michael came out of the room after Brother Tom, and closed the door.

'Poor soul, these bed sores are the final indignity. Excruciatingly painful, too. Did you see him bite his lip when Brother John moved him forward in the chair? No? It was all he could do not to cry out. It's no good being impatient with him. He's at the end of his rope I think. Let's check on the old men and have a look at Father Anselm, give Father Peregrine a chance to use the pot, then we'll collect the things we need and have him back to bed. Did you get to first Mass? Would you mind if I go to Chapter Mass, or I'll not get to Mass at all today. Thank you. I won't stay for Chapter. You can go if you like.'

'Father Chad on the fifth degree of humility, confessing our evil thoughts to the abbot? Thanks all the same, I think you need me here.'

Brother Michael frowned at him reprovingly. 'Tom, that's not the attitude. The work here sometimes detains us, but it's not to be used as an excuse.'

'Fine. You go to Chapter then. Do you good. I expect you have more evil thoughts than I do. This morning's Chapter will be just what you need. I've already had one homily this morning, from Father Peregrine. That'll do me.'

'Hush, Tom. Come in quietly to Father Anselm.

Yes...no different, look. We'll turn him over, I think; don't want *him* getting sores. You take the legs again. One, two, over. Faith, he's hot. Bed's not wet though, and it should be by now. Mmm. Not long with us, I fear, poor soul. I'll ask Father Chad to come to him this evening. Dip the cloth there into his drinking water and trickle a little into his mouth. Moisten his lips. That's right. Distressing, that wheezing, isn't it?'

Brother Michael tucked the sheet into the bed and laid the blanket over the shrunken old body. He stood with his hand on Anselm's shoulder, quietly looking down at him; took the damp washcloth that hung on a nail on the bedhead, and wiped the old man's brow, watched him a moment more. Then he replaced the cloth and turned to go.

'We'll look in on the men in bed, then the men outside. Father should be ready for us by then.'

There were only two old men left in the infirmary dorter, and both of those had to be turned over and given a sip of water.

'Oh, Father Paul, you're sodden—we'll have to change this bed, Tom.'

That took time, and then the three old men in the garden all wanted to pass water.

'I'm surprised this work doesn't drive you up the wall,' said Tom. 'Some days it must be next to impossible to get anything finished.'

'Well...you know. Anyway, we're done now. I'll get the ointments and such if you'll get some warm salted water and a few rags. He's got a towel in his room. Meet you there. He should have performed for us by now.'

Brother Michael was just before Tom into the room, carrying a tray of oils and salves.

'Oh, you've used the pot; I'm glad of that.' He put his tray down on the table, and took the bowl and rags from Tom's hands, placing them beside the tray.

'You'll be more comfortable soon; get a bit of sleep

maybe.' Brother Michael chatted amiably as he soaked a
rag and wrung it out. 'There, let Brother Tom take your
weight forward while I clean you; that's it.'

Tom loved Michael for his quickness of compassion,
the comfortable, reassuring monologue drawing a veil
over the undignified, distressing ugliness of helplessness,
its smells and pain and unsightliness. It dawned on him
that Martin Jonson intended to achieve the same result
with his aggravating patter. The difference was one of
insight, sensitivity. Brother Michael was acutely aware of
the moods and dispositions of his charges; to Martin they
were all sick and senile, and that was it.

'That's fine now. Ready to lift him back on the bed,
Brother? On his side, as he was. Lift. Good, that's lovely.
Empty that pot please, Tom. Now then, let me see; a towel
to catch the drips, a bowl of water...let's soak this off and
clean up the sore...eh, dear, we've let this get bad; that's
poor nursing. You must have felt as though someone was
sticking knives in you. Never mind, we'll soon have it
healed up.' The quiet discourse continued all the while
Tom was in the room removing the pot with its stinking
contents from the shelf of the chair, gently counteracting
the faint atmosphere of uneasiness, embarrassment.

When Tom returned, Brother Michael was carefully
lifting free the clinging fabric.

'There, that's off. Thanks, Tom. Now I'll clean it as
gently as I can. So...that's good...and dry it. Finished
with the bowl and rags, thank you, Tom. Ointment...this
is wonderful stuff for healing...wonderful. And a poultice
now.'

He laid on the place the green mush Brother John had
prepared, covering it with a square of fine linen, pressing
the edges of the linen onto the greasy ointment so that it
stuck down well.

'There now. How are you feeling?'

'Th-ank y-ou,' Peregrine replied.

Brother Michael smiled. 'No, no; I said, "How are you

feeling?" Indescribable, is it? I can believe it. All right, let me see what I can do. Let's have you on your belly then..., that's it. See my hands? Full of the peace of God they are. Some oil—doesn't it smell beautiful? Peace to you then, while I rub this into your back and legs. Lavender; for soothing, and against infection. Rose; for comfort... peace to you. Let the fear and misery go out of you. Easier said than done, well I know it, but try not to hold on to it. Feel my hands on you, rubbing the peace of Jesus in. There... on my life, Father, your shoulders feel as though they're carved in wood! Put some of it down, now. Let it go. Feel those aches easing out... there... it's the love of God soothing you now... a place to put burdens down. There now... peace to you. Be at peace... let it all go... yes... It's all right; don't hold it in... that's the way. It doesn't matter if it has you weeping. Don't try to stop it; there's no one here to see but me and Tom, and I think we know you well enough for that. There, there; that's better. Let go of it now... so... make some room for peace... and faith... again.'

He reached over and dipped his hand in the oil, carrying it deftly back without dripping any. 'Another log on the fire, Tom. It's chill to be naked. See how these knots of muscle ease out wonderfully now he's not hanging on to his woe. That's soft up here now. It was Brother Edward taught us this skill—a beautiful thing—bringing the peace of God... the peace of God to you.'

Brother Michael worked on in silence once his words had achieved their purpose, and Tom sat watching him. Although the day was bright enough outside, it was as gloomy as evening in this west-facing side of the infirmary through the early part of the day until the sun moved round. The fire on the raised hearth-stone acted as a lantern for the room. Its kindly glow reflected on Brother Michael's hands gleaming with oil as they worked methodically, firmly over Peregrine's back and buttocks and legs; slowly, carefully on the area around the sore at the base of his spine, so as not to pull at the fragile connection of skin.

The room had filled with the scent of rose and lavender oils, mingled with the heavier, earthier smell of the base oil and the fragrance of fruitwood smoke. Tom felt the silence settle around him like a mantle, a silence full of the most delicate tenderness, interwoven with primaeval, ancient strength.

Quietly, in the silence, the fear and misery that had haunted the room like shadows seeped away, displaced by a slow, deep peace; a peace of such solid personality that it arose among them with as much presence and conviction as if it had been a human face.

There was no sound in the room but quiet breathing, the occasional settling of the fire, sometimes a sound of Michael's oiled hands moving on Peregrine's skin; and two deep, shaky sighs from Peregrine as the peace that had come there breathed into him, penetrated the very depths of him, and he let go of the last drains of his anguish.

'There now.' Brother Michael had finished. 'How does that feel?'

'C-omfortable. W-onderfully comf-ortable. I . . . th-ank y-ou.' He sighed again, a long, slow sigh of contentment. 'Oh, th-at feels g-ood.'

'And on the inside? What's happened to all that misery? Mm?'

Peregrine looked across the room at the fireglow. The hard, enduring set of his face had relaxed into quietness. 'C-omforted,' he said.

Brother Michael smiled at him, pleased. 'You have a little sleep then, Father. I'll come in to you later. I'll cover you with this sheet—save anyone who comes in from the sin of Ham! Sweet dreams. Bring the things would you, Tom? I'll not touch anything with my hands this oily. Can you shut the door behind us? Lovely.

'When I've washed my hands I'll be off to chapel, if

you're happy to be left here. Oh yes, there's the Office bell now. Never mind that, I'll put the oils and so forth away. It's Mass I don't want to miss. You can leave the three in bed. If you'll just take the others a drink and see to their needs. I won't stay for Chapter. Thank you, Tom.'

Brother Tom became conscious of a rising sense of panic as he heard the door close behind Brother Michael. He would not have admitted this to anyone, and he mentally shook himself and administered a sharp rebuke. 'Don't be such a womanish fool, Brother Thomas,' he scolded himself. 'A handful of old men in your care— what's to be afraid of in that?' It also occurred to him that 'womanish' was probably not the word for it, since any woman would have faced the prospect with equanimity; but this reflection tended to make him feel worse rather than better. He went to look for Brother Edward.

'Ah, Brother, are you managing?' he asked with an air of what he hoped sounded like purposeful briskness when he finally tracked down Brother Edward, who had begun the task of measuring out the morning beakers of rich red wine that the residents of the infirmary took each day to promote their health.

Brother Edward, eighty-one years old, dim of sight and hearing, but otherwise possessed of all his faculties and as canny as ever, did not bother to hide his amusement: 'Gives you the jitters, does it, having to care for this lot?'

Brother Tom blushed. 'No,' he said, carelessly, 'I think I should be equal to an hour's nursing. It's not that difficult, is it?'

Brother Edward smiled. 'That depends,' he said. 'Ah, that's Brother Denis' bell ringing now. I expect he needs the jordan. Will you go or shall I?'

Their eyes met and the glint of good-humoured mockery needled Tom's pride. When he opened his mouth to speak, the 'Please come with me, I haven't a clue what to do' that he intended, came out as, 'Oh, I'll go, Brother. There's plenty here to keep you busy.'

Brother Edward smiled. 'As you wish, Brother Thomas. I'll finish these drinks and take them round then. Call me if you need me.'

The little bell tinkled again, rather more frantically this time, and Tom hastened out to the physic garden and Brother Denis.

'Can you help me, young man?' he asked. 'I need to relieve myself. I have a jar here, but I'm that bundled up with scarves and mittens and such, I don't think I can manage without help.'

Tom smiled brightly; a nurse's smile—the smile of a man who has the situation in hand.

'Fine,' he said, and began to extricate Brother Denis from his wrappings.

As he did so, muffled by the infirmary walls came the faint but unmistakable wavering shriek of Father Aelred: 'Aaaaagh! Aaagh! Aaaaaaagh!'

He squatted down beside Brother Denis, burrowing through the mountain of woollies, and began to lift aside the folds of his habit.

'What are you doing, Brother?' enquired Brother Denis with interest.

'You want to pass water, don't you?' Brother Tom felt instantly ashamed of the note of irritation in his voice. The continuing distant commotion ('Aaagh! Aaaagh! Aaaaaaaagh!') was beginning to worry him slightly. What if he's fallen out of bed? Tom thought in alarm. What if he's dying?

'Yes, but we have a slit cut in the front of our habits in the infirmary, Brother. Saves time you know.'

'AAAAAAAAAAAAAGH!' Then silence. Why silence? Perhaps he is dead.

'Well, why didn't you say so?' Tom sounded more impatient than he had intended.

'I'm sorry, Brother,' replied Brother Denis humbly. 'I thought you knew what you were doing. I—ooh, I'm piddling! I'm piddling!'

'Have you a handkerchief, Brother?' The educated, aristocratic voice of Father Gerald in the next chair scarcely penetrated Tom's panic. 'I don't like to distract you from your work, but I have rather a bad cold, and I can't find my handkerchief. I have a mouthful of rather nasty sputum, and I aa-a-aa-aaaSHOO!...I'm awfully sorry to trouble you, Brother, but I really *do* need a handkerchief.'

Brother Tom glanced up at the old man, the woolly rug round his knees hideously spattered with grey-green phlegm, and a long string of the same dangling trembling from his nose.

'Brother Thomas!' It was Brother Edward's voice in the doorway. 'I wonder if you might give me a hand with Brother Aelred. He's messed his bed, and he's absolutely plastered. Got the runs, I think. I've got his shirt off and cleaned up the worst, but it'll take two of us to change his bed.

'What's the matter? Is Brother Denis wet? That's not like him. Oh dear me, look at Father Gerald. He needs a hanky! Whatever have you been doing, Brother Thomas?'

Tom rose wearily to his feet. 'What am I to do about Brother Denis? I can't change him out here, he'll catch cold.'

'Put his rug back for the minute and help me with Father Aelred. I've left him naked, and if he does any more...well, he is inclined to play with it and get in a bit of a mess if he hasn't got his hands tucked outside the sheet. You'll be all right a minute, won't you, Denis? Yes, that's right—don't you let on to Brother John, though. I'll go for a bowl of water, Brother Thomas, and see you inside.'

Brother Cyprian, sitting in his chair in his favourite place beside the lavender hedge, sheltered from draughts by the infirmary wall, watched Brother Tom with inscrutable eyes.

'It's a funny thing, Cedric,' he remarked as Brother Tom passed him. 'I can never understand what they want with all these cattle. There's such a lot of cows in here today.'

Tom glanced round wildly, half-expecting to see a breakaway invasion from the farm.

'Oh, Mother of God!' he said. 'I never wiped Father Gerald's nose!'

He could have hugged Brother Michael when he walked in through the door half an hour later.

'Has everything been all right, Tom?' Michael enquired, his friendly smile and calm voice restoring a sense of sanity to Tom's ruffled spirit.

Brother Edward spoke before Tom had a chance to reply. 'He's been just grand,' he said. 'He's managed fine. Drinks are all out except Peregrine's. You'll maybe take his to him, Brother Thomas? Take some wine for yourself as well. I'll give you a call when Brother John's here, and you can get back to your ploughing.'

Peregrine was still sleeping when Brother Tom came into his room. Two of the little cats were stretched out asleep in the warmth on the floor, one with its paws up against the warm stones of the built-up hearth.

Tom sat down in the cushioned chair and sipped his wine. He reached forward for two more logs to place on the fire, and put his feet up on the hearth. The room was full of contentment and peace.

'Be m-y gues-t.'

Tom looked across to the bed. The dark grey eyes were open, smiling at him.

'G-etting un-der th-eir f-eet, were y-ou?'

Tom laughed. 'Yes. Badly. I've brought your wine. Can you drink it lying down?'

'I d-on't kn-ow. N-ot eas-ily, I th-ink. A ch-oice betw-een l-ying on m-y r-ight side and sp-illing it, or pr-opping m-ys-elf up on m-y l-eft elbow and n-ot being able to l-ift m-y hand to m-y m-outh.'

'Don't spill it. I've mopped up more mess this morning

than I hope to see for a very long time. On your left elbow, and I'll feed it to you.'

'Y-es. If it f-alls tow-ards the l-eft side of m-y m-outh, it doesn't f-all out again.'

Tom knelt beside the bed, holding the cup of wine to his friend's mouth, saddened by the helplessness, moved by the holy intimacy of that communion.

'*Calix benedictionis, cui benedicimus, nonne communicatio sanguinis Christe est?*' he whispered softly.

Peregrine lifted his face from the cup, looked at him, his eyes depths of awe, fear almost.

'I h-ave th-ought so. It s-eems too pr-esumptuous, but I have th-ought it s-o. In our s-orrow, in our d-ying, in our l-ove, is h-is real pr-esence. *"Ecce Agnus Dei."* Th-ank y-ou, T-om.'

Tom sat down by the fire again, watching one of the kittens as it yawned, white needles of teeth and a delicate curl of pink tongue contrasting with the sleek black fur. He drained the last of his wine.

'That's good: better than ale and water. Better than Brother Walafrid's strange brews.'

'Y-es. Th-ere are s-ome cons-olations to l-iving in th-e inf-irm-ary. Y-ou m-ust come and s-ee me again at this time of d-ay.'

'Mmm. I think I will. I'll fetch some more logs for this fire, shall I? Will I find some more apple logs, do you think?'

'Ask Br-other M-ichael. H-e kindl-y panders to m-y wh-ims. I f-ear you might get sh-ort shr-ift w-ith Brother J-ohn today.'

'Brother John's not back yet. That's why I'm hanging about here drinking your wine. I must get back up to the farm as soon as he returns; he'll not be long, I imagine. Anyway, I'll get those logs while I'm here; leave you with your fire well supplied.'

When Tom returned with the apple logs for the fire, he

found Brother John sitting in Peregrine's chair, talking to him. 'I'll look at that sore patch later.'

'Th-ank you.'

There was a slight tension in the air. Tom dropped the logs into the basket. 'Should I go?' he said.

'No, it's all right, Brother Thomas. I mustn't stay long. I've only just come back from my bed. I must make myself useful about the place in a minute. I've come to make my apologies, really. You used to say to us in Chapter, Father, "Courtesy is the flower of Christian charity." I don't know how many times I've heard you say that. I did listen, and I did take it in, though you might not have thought so this morning. I'm sorry. The way I spoke to you was inexcusable. I can only say that I was very tired, and you were...' Brother John's face broke into a grin '...obnoxious! Awkward? I've never known anything like it! Anyway, I'm sorry. Please forgive me.'

Peregrine smiled. 'Y-ou're s-upposed to give m-e a ch-ance to adm-it m-y own obn-oxious beh-aviour. I sh-ould listen to m-y own s-ermons. I ask y-our pardon also.'

'I've got some news for you too. I've been talking to Father Chad. He asked whether I thought you might be ready to give the homily at Chapter in early November.'

'Wh-wh-at d-d-id y-y-ou s-s-s-ay?'

'Yes. Of course.'

Peregrine said nothing, but looked at Brother John with his eyes shining. He turned his head away, and looked into the fire.

'Y-ou are n-ot b-eguiling m-e w-ith f-alse h-opes? Can I r-r-eally d-o it?'

'Yes. You really can. If you take your time, your speech is clear enough. You've had enough time to meditate and pray!'

'Wh-at ab-out th-e wr-etched inc-ontin-ence? I'd die if I wet m-yself in Ch-apter.'

Brother John shook his head. 'Not a problem. The Chapter meeting isn't that long—you could probably get

through it all right anyway; but we'll wash you till you
smell as sweet as a rose, and send you in a chair so well
padded the Great Flood would go unnoticed, just in case
of any unfortunate mishap. November 1st. Father Chad
says that day's Chapter is full of dreary stuff about exclusion from table and the oratory. "Speak about what you
like," he said. Yes?'

'Y-es. Oh, y-es pl-ease.'

'All right. I'll tell him. Now then, I must get some work
done. Brother Thomas, are you away up to the farm?
Thank you for staying so long. You've been a great help.'

'I'm not too sure about that, but yes, I must be going
now. Goodbye, Father.'

'Goodb-ye T-om.' But Peregrine spoke absently, and
did not look at him. Tom left him gazing into the fire, his
eyes burning with excitement, absorbed in thought.

VII
THE COURSE RUN

Throughout October Tom was ploughing. Brother Germanus took over the milking, the pigs and the hens, and kept a watch on the sheep, feeding them in the evenings now the growth of the grass had stopped. They had been put to the tup and were in lamb now, precious sources of revenue and meat.

Brother Prudentius saw to the apple harvest, the abbey school turning out as willing labour again. The loft above the wood store in the kitchen yard had been filled with apples, row upon row of them, green and red and russet; carefully set on the racks so that none should touch its neighbour and any rot be contained. Brother Walafrid passed his days making cider and brewing ale, tending the wines he had started in fruitful September.

Every spare minute Brother Germanus had he spent chopping wood, sawing and splitting logs. Severe frosts had held off so far, and the brothers hastened with the tasks that grew so much harder in the bitter cold to come.

By the end of October, the fields showed neat strips, ploughed, harrowed and sown. Plenty remained to be done, but they could afford to relax a little, and Brother Tom and Brother Stephen were able to spend a day mending the roof of the byre.

In the evenings, Brother Tom snatched an hour with Father Peregrine, but spent those hours for the most part

fast asleep with his feet up on the hearth. He had his own
chair in that room now, his own Office-book and ale mug.

Peregrine would talk to him as he dozed. He knew Tom
was not listening, but his mind buzzed with Scripture and
theology, his whole being dancing like a moth round the
dreadful, attractive flame of hope and fear, teaching the
brethren in Chapter again.

He must have prepared thirty sermons in the long,
empty days of waiting, his mind singing again with theology, philosophy, analogies and quotations.

Sometimes he found himself petrified before the dread
of his speech scrambling in the stress of the moment, and
sick at the thought of being wheeled in before their eyes.
He would not wholly admit his terror of appearing too
pitifully grotesque, too much a freak to be seen; but neither could he wholly suppress that fear. His sleep was
tormented and destroyed by nightmares of incontinence.
He dreamed of sitting in the abbot's chair on its dais, all
Brother John's careful padding left behind in the infirmary chair they had brought him in, fighting the sudden,
desperate urge to urinate, struggling to keep his mind on
his talk as his stuttering speech fragmented into nonsense
before the polite silence of the brethren.

Always in his dream there would be that watching,
listening, sceptical silence sitting in judgement on him, his
disintegrated speech finally stuttering into nothing as,
appalled, he felt his bladder emptying, on and on, a great
sea of it running down the floor of the Chapter House, and
the brethren in silence raising their pitying eyes from the
stinking yellow river, to watch with curiosity his tears of
mortification at the torture of his public shame.

He would wake from this dream night after night, his
bed soaked in sweat and urine, and have to force himself
to ring his bell to summon the infirmary brother, glad the
shadows of night hid his face burning with shame as he
mumbled his confession of incontinence. At first, he had
been unable to bring himself to call the night brother, but

Brother Michael had insisted gently, 'You *must* tell us. If you leave it till morning we're likely to lose the mattress as well, and heaven knows we've enough to do without spending the day making mattresses. We could come in and check you at intervals in the night, but I don't think you want that either, do you?'

And he had shaken his head, speechless in the humiliation.

'What is it?' Brother Michael had asked him. 'What's upset you?...It's this blessed Chapter talk, isn't it? You don't have to do it, you know. Would you rather not?'

And even more costly than the shame had been the admission: 'Broth-er, I w-ant to do it m-ore th-an anything.'

He tried out his ideas on Brother Tom as Tom dozed before the fire.

'D-oes F-ather Ch-ad keep th-eir v-ow of pov-erty bef-ore them? They sh-ould never forget poverty. To be p-oor in spirit...Obedience...he w-ill have spoken to th-em of obedience. It is eas-ier to talk about. Ch-astity...T-om, has h-e talked to th-em about ch-astity? Th-ey need to h-ave called to m-ind the f-ire of th-e first love f-or God, s-ingle, h-umble adorat-ion. Celibac-y w-ithout insp-ira-tion an-d tendern-ess is as soul destr-oying as C-ormac's porridge.

'H-as he sp-oken to them of th-e Tr-inity? Of pers-everance? Has he talked about h-onesty? T-om? T-om? Oh, g-o b-ack to sl-eep, y-ou usel-ess l-ump.'

'Mm? What? I'm not asleep. What did you say?' 'H-as h-e talked to th-em about l-ove, T-om; s-uffering love?'

'Pardon? Who?'

'F-ather Ch-ad.'

'Father Chad talk about suffering love? Well...he may have said something that I missed, but...I'd be inclined to doubt it.'

Tom threw another log on the fire and settled peace-fully back into his chair.

'Th-en I sh-ould talk to th-em about th-at. Th-e l-ove of J-esus. Love that gives and goes on g-iving. Th-e def-enceless, humble, r-oyal l-ove of Jes-us. Love h-as n-o def-ences, T-om. Y-ou know it's l-ove when it h-urts.'

'Mmm...good idea...you talk to them about that.'

'Y-ou th-ink so? Tr-uly?'

'What? Oh, yes...' Tom's eyes were closing in spite of his best efforts to pay attention. 'Sounds good to me...loving when it hurts...' and he was asleep, and nothing roused him again until the Compline bell rang.

The two of them spent every evening in October in this fashion: Tom working hard on the farm and bone-weary by the end of the day, Peregrine restless in the longing and dread of working again, growing more and more nervous as the first of November approached.

The night of October thirtieth Tom found him in a state of unbearable tension.

'Talk to him, for mercy's sake,' said Brother John. 'He's driving us all crazy with this talk of his. We should never have given him so much time to stew over it. He's thought of nothing else since I don't know when, and talked of nothing else either. Mind you, he changes it every five minutes. He's been so on edge today; tore Martin off a strip for some silly little thing—completely lost his temper. I'll be glad when Thursday's over and he's got it out of his system. That's if we survive tomorrow!'

Brother Tom went into the room and found Peregrine brooding, lost in thought, his chin resting in his hand, scowling in concentration.

'Byre roof's as good as new,' Tom commented cheerfully. 'And we should have a good crop of winter wheat if...'

'T-om, wh-at did Augus-tine s-ay in th-e book of h-is confessions, ab-out th-e inc-arnation? L-oving G-od in things th-at d-elight...um..."He m-ade th-is w-orld, and is not f-ar off"...oh...*M-ementote ist-ud, et conf-undam-ini: r-edite praevaricator-es ad cor*...um, it's Is-aiah, isn't it? B-ut what ch-apter? Oh, I c-an't r-emember it, and I us-ed to know it s-o w-ell.'

He shook his head impatiently, his mouth twitching in frustration. 'C-an't y-ou rem-ember?'

'What? Augustine or Isaiah? Either way, the answer's no. What do you want to know that for, anyway? You're not trying to impress the Pope. It's only a homily to a handful of monks who are weary after the harvest. All they need to know is how to find the grace to tolerate each other and stay awake through the reading of the martyrology. I guarantee you there'll not be a man in Chapter but his heart'll sink if you start quoting St Augustine in Latin.'

'Tr-uly? Do y-ou th-ink s-o?'

'No. I know it. Don't spin theological marvels for them, just talk to them about Jesus. They like it better.'

'M-aybe...I w-ish I c-ould r-em-ember it, th-ough. Do y-ou th-ink I'll g-et th-rough it all r-ight?'

'Yes. I'm sure you will. Stop worrying about it.'

'I'm afr-aid of...'

'Of what?'

Peregrine sat with his shoulders hunched, his head bent, hiding his face.

'Afraid of what?'

'Inc-ontin-ence.'

'That'll be all right. Brother John said so. You should trust him.'

'B-ut, if it's n-ot...'

'It will be.'

Peregrine sat hunched in brooding silence. He spoke only once more in the rest of that evening.

'T-om...I'm t-errified,' he said.

He scarcely looked up to say goodnight when Tom left him to go to Compline. His face was fixed in a frown, staring beyond his present reality, as he groped helplessly in his memory for forgotten teachings, sayings of the Fathers; strove in futility to remember the Athanasian Creed and the famous Corinthians passage on love. To his horror, he found he couldn't even remember whether it came in the first or second epistle. It all vanished into shadows that mocked him and eluded him. He hardly noticed Tom go.

The Chapter for the following day, October thirty-first, concerned the details of exclusion from the common table for minor faults. Brother Tom made himself as comfortable as he could in his stall, and prepared to hear Father Chad's careful dissertation on this subject. Tom could not restrain himself from the reflection that anyone who had sat opposite Brother Richard eating pottage might be tempted to commit a minor fault with the sole object of securing exclusion from the common table, but he chided himself for his cynicism, and bent his attention repentantly to Father Chad's homily, which proved to be, as he anticipated, exceedingly dull but mercifully brief.

After his homily, in the business part of the meeting, Father Chad explained to the brethren that Father Peregrine was to address them the following day in Chapter; said that this should be seen as an encouraging sign of recovery, and though they must not expect too much too soon, they might take hope from this beginning of seeing him returned to them from his long and distressing period of sickness. There was no other significant business that day.

Once released from Chapter, Brother Tom spent the morning with Brother Stephen building a rick to store some turnips and mangels for which there was no more space in the stone shed in the farmyard. They spread a layer of straw, thick enough to protect the roots from ground-frost, and then layered the roots and straw into a stack. There had been no hard frosts as yet, but winter was coming. The two men sweated as they worked, carting the roots and forking the straw, but their hands were red and rough with the cold.

That job done, they fetched the tumbrils out of storage in the barn. The air nipped with a promise of frost now, and the days were coming when the cattle would be housed in the foldyard, feeding on hay and roots, stolid, patient beasts, their breath hanging in steam on the winter cold. Their hay would be forked into the high, freestanding racks, and the roots chopped and fed to them in the wooden tumbrils, great feedtroughs that stood on tall legs near the wall of the foldyard.

After that, the morning was all but spent, and Brother Tom went into the dairy to help Brother Germanus, who had set himself the task of scrubbing it out in an effort to rebuff the sarcasm of the kitchen brothers.

'Brother Thomas!' A voice hailed him loudly from the farmyard. 'Brother Thomas!'

Tom looked puzzled. 'That's Martin Jonson,' he said. No monk would stand in the middle of the yard and shout. 'What's afoot, I wonder? They're perhaps needing me in the infirmary. Father's like a cat on hot bricks about this Chapter address tomorrow.'

Brother Germanus followed him out into the farmyard, where Martin was still calling.

'I'm here, Martin. Is something wrong?'

'Aye, I'll say there is. Father Columba's took bad: he's had another seizure. Carrying on something shocking he was this morning. We couldn't do a thing to suit him. But, "let it be", says Brother Michael, "let it be"—although I can tell you Brother John was looking pretty tight-lipped by the time we got to the morning drink.

'And there he was, would you believe, he threw his cup of wine across the room, and all because he couldn't remember how to say some ticklish business in Latin! "Well, here's a pretty kettle of fish," I says to him. "You can't have this sort of going on, not even if you've forgot your own *name*." And do you know, he swore at me something atrocious—words no man of his calling should even know, not by rights. Fair gobstruck I was.

'Still, Brother Michael, bless him, he's the patience of a saint. "Don't take it ill, Martin," he says to me, just like that, "don't take it ill," and he was on his knees by the old villain, talking to him as gentle as you please. And what we should have done if there'd been but Brother John and me there I don't like to think. Still, we shall never know, shall we?

'Any road, the long and the short of it is, he was took bad again. You should have seen him; eh, it was ghastly! Vomiting he was, and his face as purple as a pulpit cushion, his eyes turned up in his head and his mouth blowing in and out like a flapping sail.

'So I said I'd come for you. Brother Michael seemed to think you might like to know, being his friend like, so much as you brothers have friends, if you know what I mean.

'Are you all right, Brother Thomas? You don't look too good yourself.'

Tom stood with his fists clenched and his face drained of colour, staring at nothing. Everything that made up reality, the solid reassurance of his body, the breeze on his skin, the smells of beasts and hay and earth, the grey banking clouds and the mud under his feet; in that moment he lost it all. There was nothing left to him but the thunder of his heartbeat in the derelict shell of his life.

'He is...he is still alive?' he whispered.

'Oh yes, he's bad, but he's with us—just like before: helpless as a babe in arms, his face grey and his wits gone. But he's not dead. Not yet, any road.'

'I'll come,' said Tom. 'Go down ahead of me, and tell Brother Michael I'll come.' He could not bear to walk down the hill in Martin's company.

He went back into the dairy, Brother Germanus shadowing him anxiously, and like a man in a dream he picked up the yard-brush he had been using on the floor, and propped it with meticulous care and precision against the wall.

'I'm sorry I won't be able to help you finish this job,' he

said, his voice polite, remote; someone else's voice from far away.

'Don't you worry about that,' replied Brother Germanus. 'Father Columba needs you with him by the sound of it.'

'Yes,' said Tom. He was unsure whether he spoke very slowly, or if it was just that the whole universe had slowed down, stopped all its bustle and colour, condensed all its movement into one slow, agonised, wailing cry. 'Yes,' he said again. 'There may still be something I can do for him. I promised him I would do what I could.'

He stood still for a moment, Brother Germanus watching uneasily the haunted gazing of his face. Then he took a deep breath and smiled at Germanus. 'Well,' he said, 'I'd better go and see what I can do.'

He walked down the hill, cocooned in terror, aware of nothing but the nauseous fluttering of his stomach, the beating of his heart; purposing nothing but that his legs should not give way under him, should carry him into that room, where he might behold that grey, distorted face, and wait a chance to be left alone with the battle-weary, wrecked remains of his friend.

He came to the infirmary, where everything was business as usual: the old men out in their chairs encased in blankets, woolly grey bonnets framing the faces yellow and withered, or veinous purple, of their nodding, dozing heads, and Brother Edward moving among them, rousing them for their cup of wine.

Inside the building, Tom paused at the door of Peregrine's room, trying to get his body back under control, master the shaking, refuse the icy nausea. He closed his eyes for a moment. 'Help me then, help me,' he whispered; and he opened the door.

Brother John stood by the bed, bending over the form that lay there. He had his hand laid on Peregrine's brow, his face thoughtful.

'Hotter than ever,' he said, without looking up to see who had entered. 'This doesn't look good.'

He took his hand away and lifted the sick man's eyelids, one by one, moving aside slightly so that the daylight might shine in on the eyes.

They had laid him on his right side on the bed, his left arm and leg cushioned on pillows. Brother John laid his hand on the still, twisted hand on the pillow, rubbing it gently.

'Peregrine,' he said, 'Peregrine. Can you hear me?'

He waited, looking down at his patient. Tom was moved by a sudden impulse of gratitude for the look on John's face; the gravity, the respect, the sadness. Brother John looked up.

'Tom, I'm sorry. I didn't realise it was you. Martin told you?'

'Yes. Can I...can I stay with him for a while?'

'Of course. Brother Michael and I will sit with him through this morning, but I ought to get some sleep this afternoon in case he needs me through the night. Why don't you go and get a bite to eat, and come back and sit with him this afternoon?'

'Eat? Maybe...John, will he live?'

Brother John shook his head. 'Who can tell? He's very ill; burning up quite a fever now. Pulse is slow...bounding. Pulled through it last time though, didn't he?'

'And if he lives?' Tom's voice was husky. He could not iron out the tremor in it.

'Again, you can't say. How many times must a ship be dashed against the rocks before it finally tears apart? Each time is one step nearer the last time. Each battering brings further disintegration. All we can say for sure is that right up to the end, before anything else, this broken, helpless, suffering being is a living soul, a house of God's spirit, needy of tenderness, worthy of respect. I don't know, Tom. I just don't know.'

He looked down again at the man on the bed. The

sound of the slow, stertorous breathing was the only intrusion on the utter silence.

With an effort, Brother Tom forced himself to take the steps—one, two, three, four, five—that brought him round the bed where he could see Peregrine's face, clammy and colourless except for the slight, unnatural flush of fever in the cheeks. His lips vibrated with every breath, but the blowing in and out of the paralysed side of his face had been masked by lying him on his right side.

Tom gazed at him, saying nothing. Cold—it seemed so cold today. Brother John laid a hand on his shoulder. 'Get yourself something to eat, Tom. I dare say you don't feel like it, but he could be days like this.'

Tom shook his head. 'No,' he said, 'he won't.'

Brother John squeezed his shoulder. 'Have some food. You must. I can't trust you to be alert to sit with him if you haven't eaten. No one can say how long he'll be before we see a change. Go on with you. There's the bell for Sext now. Come back after the meal.'

Nobody disobeyed Brother John. He had the calm authority that went with responsibility. Tom went to chapel, then to the refectory with all the others, and forced down as much food as he could bear.

When he returned to the infirmary in the afternoon, he found Brother Michael sitting with Father Peregrine. He had a smile for Tom, as always.

'Hello, Brother. I'm glad you've come. He mustn't be left alone, and although it's quiet now, someone may need me later. We turned him only just now before Brother John went, so there's nothing to do but sit with him and keep a watch, keep the fire going and not let his lips get too dry.'

They sat, Brother Michael in Peregrine's chair and Tom in his own chair, mostly in silence. On the hour Martin came in, and the three of them turned the sick man and changed the padding and the sheet when necessary. Apart from that they just sat and kept watch.

Tom waited, the palms of his hands sweating, for the moment when Brother Michael would leave the room; leave him alone with his promise, his task. But the moment never came. For the first time Tom could remember in all his visits to the infirmary, no bell rang. The afternoon drifted by in tranquillity, the light in the room swelling to a glorious tawny gold as the day drew towards its close.

Once, Brother Edward came in to ask Brother Michael to help Martin change a wet bed. Tom's heart beat faster, but Edward said, 'I'll stay here and keep vigil with Brother Thomas till you're back. There's nothing to do for Peregrine, I know, but I'll share the watch over him a while.'

Brother Edward did not leave until Brother Michael returned, and Brother Michael stayed with Tom while Martin and Brother Edward set out the evening meal trays.

'It's a miracle how quiet it is today,' he remarked once to Brother Tom. 'Well, you know what it's like here. Some days we're rushed off our feet. I don't think I've ever known it this quiet.'

By the time the sun was sinking and the bell began to toll for Vespers, Brother John was back.

He came directly to Peregrine's room.

'No change? Ah well.' He bent over the unconscious man, making his own checks.

'We'll give him a wash, shall we, while the others are eating? Edward and Martin can do the feeders, then one of us can help settle them in to bed. No, he's not much different, is he? Still hot—I don't like the look of that. I don't think there's much point in trying to force fever herbs down him, though; not till he shows more signs of life than this. I'd hate to choke him.'

He looked at Brother Tom. 'Thank you, Brother, for staying. We'll look after him now till tomorrow. Go to Vespers and then get some supper and some rest. If you'd like to come the same time tomorrow, that would be a help.'

He saw Tom's hesitation and added, 'I will call you, don't worry. If there's any change at all, I'll let you know.'

They were waiting for him to go, Tom could see it. They didn't want the intrusion of his company while they washed and examined their patient. He dithered a moment longer, then helplessly he left. It would have to wait until tomorrow.

As he sat in the Chapter meeting the next day, Tom wondered if this was what hell was like; a grey suffering limbo of exclusion.

He listened to Father Chad's homily, but did not hear what he said, and did not take in the announcements. He registered Peregrine's name being mentioned once or twice in suitably grave tones, but nothing else.

Up on the farm he muddled through his chores, walking down the hill like a sleepwalker when the bell rang for Sext. The other men left him alone when they found their kindly questions met by his dazed, bewildered murmur, 'He's... I don't know... I don't know...'

After the midday meal, he returned doggedly to the infirmary, where he was met by Brother John.

'I'm glad you've come. I would have sent for you if you hadn't come anyway. You'll see a change in him. We must get some of the men bathed this afternoon, so I'll be glad to have you sit with him. Brother Michael will come and help me as soon as you relieve him.'

This was it then. Tom's mouth was dry and his knees turned to water as he approached the room. He felt his courage ebbing away from him, his resolve melting.

'All right, Tom?' Brother Michael smiled at him as he entered the room.

Tom's eyes were drawn to the bed, his attention riveted by the racket of breathing that filled the room.

Peregrine lay on his back in the bed, his head and arms supported on pillows. His head was propped slightly to one side, the mouth fallen ajar, his eyes half-open, dull, sightless. A vein pulsed under the scrawny skin of his neck. His face was yellow and seemed to have shrunk. Each breath he drew was a rattling labour, an unnatural, jerky heaving of his chest, separated from the next breath by an age of silence.

Tom looked in horror and sadness at the grievous, pitiful struggle; gazed without moving, without speaking. Yes, there was a change.

Brother Michael watched Tom, took in the tautness of his face, the look in his eyes that gazed across desert spaces of desolation.

Michael nodded. 'I know,' he said, 'I know.'

Tom was roused to panic for a moment, and looked at him, horrified, but Michael didn't know. 'It's the same for all of us,' he said.

And then Brother Michael left, promising to return later when the baths were done. 'I'm not sure how long I'll be,' he said, 'but you can ring his bell if you need me, or you're worried about anything. We're not turning him every hour now. No need for that any more.'

Tom watched him go, waited until the door clicked shut, gave him time to walk away. Then he moved slowly to the bedside. He put out his hand and touched the pillows that supported the unconscious man. Those under his arms were lumpy, solid, real monastic pillows, but the one under his head was filled with down, soft and light. Tom slid his hand under Peregrine's head. It felt unpleasant, sweaty. He lifted it slightly, leaning over him, and with his other hand he tugged the pillow free. He clasped it to him, holding his breath, his heart thudding as he lowered Peregrine's head back down onto the bed. Without the support of the pillow under his head, his mouth fell open even further. Tom could see inside it. There were brownish, dry patches on his tongue, and little drifts of sticky white saliva. The skin on the lips was tight and dry, cracking.

Holding the pillow in his arm, Tom reached over the bed to the bedside table, where a sponge lay in a bowl of water. He squeezed it lightly and carried it to Peregrine's mouth, dripping a trickle of water onto the parched tongue, gently moistening the cracked lips. Then he replaced the sponge in the bowl.

'It's because I promised you,' he whispered. 'It's only because I promised you.'

He stood there, very close to the bed, clutching the pillow in both hands, holding it ready as he looked down at the bleak, withdrawn, shrunken face.

He swallowed convulsively, his heart hammering and his head wobbling in uncontrollable agitation.

He couldn't do it.

After a while, he backed away from the bed, still gripping the pillow. He sat down on the low stool beside Peregrine's chair, his eyes fixed on Peregrine's face, watching the tough, insistent tic of the pulse in his neck, listening to the arduous labour of his breathing, watching the dead grey absence of his eyes, half-expecting even now to see them waken to a flicker of humour, anger, tenderness.

His grief and frozen helplessness grew until they overwhelmed him; till grief was no more part of him, but he was all grief, had become absorbed into grief, had no more being beyond this moment. Enfeebled of all power to act, he began, unawares, to rock, clinging to the pillow for comfort, past knowing or thinking, seeing nothing, hearing nothing but that face and that harsh, erratic breath.

'Oh God, give me the courage to do this thing,' he whispered in agony. 'Damn me if you like, but first give me the courage to do what I promised...oh God...for he always kept faith with me.'

He had no idea how long he sat there on the chair, clutching the pillow to him, his body rocking in grief. The golden light of afternoon filled the room and then in time subsided until the place grew dim with the violet shadows of evening, and cold. The slow, harsh breathing went on and on; a breath rasping in... the slow wheezing rattle of the outbreath...a long, long pause; impossibly long...another painful indrawing of breath. On and on.

It seemed that the diminution of human life to its last extremity was a grim wrestling with God. For did they not share the same breath, God and man? Neither, it seemed, was willing to let go, and Tom could not find the courage to come between them and break the hold that anchored this man to life.

He did not look round when the latch of the door clicked. He heard it, and yet he did not, everything in him absorbed in the slow, rattling travail of breathing that had become the heart of the cosmos.

'It's a hard, slow climb for him, isn't it?'

He glanced up then, at the sound of Brother John's voice.

'Mm?'

'Not an easy one.' Brother John looked down at Tom's haggard, distracted face. 'Shall we put that pillow under his head?' he said gently. 'It might help to make him a bit more comfortable.'

Tom sat without speaking. He looked at Brother John, then stared down at the pillow as if he'd never seen it before, dazed with grief. And he realised with slow, appalled remorse that he had missed the opportunity. His consciousness filled with the realisation that he'd left it too late. The chance had come and gone, and he had squandered it on his own distress; and now it was too late.

'I couldn't do it,' he said, gazing stupidly at the pillow. He raised his eyes, bewildered with grief, to Brother John's face. 'I promised him, but I can't...I...I've failed him...I can't do it.'

Brother John knelt down beside him and took his hands between his own. Tom's eyes searched his, yearning for refuge in John's kindness and sanity, but there was nothing, anywhere, to ease the heartache that was bursting inside him.

'Promised him what, Tom?'

Brother John's eyes looked steadily back into his, full of warmth and understanding. But warmth and understanding belonged to a dead past, to a man who had not broken his promises, failed his friend in the time of his most helpless extremity. In this cold landscape of grief and regret, warmth perished, and understanding starved; there was no comfort in all the world.

'Promised him what, Tom?'

'I promised him that... if he had another seizure... if he was helpless... dumb... incontinent... I would finish it for him. He said... he couldn't face it again. He said, hemlock, a pillow on his face, anything... and I said I would. I *promised*... but I can't... when it comes to it, I just can't... and *listen* to him...'

Brother John nodded. 'I know.'

He chafed Tom's cold hands gently between his own. 'You don't have to do it, Brother,' he said quietly. 'He's dying. This is the end now. This is it. He'll be gone before the dawn. Stay with him. You haven't failed him, Tom— far from it. Don't leave him now. I'll go and get a fresh bowl of water to wash his face and moisten his mouth. Stay with him and say whatever you still need to now, then I'll fetch Father Chad for the last rites, have them send word to his family. Help me then; let's put this pillow back under his head.'

Stiff and cold and weary, Tom rose to his feet and approached the bed. With gentle competence, Brother John slid one hand under Peregrine's head, one under his shoulder, and raised him sufficiently for Tom to replace the pillow on the bed. They both stood there looking down at the dying face, all the life in it shrunken back, conserved for the one arduous work of breath. His skin lay, a toneless shroud on the bones of his face, his eyes half-open, unfocused, dull as stone.

'Will he hear me? Does he know anything?'

Brother John looked thoughtfully, a long time, at the sick man. He put a hand to Peregrine's brow, smoothed it tenderly.

'Do you hear us, Father? Do you know we're here? Or is everything you have going into this fight for breath? We aren't sure, neither of us...but in case you can hear us, in case you know...we want you to know—we love you.

'Stay with him, Tom. Say goodbye. I won't be too long.'

He glanced at the dying fire, slipped out of the room, and went in search of Brother Michael.

'He's going, Brother. I'll go and fetch Father Chad, though I dare say he'd rather have had Theodore if I can work it tactfully. Make up the fire in case we're there through the night, and keep an eye on Brother Thomas. It's almost too much for him, I think. Oh, and you'd better take him a light. It's nigh on dark in there.'

'It won't be long now, Father,' Tom whispered as Brother John left the room. 'Brother John says it won't be long. Just a little while, and God can have his breath back, and the Earth can have her dust back, and all this hell will be over. I suppose...you won't miss me, where you're going. I don't know how I'm going to get along without you. I always did mess things up. Thank you for the help you gave me. Thank you for the man you were. Thank you for your courage, and your honesty, and your compassion...Father...goodbye. I can't tell you how much I love you.'

He reached over for the sponge and squeezed a little water between Peregrine's lips, wiped the sponge gently along his lips to moisten them. He dropped the sponge back in its bowl, and carefully with his fingers wiped away the trickle of water that dribbled from Peregrine's mouth. He lifted his hand and traced with his fingertips along the ridge of his friend's cheekbone, along his eyebrow; turned his hand over and stroked with the back of his fingers the hollow of his temple and down the sunken, toneless cheek to the bone of his jaw; a slow, rapt contemplation of tenderness.

'Father... I'll tell them what you said. "Love has no defences—you only know it's love when it hurts." I won't forget.

'Oh Jesu... Son of God, Son of Man... you have been his Lord for so long, master and man. Forgive him that his courage failed and he tried to take a way out of this long misery. Forgive me that I would have helped him but that my courage failed too. Jesus... Jesus, he loved you in Gethsemane, pleading that the cup be taken from you... he loved you for the faltering of your courage... in your utter humanity, he saw God...

'Look... Jesus, in mercy, look at him... look... oh Jesu... have mercy on your man.'

And then the night. The long, slow watch of the night: last rites, anointing, prayer of absolution from all earthly weight of sin. And the watching and waiting, the painful rattling breaths measuring out the hours of the night.

Until, as the first grey finger of day came stealing in, he drew breath, and they waited... waited... but he did not breathe again. In the dreary uncertain light of dawn, before the sunrise, he was gone.

Tom, who had thought before that those eyes looked lifeless, dull, gazed down on them now and saw beyond doubting, Peregrine was gone. Even his helplessness, his blind, broken suffering he had taken with him: those belonged with his breath, were part of the breath of God in him. They were God's helplessness, God's brokenness; and he had taken them back to himself. Peregrine had left nothing behind but this husk of flesh, a cast-off, finished corpse. And it was to that last trace of his presence among them that his brothers must now address their respect.

'Tom? Would you like to do the last offices for him, with me?'

Tom nodded in silence. He could not take his eyes from

that dead face; could not take in that this was the end...the end.

'Brother Michael, will you bring me the things I shall need? Send Martin to tell Brother Basil and Father Chad. Tell him to remind Father Chad he had family; Melissa Langton, and there is a brother still living.

'What do we do with his ring? Leave it on while he's lying in the chapel, isn't it, and take it off for burial? I think that's what we did with Abbot Gregory.

'All right then, Tom; have you ever done this before?'

'No.'

'We want everything off the bed, pillows, blankets and everything, so we can see what we're doing; that's right. Now it'll take both of us to get his clothes off—very unwieldy is a corpse. Cut the shirt. We'll burn it. No sense in heaving him about unnecessarily. Ah, Michael, thank you.

'What shall I put in his hands, Tom, to lay him in the chapel? Some men, I lay out with their rosary in their fingers, or fold their hands over their Office book, or a crucifix, depending on the special character of their devotion. I laid out Father Matthew with a copy of the Rule.'

Tom pondered the question.

'Nothing,' he said finally. 'He should have nothing in his hands. That's how he wanted to live.'

Brother John nodded. 'Yes. I think you're right. Now then, we have to plug anything that might leak—I'll do that—then you can help me wash him.'

Together they washed him, dressed him in his best habit, combed his hair. They laid him on a clean linen sheet, and folded his hands on his breast, closed his eyes and weighted them down, bound his jaw.

'Pass me that ball of thread, would you?' said Brother John as he fastened the dead man's sandals on his feet.

Tom watched as Brother John cut a length of the linen thread and tied it in a neat figure of eight round the big toes and the ankles, unobtrusively binding the feet into place.

'There. Done.' Brother John stood back and cast a critical eye over his work.

'Right then, we must set to and get this room clear. There'll be a string of people in even before we can have him lying out in the chapel, I should think. Martin can help me with that though. The fire's all but dead, but I'll souse the ashes. We certainly don't want it warm in here.' He shot a quick, appraising glance in Tom's direction. 'Will you like to sit a moment quietly with him, while I go and get that organised?'

Tom nodded, and Brother John left him, shutting the door behind him.

Left alone, he stood by the bed, his eyes travelling slowly over the motionless form of death. The ivory stillness of the toes; the misshapen fingers stark against the blackness of the habit, decorated with the opulent, bejewelled abbot's ring; the sharp, jutting outline of the hawkish nose. With his cold, trembling fingers Tom traced the line of the savage scar that ran the length of the right side of the face.

'Gone...' he murmured in amazement. 'Gone...for ever...'

Then, in the depths of his numbed, chill disbelief, he felt the first sharp stirrings of a pain too cruel to be borne, the jagged, rending legacy of love.

I don't know how I'm going to get through this, he thought as he turned away from the bed.

He stooped and untied the knotted tatter of string that had been the kittens' plaything, from the arm of Peregrine's chair. For a moment he paused. Brother Basil had begun tolling the church bell; the dolorous, repetitive tolling of the bell for the passing of the dead. He rolled up the scrap of string and put it in his pocket.

Then he left the room and, closing the door behind him, went in search of Brother John.

'Where have you put his crutch?' he asked him when he found him.

'His crutch? It's in the back room with the wheeled chairs and walking sticks and so on. Why?'

'Can I take it?'

Brother John looked at him. Brother Tom was not a man to be patted on the back and soothed like a child. If this would ease his suffering, why not?

'Yes, you can take it.'

At the funeral five days later, with its solemn requiem Mass, attended by villagers, Peregrine's family, the bishop, representatives from other religious houses and local dignitaries of all sorts, Tom stood sealed in remote, indifferent impassivity. He followed the bier with the other brethren up the winding path under the beech trees to the burial ground, and stood with the others in the raw, blowing drizzle, watching the last remains lowered into the earth, and the clay shovelled in. There had been some argument about that, because Father Chad had thought it more fitting to inter him in a vault in the church; but Brother Tom had insisted that he would have preferred to be buried with the ordinary brothers, out here on the hill, under the stars.

Tom was glad he had won that one, but apart from that, the burial had been of little consequence to him. He had said his farewell two days ago after Vespers, when he had lit a fire behind the vegetable garden, of dry, dead weeds, bean haulm and rose prunings. He had cut back the rosemary bushes and brought the trimmings green to the fire. Into the incense of their fragrant smoke he had place the little coil of knotted string and the wooden crutch. He had watched as the string charred and spurted into flame, and the crutch blackened and caught fire, the worn, shiny leather pad of the armrest and the leather pad on the foot being the last parts to ignite. He fed the fire until they were completely consumed, and stood for a long time looking up at the smoke of it rising to the stars.

Then at last, he took a stick and raked through the ashes until he found the little metal casing from the foot of the crutch, and this he wrapped carefully in his handkerchief, and he placed it in his pocket before he went to Compline.

VIII
WINTER

Father Theodore sat by the fire in the abbot's house drinking Brother Walafrid's blackberry wine. Father Chad had asked him to come and report on the progress of the young men who formed the present novitiate.

When Father Matthew died, Theodore had been a surprising choice as his successor. The obedience of Novice Master was exacting, demanding a man of considerable spiritual stature and wisdom, a man of unsentimental kindness, of both scholarly ability and common sense. Theodore; shy, clumsy and forgetful, had not been the most obvious choice. Father Chad remembered Peregrine defending his decision to some of the more sceptical among the brethren: 'I know he's a young man, but there may be good in that. The lads who come here may find a sympathy in his youth. Further to that, there is scarcely a man in this community who suffered so much in his novitiate year as Father Theodore, and so much by the fault, or at least the weakness, of his Novice Master.

'I want a man who has struggled to persevere, a man who knows what it is to bear the cost of another's weakness. I think I have that in Father Theodore. He will serve the novitiate well.'

And it had been a good choice, Father Chad acknowledged with mild astonishment.

'All is well then? You have no anxieties?' he asked him now.

'No.' Theodore shook his head. 'For the moment they are working well, praying devoutly, living contentedly. No doubt trials and difficulties will assail them, but just now we have tranquillity.'

'Good. Good; I'm glad of that. That's good.'

Theodore, experienced by now in detecting unspoken unease, gazed steadfastly into the fire, not looking at Father Chad, waiting for him to speak out whatever was on his mind.

'Father Theodore... this... this has nothing to do with the novitiate, but...'

'Yes?' Theo smiled encouragingly.

'This is a matter of confidence, you understand. I rely on your absolute discretion.'

'Of course.'

'I am not happy about Brother Thomas. He used to be such a cheerful, easygoing soul. Now he looks shut in, withdrawn from us. He has lost all his joie de vivre, all his zest for living.'

Theodore frowned in puzzlement. 'Well, he... well, naturally he has, Father. He's grieving.'

'Yes, but... this is the third week of Advent. He should be recovered by now, surely?'

'Why? Has Advent got some special healing power I haven't heard about?' said Theodore. 'I'm sorry,' he added hastily, seeing Father Chad's startled displeasure at the discourtesy of his sarcasm. 'Father Peregrine is but six weeks buried. Brother Tom will take longer than that to pick up the dropped stitches of his life again, I think. He's bound to feel a little unravelled for a while. Give him time. Perhaps he needs a chance to talk it over.'

'With me?' Father Chad sounded doubtful. And not without reason, Theodore had to admit.

'You are his abbot, for now anyway. I doubt if he will make it easy for you, but I think you ought to try.'

Father Chad nodded gloomily. 'And if I get nowhere?'

'I could have a word with him. Or Brother John.'

Father Chad sipped his wine, staring at the yellow flames of the ash logs burning on the hearth. Administering the business of the abbey had its difficulties, but it was easy compared with the pastoral care of men in grief or crisis of faith.

'I don't know what to say to him,' he admitted.

'Ask him.' Theodore spoke as diplomatically as he could. Father Chad was not an arrogant man, but Theo must not be seen to have too much of an edge over his superior in this matter of the nurturing of the souls in his care. 'Allow him to talk to you freely about Father Peregrine, about the effect on him of that loss. He loved him very much. He will be full of memories, sadness, tenderness that need to be spoken out.'

And you think if I ask him, he will be able to talk to me?'

'Yes...' said Theodore, slowly. If you ask him the right way, he thought, but he didn't say it.

'He'll be up at the farm all day. I'll catch him at Vespers. I'll try.'

With very little confidence in the usefulness of the interview, Theodore watched at the end of Vespers as Father Chad laid a detaining hand on Brother Tom's arm, beseeching his co-operation with the peculiar ghastliness of a nervous smile. He watched Brother Tom's guarded acquiescence, and saw the two of them leave the chapel with negligible hope of frank self-exposure. Brother Tom, in Theo's judgement, was about as likely to show Father Chad his soft underbelly as he was to take up embroidery. In this assessment of the situation he was right.

'Sit yourself down, Brother Thomas,' said Father Chad. He had intended a warm and reassuring welcome, but his voice slid into a disconcerting falsetto under pressure of his apprehension.

Brother Tom sat down in silence in the chair that

Father Chad indicated by the fire. He looked at the ash logs burning in the grate, then looked down at his hands with lowered head. He had a fair idea of the purpose of this summons, and he did not want his heartache forced into the open by Father Chad or anybody.

Aware that his unco-operative silence might seem more than a little rude, he glanced up with a forced and sickly smile.

'Thank you,' he said. He could think of nothing else to say. Encouraged by this crumb of compliance, Father Chad cleared his throat and began his pastoral consultation.

'I've been worried about you, Brother,' he said sympathetically. 'You haven't been your usual cheerful self at all these last six weeks.'

Tom raised his head and stared at him incredulously.

'I'm not surprised, of course; of course I'm not surprised,' Father Chad added hurriedly. 'It is quite understandable: you were very fond of Father... um...Columba.' As he came to say the man's name, Father Chad stumbled over his anxiety to do the correct thing. As acting abbot of the community it seemed more proper to refer to the deceased man by his name in religion than by the affectionate informality of 'Father Peregrine'. Tom, hearing the hesitation, wondered in amazement if Father Chad had actually forgotten Peregrine's name.

'Yes,' he said, in the pause left for his reply, which was lengthening into embarrassment. 'Yes. I was very fond of him.'

'Good. Good. Well, that's natural and right, of course.' Father Chad's voice carried the insincere effusiveness of anxiety. It matched his smile.

'However...all of us have to, um, count our blessings in circumstances like this; to...er...you know—look on the bright side and put a brave face on things and...um...so forth.'

Father Chad was a timid man, not at his best in such

circumstances as these: but he was not a fool. He struggled to repress the twinges of irritation and resentment that were awakened by the expression on Brother Tom's face. Brother Tom looked as though he thought Father Chad had all the intelligent sensitivity and discernment of an earwig.

'I *have* been putting a brave face on it,' said Brother Tom. 'At least, I thought I had. What would you like me to do differently?'

'No, no, no!' Father Chad wished he had had the humility to ask Father Theodore to join in this conversation. 'Don't misunderstand me, Brother. This is not a rebuke. It is only that, although you have not complained or given any cause for complaint in your work or prayer, nevertheless your unhappiness is very evident. I am your abbot, for now anyway. Brother Thomas, I know you don't like it, but you ought to confide in me and tell me what's on your heart. It says so in the Rule.'

Brother Tom was sufficiently self-indulgent to allow himself the tiniest twitch of the eybrows. This small twitch was so expressive that it plunged Father Chad into a sense of total inadequacy.

'So it does,' said Brother Tom. He lifted his eyes calmly to look Father Chad in the face. 'What would you like me to tell you?'

Why is this going so wrong? Father Chad floundered in desperation. I knew it wouldn't be easy for him, but why do I want to shake him and shout at him? I mustn't let him see how I feel. I must try to understand.

'Well...' he replied with forced benevolence, 'well...um...perhaps you would like to talk to me freely about Father...um—Columba, about the effect on you of that loss. You loved him very much. You must be full of memories, sadness, tenderness that need to be spoken out.'

Tom looked away quickly into the fire, biting his lip.

The hurt of bereavement was intolerably raw still. He could not bear it touched.

'He always burned apple logs,' he said at last. Father Chad smiled.

'Really? Apple logs, mm? Good, good.' There followed a silence in which Father Chad cleared his throat uneasily.

'That, um, that wasn't quite the kind of thing I was thinking of,' he said. 'I was wondering more about how you felt about him. Um, I thought you should tell me how you feel now; um, what hurts most, you know, and the memories you had of times together. That sort of thing.'

Tom swallowed. 'Oh,' he murmured, 'that sort of thing.'

'I beg your pardon?' Father Chad's face creased into the nervous smile. 'I'm sorry, I didn't quite catch what you said...'

But Tom shook his head. 'Nothing.'

He picked up the iron poker from the hearth and prodded moodily at the fire. 'What hurts most,' he said, 'is that he's dead.'

Father Chad laughed, then stopped himself abruptly, unsure if the remark had been intentionally humorous. He cleared his throat again. 'Ah yes; yes, I can understand that. Um...tell me about it.' His face twitched in alarm at Tom's sharp intake of breath. 'Are you all right, Brother? You sound as though something hurt you.'

Tom passed his hand across his face and sighed. He decided that he might as well give Father Chad what he wanted simply in order to secure his escape.

'How I felt about him? I loved him. Sometimes I was angry with him, at my wits' end with him. Sometimes he made me feel very small, very ashamed. Sometimes he tore my heart open with pity. He taught me to love in darkness, showed me that it is possible to find a little spring of hope in the most arid place of despair, just by loving; by consenting to be defenceless...permitting the pain and the wonder of loving and being loved. All that... but mostly I just loved him without knowing why. I loved his crazy smile and the way his eyes could dance with laughter. I loved the way he looked like a bad-tempered bird when things were going wrong. I loved his faith.

'And what hurts most is facing up to the fact that I will never hear that slow, careful voice struggling its way back to speech—"T-om. Th-ank y-ou, T-om." Never. As long as I live, never again. Never see those eyes smiling, "T-ell m-e about it."

'What else did you want to know? Memories? I remember the night we went out to look at the stars... the hunger and ecstasy in his eyes, the sigh in his voice, "Oh, mon Dieu; oh le bien." And the scent of rosemary. I remember lying with him in the grass below the burial ground, talking about his death, about God...I remember him lying on his bed naked in the firelight, the oil shining on his body, the sound of him weeping, and Brother Michael talking to him, quietly. I remember another time he wept, holding him in my arms, and I felt as though his pain would divide my soul in two. Those wretched blackberries. I remember holding his hand, before he learned to speak again, and the extraordinary cost of caressing it with real tenderness, such a simple thing, but it took courage to do...

'I remember how Martin used to drive him to distraction... I remember how jealous I was that it was Theodore, not me, who taught him to speak again... silly...'

Tom looked up at Father Chad, all the extravagant torment of unbearable grief in his eyes. He felt the pain of it swell relentlessly inside him; the by now familiar agony of hurting so intense he felt it would split him apart, dislocate his reason.

Father Chad was looking at him with considerable concern, clearly disturbed, shocked even, by what he had just heard. He cleared his throat and, anchoring his voice with an effort to a normal masculine pitch, began his cautious reply.

'Thank you for being so, um, open with me, er, Brother Thomas. What you have said is very moving of course, but I must, er, confess, it disturbs me just a *little* bit ... um ... concerning, er, as it were the, er, um, *nature* of your closeness to Father Columba.' He cleared his throat, crossed his legs, avoiding Tom's eyes.

'As you know, our Rule is very insistent on a most prudent modesty ... guarding against particular friendships ... against too, er, *demonstrative* forms of affection, and certainly against, er, um, nakedness. I feel I ought really to ask you whether this extreme affection was in all ways, er, in your view, quite proper?'

Father Chad would never have believed it possible for one man to pack so much contempt into his gaze. He had an extraordinary sense of having shrivelled to a state of being so cheap and so dirty that he had no rightful existence in the order of creation at all.

'What are you suggesting?' Tom asked him coldly. The simple question demanded an answer of a bald honesty that Father Chad squirmed to think of.

'Presumably you are asking me if the relationship I had with Father Peregrine was as lovers?'

Father Chad felt as though his tongue had dried up, cemented to the roof of his mouth. All he had to say was, 'Yes.' He could not bring himself to say it. It seemed to him as if some mischievous force had picked up his attempt at pastoral counselling and worried it to bits, leaving his room all strewn about with pain and indignation, disgust and distrust and distress.

He made himself look at Brother Tom. 'That, um, was what I was asking, but I see by your reaction that I may have been wrong, er ...'

'Father Peregrine,' said Tom, with a sudden, unexpected smile, 'was not that way inclined. Neither am I. We both took our vow of chastity seriously. Particular friendship... I don't know. Towards the end of his life, without friendship, what would he have had? But certainly, it was perfectly proper. He was naked because he had bedsores, and limbs deformed by paralysis, and he ached all over. Brother Michael was tending to him. There was nothing erotic about it, you may take my word.'

'Quite. Quite, I see. Good. Er, good. Well, um—oh dear, is that the Compline bell? No? Oh dear... I thought it was...'

Father Chad's hands fluttered in a small gesture of helplessness. He felt totally at sea. Perhaps, he thought, it would be possible to redeem the situation by moving on to a less critical topic of conversation.

'Has Brother Stephen told you of our new plans for the farm?' he asked brightly.

Tom frowned. 'No,' he said, with a note of surprise in his voice. It was not like Stephen to forget to mention farming matters to Brother Tom.

'Hasn't he?' Father Chad looked at Tom in alarm, wondering if he had made a blunder, racking his brains to think of some reason why Brother Stephen might have thought it more prudent to say nothing about the plans to Brother Tom. He could think of none.

'Yes, we met last week. We have decided on looking at it again that the dovecote really does need rebuilding to a larger size. Also I have been up to the buildings by the boundary, and I can quite understand from the way Brother Stephen explained it that they all need to come down. We need a good-sized barn, with three threshing floors and a granary up there, as well as new cow housing.'

Tom said nothing to this. His face was fixed in a smile of bitterness. He looked older than his thirty-three years.

'I am surprised Brother Stephen said nothing to you. Perhaps it slipped his mind.'

'Yes. Maybe so. And then again, maybe he remembered Father saying, "Over my dead body will you build a barn with three threshing floors." Perhaps he has the grace to blush. So—with what is this work to be paid for?'

Father Chad pulled a glum face. 'Well, this is the problem of course. We shall rely on selling corrodies, which I know Father—er—Columba was reluctant to do.'

'Reluctant? He wouldn't hear of it!'

'No...still, these are troubled times. Heavy taxes and so forth, you know. He was not a well man, and of course, his disability kept him rather confined here. It may be that he did not realise how common a thing it is to sell corrodies these days.'

'What ever do you mean? Of course he knew! It was seeing all the houses round about going into debt and cluttering the place up with worldly people that made him so desperate to stay free of it. I...Father Chad...please...please may I go?'

Tom got to his feet. He was shaking, his hands clenched into fists. He hardly knew how to contain his anger and grief. He knew only that he had to get out before he hit Father Chad; before he did something really stupid.

Father Chad looked up at him. He had an unwelcome suspicion that Father Peregrine, under the same circumstances, would not have permitted Tom to go anywhere. Even so, it was a relief to hear his own voice saying, 'Of course, Brother Thomas; this is not an easy time for you— you must be very tired,' in spite of the embarrassing quaver in it.

'Thank you for your time,' said Brother Tom, with a valiant attempt at humble courtesy, and left.

He did not see Theodore sitting in the cloister in the wintry darkness. He did not even register that the Compline bell was ringing. He walked swiftly along the cloister, out through the passage beside the Chapter House, and then ran up the hill to the farm; ran till the frosty night air hurt like a knife in his throat, ran till he had a stitch in his side and he gasped for breath. He stopped then, up on the hill, looking down on the farmyard in the moonlight, the silence of winter all around him. An owl floated overhead on noiseless wings. A fox's bark carried on the tingling air. He stood, his body heaving, regaining his breath.

Then, slowly, he walked down the hill again. It was too cold to stand still. The cold ached in his ears, numbed his toes.

He walked down to the farmyard. He could hear the shifting and blowing of the cows in the byre as he came alongside it. He opened the barn door and went in. The fragrance of the hay hung on the air, distilled memory of dusty summer days. Weary, numb, defeated, Tom trailed into the barn and sat in the warmth of the hay, his knees drawn up to his chest, his forehead resting on his knees and his arms wrapped tightly round his shins, contracted to a ball of aching misery.

He sat there motionless, containing the sorrow, the impossible, breaking weight of sorrow that he could not dodge or escape or put down. The spaces of the night widened away from him, until he became the beating heart of a universe of bereavement, the core of a vast, immortal, pitiless night.

Bird of death, the owl, as it came curving down on silent wings, with cool, unerring precision seizing the little grey mouse that scuttered among the hay. A small noise, a disturbance of the hay, piteous squeak of terror, and it was over. Tom raised his head and saw the owl fly through the moonbeams that shone in at the doorway, a limp scrap of frailty in its talons.

He also saw someone standing in the doorway, silhouetted in the moonlight, looking in.

'Tom?'

It was Theodore's voice. Tom watched him silently from the dark place where he crouched.

'Tom?'

It seemed churlish to hide from him. Tom felt half-inclined to call out to him; and half-possessed by the silences of an empty, finished world.

'Tom?'

Tom compromised. He shifted his position in the hay. Let him hear that if he wanted to. He heard it. 'Tom.' Theodore came into the barn. He walked forward uncertainly into the darkness.

'Theo, I'm here.'

Theodore came towards his voice, peering in the dim light afforded by the open door until he made out the blot of black dark amid the darkness that was Brother Tom.

'Tom?'

He sat down in the hay beside him. An immense, dragging weariness filled Brother Tom at the prospect of explanations, questions, futile commiseration. But Theodore said nothing. He unclasped his cloak, turned it upside down so that the wide hem of it might spread over the shoulders of both of them. Only then did Tom become aware that he had been shivering. His shivering increased, became uncontrollable, and Theodore took him in his arms, with the cloak wrapped about them, saying nothing still.

It was only there, hidden in Theodore's arms, in the sheltering cloak, hidden in the silent dark of the barn, that Tom uncovered the wound of grief that savaged the very bowels of him, and allowed his face hidden in Theodore's shoulder to wear the agonised mask of mourning, allowed the tears that ached in his throat to scald his eyes, until he clung to Theo in the sobbing anguish of his torn, abandoned soul. And Theodore did not speak, did not move, did not intrude upon that molten place of pain in which a man's soul is recast.

Eventually, it was finished. Tom sat back in the hay, drained of everything, exhausted.

'I didn't know anything could hurt this much,' he said. He lay down on the fragrant hay, his face, his throat, his belly aching from the labour of weeping.

The last six weeks had been full of the kind words and sympathetic counsel of the brethren; well-intentioned words ranging from, 'It's a blessed release for him, Brother. He's better off where he is,' to, 'I expect it's a relief to you to be free of all that extra work in the infirmary.' Theodore's company had an intriguing novelty about it in that he said nothing at all beyond the simple statement of his presence.

'D'you remember what he said about having your heart ripped open?' said Tom after a while.

'Yes, I do.' Theodore sat rubbing his ankle, easing the pins and needles that had resulted from sitting awkwardly immobile for a considerable length of time. 'He said it was part of the necessary pain of following Jesus.'

'Ripped open. That's what it feels like. Other times it doesn't feel like anything. I walk around like a man lost in the fog; things that were familiar looking alien and bizarre. My life doesn't feel like home any more. I feel as though I've been cast out of my own heart, wandering. And then the grief comes again, swelling and rising inside me till I'm maddened with it. Last night...last night I lay on my bed tearing at my belly with my hands, retching, trying to void myself of the pain of it...

'Five minutes. If I could talk to him just for five minutes. "Th-ank y-ou, T-om...T-ell m-e about it...L-ove h-as n-o def-enc-es, T-om. Y-ou kn-ow it's l-ove wh-en it h-h-urts." He...he...oh, I'm sorry...' The wash of it overwhelmed him again. He lay on his back feeling the tears welling hot in his eyes, and trickling cold down into his ears, weeping helplessly, torn open with grief.

'Psalm a hundred and twenty-nine,' said Theo. ' "*Supra dorsum meum*..." um...how does it go? "*Supra dorsum*..." '

'What ever are you talking about?' Tom's voice quavered peevishly between his tears.

'Psalm a hundred and twenty-nine. "The ploughers have ploughed upon my back, and made long furrows." '

Tom sniffed, and considered this, sniffed again. 'Yes...' he said. 'That just about says it.'

'I'll expect to see you looking like a horse with a green mane in the spring, then. And a blond hedgehog by next harvest.'

Tom felt offended by this inappropriate levity, and faintly guilty at his own, equally inappropriate, faint stirring of amusement. He was not sure how to respond. He hunted for his handkerchief and blew his nose.

'You know,' said Theo into the darkness, 'how Martin likes to have one of the brothers say grace over the food; in Latin. It has to be in Latin. He can't speak a word of Latin you know, but he thinks it's needful for blessing. I was there one day; in September, it must have been, because Father was just struggling with speech—he had it, but it was very unclear still. And Martin brought him his meal; fish, rather overcooked, and some very tough beans, the end of the season, and a hunk of Cormac's bread, chopped...and soaked to a mush. He beamed down at Father, and he said, "Now then, you be a good lad, and let's hear *you* say grace today."

'Father looked up at him, and I was a bit worried for a minute: it was so insultingly patronising; I thought he would be angry. But he smiled at Martin—the sweetest smile, and it was a bit of a relief, you know.

'He composed his face into the most dignified, sepulchral solemnity, and he said, *"L-L-amentat-iones J-er-emiae, c-cap-ut pr-im-um; V-ide D-Dom-ine quon-iam tr-ibul-or, c-conturb-atus est v-enter m-m-m-eus...in n-om-ine P-Patr-is, et F-il-io, et Sp-ir-itui S-ancto, am-m-en."* And he made the sign of the cross over his food with all the pomp and ceremony of a bishop. Martin was delighted. I couldn't figure out what he'd said at first, his speech was so stuttering and laboured still, but gradually it dawned on me. It was that verse from the first chapter of Lamentations, "Behold, oh Lord, my tribulation, and how my bowels shudder...in the name of the Father, and of the Son, and of the Holy

Spirit, Amen." I don't know how I kept a straight face. I thought I'd choke before Martin was out of the room, but he, he didn't bat an eyelid. He didn't eat it either.'

Tom smiled. It felt strange. His face wasn't used to smiling. His eyes were sore and swollen. He began to laugh, but his breath caught in a sob. 'He was awful to Martin,' he said.

'No,' said Theo. 'He took more than he gave.'

Tom wiped the cold tears out of his ears with his handkerchief. 'He couldn't always see the funny side of it,' he said, 'but we brought him up here to the farm one day, me and Stephen. It was only about the second time I'd brought him out. He was so touchy about meeting people. But he consented to come up here. The harvest was in, it was halfway through September, and Stephen and I were just pottering about doing odd jobs, so I thought it would be good for him, nice to be out of doors and have a bit of company. We wheeled the chair up as far as it would go, and then carried him to the grass beside the track up above the orchard, in the shelter of the wall.

'We left him there and came back down here to swill out the milking shed and scrub the milk barrels clean. We'd left enough chores to keep us busy round the yard for a while, knowing he would be there.

'Then Stephen and I went down to the pasture to have a look at one of the cows, she'd a bad foot. While we were there, Brother Germanus came tearing down to the field: "Brother Thomas! Brother Thomas!" he was shouting, and he as white as a sheet. We ran to meet him. He was puffing and blowing, "Oh God, come quick," he said. "Father Columba's in some kind of fit. I don't know what to do, he looks terrible."

'Stephen and I looked at each other, and we went up there at a run. I think he felt as cold and sick as I did. As we came up by the orchard, I could hear this thrashing about and garbled shouting, and when we got round the corner, sure enough there he was, rolling about on the grass, making a terrible row, calling and shouting, all nonsense. I knelt down beside him and started to soothe him as best I could, but he was pushing me away with his hand and going on and on at me, writhing about on the ground. It was odd you know, because his eyes didn't look glazed or anything, but there was obviously something badly wrong with him. He looked at my face and at Brother Stephen's and he stopped shouting, and he started to laugh. For one hideous moment I thought he'd gone insane; wondered if there was some kind of fit you could have with his illness to make you lose your mind.

' "T-om," he managed to say at last, and I was so relieved. He closed his eyes, and made a real effort to get his speech working, calm himself enough to make some sense. "F-or th-e l-ove of G-G-od, m-an," he said, "w-ill y-ou g-g-et m-e off th-is a-ants' n-est?" '

'We had to take all his clothes off and everything. They were all over him.'

Tom chuckled at the memory. 'Brother John was disgusted with us. We'd made him promise not to tell, but he was covered in bites.'

Resonant and clear on the tingling wintry air, the Matins bell began to sound in the abbey below them.

'Midnight?' said Tom, startled. 'It's not midnight already?'

'I searched for you a long time before I found you,' said Theodore. 'And you were a long time weeping.'

Tom scrambled to his feet. 'We'd better go down, Theo. They'll miss us from our beds and our places in chapel.'

Theo sat up in the hay. 'If you feel ready. There's no harder work than grieving. We can stay here if you like.'

'No.' Tom was brushing the hay from his clothes, bending over to shake it from his hair. 'No. Come on, Theo, get all the hay off you, straighten yourself up. It...it's just something Father Chad said this evening. I think I'd have a lot of explaining to do if he had reason to think I'd been out of my bed, spending half the night with you in the barn—especially you, with the novitiate and everything.

'Come on—please. I don't want another long session with him. Not just now.'

Tom fastened the barn door to keep out the animals, and they hastened down the track to the abbey.

As they approached the cloister, Tom made Theodore stop, and he inspected him anxiously in the moonlight. 'You've got hay in your hair still, look.'

'Have I? I'm surprised you can tell the difference.'

'No, I'm serious, Theo. Turn round, let me look at the back of you. Truly, I think I shall be in trouble if you appear with me in chapel looking as though you've just been having a tumble in the hay. Have a look at me. Am I all tidy?'

'Brother, you look charming. I suspect your nose and your eyes, which are rather swollen, may also be rather red, but it's hard to say by the light of the moon. Apart from that detail you look positively elegant.'

'Oh, for mercy's sake, the bell's stopped. Come on.'

Father Chad, Tom was relieved to see as he took his place in chapel, looked almost as crumpled and bleary-eyed as he did himself.

They were in silence, so Tom could not speak to Theodore again, but he sought him out the next day, climbing the stairs to the novitiate to find him in the few minutes before Vespers began, after the Novitiate Chapter. He was grateful to find him alone. The novices had already gone down to chapel.

'Theo—thank you...last night.... Thank you.'

Theodore smiled, the kindness in his eyes enfolding Tom with a gentleness and understanding that was almost unbearable. Tom bit his lip. 'Don't be too kind to me. I can't...I'm a bit shaky still.'

'Give yourself time,' said Theo. 'You can always come up and find me here if you need me. You know how it is for the novices—they spend half their lives in bits. They won't think anything of it.' He hesitated. 'Father Peregrine...'

'Yes?'

'He...he was worried about you. He spoke to me about it one day. He said that he never knew when he might be taken ill again, and he was worried once Brother Francis went away to the seminary, that if he died while Francis was away you might have no one you could turn to. He told me to look after you. He said I was to remind you, if you needed some comfort, that you'd helped him to start living again. He couldn't have faced it without you. He said that the breath of God in you is a gift of life, a holy kiss to be passed on. He said you'd know what he meant. And he said to tell you that the sorrow of grief is a bitter crucifixion, but that the loving had been joyous, and one day would be again.

'He told me to behold your grief without embarrassment, to help you not to run away from your pain. He told me...he said that it would be the comfort of my love that led your anguish out into compassion, instead of it festering to destruction. He said to tell you that a man in grief is like a man with bedsores. It costs him to reveal it, but he needs help with it. He said you'd know what he meant. And he said to remind you of the thing you said last night. That love has no defences, and you only know it's love when it hurts.'

Author's Note

In the life of the church, some people easily find an identity, a place to belong, while others find themselves marginalised, forgotten, relegated to the outside place of loneliness and aching rejection, which was how Jesus characterised hell.

This happens in part because the church community organises itself around meetings. Who cannot participate in such meetings? Children, who get bored easily. The deaf, who cannot hear, and cannot lipread or sign when seated in rows. The mentally handicapped, who may make unusual or inappropriate noises or interruptions. The incontinent, who may not be able to make it through the meeting, yet may not be able to leave quickly and quietly to reach distant toilets. It is such as these, the citizens of the kingdom of heaven, whose path into the church family we misguidedly obstruct.

The story of *The Long Fall* is about the isolating and humiliating nature of such disablement. In the story I have tried to write sensitively and respectfully of some of the most difficult, and common, aspects of human suffering. One of the problems of such writing lies in deciding just how explicit to be.

For example, it very often happens that someone who suffers from post-stroke aphasia may swear, very graphically, before the control of the rest of his speech returns. As speech returns, it sometimes happens that he may say things that would have been unacceptable to him before, of a sexual nature perhaps, or other improprieties. Along with incontinence as well as impairment of mobility, such things can make it impossibly hard to find the comfortable place in the fellowship of the church community that he once enjoyed.

Not to write about these things would compound the conspiracy of silence by which so many are excluded from the loving circle of fellowship. Yet to write too explicitly would cause offence, by the inclusion of swearwords and indecent language.

In *The Long Fall* I have tried to present an authentic picture. That is to say, a realism which includes the reality of the tender compassion of God, as well as the grittiness and tears of the reality of human suffering. It is my sincere wish that you may not be offended in any way by this portrayal of reality.

Penelope Wilcock